Isaac

fizz

nothing is as it seems

Zvi Schreiber

www.fizz-book.com

ZS
ZEDESS
publishing

Publisher's Cataloging-in-Publication data
Schreiber, Zvi.
Fizz : Nothing is as it seems / written by Zvi Schreiber.
   p.   cm.
Includes index.
ISBN:
978-0-9833968-0-2 (hardcover)
978-0-9833968-1-9 (paperback)
978-0-9833968-2-6 (ePub)

1. Historical fiction 2. History of science. 3. History of physics. 4. Popular physics. I. Title

PN45-57 2011
509   2011927076

ZEDESS PUBLISHING

First edition 20110822 v1.0.2 (BM)

Contents

for
RKEDY

The Collective

THE FUTURE: July 1, 2110.

I guide the muzzled ox across the field, suppressing thoughts of my birthday tomorrow. The ocean breeze picks up, and strands of my wavy red hair blow across my face. Pulling a band out of my pocket, I manage with my right hand to drag a bunch of hair through it, never for a second removing my left hand from the ox's blunted horn.

I turn to check on Zopp, who is steadying the plowshare with both hands as it slices vigorously through the earth. A few months older than me, he presents quite the contrast with his shaggy, jet-black hair. At over a meter eighty—a six-footer, as my late grandparents would have said— he's a little taller than me. Zopp's a great guy—bright, witty, and kind.

Looking now to the left, I sigh at the sight of several acres of freshly turned brown soil, testimony to the preceding days of mind-numbing labor, fertile and ready for sowing. I try to avoid looking to the right where an equally large expanse of cropland, still green with leftover shoots of last year's plantings, is promising to keep us working for weeks to come.

Except that I won't be working tomorrow.

A short distance ahead of us, the green-brown of the field ends, and the infinite blue of the Atlantic Ocean stretches to the horizon. Behind us, the farmland finishes abruptly at the foot of the towering, rugged, deep brown cliffs of Iceland's southern coast. The cliffs are garnished with two powerful waterfalls that naturally irrigate this small, cultivated plateau from the rocks to the beach. The field is small enough that, here at its center, I can discern the sounds of the ocean mixing harmoniously with those of the waterfalls. Each day I cross this center point hundreds of times during the plowing and reaping seasons.

"I still love this view," I shout back at Zopp.

"The view from here is better, Fizz," Zopp teases from behind me. I quite like the comment but roll my eyes all the same.

"Say, Zopp, how come we're working together again this week?"

"Luck of the draw, isn't it?" He pauses for a moment. "So, looking forward to your birthday tomorrow?"

"Hardly," I say.

"Well, yeah, I know, but looking forward to being eighteen, right?"

I don't answer.

Every few minutes, as we reach the end of the field, first at the water's edge and then at the rocks, I'm charged with steering the ox through a sharp U-turn. Between turns, I gently lead the animal's gait, digging a straight furrow, adjacent to the previous furrow, which is parallel to the furrow before that. The ox doesn't need much guiding along the straights, which leaves my mind to wander.

Birthday. The word evokes no images of colorful gifts, ribbons, candles, or cards. It provokes no thoughts about milestones of maturity. Birthday means visitation. Birthday means Dad. Dad, not only as my father, but Dad also as a portal, offering me a fleeting annual glimpse into the foreign, intriguing, forbidding world to which he belongs.

My grip of the horn slides slightly—my palm is sweating. I glance over my shoulder at Zopp, the jagged cliffs beyond him framing his muscular figure. Zopp lives two houses up the road from us with both parents and two older sisters. Over the years he has tried every possible topic of conversation with me, other than my Dad. Surely Zopp must be curious about the Outside too, yet the subject is taboo, even among us youngsters.

Especially this year. With my coming of age, and given the family history, everything about tomorrow's visit is charged. In the past I've allowed my conversation with Dad to stray where it shouldn't. This year the stakes are too high. I must play it strictly by the book: discuss family, farming, hobbies—my hobbies, not his. Keep other thoughts under cerebral lock and key.

Exhaling loudly, I force myself to focus back on the timeless sounds and smells of nature. To our community, nature is sacred, the ocean and cliffs our shrines. My reverence for this natural outdoor sanctum has been enhanced by three years of daily outdoor toiling since I graduated school at fifteen.

My attention snaps back to the field as the plow jerks on a small rock, causing the rock to shoot aside. As the lead, it is my responsibility to avoid any obstacle, as even the smallest unforeseen item can be dangerous.

"Can't focus?" Zopp raises his voice above the wind and the grinding soil. "Perhaps girls should stick to weaving."

I rise above the bait. It may be more common for guys to opt for the heavy work, but I'm quite strong enough for plowing. *Whether my mind is cut out for this endless routine is a different matter.*

I look around to survey our progress, realizing we're behind schedule. "Did you notice he's getting old?" I nod toward the ox.

"Yum," Zopp says, rubbing his tummy.

We reach the southern edge of the field, and I swing the ox around just shy of the short pebble beach. From this side of the field I can see the collection of wood-beamed, two-storied houses and thatched roofs of our Collective. A couple of hundred buildings—I know every one of them so well that the entire village almost paints itself in my mind as a single common home.

As the ox turns, I look down at some dead brown stems on the ground underfoot and clench my teeth. The rising sea's salinity is creeping in slowly but relentlessly, stunting growth, eroding the field from the south. So it's been since the middle of the twenty-first century, I've been told. The rising ocean is slowly encroaching on the small fertile area that feeds us, threatening to strangle our food supply. It's hard to pinpoint the moment, but one day this shrinking, arable flatland we're plowing will simply be too small to sustain our Collective. *And no one is doing anything about it.*

We head back toward the cliffs now. My mind continues to alternate between our labor in the field and my daydreams about tomorrow, punctuated with occasional snippets of conversation shouted awkwardly to Zopp. Minutes later, the cliffs loom above us, and I absentmindedly plan the next turn.

When it happens, I have no warning whatsoever.

The ox pulls sharply away from me to the left and bolts. It's never done anything so spontaneous before, and both Zopp and I hold on for a moment too long, finding ourselves face down in the earth, watching the plow's blade scraping across the field as the beast races away from us.

My face—and pride—have taken a beating, but Zopp and I know our responsibilities and recover quickly. A couple of seconds later we are both back on our feet, chasing the animal that suddenly seems a lot younger. Our only hope is in the plow blade, which is starting to dig itself into the earth and might soon break the run.

I feel it even as I'm running. The ground is trembling slightly. Zopp and I both slow, suddenly more worried about the rumbling under our feet than about the escaping ox. Volcanoes are not unheard of in southern Iceland. We have both heard the stories of the big one a hundred years ago in 2010. *Is that what's happening above us?* I look up at the sheer face of rock. *Or maybe an earthquake?* We're dangerously close to the rock if any stones were to shake loose. Zopp and I glance at each other but say nothing, instead nervously stepping away from the cliff. The ox is now stuck a short distance away.

The vibrations continue. We pick up our pace. A powerful crushing noise echoes down from the cliff-tops above, and we both spin around, straining our heads back as we look up toward the source of the sound.

We wait.

For a long, tense second or two nothing is visible. Then we see it: a vast block of ice and snow sliding out over the top edge of the cliff, more or less directly above us, not yet showing any signs of falling. *There must be just as much ice—if not more—that has yet to slide over, if it can balance like that,* I think. *Then again, once the majority of the ice crosses the top lip of the cliff... at the speed it's going, it could easily reach where we are standing!*

Instinct kicks in and I flee the cliff at a speed I didn't know I was capable of, heading in the general direction of the sea. My mind is totally possessed by the thought of hundreds of tons of ice dropping from the sky above me. As I run, my brain seems intent on calculating whether there is some predictable relationship between the height, speed, and weight of a falling block of ice and how far from the cliffs it will land. I try to brush the thought away and focus on powering my legs faster.

I have a vague awareness of Zopp sprinting somewhere alongside. I don't look behind, even when I think I hear the faint whistling of something large flying through the air. The threat of an imminent icy death continues to drive my heart and my every muscle to maximize my distance from the rocks in the few seconds remaining. I run right past the ox, which is struggling to free itself from a plow that is now firmly entrenched in the ground.

Suddenly we all seem frozen in time. *It's strange how the passing of time feels relative to the situation.* A few heartbeats pass, and then an impact just behind me rattles every bone of my body. Sharp, hard shards of ice shoot past me. The thing that splats against the back of my neck is not sharp though—it's warm and soft. Nonetheless, the shock of it causes my body to physically leap into the air.

Then silence—utter silence, as if the waterfalls and ocean are themselves muted.

I'm alive.

I touch my neck and look at the red on my fingers. Turning, I see the giant mass of ice resting peacefully, as if innocently, in the middle of the field, oblivious to the muzzled ox head and pair of front hoofs sticking out pathetically from below it, surrounded by a puddle of blood and guts.

Zopp and I move closer together, panting heavily, perspiring, watching the spectacle of a few smaller blocks of ice sliding over the cliff and taking dramatic nosedives in front of us. Some ice blocks survive the fall, dotting the field with punctuation marks; others explode on impact. Intermittently, we feel the rumbling of what must be a crumbling glacier above the cliff.

Doubling over with our hands on our knees, we gradually catch our breath. Still we say nothing.

I stand gazing at the ox head for quite a while. *That could have been me.* I stare for a while longer and am disturbed to realize that the thought does not really upset me. *Why aren't I more shaken by such a close scrape with death?*

Zopp straightens up and puts a hand on my hunched shoulder. "You okay?"

I shake off the hand and walk over to the remains of the ox, regarding the lifeless head for another moment. Slowly I untie the muzzle and toss it aside. The ox's body will slowly dissolve back into Mother Nature, as we all will one day.

Zopp has followed me. "Fizz, leave the stupid ox. Are you all right?"

"Yeah. Would have been unfortunate to die a day before my eighteenth." After this, my birthday should feel really significant tomorrow. *But will it?*

"It would have been murder," Zopp says. "We're not safe from the Outside, even on our very own island. What do they even do to fry our glaciers like that?"

"I think it's somehow connected to pollution from their awful SITs," I shake my head angrily.

"SITs?"

Oops. "Um, I think Supersonic Intercontinental Transits or something like that. Dreadful polluting things."

Zopp frowns. I need to be more careful—I'm not even supposed to discuss technology with Dad, let alone repeat what I hear within the Collective.

Halfway through the three-kilometer walk home, we are greeted by a party of a couple of dozen fellow Collective members marching toward us. I catch a glimpse of Mom's red hair somewhere among the heads.

Two younger boys of about twelve sprint ahead to greet us first. Soon we're engulfed with hugs. My mother finally pushes her way to the front of the pack and holds me tight. She keeps asking if I'm all right, regardless of how many times I reassure her that I am. Mom wipes the drops of blood off me with her sleeve, examines the grazes on my face and looks me up and down. For a moment I think she's about to count my fingers and toes.

For a few minutes, Zopp and I are the center of attention. Then people starts to recall their own experiences.

"I was in the community center when it happened—"

"At first I thought the kids were tipping out their toy bins—"

Most people are guessing that there was no earthquake or volcano—just a glacier finally surrendering to years of gradual warming. It seems that the two of us were the only ones in direct danger. By the time we reach the village, some people have moved on from reliving the moment to thinking about the implications.

"What happened to 'glacial' change?"

"Glaciers naturally change slowly, *this* was not natural."

"Is it safe to walk near the cliffs?"

"What will it mean for our fresh water supply?"

"Will the melting glacier raise the sea levels even more?"

I am disturbed—though not necessarily surprised—to hear words like "contingency plan" and even "reprisal" creeping into the comments.

Later we wash ourselves in the nearby hot spring and change into evening clothes. Like our day clothes, these are made of flowing natural wools, linens, and cottons, although evening outfits are more fitted, cleaner, and better preserved.

Being a Tuesday, we all meet up at the tavern for the mid-week communal evening. Perched on a hill overlooking the entire village, the tavern is a large white-washed rectangular wooden building with a sloping white, wooden roof. We group ourselves by age, with about eight to ten of us in each age group. Relaxing after the day's labors, we refresh ourselves with soft drinks, read stories, play games, tell jokes, and swap farming tips. Summer means we have an excellent range of berry juices—berries have always grown in Iceland—as well as juices of apples and pears introduced here since global warming.

It is Zopp's turn to lead an activity, and he's prepared a word game, but for a good half hour everyone ignores the game and jabbers about the imploding glacier.

Finally Zopp manages to focus us on the game. He says, "dog" which ends with "g." We have to think of a language in which the word for dog starts with a "g."

"*Gos*," I say in Catalan. Zopp smiles at me, although no one else seems sure if I'm correct. However, I am not challenged.

"*Skyli*," Toland calls out in Greek.

Language skills are highly rated throughout the "Ecommunity"—the ecological community to which our own Collective belongs. The official reason is that our members have gathered from all around the world, and even while English is encouraged as a common everyday language, we must respect the lingo and literature of all members. In particular, we respect old literature—anything written before 1800—as well as anything composed within the Ecommunity. Our studies include ancient literature, so I am not unusual in my ability to speak, in addition to English, fairly fluent modern French, German, Spanish, and Italian as well as classical Greek and Latin, plus miscellaneous words of several other languages.

As my friends shoot words at each other, filling the air with multi-lingual vocabulary, it occurs to me—not for the first time—that my community may have an ulterior motive for investing so heavily in languages. *The more time we spend accumulating linguistic skills and memorizing historical books and poems, the less time our minds have to wander where they shouldn't.* The strategy has not been particularly effective in my own case; in fact, I have come to resent it deeply.

Zeno from next door has called out something like "*inu*" in Japanese to Toland's *skyli*. Zeno had her eighteenth just last week; she of course had no visit from the Outside, and I doubt she spent even a second thinking about the legal right she technically had to visit the Outside. I've been trying not to think about it myself. *Until now.*

Now I'm back in the game, racking my brains for a language in which dog starts with a "u" sound, but soon I forget about multi-lingual dogs and survey the room. We've all known each other since birth. We might tease each other, we may have the occasional quarrel, but there is not a person in this room who would not do anything to help me if I were in trouble. Even beyond our own Collective, we can almost feel the kinship of the entire Ecommunity—the hundreds of collectives all across Iceland

and the few collectives still remaining within outside countries, all of whom passionately share our values.

Why can't I relax and appreciate the fraternity that surrounds me?

After an hour, our group joins the adults in the large community hall. The entire Collective is together, more than a thousand people. Our age group bunches toward the back, and Zopp manages to sit himself on my right, Toland on my left. The choir leads off with a couple of songs, and soon everyone joins together in a brief rendition of communal favorites.

The Dean limps onto the stage. He's in his mid-thirties, a little shorter than average, and—perhaps because he's about the only person in the room whose job does not involve manual labor—he's a little on the heavy side. The Collective has dispersed origins. The Dean traces his roots to Madrid and has naturally dark skin, making him look a lot like those of us who spend our days in the field, in fact rather darker than me. His most noticeable feature is his eyes, which absorb every detail, but reveal little more than a sparkle of passion. Although his vocation as a communal preacher may have been suited to his slight disability, he does seem to relish the role.

The Dean clears his throat. When he talks, each word drips with intensity and authority, as if it were underlined.

"We're grateful to Mother Nature for good summer fruit this year. I'd like to thank everyone for their hard work in the past months; the pear juice is particularly delicious today, and I'm already looking forward to the barley crops you are all preparing to sow."

The Dean makes a small show of folding the page of notes in his hand and stuffing it in his pocket.

"But I am forced to put aside the talk I prepared and address the painful events of today. We all live with the constant reality that even with the independence of our Ecommunity in Iceland we are not immune from the hazards of the irresponsible Outside way of life. We know that the global warming cooked in Europe, the Americas, and Asia reaches into the heart of our own island; but when it hits so close to home—directly threatening our members—we cannot and will not sit idly by!"

The Dean waits a moment for the murmurs in the crowd to die down.

"I know that other collectives throughout the island will share our outrage at the continuing blatant infringement of the Treaty of Separation, which was supposed to protect us."

The Treaty of Separation was the watershed event of 2074. The ecological community, then thirty years old, was still dispersed at that time but was growing rapidly across different countries, fueled by increasing disillusionment with the impact of technology on nature and on the quality of life. The Ecommunity had been gaining votes and lobbying vocally for independence. Some mainstream political parties started to think that they would quite like to be rid of the Ecommunity opposition. In the year 2074, the Ecological Community was finally granted independence in the island of Iceland, which was sparsely populated and the only country already independent of fossil fuels.

Independence allowed many of the collectives worldwide to come together and put some physical distance between themselves and what the community calls the "GD"—the Great Deterioration of human and natural values that was occurring all around, driven by the endless pursuit of negative knowledge and corrupting technologies that were threatening the natural human way of life and devastating Mother Nature. My maternal grandparents were old-time Ecommunity members who, immediately after Separation, moved with their collective from Bangor, Wales, to our current location in southwestern Iceland. My father's parents moved from Plovdiv, Bulgaria, to another coastal collective just ten kilometers east of here.

I focus my attention back on the Dean, who now raises both arms in the air, palms facing up, as if balancing a huge bale of hay on his head. *I can see where this is going.* His sermons usually exude love and ecology, but when he feels that our lifestyle may be threatened…

"Did we ever ask for anything from the Outside?" The Dean pauses for effect then raises his voice, pushing his arms higher. "Well did we?"

A few people mutter "no."

"Did we ever ask for help? Even during years with poor crops, even on the verge of hunger! Did we ever ask for any assistance even then?"

Several people are shouting "no!"

"Were our parents and grandparents greedy in 2074? Did we ask for community independence in the Americas? In Australia?"

Here and there a member stands up.

"Or did we ask for Iceland? Iceland, which used to be so cold it was considered inhabitable by most—that is before the Outsiders recklessly started to heat our planet. You tell me: Were we unreasonable? Iceland, which shrinks each year as they maliciously melt the polar ice and raise the sea levels all around us. Iceland, which used to host several massive

9

glaciers, some of which are already a melted memory and one of which is collapsing above us as we speak.

"Even after we achieved independence on our own island, are the Outsiders trying to curb their selfish decadence and protect our fragile environment?"

"No!" I hesitate as more and more people around me get to their feet.

"Little Iceland, which used to support puffin birds, ferns, and orchids—now wiped out by the Outside's negligent plundering of nature."

I'm standing too.

"After another invasion of our harmonious life today, will we ever accept their infringement of our ecological ways?"

"No!"

"Will we?"

"*No!*"—I'm shouting in unison with the entire Collective.

"Will we accept their blind pursuit of what they call 'progress'?"

"No, no, no!"

"I would ask each and every one of you to intensify your relationship with Mother Nature at this difficult time. And you can be certain that I will bring today's events to the attention of the Council of Deans later this week and demand that the Ecommunity's ambassador to the Outside lodge a protest in the strongest possible terms."

He's allowed his tight grip on his audience to slip briefly. I shake my head almost imperceptibly. *An audience is like an ox—you don't let go for a second.* I take my seat and so do several others. *He's going to lodge a protest—he might as well put some sticky tape on the glacier.* It would be amusing if it wasn't tragic. Admittedly, I don't actually have a better idea, but it's the Dean's job to find a suitable response, not mine, and that wasn't it.

The Dean recovers quickly, waving his hands downward, gesturing for everyone to sit as if that is what he wanted. When everyone is seated, he continues.

"I do wish to end on a more positive note. One of our members is coming of age tomorrow. We all share in the excitement of a new adult among us. This is especially significant because she is the very first of our own Collective's second-generation members to come of age and one of the first on the entire island. It's a terrific milestone, reaching adulthood entirely within the Collective, from parents who were also born into the newly independent island. Each and every day, by continuing our way of life, we honor our grandparents whose struggle against the technological society around them, back before the Treaty of Separation, allows us to live with integrity and harmony as we do today. Fizz, please stand up."

I stand.

"We are all so proud of you. Throughout your teens you have worked equally hard in the library and on the farm. Fizz, you have always channeled your natural curiosity and intelligence to pursuing positive knowledge: languages, geography, ancient literature, nature, pure mathematics. You have well understood the dangers that caused our community to reject negative knowledge, and you've been careful never to pry outside the human realm, within, without, or wherefrom."

Secretly I am cringing. *If only he knew.* I try to stare at the Dean and avoid the two thousand eyes that are watching me bask in entirely undeserved praise. I notice the quick glare the Dean shoots at Bruno when he mentions "negative knowledge." Bruno is the last person from our Collective to have "pried" and taken a brief trip to the Outside on his eighteenth birthday almost three years ago.

The Dean continues.

"Fizz, I was shocked to hear that you were in personal danger today. But I am sure that the near miss will only make you stronger, as well as provide a graphic reminder to us all of the principles of our ecological ways and the inevitable tragedies caused by so-called 'science and technology' on the Outside. 'Science,' 'technology' and 'progress'—these are nothing but euphemisms for the greedy pillaging of nature."

People are nodding in agreement.

"Fizz, we all appreciate how you and your mother are steadfast members, always contributing to others despite the difficult circumstances of a single-parent family. As every one of us congratulates you, Fizz, on turning eighteen tomorrow, we look forward to your continued contribution as a full adult member. Perhaps it won't be too long before we can celebrate our first third-generation member!"

I almost lose my balance. The floor is showing no intention of swallowing me up, so I just stumble back into my chair. I catch the Dean's eye for a second, flashing him a scolding expression, but he seems rather pleased with his quip. He leads the entire community in singing "Happy birthday dear Fizz" as my friends around me smile and slap my back. Zopp's hand lingers on my shoulder. I catch Mom's eye across the room. She is beaming as her friends kiss her warmly.

As the entire Collective dribbles down the hill from the tavern, I seek out Bruno. Working in the mill, Bruno's of average height, blonde, with a thin face. He's named after one of the historic forefathers of pantheism—worship of nature—which is the Ecommunity's religion.

"Come on, Bruno," I intone, "now you *have* to tell me about your PCC."

The PCC—Personal Choice Clause—in the Treaty of Separation grants the legal right to every eighteen-year-old in Iceland to spend three weeks on the Outside and then make their own decision about returning to the Ecological Community in Iceland. For most, it's nothing more than a legal oddity, hardly discussed and only very rarely exercised. Two days past one's eighteenth birthday, the clause expires, and no one may leave. To be accurate, if someone tried to "desert" later, they would not be physically stopped, but they could never return to the Collective—not even for a family member's birthday.

"Why do you ask?" Bruno narrows his eyes.

I lower my voice further. "Why do you think, I'm turning eighteen tomorrow, aren't I?"

He looks alarmed. "You're not considering—?"

"*Nooo*... no, of course not... but after almost dying today, I mean, I just deserve to know what I'm missing. That's all. Go on, what was it like?"

"Sorry, Fizz."

"*Bruno.*"

"Look, did you see the Dean shooting me a dirty look today in front of everyone? Three years later! I had my little rebellion and I'm still struggling to put it behind me. Don't even think about it. Anyway Fizz, happy birthday." He touches my elbow awkwardly and walks off.

A few minutes later, back in my room, I'm driven to do something that I have managed to avoid for several months now. *Why would I do this now, a short time after that congratulatory speech and a day before an emotionally loaded visit?*

I don't stop.

Walking to one corner of the room, I roll back the coarse hand-woven rug with its shades of red and brown, and gently ease out one of the bricks from the floor, carefully avoiding making any noise. Reaching into the floor, I remove an item wrapped in a long stream of linen. I quickly and just as quietly return the brick and rug to their place. *Today of all days, I should just put it back.* But for some reason, I do not. I unwrap the cloth, exposing my secret little notebook. I hesitate.

Hello, little book. It's been a while. I thought of you today. If I'd been buried under a chunk of ice you would have stayed buried under this floor forever! That just wouldn't have been right.

Drawing a long breath, I open the notebook slowly and flick through the pages of unanswered questions penned in my own handwriting—pages of my "negative" curiosity that I cannot entirely subdue, but which I have at least confined to the leaves of this book, where they will not threaten anyone else. I skim through random questions that have popped into my mind. *How old is the world? What are materials actually made of?* Today I have vividly experienced the power of heat, so I write in one new question: *What is heat?*

I close the book and think about the Dean's warm congratulations. I can still see the pride radiating from my Mom's face. Other than her work managing the cowshed, Mom has dedicated her entire life to bringing me up on her own.

I look again at the book's cover. *What a fraud I am.*

I should be channeling my thinking into the realm of human experience: languages, ancient literature, geography. I know that the questions in my notebook are a slippery slope. A founding principle of the Ecommunity is: *Prying leads to meddling leads to destruction.* I can hear the Dean's words echoing in my head: *You're merely curious about energy, then you utilize energy, next you get drunk on energy to the point that you can't control your addiction, even when the planet is overheating. As sure as night follows day.*

The words of other commonly repeated sermon themes come flooding back: *Science leads to technology leads to degradation. If we want to reject technology and recover a natural, balanced way of life, then we must reject science too.* The types of questions I am asking, the fundamental questions that I believe are known on the Outside as "physics," are the most dangerous of all—formal models for natural processes designed to help man subjugate those processes, enslaving Mother Nature instead of revering her.

And yet, what harm is there in writing down the occasional query, strictly in private, just for myself? After all, we do honor privacy in the Collective. We're told that on the Outside, in contrast, microphones and video cameras proliferate like ants, constantly recording vast streams of private information from every street corner, office and home, on endless arrays of "computers." Here in the Collective I am able to write down some private thoughts—even negative ones—and keep them private.

I wrap up the little notebook and replace it carefully below the floor, rolling up the rug on top of it. *If I can't help being curious, channeling my questions into a private notebook is the way to go.* Checking once more that the hiding place is not evident, I head to the kitchen for dinner.

Mom has prepared *fjallagrasamjólk*, a recipe the Community adopted from old Icelandic tradition, probably because its main ingredient is the bountiful Icelandic moss. Although we are farmers, we prefer to gather naturally growing ingredients where available. Even before I take the first bite, the smell of the warm food triggers the emotional warmth and security of a favorite home-cooked dish. Every aspect of this dish is familiar. I know the exact ingredients: moss, milk, brown sugar, salt. I know exactly how and by whom those ingredients were grown and picked, how Mom cleaned and cooked them, and what smell, texture, and taste to expect. I savor the first spoonful.

Mom walks over and kisses me. "I was so proud of you today, Fizz." She sits across from me and I force a warm smile. I know that Mom is even more nervous about tomorrow's visit than I am. Neither one of us will say "PCC" out loud—it is anathema. So for the rest of supper we make small talk about the farm.

After dessert, I wash up and give Mom a hug. "I'm going to sleep outdoors tonight, Mom."

"That's not a good idea," she says loosening her grip a little.

"I'm an adult now."

"Not quite yet, but—okay." Mom holds me again. "Fizz, you're my entire life. If I ever lost you…." Finally she lets go. *I know exactly what she's saying; she knows that I know.*

I go to my room and put on some nightclothes and a thick sweater. As I leave the house carrying my pillow and quilt, Mom starts playing a melancholy tune, her ten fingers slowly caressing the length of her flute as she transcribes her mood into music. Mom's life ambition was to join the Ecommunity orchestra, traveling from collective to collective spreading the gift of music. Then she became a single parent and took a job in the cowshed instead.

I walk the short distance to a sand beach, the flute's notes fading, giving way to the sounds of the waves. The evening air is typically cool. Not as cold as it used to be, as my late grandparents used to tell me.

At the beach I kick off my sandals and lie down flat on my back in the sand. Here, at one with nature, I can collect my confused thoughts at the end of a fateful day and on the eve of another. As the last of the daylight fades into the western horizon, a full Moon rises in the east and stars appear.

Looking up, I observe the vast expanse of stars, sprinkled so densely right across the sky that they almost seem to form a dome. Serene, perhaps beautiful. *Well, as beautiful as a scattering of white dots can be.* It's a timeless view that can be seen in all countries and all eras. Although on the Outside, so they say, even the features of the night sky are dimmed by light pollution from excessive artificial lighting.

How many stars are there? I make a square with my thumbs and fore-fingers and count about a hundred stars in one patch of sky. If there are some twenty or thirty patches that size in the sky, I can estimate two or three thousand stars, presumably the same number again around the other side of Earth. A few thousand—like the membership of a cluster of small collectives—fewer than I thought. *But I shouldn't think about it.* The words of past sermons again reverberate in my mind: *Confine your curiosity to the human scale. Ask not without.* The Dean has warned us not to even question about things beyond the realm of human life. According to his sermons: *First we ask about space, then we want to travel there, next we weaponize space, and eventually we destroy space just as we destroyed Earth. As sure as winter follows summer. Stick to the human scale.*

Yet what harm is there in casually observing? I notice that one bright star overhead is distinguished by a tinge of reddish color; it seems unlike any other star. Another star over the western horizon is exceptionally bright, outshining every other. What are they? A jagged stripe of sky has a slightly white hue—what's that about? What about the sky itself—is the sky a thing? Is there anything holding the stars together, or is the black sky just the nothingness between the stars?

Why all these questions? What difference can it make to my life what a star is or why that star has color?

Yet the questions keep popping into my mind, quicker than I can dismiss them. *Tonight of all nights, I really must constrain my mind to the positive.* So I recite some scenes from the epic drama *The Iliad*, in the original Greek, of course. The fallibility of mankind. The wounded pride of one warrior, Achilles, the beauty of one princess, Helen, become driving forces in massive battles that destroy thousands of lives.

Inevitably, my thoughts return to tomorrow's meeting. Dad is a virtual stranger—we meet just once a year. He lives his life in a world so radically different from mine, a world that is overwhelmingly threatening and at the same time—*fascinating*. Dad has an unfair advantage in our annual chats: asymmetric knowledge. Dad spent his childhood in a nearby collective and understands my world, whereas I have had only remote glimpses into his through our brief annual conversations or from my grandparents, when they were alive and made the occasional conversational slip about the old life. But Dad and I have one connection that transcends familiarity or common lifestyles: blood. Father and daughter. A mysterious bond, awkward but unbreakable. As if one thin vein reaches all the way from my body in Iceland to Dad in Canada, allowing just a fraction of my blood and his to mix.

An hour or so has passed when an unexpected observation focuses my attention back to the sky. Although the pattern of the stars has not changed, the entire arrangement has visibly drifted west. A few stars have set behind the western horizon while others have risen from the east. The Moon is rising further too. *I've never noticed this westerly movement of the stars before.*

Maybe I can understand this for myself. The Sun circles us from east to west during the day—the stars and the Moon must be circling us from east to west too. *How do they do that? Why is everything circling us? What keeps them moving in a circle?* It occurs to me that there *must* be some sort of physical sky in order to carry all the stars westward while preserving their perfect formation—*a physical sky carrying the stars!* I smile for a second. But then I realize that deducing the existence of a physical sky is all very well, but my conclusion invites a string of new questions: *What is the nature of the sky? How far away is it?*

My better judgment notwithstanding, I get up and walk home, leaving the quilt on the sand. I tiptoe into the house and enter my bedroom, peel back the rug, lift the brick, and carefully retrieve my notebook. Replacing the brick and rug, I grab a pencil and hide the notebook and pencil under my nightclothes, sneaking back out to the beach. I have never taken the notebook out of my room before and never thought I would. But now, sleeping under the sky, I'm faced with too many questions and feel the urge to jot some of them down.

Here, under my quilt, in the moonlight, I start a new page and write "The sky." *What are stars? How do they all move together westward? Assuming there is a physical sky carrying the stars and Moon in circles, what is its nature? What is the reddish star? Why is another star exceptionally bright? What are those patterns on the Moon?*

I close my notebook so determinedly that it accidentally drops on the sand. Brushing off the sand I open it again and open a new line of questioning on a fresh page: *Why do things fall?*

I tuck the notebook deep into my pillowcase. *This stupid little book is going to get me into trouble one day.* I dread to think what would have happened if someone had walked by just now and asked me what I was writing. What did the Dean say publicly today? "Fizz, you have always channeled your natural curiosity and intelligence to pursuing positive knowledge." Am I a liar for not correcting him? As an "adult," aren't I too old to keep secret notebooks? I try to imagine myself at age fifty penning a question in my little illicit book. I shake my head. *What choice do I have?*

If my Mom ever took the rug in my room for a beating and noticed the loose brick, the Dean might be saying some other things to the entire Collective from the stage. I should just remember my questions, not write them down. *Better still, I should forget them.*

So why do I keep asking no-good questions? There are so many more constructive ways to use my mind. Is this just a juvenile phase that will pass? Yet can it really be harmful to ask questions?

Thinking about tomorrow, my stomach tightens. I had taken it for granted that the PCC would come and go. After all, I despise the technological world on the Outside. But what if I had died today, without ever once liberating my questions from the confines of this little book?

As I tuck my notebook into the pillow, I wonder if I had died today, whether Mom would have ever discovered it.

Eventually my arms and legs start to feel like they're sinking into the sand and the tightness in my stomach dissipates. The perpetual background sound of the waves gently hypnotizes me. *Hmm, what is sound anyway?* I nod off with the question echoing in my mind.

A mysterious cold fluid drips down the arch of my neck, tickling me, causing me to wake and snap up into a sitting position. *Idiot.* The mysterious liquid is just the high tide. *Did the water line really advance by that much?* I've been having nightmares and feel shaken but can't recall them. The Moon is now directly overhead—I must have slept a good while. I grab my quilt, now soggy down one side, and walk up a sand dune and settle down.

I retrieve the notebook from my pillow. The top edge is damp, the first question or two on each page smudged and illegible. As I flick through, my eyes become as damp as some of the pages. Rubbing my eyes, I console myself that questions, unlike oxen—and probably unlike humans—surely have some sort of spiritual existence that does not depend on their being physically inscribed in my book.

In the dry lower part of a fresh page I write one more question—*What causes tides?*—before settling back into an uneasy sleep.

I'm woken a few hours later by the gentle light of dawn. *What am I doing on a sand dune?* I shake the fog from my brain and remember the previous night. Then I remember my agenda for today and immediately try to forget it.

Happy birthday, Fizz. I sigh.

Dragging myself upright, I shake off the sand, swing my sandals over my shoulder, and walk along the beach, kicking sand with my bare feet as I go. In the twilight, the Moon is setting across the water in the west while the stars fade.

Looking at the barely visible pattern of stars around the Moon, I see a bright star almost touching the Moon. I'm sure it was not there when I went to sleep. *The Moon must have fallen just a tad behind as it travelled west with the stars, revealing a star that was hidden behind it last night.* Why would the stars and Moon move west in almost perfect unison, but not quite? What keeps the Moon moving around at a slightly independent speed to the stars? *Are they not attached to the same sky?*

And then the stars are gone. Well, almost. In the blue hue of the eastern sky, I notice a lone star that has risen ahead of the Sun, so brilliant that it is clearly visible against the early morning light. Soon it has faded too and a new day—a fateful day—has dawned.

The tide is out again, and I stroll along some smooth grey rocks which are perforated with tide pools. Carelessly kicking pebbles into the sea, I watch them promptly sink. I tear off a twig from a nearby shrub and throw it in after one of the stones. The twig floats. As the rocks slope down into another sandy beach, a pale green shore crab shuffles sideways in front of my bare feet, a little too close for comfort.

The rock underfoot gives way to wet sand. The rock was solid, indifferent to the pressure of my feet. Now a different sensation ensues, as the damp sand compresses just slightly under each step, leaving a trail of soggy footprints behind me. A gust of wind sends a wave collapsing, trapping some air under it, which quickly bubbles up.

The sun's rays start to warm me, and I let my feet slip into the water. The sea reacts quite differently to my feet—the salty water instantly reshapes itself perfectly around my legs with every step. My whole body feels comfortably chilled and my sleepy mind starts to roam freely. My imagination sees not just the water around my feet, but a vast invisible ocean with my tiny feet. I imagine myself lost in the depths of the water. Will I sink like the pebble or float like the twig? Sea creatures swim by and stare at me.

My daydream is interrupted by the sound of my sandals splashing into the water just behind me. I fish them out and continue my walk on the shore. By the time I get back to my quilt, my mind is feverishly trying to catalog all the different forms of materials I have encountered during my little walk—the rock, the sea, the wind. I guess everything I encountered was pretty much either rigid or liquid. But air feels different again, although other than being much lighter, I can't quite put my finger on whether it's fundamentally different to water. But assuming it is different, I can classify everything I encountered into solids, liquids and air—or more generally, I suppose, gases. I smile. The smile soon inverts into a frown as this little insight invites a flood of more questions. *How are gases different? What really distinguishes solids, liquids, and gases? Are there other forms of matter?*

Walking home, my emotions are in turmoil. It's as if the proliferating questions are swelling in my brain, building pressure. If I don't release some of my queries, the pressure will build up dangerously and burst. I imagine myself in the middle of a communal Tuesday evening, maybe a few months from now, maybe a couple of years—when suddenly one forbidden question too many pops into my head and simply refuses to be constrained. Something snaps and suddenly I'm shouting out forbidden questions uncontrollably in all directions in front of the entire Collective.

If I don't face the stigma of the PCC now, and free some questions, I may end up as a complete social outcast later.

I try to console myself that these questions are just a passing teenage phase. But what if they're not? *Perhaps I have an innate need to understand the world I live in, a need that the Ecommunity's discipline simply cannot overcome?* Even so, I must worry not only about the stigma, but more importantly about the real reasons behind the rules—can I investigate these physics issues without getting sucked into the evil temptations of technology?

I find myself chewing my nails like a little girl. As I turn eighteen, my entire future is eclipsed by these queries. If my need to understand cannot be suppressed, I will only get one chance in my entire life to openly explore the questions in my notebook.

That chance is today.

The Visit

There is a single place in Iceland, close to Reykjavík, where islanders may meet with Outsiders. It's like a contained area which accommodates the bare minimum of inevitable contact—in a controlled environment—between two discordant worlds. This Visitors' Center feels like the seam where oil and water cannot avoid just a little bit of contact even as they stubbornly refuse to mix.

For the third year now, Laozi and I travel the four-hour journey on our own. Laozi is an Iberian breed horse—Andalusian to be precise. With her rich, dark gray coat, long, shaggy mane, and bushy, drooping tail, Laozi cuts a majestic figure as she powers me through the Icelandic countryside. The ground is uneven most of the way, but covered with a beautiful thick layer of dark green moss as soft as a thin mattress, providing natural padding for Laozi's trot, which is almost silent.

Following the tradition we set last year, Laozi and I make a brief stop at the Blue Lagoon, the Community's most sacred landmark. The mysteriously colored water bestows plentiful physical heat, spiritual relaxation, and organic health and skin care upon visitors who partake of the ritual of man submerging in Mother Nature. Just the place to "charge my batteries," whatever that means, before meeting Dad.

The rising steam broadcasts the lagoon's location to anyone approaching within several kilometers. I dismount briefly to dip my hand in the hot, sky-blue water and scoop a handful of the indigenous white cream that accumulates on the black volcanic rock all around the lagoon. A few dozen islanders are immersed in the steaming pool, meditating. For several moments I simply enjoy the scene of hot springs stirring naturally with cold water and the contrast of black volcanic rock covered with white slimy minerals submerged in cyan water. I smear my face with the thick cream and soon Laozi and I ride off through the bumpy dark-green terrain, confident that there is no one around to comment on the creamy mask covering my face.

The rest of the journey provides plenty of time for contemplation. *How did I get to the point where I'm seriously contemplating the PCC?* I try to reconstruct blurred memories of my incessant questioning as a child and the vague, evasive answers I received, and later the admonitions.

One ten-minute meeting looms large amongst all my memories. I repeatedly replay my recollection of being pulled out of class at age ten,

21

in front of all my friends, in the middle of a school day, for an urgent meeting with the headmistress. I was surprised to find my Mom already there. I looked from my Mom to the headmistress and back.

The headmistress stared at me but didn't greet me; then she turned to my Mom. "I think Fizz is a little old to be asking negative questions in class, don't you?" the headmistress addressed my Mom as if I wasn't there. "I'm very open-minded, but this irreverence for Mother Nature could contaminate other children. I'm sure you appreciate that our little school has a reputation to safeguard—we've started attracting kids from neighboring collectives, but if they hear about this kind of behavior... I... well, I trust this will stop."

That was the day I opened my little science diary and shut my mouth.

Occasional showers do little to interrupt my urgent deliberations. I grab Laozi's damp mane. If I'm ever going to get a chance to uncork all my questions, it's right now. If I don't, I will have a lifetime of plowing fields to regret it. *To resent it.* But the price is communal disgrace, and the only place to ask my questions is in the same filthy Outside that almost caused my death yesterday.

Unless...

A single spacious meeting room contains a few dozen round wooden tables, spaced just sparsely enough to allow a private conversation in hushed tones. Apparently the visiting Outsiders have a landing pad for what my Dad calls PATs carefully hidden from view in some natural cove that I've never seen. If I understood it correctly, Outsiders use PATs— something like Personal Airborne Transporters—to carry them from the larger multi-passenger SITs to individual destinations. Outsiders arrive in the meeting room carrying no visible pieces of technology. Dad told me once that he has subcutaneous microchip implants and intracranial enhancement modules, but, provided nothing is visible, they are allowed into this room to visit first-degree relatives on their birthdays.

I'm sitting at one of the tables, fidgeting, trying to avoid eye contact with anyone around. It seems impolite to look at other islanders while they're holding often uncomfortable meetings with Outsider relatives, even if the other islanders in the room do share a birthday with me, and even if I do see most of them every year. Something about my education also makes me feel very uneasy about looking other Outsiders in the eye. So I sit and twiddle my thumbs.

The pair of red doors swing open under a sign that reads: "To the Outside—strictly no islanders (except registered PCCs)." My Dad strides into the room.

He's thirty-six—younger than any of my friends' dads—tall with straight dark hair and a well-proportioned face with sharp features. He is handsome, if just a little overweight. When people see me they always recognize my mother's fiery red hair and facial features, but those who knew my Dad recall his blue eyes. I rise to greet him, but he stands looking at me for some time from a slight distance before finally approaching.

"Eighteen, I just can't believe it," he says, shaking his head. "You look great, Fizz. But it's so uncanny."

"Hi Dad," I give him a cursory hug.

He holds both my shoulders at arm's length and stares at me. "Eighteen." He shakes his head. "You know your Mom was eighteen when we uh—well, the last time I saw her; the last time before I walked out of those doors." He nods at the red doors. "Seeing you at the same age brings back such vivid memories."

"You didn't even know she was pregnant," I say.

"Nope." He pulls me into another hug, grasping me more firmly this time, before letting go and taking a seat. At the table, Dad immediately reaches out to clasp one of my hands in both of his.

"So, Fizz, how is your Mom?"

"Fine."

"Is she happy?"

"I think she's... content."

"She still hasn't—"

"No, she never married."

"A partner? Long-term relationship?"

"No." I study the expression in his eyes for a second. "Not since you." I see him swallow. "How about you, Dad?"

"No change. Several relationships. Nothing very stable. But I'm not here to reminisce. How about my birthday girl? How do you find your life, Fizz? Have you found happiness in the Ecological Community? Does the lifestyle work for you?"

I laugh nervously. "Gosh, Dad, I haven't seen you in a year. How about we make small talk for a few minutes?"

Dad smirks. "Small talk? Sure. Care to chat about the latest immersive movie? The upcoming international elections? The controversy over mood-enhancing dietary supplements?"

"How about the weather?"

"How's the weather?"

I shrug. "You can see for yourself. Cool with intermittent showers."

"Yeah." He nods, looking around for a moment before turning back to me. "So Fizz, how do you find your life? Have you found happiness in the Ecommunity? Does the lifestyle work for you?" He grasps my hand more tightly.

I roll my eyes. "You go first. How's life on the Outside?"

Dad leans back. "It's hard to remember any other way, although coming here... Yes, there is still the odd occasion when I miss the kinship of the Collective and tranquility of life island-side. Some of the things they tell you about the Outside are true—the hectic pace of life, lack of privacy, degradation of the environment—but for me it's worked out well. To be honest I've actually become quite successful in the Outside world, as a physicist."

"And inventor, yup I know. Must have been hard catching up on the Outside education."

He shrugs. "Let's get a drink."

We walk over and pour ourselves a couple of glasses of strawberry juice. This provides an opportunity to talk about farming for a few minutes. As we talk, I keep noticing how Dad is focusing on each sip of juice like it's a gourmet wine, pausing to lick his lips then focusing on the next sip. He catches me staring at his lips, which are now lipstick red.

Dad smiles self-consciously. "Okay, okay, yes this juice does bring it all back. You know, when I walked out of those doors, all I had on me was a bag of clothes—which proved entirely useless on the Outside—and a flask of strawberry juice. Some do-gooders on the Outside greeted me with a welcome kit—appropriate clothes, some unfamiliar food, and a little cash. But I remember rationing that strawberry juice, savoring the taste of home for the better part of a week."

I glance at the red doors which I myself have the legal right to walk through only once in my life, today or tomorrow. Then I look again at Dad's scarlet lips. "You were incredibly brave, walking out of there into an unknown life, on your own, equipped with nothing more than strawberry juice."

"Brave? Oh, Fizz, no, no," he says, shaking his head. He takes another sip. "I mean, in all honesty, the last thing I was is brave. I—"

Dad halts his awkward self-effacing ramble as a couple of pale, bald children are wheeled through the visitors' room and toward a different pair of doors which are white painted with a large red cross—the small adjoining clinic where volunteers from the Outside offer emergency medical treatment to islanders. Our eyes follow the poorly-looking boys almost involuntarily.

"Hypocrites," I mutter to myself not intending to be heard.

"What? Those poor kids?" Dad stares at me.

Oops. "No, no, obviously not the *kids.*"

"But?" Dad is studying me.

"Well… my community. You know how we berate the infinite evils of technology. Oh yeah, except when our children are sick." I shake my head. "Sorry, Dad, I should restrain myself."

Dad opens his mouth. Then he shuts it again.

Neither of us is sure what to say next so we walk back to the table.

"So tell me, Dad." I lower my voice to a whisper once we are facing each other again. "The invention you mentioned to me last year—the HUT," I pronounce it simply "hut" as he did last year. Any progress?"

Dad's face lights up like a full moon. I regard his intense satisfaction—his expression broadcasts a feeling of hard work paid off, a dream come true. *A world changed.*

Dad leans over the table, closer to me. "I'm keeping it strictly secret," he whispers, still beaming as he glances around the room. "But I can't think of a safer place to discuss it than here. Yes, I did it. It actually works, Fizz! I have a fully functioning prototype."

I can't help but smile back at him. *Could I ever experience that kind of satisfaction as a farmer?* For two years he has talked about "some progress, looks promising, maybe one day." What a breakthrough his innovation must be, even in the Outside world which must be saturated with technological progress. I try to imagine the implications. "The potential must be staggering!"

Dad stares into my eyes for some seconds, his own blue eyes belying his intensity. "You know, Fizz, you may look like your Mom, but I see myself in your expression. I see curiosity. Passion. I well remember my own curiosity when I turned eighteen."

My body responds with instant goose pimples. *Everyone remembers your curiosity when you were eighteen—it's pretty much the last thing they remember about you.* I find myself rubbing my knees nervously under the table.

"There's something unsettling about meeting with you, Dad. You barely know me and yet… sometimes you get me in a way that no one else does. Perhaps not even myself." I hesitate for a moment. "Well, you can imagine the dilemmas that are tearing at me. Only you could really understand." I look straight at him silently pleading for him to guide me.

Dad closes his eyes tightly and turns his head slowly from side to side. "I can't advise you, Fizz. It has to come from you, from within." He opens his eyes and looks at me again. "But I have to be honest. The curiosity never goes away. Not for me, and not, I suspect, for you. You never really suppress it, you never confine it completely to what they like to call 'positive knowledge.'"

There it is—a conversation I played out in my mind a hundred times, and was determined, at least until yesterday, to never have, now out in the open. A dreaded dilemma is on the table—a genie that cannot be returned to its bottle.

I look around the room nervously: An Outsider mother embraces her islander son; an islander father huddles with his Outsider son. I wonder if any others are having a conversation as crucial as this.

"I just cannot get the PCC option out of my mind," I say. "But it's been three years since anyone in our Collective has taken the PCC. Since global warming started killing our crops it's seen more as a legal curiosity than a legitimate option. The last eighteen-year-old who took it came back to the Collective and refuses to say a word about his experience. And even so, there is more than a hint of scandal floating over him. No one has actually left us to the Outside, since… well, since you."

"Left *them*," Dad corrects me.

"Whatever."

He draws a deep breath and slowly exhales. "Fizz, spending time on the Outside may seem tempting, but it's so very confusing—I mean emotionally—to suddenly find yourself in *such* a different environment and then to face a cardinal choice between radically different lives. I would hate to see you go through the trauma of those weeks no matter which lifestyle you would choose at the end. You're still young and impressionable, still forming your personality." Dad pauses and pinches his chin. "Then again, from the little I know you, you'll never quite be comfortable in the Collective, and you'll always wonder if you should have looked beyond. There's got to be something to be said for seeing the choices for yourself—while you can. At least that way you won't regret never seeing the alternative."

I wave my finger. "No, no, Dad. I have *no* thoughts of leaving the Collective. Mom and my friends are my whole life, and anyway—don't take offense—I hate the idea of an industrialized world. So I don't have that choice to make. But what's eating away at me is the opportunity of taking the PCC option to spend a few days on the Outside, to give myself a chance to explore some nagging questions about the universe. I can't decide if that will help me—or muddle me more—and whether it's worth the confrontation."

There is a long silence. I can't read whether Dad is relieved or disappointed that I'm not considering life on the Outside.

"Of course, Fizz, I understand. If you take that option, I will support you the whole way. I'll teach you some physics, show you the Outside lifestyle, let you try out some technologies. Give you an experience to remember for the rest of your life."

I feel dizzy. It's almost cruel—*no, it's actually cruel*—to present an eighteen-year-old with such stark choices. I can overwhelm myself with new experiences and quench my thirst for knowledge for a few days, then I'll be thrown back into the Collective I love, but my already mind-numbing lifestyle will seem even duller.

If I were blind and offered vision for one week, would I take it?

Unfortunately, I cannot postpone the opportunity. I have to exercise my right to the PCC within two days of my eighteenth birthday. That is the small window of opportunity the law permits—no doubt a political compromise hammered out by some committee in the 2070s, entirely oblivious to the traumatic nature of the emotional trap they were setting for the likes of me.

"Dad, is it true what they say about physics—about understanding the universe—that 'prying' leads to meddling?"

"There's some truth in that, yes. But science leads to so many positive things as well. It's such a complex issue. If you take the PCC I can show you the other side of the coin, the constructive aspects that they don't tell you about around here."

A radical fantasy has been tantalizing the depths of my subconscious ever since last year's conversation with Dad, when he mentioned his HUT invention. Now that he has surprised me by telling me the invention is operational, the thought is actively nagging at me. But I'm not ready to discuss it just yet, not explicitly. Not today.

"Dad, can you stay on the island till tomorrow? Please."

"Why? Actually, Fizz, that might not be so convenient."

"*Please*, Dad. I don't ask much."

Dad clears his throat. "Of course. With pleasure." He scrutinizes my face. "So tomorrow are you going to come with me for a few days?"

"If I take the PCC, Dad, you can certainly help me, but not by spending the time with me. If I take this once-in-a-lifetime opportunity of just a few days to explore all the issues that have been bothering me, I need to go much deeper than getting a guided tour of modern technology in your PAT or some SIT or watching your immersive-reality movies or whatever other gadgets you have. I have to go so much deeper."

Dad checks into the special small inn sectioned for Outsiders upstairs from the Visitors' Center. It mostly serves diplomats and approved researchers. I have four hours' riding time home to make a final decision. Yet deep down, I've already decided. The pent up frustration of hiding my enquiries is overwhelming me. *I deserve a shot at happiness.* That outweighs the fear of confusing myself and embarrassing my mom and friends.

Summer days are long and it's still light when I arrive home in the late evening. The entire ride home I tried to convince myself— unsuccessfully—to drop the whole PCC idea. *I'm going to hurt Mom; Dad won't lend me the HUT; even if he does, it's too dangerous; the trip will stoke—not appease—my curiosity; it's not worth the social stigma.* None of the powerful arguments I made convinced me to go back to my farming routine tomorrow or to keep eighteen years of increasingly urgent enquiries swept, literally, under a rug.

Mom is waiting on the doorstep. She has never discussed the PCC with me, no doubt assuming—or at least hoping—that somehow I would completely ignore the option, like virtually all the teens do, choosing to sail into adulthood. *How on earth do I break this to her?*

As I dismount, we communicate facially, as only two people who have lived together for years can do. She sees the apprehension on my face and, I believe, instantly surmises that Dad and I didn't talk about cultivating berries. I watch as expressions of shock followed by sadness— not so much anger—cross her face, almost like she's already accepted the bitter truth before I've said a word.

Mom shakes her head weakly. "I don't want to hear it. Fizz, I told you—you are my whole life. I have nothing else."

"It's just a few days, Mom."

"That's just what your Dad said," Mom whispers, then turns and sulks into the house.

I cannot sleep with the heart-wrenching sound of Mom sobbing, just audible through the walls. I join her in her bed—I haven't done that for years. As we lie alongside each other, the only noises are my breathing and Mom's sniffles. Eventually tiredness catches up with us both.

In the morning, I find myself alone in Mom's bed. I head downstairs nervously, finding Mom with the Dean. *Why did she have to bring him?* Her eyes are red and swollen. The Dean looks at me blankly. If he's decided whether his approach will be sympathetic or confrontational, his face doesn't give it away. Mom slips out to leave me alone with the Dean, which is not a good sign.

Even sitting across the low wooden coffee table from me, the Dean sounds more like he's delivering a sermon than talking. "Why would you want to spend even one day in an evil place? Why subject yourself to temptations? Why confuse yourself? Why hurt your mother? What if other teens follow your example?"

As he talks, his eyebrows are always raised, creasing his forehead, his mouth stretched wide open, almost like a forced smile. His right hand shakes up and down as he talks, while his left hand rests on his knee. "Please Fizz. Don't spend even a day in the dammed Outside."

His favorite pun seems inappropriate for the circumstances— "dammed" is a reference to coastal cities on the Outside that have erected dams against rising sea levels.

I nod my head somberly as he preaches. "Dean, I despise technology as much as you do, but I just don't get the strict ban on science. Think about it this way: I love nature so much that I want to understand it better."

The eyebrows rise again and the mouth widens. "Understand nature? That's what you call it? *Understand?* You mean dissect. Subjugate."

"No. Just understand. Look, the ban on scientific questions has been driving me insane. Now I'm eighteen and I have a non-recurring opportunity to explore some stuff. Can't you respect my decision?"

"Fizz, I can't respect your decision because you are making a harmful mistake."

"Harmful... to the unity of the Collective you lead?"

The Dean stiffens his back. "No. Harmful to Fizz. I care about you. You don't know what it's like out there: the greed, the *violence*."

My face burns and before I can stop myself I'm addressing the Dean in an entirely irreverent tone. "And you, Dean, you know what it's like out there? For that matter, do you know what it's like feeling trapped over here as you become an adult? *Muzzled!* Being told to think about this but not about that...."

He sits silently, finally relaxing his eyebrows and cheeks, giving me time to regret my little outburst.

My Mom comes back in and takes her place on his side of the table.

"Fizz," she pleads, "why are you springing this on us now, in the last minute, when we don't have time to discuss it properly?"

"I didn't plan it like this, I swear; until yesterday, when I almost died without the chance to ask my questions."

"This is because of the glacier?" The Dean's face looks like it might rip. "Surely you can see Fizz, that's all the more reason to avoid the dangers of the Outside!"

"I don't even want to go to the Outside. It's just that I can't ask my questions anywhere on the island."

"You know what, Fizz," Mom raises her voice. "Ask. Whatever you like. Just ask."

The Dean hesitates. "Your Mom... is right. It's the lesser evil. Ask us anything."

"Seriously?" I glance nervously from the Dean to Mom and back for several seconds. "Okay then, tell me, um, what is heat? How did it cause the glacier to crumble? What are the stars?"

My questions hang heavily in the air.

"You really care about that, Fizz?" Mom asks.

Now I raise my voice. "Yes, I really do!"

There is another silence.

"We—" Mom starts.

"—don't know," the Dean finishes.

I look at them both again. "Yeah, I figured. Mom, Dean, this is something I need to do. Please accept that my mind is made up. I only get one shot at this experience, and I'm taking it. I'll see you in a few days."

Neither of them answers. The thick silence filling the room is as close to consent as I'm going to get.

I walk toward the stairs.

The Dean sways his head sadly. "Fizz, be really careful out there. Please."

I pack a small canvas backpack with some clothes. Then, on a whim, I find a flask and fill it with strawberry juice before saddling Laozi and riding off. Mom does not see me off at the door. I don't stop to say goodbye to any of my friends. I'm relieved to have made my decision and to have the confrontation with Mom behind me, but as we trot past Zopp's house and then away from the Collective, I start thinking about how others will react. Now I have four hours on horseback to sell myself the lie that things will be the same when I return. *Truthfully, things will be the same when I return as they would be if I'd contracted some extra-lethal strain of leprosy.* As the tavern disappears from view, I imagine myself at a communal evening, people choosing to stand in the aisles while the seats either side of me remain empty.

A hundred thoughts and emotions assail me from all directions, but I don't look back. I experience the strangest emotional cocktail of excitement, fear, and doubt. I do not feel regret.

"How did they take it?" Dad is not surprised to hear my decision.

I exhale. "Mom is heartbroken, but I think she'll get over it when I return. The Dean really laid into me, tried to make out he was worrying about me, but I suppose he just wants everything to be plain sailing in the Collective."

"Fizz, maybe you should give them some credit." Dad holds my elbow. "There are some real dangers out there. They may be genuinely worried for you."

The intensity in his voice causes me to pause. "Dad, you sound pained."

"No, I just—" He avoids my look. "Well, sure, I've experienced the bad as well as the good, you know."

I wait but he doesn't elaborate. "What happened?"

"No, nothing specific, I'm just saying..." Dad sees my raised eyebrow and stops. "Look, we were mugged. I'd only been Outside for two weeks."

"Mugged?"

"Someone tried to rob us. He was armed with a neutron beam. I didn't even know what that was at the time, but the way he pointed the thing at us as he demanded our money, I realized it was lethal."

I swallow. "Is that common?"

"It's not all that rare."

"You said 'us'?"

"Yes, Fizz, you know I didn't walk out of those red doors alone, as you seem to assume; one of my friends took the PCC with me."

"Oh. So what happened?"

"I gave the mugger the small amount of money I'd been given when I reached the Outside. My friend—he was the brave one—he struggled with the mugger."

"Good for him. And you?"

Dad bows his head. "I never talk about this. Maybe it's time I should own up to what happened, by way of full disclosure, before you make your decision." He looks up at me. "I ran. There was a sharp noise like I'd never heard before—now I know it was a neutron beam—and I heard my friend scream. I didn't even look back. By the time I composed myself and returned to the spot, they were both gone."

I stare at him for a moment. "Did—was—was your friend—"

"I didn't know what had happened to him. I assumed the worst. But several weeks later I found out that he had been injured and survived. He went straight back to Iceland."

I consider giving Dad the good squeeze he seems to need right now but... I don't.

"So, Fizz. If you're still sure about the PCC, if you've considered the physical and emotional risks, at least spend the time with me. Let me protect you."

"Dad, no, like I said, I love you, but it's really not my goal to spend these few days with you on the Outside. However, I would very much like your assistance. I want you to lend me... your HUT."

Dad's eyebrows flick up and he tries a nervous smile but soon gives up. "F—Fizz," he finally stutters, shaking his head, "it's a prototype. We've had some successful tests but it has no safety certifications yet. I can't risk using my own daughter as a guinea pig."

I was expecting some resistance. "Would you try it?"

"Well, yes, I would. I—uh—have."

"Then so will I," I say. "This isn't negotiable. I will not spend these precious days touring the Outside to see all the awful polluting gadgets you have today or to read about physics in a library. If I'm going to unwind years of pent-up curiosity within a few days, I want to see first-hand for myself how people deciphered the universe and how the Great Deterioration came about."

Dad stares at me. "Fizz, don't get me wrong, I admire your conviction—and your courage—but no, I can't allow it. The responsibility is too much for me to bear."

"Too much for you to bear? Coming as it does on top of all the other burdens of fatherhood?" I suppose I've been saving this jab for just the right moment.

Dad blushes. "But—" He seems to be grasping for the words but finally his shoulders slump. "You're right. Of course, it's not about me. You are old enough to decide to take a calculated risk. If I'm worried, that's my problem. But what about the emotional strain on you? Spending a few days on the Outside is traumatic enough. What makes you think you're mature enough to handle time travel?"

We debate my request for quite some time. Eventually Dad capitulates and walks off to his PAT, telling me it will take him a day to make arrangements.

In the office, I sign the PCC form. The clerk is an Outsider, as if to emphasize that the Ecommunity complies with the PCC, but does not sanction it—it is administered by the Outside. Sounding rather bored, she reminds me that I have twenty-one days to return to the Ecommunity. If I choose to leave, and want to maintain the right to visit relatives on their birthdays, I must sign a cessation form, also within twenty-one days; otherwise I will be classified as a deserter with no rights to visit Iceland ever again.

What do I do till tomorrow? By now the entire Collective will be gossiping about me and my "cowardly" decision. Going home is out. So instead, Laozi and I spend a day hiking around the hills and hot springs in the area and then I spend a sleepless night in a local bed and breakfast. *Could I really be time traveling tomorrow?*

I start considering the more practical questions. Will I be able to communicate with people in the past? Whom should I choose to converse with, and will they talk to me? What will I eat? *Should I have thought about all of that before signing up?* These same thoughts are still lapping around my mind for the thousandth time, no closer to being resolved, as I go back to the meeting room the next morning to wait for Dad's return.

It is evening again by the time Dad walks in looking tired and frazzled. He smiles at me, but it's a strained smile.

"You got it?"

He nods. "It wasn't easy. There were many arrangements to make in a short time. I don't work on my own you know. My colleagues and lab assistants didn't want me taking the machine away. But I explained to them that there was an opportunity for a test-journey without all the normal regulatory oversight of health and safety."

"Did they buy it?"

"Reluctantly. In the end there are some advantages to being the boss."

Dad uses his back to hold open wide one of the pair of swinging red doors. He stands there watching me. I hesitate for a second, then pull my shoulders back and through the doors I walk—attempt to stride actually—ignoring the stares that are doubtlessly following the rare site of a girl in communal clothes exiting through this doorway.

Dad leads me to the docking pad and I stop to get my first-ever view of Outside technology: a row of parked PATs. I stand mesmerized for a long while, and Dad waits, trying to be patient, but fidgeting, as I watch a take-off and a couple landings. The machines I have only ever heard whispers about are now flying around in front of my eyes. My nose turns itself up at my first ever whiff of what must be "pollution," but the rest of my senses are tantalized.

I stand like some demigod in an ancient myth, privy to the impossible sight of powerful dragon-like creatures flying in and out at great speeds, breathing fire in all directions, their metallic bodies gleaming, true to the original Greek etymology of "*drakon,*" which I know means something like "that which gleams." Only these dragons—more like Trojan horses—conceal within them visitors from an alien culture.

Standing here, I feel like I've been thrust into the myth halfway through act three, ignorant of what has transpired hitherto, unsure whether these technological dragons are allies or, as I have been told all my life, foes. I remind myself that the little fires they are breathing are somehow melting the ice that almost killed me. I have to battle the feeling that, by not drawing my sword and slaying every one of them, I am failing my own people and betraying myself. No matter, soon I will be elsewhere. *Indeed, elsewhen.*

Minutes fly past, and Dad finally clears his throat.

"Before we go, just tell me Dad, do you feel those terrific speeds when you're sitting inside those things?"

"You can feel the initial acceleration and any air turbulence—fluctuations of the wind. But when the journey is steady you don't feel a thing."

Dad leads me to a small shed. He looks at me and lets out a small laugh. "Funny how you're going to skip in one day from manual farming to time travel."

"Pleased you find it amusing. So your HUT time machine fits in that shed?"

He looks at me confused. "The time machine," Dad says, "*is* the hut."

I smile. So HUT isn't an acronym for Hypersonic Ultra-cool Time-machine or anything like that. Well, a small wooden hut could be a very practical timeless disguise. At this moment, I find some comfort in the knowledge that my home for the next few days of time travel at least looks somewhat familiar externally.

Dad and I step inside to find a small bedroom with a bed, clinically made up with white sheets, a metallic desk and chair, a shelf overhead, and one closet with a mirrored door.

There is a second closet—big enough to stand in, but most of its floor space is taken up with a sizeable rimmed bucket, some water at its bottom, attached firmly to the floor. There is also a small metal bowl attached to the wall and a small pipe arching above it.

I try to shift the bucket with my foot but it won't budge. "How can I use that bucket if it's attached to the floor?"

"That's the toilet."

"The—urrgh—I'm not going to excuse myself inside my own home."

"You'll get used to it. It flushes clean when you press this button." He demonstrates, and a flourish of swirling water materializes with a strange swooshing noise. "Also I think you'll enjoy having running water on demand." He turns a knob on the pipe and water flows into the bowl.

"Yeah, that's awesome!" I turn the knob on and off a few times; each time water flows into the bowl then somehow just disappears down it. "Where does the water come from?" I continue turning it on and off.

"Some is condensed from the air. Some is recycled and filtered from the drain. Fizz, you'll have plenty of time to play with that."

I close the knob and walk back into the room. The only other visible gadget in the hut is a small display screen over the desk. I run my finger over it. Can this little bedroom in a hut really time travel?

"So, how do I pilot this thing?"

"It's quite user-friendly," he says.

"User-friendly?"

"Straightforward. Voice activated. The onboard computer can take you to times and places based on your specific verbal description."

"You're kidding—I just say out loud where I want to go? That sounds way too easy."

"Hah, maybe for you. It took years of innovation and development and it takes considerable investment to organize each trip. The initial passage back in time is very complex to arrange. You can only travel back once. Then you can time-travel forwards a few times. The 3D printer concealed under the desk can create clothes and other simple items, pixel-by-pixel, based on your verbal description. It has a reasonable supply of raw material, but if it runs out, then recycle your items back in that little chute." Dad points under the desk.

I stare at him a little blankly but he continues.

"One rule, Fizz: Never share knowledge or items from one period of time with people in another period. That's pretty much all you need to know."

"Great. This might sound strange but I've been wondering, what happens if I meet myself in the past?"

I am totally unprepared for the reaction. Dad turns red and lifts up his hands. "Absolutely not, Fizz, that would be incredibly dangerous—unpredictable—look Fizz, maybe we should forget the whole thing, maybe—"

"Dad—"

"—perhaps you're not ready for this—the entire idea—"

"Dad! I get it. No problem." I grab his arm and look in his eyes. "It's ok. I won't even think of traveling to any time when I'm alive."

Dad gradually controls his breathing.

"And before I entrust my life to this thing," I say, "can you tell me how it works?"

"A combination of time dilation and wormholes."

"What?"

"Fizz, it's to do with the theory of relativity, but right now you know zero physics. Maybe when you get back. Oh, and Fizz, there's a small budget of tiny gold nuggets in the desk drawer."

I shake my head firmly. "Dad, I don't want any help. This is my own journey of discovery."

"You're... borrowing my time machine."

I cringe slightly. "True. Ok, I don't want any additional help."

"Don't worry, young woman. Arriving in the past, you're going to have enough challenges to tackle independently. I don't think a bit of pocket money constitutes interference. Before you go, I want you to read this." Awkwardly, he tries to hand me a letter.

I'm touched that he is so invested in this, and at such short notice, but I don't take the letter immediately. "Dad, if there's something you want to say to me, please say it in person."

He turns red again. "No, I—um—err—I kind of need you to read and sign this. It's a disclaimer. It says that you understand the risks and that I won't get—um—sued. Liability is a big issue on the Outside."

"You want a disclaimer from your own daughter?"

"I'm not asking for anything, Fizz. This was your idea."

I take the paper and sign it. *Well, I didn't want a big emotional goodbye and I'm not getting one.* Still, even through the embarrassing moment I can see the pride and apprehension in Dad's eyes. No doubt he can see the nervousness and anticipation in mine. I kiss his cheek, take a deep breath, and usher him out of the hut.

"See you in three or four days," I say.

"Break a leg," Dad says, as I close the door.

I sit on the bed and lay down my little backpack beside me. Ironically, this small windowless room is supposed to represent freedom—freedom from the constraints of time and space, freedom from the classification of knowledge into positive and negative. A safe place where I can ask what I want, where I want, and "when" I want. *A dangerous place that could get me killed or stranded in any number of ways.*

The curiosity that has so far been channeled into a small concealed notebook may now run wild for just a few days. A lifetime of questions must be carefully crammed into my short trip, giving my curiosity a lifetime of satisfaction.

Opening my backpack I take out the small flask of strawberry juice and take my first sip. I know where I want to start. The questions in my little notebook pretty much fall into two groups: about the night sky and about the nature of materials here on Earth. My goal is to get some insight into both realms.

I draw a deep breath.

"Computer, find me an early historical figure who systematically studied the physical world. I'm interested both in the matter down here and in the stuff we see up in the night sky."

With that simple instruction, I am supposedly untethered from my own space and from my own time and cast off into the unknowns of the past. I look around, waiting for some feeling of movement or shift in time. Everything remains the same. I sit on the bed a few moments longer, waiting, but all I feel is a sudden heaviness, an urge to lie down. *All the emotion of the last few days is catching up on me.* I lie back hoping to meditate about the upcoming experience, while the computer does its work. Before I know it, I'm drifting off to sleep.

Greek to Me

Day 1. 343BC. Greek Isle of Lesbos, the Aegean Sea.
Waking up the next morning, surprised by the realization that I have slept soundly, I squint at the small control panel in disbelief. Could the Collective girl from Iceland, who has never traveled further than a horse-ride from home, really be on a Greek island? *In the fourth century BC?* I stare at the screen for a good while and then, despite myself, burst into a nervous laugh. If it's true, the computer could hardly have chosen a more remote time and place to drop me in on my first day. *On the other hand, the level of technology in Ancient Greece should be just about comfortable for an Ecommunity girl.*

I recall protesting loudly, when I was twelve years old, that learning ancient Greek was completely pointless. I demanded to know what possible use I could ever have for the language. Whatever answers I received then were not nearly as convincing as the one now staring me in the face. In fact, after this I may owe a couple of apologies. Mind you, if the Ecommunity taught me languages to keep my mind off science, that strategy is backfiring pretty badly today.

Mom and the entire Collective are probably imagining me flying around the modern world in a PAT. Instead, I'm going to be walking around an ancient civilization practicing my Classics. *If that little screen is to be believed.*

I take a minute to stretch and orient myself, looking around my time machine hut.

I sit up quickly when I notice that the small shelf just under the ceiling over the bed is not empty. I finally stand up on the bed and see a box labeled *Open If Needed.* That's slightly annoying. *I told Dad, no help.* I push the box to the very back of the shelf, but do wonder what help Dad would *think* I need.

I open the front door, just a crack. Warm air flows in, carrying the familiar sounds and smells of the sea. I see sand, but no people. I stick my head out. Yes, a deserted beach. Finally I swing the door wide open and step outside. As the door closes behind me, I see a small sign, "Fizz's Place," affixed to the door. *Cute, Dad.*

The sun shines brightly from a cloudless sky as gentle, deep blue waves lap up against the sand. Inland, I see a mountain range carpeted with forest all the way up to a couple of fairly impressive peaks. *I'm not in*

Iceland. There aren't that many sandy beaches in Iceland, and the color of the sand seems distinct. The air feels too warm for an Icelandic morning. The small trees are unfamiliar with their dark, intricately twisted trunks surrounded by millions of tiny narrow long leaves—I have never seen such trees but they do resemble the trees in some ancient Greek etchings, and the color might certainly be described as olive green. In the Classics, I recall, Athena gifted the olive tree to the Athenians to provide wood, oil and food. *Perhaps this really is Greece!* Still there is nothing to confirm the time period.

I jog along the sand looking for some civilization. I need to find some people to orient myself.

After about ten minutes, I see a small coastal village in the distance. The village slopes up the hill away from the bay, giving me a clear view of many of the houses. I slow to a nervous stroll, watching boats swarm in the nearby sea. The boats have square sails familiar from illustrations of Greek dramas. I come to a standstill and stare, my lower jaw descending.

Tiny whitish dots shift around. *People.* Real Ancient Greek people. Suddenly I find myself breaking into a sweat and, without any conscious decision, I flee back to the hut. *Why am I panicking?* This is not like me! What am I actually afraid of? That the time machine could fail and leave me stranded alone in this place? That the people will lock me up as a curiosity—or worse, a threat?

When I get back to "Fizz's Place," I slam the door closed and collapse on the bed. I'm out of breath, hot, and damp. I would be so much happier if I could go home, just to check that I can actually get home, then come back here. But Dad was very clear, only one trip back in time. It's now or never. I look down—*oops*—I'm wearing Ecommunity clothes. *Oh great, my first step outside and I have already broken the only rule that Dad set for me.* I'm actually in ancient Greece—I'd better behave appropriately.

"Computer, print me a garment for this time and place."

The screen says **Printing Greek chiton with zoster belt**. To my amazement, a piece of woven woolen cloth emerges very slowly from under the desk. *Awesome.*

The chiton—which I think means a tunic—turns out to be nothing more than a large rectangle of cream-colored wool with a second strip of woolen material which must be the zoster belt, plus a couple of pins and a pair of sandals made of tooled leather.

No one has taught me how to wear a rectangle. *This constitutes clothing?* After trying a few variations I fold it in half, sideways. If I could somehow get in between the two halves, it might resemble a garment. Standing naked in front of the mirror, I hold the two top corners in one hand high over my head off to one side and somehow slither in between the two folds. Then I lower it to shoulder height and the bottom edge reaches my ankles. Awkwardly, I pin two corners over one shoulder and then the other and it seems to somehow stay up. I pin the open side as best I can and tie the "belt" around the waist.

The chiton now seems firmly in place although it droops fairly low at the front and back and is not exactly hermetically sealed down the entire length of my right side either. I worry for a second whether people might get a glimpse of my stomach through the slit on the side—I have a slight mark on my tummy which I'm self-conscious about.

Well, whomever I meet today, I'll never meet again, so here goes!

But I haven't gone. I feel horribly insecure, which is an unfamiliar emotion. *Am I dressed right? What will they make of my pale skin and flaming red hair? Even if I'm received well, how will I find the person who can help me understand the universe, and will he or she speak to me?* I feel somewhat annoyed with myself for feeling so insecure. Still, these are surely extenuating circumstances. Pacing the length of my room in the chiton, playing for time, my eye falls on the box again. *Open If Needed.* Why should I need it? Why did Dad presume? *Still, I could just take a peek…*

Placing the box on the desk, I reach in and remove a glass jar full of brown powder, probably soil. *What is that for?* Some kind of clue to guide my understanding of the universe? I remove a glass bottle full of water. *Is there some kind of hidden meaning? Is this some sort of apparatus?* I take out a paper bag. I look inside: completely empty. What am I supposed to learn from an empty paper bag?

Next I retrieve a metal container that feels surprisingly warm. How could it stay warm after a whole night? What do I do with a warm can? I stare at the four artifacts for a few moments. How are these supposed to help me when I discuss the universe with ancient Greeks?

There are some smaller items in the box: two stones—a rough black stone and a bright semi-transparent, orange-yellow stone that reminds me of my grandmother's broach—I think it is amber. I bring the amber to my eye. The world looks blurred and yellow through it. Finally, I find a small glass disk. Through the glass disk, the world appears distorted.

Whatever can it all mean? Perhaps my discussions today will shed light on these odd articles. Speaking of which...

Walking toward the village for a second time, my mind is full of doubts. Yesterday in Iceland, this seemed like a genius plan. Right now, I feel that I have upset my community and friends and taken a big risk, and I'm no longer clear on what I hope to achieve in return. I try to focus: *Discover the explanation of the universe that I've always been secretly curious about.*
Backup plan: *Try to enjoy the unique experience of popping into Ancient Greece.*

I walk into the village dressed in a folded sheet and am pleased to find everyone else in similar attire. This chiton must be very convenient at bedtime—you're already in a sheet, maybe you just unpin it for the night and pin it up again in the morning!

My skin is naturally very light, but fortunately it's tanned. I am relieved to spot at least one boy with red hair and freckles. People glance at me oddly, perhaps they can spot I'm foreign, but no one seems overly amused or threatened. Gradually I feel my shoulders relaxing.

People, mostly men, are walking to and from boats carrying bags of fish, pitchers of water, and other supplies. I stroll into the port, clearly the hub of village life, trying hard to act casual although I've never been more self-conscious. It doesn't help that just as I join the crowd a gust of wind bellows my flimsy chiton, uncovering my knees and threatening to expose me, but I reflexively drop my arms to my side so the awkward moment passes quickly.

Can I communicate? I choose a young man. "καλημέρα" I say in what I think is a passable classical Greek. Pronunciation is difficult as we mostly studied Greek in writing.

"Good morning," the man replies.

Kaliméra. I rehearse his pronunciation. He looks me up and down for a second and walks off. Not much help, but it's an achievement that I could greet this man who predates my time by more than two millennia.

An older woman is walking past a little slower, carrying a basket of olives.

"Good... morning" I try again. "Who... around... here... knows... about... physics?" I ask awkwardly. "I... mean... natural philosophy?"

She stands and appraises me for a good minute. Finally, the woman raises her arm unsteadily and silently points at a bearded man, who seems about forty years old, sitting on a chair at the edge of the port. Approaching, I see the man examining each fishing net as it's dragged into town and writing notes on a scroll. What would a harbormaster know about physics?

Sneaking up from behind, I'm surprised to find a pile of dead sea-creatures next to the man's chair—octopuses, catfish, all manner of bizarre aquatic animals other than fish—apparently donated by fisherman from their nets. Then I see that his notebook isn't cataloging fish hauls at all. He's meticulously sketching the animals with intense concentration. Even so, what help will I get from someone studying marine wildlife?

"Um, excuse me, kind sir." I clear my throat. "If I could trouble you for just a second, have you perhaps studied natural philosophy?"

He glares at me quizzically for several long seconds. "I believe that after twenty years in the Academy of Plato, student of Socrates, near Athens, you could say that I have studied natural philosophy. Who is asking?"

"My name is—err—Fizzos. Well sir, I hate to impose, but is there any chance we could have a brief discussion about the nature of the universe?"

He surveys me like I'm a statue. "Pardon me? Look here, I do not know who you are or from whence you hail, but these are not topics for commoners, much less for women."

"And why can't women study natural philosophy?" I snap before I can stop myself.

And he called me a commoner. I now notice that the man's chiton is distinguished by a lining of silver and gold threads. He wears rings on his fingers and wears his hair styled shorter than most. I recall from my literature studies that many societies, unlike my own, have classes often distinguished by dress. Perhaps next time I should be more specific in asking the computer for clothing appropriate to the educated classes.

He turns back to his sketching as he talks. "Well, there is no cause for umbrage. This is a natural consequence of women being a lower form of life than men." He picks up a damp leg from a dead octopus and examines one of the suckers closely.

Oh, fair enough then, it's because we're a lower life form—silly me for thinking I was being patronized unfairly. "So what gave us away—how did you discover that women are a lower form of life?"

"This is apparent from the fact that females are colder and have fewer teeth than males," he says matter-of-factly.

I bite my tongue with my "fewer teeth." *I cannot have travelled back twenty-four centuries just to hit a wall because of this guy's misogyny.* The philosopher is now delicately caressing the dead octopus' tentacle with a finger, writing notes with his other hand. *Think of something, Fizz.*

"Um, sir, your powers of exposition are famous. I have travelled from far, far away because word reached me that you are the only person in the world whose clarity of thought could make natural philosophy understandable even to a commoner girl."

He finally looks up from the sea creature. "Make natural philosophy understandable to a female?" He chuckles. "Well, that would certainly be a challenge."

"A challenge you would rise to?"

He shakes his head. "Not I." He pinches one of the octopus's eyes and starts to tug at it.

"Sir, perhaps a woman could at least understand the nature of matter. I noticed that the ground is firm," I stamp on the ground, by way of frustration as much as demonstration, "while the seawater is completely pliable. Air seems different again. Do these differences tell us anything about their composition?"

I listen to my own voice in amazement. I've blurted out a question I have never been allowed to ask out loud. What made it easier is that I am not sure anyone is actually listening or minded to answer. But soon the philosopher looks up quite suddenly—perhaps he is listening after all.

"That is perceptive. Well, two hundred years ago, Thales said that everything is made of one element: water. What would you think of that proposition?"

"I find it unlikely that air could be made out of water which is so much heavier than air."

"Yes," he strokes his beard, "I concur. Then Thales' student, Anaximenes, agreed with Thales that everything is made of one ingredient, but Anaximenes believed that the one ingredient of everything was in fact air. What say you?"

I think for a second. "I would wonder how air which cannot hold any shape would form the ground or your chair, which clearly have firm shapes."

"Indeed." The man strokes his beard again. "Much more recently, Democritus, who died when I was a child, came up with the more fanciful idea that matter is comprised of small particles called atoms which, he thought, come in different shapes and sizes. 'Atom' means indivisible, and Democritus conjectured that these indivisible particles are constantly in motion and that there is empty space between the atoms."

I consider this. "I would ask whether we can observe these atoms and whether atoms can explain the differences between solids and liquids. In any event sir, I travelled here to learn your own view of the nature of matter."

I catch myself glancing around to check that no one is listening. The words of so many sermons haunt me. *Ask not wherein. First you pry, then you modify…*

"I have discredited the idea of a single ingredient and the idea of atoms. Instead at the academy we concluded that matter is made of four elements: *Earth*, which is cold and dry, *Water*, which is cold and wet, *Air*, which is hot and wet, and *Fire*, which is hot and dry. They are naturally ordered in this way—*Earth* is the lowest striving to the center of the universe, above it *Water*, above it *Air*, above it *Fire*."

Air, Water, Earth. So simple and elegant. I'm almost minded to say "I called that." In honesty though, while I noticed the different nature of solids, liquids, and gases, I didn't have the thought that these must be the three fundamental ingredients of everything.

Fire is a little more confusing. What kind of element is that? Perhaps fire means *heat*. I guess heat behaves like an element contained within matter. It flows from a hotter object to a colder object. Heat can seep slowly into a glacier. So now I know, *heat is a fundamental element.*

Suddenly I recall the box. There was earth and water. And of course—the paper bag isn't an empty paper bag—it contains… air! And the warm can contained heat—fire! I smile at the thought of Dad leaving me clues for knowledge that I was able to gather by myself in one morning—from a student of Plato, no less.

My mind flashes back to the solid twig I saw floating on top of water in the sea two days ago and then to my solid chiton briefly lifting above the air this morning. This man spoke of the layering of air above water and water above earth. So what gives with the floating twig and rising chiton? I suppose these are just minor little exceptions to a profound theory.

But what could he mean about air being "hot and wet"? As I ponder this, I wipe a little perspiration from my forehead with my bare arms. I smile.

"Is something amusing?" he asks.

You'd have some other adjectives for air if you came from Iceland! "No, no," I say, "it's beautiful. I appreciate the elegance of explaining matter in terms of those four elements and I like the way you've ordered them. I hate to further call on your generosity but might you be able to tell me about the world," I hesitate to ask another forbidden question, "up there?"

He looks confused.

"I mean… the night sky?" I suppress the urge to verify that no one is listening.

"Young girl, just because you were able to understand a little about the nature of matter, you presume to comprehend the lofty and perfect celestial world? This was an interesting challenge but I should say it has gone far enough. Good day."

He tugs sharply on the slimy octopus eye which finally pops out in his hand.

"Sir, I come prepared for the discussion. Back in my distant island home I have observed the night sky." *For one night, but it's worth a try.*

He continues to slowly rotate and examine the eye for a second then suddenly seems to have a thought.

"This distant island you come from, might it be considerably north or south of here?"

"Yes, considerably north of here. And west."

"Aha. You say you have studied the night sky. Have you memorized the constellations?"

"What?"

"The patterns of the stars, girl, have you committed them to memory?"

"Some. Why?"

"I see. Then you may visit my home before sunset." He points at a building a hundred meters up the hill but offers no explanation for his change of heart.

"Oh. I thank you. What would you suggest doing before then?"

"Do as you please, stranger, go climb Mount Olympus," and he gestures at a peak behind us.

It's too hot for climbing, so I walk around for several hours, becoming acclimated to the unfamiliar surroundings, weather, and language while wondering what prompted the man to invite me to his home. From the small port, mud brick houses of various sizes sprawl uphill. Some have slanting tiled terracotta roofs supported by thick wooden beams; a couple of fancier buildings boast proud rows of marble columns. The narrow sloping streets offer an ever-present view of the port, bustling with simple sailboats. I chat with passing fisherman and housewives and learn the differences between an Athenian *obol*, *drachma*, and *mina*—currency that seems to be quite popular here in Lesbos. *In many ways this village is not that different from the fishing collectives in Iceland.* At midday I see the Sun almost directly overhead—I have never before in my life stood in the sunlight and not cast a shadow. By mid-afternoon my eyes are aching from the overload of sunlight reflecting in all directions off the white stone and marble.

The man's house seems grander than most. From the street, I enter his open-air courtyard with the rooms of the house surrounding me and wait in the doorway, nervous to call upon his somewhat reluctant hospitality. In the courtyard I note some pillars and a stone edifice that, judging by the bloodstains, might be an altar. One part of the floor boasts an intricate mosaic of colored stones. A small sign on the wall reads *Home of Aristotle*.

Aha, Aristotle! I don't know very much about him, but I've heard his name in my study of the Classics, two thousand four hundred years hence, so he must be quite an authority. *I've done well to find him.* As he appears in the courtyard I wonder if he has any inkling of how famous he is destined to become!

My host greets me with great warmth, taking my right hand and leading me in. I look at him—this can hardly be the same person who seemed distant and patronizing this morning in the port.

Aristotle brings a bucket and personally kneels in front of me and washes the dust off my feet as I look down at his head, confused. Soon I recall from *The Odyssey* how Telemachos unconditionally welcomes a total stranger, and how this proves to be very politic as the guest turns out to be the goddess Athena disguised as a mortal. Interrupting Aristotle's work earlier was unwelcome, but now that I am visiting his home, I realize to my delight that he is bound by *xenia:* ritualized friendship toward guests. For all Aristotle knows, I may be a disguised god dropping in to test his hospitality, and so the great Aristotle himself, taking no risks, is giving me a welcome fit for a deity! It doesn't seem appropriate to disillusion him by professing my mortality.

Of course, I still have no idea why he invited me here in the first place.

Once my feet are clean, Aristotle leads me past a kitchen where a couple of servants are working over a stone oven surrounded by earthenware and metal pots. My rumbling stomach catches a whiff of cooked fish. If my albeit limited insights into the local culture are correct, I may have a good shot at tasting that food. Through the kitchen I notice a small, dark storeroom. We walk past the kitchen and into a dining room surrounded with decorated tiles. Aristotle reclines on one couch and invites me to recline opposite him on another. We each have a small personal table in front of us which, as hoped, is soon laden with bread, wine, fish, and olives. Aristotle dips the bread in the wine and eats it. I do the same, finding the wine to be quite diluted but pleasant. He then eats the fish, breaking off a bite-full at a time with his hands; I follow suit. Like Telemachos, Aristotle is careful to prove his unconditional hospitality by asking me no personal questions during dinner—*fortunate given the circumstances*.

After this early dinner, Aristotle leads me into a living room that is lined with bookshelves—or, more accurately, scroll racks. As we walk toward the chairs, I take in the compact but varied library with its carefully labeled shelves: anatomy, astronomy and astrology, economics, embryology, geography, geology, logic, metaphysics, meteorology, natural philosophy, philosophy, and zoology. The philosophy shelf is divided into subsections for aesthetics, ethics, government, metaphysics, politics, psychology, rhetoric, and theology.

"Fizzos, I wish you to examine something." Aristotle brings to the table one large scroll and four huge tightly tied bundles of documents. I gawk at the heavy bundles. *He's going to make me read all of that Greek?*

I'm relieved when he spreads out the large scroll and uses the four bundles to weigh down the corners:

A chart of constellations

The chart on the large scroll is like nothing I've ever seen before—*like nothing I've been allowed to see before*. Every single star has been enumerated, creating an expert cartography of the night sky. Strangely though, lines connect the stars in groups rather like a child's draw-by-numbers.

"What are all these lines and borders?" I ask.

"Why, these are the constellations. We divide up the stars into forty-eight territories—imaginary territories—for convenience."

I look for a while. Each constellation has been given a creative label: Leo the lion, Ursa Major and Ursa Minor the bears, the mythological hunter Orion, Cancer the crab. In some cases there is a slight recognizable resemblance between the lines and the name, but thinking of the crab I saw on the beach the other day, I realize that most of the names of these constellations exhibit, to put it delicately, creativity.

"So did you guys get pretty bored in the long dark evenings at Plato's Academy?" I ask.

"I beg your pardon?"

"I mean did Plato lie on his back on the grass late at night, with his disciples lying around him, and say 'behold that group of white dots is a sea goat,' and then you said, 'no, no, my esteemed philosopher teacher, can you not see that those white dots are surely a virgin?'"

He stares right at me for a long moment. *Drat, I've blown this.* And before we've even started discussing the sky—me and my big mouth. Wasn't I taught how past societies had hierarchy, class, and personal distance? Aristotle and Plato are not local teachers or deans from neighboring Ecommunity collectives. I look at him and smile weakly. Aristotle continues to stare back at me.

Suddenly he bursts into a booming laugh, and I join in with great relief. *I made Aristotle laugh.* I can't imagine that many people have had such an opportunity.

Finally he looks serious again. "Well, the constellations give us a language. They are a convenient convention, like city names. Now I may tell you where the heavenly bodies are located in the sky. For example, 'the Moon is in Sagittarius.' And here is my question to you—think carefully before you answer: In your northern residence, did you observe any variance in the constellations?"

"My observations were—well—they took place during a different year," I say.

"That is of no consequence," he waves aside my comment. "The celestial world is eternal and never changing. Do you notice any discrepancy? Focus on the southern horizon." He points.

"I—I'm not sure I can recall in such detail."

He pulls back. "For how many years did you study the sky?"

"Not that many, err, years—oh, wait, yes, I do recognize a few of the patterns." I close my eyes and try to replay snippets of my star gazing two nights ago. "Yes, I don't think I saw this most southern constellation, I believe I recall the horizon cutting off this lion constellation here." I trace a line through a constellation labeled Libra with my finger.

Aristotle beams and slaps the table. "Just as I thought. You see, Fizzos, the ever-changing terrestrial world and the perfectly immutable celestial world may be quite separate but that does not preclude the one teaching us about the other."

"How so?"

"Sometimes things are not as they seem. For example, would you believe that the Earth we live on is round like a ball?"

"Yes, I knew that." The roundness of the Earth was considered within the realm of human scale back home.

"You do?" He seems taken aback. "And how do you know that?"

"I'm... not sure."

Aristotle walks to the window and points out. "Look at that distant sail on the horizon. Where is the boat's hull?"

It does seem reasonable to expect the sail to be attached to the body of a boat. "I see. It must be hidden behind the curvature of the Earth! Is this your own discovery, that the Earth is round?"

"Pythagoras speculated about a round Earth already two hundred years ago, but I have attempted to solidify the arguments. I think the reason why the Earth is round is because all earthly material is striving toward the center of the universe causing it to compact into a ball around the center of the universe."

"Striving toward the center of the universe?"

Aristotle picks up a pebble from the shelf and drops it to the stone floor by way of demonstration. It's interesting to hear him talk about not just *what* the world is but *why*. I think my own questions in my little notebook have been more about what, and maybe how, but not much why.

My eyes fixate on the pebble. Suddenly it strikes me that the pebble actually resembles the black stone in the box back in Fizz's Place. Perhaps the stone artifact represented this observation about matter striving downward!

"You see," Aristotle says, "all earthly matter wants to be at the center of the universe. Heavier items fall faster in proportion to their weight because they strive more strongly to be at the center. As everything pulls toward the center, you get a spherical Earth."

"You said that the celestial world can teach us about the terrestrial world?"

"So it can. By studying the sky I have found two further indicators that the Earth is round. When there is an eclipse of the Moon, we observe the Earth's round shadow crossing the face of the Moon."

I saw an eclipse of the Moon once, but have to admit to not noticing that detail. I sigh. *Even if I'm naturally observant, my skills of observation have been consistently discouraged, never honed.* At least, that's my excuse.

"And today I have found a second celestial indicator confirming the roundness of the Earth," Aristotle says.

"Today?"

"Yes, today. Thanks to you, Fizzos. It would seem that people from more northern lands cannot observe the most southern constellations. That indicates that the Earth is curved causing northern lands to have a different perspective on the sky."

"Cool!" He raises an eyebrow—I've translated the word literally. "I mean, I like that. You've used observation of the remote sky to deduce that the Earth under our feet is round. Could you tell me more about the celestial world?"

I cringe, but only slightly. It's amazing how in the space of one day I'm feeling a little more comfortable asking questions that are anathema back home. *What possible harm could come of such discussions?* I have to wonder, was there actually any good reason for the Ecommunity banning this type of enquiry?

Aristotle gathers his legs up onto the couch and reclines sideways propped on an elbow. I'm too excited to sit and remain standing over the scroll.

He looks at me, then speaks. "As you have brought me some important information, I am willing to attempt to explain the celestial world to you. The celestial world from the Moon outwards is perfect. The only shapes in the celestial world are precise spheres, and the only movement is perpetual movement in perfect circles. The Moon itself is slightly contaminated by its proximity to Earth which is why—although the

Moon is perfectly round and smooth—it does have dark patches as well as phases of darkness. The entire celestial world is made of a fifth element, the *aether*, also known as *quintessence* for fifth. In fact the celestial world, even the gaps between the heavenly bodies, are filled with quintessence. There can be no gaps in the aether, as nature abhors a vacuum. There must always be something. The celestial world of quintessence is incapable of change."

Nature abhors a vacuum. I smile as I recall sucking some air out of a bottle as a child, till my face went red. Then I ran around our yard with the bottle dangling from my lower lip, nature sucking my lip far down the bottle's neck, in an attempt, I suppose, to fill the abhorrent vacuum I had created.

So the universe up there is full, and it is incapable of change. *There's something comforting about a timeless night sky.* Glancing again at the chart, I think how the night sky is the only view that will be with me wherever and whenever my travels carry me. Then I think about the box. Could the aether be represented by the beautiful yellow amber in my box, which somehow resembles the Sun? That would explain all but one of the artifacts in the box.

"I noticed that the pattern of stars moves from east to west. I was wondering whether there must be some sort of physical sky to carry them."

"Indeed the stars rotate around us once a day on the outermost *celestial sphere*. The celestial sphere is perfectly round and transparent and carries the constellations."

Round and transparent... that reminds me of something—of course, the glass disk. *I've discovered all seven clues in the box!*

The Sun hangs low over the village, and through the windows I can see the port filling up with boats mooring for the night. I look back at Aristotle with growing wonderment. This philosopher is able to talk with authority on all aspects of natural philosophy. He has touched on all seven artifacts in the box, confirming that my mission to answer my questions about nature is nearing completion. However, some details of the sky are missing and time is short, I must make it to the hut before dark—not to mention that I believe it is my duty as a guest to avoid being a burden. If I can keep the conversation focused I could actually see myself gaining a complete description of the universe already on my first day!

"What about the rest of the sky?"

"Within the sphere of the constellations of stars, there are seven other spheres."

"Seven?"

"Yes, seven. They were enumerated by Plato and others before him. Is seven too many for you to comprehend?"

"*No.* It's just that I wasn't expecting that many. But please do tell me about them all."

"Very well." He takes a second smaller parchment out of one of the bundles and opens it on top of the first:

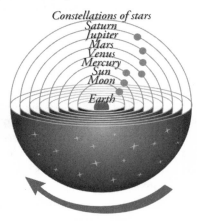

Celestial spheres

"The sphere of the constellations of the stars is outermost. Within it, from the outside in, are concentric spheres all circling the Earth carrying, respectively, the seven heavenly bodies of: Saturn, Jupiter, Mars, Venus, Mercury, the Sun, and the Moon."

Those names sound oddly familiar. *Ah yes—the seven days of the week in several European languages.*

"I saw a red dot in the sky?" I ask.

"That is Mars. It is associated with masculinity."

Red for blood, no doubt. *Men!*

"So why all these separate spheres? I get that the thousands of stars in the constellations form a sphere. But that little red dot called Mars has its own vast sphere extending all the way around Earth?"

"Firstly, what you refer to as a 'dot' is correctly termed a *planet*. Each of the planets circles us at a slightly different rate. All the spheres circle us approximately once in twenty-four hours but each sphere is just a little bit slower than the one outside it."

"So it's about movement!" I say. A tiny little dot like Mars has its own independent movement, circling the Earth in the sky at a slightly independent rate. To make circles around us it requires a celestial sphere to carry it, and if it has its own movement it must have its very own sphere. *I think I get it.*

"Allow me to write some brief notes about the spheres for you," Aristotle says picking up a quill and writing furiously.

I read over his shoulder as he writes. *Saturn—its rotation is almost perfectly aligned with the stars, but it falls behind by one rotation every thirty years.*

"What does Saturn look like?" I ask.

"Actually it looks rather like an ordinary star. You need to track Saturn carefully for months to even notice that it shifts its position against the constellations. It appears in the constellation of Libra this year."

Thinking for a second, it seems like quite a coincidence that Saturn tracks the stars' movement so perfectly, falling behind by just one lap in thirty years. *Strange.* Thirty years multiplied by three hundred and something days per year—that would be more than ten thousand days! So the stars go around us some ten thousand times before getting ahead of Saturn by just one rotation!

I imagine a circular athletics running track where several runners—the stars—set the pace and another runner follows their pace so perfectly that they complete ten thousand circuits before he falls behind by just one lap!

"Aristotle, sir, are you really saying that the stars and Saturn's speeds are so perfectly aligned that they rotate around us every day for thirty years before Saturn gets lapped once? Isn't that an incredible coincidence?"

"Hmm, that is an insightful thing to notice. I believe you are absorbing some of this. However, on another level it is an ignorant comment since you cannot argue with the facts. If you wish, you may track Saturn for yourself and see it rotating with the stars each night. After a couple of years you shall observe with your own eyes that Saturn has slipped back into the next constellation—Scorpio."

I glance outside—the sun has dipped lower. "I believe you. Please carry on."

Jupiter—appears as an extremely bright dot; falls behind the stars by just one cycle every twelve years or so.

Again, almost identical speeds. Jupiter must have been the exceptionally bright star I noticed the other evening. *No, not a star, a "planet"—carried by its own sphere.*

Mars—the reddish one, loses one cycle every year or so.

Venus—actually follows the Sun around; sometimes faster than the Sun sometimes slower. Appears very brightly either rising before the Sun as the morning star or setting after the Sun as the evening star. Associated with femininity.

That must have been the bright "star" I saw rising ahead of the Sun on the beach the other morning. Other times I have seen a bright star following the Sun down. So the "morning star" and "evening star" are one and the same—Venus. *But why is that particular white dot considered feminine?*

I look again at Aristotle's notes. The pattern seems to have been disrupted at this point. The spheres were supposed to get slower and slower from the outside in. But now Aristotle has written that Venus is not in fact consistently faster than the Sun. Rather, it tracks the Sun, sometimes getting ahead, sometimes behind.

Mercury—similar to Venus; tracks the Sun even more closely, appears very briefly just after sunset or just before sunrise.

Then the Sun—falls behind the stars by one constellation every month, by one cycle or lap, precisely once a year.

"Does the Sun travel through all the different constellations?" I ask.

"No, in fact all these heavenly bodies travel along one very specific ring in the sky, called the *ecliptic*, which crosses through just twelve constellations."

Aristotle sits up and peels back the chart of the planets and celestial spheres and refers back to the chart of the constellations—the outermost sphere. He traces his finger along a curved line in the chart through twelve constellations. I recognize those constellations from ancient literature—the zodiac. So all the heavenly bodies follow the "ecliptic" through the twelve constellations of the zodiac.

"This month the Sun is in *Gemini*," he says.

I look out of the window at the Sun, then turn back to Aristotle. "How can you even see which constellation the Sun is in?"

"Did you see the constellation of *Taurus* rising in the east just before the sunrise this morning? The Sun was rising in the next constellation east of Taurus. By the time the Sun rises, the stars are not visible, but we can confidently infer that the Sun was here." He plants his finger firmly on the star chart on the constellation just east of Taurus. "Gemini," he repeats.

"I'm a 'Gemini'," I say.

"Good for you. Happy birthday."

"What?"

Wait. The Sun moves through one constellation each month. I've been called a "Gemini," but I didn't even know what that meant—Gemini must be the constellation which the Sun appeared in front of when I was born.

"Thank you," I correct myself.

"Which year?" he asks.

"Two thou—" I stop. "You know, I'm a bit sensitive about my age."

A slight movement distracts me. I look out to the courtyard and see a little girl crouching just outside the doorway. She catches my eye and puts her finger to her lips, somewhat urgently. The girl seems to be carefully positioned to avoid Aristotle's line of sight. I wink at her; I have no idea if she understands the gesture although perhaps she does since I understood hers.

Aristotle pens a final line.

The Moon—it is the innermost sphere, closest to us, and the slowest, losing one cycle each month, completing just twenty-nine circuits around us while the stars complete thirty each month.

I smile. So that's why I could see the Moon's position shifting just slightly against the constellations in the course of one night.

I lean back, still smiling. Aristotle has given me a complete consistent picture of both the terrestrial and celestial worlds. In both cases he layered and ordered the contents. I try to check mentally whether any of the questions in my notebook are unanswered. I haven't touched on the third taboo pillar of negative knowledge, *Ask not wherefrom* and this time I barely hesitate before asking.

"One more question. How old are the stars? How old is the world?"

Aristotle frowns. "Young woman, perhaps you were not absorbing all that I said. The celestial world is never-changing. That implies that it has been around for an infinitely long time and will remain for infinitely long."

I glance at the young girl and make what I think passes as an "oops" face. She smiles.

"So Fizzos, I hope that the mission that brought you to my humble home has been successful?"

"Astoundingly successful. I would like to ask you something more personal about natural philosophy. Are you the first to explore natural philosophy? Do you see any dangers? Can these studies alter the way humans live?"

"I am not the first," Aristotle answers, "but I have aimed to build up a more complete understanding. My approach is a little different. Plato was very interested in forms or concepts. To him an actual physical dog was just the shadow of an idealized concept of 'dog.' I, on the other hand, am interested in studying the physical world directly. I am also most interested in the final cause—namely, why things happen. For example, the material cause of rain might be water, but the final cause of rain is providing water for crops."

He glances at me. I smile and encourage him to continue.

"Natural philosophy serves to allow a man to understand the world. It does not change the world in any way. As to danger, I am afraid that only a woman could see danger in a man seeking to understand the world he lives in."

If only you knew of my world. "Thank you," I say. "I am so grateful that you were able to condescend to explain these concepts to me."

"Well, Fizzos, I thank you. I was quite interested to see you grasp some of this. Perhaps it is fortunate your interest is in natural philosophy because you could not possibly understand the formal logic I am developing for reasoning about the world."

Getting up, my momentary annoyance is interrupted as I notice a small bust on the shelf labeled *Pythias*, apparently commemorating a grown woman with a striking resemblance to the girl lurking outside. He catches me looking at it sadly.

"Your wife?"

"Yes. I have a daughter named Pythias after her."

"Do you? Does she take an interest in philosophy?"

He snorts. "No, of course not."

"Who knows? Maybe she is more interested than you realize. In any event, I thank you for your kind hospitality and wish you and little Pythias a long and happy life in Lesbos."

"I accept the first part of your wishes, but Pythias and I are to depart shortly to Macedon."

"Macedon? May I inquire why?"

"I am to head up the Royal Academy and tutor the king's son, Alexander."

"Alexander? Oh—you mean Alexander the Great?"

"Pardon? Well I hope Alexander has a great future ahead of him. Before you go—it is traditional to give a gift to a visitor, and I hope you might accept the gift of a shared experience."

He walks to the doorway, and I notice little Pythias scampering away. I expect him to retrieve a souvenir, but instead he shutters the door securely. Confused, I watch as he walks to the window and shutters it too. It's completely dark inside. I freeze in panic. *What kind of experience does he have in mind?* I'm in a dark secluded room with Aristotle, a widower whom I have found to be a gracious host but not a great respecter of women. My pulse quickens. *Am I finding out about the real dangers of time travel in my first day in a strange land and place?*

"Um, Aristotle, sir—what are you doing?" I try to sound calm but my voice is quivering and my light-adapted eyes cannot discern his response in the dark.

"Relax." I can hear him walking about in the dark. Suddenly he removes a small plug which I had not noticed, revealing a small aperture in the wall. Light floods the dark room and a beautiful view of the outside village is projected through the small hole and onto the opposite white wall, where it appears clearly, albeit inverted.

Aristotle is just about visible now and I see him smiling with pride at what must be a breakthrough optical development. I let out a deep sigh, trying to put the brief terror behind me as I take in the entrancing effect. I see a beautiful upside-down image on the wall of the village's trees and buildings in the warm afternoon light, and I get a live view of people moving around, sails flapping, clouds drifting across the orange evening sky. All it takes is a pinhole and a darkened room. I recall the Latin term for a dark room—*camera obscura*—which I believe lent its name to the cameras used on the modern Outside. So even in this pre-technological age, Aristotle is experimenting with a simple technological effect.

"How does that happen?" I ask.

"Observe," he says passing me a diagram:

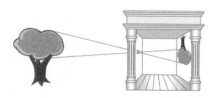

Image through pin-hole in Aristotle's dark room

I thank Aristotle profusely. As he walks me out to his courtyard, I recall that one detail in his elegant model of the celestial spheres seemed out of place.

"Just out of curiosity," I say, "I thought you said that, from the outside in, each sphere is slightly slower than the one beyond it. But then did you not say that Mercury and Venus are beyond the Sun but *not* consistently faster than the Sun—rather they track the Sun and stay close to it in the sky, sometimes speeding a little ahead, something falling behind?"

"True, very true. For this reason some of my colleagues at Plato's Academy argued that Mercury and Venus may be below or *within* the sphere of the Sun, not outside. It remains an unresolved issue. Anyway, goodbye young stranger." With that, he shows me out to the street where I thank him once more.

Elated, I float around the nearest corner and hover for a moment, reflecting on my dreamlike experience. *My mission is a resounding success.* My questions are answered; I do think my curiosity is appeased. One can see why Aristotle is one of those extremely rare people who will be remembered in the distant future. How impressive is his calm, orderly grasp of all aspects of nature. It was smart to ask the computer to meet one person who could advise me on both the night sky and the nature of matter. Now I'm walking out of a single encounter with a complete description of both aspects of the universe.

My self-congratulations are interrupted when a horse-drawn two-wheel chariot comes flying toward me, vibrating on the uneven street, forcing me to quickly back right up against the wall behind me.

Scurrying out of the village, I start walking "home." I may have satisfied my curiosity but there is something disturbing about today's revelations. Aristotle explained the world "without"—the celestial; the world "within"—the ingredients of matter; and "wherefrom"—the origins of the world. In one day I have learned about everything I have been taught not to think about. Is human lifestyle going to change tomorrow because of his thoughts? Based on my study of the classics, I know it's not. Is the Earth in peril because this man satisfied his inquisitiveness and thought about the nature of the universe? I cannot see how. Could it really be that all along these have been harmless legitimate questions—that it is, after all, only human nature to make such enquiries? Look how the legendary Aristotle and little me, in entirely different times and environments, pondered some of the very same issues. *Surely that proves that these questions are innate.*

In some ways, I feel like a person who has been unable to see their whole life only to discover one day that I'm not blind, just blindfolded.

As I finally see "Fizz's Place" in the distance, the Sun has set and the bright dot of Venus is following the Sun down in the western sky. Where are you, you "feminine" white dot? *What was that about Mercury and Venus sometimes appearing to be below, or slower than, rather than above, and faster than the Sun?* What about the solid twig floating in water or the chiton blowing up in the wind? I love having the world in ordered layers, but these few quirks—a couple of planets and a twig—are spoiling an otherwise perfect ordering.

In the hut I smile at the artifacts: the earth, water, air and "fire" as well as the symbols representing celestial spheres, quintessence and the pebble representing the tendency to fall to the center of the universe. *I'm way ahead of you, Dad.*

I fill a cheek with strawberry juice and as I swallow it, very slowly, I consider going home. But it's been just one day. I should take another day or two to resolve the remaining problems and check whether Aristotle's "prying" did lead to any "meddling." Today I achieved a fantastic overview. Tomorrow I can focus on filling in the remaining details.

"Computer. Take me to someone who can explain the positions of Mercury and Venus." I say to the control panel and collapse into bed. I won't object if my next stop is somewhere less "hot and wet."

Fizz's Place is humming and vibrating around me, but I rapidly fall into a deep sleep.

Center of the World

Day 2. Year 1514. Vistula Lagoon near Frombork, Prince-Bishopric of Warmia, Kingdom of Poland.

I awake and stretch—my bed feels a bit hard—where am I? Oh, that's right, I could be anywhere really. I glance at the panel and break into a grin. I'm in Poland in 1514!

Have I had to skip eighteen centuries forward to find someone who can explain the position of Mercury and Venus? Relative to yesterday, I'm almost home! But I can say nothing more than "good morning" in Polish. Maybe I can hire an interpreter.

"Computer, get me some clothes for Poland—clothes appropriate for an educated person."

Printing Hungarian-Polish szür.

I watch mesmerized as the 3D printer chugs away for a few minutes. *This printer thing is just awesome.*

"Computer, after this, while I'm out, print me a second pillow and a stuffed horse. Make it Andalusian."

The szür is shaped a bit like a coat—white with decorative, colored embroidery along the hems and sleeves. An oversized, rectangular collar hangs halfway down my back and then flows over the shoulders draping down as huge lapels either side of the front buttons. I regard myself in the mirror and chuckle. I've never worn anything nearly this ornate. *This is for dolls, not people.*

Stepping out, I see a blue lake—must be the Vistula Lagoon— extending to the horizon. The weather is overcast and bitterly cold. It's enough to make me miss Aristotle's "hot and wet" air. *I wonder if it's healthy, time traveling between such extremes of weather.* A town, presumably Frombork, looms a couple of kilometers inland from the lake.

Frombork is dominated by a magnificent, red brick Gothic building with a steep sloping red tile roof supporting spires in the center and on each corner. This could be a cathedral, although it's way grander than the old cathedral building in Reykjavík, which now houses the Council of Deans. The imposing building and its grounds are surrounded by a matching red brick castle wall. The cathedral seems out of proportion to the small town it serves.

Frombork Cathedral with Vistula Lagoon in background

"*Dzień dobry,*" I say to the first woman I meet upon reaching the town, a middle-aged woman dressed more simply than I am. My entire Polish vocabulary—two words—condenses into visible steam in the frigid air in front of my face. I wonder if I should offer to shake hands, but I have no idea if it's appropriate, and anyway there's just no way I'm taking my hands out of my pockets.

"*Guten morgen,*" she replies, almost spitting the words.

A stroke of luck—perhaps German is common or even preferred around here.

"Would you mind just telling me," I say in German, "how big is Jupiter?"

"Pardon? Of all the strange questions!" the woman looks at me cross-eyed and turns to leave.

"Don't worry. You don't need to answer," I smile at her. "I just love the fact that I can ask."

In a bakery, I point at some sort of bread-cake and, rather nervously, hand over a gold nugget. *This must be overpaying but it's all I have.*

The baker, beaming from ear to ear, retrieves a tool and files off some gold dust, then returns the remainder of the gold lump and cuts me a generous chunk of the bread-cake.

"You use gold to buy babka?" he asks, still smiling. "Come every day."

The "babka" is still warm, and I need it to thaw my hands as much as for nourishment.

Hanging around the bakery, I throw some more forbidden, negative questions at the baker and some fellow patrons. They think I'm crazy but take it in good humor. I did pay in bullion, after all.

I spend several hours walking through the town. The only technological progress I notice is a mechanical clock on a tower, which seems harmless, and a workshop for making rifles, which perhaps are not. I'm not even sure if there was anything in the natural philosophy of Aristotle that could have helped the invention of the clock and gun. The occasional horse-drawn carriage coasts by, and I notice the axles are only slightly improved compared to those of the Greek chariots I saw my yesterday. Clothes boast buttons; building techniques show marginal progress. But my overall impression is that, contrary to everything I've been taught, Aristotle's investigations—his "prying"—has not led to any significant meddling with nature for the better part of two thousand years.

In the early afternoon I decide to focus on my unanswered questions. I head toward the cathedral, clearly the epicenter of this place. Walking up the hill, a beautiful view of the lake and surrounding area opens in all directions.

Soon a man is walking beside me. "*Guten tag*," I say. "Tell me, please, is there an astronomer I can meet around here?"

"*Ja*, you must be looking for, Nicolaus, one of our canons. If I may say, do not waste your time."

"Why not?"

The man looks at me. "Already in his late thirties."

I shrug. "And?"

"I suspect he is a committed bachelor."

Fortunately my face is too cold to blush. "Um, no, I actually want to ask him about astronomy. Where can I find him?"

"Who are you? Where are you from?"

"I traveled here from a distant land because I heard there were some new ideas in astronomy coming out of Frombork."

The man stops walking. "Out of our little Frombork? I think not. I work for the Bishop and do not recall him approving any new astronomical ideas."

My step falters. This man must be some kind of clergyman and I think I've said the wrong thing. "Oh. Perhaps I'm mistaken."

"Most probably. Then again… Nicolaus is a strange fellow. This does not sound entirely unlike him. I shall accompany you to make certain.

He lives in one of the towers of the cathedral. Follow me. I am Krystian, how do you do."

"I am Fizz." I pronounce the two z's as in *pizza,* making my name sound like "fitz."

"Fizz? What kind of a name is that? Which date?"

"Pardon?"

"The saint you are named after, on which date is their feast?"

"Well Fizz isn't a saint's name per se, I suppose it's shortened—"

He holds up his hand. "Wait, do not tell me." Krystian continues walking, apparently in deep thought, then smiles. "Ah, diminutive perhaps for F. Pattrizzi? May 12?"

"Yes," I smile. "On the island I come from, we're lazy about long names. So what is this astronomer like?"

We walk through the imposing red castle walls and onto the damp lawns of the cathedral grounds. I'm forced to risk removing my hands from my pockets in order to service the greater need of rubbing my ears.

"Well, Nicolaus is well connected around these parts because, when he was orphaned of his father, he was brought up and sponsored by his uncle—the former Bishop, no less. His Excellency sponsored Nicolaus' education in law and medicine and personally arranged some engagements for him advising the government of Warmia on economic issues. But the Bishop died a couple of years ago, and now Nicolaus is rather a loner."

We pass the entrance of the main cathedral building, and I catch a glimpse of the seemingly endless checkered black-and-white floor with an intricate organ just visible at the far end under a decorated ceiling. A minute later, we enter a round tower, made of the same red bricks as everything else, and start to climb the tight spiral stone staircase.

We reach a landing several stories up. "Nicolaus!" Krystian pants. He knocks on a wooden door.

A man opens a face-sized hatch in the door and peers out at us. Nicolaus wears his wavy black hair long, completely covering his ears, with bangs on his forehead. The bottom half of his face is drawn narrow and supports a long, slightly downturned nose.

"You have a visitor. She says something about you having some new ideas—how come this stranger has heard about it before the Bishop and I have?"

Soon the three of us are sitting at Nicolaus' plain wood table.

"Actually," I explain, "I specifically wanted to ask you something about Aristotle's astronomy. Might you have some new insights into the orbits of Mercury and Venus?"

Nicolaus regards me suspiciously. "How would you know that?"

"Well you're famous—"

"Famous?" He narrows his eyes. "No, I have only ever discussed that with a few close friends."

Krystian is following our conversation with raised eyebrows.

"Oh—um, I think one of them told me that you *should* be famous—I can't remember who it was."

"So one of my so-called friends said you could have a good laugh by securing an audience with Nicolaus and his eccentric ideas, did they?"

"No, no, not at all, err, I think they said 'very intriguing' or something like that."

"Did they?"

"Yes. And I was wondering if you might wish to discuss the ideas once more."

"I think not."

Krystian stiffens. "I rather think you should." It sounds almost like an order.

Nicolaus all but rolls his eyes. "Very well."

"Just by way of background first," I say, "can you tell me, is Aristotle's natural philosophy still popular?"

"Is Aristotle's philosophy popular?" Krystian almost falls off his chair. "Have you even heard any alternative natural philosophy?"

"Well, no."

"Then I suppose it is popular," Krystian concludes more calmly, and—I have to say—quite reasonably.

"So how has natural philosophy changed in the eighteen hundred years since Aristotle?" I ask.

Nicolaus jumps in. "In the second century AD, the Egyptian-Greek-Roman astronomer Claudius Ptolemy added some details about the spheres to help accurately predict planetary positions. He finalized the constellations. Ptolemy put Mercury and Venus below the Sun, while Aristotle had them above the Sun, so Mercury and Venus continued to cause confusion. And, of course, the Church has revised the age of the universe from infinite to five and a half thousand years." He glances at Krystian. "Other than that, nothing has changed."

I shake my head in amazement. *Two millennia of thought summed up in a couple of sentences.*

"Okay," I say, "allow me just one more question before we talk astronomy. Have there been any recent changes in technology?"

"What?"

"Well, for example advances in machinery? Any new types of products?"

"There is Gutenberg, of course," Krystian says.

"Gutenberg?"

"Gutenberg's new printing press with its movable metal type is allowing books to be printed in a fraction of the time and cost. I can tell you, Miss Fizz, the world will never be the same again," Krystian sighs almost dreamily. "We are entering a whole new era of information. Soon a scholar will be able to write a book in Paris, three months later it will be at the censorship in Rome, and within six to nine months the clergy might be reading prints of the book in a library in Krakow or even in London. The implications are incredible. God's word will be spreading instantly."

"And," Nicolaus adds, "one Leonardo da Vinci invented the ball bearings that might make future carriages travel more smoothly."

"Da Vinci?" says Krystian. "Is he not the one who fantasized about some flying machine?" He spins his arms around his head like a windmill and they both smile.

Confusing. I noticed almost no technological changes, but these people consider changes like the printing press to be revolutionary. People—or at least one person—has already dreamt about a flying machine, which he has no possible method of constructing or powering. Are these the first seeds of future progress—and of future deterioration? Do they have any connection to natural philosophy? I remind myself that I came here with a specific question.

"So," I say, turning pointedly to Nicolaus, "what's your idea for resolving the issue of how Mercury and Venus always track the Sun instead of circling us independently like the other planets?"

"Is that," asks Nicolaus, "the only oddity in Aristotle's astronomy? What about the speeds of the heavenly bodies?"

I think for a second. "Oh yes! I did think it was kind of a coincidence, all the spheres rotating independently and yet all almost precisely once in twenty-four hours. But as Aristotle pointed out to me—I mean, I read that Aristotle pointed out that you can't argue with the facts."

"You can read?" Nicolaus narrows his eyes, then continues. "In any event, sometimes the facts are deceptive. I have a thought that the daily rotation of the heavenly bodies might not be as they seem, but I do not like discussing it much—"

"Not as they seem?" Krystian challenges. "We can see the rotations very clearly with our own eyes."

Nicolaus remains quiet.

"Please do explain, Nicolaus. I've come such a long way."

He hesitates. "All right. Stand up, both of you, and turn around on the spot, slowly."

Krystian folds his arms across his chest. "We are your visitors. I wish to hear your ideas and report to the Bishop. We did not come here to make fools of ourselves."

"Why not?" I say, shrugging. I turn to Krystian. "Come on, let's try it—for the sake of the completeness of your report."

Krystian and I both stand and slowly turn counter-clockwise on the spot, Krystian pulling an indignant face. While turning I get a good look at Nicolaus' spacious but austere single-room home; I see the dark wooden dining table with four dark chairs that we have been sitting on, and a slightly lower dark wood desk with three reddish wooden stools. There is one side unit, a wardrobe, and a small corner that might be described as a kitchenette. Some logs are smoldering in a fireplace. The windows are deeply inset into the thick tower walls.

"So what is the point of this humiliation?" Krystian asks.

"Look at the walls," Nicolaus says. "Imagine the flecks on the wall are the constellations. Try to forget the fact that you are rotating—how do the walls appear to you?"

I stop and clasp my hands together. "They appear to rotate clockwise!" I say.

Nicolaus smiles.

I look at him. *Could it really be true?* I must savor this moment—how often will an unexpected insight completely overturn my perspective of the world in which I live? I sat for hours watching the stars, planets and Moon stream gently across the sky the other night and it didn't once occur to me that it could be me who was rotating! *Neither, I suppose, did it occur to hundreds of generations since the ancient Greeks.* For Nicolaus and his age, the whole idea must be entirely radical.

"You cannot seriously be suggesting—" Krystian starts.

"Yes, I do think that our Earth might be rotating eastward completing a cycle every twenty-four hours, thereby creating the illusion that everything is rotating westward around us. Now keep turning there for one second..."

Krystian stops turning and stares at Nicolaus while I continue. As I rotate counter-clockwise, Nicolaus starts strolling very slowly around the outside of the room also counter-clockwise. "Now look," he says, "I am Saturn. I make a full rotation eastward once in thirty years, rather than westward once a day! I appear to be rotating westward daily with the stars but that is just an illusion caused by your own eastward rotation. And the reason why I appear to slip behind the stars by one lap every thirty years is because I am in fact orbiting slowly eastward in front of the stars, which are stationary."

Krystian looks apoplectic. "You are talking like a madman and in front of a foreign guest. The Earth is the stationary foundation of the universe. We are standing right here on the Earth and can feel for ourselves that it is quite still!"

"Well," says Nicolaus, "the Earth is large. Just like you cannot see its curvature, you would not necessarily feel turning around such a large gentle curve."

"What would even make you think such a thing?" Krystian's voice rises an octave.

"It is the principle of *Ockham's razor*," Nicolaus says, keeping his calm.

"Oak hams razor? It slashes common sense?"

"No... Ockham is the name of an English monk and logician, William of Ockham. Early 1300s. He said that the simplest idea is best. It may not be intuitive that the Earth under our feet is rotating but it is the simplest idea because it explains what we see by assuming only one daily rotation of the Earth instead of having to assume that eight spheres—the stars, Sun, Moon, and five planets—each rotate coincidentally at almost exactly the same speed of once in twenty-four hours. It is the more elegant configuration."

"And you are proposing," Krystian says, "that we are all living on an oversized spinning ball because you find that crazy idea somehow more *elegant?*"

I peek out of a window while Nicolaus pleads with Krystian to keep an open mind. *Why can't I think with that kind of creativity?* I scratch my neck. *Then again, why did no one else for eighteen centuries?* Some more mundane thoughts occur to me about food and drink. Either medieval

Polish culture has more lax rules of hospitality, or—and this seems somehow credible—Nicolaus disregards the relevant social conventions.

Up this tower we must be a few tens of meters from the ground, and from here I can overlook not only the green cathedral grounds but also beyond the castle walls to the town roofs and the lagoon. At the far end of the lake is more land.

"What's beyond the lake?" I attempt to interrupt a conversation that is going nowhere.

"That is the Vistula Spit," Krystian says. "It is a narrow finger of land eighty kilometers long and just one or two kilometers wide separating our fresh water Vistula Lagoon from the saltier Baltic Sea."

Having created a brief opening, I dive back into the conversation. "So what about Mercury and Venus?" I pointedly face Nicolaus. "Why do they always appear fairly close to the Sun's position in the sky?"

"Ah. This may sound strange." Nicolaus hesitates. "Or... impossible, but hear me out for a moment. What if Mercury and Venus are not circling the Earth at all, but are circling... the Sun? Would that not explain why they always appear proximate to the Sun in the sky?"

For a moment, Nicolaus' second bombshell hangs in the air as I absorb it, while Krystian stands still, dumbfounded.

"What?" Krystian finally screeches, clearly having recovered his power of speech. He shakes his head. "All the planets circle the center of the universe. They circle the Earth."

Nicolaus tilts his head. "Or so we thought. What if all the planets do circle the center of the universe but the Sun is the center of the universe, not the Earth?"

I clap both hands over my mouth. *Nicolaus is turning my universe inside out—again!*

Nicolaus smiles. There's something odd about his smile, especially in the face of obvious adversity.

Meanwhile, Krystian looks quite incredulous. "The Sun the center of the universe? And where are we?"

"I think the Earth is just one of the planets circling the Sun. I know, it sounds surprising, but please take a look."

"The Earth—a planet?" Krystian spits out the words.

"Let's give him a chance." I rest a hand on Krystian's shoulder, hoping to prevent him from physically pouncing on Nicolaus.

Nicolaus picks up a sheet of paper and grabs a quill. "My proposal is that the Sun is the center. In fact it is quite fitting; the lantern of the universe sits on its centric throne from where it can best illuminate the planets that surround it, which are, from the inside out"—he draws concentric circles on the paper—"Mercury, Venus, the Earth, Mars, Jupiter, Saturn, and the stars. This explains why Mercury and Venus always appear near the Sun in the sky: they are circling the Sun and are closer to the Sun than we are. Only the Moon is circling the Earth."

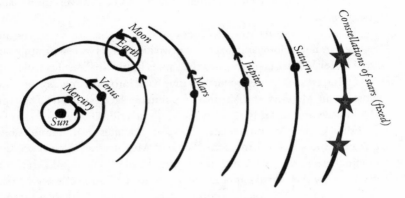

Sun-centric ("heliocentric") model

Nicolaus rests his quill. I notice the elegance of his model. Now all the vast spheres rotate slowly and calmly, and their speed is truly ordered, with Mercury having the quickest circuit and Saturn the slowest—no exceptions. The stars are not rotating at all. Yet in one respect this model is more complex. Not all the spheres are concentric anymore. The Moon is circling the Earth while the Earth circles the Sun—circles around circles.

"All this madness just to explain where two little white dots appear in the sky?" Krystian shakes his head and crosses his arms once again. "I think not."

"Every detail is important." Nicolaus raises his chin a little. "In fact, this ordering was already proposed once by the Ancient Greek Aristarchus but largely rejected and forgotten. We must face the facts with both eyes open. In addition to explaining Mercury and Venus, sometimes we see the other planets in a retrograde movement for just a few days— drifting west ahead of the constellations instead of always trailing to the east—that too is explained by the fact that we are observing the planets from the vantage point of a moving Earth." Nicolaus leans back. "Yes, this scheme right here is suggested by the systematic procession of events. It captures the harmony of the whole universe."

"Harmony?" Krystian sputters.

"Indeed, harmony," Nicolaus says firmly before Krystian can erupt into another tirade. "I am relieving all heavenly bodies of the onerous duty of completing vast circuits around us in near unison each and every day. I am allowing the stars to rest peacefully in their place and the planets to complete leisurely circuits over months and years while, instead, it is we who rotate once a day."

"This is truly amazing," I say. "It's shocking, but it explains all my open questions. Nicolaus, can you say, with authority, that this is the way the Universe is?" I point at the paper.

"After years of observations from the roof of this tower," Nicolaus says, "I believe I could say just that."

"What? This nonsense, authoritative?" Krystian is turning bright red. He suddenly turns to me, takes a deep breath, and smiles. In a calm, almost pleasant voice, albeit through clenched teeth, he says, "Fizz, you had best leave now. I do apologize for us subjecting you to this on your visit to Frombork. I would kindly ask that you repeat nothing that you have heard in this room." He then ushers me out the door.

I try to mutter "thanks" to Nicolaus over my shoulder as the door slams behind me. Despite the inauspicious end to the meeting, I'm thrilled to have a completely surprising solution to the problems that were bothering me as I left Aristotle's home. I decide to return to the hut and write some notes. I've had an interesting first-hand taste of history for a couple of days and I've come away with a good, consistent description of the universe. I can almost feel my curiosity being tamed. *I should return home—that would certainly be a relief for Mom.*

As I step away, some raised tones from the room behind draw me back and I linger, listening—well, eavesdropping—at the door.

"The old Bishop must be turning in his grave," Krystian is shouting. "He is probably reciting 'The world is firmly established, it cannot be moved,' or maybe 'The Sun rises and sets and returns to its place.'"

"Krystian, if you wish to distort scripture to your own purpose, to assail my work, while overlooking the evidence, then your rash judgment is of no importance to me. I believe the purpose of Holy Scripture is to guide us how to go to heaven, not how the heavens go!"

"Overlooking the evidence? What evidence? People spinning around like fools in a tower and some imaginary razor blade? You put such evidence ahead of the Book of Genesis, which has the Earth created first, and the Sun and the Moon around it? You deny that our Earth and the people on it are the *purpose* and therefore the epicenter of creation? Nicolaus, you are placing the entire Copernicus family at risk of excommunication."

I listen with increasing sadness. The man who a moment ago was waxing philosophical, confidently nullifying age-old wisdoms and proposing new world orders, is now reduced to defending himself like a naughty schoolboy, somehow hiding behind the implicit protection of his dead bishop uncle.

"Well," I hear Nicolaus saying, "perhaps Rome will not take my ideas too seriously."

"*That* is the first thing you have said with which I agree; I do not think anyone is going to take you seriously."

I leave quickly, feeling rather guilty for getting Nicolaus into hot water, and make my way down the tower into the freezing evening air. As the Sun sets in front of me, I spot a white dot suspended just over the horizon, visible before any other stars have come out, like a white spot on the sky's blue face. *Mercury*. Minutes later, it sets after the Sun.

Nicolaus' idea is beautiful in its simplicity. Mercury always appears near the Sun because it *is* near the Sun—circling the Sun at a much closer distance than we are.

Walking, I think about Nicolaus. *What a fascinating man.* He was initially nervous of Krystian, but once he got into the swing of his ideas, there was no stopping him. I think about his smile even under attack by Krystian. What did that smile mean? It could almost mean something like "I am cleverer than everybody else in all of history. Everyone up to now lived under an illusion that I have exposed. Every human being until this moment has always thought they were residing on the stationary foundation of the universe. Now I, Nicolaus Copernicus, having meticulously plotted the movements of the planets, have the confidence to stand up and say: Contrary to everything you believe, you are all living on a spinning ball that is flying in circles around the Sun!"

That's what Nicolaus meant by things being "not as they seem."

I wonder what will become of this Copernicus. By now Krystian has probably left. Is Nicolaus bravely planning the publication of his breakthrough, the greatest exposé ever of the world's secrets? Or will he retract further into his seemingly solitary life up some forgotten tower of a little known Polish cathedral. I smile wistfully to myself. *Will he too hide his ideas in some notebook under the floor?*

And for that matter was he really the first, or did other people before Nicolaus take similar maverick ideas with them to their graves?

Either way, perhaps I should try to learn not only from his conclusions but also from his process. How did Copernicus do it? I realize that he paid great attention to the anomalies in Aristotle's model and did not allow himself to "get used to" Mercury and Venus being a bit odd or to "learn to accept" the occasional retrograde movements of the planets, as everyone had before him.

After focusing on the anomalies, Nicolaus must have thought laterally about alternative models that could better explain the evidence. He seems to have had the amazing ability to suspend all normal human intuition— even the intuition that the Earth under our feet is stationary—when exploring alternative models.

Finally, Nicolaus placed much emphasis on the elegance of the model, choosing the theory with the fewest assumptions.

By the time I reach the edge of the town, my teeth are chattering. A roaring noise makes me jump. Thunder. *What is thunder?* Seconds later the skies open up and the rain buckets down. I break into a run, trying to avoid slipping in the mud. My limbs are numb, like my mind. Finally, I reach Fizz's Place soaked to the bone and shivering uncontrollably.

I'm going home.

By this time tomorrow, I will be back in the field, guiding a new ox, cursing the rising sea.

But… would it do any harm to make certain that I've fully answered my questions? After all, Krystian had a point about Copernicus presenting limited evidence. Will more solid evidence emerge to support Copernicus' radical new model? Why indeed don't we feel the Earth's movement? Even if the rotation is too gentle to detect, what about our planet whizzing around the Sun—shouldn't we sense that? And speaking of not experiencing things, now that Aristotle and Copernicus have studied the physical world, where are the negative repercussions? And when the Great Deterioration eventually occurs, will Aristotle and Copernicus have played any role in bringing it on? Will the conversations that seemed so innocuous yesterday and today somehow seem malignant in retrospect?

I'll invest one more day.

I print some dry nightclothes, but I'm still shivering. I think of home—of Mom, of Zopp, of my neighbors, even of the Dean. They're so far away in space and in time. I miss the familiarity of the Collective, of home-cooked food. I think of the warm feeling I had eating Mom's fjalla-grasamjólk the other evening. What a contrast to sixteenth-century Poland, where pretty much nothing is familiar.

How did my curiosity about some obscure questions like the nature of matter or the movement of stars drive me so far from home?

Then it hits me. This is exactly why it's so very natural to ask about the world—what's inside matter, what's beyond the Earth, where it all came from. We seek familiarity. If we can understand the world, we feel more comfortable in it. Physics offers us the promise of the comfort—even in strange times or places—of really understanding the night sky or the composition of matter, of really knowing them, what they are made of, where they came from, just as well as I know the harðifiskur fish dish we eat at home.

Suddenly, at this moment, I understand my own curiosity better than ever before. We are all born into a big, unmapped mysterious universe. What could be more human than wanting to know a little about our surroundings? Surely it is right to know something about the materials we interact with, the matter we ourselves are made of, and the sky we sleep under. *Isn't it?*

I stand up and pace. How can I encapsulate the familiarity I created with my surroundings yesterday and today? I think again of homemade food. Food products back home are sold with a simple hand-written label. Nobody wants to buy a pie without knowing just a bit about what's in it and where it came from. *A "product" as complex as our universe surely deserves—at the very least—a label!*

In fact, I wonder how I even step outside the door of my familiar little hut without the vaguest knowledge of the nature of the world I'm stepping into. *It's practically madness to live in a world we know virtually nothing about!*

I print myself a poster-size sheet of paper and a marker, sit down at the desk and, steadying my still-cold hand, I write:

<u>ROW Label</u>

Date of manufacture: 5–6,000 years ago

Contents: Sun at center surrounded by rotating spheres with Mercury, Venus, Earth (plus sphere of Moon around Earth), Mars, Jupiter, Saturn and finally the stationary sphere with constellations of stars (NB: The details of the stars are available in star charts).

Ingredients:

<u>For terrestrial world:</u> In ascending order: Earth, Water, Air, Fire. Terrestrial matter is naturally stationary and strives toward the center of the Earth.

<u>For celestial world:</u> Aether—immutable, eternally moving in perfect spheres and circles.

I fold the ROW Label in half and am about to fold it again when I stop myself. This little hut is a place of freedom. Unfolding the poster, I smile as I proudly hang it full-length on my door. Now I can look at it each time I step out from the intimacy of my hut into the more foreign *Rest of World*. Hopefully with this ROW label, the rest-of-world will seem a little more intimate—perhaps through physics I can strive to make the rest of the world almost as familiar as my room back home or as familiar as "Fizz's Place" is starting to become.

Sitting on the bed I look up and down the label. It reflects the considered worldview painstakingly debated and formed by famous philosophers and accepted universally over the centuries. Yet one key issue—the earth-centric versus the sun-centric model—is still a matter of fierce debate. I have limited evidence for Copernicus' model. So I add to the label:

Alternative Contents: Earth at center surrounded by rotating spheres with Moon, Mercury, Venus, Sun, Mars, Jupiter, Saturn, and finally the sphere of the constellations of stars.

Hmm, would I be willing to buy a cake if the supplier gave two completely different alternative labels for how it was made?

"Computer, take me to someone who found evidence to resolve the Aristotle v. Copernicus debate."

While the room around me starts to vibrate, my fingers are finally recovering their color, and I lie in bed gazing at the label.

My mission is clear. When I get home tomorrow evening to Iceland in 2110, and walk out of that door for the last time, the Rest of World I walk into will have a clear label allowing me to enter it with confidence.

Humming Collective songs, I soon start feeling heavy and nod off.

Father and Sun

Day 3. 1610. River Arno, Grand Duchy of Tuscany.

I jump out of bed, walk across to the desk, lean over it, and actually kiss the screen.

I laugh at myself. Waking up some one hundred years after I went to sleep, is almost mundane relative to the time jumps of the previous two nights. It's amazing how quickly I'm acclimating to a lifestyle of time travel. I print and climb into a long dress surrounded by many layers of flowing colored fabric, pin my hair up, and insert a jeweled comb into the bun. Around my neck, I fit a ruff—almost like a decorative dog collar.

I regard myself in the mirror. I'm even more dolled up than yesterday. *That's saying something.* Looking at myself, dressed to the nines, I smile with mild amusement but don't feel any particular pleasure. *If I've got to carry this dress all day, I should at least get a kick out of it.*

In my heavy gear, I step out of the hut, which once again seems to have picked itself a discreet location surrounded by trees, just outside a built-up area. I follow what must be the Arno—wider than any river I've seen before—a short way into a walled city. Now the waterway is flanked by a dense sequence of tasteful three- and four-story stone buildings, each plastered in its own unique shade of yellow, orange, or red.

I kick some pebbles as I go, feeling a little embarrassed for kissing the screen. I upset my Mom and friends in order to relieve my crushing curiosity, not to have fun century-hopping. *Then again, I never promised anyone that I wouldn't enjoy myself a bit.*

Gradually dusting off my Italian, I ask passers-by for a university or place of study, and am directed over the gentle arch of the *Ponte Vecchio*, or old bridge, one of two available bridges. From the bridge I have an excellent view of crates, laden with fruit and vegetables, being pulled up by rope from barges and delivered directly to the market stalls in the *Piazza Cairoli*, an open square which is nestled between the river and the warm colors of the plastered buildings.

After crossing, I follow the river's northern bank for about a minute, then turn right, away from the river into a narrow street, walking just a few tens of meters until I come across the entrance of the *Palazzo della Sapienza*, or Palace of Wisdom. This aptly named yellow-orange plastered structure is built around a courtyard with arcades surrounding the lower two levels and a simpler arch-less third story. The "palace" is the single-building campus of the *Stadium,* which—as far as I can tell—is equivalent to what the Outside would call a "university." At reception I enquire who might be interested in astronomy and am directed to a second-floor office.

The man who greets me is almost as dressed up as I am, with his decorated baggy sleeves, puffed knee-length breeches ending at his boots and, yes, he too has a ruff tied around his neck.

"*Buon giorno, signore.* Perhaps I can volunteer as your laboratory assistant today?" I say in my unpolished Italian to the man who looks like he's in his mid-forties. He wears his dark hair flicked back from above a forehead that is extended by a hairline receding at the temples. His frizzy reddish beard, with just a few telltale white hairs, is trimmed neatly to a square.

"As my what?"

"As your laboratory assistant," I say. "This is your laboratory isn't it? Don't you require a lab assistant?" Dad referred to his lab assistants, so it seems like the perfect cover.

"Do I?"

"I would think so. Don't other laboratories have an assistant?"

"Other laboratories?" He looks confused.

"Oh." I hesitate. "Well I would think that other *future* laboratories would be pleased to follow your example and employ lab assistants."

"And you think these laboratory assistants will be girls?"

"Yes. I do," I say with as much confidence as I can muster. *I actually have no idea if and when it will become common to employ women in labs.* "Especially if, like me, they come qualified with an understanding of natural philosophy. I have, um, studied both Aristotle and Copernicus."

He smirks.

"Oh. Is that funny?" I ask, cringing slightly. "Would you say that Aristotle's views are not as popular nowadays? Has Copernicus not been accepted?"

"Yes, yes, Aristotle is universally accepted. But—we shall see," he says. *We shall see what?*

"As for Copernicus and his heliocentric model," the man continues, "only a select few have championed his cause, such as Bruno here in Italy."

"You mean Giordano Bruno? One of the forefathers of pantheism?" *I know someone named after him.*

"Pantheism?!" The man squints at me.

"Worship of nature?"

He nods. "Well, that sounds like him."

"Great! So how's Bruno faring, championing heliocentrism?"

"Not so well." The man stares at me for a moment. "Bruno was burned at the stake in Rome on charges of heresy."

The words pierce my brain and I grab my head tightly with both hands almost dislodging the comb. Executed for supporting heliocentrism? Murdered! The one and only question open in my ROW label—in my understanding of the world—is whether the planets revolve around the Sun or around the Earth. Whether Earth is the foundation of the universe or just a planet.

Fizz, you idiot, you've traveled from a time when scientific questions attract a conference with the headmistress and social stigma, to a time period when scientific questions could get you burned at the stake in front of a cheering crowd!

"Err—oh," I eventually stutter, "Sorry. I was actually kind of, somehow, hoping you might be studying that very issue. But in the circumstances—"

He puts a hand on my shoulder and smiles warmly. "Do not be distressed, young woman. I am a devout Roman Catholic and am not afraid to study Copernicanism. When I find sufficient evidence, my Church will see the light."

I gaze at him. *What gallantry!* "In that case sir, it would be a great honor to volunteer as your lab assistant. My name is Fizzella." I'm careful to again pronounce the *zz* as in *pizza* and to emphasize and elongate and emphasize the *e*.

"But Fizzella, Pisa is no longer my main laboratory. In recent years I am but a visitor in my own hometown of Pisa."

"Really? The plaque on your door listed your title as Chief Mathematician of the University of Pisa and… err…"

"And Philosopher and Mathematician to the Grand Duke of Tuscany. Yes, I am Chief Mathematician of the University of Pisa. In Padua."

"Padua? Is that even in Tuscany?"

"I have promised to move to Florence."

"Well perfect, I'm only in Pisa for a short stay myself—I shall assist you while we are both here."

He kisses my hand. "We shall give your proposed arrangement a try. Call me Galileo."

I'm relieved—the full name on the door was Professor Galileo di Vincenzo Bonaiuti de' Galilei.

Galileo Galilei

We sit at his desk where I dodge some questions about where I came from and how I travelled to Italy. "So, Galileo, I may have missed some developments while I travelled. Have there been any interesting new inventions recently?"

"Ah yes, there is a report that one Sir John Harington has invented a water closet. Not that I expect that idea to spread outside England."

I have one of those now—they're more convenient than they sound.

Amazing. Another hundred years and the only noteworthy new invention is the toilet. Somehow that does not seem like a threat to the well-being of the planet.

"And would you say that anything has changed in natural philosophy since the ideas of Aristotle and Copernicus?"

"The ideas have not changed, but the world has changed since the so-called immutable skies sprouted the nova. Now the ideas must change too."

"The… nova?"

Galileo frowns. "*Signorina*, you represented that you are well-studied. The nova is the new bright star that suddenly appeared in 1604. There is no record of a new star ever materializing before. Of course, following Aristotle, almost all thinkers denied it could be a new star at all, since the celestial world is 'immutable'; most philosophers claim it must be some phenomenon within the Earth's atmosphere."

"And is it?"

"It was Johannes Kepler who pointed out that everyone sees the nova in the constellation of Ophiuchus!"

How does that answer my question? I play for time. "Kepler?"

"*Sì*. Johannes Kepler. German mathematician, astronomer, and astrologer at the University of Graz in Austria. Kepler's father, a mercenary, abandoned the family when Johannes was young and is presumed dead. His mother is a healer and herbalist and is fighting witchcraft charges. Despite his, let us say, inauspicious circumstances, Kepler developed a keen interest in astronomy, possibly sparked by his seeing a comet in the sky as a young child. Now he is continuing the work of his mentor, a well-known Dane named Tycho Brahe, in making extremely detailed records of planetary motions."

So why did Galileo tell me that everyone sees the nova in the same constellation? In my mind's eye I picture two people observing a nova that is close to Earth:

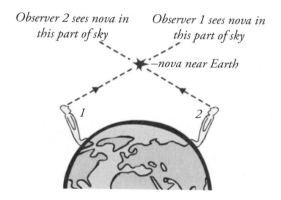

Observer 2 sees nova in this part of sky *Observer 1 sees nova in this part of sky*

—*nova near Earth*

Of course! If the nova were indeed nearby, people in different countries would see it from different perspectives and would have to observe it against the background of different constellations.

"Kepler has been quite provocative," Galileo smiles. "He is challenging all the Aristotelians, asking whether they are going to fit the facts to their philosophy or adapt their philosophy to fit the facts! His supporters—few as they are—are calling it Kepler's Nova."

Another attack on Aristotle's ideas—based on what Galileo's saying, possibly the first significant attack in the century since Copernicus. *It's almost as if humanity has been in mental hibernation for almost two thousand years.* Last century, Copernicus attempted to wake everyone up but roused only a select few, such as Bruno, Kepler, and this Galileo. Now they're trying to leverage the chance occurrence of an unexplained nova—which materialized literally out of the blue—as a wakeup call for everyone else.

But how far is Galileo willing to go?

The computer must have had some reason to bring me here. "So, Galileo, what evidence have you found for heliocentrism?"

"Tonight."

"Tonight?"

I have plans for tonight—namely time-travelling home, equipped with fresh evidence for the Sun being the center of the universe. Shall I spend another night in the past, my first night out in the ROW?

"Tonight. Well, maybe today as well. But not here. Perhaps by the sea."

"The sea? I was quite hoping... to spend the day in your lab?"

"Are you my assistant?"

"Well, yes—"

"Interested in heliocentrism?"

"Yes, but—"

"The sea."

"Okay. May I have a quick look around the lab first? *Per favore?*"

He looks at me for a second. "Of course. Follow me."

Galileo leads me from his study room into the actual lab. Thinking back to Aristotle and how he sat and discussed the world, I realize that Galileo's idea of performing experiments in a room must be entirely novel.

As we walk in, my head nearly hits a metal sphere dangling from the ceiling. The health and safety regulations for laboratories, which are—*will be?*—a burden to my Dad, must be quite lax at this time. I walk around the weight and give it a push. It duly sways back and forth.

"Do you see," Galileo asks, "what happens to the time between the pendulum's oscillations?"

I watch the fading to-and-fro motion for a while. The oscillations get smaller, but don't appear to get faster or slower. "Nothing?" I suggest.

"Correct, nothing. The time of the oscillation is the same regardless of the width—or *amplitude*—of the oscillation. Based on this discovery, I think pendula could be used for—"

"No, no," I make a pained face.

"No, what?"

"If you don't mind... let's just understand the world. Let's not worry about applications."

Ignoring his confused frown, I quickly move on to the next item on the desk, a brass plate finely engraved with hundreds of parallel grooves, a chisel resting across it. I pick up the chisel and casually scrape it gently across the grooved surface and hear a sound similar to a single musical note.

"Fizzella, do you mind, um..." Galileo starts holding out his hand forbiddingly.

I scrape the chisel faster over the grooves and get a higher pitch note. "What?"

"Well, oh, I suppose it is acceptable. I am just not used to people toying with my instruments. So what do you think is the physical difference between a high pitch sound and a low pitch sound?"

"I... never even thought to ask that."

"Two thousand years ago Pythagoras found that pairs of strings that have their lengths in simple ratios, like one to two, or two to three, make sounds that harmonize. But nobody ever knew what sound actually is. No one has ever understood the physical difference between sounds that we perceive as having high or low pitches. Can you suggest an explanation based on that little experiment you just performed?"

I brush the chisel back and forth a few more times along the hundreds of tiny grooves at varying speeds. "Well, the pitch seems to vary with the number of grooves scraped per second," I say. "Is pitch related to the number of, let's say, agitations of the air per second?"

"*Corretto*," he smiles. "I think sound is actually oscillations of the air—air physically edging back and forth many times a second. The pitch is just the *frequency*—that is, how many times per second the air is sloshing back and forth. For example, when you say one note is an *octave* higher than another, it simply means that the air is oscillating twice as many times per second—a frequency of two thousand air oscillations per second sounds one octave higher than a frequency of one thousand oscillations per second."

As I listen to Galileo's voice, I realize that he is the first person in history to understand how the miracle of hearing even occurs—oscillations of the air. His throat is agitating the air back and forth and that pattern of air oscillations is somehow relayed through the air to my ears. Galileo, with the simplest of apparatus—a chisel and fine grooves—has deciphered the phenomenon of sound. He explains it, though, with all the casualness usually summoned up for a comment on the weather.

I recall how Mom takes her flute up an octave by opening a hole which I guess effectively halves the flute's length—I wonder if I should ever tell my Mom what an octave actually means.

On the next desk along I find two lit lanterns, each with a shutter. I flick the shutter of one of them open and closed a few times. "What's this for?"

Galileo takes a sharp breath. "All right." He grabs the second lantern walking with it to the opposite side of the room. He faces me. "Open your shutter."

I face him and open the shutter on my lantern. Immediately as he sees me opening the shutter, he does the same.

"Did you notice any delay?" he asks me.

"Um, I don't think so—maybe just your reaction time."

Galileo shrugs. "I am trying to measure the speed of light but I have not managed to detect any delay, even when I try these lantern shutters between distant hills at night. Light is either extremely fast or perhaps instantaneous."

I pause and glance back at the instruments I've just seen, and survey all the devices yet to be explored. Exhaling slowly, my shoulders slump as fascination turns into desperation. Galileo is clearly throwing the world of natural philosophy into pandemonium, not to mention wreaking havoc with my own travel plans. Could it really be that the great Aristotle, or the nonconformist Copernicus, were barely scratching the surface of the natural world? They thought about a few big-picture issues and never worried themselves with the extensive small print of the universe, like the oscillations of a pendulum, the nature of sound, or the speed of light.

For two days I've been industriously and confidently climbing a hill toward the satisfaction that I know is waiting for me at its peak. On the third morning, as I reach the summit, what do I find? Galileo Galilei standing there casually, almost flippantly, pointing at a vast, rugged mountain range of new avenues of exploration and unanswered questions, stretching way beyond the horizon. *Where does curiosity end?*

"So, regarding the sea," Galileo brings me right back to the present.

I go to the sea every day; I only get to see Galileo's lab once in a life-time. "What's this?" I try, shaking a sealed glass tube of water containing many little weights—some floating, some resting at the bottom.

"Take it over there. Carefully." Galileo gestures at a small fireplace in the corner.

I delicately rest the glass tube near the heat of the fire. After a couple of minutes one of the floating weights sinks. Then another.

"I call it a *thermometer*," Galileo says. That must be from the Greek *thermo* for warm. "I designed it to measure temperature. As the water heats up, it expands and becomes less dense, whereupon some of the weights will be denser than the water and will sink, based on Archimedes' principle."

"Um, remind me, Archimedes' principle?"

He rolls his eyes. "An object submerged in water feels an up-thrust equal to the weight of the water it displaces. If the object is denser than the water then its weight is more than the weight of the water it displaces, so it sinks. Otherwise it floats."

"What's that got to do with temperature?"

"Warm water expands; it is less dense."

I think for a second. "Wow," I say, "you managed to arrange all those little weights so precisely that each one is as dense as a different tempera-ture of water?"

For a second I also wonder why water expands as it heats up.

"*Si,*" Galileo says. Then he chuckles. "Actually the same Archimedes' principle won me a public debate about why ice floats. The accepted Aristotelian view is that ice is heavier than water—"

"*Water* above *Earth.*"

"Right. So Aristotelians believe that ice is heavier than water and that it only floats because it cannot penetrate the surface of the water. For dramatic effect, I spent a few minutes of the debate amplifying my opponent's arguments, as if I supported them." Galileo smiles ruefully. "Then I pushed the ice to the bottom of the water tank and held it there. With my hand still on the ice, I took a moment to look around the audience and eye-ball my interlocutor."

I imagine this man standing there in front of an audience of Italian intellectuals, holding solid ice—*Earth*—just where it belongs, below *Water*, building drama for the moment when he releases it.

"Then I let go of the ice and it popped right back up over the water. The debate was over."

Nervously, I smile. *Was Aristotle wrong? What does that mean for the order or elements on my ROW label?*

"Anyhow, Fizzella, understand this about the thermometer. *Measuring* is central to what we do in this laboratory. We measure time, length, speed, and temperature. I am not satisfied with the Greeks' qualitative descriptions of the world. I am looking to measure phenomena and build a *quantitative* model."

I'm not actually sure what he means, but it sounds like some kind of radical rethink of the very goals of natural philosophy. I've been in the job for less than an hour, and don't feel I can push my luck any further in asking him to explain himself. I certainly don't want to risk getting fired before I've even explored the question that brought me here—evidence for heliocentrism.

But I'm fascinated—and apprehensive—to understand what is driving him to this fresh thinking. What sparked the beginning of science, the beginning of the process that the Ecommunity considers to be so destructive? What drove this man, in this lab, to germinate the seeds of "negative knowledge"?

"So, Galileo, if I may ask, what gives you the confidence to challenge Greek philosophy that has stood up to almost two thousand years of scrutiny?"

"Here, take a look." He hands me a pebble and a rock. The pebble is light, the rock obviously much heavier.

I regard them. "Err... the rock is the Greeks," I try, "the Goliath—substantial, solid, but unwieldy—the pebble is you, Professor Galilei, the David—light-weight but nimble and fresh in your thoughts?"

"*Pah,*" he almost spits. Galileo takes the stones back from me. He climbs up to stand on a chair, apparently unaware of how un-professor-like he appears. He holds out the pebble in one arm and the rock in another. "So, which will land first?" he asks.

"The rock," I say, resisting the temptation to add "duh."

Galileo drops them both and they hit the floor simultaneously.

"Um, Galileo... how did you do that?" I'm not easily fooled and my mind is racing. Perhaps he gave the pebble a flick of the wrist to compensate for its lighter weight? Did I not notice him releasing the pebble a little earlier or maybe from slightly lower?

"Try it," he says.

I pick up the two stones and climb on the chair. I drop them, taking care to do so at the same moment from identical heights. The pebble and rock descend away from my hands and hit the floor in perfect unison, the single thump reverberating through my mind. *How could it be? Aristotle told me heavier things fall faster. I know that heavier things fall faster.*

I'm frowning. Galileo is smiling. I've seen that smile before! "Fizzella, stop thinking so hard. That is just how the world is; heavy things and light things fall at the same rate. In a vacuum the rate is identical. Even in air, the speeds are virtually the same, regardless of weight, except at high speeds or for very light, wide items like a feather or paper which are influenced by the drag of the air. But fundamentally, air resistance aside, the speed of falling objects does not depend at all on their weight."

"But Aristotle said that the speed of falling is *proportional* to the weight—this rock should be falling ten or twenty times faster than the pebble!"

"It sounds right, does it—that the speed is proportional to the weight?"

"Yes," I say.

"And yet it is utter nonsense."

I'm amazed at his caustic irreverence toward the dominant intellectual authority of the last nineteen centuries.

"Galileo, Aristotle explained philosophically *why* heavy objects pull more to the center of the Earth. They strive to be at the center of the universe."

"You know, Fizzella, I am not too worried about the philosophy of *why*. I certainly want to describe the *what*—the facts—accurately. If I can fathom the *how*, all the better. By the way, if you are going to work here, never forget that the center of the Earth is not, after all, the center of the universe."

"Oh right, sorry."

"Now never forget this: We seek evidence, not intuition. At times intuition can guide us and we back it up with evidence; at times it can misguide us. But good intuition depends on having the right perspective on the issue."

"How can intuition both guide and misguide us?"

"It was intuitive to you that a stone that is twice as big falls twice as fast, yes?" Galileo scrunches his short beard.

"Yeah, I admit that felt right."

"Now think of it a different way. If two stones were falling, side by side, and they happened to join together while they fell, do you think—

intuitively—that they would suddenly double the speed of their fall just because they were joined, one to the other?"

"Err… no… when you put it like that, why should they?" I adjust the comb in my hair bun. "So, Galileo, are you telling me that pretty much everyone, throughout human history, has thought that heavy things fall faster, and no one throughout the eons, until now, has ever said 'let's stand on a chair and drop some stuff'?"

"Welcome to my lab," Galileo grins.

I take a moment longer to glance around at the apparatus and notebooks. This is way beyond any kind of curiosity I ever had. *This is more like a torture chamber for the universe—subjecting the physical world to a battery of tests never before attempted—forcing Mother Nature to reveal her deep, long-kept secrets.*

"So, Galileo, if you're into measuring stuff, how about today we measure the Earth's spinning or the Earth's movement around the Sun and finally vindicate Copernicus?"

"Regarding that. Time to visit the sea."

"No, no, my point was, don't you have some brilliant experiment to do here in your lab?"

"The sea."

My face drops. "We can measure the subtleties of sound and temperature in this room but we can't measure the powerful spinning of our planet?"

"All right, look. The Earth must be moving some thirty kilometers per second in order to orbit the Sun in a year. But every experiment that I have tried to detect or measure that incredibly fast movement has, well, failed. So, no, I have no brilliant experiment to measure it in the laboratory. So today we will gather data about the tide levels. The sea is ten kilometers down the river. We shall each polish a lens as well." Galileo picks up two glass lenses, which seem well shaped but a little rough, and two polishing cloths, and he hands me one lens and one cloth. "I will polish this other one. Report back at sunset."

"Report back? You're… not coming with me?"

"No."

"Ten kilometers! In this?" I look down at my clothing. *I'm used to walking long distances, but really!*

"I told you I did not think this was a job for woman, but, no, you insisted—"

"Okay, okay, consider me gone. What exciting experiments are you going to be doing while I march to the sea and sit watching the tide?"

"Now that I have a laboratory assistant, I rather think I will spend a bit of time today with Marina and the kids before working again tonight. Won't they be surprised to see me."

"Ah. Marina is your wife?"

He glances at his feet for a moment. "Well, kind of. Good luck today."

It's a bright day, warm but not hot. I walk through the city's narrow streets—many of them paved with rectangular black slabs of sandstone—slaloming between pedestrians and horse-drawn carriages. In the *Piazza Cairoli*, I sell about three or four grams of gold for a gold florin coin then change the gold florin for a handful of silver lire. One lire buys me some fruit.

Next, a minute's walk brings me to the grain market and then the coal market, each supplied by pulleys from its own dock on the Arno. Then the meat market. One stand offers pork and beef, another sells pigs' blood that, I'm promised, is perfect for black pudding. The surrounding streets have stalls too, lining the shaded arcades under their cross-vaulted arches, almost everything plastered in warm colors. At a bakery at the side of the market, patrons are collecting bread for lunch. Each customer seems to identify his or her own unique loaf, baked, I suppose, from the dough they dropped off in the morning.

A small stand is offering a taste of a new exotic drink called *caffè*. Coffee! How often did my grandparents moan that we have to find a way to grow coffee in Iceland—that they can't start the day without it? I pay one giulio and the stall owner reassures me that Pope Clement VIII has permitted the consumption of coffee.

I take a sip of the bitter brown drink. *What was all the fuss about?* Maybe the Pope sees this as some kind of penance.

I purchase a pitcher and shoulder strap and ask the shopkeeper where to get safe drinking water. He points at a marble fountain in the center of the piazza.

"Is that from the river?" I ask nervously. The shopkeeper patiently explains with obvious pride how the royal family of Tuscany—the Medicis—conquered Pisa and made it the second capital of Tuscany, funding an ambitious aqueduct project that supplies fresh drinking water from the mountains to the city.

The aqueduct is not the only new construction in Pisa. A two-minute walk north takes me through the spacious triangular *Piazza Cavalieri*, evidently the headquarters of the Medicis' sailors, the Knights of the Order of Saint Stephen. Hundreds of workmen are plastering new façades on old buildings. One palatial brick building is being covered in off-white plaster decorated with elegant graffiti, depicting, among other images, the signs of the zodiac, which Aristotle explained to me. Within the piazza, the order has its own beautiful church alongside the barracks.

I walk back to the riverbank and follow the water flow out of the walls and toward the sea. I have a couple of hours of walking ahead of me to reflect on this morning's discussion, polishing the glass lens obsessively all the while. *What is this lens for?*

Is it really the case that Aristotle's views have been accepted for almost two millennia—with the single exception of Copernicus' proposed modification to the spheres—and nobody has ever thought of putting them to even the simplest empirical test? Is the description on the ROW label, which I thought was fairly comprehensive, in fact barely surface deep? The difference in approach is stark. If Aristotle were a woman, she would size up a guy by taking a cursory glance and would then sit in a room and wax lyrical about him. Galileo as a woman, on the other hand, would systematically inspect every centimeter of the guy's body, clothing, possessions, background, and friends.

What made him this way? How much of his confidence came from the serendipitous wake-up call of the nova?

And what of my mission? I could perhaps extend it a couple of days to try to dig deeper. Would that even be enough?

I hike along a path with the river on one side and vines and olive orchards on the other, heading toward the distant sea. The occasional barge floats by. Eventually the river spreads out and pours into what must be the Mediterranean Sea. I find myself a rock to sit on, and after an hour or so I start to notice that the tide has gradually receded. What could cause an entire ocean to rise and fall in a matter of hours? I sit some more.

Loneliness sets in. Somehow my clearly defined mission kept me company for the first two days. *Plus the novelty of it all.* Now that the goal of understanding the universe has been expanded by Galileo to the point where it seems unattainable—at least during a short trip—and I begin to miss home all the more. Closing my eyes and listening to the waves, I can almost imagine I'm back at the beach in Iceland. As I polish the lens, I try to picture my hands sifting grain, back in the warmth of my Collective family.

"You all right, *signorina?*"

I hear a male voice and smell the stench of fish. I open my eyes.

"I guess. Oh, you must know something about the tides. Could you tell me about them?"

"What?" says the fisherman.

"The tides, tell me all about them. I want times, measurements, patterns, rules."

"Two high tides a day, two low tides, miss."

"That's it? What time? How high?" I demand.

He regards me doubtfully. "Times keep changing. At the moment high tide's about an hour after sunrise. Maybe 'bout so high." He holds his hand over his head.

That will have to do. I start the long walk back to the city, this time climbing gently all the way, unsure if I have the information that my new boss is expecting from me. My right hand and elbow ache from rubbing the glass.

The Sun is setting over the sea behind my back, casting a long shadow in front of me as I walk, beyond which I can see the city brick walls bathed in the beautiful evening glow. Eventually, worn down by hours of walking and polishing, I enter Pisa and buy myself another small measure of that awful bitter substance—coffee. It perks me up a bit. *I'm starting to get it.*

"Here's your polished lens," I say to Galileo. "Not sure why you need two lenses—if you want to start two fires, you can use the same lens twice, you know."

He pulls a face. His lens is polished too. Galileo retrieves a leather-bound tube from a shelf and removes two old lenses, mounting the two fresh lenses in their place at either extreme. The leather is decorated with delicate gold leaf patterns. He leads me up to the roof of the Stadium. Here Galileo peers through the tube at some distant site. Then he makes some adjustments and tries again.

"What is this?" I ask.

"I am one of the very first people to construct this new invention out of the Netherlands, the *telescopio*. Some Dutch optician discovered it—probably by pure accident playing with two spectacle lenses. I have already constructed one that magnifies three times, and I have designed these two lenses to magnify by a record thirty times. Hopefully. So what did you discover about the tides?"

"In and out twice each day," I say. "The times vary. Currently the first high tide is shortly after sunrise. Is that what you wanted?"

Galileo holds his beard. "That is not the answer I was hoping for. You see, you asked about evidence for heliocentrism," he sighs. "I have failed to detect the Earth's rapid movement through space around the Sun but I was hoping to find evidence of the Earth's rotation around its own axis. I have an intuition that the tides are evidence for the Earth's rotation."

"Ah, yes! I was wondering what could shift an entire ocean. I suppose the spinning of the planet could be the culprit," I say. "But—if so why are there two tides for each single rotation of the Earth?"

He shakes his head. "As I said, it was not the answer I was hoping for. Yet I am still certain that tides are a consequence of the Earth's spinning."

Finally Galileo seems pleased with his calibration of this telescope thing, and he hands it to me. I point it out at the city and apply my eye to the decorated narrow end as I saw him do.

"Awesome!" Through the peephole, the world magically comes to me. I swing it left and right. I try my other eye. I rotate the telescope and look through the other end, but that makes things look more distant.

Looking the right way again I point the telescope at a grand white marble building and see what might be the city's cathedral as if I were standing near it, a mountain range looms majestically as a backdrop behind it. Alongside the cathedral is a prominent, ornate bell tower.

An eye piece of one of Galileo's telescopes
and view of the cathedral and tower from the Medici Palace

I let out a long whistle as I admire the view. "Galileo. At the risk of being pedantic about your instrument, it makes that tower look a little crooked," I say.

"Fizzella, I am disappointed in you. Your polishing must have been lopsided."

My face burns until I notice that Galileo is chuckling cryptically.

"Maybe you should try dropping some weights from up there," I suggest.

"It will be dark soon. Follow me."

"But Galileo, what use could you have for this thing in the dark?"

I follow Galileo out of the Stadium and we take a short walk along the river to the *Palazzo Reale*. Like many of the surrounding riverside buildings, its three-story walls are plastered in a rich yellow-orange color, topped with a gently sloping red-tiled roof. The building appears plain for a *palazzo*, but its sheer size is palatial and it boasts an impressive beige tower above its roof. A pigeon flies over the tower.

The Medici Palazzo Reale, and the tower from which Galileo observed

The butler recognizes Galileo. "I am sorry sir; the Grand Duke is expecting you tomorrow night."

"I know. May we carry out a practice run up the tower tonight?" Galileo says.

The butler bows, and Galileo leads me up the stairs.

"The Grand Duke?" I enquire.

"The Grand Duke of Tuscany, Cosimo II de' Medici. I tutored him when he was a child." He lowers his voice. "It has proven worthwhile to have connections in the House of Medici. Their influence extends well beyond Tuscany. The previous pope was a Medici, and the current pope is pro-Medici too."

The two of us climb a narrow, dark rectangular stone staircase to the Medici's private bell tower. Each level is illuminated by one small window, and each windowsill seems to be home to a pigeon's nest.

"Something you said when we met," I catch my breath, "that with sufficient evidence your church—the Catholic Church—will accept your view. You really think so?"

"Absolutely. I shall present the evidence and campaign for its acceptance."

As we alight at the top of the tower, six large arches afford panoramic views in all four directions. Through these we watch the sea of red roof tops below disappear as the constellations above emerge.

I still have no idea why Galileo brought his telescope here. *Surely a white dot through a telescope is still a white dot?*

Galileo points his telescope at some random constellation. A moment later, his mouth drops open. I remain silent, not wanting to ruin this moment for him, whatever it is. Finally Galileo hands me the telescope and starts pacing around the platform excitedly.

I point the telescope more or less at the same constellation I think Galileo has been observing. I gently press my eye against the leather rim of the telescope's narrow end.

"Um, white dots?"

I look back at Galileo. He's bursting with excitement.

I sigh and look through the telescope again. "Oh!" I finally say. We look at each other. The view in the telescope is indeed white dots—the familiar pattern of the constellation. The big surprise is that there are many extra white dots!

"So—"

"Yes," Galileo says, "more stars."

"—being observed tonight for the first time ever," I add.

We spend some time pointing the telescope here and there. Wherever we look, extra stars make their début. So, it turns out, the "immutable" constellations proudly documented by the ancients—which I saw two days ago—were just those stars that happened to be bright enough for the naked human eye to see. *Things are definitely not as they seem.* With a slight visual aid, thousands more stars finally get to say: "yeah, I'm here too, about time someone acknowledged me."

As we probe the night sky, my upbringing comes flooding back. I feel dizzy. *Ask not whereout—do not pry beyond the human scale.* It was one thing chatting with Aristotle and Copernicus about their casual observations—but Galileo is now using instruments to actively expose hidden worlds. Is this a benign extension of natural, healthy curiosity or is this, right here and now, the moment where humanity tips from observing to prying?

How can my journey have a happy ending with the cascade of Galileo's discoveries showing no sign of converging to any kind of conclusion? Every minute I spend with Galileo, the goal of a complete ROW label seems further away!

The thought slaps me—*should I rethink my goals?* If Galileo thinks he can change the Church, why shouldn't I try and change the Ecommunity! Campaign for openness to scientific observation of the world in the Ecommunity! We could do that while of course maintaining the ban on use of harmful technologies.

I try to imagine myself, armed with first-hand knowledge of Aristotle, Copernicus, and Galileo, arguing that studying and analyzing nature are natural and positive activities—that you can and should explore, without meddling. I picture a life of writing political essays, making impassioned speeches, gathering petitions, giving expert testimony to committees of deans, slowly enacting reform in the Ecommunity. I can almost see the placards: *Science in, technology out. Explore, don't meddle.*

Reality check: Deans are elected by each Collective for life—until the retirement age of fifty-five. I'm not sure how much incentive they have to experiment with change.

"Fizzella," Galileo rudely interrupts my runaway imagination, "let us take a look at the *Milky Way*," Galileo aims the tube at the milky-white strip I had previously noticed across the sky. "Stars!" he exclaims simply and hands me the telescope.

I take a look, shocked that the silky white of the Milky Way is in fact the accumulated whiteness of vast numbers of distant stars, too densely packed for the eye to resolve!

A panorama of the Milky Way

"Goodness, thousands more stars," I whisper.

"Thousands? Millions. You know I have an idea for improving this telescope further."

Galileo is exposing millions of hidden stars and already all he can think about is exposing yet deeper layers of the universe. *There is at least some truth in the Ecommunity's warning about curiosity being addictive.* But is it harmful?

Galileo keeps examining the white dots. "Did you notice in the telescope that the stars are not just infinitesimal dots? I can see that they have some size. *Varying* sizes, in fact."

I take a look. Yes, I can just about discern that some stars are a little wider than others.

"You know what varying sizes means?" he says.

It could simply mean that there are big stars and little stars. *Or—* "Different distances?"

"*Bravo.* I do think so."

In my mind, I can almost feel the cacophonous shattering of Aristotle's vast celestial sphere of constellations. "So there is no celestial sphere?"

"After all, why should there be?" Galileo smirks.

Why should there be—what does he mean? I think of my night on the beach in Iceland. When I saw the constellations circling around us in perfect formation, I thought a physical sky may be required to carry them. Aristotle believed in celestial spheres for exactly that reason—to explain the movement of the stars. But since Copernicus suggested that the stars aren't in fact moving around us at all, what need is there for a celestial sphere of the constellations? *Old habits die hard.* Even a maverick like Copernicus who made the celestial sphere of the stars redundant never thought to question that the sphere exists.

I take a second to reflect, but Galileo's mind waits for no one: "In fact, I rather suspect that each star is a sun, just like our Sun."

Suns? *Nothing will stop this man.* I feel queasy at the suggestion that there are thousands—*no millions!*—of suns as powerful as our own Sun looming above us. What reserves of creative energy is he calling on to suggest that the blinding sun and a white speck are one and the same.

Soon it occurs to me that Galileo's proposal is another radical attack on the human view of nature and on the religious view of humans as the purpose of nature. Copernicus said our Earth is just a planet, an opinion which a hundred years later is still highly controversial. Even before that is resolved, Galileo is now questioning whether the Sun is the center of the universe or just one of many stars. *If we don't live on a special planet and don't orbit a special star, are we humans even important?*

I rub my temples and pace the short length of the tower's platform, peering out at the dark city of Pisa while Galileo keeps peering upward. Candlelight is still flickering in some windows, but most of the city is in slumber land. Those sleeping Italians are completely unaware how the universe is expanding around them as they sleep. I wonder how many will take an interest in the transformational discoveries occurring tonight up this tower.

I look at Galileo still observing intensely. He will no doubt become famous. *Is he earning his fame tonight for his brilliant abilities of observation and reason? Or because he happened to be the first person to point a tele-scope—a brand new invention—upward?* Brilliance or luck? Perhaps a bit of both.

As for me, my mind is in turmoil. Galileo's excitement is contagious, but I've been trained to be wary of exploration beyond the human realm. I don't necessarily object to Galileo using instruments to expose the universe, but boy does it make me uncomfortable.

After several minutes, I stop pacing and rejoin Galileo. "So what revolutionary new observations have you made in the last few minutes?" I ask nervously.

"Take a look at Jupiter," Galileo says pointing his telescope at the brightest dot in the sky. "There are three more dots right around it—in fact maybe four. I think those dots are moving through the constellations with Jupiter!"

Jupiter and its four "Galilean" moons through a small telescope

I swallow the lump in my throat. *Moving through the constellations!* "New planets?" I ask.

"Yes and no. Those are clearly not fixed stars. But what if they are indeed circling Jupiter, not circling the Sun—what shall we call them?"

"Wow. The Moon is the only other celestial object that circles a planet, right?" I say.

Galileo nods. "Correct. *Si*, let us call them 'moons.' I think I shall name these moons of Jupiter for my sponsors the Medici royal family. Copernicus would have loved to see this."

You could say that again. This new evidence proves beyond a doubt that not all the orbits are concentric as Aristotle's supporters still insist.

Galileo points the telescope at the fainter white dot of Saturn. He squints at it for quite some time. "There seems to be something around Saturn, but it is not clear. Possibly moons on either side."

I take a look. "It's really not very clear. Are you ready to gamble that those are really moons?"

"Hmm. What to do?" Now Galileo is pacing. "Telescopes will be spreading rapidly now. If I do not publish this discovery someone else will get credit for all eternity for discovering the moons of Saturn. If I publish and I am wrong, I shall be ridiculed, eclipsing my other triumphant discoveries. Certainly there are enough people looking for an opportunity to discredit me."

Galileo is still debating the issue when our very own Moon rises majestically in the east, bathing the expanse of red tiles all around us in gentle moonlight. Galileo immediately observes the lunar sphere through the telescope.

"The Moon as never seen before," Galileo says, handing me the telescope.

I look through it to see a beautiful view of circles of varying sizes and light and dark areas, a patchwork of intricate lunar detail that has been veiled from human view until tonight.

"Stunning," I say.

"Shadows," he replies.

Shadows? Of all the interesting details, who cares about shadows? *Oh.* "So it's not a perfectly smooth sphere after all!"

Aristotle's philosophical principles—the world's philosophical principles for two thousand years—are toppling like dominoes tonight. The Greek map of stars was far from complete; the stars are at different distances, so they cannot be resting on a celestial sphere; Jupiter has moons that do not orbit the center of the universe, and our Moon is not a sphere. "Amazing. But Galileo, for all these discoveries, have we actually found any direct evidence that Copernicus was right—that the planets circle the Sun?"

"Patience, young Fizzella, the night is still young."

We observe the sky all night. I try to memorize carefully the many changes I need to write up on the ROW label when I finally get back to the hut. While I've not yet seen any evidence that science leads to technology, I am certainly witnessing one small piece of technology revolutionizing science.

"Ah," Galileo says.

"Ah, what?"

"My dilemma—the fuzziness around Saturn."

"You're still worrying about that?"

"I shall publish an anagram," he waves his finger.

"An anagram?"

"Yes. I shall take the sentence 'I observe the highest planet to be triple-bodied,' mix the letters beyond recognition, and publish it. If the discovery proves correct, I shall later reveal the deciphered version of the sentence, proving that I was the first to discover the moons of Saturn. If not, my error shall remain scrambled forever."

I laugh. Clearly Galileo's ingenuity extends beyond scientific discovery into the realms of what must be some sort of academic politics.

Finally as the first hints of dawn appear in the east, Galileo says, "Now let us settle the matter of the planets' orbits." He is gazing at Venus, the bright "morning star" that is rising in the east like a footman foretelling the approach of the Sun.

"Venus revealed," he says handing me the telescope with a grin on his face.

I look through the new invention. Venus doesn't look like much, still a smallish white dot. *No*, it isn't a round dot at all—it has a tiny crescent shape—a banana shape, just like a new Moon.

"You know why Venus appears as a crescent?" Galileo asks.

Why is it a crescent? Well, why is the new Moon a crescent? *Think, Fizz...*

"It must mean," I say, "that Venus is closer to the Earth than the Sun—in fact it is more or less in-between the Sun and the Earth right now. The Sun is mostly illuminating the other side of Venus—we are seeing the dark Venus night and just a crescent of Venus day—where Venus morning has broken." I recall my conversation with Copernicus.

"So I suppose that Ptolemy's theory was right—Venus is closer to the Earth than the Sun, not further than the Sun as Aristotle had it."

"Right now Venus is closer than the Sun…"

Oops! Indeed right now it is closer, but Aristotle and Ptolemy might both be wrong…

"…some weeks ago with my old weaker telescope I saw Venus as a full circle—so it was beyond the Sun then, but between us and the Sun now."

"Aha," I say, "evidence that a planet—Venus—is circling the Sun, not the Earth!"

"Incontrovertible," Galileo confirms.

Finally, the thing I actually came for: evidence for Copernicus' Sun-centric model.

Soon the Sun rises. I'm getting rather drowsy.

Galileo immediately points the telescope directly at it. "Spots!"

Taking the telescope I squint through it at the Sun. The blinding light startles my droopy eye—I wonder if this is even healthy for my eyes. "Huh, Sun spots? So the Sun isn't a perfect sphere either?"

"And now," he says, leaping one step ahead yet again, "we can track those spots to determine whether the Sun is rotating. I had better sketch them."

Galileo removes a notebook from his pocket and pencils a careful sketch, labeling one prominent sun spot *A* as a marker he can now track.

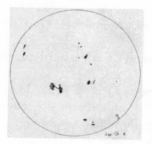

Galileo's sketch of sunspots

If his hunch is right and the Sun is rotating, it will be more evidence that the Sun is not the stationary foundation of the universe after all. The Sun may be the center of our system of planets—I guess you could say the *solar system*—but in the bigger scheme of things the Sun may be just another star.

"Well, the Sun is up, it is a new day," Galileo says, "let us get back to work in the lab."

I stare at Galileo, physically and emotionally drained. "I think," I slur, "that I have gotten what I came for, a key missing piece in my understanding of the universe—evidence for heliocentrism... and many other exciting discoveries... with your permission I will go and rest." *Maybe go home*, I think. Or maybe rethink my quest.

"Well, Fizzella, you may think you got what you came for," he says brightly, "but you are mistaken. You have much more to understand about the world. Come with me."

Reluctantly, I stagger behind Galileo down the stairs of the tower and back to his lab in the Pisan Stadium. He has exposed new moons, new suns, new features of our own Sun and Moon—a whole new reality. *What more could he possibly be planning to explore?*

Nature's Beat

Day 4.

"So *buon giorno*, Fizzella. Your work for this morning."

Back in the lab, Galileo hands me a pebble. If he's as tired as I am after a night of observations, he doesn't show it. "Perform an experiment where you drop this pebble and see how far it falls after different intervals of time. Look for a pattern."

In addition to being fatigued after days of time travel and a night without sleep, I am now assigned menial tasks like timing the fall of a pebble. *This is not how I imagined spending my precious few days of exploration.*

"Didn't you already demonstrate the principle that the speed of falling doesn't depend on weight?" I try, but he waves me out.

I splash some water on my face and take the pebble in turn to each of the three floors of the stadium's home, the *Palazzo della Sapienza*. Perhaps this is what he meant when he commented that he is seeking a "quantitative analysis" of the world—not that I quite see the point.

Throwing the pebble out from windows of different heights with my right hand, I touch my neck with the left hand, using my pulse as an approximation for counting seconds. I measure, at least roughly, the time taken for the pebble to fall from each story.

A professor sweeps along the second floor arcade in his imposing academic robes. I realize for the first time that Galileo is omitting—perhaps refusing—to wear the robes that adorn the other scholars.

"Young girl, what are you thinking, throwing stones around this distinguished place of learning?"

"I'm assisting Galileo Galilei."

"Ah," he gives me a knowing laugh. "Continue."

Unfortunately the third and top floor of the Stadium seems just some ten meters from the ground and pebbles fall from it in just over a second, giving me a very limited range of measurements. I go back to the lab and complain to Galileo.

"Find somewhere higher."

I have an idea. Exiting the *Palazzo della Sapienza*, I walk north for ten minutes.

Emerging from a dingy narrow road, I enter the vast expanse of the *Piazza dei Miracoli* and am awestruck by the sights before me. The three white marble buildings that I had glimpsed through the telescope now sparkle down at me like two elephants and a giraffe regarding an ant: the grandiose round domed Baptistry, the colossal cathedral, and the stunning bell tower. I swing my arms out like an oversized letter T. Finally I get to smile at Galileo's joke from yesterday evening: The bell tower really is wonky. It almost looks as if the tower is frustrated at having the cathedral blocking its view of the Baptistry—it leans precariously to the side, hoping to get a peek.

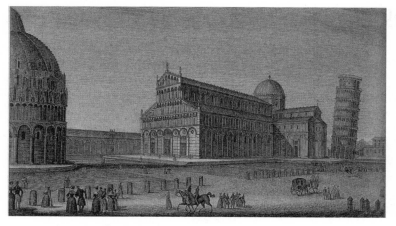

Pisa's Piazza dei Miracoli: Baptistry, cathedral, leaning bell tower

Walking under three rows of decorative arches, I enter the cathedral—the *Duomo*. A gilded ceiling way above me, flanked by two more rows of marble arches, draws me along the long section of the church to the intersection of the cross-shaped building where I find myself under a frescoed dome.

A janitor on a ladder is lighting the candles of the central chandelier. Stepping down, he leaves the chandelier swinging gently. I smile to myself. *Might this be where Galileo, perhaps while he knelt in prayer, noticed the regularity of the swings of a pendulum?*

Emerging from the far end of the cathedral, I find myself literally in the mid-morning shadow of *La Torre di Pisa*—the leaning tower. Grabbing a handful of pebbles, I start to spiral my way up, dropping a pebble from the leaning side—one at each level—counting pulses.

As I get higher the time of the drop starts increasing surprisingly rapidly. I take copious notes. Some of the results are confusing, but luckily I have some spare pebbles so I repeat the measurement from the same level a second and third time. Each time, the very same fall takes fewer pulses. I scratch my head.

Then I laugh at myself. My pulse is a bit of a crude timer at the best of times. But walking up stairs is not the best of times! However, what better timer is available? After racking my brains for a minute, I start singing, and even as I walk up and down releasing pebbles from different heights, I never stop singing the song, again and again.

We MARCH in TUNE with NAture's BEAT
Our enVIronMENT we WON'T misTREAT
MAN in HARmoNY with EARTH
SusTAINing NATURE from birth to BIRTH

My own singing provides a timer of about two beats per second. Even if the number of seconds isn't accurate, at least the beats are pretty consistent. I try to ignore the irony of singing an Ecommunity song while making forbidden measurements of Mother Nature.

After an hour or two I summarize my best results:

Time fallen	Distance fallen
1 second	5 meters
2 seconds	20 meters
3 seconds	45 meters

Amazingly, the pebble falls from even the highest level in just over three seconds so my measurements go no further than that. I try to focus my droopy eyes on the numbers. If there's a pattern here, I'm too tired to spot it.

Back in the lab I slump into a chair. Galileo comes over, takes my results, smiles, and hands my notes back to me.

"Say, Galileo, how come you don't wear academic robes like all the other professors?"

"*Pah.* The academic toga is the disguise of the empty-headed. I would rather go naked."

"Yeah, we're not big on uniforms where I come from either, but what's the harm?"

"As well as being pointlessly pretentious, recognizable academic dress makes it impractical to visit brothels." He doesn't flinch as he says it, and I try to hide my surprise. "So, Fizzella, you identified the pattern?"

I didn't and I'm still not sure why it matters. *Concentrate, Fizz.* Okay, in two seconds, the pebble fell four times more than in one second. In three seconds, it fell nine times more than in one second. Two times two is four, three times three is nine. Through my exhaustion I feel a moment of satisfaction as my brain takes charge of the seemingly random numbers and marches the numbers into an orderly formation.

"Galileo, if I may use a geometric analogy, I think the distances grow like a square—if you double the side of a square the area grows by two times two, or four times. Here it's the same. If you double the time of falling: the distance fallen is four times more. If you triple the time, the distance grows nine times."

"Good. There is a law of nature for you: The distance fallen varies with the square of the time of the fall. So, Fizzella, can you use this law to predict what would happen if I dropped the pebble from higher still?"

I rub my eyes hard. *Predict?* Suddenly I understand what he said yesterday about seeking quantitative laws. I suppose this law could be used to make specific predictions. *Wow.* It's a whole different level of ambition compared to Aristotle's qualitative predictions like "water will strive to be above earth." Okay, in four seconds the pebble would fall four times further than in two seconds or sixteen times further than in one second.

I grab the sheet of paper and scribble one more number:

Time fallen	Distance fallen
1 second	5 meters
2 seconds	20 meters
3 seconds	45 meters
4 seconds	80 meters (predicted)

"Fantastic, Fizzella. Look, you have made a quantitative prediction about the world. Very few people have ever even attempted that. Now let us analyze. How is it that the distance increases like the square of the time?" Galileo asks. "How does twice as much time give four times more distance?"

"I… Galileo… I really don't know. I thought you said you were only interested in *what?*"

"*Corretto*, very true, Fizzella. I am not interested in 'final causes.' I want to find the laws governing the falling; I care little to speculate why the stone chooses to fall. But I told you that, where possible, I want to look beyond *what* to *how*—to find the more fundamental underlying law. I think this law of distance fallen varying like the square of the time, is just a symptom of a deeper law of the universe. Stay with me. What was the average speed in each second?"

I am amazed how Galileo takes only the briefest satisfaction in his revolutionary discovery. Already he is digging deeper. I suspect my Dad is a bit like that. *Am I? Is the key to being a successful scientist as much drive as intelligence?*

I shake my head lethargically and return to the question. The pebble fell five meters in the first second, so the average speed in the first second was five meters per second. In two seconds, it fell a total of twenty meters, so it must have fallen another fifteen meters during the second second. I turn over the sheet of paper and, using the change in the distance during each second, I calculate the average speeds:

Time interval	Average speed
1st second	5 meters per second
2nd second	15 meters per second (fell from 5 to 20)
3rd second	25 meters per second (from 20 to 45)
4th second	35 meters per second (predicted)

"So what is happening to the speed?" Galileo says.

"Um, well, the speed is increasing at a constant rate—by an extra ten meters per second each second."

"Do you see?" Galileo asks. "Now we have a fundamental law. The speed of a falling object increases by ten meters per second each second. We can also say that a falling object *accelerates* downward at ten meters per second per second. By acceleration I mean the rate at which the velocity changes."

Through my sleepiness, I'm vaguely aware that I'm participating in a revolutionary thought process. What he's doing is using mathematics to find patterns in physical behaviors and then analyzing those patterns—in this case looking at the rate of change—to find more fundamental patterns. He is, right here and now, marrying mathematics to physics for the very first time, and I've been invited to the wedding.

Unfortunately I was up all night at the bachelorette party.

"If speed is increasing constantly," I ask, "why did we find that distance is increasing like the square of time?"

"Do you not see?" Galileo opens his arms. "When you double the time of falling, say from one second to two seconds, you get both twice as much speed and twice as much falling time. And two times two is?"

"I get it," I say. "Twice as much time and twice as much speed gives a four times longer fall. Galileo—I will never forget this experience. Analyzing the world numerically, finding a pattern, making predictions, scrutinizing the pattern of the distances to find an underlying pattern of the speeds—but would it please be possible for me to sleep now?" I start staggering toward the door.

"But you have missed the underlying point," Galileo insists. "I believe our finding about how the speed changes, tells us something quite fundamental about nature. What is the natural state of matter?"

"Um, I know this… matter is naturally stationary?" The room is starting to blur.

"That is the accepted view, ever since Aristotle: matter is naturally stationary. But how then do some things keep moving for a long time with no force pushing them. For example how can a pebble slide smoothly on ice? No, I think the very opposite of Aristotle. I think the natural state of matter is one of continuous motion. I shall call it *inertia*: absent any external forces, matter tends to continue moving at constant speed in a straight line. There is nothing natural about slowing to a stop—slowing, like any change of velocity, requires a force."

"Then why do objects all around us tend to stop?" Right now the room is waving in front of me—I would rather like *it* to stop.

"Because there are almost always frictional forces," Galileo says. "But without friction and other forces, a moving object will continue to move in a straight line at the same speed, forever. Inertia."

"You mean like Aristotle?"

"Aren't you listening? This is the very opposite of Aristotle's view. He thought matter stops."

"No, I mean like Aristotle's ideas had inertia. His ideas didn't change for centuries, not until you applied the force of fresh thinking."

Galileo laughs appreciatively.

I wish I was fully conscious to appreciate all this rethinking of age-old wisdoms. "B-but, Galileo, where did that stuff about inertia come from? What has it got to do with the falling pebble?"

"Ah, do you not see? Aristotle thought that matter is naturally stationary. So he thought you need a force to *change position*. My principle of inertia states that matter naturally moves with constant speed and direction. So the role of a force is *to change the velocity* of an object—to *accelerate* it. Once started, the pebble can keep falling all on its own. But the pull of the Earth has the effect of making the downward speed accelerate. So you see the idea: force creates acceleration—force changes speed."

"Galileo, this has been great. You not only found the first evidence for heliocentrism but also a plethora of other discoveries, astronomical and terrestrial... introduced new techniques... I will treasure my two days with you and my new understanding of the universe...." I start swaying toward the door.

"But Fizzella," Galileo is saying, "what new understanding of the universe? We only completed measurements of one phenomenon, the law of a falling object, and some astronomy—"

Visions of my bed in the hut come to mind...

"—with this new approach of experimentation, with the new discipline of applying mathematics to the quantitative analysis of the world—"

...I think of my very own bed back in Iceland...

"—we can quantitatively explore many more forces: frictions, materials, springs—"

...as I start to falter I think of my Mom, Zopp, I even see images of the Dean...

"—analyze the flow of liquids, the effects of temperature, not to mention that with bigger telescopes—"

I collapse.

In my dream, I'm walking on the beach in Iceland. Aristotle is walking next to me, stroking his beard. "You're not allowed here," I say. "I just want to describe the world I see," he says. I point at the sea, to a floating iceberg surrounded by thousands of floating twigs. He's not allowed here. *Go away.* I can see my village in the distance. I won't be welcome there with Aristotle, who is oozing negative knowledge. "I've heard all about the universe, please go away," I say. "You know nothing, Fizzos," I hear.

"Yes, I do." The voice is changing. "Nothing real... almost nothing validated..." "Neither do you." "You know almost nothing quantitatively... Fizzella... you know almost nothing..."

Now Galileo is shouting: "Fizzella! FIZZELLA!"

Waking up startled, I swing my arms around me. I'm on the floor of the lab, with Galileo crouching over me, holding the bottom half of a shattered glass of water, a piece of glass hanging from his beard and water all over his clothes. Fortunately, neither he nor I are cut, and I won't have to go down in history for hurting Galileo, whom I'm betting becomes pretty well known. He sets down the glass fragment and turns back to me.

"Fizzella, are you okay?" Galileo holds my hand, helping me to sit up while using his other hand to flick away some shards of the glass I must have just broken.

"Um, what, yes, yes, I think so. I just need sleep. Time to absorb. Thank you, Galileo." I stand up slowly, still in the dress from yesterday. There is a softness in Galileo's expression that I have not noticed before as he helps me to my feet, but I'm feeling too overwhelmed to think about anything other than getting home. Not just home to the hut— *home to Iceland.* Returning within four days will minimize the scandal, and I've achieved a lot in that short time. Once I get home, I can think about planning my political campaign. I gather the jeweled comb from across the room and stuff it randomly in my hair, curtsey, and take my leave.

The Sun is directly overhead as I trudge through Pisa. Safely back in Fizz's Place, I slide into bed and fall asleep for several hours. When I wake, it's evening. I feel somewhat rested but disorientated, confused, and intensely lonely, as if my brain has been dragged through a nasty storm. I sit on the bed for some time, visualizing our communal evenings. In fact, I left home on a Friday and, if my count is correct, it's Tuesday evening in the Collective right now. *I'm going home.*

I glance over at the door and the ROW label. That label is to be my memento from these four days of time travel. I have visions of folding it and keeping it under the floor with my notebook; from time to time, I'll retrieve it to remember—maybe even relive in a way—my few days in ancient Greece, in the middle ages in Poland, and in early Renaissance Italy. If my campaign for openness in the Ecommunity is successful, I will eventually unfold the label and put it on the door of my room at home.

I sigh and sink further onto the bed. The only tiny imperfection with this plan is that Galileo has pretty much destroyed the validity of every single fact on my label. Not a single statement on that label has been verified by experiment in the way Galileo taught me yesterday and today. In fact, most of the statements have already been destroyed by Galileo's experiments. Not one quantitative law is included on the label—no laws that can be used to make predictions, no laws that constitute what I suppose will in the future be described as *science*.

The label as it is now would, in all honesty, be testimony to a failed trip.

I rip up the ROW label and make another attempt at describing the Rest Of World beyond the hut door. Based on Galileo's teachings, I leave out any natural philosophy that is not confirmed by experimental evidence.

ROW Label

Date of manufacture: ~~Infinite 5-6,000 years~~ No evidence!

Contents: ~~Celestial spheres...~~ Sun (with sun spots) surrounded by the orbits of Mercury, Venus, Earth (plus cratered Moon orbiting Earth), Mars, Jupiter (plus four moons orbiting Jupiter), Saturn (with something indiscernible around it). Millions of stars at different distances, each of which may be a sun.

Ingredients: ~~Four elements...~~ No scientific evidence!

Laws:

Natural state of matter is moving at constant speed (inertia).

Falling objects have constant downward acceleration.

Err, that's it.

WARNING: DOZENS OF QUANTITATIVE LAWS FOR PREDICTING PHYSICAL PROCESSES PROBABLY MISSING!

I look down at the label sadly. *Pitiful, Fizz.*

I actually blame Galileo. He has toppled pillar after pillar of human knowledge, using nothing more than a couple of lenses in a tube, and a sharp and open mind. Time after time, Galileo said to the world that nothing is as it seems. *Yet he's destroyed much more than he's created.* Galileo held a mirror up to his fellow thinkers, showing them that the world in 1610 has almost no knowledge at all—no real tested and quantified knowledge.

Come to think of it, I didn't fully get the one thing I was actually looking for when I came here yesterday. Galileo has no direct evidence for the Earth's rotation and movement! True, I saw evidence that Venus circles the Sun, and maybe the tides hint at the Earth's rotation, but if the Earth is spinning and orbiting there should surely be direct evidence for it. The very question that brought me to Italy is still at large.

I glance at the seven artifacts from the box. I'm not even sure what Dad was hinting at any more. There is no evidence for earth, water, air, fire or aether as the elements of matter and there are no celestial spheres, at least not for the stars. So what do those artifacts even mean?

I scrunch up my hair with both hands and stare at the nearly empty flask of strawberry juice. If I go home now, I will minimize the scandal, but I'll have even more open questions to drive me completely insane during a long life of husbandry. If I stay a day or two—*even if I stay the entire three weeks!*—I'm not sure I could investigate every aspect of nature in the thorough way Galileo has taught me.

I certainly wouldn't mind the chance to discuss this with someone right around now—Dad would be the only appropriate someone.

After debating with myself for some time, I decide on the compromise of investing one more day in my journey. I can get another look at how Galileo's seminal thinking develops. Tomorrow evening I'll head home with at least a somewhat more complete understanding of the roots of science that Galileo is planting. Maybe I can fill out the label a little more and gather more ammunition for my political campaign. At the very least, perhaps I can solve today's biggest mystery: If the planets are moving around the Sun—and we saw that clearly now, at least for Venus—why have all attempts failed to detect the rapid movement of the Earth under our feet.

"Computer, take me to a time when Galileo resolves the issue of the Earth's movement."

Relative

Day 5. 1633. Arcetri, Grand Duchy of Tuscany.

1633? I was expecting to jump a few months forward, not twenty-three years! Galileo must be seventy years old by now. I hope he's had time to find scientific laws for many phenomena. Perhaps I have a chance of going home this evening with a significantly expanded label.

Suddenly I pause and close my eyes tight. Galileo's going to expect me to be forty! What can I do? Do I protect the secret of the time travel and not go to meet him today? Or hope he's forgotten me in the intervening two decades?

I'm dying to see what has happened in all those years. Here I am, in 1633, Galileo presumably a short walk away—surely I can't be expected to just leave.

So how do I age my appearance?

Stepping outside, I'm traversing a splendid grassy hill, checkered with trees which alternately bear olives and pink blossoms. I walk for a few minutes, pressing olives into the earth with every step, leaving small patches of olives behind me. At the edge of the orchard, still in yesterday's clothes, I find myself in a small country village capping the lush hill, and as I turn a corner, without any warning, a panoramic view of a city unfolds below—spanning a large valley all the way from the foot of the hill I'm on, to some distant hills near the horizon. A green river crosses the city and is in turn spanned by stone bridges.

For a moment I think I'm back in Pisa. A cathedral, bell tower, and another domed building—presumably a baptistery—overshadow the city center. But even from this distance I can see that the marble bell tower is square, not round, and perfectly vertical. The expanse of red roofs and orange plastered walls below me is not Pisa.

I look back at the village. Again, even after Galileo introduced techniques of scientific rigor into natural philosophy, I see no new technology. Where are those destructive consequences of physics?

Unlike technology, fashions have evolved. Most notably, many men are wearing their hair long and curly. I'm the only one in a ruff, others now wear softer, more practical, lace collars.

After watching passersby for a moment, I stop a middle-aged woman and while she informs me that the city below Arcetri is *Firenze—*

Florence—also on the River Arno, I'm busy studying what she looks like and how she's dressed.

Suddenly I let out a small gasp. Amongst the light foot traffic are two sinister figures—I actually have no idea how old they are, or whether, for that matter, they are men or women. The two of them are sweeping through the quaint streets in long, black, hooded capes, topped with three-cornered black hats. Believe it or not, their faces are completely covered with milk-white masks. These masks are not cream from the Blue Lagoon—they appear rigid, obscuring all facial expressions, and are decorated with delicate, golden patterns.

As the two black cloaks flap in the breeze, silhouetted against the backdrop of bright Italian stone walls and green olive trees, the concealed faces look disturbingly spooky to me but no one is screaming or running for their lives.

"Computer, print me a black cape, a three-cornered hat, and a white gilded mask. Yes, seriously."

Printing Bauta disguise.

The first man I ask directs me to Galileo's home—Villa il Gioiello—without so much as a comment on my masquerade. A coach is waiting just outside the elegant, U-shaped, white villa, the driver restraining two horses which seem to be chomping at the bit.

I walk up to the arched, dark-wooden front door, which is right on the small street, and pull a chain to ring the bell.

A maid ushers me in. She holds out her hand offering to take my mask. Behind the mask, I cringe. _This was a crazy idea—being disguised in the street is one thing, but why should he agree to receive me like this._ I nod sidewise and the maid just shrugs and leads me to his office.

"_Buon giorno_, Galileo."

Galileo

What an experience to see someone age over twenty years in just one of my days. His hair is now completely white, his stature hunched—he looks poorly. The years have softened his features—I feel a little extra warmth emanating from him, with a little less intensity.

Judging by the watercolors hanging on the wall, he has continued making observations with his *telescopio* in the intervening years:

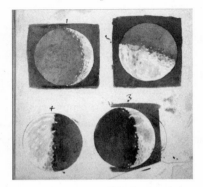

Galileo's sketches of the lunar phases

Sitting at a small desk, a wooden globe by his side, Galileo looks toward me, but not quite at me, frowning for several seconds. *Here it comes: Would you mind removing your mask when you enter my office.*

"Could that be... Fizzella's voice?"

I didn't even think of that. *After twenty years, he recognized my voice!* I remove my mask and push my hood back, liberating my signature red hair. "Yes Galileo, it's so good to see you. You've aged well," I lie.

And you haven't aged at all.

But he's not even looking at me. "Fizzella. I cannot believe it. Your voice has not changed a bit. How time flies. It seems like just yesterday that you collapsed on the floor in Pisa and then woke up and shattered the glass of water I was holding for you. Unfortunately, you are finding me on my way out. I am departing to Rome." He stops for a fit of coughing, which sounds pained.

"To Rome. Why?" It seems unlikely he would be traveling for pleasure in his condition. And still no comment at all on my appearance.

"I wrote a book, *Dialogue Concerning the Two Chief World Systems.*" Galileo talks a little slower than he used to, but there is still wisdom in every one of his carefully chosen words. "It presents balanced arguments for geocentrism and heliocentrism. I wrote the book with the approval of His Holiness the Pope. I need to go to Rome to, um, discuss it. It is a long journey and I may have to stop along the way for some days of quarantine."

"Oh, I see." I try to hide my disappointment. *So much for the finale to my once-in-a-lifetime tour of the past.* Why did the computer bring me here on a day when Galileo's leaving? Still, I can hardly blame the kindly elderly man. "Well, Galileo, I wish you a safe journey. But please tell me, how do you feel your ideas have fared in the intervening decades?"

"As you undoubtedly know, Fizzella, it has been a constant struggle. I have been greatly honored by some, chided and reproached by others." He slouches into the chair. "Aristotle has many loyal followers. No, not followers—worshipers! I swear that if Aristotle himself rose from the grave he would honor the evidence of his senses, but these so-called followers refuse to even peer through a telescope! They wish never to raise their eyes from the pages of Aristotle's works, as if the universe had been written to be read by nobody but Aristotle; as if Aristotle's eyes had been destined to see for all posterity! Then they accuse me, as if I reached into the sky and mischievously placed up there the stars and moons that Aristotle's eyes did not observe!"

I smile at his eloquent description of his own struggle with his critics. Many in my Collective choose to see the world only through the eyes of Ecommunity's forefathers. *Can I change that?*

"May I ask you one question before you leave?"

"*Si, si*, Fizzella. I am delighted that you are still asking questions. Go ahead."

"In all the intervening time, did you ever manage to detect the Earth's movement?"

"Ah. No, I did not. But I have pondered the question all my years. I think I have understood why we do not feel the Earth's rapid movement. Allow me to explain." He leans forward, awkwardly avoiding eye contact. "Imagine for a moment, Fizzella, that you were in the hold of a ship and the ship was sailing at constant speed and constant direction on a calm sea. Down in the hold, with no windows, do you think you could tell whether the ship was moving and how fast?"

I recall Dad saying that you don't feel the speed of a PAT when the journey is smooth. But could that be right—could I really be in the hold of the ship completely oblivious to the ship's movement? "Well, what if I dropped something? Wouldn't it land slightly behind me on the floor since the ship and I would be moving forward while the item falls?"

"No Fizzella, try it. The item would not land behind you as it is already moving along with you and the ship. As the item drops it will also continue its forward movement, along with you and the ship and it will land on your feet whether the ship is moving or not. Here look:"

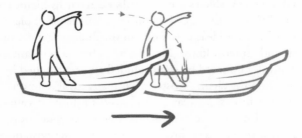

An object dropped inside a moving ship still lands on the man's toes

"I see, but surely some other experiment could help me discern whether the ship is moving?"

"I believe not," Galileo says. "I call it the *principle of relativity*. My principle states that all the laws of nature will work identically in a moving environment as in a static one. You cannot tell that you are moving without looking outside."

Strange, Dad murmured something about "relativity" when I asked him how the hut works. But I'm pretty sure he said *theory of relativity*.

"Why do you call it the principle of relativity?"

"My principle is much broader than just a law—it is like a *meta* law. The principle states that *all* the laws of the natural world must comply with this overriding principle. All laws of nature must work equally well whether you are in a stationary environment or in a moving environment like the hold of ship."

"Why the principle of *relativity*?"

"Do you see, Fizzella, my principle is not just saying that you cannot tell if the ship is stationary or moving. No, the principle is much more profound than that. It is saying that 'stationary' and 'moving' are equivalent—they are one and the same thing. We might like to consider that the ocean is stationary and the ship is moving, but it is just as valid for the passenger to think that he and the ship are stationary and the Earth and ocean are moving. Relative to the Earth, the ship is moving; relative to the ship, the Earth is moving. 'Stationary' and 'moving' are relative concepts. Nobody can say what is truly stationary and what is truly moving."

He leans forward, preparing to leave, but I really want to understand this principle.

I imagine myself floating alone in deep space. Yes, who's to say if I'm moving or not? I suppose I'm entitled to think of myself as stationary. If someone else floats by, who's to say if I'm moving past them or they are moving past me.

In fact, standing here in a suburb of Florence right now, am I standing still? Or am I flying around the Sun? I suppose all I can really say, to be accurate, is that I'm stationary *relative* to the Earth.

Aristotle told me that all matter is naturally stationary. Now Galileo not only says that things naturally keep moving, but he dares to say that there is no such objective concept of stationary at all!

Hmm. I wonder whether the Church will accept this principle of relativity as justification for not feeling the Earth's movement—or might the Church dismiss it as an excuse?

"Tell me Galileo, in the last twenty years, did you find quantitative laws for other physical processes besides falling objects?"

"Alas, Fizzella, it is of utmost importance that I take my leave right now. My bags are packed and my coach is waiting. But there is something I want you to have."

Rising from his desk, Galileo slowly shuffles toward the wall. Now he hugs the wall and pigeon-steps along the edge of the room toward the bookcase. For a moment I think he needs the wall for support but it seems his hand is only brushing the wood paneling gently as he progresses. I gaze at him sadly as he progresses slowly.

A handful of old telescopes are on the shelf. Galileo feels each one clumsily with both hands and finally picks one up. "Where are you Fizzella?"

My eyes are welling up. I walk toward Galileo. I'm still holding the mask in one hand—with my other hand I take his free arm and whisper, "I'm right here."

Galileo takes my hand off his arm and puts it on the telescope. "I want you to have this. You know, we changed the world with this little telescope."

The generosity of the choice of word "we" stirs me. I drop the mask and take the telescope with both hands.

One of Galileo's telescopes

Through my tears I look at the telescope, then I study Galileo's eyes, which are darting around, unable to make proper eye contact.

"Is this," I sob, "the telescope with which you observed the Sun all those years ago?"

"It is."

"Do you ever... regret it?"

"I regret nothing. We explored the Sun and so much else. In many ways I think that this, here, was the first ever scientific instrument. It allowed us to reveal many hidden truths." Galileo holds my head in two hands and kisses me on the forehead, knocking my triangular hat off. "I hope you will take away this one lesson from our brief work together, Fizzella, all that time ago: Always pursue the truth. Always. And now I must depart."

Suddenly, more than anything in the world, I want Galileo to stay. For a moment I have the overpowering feeling that if Galileo would stay here now, I would stay right here with him and not return to my Mom.

Holding Galileo's arm, I guide him out to the corridor. I know what I'm feeling, but I wonder what prompted him to bequeath me such a touching, precious gift. At the door, Galileo gently removes my hand from his arm and heads out of the front door on his own, stroking his hand along the wall the whole while, leaving me standing in the doorway of the empty office. Holding the telescope in my hand, I watch his back until he disappears around the corner.

I touch my forehead as if to hold his kiss in place. Slowly I walk back into his office. Many of the artifacts from the Pisa lab are here: the pendulum, the lanterns with shutters, the chisel, the thermometer. Many more instruments have been added over the years—since my yesterday— an inclined plane some six or seven meters long complete with little bells along its length which I assume aid the timing of descending balls, other optical arrangements which seem to be for examining small details from close by, detailed charts for the orbits of the four moons that he discovered around Jupiter:

A fragment of Galileo's records of Jupiter's moons

I spend some minutes toying with the instruments.

This sad goodbye may be my final encounter with the historical world. As I leave, I glance at Galileo's desk. On the top of a pile of papers I see correspondence from Johannes Kepler—Kepler of *Kepler's Nova*. The letter is spread open so I read it without actually touching anything.

My dear Galileo,

Enclosed are some tables with detailed daily observations by Tycho and myself of the planets' motions through our telescopium.

I have found some interesting patterns and laws. I can confirm, as you would expect by now, that all planets are circling the Sun. I have found three mathematical laws that completely describe the planets' motion:

1. *The planets' paths around the Sun are not perfect circles—they seem to be ellipses! For example, the Earth is closest to the Sun in January and furthest in July.*

2. *The speed of a planet's movement around its orbit increases when it is nearer to the Sun (on the narrow part of the ellipse) and decreases when far from the Sun.*

3. *The time the planet takes to complete an orbit depends on its distance from the Sun. My formula can predict why Mercury circles the sun in eighty-eight of our days, Earth in one year, while Mars, which is further, takes almost two of our years.*

Incidentally, that last formula works both ways—I know Saturn takes almost thirty years to orbit the Sun but I do not know its distance—now I can use my formula to calculate how far away Saturn is.

The ellipses take me back to my childhood observations—this finally explains how comets can sometimes be very close to the Sun and then invisibly far for some years.

Sincerely,

Johannes

PS I enclose a story about traveling to the Moon for your entertainment.

PPS Speaking of the Moon, I have been studying the tides—I have discovered that tides are determined by the position of the Moon!

I read the last lines again. *A story about travel to the Moon?* What is propelling Kepler, who will never travel further or faster than a horse and carriage can carry him, to write fiction—I suppose you could call it science fiction—about traveling to the Moon? *What a strange genre of writing.*

Kepler has also attached a small diagram about comets and their elliptic orbit. I recall my grandparents telling me how they saw Halley's Comet as children, in 2061, I think they said. So that's why comets appear for some months then disappear for many years—*orbits are elliptical!*

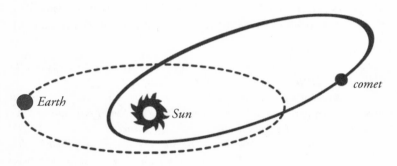

Kepler's theory of elliptical orbits

But he's saying that the planets travel on ellipses too, not circles. That means that although the planets are moving, they too, like the stars, could not possibly be carried by spheres! So what is keeping planets moving in an orbit? The planetary orbits are now a complete mystery.

It's exciting to see Kepler adopting Galileo's methodology and searching for specific mathematical patterns in experimental data about natural phenomena. Maybe it could be taken a step further, as Galileo taught me; I wonder whether these three laws could also have a simpler, more fundamental underlying law.

Galileo has written some notes in the margin. Opposite the first law about ellipses, Galileo has written, "*Nonsense—circles are the perfect shape for orbits.*" I'm not sure why Galileo rejected Kepler's seemingly meticulous measurements of the orbits' shape.

Galileo has also scribbled an Italian equivalent of "gibberish" by the PPS about the Moon being the cause of the tides. I glare at the scribble for a moment before it hits me—we cannot detect the Earth's movement around its orbit because of Galileo's principle of relativity, but at least

Galileo thought he had found evidence of the Earth's *rotation*—in the tides. The tides were his star witness in his case for heliocentrism. But now Kepler is proposing a competing explanation for the oceanic ebb and flow!

My shoulders slump. That means that Galileo is left with no direct evidence at all that the Earth is spinning and no direct evidence that the Earth circles the Sun. He has some astronomical evidence that Venus circles the Sun, but the Church is not going to accept that indirect evidence over the word of Scripture! I wonder how his discussions in Rome will play out.

Also on the desk is a thick book by Copernicus, *De Revolutionibus*, dedicated to Pope Paul III. I open the cover and see that it was published in the year of Copernicus' death, 1543—after what must have been decades of hesitation. So he did publish! I wonder if Copernicus saw this book in print before he died.

Again I see Galileo's notes in the margin, but several passages have also been scribbled out. Why would Galileo deface the book? *Oh.* I can only guess that he made these modifications at the directive of the Vatican's censorship. I smile as I notice that Galileo has crossed out the censored passages with a light touch; the print underneath is still just about legible.

Copernicus' Latin book seems incredibly heavy and complex—I wonder how many people will read it. It includes detailed appendices documenting Copernicus' painstaking observations:

Page from De Revolutionibus *by Copernicus*

Alongside this is a copy of Galileo's own book, *Dialogue Concerning the Two Chief World Systems*. Unlike Copernicus—and unlike the other academic books on the surrounding shelves—Galileo writes in Italian, not Latin, perhaps aiming to attract a broader audience to science:

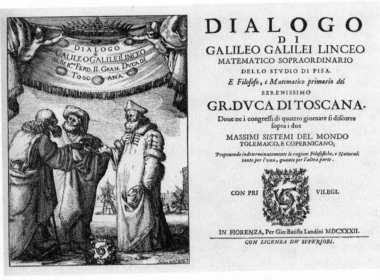

Galileo's Dialogue of Two Chief World Systems

I see that Galileo has also dedicated his book to the reigning pontiff, Pope Urban VIII, and published it with the permission of the Roman Catholic Inquisition set up by the same Pope Paul III whom Copernicus honored. As Galileo mentioned to me, he's been very politic in presenting the book as a dialog between two views. Hopefully he can't get into trouble for presenting a discussion between two opinions if he doesn't take sides.

But looking more carefully through the pages, I note that the "impartial" dialogue, or *Dialogo*, is presented between a supporter of heliocentrism named Salviati and a supporter of Aristotle's geocentrism—which is also of course the view of the Church itself—represented by *Simplicio!* Worse, leafing through the pages I get the impression that Salviati gives reasoned and illustrated arguments whereas Simplicio answers with brief babblings.

Amusingly, Galileo has included printed side comments in the book, saving the reader the trouble of making the kind of marginal notes that Galileo himself is in the habit of penning.

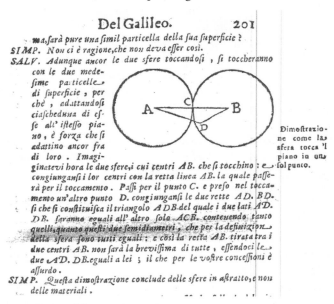

Del Galileo. 201

ma, farà pure una fimil particella della sua superficie ?
SIMP. *Non ci è ragione, che non deva effer così.*
SALV. *Adunque ancor le due sfere toccandofi , si toccheranno*
con le due mede-
fime particelle
di fuperficie , per
chè , adattandofi
ciafcheduna di ef-
fe all' istesso pia-
no , è forza che si
adattino ancor fra
di loro . Imagi-
ginatevi hora le due sfere, i cui centri *AB.* che si tocchino : e sol punto.
congiunganfi i lor centri con la retta linea *AB.* la quale passe-
rà per il toccamento . Paffi per il punto *C.* e prefo nel toccamento un'altro punto *D.* congiunganfi le due rette *AD. BD.*
si che si conftituifca il triangolo *A DB.* del quale i due lati *AD.*
DB. faranno eguali all' altro folo *ACB.* contenendo tanto
quelli, quanto quefti due femidiametri , che per la definizion
della sfera fono tutti eguali ; e così la retta *AB.* tirata tra i
due centri *AB.* non farà la breviffima di tutte , effendoci le
due *AD. DB.* eguali a lei ; il che per le vostre conceffioni è
affurdo .
SIMP. *Quefta dimoftrazione conclude delle sfere in aftratto, e non
delle materiali .*

*Dimoftrazio-
ne come la
sfera tocca 'l
piano in un
sol punto.*

Page from Galileo's Dialogue *between Salviati and "Simplicio"*

I look around Galileo's stacks of files of correspondence. One file is resting in the middle of his desk as if he were in the middle of reading it. *More likely having it read to him.* The original title of the file, *Cardinal Maffeo Barberini,* has been crossed out and below it is written importantly *Pope Urban VIII.* Galileo's correspondence with the Pope! I hesitate. I open the file, just for a really quick peek.

It seems that Galileo and the Cardinal-cum-Pope have had a relationship of many years. The correspondence dates back to 1611, the year following the one I visited yesterday. Galileo had been visiting Rome with his telescope, showing off his recent discoveries. The letter suggests that Cardinal Barberini was impressed by Galileo's astronomical discoveries and even more taken by Galileo's convincing demonstration, at a dinner party, that ice is lighter than water. The Cardinal wrote, "I pray the Lord God to preserve you, because men of great value like you deserve to live a long time to the benefit of the public." The correspondence continues over the years, with some of the letters signed by the cardinal, "as your brother." I read that Galileo visited him, now as Pope Urban VIII, in 1623 and was honored with no fewer than six private Papal audiences, after which His Holiness wrote of Galileo, "We embrace with paternal love this great man whose fame shines in the heavens and goes on Earth far and wide."

I smile at the warmth of the correspondence.

As I leaf through, nothing prepares me for the sudden and atrocious change in the nature of the correspondence since last year. I realize that was the year in which the *Dialogue* was published, dedicated to the Pope and published with the Pope's approval, but with the Pontiff's own ideas placed rather patronizingly in the mouth of Simplicio.

AD 1632. Professor Galileo Galilei... You are hereby summoned to Rome to appear before the holy Catholic Inquisition accused of the capital offense of heresy...

As my entire insides freefall, I read Galileo's petition, endorsed by three physicians, to have his Inquisition trial moved to Florence on account of his fragile health. A meeting of the Inquisition personally chaired by the Pope rejected the petition. I read an official notice informing Galileo that if he does not present himself in Rome he will be brought to Rome in chains.

I freeze and simultaneously break into a sweat. I imagine Bruno burning alive at the stake on charges of heresy. Galileo has gone to the Holy See to fight the indictment, but bears no direct evidence that the Earth is moving—and based on his own principle of relativity he will never have such evidence. No doubt Galileo will call upon the oceans to rise and bear witness to the Earth's movement, but no lesser an authority than Kepler has disputed the connection between the tides and the Earth's rotation! True, Galileo has observations proving that Venus circles the Sun, but that in itself creates no problem with scripture. The Church, if it even bothers to assess Galileo's arguments, may concede that Venus circles the Sun and still convict Galileo for the heretical view that the Earth circles the Sun.

Galileo has dedicated his entire life to understanding the world—to *really* understanding the world—dispelling historic myths and exposing deep hidden truths. His focus has always been to seek the truth. And now at the age of seventy, after a lifetime of service to humanity, the Church he has always loved and served, headed by Galileo's life-long personal friend, has ordered him to Rome—not to thank him, not to reward him—but to publicly threaten and bully him, and quite possibly to take his life.

And I watched him leave some minutes ago, stooped with age, unwell, obviously blind, but exuding dignity, ready to pit his wits against his accusers with honor.

With a small old telescope in one hand and a file of Inquisition summonses in the other, I lay my head on the unoccupied desk of the frail and visually impaired Professor Galileo Galilei here in Arcetri, outside Florence, and weep. I do not know how much time has passed, but when I finally catch my breath I notice a small patch of salty tears on the beautiful teak desk.

Eventually, I sulk back to Fizz's Place in a dizzy spell. My mind is ruminating on my three days with Galileo, replaying each minute again and again, with one moment in particular reverberating through my consciousness. "Always pursue the truth. Always," Galileo said as he kissed my forehead. He said it so simply—tenderly protecting me by not adding the words he must have surely been thinking: even if pursuing the truth will cost you your life.

The truth. Always the *truth*. That word echoes through my mind. It's not about curiosity. All along, it was never about greed. *It's about truth.*

Back in the hut, I realize my first truth: Galileo enquired into the world honestly—he didn't "pry" and it didn't lead to "meddling" or in fact to any technology at all. It just led to people better understanding the world that is our shared home. He was willing to risk his life to continue his honorable enquiries, even as a blind old man.

Another truth: After five days of time travel, I may have some understanding about how people like Aristotle started enquiring into the world, and I may have some feeling for how Galileo pioneered a more scientific approach, but I know almost no science because—now that Galileo has started to define what science means—it is apparent that the entire world has almost no scientific knowledge as of 1633.

Indeed, in truth, if I return to the Ecommunity right now, I will never know any science.

And the most painful truth: The ecological community that I live in and love may have misled me. Galileo has shown me that scientific enquiry is not necessarily motivated by greed and does not inevitably lead to the ruin of nature. Scientific enquiry can be a noble pursuit of the truth.

I touch my forehead and replay the moment yet again, then I think back to the satisfaction that Galileo derived each time he unraveled a new hidden truth about the world. I think how minutes after each discovery the exhilaration passed and he was already seeking the next truth.

I resolve not to end my trip now. I resolve to continue my time travel—for the entire three weeks if necessary—and fully understand the universe as deeply as humanly possible.

I resolve to dedicate my life to the pursuit of truth, to reforming the Ecommunity, to freeing scientific thought while still shunning technology, to allowing others in my community to pursue their own yearning for truth, their own passion to understand the world.

At the top of the ROW label—which, if it were a glass of wine, would be no more than a small taste, much more empty than full—I add the words "*To Galileo*" and collapse onto my bed.

"Computer, take me to see Galileo's fate."

But hearing my own voice, my instruction doesn't sound appropriate. My mission is to understand Galileo's legacy, not his personal destiny. Galileo himself would want me to continue my enquiries, not to follow him. I shouldn't abuse the privilege of these days of time travel.

"Computer, cancel that. Take me to whoever implemented Galileo's program for finding mathematical models for the world."

I take my flask of strawberry juice and down the final mouthful.

Them Apples

Day 6. 1667. The River Cam, Cambridge, England.

I jump out of bed, dress, and march out of the hut to find the nearest university.

The short, wide, cobbled pathway from Trinity Street to the college entrance is flanked by dark brick walls. Vegetation creeps over their tops, hinting at gardens beyond. But I'm awestruck by the gateway itself: a mini-castle towering above me, several stories high with octagonal columns in each corner and a turreted roof. What grandeur. *Or maybe pomp.*

A lone stone statue gazes down at me from the second story of the tower's façade, reminding me briefly of the Dean looking down from the tavern stage. The statue depicts a plump bearded king holding a golden orb in one hand and a golden scepter in the other. Above the statue, a decorative stone and gold cage forms a kind of oversized crown, whilst below it a blue, red, and gold coat of arms is held by two unidentifiable stone animals.

Great Gate, Trinity College, Cambridge

Passing through the archway in the gate, I find myself in a vast formal courtyard. Drawing a deep breath, I scan my surroundings. The courtyard stretches some one hundred meters on each side spanned by lawns that seem to have been manicured with nail scissors, interrupted by one cross of paths through the middle of the courtyard with another pathway circling the periphery. Along the north side I find the college's grandiose private chapel. Attached to the far end of the chapel stands a beautiful clock tower with another statue. Opposite the entrance, to the west, is a proud building with sloping tiled roofs. In the center of the courtyard stands a water fountain that, although not small, seems somehow dwarfed by the magnificence of the surroundings.

Where to start?

I retrace my steps. Within Great Gate itself I had passed a doorway labeled *Porters' Lodge,* and in it I now find a couple of "porters," complete with black suits and bowler hats, wielding big chains of keys. Like most men I have seen walking here this morning, they wear their hair long with curls falling below the shoulder. I suspect at least one of the men's curly hair is actually a wig. Also, like other men I passed, the porters smell awful, but they look quite like they own the place, so I request some background information.

"Great Court," one of them explains to me, "is the largest enclosed courtyard in Europe. It was built by King Henry VIII when he founded this college in 1546." He glances at a portrait of King Henry VIII, whom I recognize from the statue that greeted me a moment ago.

"Beautiful," I say.

"Indeed," says the porter, "it is the magnificence of this college's architecture that attracts the cream of society to come and study within its walls."

"Ah yes, the cream of society," says the other porter, "rich and thick."

I chuckle politely, wondering how many times they've cracked that joke. But I have a job to do and enquire about experts in natural philosophy.

The porter smirks. "Madam, Trinity College is one of sixteen colleges in the University of Cambridge, several dating back to the twelve and thirteen hundreds. I think that more than one professor around here would be considered an expert on Greek natural philosophy."

So much for all the grandeur. So this university is stuck on Greek philosophy. "Well, might you have any experts on alternative natural philosophies?"

"Non-Greek? That is much less common. There is that new young fellow—I heard he studies radical ideas. Let me look him up for you." The porter leafs through some lists. "Here we are—Isaac Newton lists his interests as Galileo, Kepler, and Descartes."

My heart skips a beat, then another. "Galileo! Whatever happened to him?"

"Madam, I have no idea what or who Galileo is. It just says here that this new young professor is interested in that topic. It also notes that he has a private lab—" he leafs through his notebook, "strange—it says somewhere behind this porter's lodge. Newton moved back here very recently."

"Back from?" I ask.

He consults the list again. "Back from Woolsthorpe-by-Colsterworth, Lincolnshire. A small farming hamlet, I think somewhere north of here. After graduating he went home for two years. He just returned when the university reopened."

"The university—reopened?"

"You know, once the great plague subsided a little."

As I stare at the porter blankly, pondering this information, I hear a student sneeze in the distance.

Another danger of time travel that I never even weighed. The threat of contracting a terrible disease so far away in time and space from my family causes my throat to contract. For a second I wonder if it's too dangerous to hang around here. *But if Galileo was not afraid of death, I suppose I should brave the plague too.*

I smile at the porter weakly. "So how do I get to this laboratory?"

"I actually have no idea. No precise location is listed. There is no back door here in the lodge so maybe 'behind the lodge' is incorrect. You will have to find it yourself."

I head off in search of a passage that might take me behind the porters' lodge. Before entering the college I saw plants growing from behind the wall—there must be a garden somewhere back there. But past the lodge I find myself in the fully enclosed Great Court. A stone dorm building runs all the way from the lodge to the chapel. I enter the dorm building looking for a way through to the garden that ought to be behind it, but find none. I enter the chapel and walk its entire length. The long black-and-white-patterned floor reminds me of the Cathedral floor in Frombork, but no openings connect the chapel to the garden.

I retrace my steps again—the long chapel, the dorm building, the porter's lodge, and the wall on the street form an apparently impenetrable square—none of them have a doorway to the garden that I know must be enclosed between them. *What kind of lab would be concealed in a walled garden with no obvious access?*

Trinity College Cambridge in the 1600s

Finally I return to the chapel and, balancing rudely on a wooden pew, I climb up and peek through one of the huge arched bay windows. At last I can see the meticulously kept garden. A narrow stairway leads down from the second floor of the dorm building into the garden. *Success!* Strangely it seems you can only access the garden via the second floor of the dorms, so that's where I head. The second floor corridor is cloistered, with an open view of the garden, interrupted by posts. At the far end I find the staircase I had seen.

The smallish garden is a mixture of grass, plain earth, shrubs, and flowers shaded by some trees. At one end I notice a water pump. On the north side, the chapel building steps in and out, creating three bays, set within the chapel wall. Nestled inside the far bay is a small stone building, not much bigger than my own time-travel hut. *What a bizarre secretive place for a little physics laboratory—in the corner of a barely accessible yard.* I walk over and knock on the door.

"No!"

I want to protest that I've come all the way from Iceland in 2110 to explore the development of science, but instead I just ease open the door. "Mr. Newton?" I try to smile though the crack. I'm surprised to see he's in his early twenties, not much older than myself. "Isaac?" I try.

"I said *no!*"

Newton is dressed in a ruffled long-sleeved white shirt with a coat, waistcoat and breeches. Under his wavy, platinum blonde wig he has a narrow face that could only be faulted for a slightly pronounced nose, and, at this moment, a venomous expression that does not invite any negotiation.

From a shelf above his head, *Dialogue Concerning the Two Chief World Systems* beckons to me, and next to it is another book by Galileo, *The Starry Messenger. This is my guy.* I have to find some way to connect.

"I had some thoughts I wanted to discuss about those very books on your shelf. Do you have a minute?"

"No."

Having exhausted the tasteful options, I decide to attempt an age-old tactic that I've seen some of my girl friends back home use effectively. Turning one shoulder toward Isaac, I flash him a coy smile. "Isaac, I'm sure you could do with a little company while you do your research." In the confines of the tiny lab, his body odor refuses my attempts to ignore it, but I breathe through my mouth and strain to hold an attractive smile.

I think I spot his face relaxing just slightly. "What is your name?"

"I'm Fizz."

"Then go away, Fizz. Now."

Through my anger at his rudeness I'm vaguely aware that it is I who has humiliated myself. Be that as it may, going away is really not an option. Thanks to a brick charcoal furnace in one corner, the lab is baking hot. On the small span of desk between myself and Isaac, I notice a glass pitcher filled with the most curious substance. It looks like a shiny metal, but fills the pitcher like a liquid.

"So what are you doing with this?" I say, reaching to casually pick it up. The liquid's weight takes me by surprise—*it's as heavy as lead!*—and, to my horror, instead of lifting it, I tilt and spill some of the silvery fluid all over the desk. The liquid doesn't splash, but rather groups itself playfully into a handful of globules, each of which curls into a small ball. Every ball quickly comes to rest, suddenly regaining the appearance of solid silver. Fascinated, I reach out instinctively to poke the whimsical fluid, then immediately stop myself. I look at Isaac in desperation, my skin becoming damp.

"How dare you! Leave that mercury alone," Isaac's shouting reverberates through the tiny brick room. "Get out of here this second."

"Look I'm really, really sorry to disturb your work and I didn't mean to spill your substance. I'm just genuinely interested in what you're doing."

I wait for him to physically throw me out, but instead he stops and stares at me. "What do you mean interested in what I am doing?" He narrows his eyes and talks more slowly, now sounding more suspicious than angry. "What is the nature of your interest? Why are you interested? Who sent you to check on me?"

"No, um, I'm just fascinated."

"It is none of your business, not at all. Nobody comes in here uninvited." He sighs, as if realizing that I won't leave without some explanation. "In any event, I was just, well, about to perform an experiment. In fact, I was going to... reproduce Pascal's experiment. Yes, that is what I was going to do with this mercury. Perform Pascal's experiment. You've got your explanation. Now go."

I regard him without moving. I have no idea who Pascal is and what experiment is named after him or her, but I would bet that people who are busy reproducing Pascal's experiment don't have to worry about spies. *If his original plan for this mercury stuff was really Pascal's experiment, then*

I'm the Chief Dean. But what could he really be doing? Perhaps I can use his suspicion to my advantage.

When did I learn to think this way?

"Well that's all in order then," I'm shocked to hear myself saying. "I'll just have to see the experiment you were going to perform, of course, with an explanation, and then I'll be on my way. So who is Pascal?"

My muscles tense and I bite my tongue. I'm not sure if it's nervousness or pangs of guilt about deceiving him in a way I don't even understand.

Newton eyes me, visibly steaming. "So be it. Frenchman, Blaise Pascal. I shall fetch some equipment and show you the experiment. Then you leave."

Newton doesn't seem to have any of the necessary equipment prepared and flusters around a while, collecting it. He locates a funnel and a very long thin glass tube closed at one end. It must be about a meter long. Using the funnel he fills the long tube with the playful mercury stuff. Then he quickly flips the tube to point upside down at a forty-five degree angle into the beaker of mercury. He does this fast enough that no mercury has time to spill. The tube remains full. I suppose it can't flow down into the beaker while the tube is sealed at its top so there's no way for air to get in. Isaac slowly pulls the long capillary up into a vertical position. Strangely, the mercury no longer reaches the top!

"That is the experiment," Isaac says. "The mercury in the tube never extends higher than 76 centimeters."

"Strange." I point at the gap above the mercury. "How did air get in there?"

"It did not."

"No air? But doesn't nature abhor a vacuum? There must be something there."

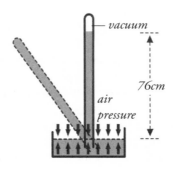

Pascal's experiment

"You barge in here and then you quote Aristotle?"

He has a point. I suspect that particular assertion of Aristotle was backed by no more evidence than any of his other statements. This demonstration of a vacuum is quite convincing. *Perhaps nature only mildly dislikes a vacuum.*

"But if nature doesn't abhor a vacuum," I pinch my lip, "why is it so difficult to suck the air out of a bottle?"

"There is no difficulty at all in sucking air out of a bottle. But what are you doing with that air as you extract it?"

"I suppose—"

"When you pump the air out of the bottle you are pushing that air *into* the Earth's atmosphere, are you not? Or if you breathe it your lungs are expanding and your chest has to push hard to lift up the Earth's pressurized atmosphere just a little bit. *That* is what is difficult."

"Wow—not what it seems," I say out loud although mostly to myself. "So people have always thought that nature resists sucking air out of a bottle whereas all along nature was actually abhorring the effort to push more air into the Earth's atmosphere."

"Yes. But air pressure has its limits, that is Pascal's point," Isaac points at the tube grudgingly. "Mercury is heavy. The air pushing down on the beaker can support the weight of a seventy-six-centimeter column of mercury. Anything higher than that cannot be supported by air pressure, and a vacuum is formed above it. There you are, Pascal's experiment."

"Always seventy-six centimeters?"

"Almost exactly. Evangelista Torricelli in Italy recently showed that there are some small changes to the height of the column from one day to the other or at different altitudes. Torricelli calls this arrangement a *barometer* and uses it to measure the Earth's atmospheric pressure. And Otto von Guericke in Germany discovered that a small drop in atmospheric pressure—a drop in the mercury in the barometer—is a predictor of rain."

"Back home, we used sitting cows as a predictor of rain."

"We did too," he says curtly.

I smile. "So, how did you like growing up in a farming community?" He rolls his eyes. "Not at all."

"Oh. So can we feel this atmospheric air pressure?"

"You saw the experiment." Isaac points at the door.

"We agreed to the experiment with a full explanation."

Newton exhales loudly while I briefly hold my breath. *How much will he invest in covering up whatever it was he was doing?*

"All right. The total atmospheric pressure on both sides of your body exceeds the weight of an elephant. But it is applied evenly from all sides and you are used to it so you are not aware of the pressure."

"So we live our lives immersed in a crushing soup of air, without even realizing it?"

"Yes. Did you read about the demonstration by that same Otto von Guericke at the court of Friedrich Wilhelm I of Brandenburg in Berlin? You did not? Von Guericke took two copper hemispheres of about fifty centimeters in diameter and touched them together, with no adhesive, to make a sphere, then emptied the air from between the hemispheres using a vacuum pump that he invented. He harnessed a dozen horses to each hemisphere. Those twenty-four horses could not pull the two hemispheres apart on account of the air pressure on the outside of the spheres. Again, it was not the vacuum sucking the hemispheres in, but rather the outside air pressure pushing them in."

"Explain."

He sloppily sketches a quick diagram. "Here:"

Otto von Guericke's experiment

Twenty-four horses! That Otto von Guericke obviously has a flair for dramatizing physics. Interesting that he should be willing to flagrantly ridicule one of Aristotle's beliefs in such a public way.

"So," I say, "some natural philosophers are continuing Galileo's tradition of using experimentation to challenge ancient beliefs."

"Yes. The importance of experimentation was famously espoused by Sir Francis Bacon, who studied here in Trinity College. You could say that Bacon died experimenting—it was his exploration of the effect of snow on preserving meat that led him to catch a fatal pneumonia."

"So what *is* this air pressure anyway? Why should air push things at all?"

For a second I think he is actually looking at me, not through me, as if surprised by such an intelligent question. "Well, no one fully knows, but Boyle offers an interesting insight into air pressure."

"Who's Boyle?"

"Ah. My good friend, Robert Boyle, born in Ireland to an aristocratic English family. In 1641, as a teenager, he visited Florence and was so inspired by being in the proximity of the elderly Galileo Galilei that he became an important scientist."

Suddenly I'm not in an overheated little brick lab in a secret garden in Cambridge sparring with an unpleasant young English professor, but back in Pisa and Galileo is kissing me and handing me a telescope. I close my eyes and slump into a small chair as waves of relief wash over me. "Galileo was alive in 1641?"

"Yes. Under house arrest, blind, prohibited from studying or support- ing heliocentrism, his books banned. But he was alive and still thinking about science. Galileo died aged seventy-seven at the end of that same year, 1641; mind you, it was already 1642 on the Gregorian calendar they use over there. Actually I was born at the end of 1642.

My eyes still closed, I touch my forehead. Galileo made it. He lived on to die a natural death. *And his spirit is clearly living on and thriving in the likes of Pascal, von Guericke, and Boyle, who are systematically exploring nature and flamboyantly challenging Aristotelian dogma.* I'm almost giddy with relief.

"Woman, do not make yourself comfortable." When I make no move, he continues. "So do you wish to hear about Boyle before you leave?"

"Yes." I open my eyes and focus.

"He is the author of the book *The Sceptical Chymist*—a pioneer in applying new scientific rigor to the field of chemistry." For a brief moment the unwillingness is gone and I think I see a hint of admiration in his expression as he talks about Boyle. "But you asked about his insights into gases. You know that you can change the volume of a gas— expand or contract it?"

"You can?"

Isaac rolls his eyes. "Yes. You can expand or contract a gas. That is the definition of a gas, what distinguishes it from a liquid. Boyle experiment- ed with changing the volume of gases. He found a law that the pressure of a gas is *inversely proportional* to its volume. So if you compress a gas to half the volume, its pressure doubles. If you expand a gas to double the volume, the pressure drops to half."

"Interesting. But again, what is this gas pressure? Can Boyle explain how it is that a gas keeps pushing at everything around it? How the pressure changes inversely to the volume?"

"No. Boyle and I have no explanation for that."

"So you and Boyle collaborate?"

It seemed like an innocent question, but Isaac instantly squints at me. "What is that to you? Is that any of your business? I showed you the experiment with the mercury—have you quite finished interrogating me?"

"Of course, you're right. It's none of my business, I was just being curious."

"Damned right it is not. Boyle and I are both members of the Royal Society of London for the Improvement of Natural Knowledge. We collaborate on physics at the Royal Society. So I showed you the experiment I was performing. Now go." He stands up, his head almost touching the low ceiling, and points toward the door.

I glance at a stack of papers at the end of the lab desk, seeing a familiar name jump up from the covers. *I can't leave without even finding out what this objectionable young man has contributed.* "You know, I'm familiar with Kepler's laws of planetary motion," I gesture at the papers. "Based on Galileo's technique, I was thinking that the three patterns Kepler found in the orbits of the planets might hint at an underlying fundamental law. Might you have any thoughts on that?"

"Perhaps I do."

For one second I think I may have piqued his interest, but he starts advancing toward me to physically push me out. I feel indignant at his rude selfishness, but I'm out of ideas for extending the conversation and am forced to leave.

I take a walk around Cambridge and slowly unwind in the mid-morning air. I try to remind myself that Isaac doesn't owe me anything. I barged in. He doesn't know my circumstances—that I need to understand physics quickly in order to sort out my life. He was perfectly entitled to refuse to talk to me. *Jerk.*

Why did he entertain me at all? It clearly wasn't willingly. Now how can I entice him into further conversation?

Touring around a while, I find that all sixteen colleges are in close proximity and mostly built in similar styles around formal rectangular courtyards. The oldest is Peterhouse, founded 1284. The newest is

Sidney Sussex founded in 1596 by a woman—Lady Sidney, countess of Sussex. King's College has a more ornate Gothic architecture than the others with many dramatic turrets along the imposing college chapel which is flanked by twelve massive stained glass windows. This private college chapel would shame the cathedral in Reykjavík.

Gradually I build up the courage to make another attempt to communicate with Isaac. Perhaps a better tactic is to catch him when I'm not trespassing on the privacy of his semi-covert lab. A three-minute walk down King's Parade and Trinity Street takes me back to Trinity College, where I linger on the second floor of the dorms, leaning against one of the pillars with a bird's eye view of the small walled garden. From time to time I pace the length of the loggia, then return to lean on one of the pillars.

Air pressure—I take a breath and watch my chest rise. Twenty-four horses. Every one of us experiencing the weight of an elephant. And we're not even sure what air pressure is. Mercury. Heavy enough that seventy-six centimeters of the silvery stuff can overcome air pressure. *But what was he really doing with that mercury that would make him almost paranoid?*

An hour later, Isaac emerges from the lab. I climb a flight of stairs to hide on the third floor while he climbs up to the second floor and then down again into Great Court. I descend and follow him across the full length of Great Court and past the college's formal dining hall into a second courtyard, signed "Nevile's Court." Nevile's Court has just three built sides, with the far side opening into a small informal meadow. According to another sign, this area is referred to as the "backs" of the college. The ground slopes down some tens of meters and ends at the artificial brick bank walls of the river Cam. The backs are dotted with willows, bursting with slender green leaves, weeping far out across the water. Isaac strides across the lawn and takes the college's stone bridge over the water continuing into the Avenue, a lane beautifully demarcated on both sides by a colonnade of formally spaced lime and cherry trees.

Trinity College's extensive grounds seem to continue with formal gardens here on the west side of the river. A duck flies past—*another example of what Aristotle would consider an anomaly of Earth rising above Air.* As the duck splashes down into the Cam with a quack, I wonder how birds fly.

Isaac breaks off from the Avenue and into the gardens. I follow him even when he passes a little wooden sign, hammered into the lawn, reading, "Fellow's Garden—College fellows only." Finally he sits down on the grass and leans against a tree, takes a notebook out of a pocket, and starts writing.

Newton's absorption seems total. Not for a second does he take his nose out of that notebook to take in the picturesque scenery. After an hour, I've not had a single opportunity to catch his eye. His intensity is trying my patience. Finally, I pick an apple off one of the trees near me and lob it into a high arc, successfully landing it just in front of him. It hits the ground with a small thud. Sure enough Isaac finally extracts his face from his notebook to stare at the apple for a while. Then he picks it up and glances up at the apple tree that's shading him.

Seizing the moment, I stroll past.

"Oh, hi Isaac."

"How did that apple fall just now?"

My body seizes up.

"How *did* that apple fall?" Isaac repeats sharply.

"Well, um, what apple? Oh that apple... well I assume..." I gesture at the tree above him.

"I know where it fell from, idiot, but how?"

"Oh, how?" I smile. "It looks ripe. Apples fall when they're ripe, don't they?"

"Silence. I am thinking."

I frown and shut up.

Eventually he continues. "What would have happened if the tree were higher?"

"What?"

"If the tree were five miles high, what would have happened?"

"Well I'm not sure the bees would pollinate it at that altitude." At least I know a bit about farming.

"Focus, you imbecile. Would the apple fall?"

"I suppose."

"Indeed, I suppose too. Now what if the tree were higher still?" He points directly at the sky.

"Come again?" Following his finger, I notice that he's not pointing randomly at the sky—he's pointing at the semi-circular Moon overhead.

"Well, would the apple fall?"

I've got an awkward feeling that these questions are rhetorical—that he's using me as a sounding board because I happen to be standing around when he wants to talk himself through a complex thought. That's not going to stop me from trying to turn it into a dialog.

"You mean if the tree extended up to the Moon? Isaac, back up a bit."

"If the Earth can pull an apple... might it be pulling the Moon?"

I shake my head. "That's insane. Isn't the Moon up in the lofty celestial world, a world that works independently of the forces affecting materials here on Earth? Fortunate really. We wouldn't want the Moon falling toward us like an apple."

"I am thinking maybe the Moon is falling toward us right now."

Have I been following a lunatic—literally?

He persists. "Stay with me, whatever-your-name-is... I need to work this through. What is the natural state of motion?"

"Fizz."

"What?"

"My name is Fizz."

"What kind of a name is that?"

"Err, short for Fitzpatrick."

"Miss Fitzpatrick. What is the natural state of motion?"

"According to Galileo, matter has 'inertia' to continue in a straight line at a constant speed."

"Right. So left to its own devices, the Moon would float off in a straight line, yes?"

"Well I don't quite know if inertia applies to the Moon, but if it does, then yes."

"Okay," Isaac says. "So now imagine the Moon is floating in a straight line but the Earth pulls it just a bit."

"The Earth pulls the Moon?" I glance around to see if anyone else is hearing this, but no one is close. "Just a bit? Oh! You mean just enough to pull the Moon into a circular path!"

"Yes, or an ellipse. You see, I am thinking that the Moon is actually being pulled by the Earth and it may be constantly falling toward us and yet it would never get any closer to Earth if the amount it falls is always *just* enough to bend it from a straight line to a circular orbit—no more and no less."

Isaac takes his notebook and sketches a diagram:

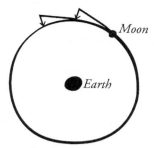

The Moon's orbit may be thought of as motion in a straight line combined with falling toward the Earth

I stare at the diagram as he continues.

"So perhaps the reason that the Moon keeps moving is not because of a rotating celestial sphere, or a Greek god, or magnetism as Kepler speculated. The Moon keeps moving because that is what objects do naturally—they keep moving—inertia. There is no friction up there, so the Moon does not slow down. But why does the Moon travel in a circle rather than a straight line? Because the Earth is continuously pulling the Moon, just like it pulls an apple, and the pull happens to be *just* enough to always keep the Moon traveling around a circle. It could be exactly the same reason that the planets circle the Sun—the planets keep moving straight due to inertia and the Sun keeps pulling at them just enough to pull them into a circular or elliptical orbit."

"That's an astounding thought. But for that to work," I protest, "wouldn't each planet's distance and speed have to be perfectly matched to the Sun's pull—if the Sun really has such a pull—so that there is just enough pull to keep the orbit in the precise circular or elliptical orbit? I mean, imagine if a planet were moving too fast, it would... it would... oh, I see, it would drift up to a larger orbit where the speed and pull were balanced! Yes, too slow... it would be pulled down into a lower orbit, closer to the Sun, where the speed and pull were again balanced. I think I get it: The planet naturally ends up at a distance and speed such that the Sun's pull is just right to bend the 'inertial' straight path into an elliptical orbit. But what if a planet was going much too fast or much too slow?"

"Such planets are gone," Isaac says simply.

Yes, of course. Any planets that were much too fast would have escaped the Sun's pull and flown away, while any that were much too slow would have been overcome by the Sun's pull and crashed into the Sun. We're left with the planets where the pull is in the right range to hold them in an orbit.

"So that balance explains Kepler's second law of planetary motion?"

Newton nods. "Indeed. That is the reason behind the mathematical law that relates the size of a planet's orbit to the speed of orbit. The Sun's pull must be matched to the size and the speed of the orbit so that the pull is just enough to bend the movement into a circle or ellipse."

"But Isaac, what is all this pulling: The Earth pulls an apple? The Earth pulls the Moon? The Sun pulls a planet? Is there some law, governing which objects are attracted to other?"

"I am thinking about that." Apparently Newton means right this second because he stands up to walk away without a word of parting.

"Isaac!"

"Yes?"

"Just before you go—"

He sighs loudly. "Yes?"

"If I may, now that we've had a couple of conversations, may I ask a personal question?"

Silence.

I take a deep breath then go on. "How did you get to be like this?"

"Like what?"

"Well, a brilliant, fiercely independent thinker on the one hand, but— may I say—just a little insecure and jumpy on the other."

"No, you may not."

"I share some of those characteristics you know, not perhaps your genius, but I can be pretty independent."

"So?"

"OK. Don't take this the wrong way, but I grew up without a father. He abandoned my mother and, unwittingly, the unborn me. You?"

He stares through me. "My father did not abandon me." With that he turns and walks off.

"I didn't mean specifically—" I call after him, but he doesn't turn around. "Please excuse me," I shout at his back, "just taking a friendly interest."

By now Isaac is out of earshot striding toward the adjacent backs of St. John's College. I take the apple and stroll back toward Nevile's Court. I rotate the apple around in my fingers as I walk.

Isaac certainly shows the kind of maverick thinking that I admired in Nicolaus Copernicus and Galileo Galilei. I smile. The Dean would probably call it "irreverence"—they all disrespected the authority of Aristotle. Galileo was also irreverent toward academic dress and the Church. Newton is irreverent not only toward Aristotle—who according to the porters is still the dominant intellectual authority in Cambridge— but also toward the mighty planets—seeing them not as some sort of immutable celestial gods but as mere balls, subject to the same laws as an apple!

How apt that Newton was born in the year that Galileo died.

On a personal level though, Isaac Newton seems so different from Galileo. Where is the self-confidence, charisma, the warmth? Newton seems anxious, temperamental, bordering on paranoid. If I meet him when he's old, Newton's not going to kiss my forehead or present me with any sentimental gift. So how *did* he turn out like this?

The apple in my hand draws my attention back to physics. I hold it in front of me and toss it up a few times. "It would not be an exaggeration," I say to the apple, "to say that you triggered the unification of the heavens and the earth! People have treated the terrestrial and celestial as detached realms until today, when Isaac Newton saw you fall, and suggested that the very same forces, and the same principles like inertia, govern an apple and a planet."

And I had planned to distract him!

I take a bite of the apple and cross the bridge back toward the college. The river Cam smells awful—as well as being a major supply route for the town, it seems to function as the official sewer and rubbish dump. I look at the apple core. If an apple triggers such insights, what else can Isaac teach me—teach the world—about the workings of the universe? I toss the core into the river and as I watch it drift off, I decide to stay in Cambridge another day in the hopes that one obnoxious young man can take me another step closer to the truth about the world—a step closer to being ready to embark on a mission of change in my Ecommunity.

But every day of my PCC is precious: Isaac had better be in a more talkative mood tomorrow.

Instant Attraction

One week. Mom must be having kittens. *Well, she'll put it behind her once I get home.*

As the clock in Great Court strikes 8 am, I arrive at Isaac's secret lab hoping he starts work early. After the more cordial conversation under the apple tree, perhaps his initial suspicion has subsided. *Assuming I didn't spook him with my personal question.*

"Morning, Isaac. Just curious if you had any luck analyzing what we discussed yesterday." He's sitting at his desk toying with a long, triangular chunk of glass, rotating it in the sunlight that streams in through a small window in the brick wall. The furnace is thankfully unlit. Unshaven, in crumpled clothes, the young man looks a bit of a mess.

"Oh, you," he says.

"Isaac, excuse the question, have you slept since we met yesterday? Or... eaten?"

"Been thinking about gravity."

"Gravity?"

"From the Latin *gravitas*." He doesn't look up. "That is what I am calling the force that pulls the apple—and the Moon." He turns the prism and it casts a small rainbow on the desk.

"Ah, have you figured it out then? Isaac, stop playing with that glass for a minute."

"This prism is interesting. The white daylight *refracts* through the prism and decomposes into a spectrum of colors. Do you realize that with a second prism I can take all these rainbow colors and combine them back into white light?"

"That is interesting. What do you mean, the light 'refracts'?"

He fumbles around with the prism some more. "Light changes direction when it passes from one material to another—here light changes its angle when it passes from air into glass. The same is true from air to water. But the different colors of light, which enter the prism mixed together as white light, refract to different extents, causing them to exit the prism at different angles. The rainbow here reveals to us that white light is in fact a mixture of the colors of the rainbow."

I think again of Galileo. Mundane objects such as a chisel, lamp, or a triangular chunk of glass in the hands of a Galileo or a Newton are transformed into surgical instruments for incisive probing of nature. Yet Isaac reports his discovery with a tone more appropriate to announcing the discovery of a chocolate chip in his cookie.

"So white light is a cocktail of colors. But what *is* light?" I think of the *Ingredients* section of my label—I never thought of light as an ingredient of the universe before. *Perhaps I've done light an injustice.*

"Light is made of *corpuscles*—special particles of light. That best explains the refraction. And there appear to be seven different colors of corpuscles. This disproves the theory of those dunces Hooke and Huygens, who claimed that light is some sort of wave."

I wonder if I should know something about those "dunces."

"Hooke?"

Isaac finally looks up. "Robert Hooke at Oxford. A short man, disfigured and hunched by smallpox. He has coined the term 'cell' for the basic unit of life. Should stick to the work of sketching bugs through a microscope. Besides his fantasies about light being a wave, he has also found some minor law for the *elasticity* of materials—he found that the tension force in a spring or an elastic material increases proportionally to the amount it is stretched. All he is saying is that if you stretch a piece of rubber twice as much, the tension force pulling the piece of rubber back is twice as strong."

"That doesn't sound so minor. And Huygens?"

"What is this obsession with unimportant natural philosophers? Christiaan Huygens—Dutch. Also a member of the Royal Society—I met him in London. He has continued Galileo's work—exploring the nature of sound pitch, analyzing the oscillations of a pendulum, observing the planets."

"Huygens sounds like an important unimportant natural philosopher."

Newton sighs. "Well, Huygens also gets credit for some work on 'centripetal force'—the insight that circular motion can be caused by a force pulling toward the center of the circle, a discovery which I used in understanding how gravity can drive the orbits."

"So what's his theory of light?"

"Absurd," Isaac dismisses it with a sweep of his hand. "Huygens thinks he can use a wave theory to explain how light is *reflected* by mirrors and how light is refracted when moving from one material to another. His theory is elegant, but wrong."

"Oh. So what about your 'gravity'?"

"Two objects attract each other depending on just two criteria: how massive the bodies both are, and the distance between them. The dependence on distance is *inverse square*, meaning that if you double the distance between two objects you get four times less gravitational attraction between them. If you triple that same distance you get nine times less gravitational attraction. So even though the Sun may be more massive than the Earth and has more gravitational pull, the apple falls to the Earth, not the Sun, because the apple is much closer to the Earth than to the Sun."

"You sound very sure. How do you know the attraction varies in that particular way—inverse square?"

"I analyzed the math. An inverse square law of attraction explains Kepler's three laws for the planetary orbits."

Just as I thought—Kepler's three laws are indicative of a deeper law. Now Newton is following Galileo's approach, analyzing Kepler's laws of planetary motion and looking for a simpler underlying mathematical rule to explain the patterns that Kepler observed in the sky.

"Great. But what do you mean 'attract each other'? After all, it's the Earth that pulls the apple and the Moon."

"No, err, Fizz, they pull each other. The Moon pulls the Earth as much as the Earth pulls the Moon."

"What makes you think *that?*"

"The tides, for one."

"The tides?"

"The tides," Isaac repeats. "Kepler was right, Galileo was wrong—the Moon causes the tides. Now we know why. It is the Moon's gravitational attraction that tugs the ocean up—just a little—toward the Moon."

I smile. "I wondered what could cause an entire ocean to shift. So it's this 'gravitational' attraction of the Moon! But, Isaac, I don't think it adds up. Did you know there are two tides a day? Explain that! Do you realize that neither Kepler nor Galileo could."

"You know a lot about tides," he says. "But it's obvious; there have to be two tides. If the Moon is overhead say here in England, the ocean here is closer to the Moon than most of the Earth so it gets pulled more strongly toward the Moon so—"

"High tide. That's exactly what I said. We should expect one high tide a day when we rotate under the Moon."

"But think about a place diametrically opposite to England. Say, New Holland. When England rotates under the Moon and New Holland is furthest—"

"New Holland?" I interrupt him.

He looks way up at the ceiling. "Yes. A large land mass east of Indonesia. Anyway, when—"

"Australia?"

"What?"

"Never mind."

"Anyway, when the water around New Holland is furthest from the Moon, it gets pulled less strongly than most of the Earth, thus it bulges away from the Moon, so..."

I shake my head. "Can you draw it for me?"

Isaac makes a quick sketch:

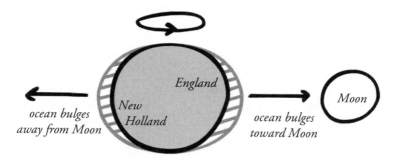

Two tides a day

"Ah, another high tide!" I rub my hands together. A problem that baffled the great minds of Kepler and Galileo, not to mention philosophers and seamen over the ages, solved in a stroke. We get a high tide when we are closest to the Moon and again twelve hours later when the Moon is furthest and the sea bulges up to move *away* from the Moon.

"Okay, the tides are evidence that the Moon is attracted to the Earth. But how does the apple pull the Earth?"

"I surmise that the apple attracts planet Earth just as strongly as the Earth attracts the apple. But there is a caveat—I have inferred that the effect of a force, any force, varies *inversely* with the mass. If something is ten times more massive—that is ten times heavier—it has ten times more inertia, and it takes ten times more force to accelerate it. So although the Earth attracts the apple as much as the apple attracts the Earth, the apple—which is light—accelerates rapidly toward the Earth, whereas the very same force induces a negligibly small acceleration of the Earth toward the apple."

"Huh—weird," I say. "The Earth and the apple are actually falling toward each other! Not what it seems. But what is it about the Earth, or even the Sun, that makes them have this attractive force?"

"Nothing."

"Nothing?"

"Nothing special about the Earth or Sun," Isaac says. "*Everything* attracts everything. Gravity is universal."

"What? So you are saying that an apple can attract another apple? I've never seen such a thing. A person attracts an apple? Do I... attract you?"

The tease, such as it was, goes right over his head. "Correct. But gravity is extremely weak."

"Weak or not," I say, "this universal gravity is an astounding discovery. Do show me."

"No."

I frown. "No, you won't?"

"No I can't demonstrate it. Gravity between everyday objects is far too weak to be detected. Humanity might not have ever noticed that gravity exists at all if we didn't happen to live on an extremely massive planet."

So there could be other forces of nature that we still haven't noticed.

As I absorb what he's said, I stand marveling at Newton open-mouthed. "So, Isaac, let me get this right. You had some epiphany about explaining planetary orbits and falling apples with one common cause, and you feel so passionate about the elegance of that explanation that you're not afraid to predict a pervasive force of gravity between every pair of everyday objects, something that you've never even seen?"

"Right."

I shake my head in admiration for a minute trying to grasp the significance of the thought process I am witnessing first hand. "You know," I finally say, "it's a whole new level of truth."

"Truth? How do you mean?"

"I mean Aristotle made vague predictions that no one ever bothered to test. Galileo made much more rigorous predictions, but very narrow predictions—the acceleration of a dropping object, the period of a pendulum—Galileo espoused truths that he had already thoroughly tested himself."

"Yes."

"But you, Isaac, you are making predictions way beyond what you've actually observed, universal predictions that are unverified, purely motivated by elegant reasoning. You are making radical forecasts that others will be free to test and confirm or refute. A broad but testable truth. You know, I'm really inspired by your independence and originality." I look in his eyes. "I know you don't want to discuss it, but I really want to know where it comes from."

"Well, since we are on the subject of truth—" he looks away to the side.

"Yes?"

"When you asked and I said my father did not abandon me—"

"Yes?" I try to sound encouraging.

"To be accurate, my father died before I was born."

"Oh. I'm very sorry." I glance at his hand for a moment but don't take it. "Different circumstances, but we both grew up without fathers around, although neither of our fathers intentionally left us. You get really close to your mother, don't you, when it's just you and her?"

Another silence. He turns his head further to the side then continues, slowly. "If you must know, it was my mother who abandoned me."

I'm speechless for a moment, then squeak out, "That's awful. How come?"

"Left me as an infant, after she was widowed, for her new husband and his family—there was no room for me there. Left me on Grandma's farm." Finally he looks at me. "So any more questions about gravity?"

Now I do try to place my hand on his, but he shakes it off sharply. I can almost feel the brief window into his personal life slamming shut.

A torturous silence follows until I finally break it. "Yes. You said gravity was not at all strong. Just how strong or weak is it?"

"Actually," Isaac says, "I have no idea. I know the pattern for gravity. But I have no baseline to measure the actual strength of gravity. If I could, just once, measure the gravity between two known masses, it would give me a baseline for gravity's strength. You could call that strength the *universal gravitational constant*—one number telling us how strong gravity is based on just one canonical case, such as two one-kilogram masses one meter apart. But I do not know the number."

It's ironic, like knowing all the prices in some currency but not knowing how much the currency itself is worth. How does Isaac know everything about gravity except the most important detail of all—namely, how strong gravity is? I suppose he can measure the gravitational attraction of the Earth, Moon, or Sun, but he does not know their mass. Meanwhile, for items whose mass is known, like weights in the lab, gravity is too weak to detect and measure.

As I digest this, something else seems very discomforting about this "gravity."

"Isaac, how does this gravitational attraction propagate? How does the pull of Earth reach the apple, or the pull of the Moon reach the ocean? And how quickly?"

"Instantly."

Nooo! It's unimaginable—a million everyday objects and planets and stars reaching across space and exerting an instant pull on one another. *Exerting a pull on me.* I feel physically dizzy just thinking about it. How can the attraction possibly be transmitted instantly? When a man in Australia—or New Holland—takes a step, if I'm sensitive enough, will I really feel the shift in his tiny gravitational attraction simultaneously?

"How?" I say, somewhat weakly. "How can something moving on the other side of the universe effect me at the very same moment."

"I call it *action at a distance.*"

"But Isaac, where do you get such an astonishing idea—that something changing here can influence something millions of kilometers away with no delay and with no method of propagating?"

Suddenly, his suspicion reappears with a vengeance. Any goodwill built up over two productive conversations dissipates as quickly as gravity acts. Newton glares at me for several discomforting seconds. "I think I was right the first time," he says very slowly. "You are spying on me. What are you implying? Where are you suggesting I obtained the concept of action at a distance? For your information, I got the idea from analyzing Kepler's equations of motion—not that I owe you an explanation. Now depart."

"But why?" I plead.

"Go."

I'm blinking heavily as I involuntarily leave. *What did I do to unwittingly pluck some raw nerve?* My mind is racing. How am I periodically provoking these reactions?

As I leave, I mentally list the taboo subjects: mercury, Robert Boyle, action at a distance. Is there a pattern? *The substance of mercury, the physicist Robert Boyle, and the concept of action at a distance.* Try as I might, I cannot think why these might be sensitive subjects or what they may have in common, or why anyone would want to spy on Isaac. Sure he's paranoid, but what is he paranoid about?

Eventually my mind returns to the physics. *Action at a distance*—a strange world. The universe seems like a sane place where things traveling from A to C pass through B on the way. Yet perhaps once again the universe is not at all as it seems.

I stroll southbound along the River Cam, which winds peacefully past the backs of the grand Gothic colleges: St. John's, Trinity, Gonville and Caius, Trinity Hall, Kings. Each one has its own courtyards and informal "backs" on the east of the river. Most have their own stone bridge leading to beautiful fellows' gardens, lush with colorful flowers, to the west of the river. I realize that my eyes observe these ostentatious sights because various mixtures of the seven different colors of corpuscles—light particles—are reflected off the college buildings, trees, flowers, birds, and water into my eyes. Regrettably, something is also making its way from the river into my nose, and that stench is even more intense at the end of a hot, sunny day.

I place one foot in front of the other on the ground. The very act of walking has taken on new meaning now that I know how walking is possible—how the ground and I attract each other and stay firmly in contact. I'm not "striving" toward the center of the universe. Planet Earth does not have some special pull. Rather, all matter attracts all other matter; the Earth is massive and nearby, so it attracts me more than most, allowing me to walk its surface. *Gravity.*

What about the terms Isaac used? He kept talking about the "mass" of a body. *Why didn't he just say weight?* If I understand correctly, mass is an actual measure of the amount of material in the body whereas weight seems to refer to the downward gravitational pull that the Earth exerts on the mass. So while the mass—the quantity of matter—is inherent to the object whether it is on Earth or on the Moon, I suppose that the weight would be lower on the Moon as the intensity of gravity is lower. Mass is a measure of the amount of material; weight is the gravitation force that may pull the mass.

It's intriguing how Isaac uses terminology so carefully and precisely.

I pick up a small pebble and a larger rock and drop them into the Cam, reliving the simple experiment that Galileo used—just three days ago for me—to ridicule Aristotle. *Something doesn't add up.* Isaac said that the amount of gravity between objects varies with the mass of the objects. A massive rock feels a greater gravitational attraction to the Earth than a pebble, which is why it feels heavier. *So why do they accelerate downward in unison—how could the new theory of gravitation explain that?*

But Isaac said something else about mass. He said that the same force has less effect on a more massive body. *That makes sense.* If I were to push an elephant and a mouse with the same force, the elephant would accelerate less than the mouse.

I smile as it dawns on me how these two definitions of mass may actually balance each other out perfectly in the case of falling objects. The rock may be ten times more massive than the pebble, and it experiences a ten times larger gravitational force, but it also requires ten times more force to accelerate it. *Bottom line: The rock and pebble end up with the very same downward acceleration, falling side by side.*

I roll my head a little. *Different forces, but the same result—an elegant explanation or an implausible coincidence?* I can't quite decide.

Walking around Cambridge absent-mindedly for a while, I finally head back to Fizz's Place and pen one more law on the ROW label:

> <u>Universal law of gravitation</u>: Any two objects in the universe attract each other, <u>instantly</u>. The attraction is proportional to both objects' masses and inversely proportional to the square of the distance between them.
>
> The actual strength of gravity (the universal gravitational constant which provides a baseline) is unknown!

I think again of this instantaneous action at a distance. Everything attracting everything else, even across vast distances, with no mechanism for carrying the force between them. *How can such a magical idea appeal to a rational scientist like Isaac?* A product—the universe—that exhibits such strange behavior requires a suitable warning on the packaging so I add one to the ROW label:

> WARNING: Instant action at a distance.

Gravity is just one law, but it helps me solidify several ideas that I've been forming since working with Galileo about the new scientific method that Galileo—and now Newton—are pioneering. I jot down some notes:

Recipe for breakthrough physical theory:

— Make detailed observations and measurements of physical processes.
— Enhance the observations using instruments wherever advantageous.
— Look for patterns and model them mathematically.
— Think creatively of simpler, more fundamental laws that explain multiple patterns.

Convinced that Isaac has more to offer, I decide to brave another conversation with him. *If I can somehow wiggle my way into one.*

Fluxions

It's early afternoon and Isaac isn't in the lab. I don't find him in the gardens. He may be in his rooms, of course. He threw me out of his lab—what chance do I have of negotiating my way into his dorm? *I'm not going back to Iceland without trying.*

I walk back up to the dorm building overlooking the secret gardens. The door labeled "Newton, Isaac" has an "in/out" slider that is set to "in." I knock.

"Go away!"

Here we go again. I open the door slightly. "Isaac I'm sorry to barge in. Look, I'm not spying on you, but I do need to speak to you. Please give me a moment."

Isaac is reading at his wooden and leather desk. Alongside his book is a curved mirror with some polishing equipment strewn around. He slams the book closed and shoves it hurriedly into a drawer in the desk. "I said *go away!*"

I stand there trying to think of an angle. Every day of time travel is precious. I can't just walk away from the chance to learn more from Newton. He keeps staring me out.

"My God," he says a few seconds later, slumping back in his chair, "you saw it, didn't you?" He rubs his eyes with the base of his palms. "Congratulations. Your spying has finally borne fruit. I should have paid more attention to my first instincts. A girl hanging around Cambridge asking about natural philosophy—such a strange cover that for a time I thought it might be real. So for whom are you working? What do they want from me? How will you leverage your exposé?"

I stand speechless for a moment. Then I talk slowly.

"Isaac, I'm interested in your natural philosophy. That's all I want to talk about. If we can just discuss natural philosophy once more," I hesitate, "I will forget all about… the book. Just one day. Or, of course, we could talk about the book. Which do you choose?"

He glares at me menacingly. It feels like everything in the room is glaring at me. Isaac says nothing. I feel awful, but I don't back off.

I decide to try humor. "So, Isaac, what is that curved mirror for? Hoping to apply your makeup more accurately?" My attempt at breaking the ice falls completely flat, not only because he's fuming, but also because I suspect that he does in fact wear makeup.

"Telescope."

"You want to make a telescope with a curved mirror? Why not use lenses?"

"Avoids the color separation that occurs in lenses," he says, somehow intonating a grudge in every single word. "Refraction by lenses causes a slight separation of the colors, like in a prism, leading to a bit of blurring of the image in the telescope. A curved mirror avoids that. Also, by bouncing the light back and forth inside the telescope, you can keep the telescope shorter."

"Where's the telescope?"

He points at a shelf:

Newton's reflector telescope

"Great. So tell me, I wonder, have you been analyzing any other forces besides gravity?" I try to sound upbeat.

"Working on a framework for all the forces and how they affect motion," he mutters through clenched teeth. This is going to be a painful conversation if he doesn't open up a bit.

"Framework?"

He opens a notebook and passes it to me silently, avoiding eye contact. I turn the notebook around and find he has scribbled the title *Philosophiæ Naturalis Principia Mathematica*. The Latin notes translate along the lines of:

Three laws of motion
Law 1: Inertia: Absent any forces, an object moves in a straight line at constant velocity.

I recognize that from Galileo.

Law 2: The force required to accelerate a body is proportional to its mass.

We discussed that yesterday—it takes more force to accelerate a more massive body.

Law 3: Forces come in pairs: Action and reaction are equal and opposite.

I think about the last one. "Isaac, I remember that the Earth pulls the Moon and the Moon pulls the Earth. But are you saying that all forces come in pairs of action and reaction?"

"If I push you hard, I recoil too. Shall I demonstrate?" he asks.

I smile nervously and shake my head sideways.

"The floor supports my feet," he continues, "but my feet also push down on the floor. Forces always come in equal and opposite pairs."

"Hmm, there's something very balanced about that. So let's get started, tell me all about the other forces, besides gravity."

"I know nothing about the other forces, honestly I do not. It will take future effort to fill in laws for the other forces in order for this framework to be used to make predictions."

I grab a seat. Hopefully Isaac's natural interest in the subject will gradually override his spite at the circumstances. "So you can use this to make predictions for the movement of any bodies?"

Isaac points to a page in his notebook.

Predicting movement one moment at a time—Sun, Earth and Moon

"Explain the example." It isn't a request.

He blows out some air. "All right. Assume that at some point in time you know the position, speed and mass of some objects. For example the Sun, Earth, and Moon."

"Okay."

"You can use my universal law of gravitation to calculate the *forces*— the attractions between the Sun and Earth, Sun and Moon, and Earth and Moon."

"But what about other forces besides gravity?"

"Those too, assuming they were known, but in this particular case gravity is the dominant force. Once you calculate the forces, my second law of motion tells you how to use the forces to calculate the accelerations."

I flick back a couple of pages and look at the second law again. *Yes, force determines acceleration.* "Okay, I think I follow. So now I know the position, speed, mass, forces, and acceleration, for each body. So what?"

"Voilà!" Isaac points to the second frame. "Now you can make a prediction. The speed at the first instant tells you how the position will change in the next instant. Meanwhile, the accelerations at the first instant tell you how the speeds will change at the next instant. So you may predict the new positions and new speeds for each and every body in the next instant."

"So after all of that, you can only predict one instant into the future?"

"Right, because as soon as the positions have changed, the forces change, so you have to calculate everything all over again."

"Wow," I thump the table with excitement, "now that I've predicted the positions and speeds for the second instant I can start the same process all over again and predict the third instant and so on and so forth! Right? Amazing—give me a moment to get this clear."

Pushing down on the floor with my toes, an equal and opposite force tilts my chair right back on its hind legs as the wood creaks in protest.

Masses, forces, and acceleration sound so abstract. I want to ask him what we are really talking about: The planets' orbits? Water falling in a waterfall? A tree swaying in the wind? A soufflé gently rising in an oven? Small droplets shooting out when a giraffe sneezes?

I don't ask because I think I know the answer; right now he's talking about all of the above! Newton is talking about every type of motion in the universe and dissecting it to infinitesimally small slices, paring it down to its most fundamental: Masses move around, exerting forces on each other, which results in accelerations—in other words, changes to those movements.

I look at the page again. *It's true—Newton's Equations of Motion are nothing less than a physics recipe for predicting the movement of any set of objects, one instant at a time!*

I rip another sheet of paper out of his pad and grab a quill, sketching myself a conceptual diagram of how to predict the future using the laws of motion:

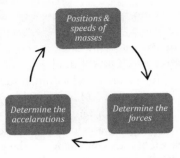

How the universe ticks according to Newton's laws of motion

It's profound, but, well, esoteric. In practice it sounds too difficult to gather the perfect information about the initial positions and speeds and then perform the calculations again and again, instant by instant. Hmm, maybe with the kind of computers my Dad told me about in the future someone could actually perform these calculations.

"The problem," Isaac says, as if reading my mind, "is that to make accurate predictions you have to add up infinitely many instants and infinitely many forces. For example, each point on planet Earth exerts its own gravitational force."

My face drops. "How can we calculate anything if we have infinitely many forces and have to repeat the calculation over infinitely many instants?"

"Well," he says, "you can always make approximate predictions by considering just the most important bodies and by considering just a finite number of instants. But I am working on some mathematics that might help."

"Help to add infinitely many things?"

He shrugs. "I'm working on it."

I glance at the desk drawer.

"Look, whatever your name is, I will tell you about it later. If you guarantee it is the last I see of you."

"At dinner?"

"Whatever."

"Do you think," I wonder out loud, "that our minds might have an intuitive ability to analyze your equations of motion and predict future movements, at least in some simple cases?"

"How do you mean?"

"For example," I say, "do you think my mind would be able to predict the trajectory of an apple accurately enough that I could throw it at the right speed and angle for it to land where I want it to?"

He gawks at me, then cracks a hint of his all-too-rare smile. "I suppose you want to share the credit for the universal law of gravitation, do you?"

"Not at all. But I'm pleased I helped."

"You might also like to know," he says, "that there exists a calculating machine that can analyze the equations of motion instant-by-instant and play out the positions, speeds, forces, and accelerations of all objects way out into the future, with perfect accuracy."

A machine that can calculate the future? "No kidding?"

"Yes. I call it 'the universe.'"

College dinner is pretty formal. The dining hall is the long, extravagant building with a sloping tiled roof that partitions Great Court from Nevil's Court. Climbing a flight of stone steps and entering the large wooden doors, I'm greeted by yet another portrait of King Henry VIII, full length, hanging at the far end of the hall. *That king clearly wanted to leave no doubt whatsoever as to who founded this college.* The dining room walls are covered in ornate woodwork under a hammer-beamed ceiling. Three long wooden tables with molded benches run parallel along almost the entire length of the hall, leaving room for the head table across the width at the far end. Each place is set with silver cutlery, two china plates, a side plate, and three crystal glasses. Everyone except the odd guest is wearing blue college robes as they sit to dine. No one here seems to share Galileo's objection to academic gear. Then again, these robes are worn over normal clothes and may be easily slipped off.

I find Isaac at the far end of one of the long tables. He's sitting solo, writing in his notepad as I take my place on the bench next to him. I wonder if he always sits far from his colleagues or whether this was in honor of the fact that he's expecting me.

"So how do you add infinitely many things?" I reach for some bread.

"Ahem," he says and looks over to the head table where an older gentleman starts talking.

Benedic, Domine, nos et dona tua, quae de largitate tua sumus sumpturi,... per Christum Dominum nostrum.

After this Latin grace, Isaac grabs a roll and devours it while I nibble on mine. Then he takes a second roll and almost swallows it whole.

Finally, he finishes off the last crumbs and takes a few seconds to catch his breath.

"Once I tell, you promise to disappear?"

"I promise. I will keep hundreds of years away from you."

"By way of example, consider the gravitational pull of this long table on me," he taps the table. "The challenge, just as with the gravity of planet Earth, is that each infinitesimally small slice of table is at a different distance from me so, based on my universal law of gravitation, each and every imaginary slice of table exerts a different gravitational force determined according to the inverse square of its distance. To predict the total gravitational pull of the table, I must add up the pull of each of the infinitely many infinitesimal slices. Do you see?"

He sketches it for me in his notebook:

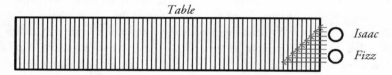

*Each imaginary slice of the table is at a different distance,
thereby exerting a different gravitational pull*

"Hmm, I guess."

"So," he says, "how do we add the gravity of all of those slices together to predict the total gravitational pull of the table on me—or of planet Earth on the apple? I have found that in order to add up infinitely many slices in a single stroke, we must use... fluxions."

"Fluxions?"

"Fluxions."

"What are fluxions?"

"That is the name I am using for my method of calculation."

"Um, Isaac, maybe find a better name. If it's a method of calculation, why not call it calculus?"

"What is the difference?"

"It sounds better. So how do you do it?"

"I call the adding of infinitely many quantities *integration*. Instead of calculating the gravity for this specific table, we seek the pattern for the gravity of all lengths of table."

"All different lengths of table? Isaac, you've just made the problem even harder!"

He pauses as a waiter leans graciously between us and serves a dish. "Roasted pullet in a sauce of butter, egg yolk and lemon," the waiter announces.

"Sometimes harder is easier," Newton continues as the waiter retreats. "Imagine for a second that we knew the pattern for how much gravity a table exerts on us, for all lengths of table."

"But Isaac, the whole point is that we don't know that, not even for this one table!"

"Yes, Fizz, that is why I said 'imagine.' We do not know what the pattern is. Just imagine we know the pattern, if it is not too much trouble."

"Okay..."

"The one thing we do know is how the pattern must change. If I add just a tiny little bit to the length of the table I know that the increase in the total gravity of the table will be from the gravity of the slice I just added. So I know how the pattern changes when the length increases slightly."

"I suppose that makes sense, if you make the table a bit longer, the change in gravity comes from the extra slice of table. So what?"

"So we do not know the pattern for the gravity of tables of different lengths, but we do know how that pattern must change when the length is increased just a touch. Now we can take lots and lots of different mathematical patterns and calculate their rate of change. I call that the *derivative* of the pattern. When we find a pattern—or *function* in mathematical nomenclature—with a rate of change—or derivate—which is just right, then we have our answer."

"Isaac, you've got to be kidding me. Do people even know how to find the rate of change—or this 'derivate'—of a pattern? Without that, what is the point of the entire analysis?"

"Yes, I invented a method for finding the derivative of a pattern. I call that process *differentiation*."

I sigh loudly. "Oh, of course you did. I suppose you figured that out yesterday?"

"Last week," he says, not looking up from his food.

"So let's see if I got this right. You've invented two fundamentally new mathematical processes, the calculus of differentiation and integration, which allow you to find a pattern for adding up infinitely many things using a cunning trick involving looking for a recognizable rate of change of the desired pattern."

"Yes. I can similarly add up infinitely many instants to predict the future. For example, I can add up the instant-by-instant predictions for the path of a flying apple and predict that it will follow a shape called a parabola. But calculus only works for some of the simpler scenarios."

"Wow. Your paper will be a watershed."

"No," he says.

"No, your paper won't be significant?"

"No, I'm not planning to publish it."

More secrets. *Why wouldn't he publish such an important new branch of mathematics?* Unless... "This calculus, Isaac, is it, well, original? Uniquely yours?"

"Of course." He turns quite red. "Although some German cad, Gottfried Leibniz, has plagiarized it."

"Leibniz? *The* Leibniz?"

"*The?* Hardly!" he tails off.

"I mean the Leibniz who was—is—one of the first people to think about pantheism? In fact wasn't the word 'pantheism' first suggested in a letter to Leibniz?"

"I—you—what is pantheism? Why on earth should I care? Whatever philosophical thoughts Leibniz has are probably plagiarized too."

"Um, Isaac, how could Leibniz plagiarize something you've not actually published? Is it not possible that he had the same idea independently?"

"*No!* The Royal Society will determine that Leibniz stole calculus from me."

"Oh. How can you be so sure?"

Newton hesitates. "I have written the report."

While the waiters bring a dessert of countesse cakes, a few of Isaac's acquaintances stroll over in their blue gowns. They appear to be my age or a couple of years older and seem surprised to find Isaac with a girl. One of them gives Isaac a slap on the back and lets out a whistle. It's my first encounter with any of his colleagues and, as I look at them, I wonder if they know whatever secret Isaac thinks that I've discovered.

"Who is the girlfriend?" one asks.

"This is, um, Miss Fitzgerald or something like that," Isaac says. *"Not* my friend. We were discussing mathematics."

"Of course you are."

"Discussing multiplication, no doubt," says another.

"In fact, she was just leaving," Isaac says.

I stay. Three friends sit around the table from us.

"So, Newton, are you still trying to reduce the world to a deterministic machine? Everything in your world is determined by equations, no room for God or for humans' free choice?"

Hmm, I haven't considered that perspective. Words from an Ecommunity sermon come flooding back: *The world is a machine to them. They analyze it to death. They treat the natural world like their own personal device to use and abuse.*

"That is not my intention," Isaac frowns.

"And why ever not?" says another. "Perhaps that is exactly what the world is: a big, complex, but predictable machine." He sits down and pours some wine. "You know, I have been reflecting. Your work, Newton, completes a revolution. I would call it the *scientific revolution*— with the new emphasis on experimentation and mathematical analysis, we can now strive to model all the laws of the universe."

He raises his wine glass toward Isaac. "To Isaac. I think it would not be an exaggeration to say that our very own Isaac Newton here has set the stage for the future of science. I believe Newton's equations of motion will be the platform on which all future investigation of the laws of nature will be played out, far into the future."

There is an awkward silence. Everyone looks at Isaac.

"Well, if I have seen far," he says, "it is by standing on the shoulders of giants."

"Pompous git," someone teases. "And would you take a break from poking fun at Hooke's small stature?"

Everyone smiles.

It's amazing to hear the importance some people are attaching to the equations of motion. "But," I protest, "the equations of motion are like having judge and jury yet only one law, the law of gravitation. The world's other forces aren't modeled yet."

Some eyebrows lift. "True, very true," one of the friends says, "John Donne at St. John's College next door summed it up quite nicely:

> 'The new Philosophy calls all in doubt,
> The Element of fire is quite put out;
> The Sun is lost, and th'earth, and no man's wit
> Can well direct him where to look for it.'"

"Yes," another friend answers, "the scientific revolution has not yet rebuilt all the ideas that it has disassembled, but surely now it can only be a matter of time until we replace Greek speculation with scientific laws for all the forces of nature."

My time is metered. I take this as my cue to excuse myself and leave.

Back in Fizz's place I take the ROW label to the desk and try to synthesize what I've learned. Under *Ingredients* I write *Light—made of corpuscles of seven colors.* I now know more about the composition of light than I know about the composition of simple matter like a glass of water or a potato.

In the *Laws* section, I reproduce Newton's three laws of motion:

Laws of motion:

Absent any forces, an object moves in a straight line at constant velocity. (Inertia)

The force required to accelerate a body is proportional to its mass.

Forces come in pairs—action and reaction are equal and opposite.

An amazing framework, but it's only as good as the forces we understand. *Where to start?*

Dozens of avenues of exploration suggest themselves. I could investigate sound, light, friction, the composition of matter—almost anything. Suddenly I feel quite lost in the sea of choices that face me. I have the computer to navigate, but what directive shall I give it? How will the post-scientific-revolution world start to fill in all the gaps?

I scratch my head. *My quest is really only starting now.* Now that I know the methodology—keen observation, scientific rigor, mathematical analysis, the program to model the world through laws of forces, testable predictions, plus one showcase law of gravity—I can start to understand the specific phenomena of the world and the laws that govern them.

I now have the ox and the plow—where shall I dig the first furrow?

My eyes fall on the box. At first I resented there even being a box. After visiting Aristotle I flippantly dismissed all seven artifacts as "been-there-done-that." Maybe a little guidance would not be unwelcome at this point—if I can just understand it. I decide to reconsider each of the artifacts, one at a time.

Brown powdery material—perhaps I took this too literally as "earth." It must represent matter. Yes, this is perhaps the most fundamentally open question of all: What is matter composed of? What are the ingredients of the universe?

Water—this must represent liquids—no one has yet analyzed how liquids move and behave.

Bag of air—I must understand how gases behave.

Hot jar—We have dismissed Aristotle's element of Fire and require a scientific theory of heat and temperature to replace it.

Glass disk—I play with it for a few moments and hold it to my eye again. The world looks distorted. *Duh.* It's not just a glass disk, it's a lens. *Light.* I must finish understanding light and how light is refracted by lenses.

Then the *amber* and the *pebble*—what are they?

I turn the pretty amber over in my hands. I polish it a bit on my sleeve and turn it around some more, enjoying its orange brilliance. Cut right, it could make a beautiful pendant for a necklace. Aristotle's ether has been discredited. *Amber, what do you mean?*

Fumbling with the amber, I experience a slightly odd sensation as it brushes past the back of my hand. *What is that feeling?* I rub the amber some more on my sleeve and hold it right over the skin of my hand. Now the sensation is a little stronger. I look very closely. The fine hairs of my hand are standing on edge whenever the amber is close! *How strange!* I use my woolen clothes to shine the amber vigorously, then hold it over the back of my hand again. This time a small spark flies between the amber and my hand, giving me a tiny shock.

I could really kick myself. Amber. Ἤλεκτρο in Greek—*electro*. "Electricity" must come from the Greek for *amber-like*. I wonder if this is how electricity was first discovered, by rubbing amber on wool. *Dad is reminding me that I must study electricity!* All my education had to say about electricity was that it was the very bloodline of the Great Deterioration.

So Dad has laid it all out for me. Somehow, with the solid foundations I have acquired on my own and with so much uncharted territory to explore in less than two weeks, I don't resent this little bit of direction.

Only the pebble remains a complete mystery. I pull a thread out of the seam of my dress and tie the pebble from the shelf over my bed so that I'll be reminded to decipher this clue, each time I wake up and see it dangling above me.

Seven forces of nature to explore. But before I continue my future-bound travel, there is just one mystery that can only be solved now in 1667 and only under the cover of night.

Carrying a small lantern, I creep once more through Great Gate and into Great Court. Everything is dark except the small area illuminated by my lantern. Only one or two other people are walking around with lanterns of their own. I tiptoe up one floor in the dorm building and along the corridor. The garden below is invisible in the dark. I draw a deep breath as I pass the room labeled "Newton, Isaac." Everyone seems quietly asleep, although I worry that Isaac is quite capable of working through the night. At the far end of the corridor, I glide down the wooden staircase into the secret garden and make my way along the damp grass, between the shrubs, to the small brick lab nestled in a niche between the dark walls of Trinity College chapel.

After looking around, checking that the coast is clear, I very carefully try the door handle. *Locked.* I feel for a key above the door—nothing. I crouch down slowly, rest the lantern on the floor, and feel around the doorstep. Zilch.

In the flickering light of the lantern, I notice some subtle signs that one small patch of earth has been recently turned. I never thought my experience with plowing could be applied to crime! Digging with my hands through a couple of inches of earth, I find a buried key. Unlocking the door, I ease myself into the lab.

Unfortunately, there are no shutters or curtains for the windows, so I must be quick as the lantern light might be spotted from the outside at any moment. I open a cupboard and hold up the lamp. I find many labeled minerals: mercury, gold, copper, arsenic, and zinc. I wonder how these relate to Isaac's studies.

I find nothing unexpected on the bookshelf: books by Copernicus, Descartes, Kepler, and Galileo and papers by Hooke and Boyle.

As I pull *Principia Philosophiae* by Descartes I notice that my hand is shaking. I flick through its Latin pages. Descartes espouses a "rationalist" approach to science but also supports a "dualism" in which the human mind is separate from the physical body and not subject to the laws of science. He delves into pure mathematics too, and I notice an intriguing proposal to model our three-dimensional space using x-, y- and z-axes. *I didn't come here to study mathematics.* I close the book gently and reach to return it carefully to the shelf.

Then I see it. From the back of the slot where Descartes' book had been, another book is peeking out. I stand on a chair and discover that the entire bookshelf is two books deep! I hold up the lantern and squint to read the spine of the book that was hidden behind *Principia Philoso-phiae*.

Alchemy: The Philosopher's Stone.

What's *that* doing here? Does Isaac Newton, key proponent of the scientific revolution, have a passion for magic? And, if so, why is he so secretive and sensitive about it?

I take some time to look through all of the hidden books, removing and replacing them one at a time. There is a rich range of books on alchemy. I read how the Philosopher's Stone will turn lead into gold and provide an elixir of life. Mercury seems to be an important element to alchemists. I find dozens of articles by Newton himself such as a work with the not-so-snappy title of *Nicholas Flammel, His Exposition of the Hieroglyphicall Figures which he caused to be painted upon an Arch in St Innocents Church-yard in Paris, The secret Booke of Artephius, And the Epistle of Iohn Pontanus: Containing both the Theoricke and the Practicke of the Philosophers Stone.* I find a file of Newton's correspondence with physicist and chemist Robert Boyle. There is almost no physics or chemistry in the correspondence; it is all alchemy. I find writings on alchemy by Tycho Brahe, who mentored Kepler. I come across references to the occult concept of *action at a distance*, which Newton has evidently appropriated to physics.

Why didn't he tell me where he got that concept? If he likes alchemy why is he so secretive about it?

I also find dozens of works by Newton on obscure codes in the words of the Bible, which he refers to as biblical hermeneutics. Newton's own articles include *Rules for interpreting the words & language in Scripture* and *The Temple of Solomon.* Newton seems to consider himself to be a divinely chosen prophet tasked with decoding the Bible.

So why the paranoia? *Oh.* I come across a convincing explanation in a copy of a letter from Robert Boyle to King Charles I, beseeching His Majesty to repeal the tortuous death penalty for the practice of alchemy. His Majesty no doubt worries that the multiplication of gold would devalue the royal coffers, Boyle acknowledges, but he argues that it would be in the king's interest to allow alchemy and simply confiscate any gold produced. Leafing through the papers, I find no indication that the death penalty has in fact been repealed.

So Newton was another scientist willing to risk his life—although for a rather less worthy cause than Galileo.

I hear a sound and freeze. *Footsteps.* Who would be walking in this isolated garden in the middle of the night? Through the thin walls I suddenly hear a familiar man's voice shouting, "Stop thief! Call the watchman! Stop thief!"

I spin around so violently that I knock the lantern to the floor. Without stopping to pick it up I dart outside only to come to an abrupt stop, face-to-face with Isaac Newton and his lantern. He stands to block my path and continues screaming "Stop thief!" although he makes no immediate move to physically attack me.

No one has answered his screams yet, but it can't be long. His menacing gaze locks with mine.

"I'm not a thief. I didn't steal anything," I choke out, "I was just exploring."

Suddenly Isaac looks away from my eyes and over my shoulder and his jaw drops from his furious face. His face becomes more brightly illuminated. I spin back toward the lab to find it up in flames. We both run toward the door, but it is too hot to enter. No one has arrived yet, but just in case Isaac hasn't shouted loud enough, a dog is awakened by the commotion and starts barking furiously. The damage is irreversible, and I'm sure reinforcements will come soon.

I stand there crying in the light of the fire. I feel horribly shamed at the unthinkable damage I've caused, but my mind is overcome with more selfish thoughts of growing up in a crowded seventeenth-century jail, overrun with rats, rampant with plague, with a small bucket for a toilet. How long could I survive? Would I ever in my entire life manage to get free for long enough to run to the hut? *Should I run for it right now?*

Two large porters come marching down the only staircase into this walled garden, answering my question for me. One runs toward us while the other heads directly to the water pump on the other side of the small garden.

"What happened, sir?" the porter is shouting from across the garden.

"Please," I plead to Isaac in a whisper. "I'm so, so sorry. It was an accident. Maybe I deserve to be punished, but I'm just a kid. I can't face jail."

"You do not have to worry about that."

I'm in a deep, dark pit and for a second there seems to be a speck of light opening above. "I don't?"

"No, you do not have to worry about jail. We hang thieves." Isaac turns to the approaching porter. "She did it, she broke in and started the fire."

The porter looks at me and grabs my arm. He addresses Isaac. "We will apprehend her. She will pay for the damage she has caused. What did you have in there, sir?"

Silence. Isaac and I stare at each other.

"I can tell you," I manage to choke out.

Isaac is bright red. His temper is clearly boiling over, yet he is trapped and he knows it.

The dog moves closer toward us, barking menacingly.

"Let go of her," Isaac blurts out. "Did you not hear me? She did it," he says, now pointing at the dog. He is gritting his teeth so hard they could chip.

The porter releases me and I scramble away, fleeing Trinity College as the sculpture of King Henry VIII glares down at my back, disapprovingly. It occurs to me that I learned something about that king, but I can't remember what it is. *Not now, Fizz, just get out of here.*

My body is shivering violently. Soon I break into a run and don't stop or look back until I reach Fizz's Place.

Still shaking from the ordeal—not to mention the cold English night—I hold the warm can in both hands and slowly steady myself. I sit breathing heavily, sweating and shivering at the same time. I resolve to never again resort to blackmail, trespassing, or any crime in my pursuit of the truth. It was wrong, it wasn't truthful, and it was extremely stupid. My passion for making an informed choice between the Ecological Community and the Outside in 2110 almost got me hanged in the 1600s.

I wonder about the damage I've caused. The books may be replaceable, but what of Isaac's notebooks? The only conciliation is that I doubt Isaac's unique brain forgets anything at all.

Only much later do my hands finally warm up and become steadier. I force myself to think about tomorrow. The warm can is still in my hands. That's as good a place to start as any.

"Computer, find me someone who understands heat."

Take me to a faraway place and a distant time, I almost add.

Tossing and turning myself to sleep, I try hard to put my second close encounter with death behind me. I attempt to convince myself that I have nothing to feel guilty about. *I'm not at all convincing.* Yet of all the strange things I encountered today, the person who most occupies my fading thoughts is the late King Henry VIII.

Fluid Situation

Day 8. Basel, Switzerland, 1739.

I glance at the screen and go back to sleep. When my eyes next open, I try to snooze some more, but my thoughts won't let me sleep any longer. I'm relieved to be seventy years ahead of yesterday. *I won't be meeting Isaac Newton today.* Yet I'm also surprised—with the framework of Newton's laws of motion, I had expected rapid year-by-year progress.

Finally giving up on my efforts to sleep, I print and drag myself into some clothes and sulk out into a wooded section of one of Basel's parks—Schützenmattpark, according to a sign. My eye gravitates toward a dominant edifice along the architectural horizon, possibly a cathedral—red sandstone walls topped with a playful patchwork of colored roof tiles and dramatic turrets pointing skyward. I drift through the streets in that general direction.

I find no new technology. The horse-drawn carriages crisscrossing Basel today would not create any dramatic scandal if one of them turned up in Ancient Greece. One music workshop is offering a piano and tuning forks, which I have not seen in earlier times. These don't seem likely to devour the planet. *So much for the scientific "revolution"*—its impact seems limited to the ivory towers of a handful of small European universities. I think about all of those Ecommunity sermons about prying leading to meddling as sure as reaping follows sowing, and I shake my head.

While walking, my mind is struggling to reconstruct obscure snippets of British history that may have renewed relevance to my situation. I remember that Wordsworth's *Preface to the Lyrical Ballads* was the last major literary work to make the Ecommunity's literature cutoff at the year 1800. The work was lauded for its pantheistic tendencies. In school, we memorized the line "the passions of men are incorporated with the beautiful and permanent forms of nature." Yet I also remember being warned that Wordsworth was by no means a pure pantheist; rather, he was loyal to the Church of England, which had broken away from Catholicism in one of those bloody wars that plague the Outside's non-naturalistic religions. I'm pretty sure that schism was led by some King

Henry who had a V and some I's after his name. The more I think about it the more I believe it was Henry VIII.

So Galileo died as a banned man in Italy, and within the year Isaac Newton was born in Protestant England, eventually attending the college founded by Henry VIII. It was there—in one of the few non-Catholic European countries—that Newton picked up and carried forward the torch of science that Galileo had ignited.

Galileo failed.

Soon I find myself under Basel's Münster, the cathedral. The architecture and coloring are quite a contrast to Hallgrimskirkja—the old cathedral in Reykjavík—but it has the same style of plain crosses without the crucifixes I saw in Frombork and Pisa. *Basel is also Protestant.*

I scratch my forehead.

Get real, Fizz. You can't reform a community that doesn't want to be reformed.

"Professor Bernoulli will see you for a few minutes in an hour."

"*Danke schön,*" I mutter back rather apathetically.

I'm in the University of Basel, just ten minutes from the cathedral, northbound along the river Rhine. The university was founded by the order of Pope Pius II in 1459 and occupies a single spacious, rectangular, bright off-white building. The receptionist informed me that Dutch-Swiss Daniel Bernoulli is the eminent natural philosopher in residence. Born in the Netherlands in 1700, so now approaching forty, Bernoulli apparently studied mathematics, which is the family tradition, but he has also held chairs in medicine, metaphysics, and natural philosophy.

I head to the university library, resolved to refocus my mind on preparing for the meeting. Instead, I find myself reminiscing, and I do some research on Isaac Newton, with whom I spent my last few turbulent days. I discover that, since my yesterday, Newton has become warden of the Royal Mint and a Member of Parliament, eventually dying as Sir Isaac Newton in 1727 at the impressive age of 84. As Member of Parliament for the University of Cambridge—yes it seems the university has its own Member of Parliament—his only comment on record was a request to close a window in the chamber as he didn't like the draft.

Newton apparently wasted many years in his bitter dispute with Leibniz over priority for calculus. He eventually published his *Principia,* but I find no record of further revolutionary contributions to physics. By all the accounts I read, he became even more eccentric and bad tempered, which some have attributed to the high levels of mercury found in an autopsy of his body.

Despite his odd personality, the obituaries wax lyrical about the greatest mathematician and natural philosopher of all time and hail his lasting legacy to humanity. Many of the eulogists omit—or are ignorant of—the fact that Newton wrote more about alchemy and biblical hermeneutics than physics.

I ask the librarian which of Newton's works they have. "Many of his works were lost in a fire you know," he says, callously oblivious to the stabbing effect his words are having on me. "We have one copy of *Principia* right here."

As I take the book to the desk and flip open the cover, I suddenly find myself face to face with Newton once more. We stare at each other. His picture looks at me accusingly.

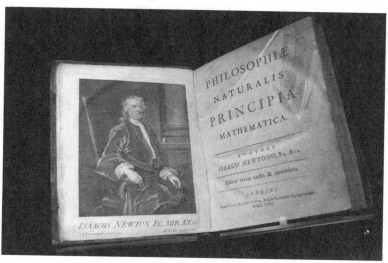

Newton's Principia

You talk about "truth" but you blackmailed me, trespassed on my property, burned my works, he says.

Solemnly, I hesitate. *You weren't exactly truthful yourself, hiding your alchemy and hermeneutics,* I try to respond. But my response sounds defensive and unconvincing. *He's right.*

Newton holds his cold accusing expression. I want him to go and look at someone else, but he refuses to relent. Finally, under the spell of his censuring stare, I break down and cry.

I'm not actually crying for Newton, though. I'm crying for Galileo. I'm crying because I failed Galileo. Galileo taught me to seek the truth; in my efforts to seek truth, I resorted to lies.

I'm also crying because Galileo failed me. He promised me that the truth would win out—that he would reform his church, but instead he died under house arrest, his truths censored. The science he founded rekindled itself with a vengeance, but not within Galileo's community, as he promised.

I wipe my eyes and nose on my sleeve. *Why am I still crying?* The truth hits me like a chunk of glacier hitting an ox: *My own pursuit of truth may be impossible within my own community.* My mission to learn science and to reform the Ecommunity may be doomed. *I may have to leave.* I've never, ever admitted this to myself.

A clock's chime interrupts this tornado of introspective thoughts. My meeting is in fifteen minutes. I move to the "B" shelf and retrieve Bernoulli's book *Hydraulica,* printed a few years back in 1732. *Strange.* I requested an explanation of heat, and the computer has brought me to a pioneer studying the motion of fluids. Of course, if he can explain the dynamics of water, that covers one of my artifacts too.

I look at the book more carefully and spot my mistake. *Hydraulica* is written by Johannis Bernoulli. Next to it on the "B" shelf I find the book *Hydrodynamica*, freshly published last year by Daniel Bernoulli, whom I am visiting. In his book, he introduces himself as "son of Johannis," which seems very respectful.

Flicking through both books, I'm surprised to find a lot of overlapping material, but despite introducing himself as "son of Johannis," Daniel makes not a single mention of his father's earlier and similar work.

I look from one book to the other. *What kind of ungrateful son would plagiarize his own father's research?* I think about my own Dad. Perhaps I don't have a whole lot to thank my father for, but I can't see myself going around claiming that his time machine was my invention! In the name of truth, I decide to challenge him about this—*after* he explains hydrodynamics, of course.

DANIELIS BERNOULLI Joh. Fil.
MED. PROF. BASIL.
ACAD. SCIENT. IMPER. PETROPOLITANÆ, PRIUS MATHESEOS
SUBLIMIORIS PROF. ORD. NUNC MEMBRI ET PROF. HONOR.

HYDRODYNAMICA,
SIVE
DE VIRIBUS ET MOTIBUS FLUIDORUM
COMMENTARII.
OPUS ACADEMICUM
AB AUCTORE, DUM PETROPOLI AGERET,
CONGESTUM.

ARGENTORATI,
Sumptibus JOHANNIS REINHOLDI DULSECKERI,
Anno M D CC XXXVIII.
Typis Joh. Henr. Deckeri, Typographi Basiliensis.

Daniel Bernoulli's Hydrodynamica *title page*

Given what I've uncovered about him, it's surprising that Bernoulli receives me with perfect courtesy, or in fact that he receives me at all. He wears another of those ridiculous, long, curly platinum-blonde wigs, making him look older than his thirty-nine years. While noting that his nose is just a touch too long, I almost skid on a puddle. Pipes are strewn all around his lab, and even the ceiling is a patchwork of water stains.

Daniel Bernoulli

After introductions, Daniel quickly gets to the point. "Fluids, both liquids and gases, exert a certain *pressure* at every point. The pressure is always the same in every direction. Pressure really means that there is a certain *force per unit area,* the same force on each square meter."

"Is the pressure the same at different points?" I ask.

"Not when the fluid is flowing. I have discovered a relationship between pressure and speed. In fact, the pressure in a fluid is *lower* where the speed of flow is *higher.*"

"And this discovery of yours, the relationship between speed and pressure in a fluid, was it… your own discovery?"

"Certainly. Why do you ask?"

I shrug. "It's not important." *I'll seek the truth, but there is time for that after I've learned what I came to learn.* "So you found that the pressure is lower where the speed is higher—that's really unintuitive. Wouldn't the pressure be higher?"

Last year my Dad said something about learning to enjoy the "pressure in the fast lane," but here Bernoulli claims that, as far as fluid dynamics goes, pressure is lowest in the fast lane.

"Ah, *nein.* To see why, perhaps imagine that you are underwater in a river, flowing with the current."

I close my eyes and imagine myself back in Iceland. Our collective is near several streams of snow-melt waters and other streams of hot geothermal waters. At a few highly desirable points, these streams mix, creating the natural flows of beautifully warm water in which we all bathe, the days alternating between men and women. I imagine myself now swimming in one of these, being swept toward the Atlantic.

"Now imagine," Daniel continues, "that you are at the transition of the river from a wide deep part to a narrower shallower section. What happens to the flow?"

I remember how the river gushes most where it's narrow. I close my eyes for a second and immerse myself in the warm water flow—a slower gentler flow in the wide section behind me, the clear water gushing through the narrow section in front of me. I can smell a hint of rotten eggs from the hot spring water as I anticipate the brief thrill of being swept into the faster narrower section ahead.

"The flow gets faster in the narrow part ahead of me," I say. That's how the narrow river section manages to carry as much water current as the wider section."

"Correct. So how do you—and how does the water around you— accelerate as you transition to the faster flow?"

"Well," I say, opening my eyes, "the water *must* get faster in order for the same amount of water per second to fit through the narrower river stretch ahead."

But listening to myself, I hear Aristotle. *What would Galileo say if he heard me?* That answer would have been appropriate a week ago, but not now. Things don't get faster because they *must*. Things get faster if a force accelerates them.

"No," I correct myself, "according to Newton, the water accelerates forward if there is a net forward force on it." I close my eyes again and imagine myself with the slow current behind me and the fast current ahead. What force could be accelerating me forward into the faster flow? The slow water behind is pressing me forward, and the fast water in front is exerting pressure backward. So the forward pressure from behind is greater than the backward pressure from in front, resulting in a net forward force accelerating me forward.

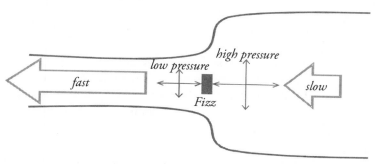

The Bernoulli effect: pressure is lower where liquid flows fast causing Fizz to accelerate into the faster, narrower flow

I smile. As Galileo taught me, clear logical thinking trumps intuition. "Okay, I get it. The slow water has higher pressure than the fast water. That difference in pressures accelerates the water—or me—forward from the slower flow into the faster flow!"

I admit that it's a clever insight. *Which he inherited.*

"Right," Daniel smiles. "A similar effect occurs in gases like air."

"Is that how birds fly?" I try to imagine myself floating through the air.

"I believe so. Their wings must be shaped so that the top curve of the wing is longer than the bottom such that the air on top is traveling faster. That way the air pressure below the wing is greater than the air pressure of the faster air above it. It is this differential in air pressure that creates a *lift* force on the bird. The same principle might apply to sails propelling ships. Let me draw it:"

Bernoulli effect generates lift on wing

"That's enough to hold a bird up? Is the difference in air pressure substantial?"

"At most a few percent."

Just a few percent? Then I recall Pascal's experiment and Newton's description of how dramatically forceful air pressure is—like the weight of ten tons on every square meter. So I guess even a few percent difference in pressure would amount to a significant lift.

"So now we know how birds fly! Do you think the same principle could be applied to implement"—I almost say PATs—"um, Leonardo da Vinci's dream of a flying machine?"

"Well," Daniel chuckles, "you only get this lift from the fast and slow air flows if you are moving rapidly through the air—da Vinci's machine would need to be propelled forward before the wings could hold it up."

"But all this talk of low pressure, high pressure," I look right at him. "It's so abstract. What is this pressure in gases and liquids? Why do fluids push outward?"

"I do have a theory, although it is… speculative. You see, I wonder if liquids and gases might comprise randomly moving microscopic particles. Then the pressure might simply be the effect of the particles bouncing off the container."

He shows me a diagram:

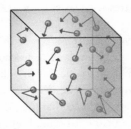

Kinetic theory explains pressure and heat in a fluid

I frown at the diagram. "Wait a second. You're really suggesting that a liquid is not continuous? That it contains particles with gaps? You really think that air pressure, equivalent to the weight of ten tons on every square meter of my body surface, could be just the effect of invisible tiny particles bouncing off me?"

"That is my theory," he says. "I call it *kinetic theory*—kinetic for movement—the theory that pressure is caused by the movement of particles."

Twenty-four horses unable to pull apart two hemispheres, PATs gliding through the air—all because some invisible particles are bouncing off the outside of the hemispheres, or off the bottom of the wing.

If I've learned one thing this past week, it's that surprising does not mean impossible. *I should see if I can apply the scientific method.*

"So do you have evidence for your kinetic theory—or rather for *this* kinetic theory? Can it at least provide an underlying explanation for known features of a gas? For example, can kinetic theory explain Boyle's law of gas pressure, that when you compress the volume of a gas, the pressure increases in inverse proportion—oh, wait... okay, maybe I can see that myself. If you force the same randomly moving particles into a smaller volume, then they are packed more densely and bounce off the vessel more frequently, creating more pressure!"

I turn over the sheet of paper he had used and sketch it for myself:

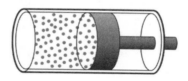

In a smaller volume the densely packed particles bounce off the container more frequently creating higher pressure—kinetic theory explains Boyle's law

"*Ja,*" Daniel says smugly. "What is more, if fluids really comprise randomly moving particles, this suggests an explanation of heat. Heat might simply be the movement of the particles. If that is true, then a higher temperature just means faster moving particles."

Heat! So the computer did have a reason to bring me to eighteenth-century Switzerland after all. This man—or his father—does have a theory of heat, at least a hypothesis. Analyzing the pressure in a liquid or gas has led to the hypothesis that the pressure might be caused by moving particles, which then suggests an explanation for the age-old mystery of the nature of heat.

Yet again one underlying theory—the kinetic theory of moving particles—provides an underlying explanation for multiple phenomena, such as Boyle's law of gas pressure and the nature of heat.

"But," I ask, "are you suggesting that all materials are made out of particles? Like, resuscitating Democritus' ancient discredited theory of atoms?"

"*Neinstimme*. I have no evidence of that. I only have evidence that the idea of randomly moving particles provides a good model for understanding the pressures in fluids."

"Well, I'm very grateful for your time and insights." I hesitate. "Actually, I did want to ask you a more personal question, if I may. These ideas about the pressure varying with speed in a moving fluid and the kinetic theory, are these really your own insights?"

"Surely." He sounds irritated.

"Well forgive me, but I guess I do have to ask you. Did I not see in the library some similar ideas published by your own father, Johannis, back in 1732?"

Daniel Bernoulli glares at me silently. Then he looks down at his feet. I try to read his expression—he looks neither embarrassed nor indignant. If I had to describe it, I would have to say he looks… sad; yes, deeply sad. I immediately regret challenging him. I'm seeking the truth, I'm not breaking any laws. *But is it really my job to appear from nowhere and judge a complete stranger, someone who has just done me a favor?*

"Well," Daniel Bernoulli says very softly, rubbing an eye, "this is how it has been since 1735."

His answer makes no sense, given that he was asked about 1732. However it is not my place to upset him more so I say, "Sure, I'm really sorry to hear that." I thank him and awkwardly take my leave, still feeling awful.

On the way out, I pass by the librarian who helped me earlier.

"Tell me, please," I ask with exaggerated casualness, "any idea what may have happened to Professor Daniel Bernoulli in 1735?"

"1735? I think that was when he won one of his prizes from the Paris Academy of Sciences."

"One of? Was there something special about that year's prize?" I say.

"*Ja*. That was the year when the Academy awarded it jointly to Johannis Bernoulli and Daniel Bernoulli."

I smile. *If I can bring myself to leave—would my Dad and I ever get to do science together?*

"How special. Johannis must have been very proud."

The librarian lowers his voice. "It is said Johannis was so ashamed at having to share the prize with his son that he threw Daniel out of the house and has not spoken to him since. The preeminent Swiss mathematician, Leonhard Euler, has tried to reconcile the two of them without success."

"Well, actually I might have an idea why Johannis was so upset with his son." I lower my voice to the softest whisper. "Did you know that much of the work of your Professor Daniel Bernoulli was actually plagiarized from Johannis?"

The librarian seems to experience a small involuntary shiver. "*Nein, nein,* you are sadly mistaken."

"Mistaken?"

"It was Johannis, overcome with jealousy over his son Daniel's success, who plagiarized his son's *Hydrodynamica.*"

"No, I checked that. *Hydrodynamica* was only published last year. 1738."

"*Ja,* and Johannis wrote *Hydraulica* this year, 1739, and backdated it to 1732!"

Later, back in Fizz's Place, still keeping the lid on my disturbing thoughts from this morning, I move three artifacts from the shelf and place them on the desk.

The paper bag—does this bag really contain billions of particles constantly flying around? I seal the bag closed and try to compress it between my hands. I have to exert myself to compress it just a little. Are bouncing particles really able to produce the huge air pressure that my farm hands can barely overcome?

The hot can—Bernoulli speculated that heat in a gas is just a name for the internal movement of the particles. But is his speculation correct? And how do we explain heat in a solid?

The water—I didn't ask to explore liquids, but Bernoulli has provided an explanation. Now I have a doubt: Is his hydrodynamics a fundamental law of nature or merely an application of Newton's laws of motion to fluids? *Shouldn't each artifact hint at a fundamental law?*

I stare at the other artifacts on the shelf and almost feel them staring back, holding out on me. I have some information about heat, liquids, and light, but I don't feel that I've mastered any one phenomenon of nature.

There is one artifact that I've not even touched on, and I believe it becomes important to later Outside developments. I will never understand how technology developed, and whether it is desirable, without understanding this sign.

I pick the amber off the shelf.

"Computer, find me someone who studied electricity."

Settling down for the night, I look again at the artifacts, but now I find myself looking right through them, thinking about the man who carefully prepared these clues for me. The man who may become the only relative in my life—except on Mom's birthday, when I can visit her—if I find that the scientific process continues to develop as a positive quest for truth, if I find that I cannot pursue my own truth within my community, if I continue to find that my community lied to me about the connection between science and technology.

The thought of trusting my life to Dad is creating some sort of negative pressure inside me, physically causing my insides to contract. *Do I even know if my father wants me to live with him on the Outside?* I mean, how much does Dad actually... love me? Is a father's love innate, something to be taken for granted? *Apparently not!* If I were ever to be successful on the Outside, do I risk him becoming jealous of me? If not actually jealous, resentful of the distraction I would be to what he calls his "career"?

I look around. To Dad's credit, he did lend me his time machine. Then again, that could be due more to guilt than love. *If Dad really loves me, wouldn't he have refused to put me in danger rather than just warning me about it?* Maybe when Dad said his colleagues were pleased to have this thing tested without the usual regulation, he actually meant himself.

The artifacts somehow seem to be staring at me again. This time the strange assortment of objects are actually whispering a personal message in my ear: *It's always possible, Fizz, that you bullied your Dad into lending you his time machine, playing on his guilt of absentee fatherhood. But he handpicked each of us, didn't he, to help guide you on your quest. No one asked him to put us here. Isn't that pure paternal love?*

Perhaps.

And still one of those objects has not helped me at all. As I settle down to sleep, I spin the pebble hanging over my head. *What do you represent?*

Waving

"*Non.*"

The receptionist here at the Académie Royale des Sciences has informed me that the senior mathematician and natural philosopher in Paris is Jean le Rond d'Alembert, permanent secretary of the Académie Française. He has assured me that Jean and his students are the new torch-bearers for the Newton-Leibniz tradition of mathematical physics—using mathematics, in particular calculus, to model the physical world. Apparently d'Alembert is also the scientific editor of the *Encyclopédie*. If anyone can help me understand electricity, it must be him.

However, on the subject of getting an audience with d'Alembert, right now all the receptionist will say is "*non.*"

After my embarrassing misjudgment of Bernoulli, I was careful to ask for some personal background on d'Alembert. Born out of wedlock, Jean was apparently abandoned by his mother on the church steps. He lived in an orphanage before being adopted by a glazier.

Is there is some reason why so many of the physicists—Copernicus, Kepler, Newton, d'Alembert—grew up without fathers? *Does it bode well for me in case I opt for the Outside?* Or is it pure coincidence? Perhaps in the centuries I'm visiting, it's not so rare to lose a father to war, disease, and abandonment.

From his humble beginnings, d'Alembert rose to prominence. He studied theology and then law—the rumors are that d'Alembert's biological father secretly paid for his studies, the receptionist whispered. Jean then tried his hand at medicine before finally turning his hobby of mathematics into a profession and earning a position here at the Académie Royale des Sciences. In fact, he is so prominent that even his receptionist will barely talk to the likes of me.

I'm wearing a low-necked gown in shades of ivory, elaborately decorated with beads, the sleeves ending in a lacy ruff at the elbows. Under the gown I'm wearing a long smock as underwear, bound in a tight corset. I imagine that the corseted ladies of Paris must wear extra rouge to cover up the blue of asphyxiation. And yet, I can't argue with the results; my waist has never been this thin or my bust this full. Even this outfit is at the low-end as I discovered while walking here along the right bank of the Seine. Losing myself for a while in the elegant streets of Paris, of which my grandparents had occasionally whispered, I studied the fashionable women walking around in elaborate gowns, with panniers creating the effect of a skirt exploding outwards from their tightly corseted waists. I observed genteel ladies in dresses spanning the entire width of the generous sidewalks, sweeping past, oblivious to the poor beggars all around, some of whom seem to live on a patch of sidewalk smaller than the dresses. *Talk about having a presence.*

Just before arriving here at the Académie Royale des Sciences, I had the pleasure of seeing the magnificent royal Palais des Tuileries, although I was told that King Louis XVI now lives in Versailles. Immediately after Tuileries, I entered the expanse of a three-sided courtyard of the majestic Louvre Palace and stopped to look around and draw a deep breath. I found the courtyard to be almost too big and open; Great Court in Cambridge has a fountain; perhaps the Louvre could do with a focal point too.

It is here inside the Louvre Palace, that I am failing to gain access to the Académie.

"What do you mean '*non*'? Surely given the background you described, Professor d'Alembert has an interest in discussing physics?"

"*Oui*, the professor is interested in discussing physics."

"And given his background, surely he's not above a quick chat with a visitor?

"Not at all, the professor will see anyone."

"So what's the problem here?"

"But you—I mean you are—" The receptionist waves his hand toward my gown.

"Female?"

"*Oui*," he confirms.

Now he says, "*oui*."

An hour later, in a different outfit and approaching a different receptionist, I secure an audience with Jean le Rond d'Alembert. He appears to be in his sixties and exudes the quiet confidence of someone who has risen steadily from the most modest beginnings to become the patriarch of French science.

I walk in on a heated political debate. "He may be foreign, but director-general Necker is absolutely right," d'Alembert is saying confidently, "we must tax the nobility to close the country's exploding deficit—"

"I am not saying we do not need to," his guest raises his voice slightly, "I am saying the King will not do it, and then, well, there is no saying—"

They don't seem to notice me standing in the doorway, fidgeting nervously. This time I'm wearing tight breeches with a cloth stuffed in to pad the crotch. Under it I'm wearing silk stockings ending in buckled shoes. On top I'm wearing a coat and waistcoat; together these two layers hopefully obscure the shape of my chest.

Again I decided to pass on the recommended wig and instead powdered my hair and tied it back with a black ribbon under a wide-brimmed three-cornered hat which is heavier but less ridiculous than the tiny woman's hat I had earlier.

It was actually worth dressing as a man just to get out of the corset—but will I fool them?

The political chatter goes right over my head. "Ahem," I clear my throat in the lowest tone I can manage. *I bet in the dress from earlier I would have distracted them immediately.*

"Ah yes, I have a visitor from abroad," Jean closes the discussion. "It will be good to get back to physics for a few minutes." He consults the note from the receptionist and turns to me, "Fizzet, bonjour. You are interested in hyperbolic partial differential equations?"

As d'Alembert looks up at me, both my fists clench.

Will he notice my feminine face? Is he glancing at my bust? Will my voice give me away?

"Um, hyperbolic what? Not so much, I was wondering if you are studying electricity."

Talking French is hard enough without having to remember to use the masculine tense and a male voice.

"Electricity—why?" he seems slightly hurt. "You do not like hyperbolic partial differential equations?"

I don't think he suspects anything. My fists start to relax.

"I'm on kind of a personal mission to understand the universe and how physics impacts people's lives. I'm somewhat less interested in the detailed mathematics." I try a weak smile.

He walks to the cupboard and comes back with a long elastic string.

"Grab the other end of this string," Jean commands, handing me one end.

"What?"

"Do as I say. Grab the string. I do not like performing experiments, but if you cannot appreciate the pure mathematics, well, you leave me with no choice."

Jean then takes a few paces back holding the string taught between us. He gives a flick of the wrist creating a shape in the string. The shape travels toward me:

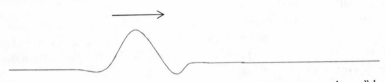

"You watch how that disturbance is preserved as it moves along," he says.

I see the pattern traveling along the string toward me, intact. "So?"

"Well, do you not see, this is how *l'information* travels around the universe. In a *wave*. A wave is just some pattern—some *disturbance*—in a *medium*. Here the medium is the elastic string and the disturbance is the sideways movement of that string. A wave is a pattern that travels through a medium while preserving its shape. The pattern can carry information, *d'accord?*"

This idea of transmitting information triggers another memory of a sermon. *On the Outside they transmit unimaginable quantities of data, of information, every second of every day, completely overwhelming our natural ability to gather information on a human scale…* In fact information is one of the two "core evils"—artificial energy and artificial information.

"Now, let me combine two patterns." He waves his arm up and down while vibrating his wrist. "Do you see how the two patterns are added to each other?"

Yes, I can indeed see a coarser wave and a thinner wave added together. "And therefore?"

"And therefore? Is the significance not obvious? Look how much information the wave can transport: the information in the big wave and the information in the small wrist-wave added together and transmitted to you all at once."

Unimaginable quantities of data. I might have been expecting to discuss electricity, but I'm beginning to see why d'Alembert considers waves to be important. "But information doesn't move around the world in vibrating strings?"

"We will see soon. Now let us combine a course and fine wave again, but this time moving in opposite directions," he says. "One... two... three."

D'Alembert makes several quick small waves with his wrist. I make a couple of bigger waves with my arm. The two patterns head toward each other.

"So what will happen when the two patterns meet?" he asks.

As the patterns meet, they become intermingled.

"Look how my pattern and your pattern are being added together. We call the addition of waves, *interference*. The waves are added to each other at each point and at each time. When your wave is displaced upward and mine is also up, we get a big upward displacement of the string. When your wave is displaced upward but mine is down they cancel each other out at that point."

Sure enough, while he speaks the two waves add together to give:

Then, from the messy interference of our two patterns passing through each other in opposite directions, both patterns magically emerge, unmodified, with each pattern reaching the other end.

"Hmm, I think I see. But isn't interference the wrong word? The two waves seem to mix together but not interfere with each other at all. They both emerge unchanged at the other end!"

"Never mind the word. How?" Jean says.

"How?"

"Yes, how? Each little piece of string is not aware that I want to send you a pattern with information. The little piece of string certainly does not know that it is supposed to transmit two patterns simultaneously. All that each tiny segment of string is aware of are the *tension* forces it feels from the neighboring bits of string pulling it. Yet somehow from all those microscopic tension forces emerges a big string with an impressive capability of transporting multiple patterns, in both directions simultaneously. So, Fizzet, I repeat, how?"

He has a point. How do the simple dynamics of each of the bits of string fit together to transmit patterns? "I give up, how?"

"Aha, so now that I wave a string around, suddenly you are interested in second-order hyperbolic partial differential equations?"

"I think maybe there is a marketing issue here. Can't you just call it the 'wave equation'?"

"Call it what you wish. You see, each displaced point on the string is pulled back by an amount proportional to the curvature of the string at that point."

He grabs a piece of paper and draws me a diagram:

"Do you see the string is curved at this point? That stretches the string and causes the point to be pulled back down. With the help of calculus, I add up the behavior of all the infinity of points. *Voilà!* My equation shows that this behavior of each point—resisting curvature—leads to the aggregate behavior of the string, which is to transport patterns. Calculus helps me relate the local behavior at each point to the global behavior."

"Cool. So that's how lots of little bits of string collaborate to transmit patterns. But how does your wave equation explain phenomena of waves, like reflection?"

"I suppose that showing you the equations will not be of interest, so tie your end to that chair. Go ahead."

I tie one end of the string as instructed. Jean waves his wrist flamboyantly, sending a pattern of disturbances toward the chair. As it reaches the chair, the pattern comes reflecting back, intact but inverted.

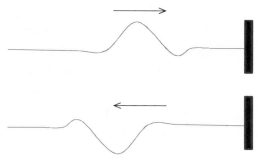

Reflection of a wave

"Okay, I see the reflection, but how does it happen?"

"Do you not see?" he says. "When one end is tied to the chair, it is *constrained*. The total wave at that point has to be zero because the string is tied to the chair and unable to move. So how can the disturbance be zero if I am sending a wave toward it?"

Hmm. "Ah," I point at the chair, "I suppose it could only be zero if an equal and opposite wave is emerging back from the chair even as the first wave comes in. So the reflection is an equal and inverted wave emerging from the chair, ensuring that the total of the two waves at the chair—the wave coming in plus the reflection—is always exactly zero!" For just one second I smile proudly, then, remembering I'm supposed to be a man, quickly wipe the smile off my face. "But, as I said, information is not often conveyed by strings, is it?"

"A string is an example of a one-dimensional medium carrying waves. Since you clearly do not like equations, I shall be forced to demonstrate to you waves in two and three dimensions."

Jean takes a tray from a cupboard, then walks off and returns a minute later carrying a bottle of water. It actually bears an uncanny resemblance to the bottle of water from the box in my hut. Suddenly I wonder if that bottle never represented the dynamics of liquids; more likely it represented the phenomenon of waves! Maybe this guy doesn't know electricity, but he's going to solve one of the other artifact riddles for me.

Jean dips two fingers in the two-dimensional surface of the water. Immediately we see how the resulting two-dimensional ripples have the same ability to travel through the medium while preserving their shape and to pass through one another and interfere, yet emerge intact.

Two-dimensional waves: two sets of water ripples interfering

"Got it. What about three dimensions?"

Jean shouts out loud: "Pierre-Simon. Joseph-Louis." The shouting seems out of place in the distinguished setting of this academy in the Louvre. A minute later two younger men stroll in wearing rather expensive-looking versions of the outfit I'm in.

My fists tighten again as the men enter the room and we all say, "*Bonjour.*" Any one of them could notice the contours of my breasts—even under the waistcoat—or suspect my voice, at any moment.

I force myself to relax. *Stop worrying Fizz—you're not a woman now—the men simply won't be looking.*

"Did you see my demonstration?" Jean asks me.

"Demonstration—what demonstration?"

"The effects of waves in three-dimensional space." he says.

"What waves? Oh, you mean sound waves!"

"*Correcte.* I created a disturbance in the air by generating vibrations in my throat and mouth, representing the information of two names. The next moment the specific two students owning those very names enter this room. The universe communicating information via waves—sound waves in three dimensions—emitted by throats, carried by air, reflecting off walls, refracting through doors, detected by ears. Waves are one of the miracles of physics."

"Or one of the tragedies," one of the students laments.

I recall Galileo first discovering that sound comprises vibrations of the air. Now this wave equation analysis helps me understand how the properties of each little air particle—if they are in fact particles, as Bernoulli suggested—accumulate to give air the overall ability to transport complex patterns of speech and other sounds in all directions. The wave equation teaches me how two sounds may cross paths in the air, yet both emerge unmarred by the interference.

"*Merci*, Professor. It's kind of exciting to see how you applied Newton's calculus to reveal the relationship between the dynamics of each point of string, or air, and the overall behavior of transporting waves."

I turn to the two students.

"You are not in England," Jean says.

"Pardon?" I turn back to him. "Oh, I'm sorry, no doubt you must be using Leibniz's version of the calculus."

"Now," Jean says, "introductions. Pierre-Simon, Joseph-Louis, this is Fizzet."

We all bow and sit. I feel bad using deceit to get an audience with these eminent physicists, but, well, I'm not breaking any laws.

"One final demonstration of sound waves." Jean takes a look at me, then shouts: "Three coffees and a hot chocolate, *s'il vous plait.*" Then to me he says, "Fizzet, I shall get back to work. Feel free to chat with my students."

"Actually, we have not been 'students' for some time now," Pierre-Simon says as soon as Jean d'Alembert is out of earshot.

"So who are you?"

"I," says Pierre-Simon, "am the Marquis de Laplace."

"Enchanted, I'm sure. And you?"

"Joseph-Louis Lagrange. I am at the École Polytechnique."

His accent is not French, it reminds me of Galileo. "And previously you were…?"

"Giuseppe Lodovico Lagrangia. And you, where are you from?"

"Iceland."

"Iceland? So all this is your fault!"

"What is my fault?"

"The weather."

"The weather?"

"A joke. Unimportant."

The joke goes right over my head. "So, you are also both in mathematical physics?"

"That is us," says Pierre-Simon, "using mathematics to model the universe."

"Do you think we will ever have a complete mathematical model of the universe?" I ask.

"*Oui, oui.* I am a big believer in *causal determinism*—that every detail of the future unfolds based on rigorous laws of nature. You know if some superior being, say a theoretical demon, could collect perfect information on today's world, and if the demon had sufficient intelligence to calculate the laws of motion, it could calculate the entire future just perfectly."

I remember discussing the idea of predicting future movements with Newton and his friends. *But I never fully absorbed that it could be taken to this extreme!*

"Wait a second, Pierre-Simon." I lean toward him and bring my fingertips together. "You're not saying that the entire universe is a purely predictable machine, just ticking away mindlessly according to the formulae of Newton's laws of motion?"

"I'm not?"

"Well, I can't talk for you." I pause to frown. "But I'm quite capable of making my own decisions. I'm not some deterministic machine."

"You are not?" he looks at me searchingly.

"I… don't think I am," I say.

Then again, how did I just choose to say that—my brain is after all made of materials moving according to the deterministic laws of physics, just like everything else in the universe!

Laplace is following my facial expressions with an air of mild amusement. I feel anything but amused. The thought of being just a piece of material playing out the equations of motion makes me feel emptiness—almost as though Laplace's demon is sucking out my soul, attempting to reduce me to some automaton that obediently calculates Newton's equations. *But is this emotion of emptiness just some deterministic response of the materials in my brain?*

Brrrrrr. I shake my head vigorously to break up the thought.

"Joseph-Louis, what are you working on?"

"I have an alternative approach to Newton's equations of motion."

"An alternative approach?"

"*Si.* Consider trying to predict the path of a kicked ball. Newton's methodology was to use the forces to predict the positions, speeds, forces, and resulting accelerations, moment by moment. My approach is to look at the entire path of the projectile through time. I have derived an equation that can consider all the possible paths through space and can pick out the correct one. In this case, it turns out to be a parabola."

He sketches it:

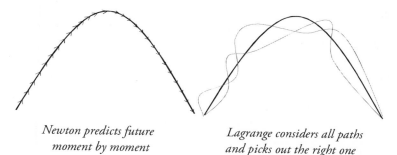

Newton predicts future
moment by moment

Lagrange considers all paths
and picks out the right one

"Interesting," I say, "so your way gives some insight as to how the ball ends up along that particular path—a parabola."

I look back to Pierre-Simon. "Now your demon, Laplace, has two choices: She can calculate the future one moment at a time, or she can map out all future scenarios—whether they obey the laws of physics or not—and use this Lagrangian approach," I glance at Lagrange, "to pick out the true physical future! So how about you, are you doing any mathematical work to help your demon calculate the future?"

"Well," says Pierre-Simon, "I have a new simpler way to model gravity."

"Gravity? You're both revisiting fields that are already plowed!"

"I call it *potential*. Potential is a generalization of the concept of height, or altitude. On Earth, for example, one simple way to model gravity is to note the altitude of each point. Then the law of gravity may be stated as: Gravity pulls from high altitude to low altitude.

But if there are two planets exerting gravitational pull, you cannot just describe the altitude. So I introduced the concept of the potential, which is a number at each point such that gravity will always pull from high potential to low potential."

I sip my cocoa and look at them both. They've taught me something: *There can be two entirely different yet equivalent ways of looking at the very same aspect of the world.*

I think more about this potential. Gravity always pulls from high potential to low potential, as in the case of Earth's gravity, where gravity pulls from high altitude to low altitude. I try to imagine Earth as a well of low potential. Every time I climb stairs I exert effort to reach a higher potential. It is as if the lower potential is trapping us, or at least making it hard for us to escape. But it seems abstract. Just what is the potential?

As I think about climbing stairs, a thought is forming in my mind, a dark thought. How deep can a well of potential be? Could there be a place where the potential around was so high that I simply couldn't climb out of that place? For example, a really massive planet might have such strong gravity that it creates a steep potential gradient analogous to an unscalable wall. *Could it be so steep that nothing could climb out?*

"Pierre-Simon, just how steep can the changes in potential be?"

"I am not aware of any limit," Laplace says.

"This may be a strange question, but could there be a planet so massive that I could never climb out? Or even a planet so massive that nothing could climb out?"

The two men look at each other.

Laplace nods enthusiastically. "Yes, that is a profound thought. I have been starting to think about this myself. I wonder if there could be a place where nothing—not even corpuscles of light—can escape the gravity. I would call it a *black hole*."

My thought was literally a dark thought! This might be a good time to get back to the topic that brought me to Paris.

"Thank you both for your fresh perspectives on mathematical physics. But is either of you working on electricity? I have a particular interest in that topic."

"*Non.*"

"Hmm, any ideas as to who might be studying electricity in Paris?"

"You could try the Good Doctor."

"The Good Doctor?"

"That is how everyone knows him." They explain how to find the Good Doctor.

"Great, thank you both for your time."

"It was a pleasure, *monsieur* Fizzet."

"*Mademoiselle*," I correct them with a rueful smile.

"I think you are confusing your French, Fizzet," Laplace smirks. "We use *mademoiselle* to address a girl."

"No matter, I used to confuse the French genders too," Lagrange says kindly.

I stick my hand straight down the front of my awful tight breeches and remove the cloth. I take the triangular hat off my head and pull open the pony tail liberating my hair which I give a good shake. Pulling apart my coat and waistcoat I liberate my man's shirt complete with pansy lace trims. I hold my chest out proudly.

"*Mademoiselle*," I repeat watching closely for their reactions.

Pierre-Simon and Joseph-Louis are frozen in place looking rather like they are impersonating fish. I'm kind of pleased to have shocked these misogynistic French academics.

"B–b–but why?" Pierre-Simon finally mumbles, waving his hand vaguely at my gentleman's outfit.

"Well, the receptionist told me you professors here don't welcome women. Maybe you think woman can't understand your lofty ideas. Yet I believe that I have."

After a few tense seconds, Joseph-Louis bursts out laughing. We all laugh for a minute and finally they both kiss my hand.

"So why are you all men anyway?"

"Actually this is how I was born," says the Marquis de Laplace, tugging lightly at the belt of his own breeches.

Joseph-Louis Lagrange nods in agreement.

"Yeah, I know that. I mean why are all physicists men? And why won't you discuss physics with a woman?"

"Oh, we like discussing physics with women," Joseph-Louis says as he sees me through the door, "but our receptionist has his own ideas."

The Good Doctor

In the hut I change back—reluctantly—into the heavy, gender-appropriate outfit that I earlier left strewn across my little bed. I check the mirror. I wonder why I can't take more pleasure in seeing myself in this gorgeous outfit.

Still regarding my reflection, my thoughts drift back to this morning's encounter with d'Alembert and his fatherless background, then to all the other fatherless physicists I've met. *How has it affected me growing up without a Dad around? Did I suffer from never having a male role model to help me understand men? Am I missing the confidence that would have come from having a Dad to tell his little girl she's beautiful?*

I look around me still thinking about Dad. Why did he even invent this time machine? *To be successful, rich, and famous in the eyes of the greedy world he lives in, no doubt.* But of all the things he could have invented. *Unless...*

"Computer, can you display a log of previous journeys?"

The screen flashes a series of messages.

Log:
1950. Stayed 3 hrs. Return to 2110.
1900. Stayed 6 hrs. 2092. Stayed 5 mins. Return to 2110.
1850. Stayed 9 hrs. 2092. Stayed 20 mins. Return to 2110.
1800. Stayed 1 day. 2092. Stayed 12 hrs. Return to 2110.
-343. Stayed 1 day...

My own travel log follows. It's just like my Dad to systematically test earlier and earlier times with longer and longer stays. *Yet given that he warned me sharply against visiting times when I am alive, why did he keep making stops at a time when he was alive—2092?*

I hire a coach for the few kilometers to the Hôtel de Valentinois in Passy, just outside Paris on the road to Versailles. I suppose my morning in Paris has been worthwhile, learning about waves and seeing how calculus is expanding and providing new insights and alternative ways to model the world. Yet no one I have met here has come up with the kind of *wow* insights I heard from Galileo, Newton, or even Copernicus. *I've gotten spoiled.*

The weather is still depressingly foggy for the middle of a summer's day as we drive through squalor and back into affluence. I don't know if it's the dull weather but I just can't escape the feeling that my carriage is—or maybe I myself am—haunted by that demon Laplace spoke about, that everything in my life may be predetermined by the cold rational laws of physics. *If so, what significance does my life have?*

I'm shown into the Good Doctor's room, but he is not present, affording me some time to take in the room's rich and varied contents. The office hosts a harp, a violin, a guitar, and notebooks of the Doctor's musical compositions. There is a chess set and his own writings on chess. According to the certificates on the wall, the Doctor has run a printing business, established a fire-fighting company, and served as Justice of the Peace and as an elected politician. I see souvenirs from time spent in London and from a stint as deputy postmaster-general. I'm looking forward to meeting this man.

There are no leeches around. He seems to have earned the title "doctor" by way of an honorary doctorate from the University of Oxford. The Good Doctor also boasts honorary degrees from Harvard and Yale.

The shelves include writings in his own hand, such as *A Scheme for a new Alphabet and a Reformed Mode of Spelling* and political essays such as *Rules by Which a Great Empire May Be Reduced to a Small One* and *A Dissertation on Liberty and Necessity, Pleasure and Pain.* I find some prayer books he has edited, including a six-minute funeral service shortened to "preserve the health and lives of the living."

There is even a cooking utensil on the floor in one corner. About the only hobby not in evidence in the Good Doctor's floor-to-ceiling shelving is physics.

The eclectic collection of professions and hobbies gets me thinking: Why does my Dad call himself a "physicist"? Why am I a "farmer"? *Why can't I be tons of different things like this guy?*

"Ambassador Doctor Benjamin Franklin of the United States of America," the secretary finally announces. "He will only have a few minutes." Franklin walks in awkwardly. Well into his seventies, he is stout and partly bald. He's about the first gentleman I've met in Paris who is wigless, the natural gray hair from the back half of his head waving all the way down to his shoulders. His clothes are gray and more sober than the Parisian norm. After sitting, he puts on a pair of spectacles with the lens split horizontally in a way I've not noticed before. In his own understated way, there is something very distinguished about Franklin's presence as he sits behind his desk as representative of the newly independent fourteen states.

Benjamin Franklin

"You are my first visitor from Iceland. You certainly brought the weather with you."

"The weather?" I squint at him. "Why is everyone blaming me for the bad weather today? We don't have summer fog like this in Iceland."

He laughs. "This year you do."

"What's special this year?"

He looks quizzical. "Well, do you not know? The Laki fissure volcano has been erupting for weeks. Covered all of Europe in soot, creating this damned fog."

"Oh, I see," I smile.

"This is anything but amusing. The lack of summer sun could damage crops and cause famine. I mean, what you spew into the atmosphere in Iceland effects us here in Europe, you know."

Little do you know, Franklin, how what you spew into the atmosphere in Europe is going to affect us in Iceland.

"Anyway, my secretary said you have an enquiry about electricity." Now he smiles. "It has certainly been many years since I have had any visitors on that topic." Franklin leans back in his ambassadorial chair, "but I could welcome a brief distraction from the war."

The word *war* sends a shiver down my spine. *We've been warned about the wars on the Outside.*

"Thank you. So what have you discovered?"

"I built on the work of others. It was actually Charles du Fay here in Paris in 1733 who discovered that there are two types of electricity. He found that the electricity created by rubbing amber with wool is different from the electricity produced by rubbing glass with silk. When combined together, they cancel each other out, so you could say that the two types of electricity are opposite.

"In order to capture the fact that these two forms of electricity add to zero, it was I who proposed, some years later, to call the electricity produced in glass *positive* and the electricity produced in amber *negative*."

"Why that way?" I ask.

"Tails," he says.

"Pardon?"

"The coin came up tails. Du Fay and I found that in electricity, as sometimes in life, opposites attract. So a positive electricity—a positive electric *charge* attracts a negative electric charge but repels another positive charge."

I place my hands on the ambassador's desk. "But what are these invisible 'charges'? What is it inside the rubbed ambers that causes them to repel? What causes rubbed amber to attract rubbed glass?"

"No one actually knows what the electric charge is."

My fingers drum the table. It's frustrating that words like charge are being used to cover up the lack of a real understanding for what is going on inside the electrically charged amber or glass. I also have an idea that electricity is used on the Outside in my own time period on a scale much bigger than that of rubbing amber or glass.

"Does electricity ever appear on a scale bigger than tiny sparks in rubbed materials?"

"Ah," he says, "yes. I suggested, back around 1750, that the tiny spark seen when charged amber is brought close to a metal might represent the same electric effect seen in, well, a much larger spark."

"Which is?"

Ambassador Franklin looks at me. "You guess."

A larger spark? I don't think I've ever seen a larger spark than in the amber. "How large?"

He extends his arms pointing way up and down.

"Oh… lightning?"

"Right," Franklin smiles.

I look at him with renewed admiration. This man saw a spark in a rubbed piece of glass, and a clap of lightning, and had the imagination to suggest that they are the same phenomenon! Once again, that thirst for unifying disparate phenomena.

"That's wild. Could you ever test such a hypothesis?"

"I have proposed an experiment to do just that. You could fly a kite in a thunder storm with a piece of metal tied near the kite, maybe a key, and with the bottom of the string tied to a Leyden jar."

Cool. "A Leyden jar?"

He picks up the bizarre cooking utensil from a corner of the floor. "Invented in Leyden, the Netherlands. It is a *capacitor* that can store electric charge quite effectively."

Leyden jar for storing electric charge

This room contained physics apparatus after all. I look at Franklin and try to imagine the old man standing in the gusting winds, sheets of rain smacking his face, risking life and limb to fly a kite in a thunderstorm, hoping to tap into the mighty lightning and bring home just a small sampling of its fearsome electric charge, trapped in a jar, almost like a mythical hunter who brings home one scale from the skin of a slain dragon.

"Well? Did you perform your experiment—did you fly a kite in a thunderstorm?" I look at the Leyden jar and smile. "Does that Leyden jar right there, perhaps, preserve a little electric charge, a small trophy from a clap of thunder, years ago, which was deafening one second and forgotten the next, all except for that little bit of charge?"

Franklin laughs. "Since then, others have taken over the research to fully understand electricity. I assume you are going to meet Coulomb? Reluctantly I do need to get back to matters of state—"

"Do you think Coulomb will see me?" I guess I'm feeling less secure after having to fight for a meeting this morning.

Franklin writes a quick note of recommendation on the back of a small card that bears his name and title. He hands it to me. "I think he might."

"Another inverse square law?"

Charles-Augustin de Coulomb is in his forties. I have learned that he spent several years abroad surveying coasts and constructing forts, reaching the rank of Captain before returning to Paris and to physics.

"*Oui*, just like gravity. The force between two charged objects—say the attractive force between amber and glass—varies as the inverse square of the distance. If you double the distance between them, the force reduces to one quarter. As with gravity, the force also depends on how much charge there is in each object—*charge* is the equivalent of mass. More electric charge gives more electric force, just as more mass gives more gravitational force. However, unlike gravity, charge may be positive or negative, and the electric force can not only attract but also repel. Here." Coulomb pulls out a small chart:

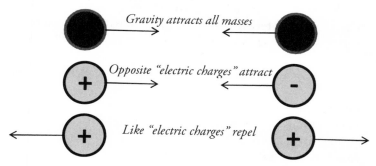

Gravitational and electrical inverse-square laws

"Great," I smile. "I love it when the same pattern reappears in different natural phenomena—I saw that with waves just this morning. But what's the significance of this inverse square pattern?"

"That is what we observe."

My smile fades a bit—*if the same pattern appears multiple times, there ought to be an underlying reason.* "So you discovered this inverse square law of electrical charges?"

"I did, although I must admit that there are rumors that Henry Cavendish in Cambridge worked on it first—but he has not published anything."

"Why not?"

"I have no idea."

Perhaps he takes after fellow Cambridge-man Newton.

"And the electric force—how is it transmitted from one charge to the other? I hope you have a better answer than Newton did for gravity."

"Instant action at a distance. I believe each charge responds instantly to the influence of other charges."

I think again about the eerie concept of masses—and now also charges—across the universe exerting a small but instantaneous pull on me right here in this room.

"I wish you hadn't said that. But tell me, Charles-Augustin, what actually is this charge?"

"We do not know. It is the word we use to describe the state of any body when it exerts and experiences an electric force."

Come on. I've been gaining insights into electricity, gravity, heat, waves, fluid motion, but no one can ever tell me what's really happening deep inside. What is the mass made of? What are the charges? Is heat really the movement of particles, and what are those particles?

Ask not within... The Collective didn't want me to ask what is within matter. Increasingly I see that that very question is the key to everything. Perhaps that's why it's forbidden. It is time to focus on that fundamental unknown.

"Coulomb, is anyone in Paris investigating the composition of matter?"

"Of course. Antoine Lavoisier."

"Do you think he'll see me?"

"I did," he says reasonably.

"And I appreciate that. By the way, why did you?"

"You had a note from the Good Doctor."

"Yes. Even so?"

"Well, I do not often get visited by beautiful young women asking about physics," he smiles.

For an awful moment my mind flickers through all the other physicists I have met. How many of them spoke to me not despite, but because I'm a woman? How many were checking me out while we spoke? How many of them glanced at my bust as they espoused their theories or gazed after me as I walked away?

"Oh. That's why?"

Then again, I reassure myself, three of the physicists I met thought I was a man, Newton seemed completely asexual, and Galileo was surely— I absolutely have to believe—too paternal to have any sort of sexual interest.

"I—" Coulomb says slowly, more seriously, "well truthfully, no. I actually do not get that many visitors at all." He runs his hand through his hair. "Ours is a lonely profession. Here we are deciphering the secrets of our universe—it is always gratifying when, once in a while, one of the universe's inhabitants appreciates the service."

It is evening, and, armed with a brief letter of introduction from Coulomb, I fit in one more meeting with Antoine Lavoisier. Antoine is in his late thirties. Coulomb told me that he inherited a fortune upon the death of his mother when he was five, allowing him to finance a substantial lab. *Another orphan.* His much younger wife, Marie-Anne, apparently married to him since she was thirteen, is his scientific assistant. So at least a woman will be playing some active role in this lab.

Coulomb also told me—and I truly wish he hadn't—about Lavoisier's day job.

After one of their servants announces a visitor from Coulomb, I enter the room and find Antoine making notes on some concoction bubbling away in a large glass container in front of him. Marie-Anne is leaning over his shoulder discussing the work. As I walk in, she turns her head toward me and smiles gently, possibly pleased to see that the visitor referred by Coulomb is a woman.

Antoine and Marie-Anne Lavoisier

Marie-Anne actually makes me feel underdressed with her multi-layered long cream muslin gown and her voluminous curly blond wig.

I catch myself glaring accusingly at Antoine and quickly force myself to smile and thank him for receiving me. I try to focus my mind exclusively on his scientific work.

"You could say I am an accountant. An accountant for matter. You know, when one imposes meticulous accounting, one never knows what one may uncover."

I cringe. *That's not all you're an accountant for, is it?* "Accounting?"

"In a way. I have discovered a *law of the conservation of mass*. You may dramatically change the nature of materials by chemical reaction—mixing chemicals, heating them, waiting for them to interact—but the total quantity of mass always remains just the same; rather like how money in must always match money out. Whenever the mass appears to change, it is actually hinting at a deeper undiscovered process."

"That reminds me of something in the classics," I say. "Didn't the ancient Greek Epicurus suggest that the total amount of substance in the universe never changes?"

"Perhaps, but little did he understand the subtleties of defining and tracking mass. The conservation of mass based on modern experiments has been suggested by several scientists, such as Henry Cavendish. Now I have demonstrated it conclusively by meticulously measuring the total mass—or weight—before and after a vast array of different chemical reactions."

This is second time today I hear that name, Henry Cavendish. I wonder why the computer never took me to meet him.

"So what do you mean by mass appearing to change?"

"Take combustion for example. Fire is probably the oldest and most important process used by mankind—it is the process that feeds us. Chemists have long believed that what actually burns is an element called phlogiston inside flammable materials. They think that phlogiston is consumed by fire. But careful accounting shows otherwise."

"How so?"

"In some cases, the total mass—or weight—of burned materials, is greater than the mass before the process."

"Really? So much for the phlogiston theory. But I thought you said mass is always conserved. Surely the mass of the burning materials shouldn't change either way!"

"Ah, you see? An accountant must track absolutely everything."

"Everything?" *Every penny from every farmer*, I think.

"Everything. Even, would you believe, the air! If you weigh the air, you find that the mass of the air decreases when the mass of the burnt solids increases. From this I have discovered that flames are not fed by phlogiston in the material; rather, they are fed by some constituent of the air! I have named it oxygen."

"Oxygen? Is it sharp?" I ask, recognizing the Greek *oxys*.

"Well, it creates acidity which has a sharp taste." He bows his head. "There are other constituents of the air too—another was discovered by Henry Cavendish. I have named it hydrogen."

Water-former in Greek. "All right," I say, "now we're getting somewhere. So the ancient Greek element of 'air' is being broken down into constituent parts! What other fundamental ingredients are there in matter?"

"So far I have identified the elements of oxygen, nitrogen, hydrogen, phosphorus, mercury, zinc, and sulfur."

"Is that it? Is everything made of those," I count on my fingers, "seven elements?"

"Not so quickly. This is a work in progress. I suspect there are more. I do know that, in addition to the material elements I am investigating, there are two special elements in the universe: light and caloric."

"Caloric?"

"Caloric. Heat. It is an element. Caloric is also conserved—when heat flows from a hot body to a cold body, the total amount of heat is unchanged. So mass is conserved—never changes in total—and caloric is conserved too."

"Hmm. But how about Bernoulli's theory that heat represents the movement of particles?"

"We may discard Bernoulli's kinetic theory. The conservation of heat suggests that heat is an element—the caloric. That best explains how heat flows from one body to another but is not created or destroyed."

"So you're bringing back Aristotle's idea of fire—heat—as a fundamental element!"

"Excuse me, but I do believe that my idea is based on scientific experimentation, not philosophical speculation."

Why did the computer take me to Bernoulli when I asked to understand heat, if this Lavoisier has a later and superior theory of heat? It crosses my mind that I've been putting a lot of trust in that computer.

Mind you, today in Paris, for the first time, I have navigated from one physicist to the next pretty effectively on my own.

"Yes, yes, of course. What about cold?"

"Some think cold is another element called *frigoric*, but cold may just represent the lack of caloric."

I find myself glaring at Lavoisier again, recalling the snippet of d'Alembert's conversation about the king refusing to tax the nobility. "Antoine, look at your talent. You've identified some of the fundamental ingredients of matter, something Aristotle himself tried but messed up! You've deciphered the age-old mystery of fire, the process that feeds us and heats us. You could be one of history's great men! Why not invest all your resources in your groundbreaking science? Why on earth would you choose instead to be a partner in a tax-collecting consortium that extracts the crown's taxation, presumably using the threat of violence, from poor farmers, while the nobility get off scot-free? Marie-Anne, can't you tell him?"

I don't actually say this, of course, but, especially if I do go back to toiling on a farm in my collective, I'll probably wonder every single day whether I should have.

Instead, I force my mind back to the scientific question that is bothering me most. "Monsieur Lavoisier, all these elements you are identifying and investigating: What are they?" He looks confused. "I mean, what's inside them? What are the elements themselves made of? What is... *within?*"

Back in the hut, not that much closer to understanding the "within," I add some new notes to the ROW label.

Law: The **wave equation** explains how information travels and how waves interfere, reflect, and refract; the very same wave equation explains elastic string vibrations, water waves, and sound.

Law: **Coulomb's inverse square law** for the attraction and repulsion of **electric charges**.

Law: **Conservation of mass**—total mass never changes.

I make a mental note that calculating the future may be aided by the Lagrangian method of considering all possible paths, and by Laplace's idea of potential as a generalization of altitude. However, I would still like a better way to understand the abstract idea of potential.

I cross out the old sentence about heat and write:

Heat is a fluid called caloric. Heat (caloric) is conserved.

Under the warning about action at a distance, I add another:

Warning: The universe may be one big deterministic machine, the future entirely predictable, in principle, by the likes of Laplace's demon.

Every one of these scientific theories is undermined by the lack of understanding of what is inherent within materials. Understanding the "within" really ought to underpin everything else.

"Computer, find me someone who figured out what matter is made of. Oh, make it a woman if you can."

As I lie down at the end of an intensive day in which I met six physicists in four locations around Paris, one thought echoes in my mind: *Why are they all men?* Are men somehow silencing potential female scientists or depriving them of the necessary education? Are they burdening women with other tasks, such as housekeeping and childrearing, preventing them from having a chance at anything else? Will this chauvinism change in other periods? In the Ecommunity, jobs are mostly traditional, with most men doing the heavy field work and most women working indoors. But we allow exceptions, like me, and both sexes play equal roles in communal leadership and policy setting. In a more egalitarian society, will there be as many woman physicists as men?

Or could women be innately less analytical?

Coulomb's words are ringing in my ears. *A lonely profession.* He has no idea what it means to be a lonely scientist! *Not one of the physicists I met has experienced the kind of social backlash that I'm risking.* I gently bite my tongue. *Except, of course, Galileo.*

Still, is Coulomb getting at something? Does connecting with the physical universe somehow compete with connecting socially? Are most people, perhaps especially women, more interested in people than in the science of the universe? Is my own interest unusual? Is it *masculine?*

Turning over on my side and curling up to sleep, I think of my Mom. I think of Toland, Zeno, and my other friends. I think of Zopp, a gorgeous guy who's been hitting on me for two years without any success. I miss them all. I really miss them all.

But, after ten days away, do I really really *really* miss them all?

Before closing my eyes, I reach up and give the hanging pebble another spin.

In a New Light

Day 10. Manchester, England. 1800.

So that's all the 1700s had to offer? Coulomb's law for the force between electric charges, some chemical investigation of the elements by Lavoisier, a few advancements of calculus techniques—good stuff, no doubt, but not much of an encore to Galileo and Newton's performance in the 1600s.

Here I am in 1800. Under the cover of night I have slipped across the official cut-off year of the Ecommunity and into the era of irreparable degradation. Now I stand at the very edge of the abyss, the point of no return—at least no return until the Ecommunity decided to return all the way to square one. This is the moment when deterioration became—or is becoming—so bad that not only all technology but also all literature from this moment on will be banned. For the first time, I'm now officially visiting the Great Deterioration.

Sure enough, the technological progress which has eluded me up to now, has broken out like a plague of mushrooms after a storm. Manchester in 1800 is booming—literally booming, as factories are under construction all around. Homes are being thrown up around the factories to house the erstwhile farmers who are flocking to the city to work in manufacturing. Horse-drawn carriages noisily crisscross the filthy cobblestone streets carrying people, coal, and all manner of goods in every direction. Garments seem more sophisticated. Shops boast a variety of products at lower prices than I've ever witnessed before, and the package-laden customers love it.

Navigating around the record accumulation of horse dung on the streets, I can smell the economic growth in the air.

On the Outside they are driven by insatiable greed for more goods, more services, more efficiency. Does it bring them happiness? No! It is greed for greed's sake, and, once started, it is insatiable, which is why the founders of our Ecommunity had the foresight to dam greed at the source...

I keep gazing around, with feelings of excitement and discomfort doing battle in my mind. Now that I'm at last experiencing all this dreaded development, how do I actually decide if I want some?

Fashion has relaxed a little. I'm wearing a high-waist gown with a soft flowing skirt of white muslin. No corset. My hair is gathered under a bonnet. The men have hung up their periwigs, although they still wear hats outdoors. Their breeches have morphed into pants, or "trousers" as they're known around here, often tucked into their boots.

Near the hut I find the Manchester Literary and Philosophical Society and am directed to the Secretary, John Dalton. Despite my special request of the computer, John does not appear to be a woman. I find him balancing precariously on the windowsill, the window wide open, apparently measuring the weather. Son of a weaver and a former school-master, John is in his thirties, wearing round spectacles on his roundish face that has a slightly protruding chin and is topped with dark, receding hair. The notebook of meteorological measurements in his hand is matched by hundreds more like it on a nearby shelf. I've noticed that the British like talking about the weather; this guy has taken it to a whole new level with his library full of meteorological notes.

"So what are you doing here?" I ask John.

"I work here. I am the secretary—I perform chemical research."

Dalton walks back from the window to his desk, turns his chair to face me, crosses his legs, and lightly supports his head with one finger. A curl of hair falls across his forehead.

John Dalton

"I realize that. I mean, what are you doing here in some Manchester society? Shouldn't a scientist like you be in one of the universities?"

While I speak, Dalton puts the full weight of his head on his hand, pinching his cheeks and covering his mouth. *Ouch.* Something inside me hates to see his mouth covered, I have no idea why. I actually feel relief when a couple of seconds later he uncovers his mouth to answer my question.

"There is an academy for dissenters in Manchester. We are not welcome in Oxford and Cambridge."

"Oh. Their loss, I'm sure. What's a dissenter?"

"I belong to the Religious Society of Friends." He spots my confused look. "A Quaker," he adds, not altogether helpfully.

"So your community prevented you from studying science?" I scrutinize his face.

"Not really. It is Oxford and Cambridge that reject admissions from my community."

"Yeah, but same result, right? Being part of the Quaker community shut you off from the scientific world, didn't it?"

"To some extent."

"Do you mind if I ask you something? Did you ever consider leaving?"

"Look here, young lady, I just met you two minutes ago. I was told you wanted a quick discussion about the elements."

"Sorry for my directness. It's just that I come from a restrictive community too, so I've got a keen personal interest."

"I see. Which community is that?"

"I prefer not to say."

"Yet you enquire all about my choices?" Dalton lifts his eyebrows.

"Apologies. Of course you're right; I'm—err—Amish." I don't actually know much about the Amish, but I know that their lifestyle—although certainly not their belief system—was part of the inspiration for the Ecommunity's radical back-to-basics.

"Amish? In England?"

"No, I'm from… Switzerland."

"I understand. I cannot deny that the idea of leaving has crossed my mind more than once when I saw the opportunities that opened up to those who left. Yet, as you can see, I have managed to remain a Quaker while pursuing science here at the Lit. and Phil."

I look around at all the scientific apparatus feeling a moment of elation. "So you really did it—the best of both worlds!"

"Then again, my community is not all that restrictive. The Amish are a different story all together. Your community must be having a hard time with all the development going on in the cities."

"Don't remind me—you can't even imagine," I throw my hands up. "Personally, I'm not even sure if I object to it all or not, I'm just struggling to understand it. Can you shed any light on what prompted this sudden explosion of factories at this moment in history?"

"Indeed, development is everywhere." John nods. "A French envoy to London referred to it recently as the *industrial revolution*. Steam engines are powering mines, mills, and factories that are producing an ever-growing range of goods employing ever-less labor per product. We are no longer depending on rivers and horses as sources of power. The result is an unprecedented increase in personal wealth. More is to come. Would you believe that there are prototypes of motorized carriages—nicknamed cars—powered by coal and steam!"

Prying leads to tinkering. Analyzing leads to changing. Nature cannot survive the onslaught.

"So this industrial revolution is the result of the scientific revolution!" I say.

"Is it? No, I do not see how. Innovation was a factor, no doubt. Thomas Newcomen in Dartmouth, England, invented the first practical steam engine around 1712, though it was extremely inefficient. Things really took off when James Watt in Scotland revamped the design in the 1770s. In fact, to date, the only supplier of efficient steam engines is Boulton and Watt, although their patent will expire this year. Earlier innovations played a subtle but important role too. In fact, looking back, you could say that the invention of the mechanical clock in the Middle Ages introduced the discipline of time-keeping, which is vital to the new industries."

"But if these inventions were so pivotal, why would you say that science played no role?"

"Science?" John squints at me. "Industry has no connection with science. There exists no scientific model for the conversion of heat into motive power, no scientific guidance for building steam engines. Engineers like Newcomen and Watt are guided by their intuition and trial-and-error."

"Is that right?"

There it is—proof positive. Not only did Aristotle, Galileo, and Newton not cause any degradation, but even right here in 1800, there is no connection between John Dalton's science and this James Watt's technology. One of the founding axioms of my community has been shattered. If I go back home I have evidence—from 1800—to justify my own private pursuit of science, maybe even to persuade others, although... I've all but discounted that plan. If I leave, it will be because my community seriously misled me.

"On the other hand, there were many social factors besides technology fueling this industrial revolution," John offers.

"Social factors?"

"In Britain, agriculture became more efficient, contagious diseases were contained, and feudalism ended. As trade barriers come down, one big home market emerged. In France, on the other hand, each region still has its own tariffs and tolls dampening trade. The patent system here has also given a good incentive to inventors like Watt by granting them a monopoly for some years in exchange for publishing their ideas."

"Amazing. Anyway, back to science. I see you've got a list of elements… that looks like it's expanded quite a bit since Antoine Lavoisier." I point at a chart on his wall:

John Dalton's list of elements

"Ah, Antoine Lavoisier. As Laplace said, it took just a moment to chop off his head, it might take France a hundred years to produce another such head."

My stomach lurches. The man I met my yesterday—beheaded! I must be turning a bit white because John adds, "I am sorry, I assumed you must know. Of course the French Revolution claimed so many innocent victims. The judge determined that 'The Republic needs neither scientists nor chemists.' Ironically, they exonerated him a year and a half later. Well, as to the elements…"

Whew, if I'd confronted Lavoisier my yesterday evening I would feel terrible right now. I try to focus my mind back on the issue at hand but it's a nasty reminder of the oddities of time travel: Tomorrow—my tomorrow—the man I'm talking to right now may be dead. And what a strange comment: "The Republic needs neither scientists nor chemists"—*almost like the Ecommunity!*

"The elements comprise atoms," John's answer makes it to my brain with some delay.

"Atoms? Surely not. Wasn't it Democritus who speculated about atoms, only to be discredited by Aristotle and others? Then Bernoulli hypothesized that moving particles carry the heat in fluids, but Lavoisier rejected that. Why would you want to flog that dead horse?"

Dalton's eyebrows flick up. "Well then, you judge for yourself. You know Lavoisier's law that mass is conserved, which I call the first law of chemistry?"

"Sure. And yeah, that's consistent with atoms, but it doesn't prove that the mass is made of atoms."

"I agree. But consider what I call the second law of chemistry: the *law of definite proportions* by French chemist Joseph Proust. When you react, by way of example, nitrogen with oxygen to make nitric acid, you always consume exactly the same ratio: Sixteen grams of oxygen to fourteen grams of nitrogen, never more, never less. So why do you think that oxygen and nitrogen mix in that very specific proportion to make nitric oxide?"

I consider for a moment. *Why would the oxygen and nitrogen always mix in a definite ratio?* "Well, I think that you think that it's because nitrogen is made of nitrogen atoms and oxygen is made of oxygen atoms. Then nitric oxide might be made of a compound particle with a pair of one nitrogen atom and one oxygen atom. And I guess the ratio of fourteen to sixteen is just the ratio of the mass of an oxygen atom to the mass of a nitrogen atom."

"Right," John smiles, "I do think that. I call such a compound particle a *molecule*—a cluster of very specific atoms bound together."

"I like the argument, but to me it's still not conclusive. It could be that nitrogen and oxygen are not made of atoms. Perhaps they are smooth, continuous materials, and maybe there is some other reason that they like to mix in the ratio of 14:16."

Dalton nods. "Perhaps. But then comes the third law of chemistry, my own *law of multiple proportions*. You see, nitrogen and oxygen can mix in other proportions too. You can also mix fourteen grams of nitrogen with thirty-two grams of oxygen to make this toxic red gas." He shows me a test tube. "Explain that!"

"Brown."

"What?"

"Your toxic gas looks brown, not red," I say.

"Whatever. How do you explain that?"

I think for a moment. "Yeah, I get it. You can mix oxygen and nitrogen in the ratios 14:16 and 14:32 because you can have a molecule with one nitrogen atom and one oxygen atom or a different molecule with one nitrogen atom and two oxygen atoms. But you can't mix other ratios in between, since the atoms can't match up."

"Right. So I abbreviate nitric oxide as NO, whereas this new substance, which we can call nitrogen dioxide, can be written NO_2. Try and explain that if oxygen and nitrogen are continuous."

Nitric oxide NO   *Nitric dioxide NO$_2$*

I lift my hands up in surrender. If continuous materials, not made of particles, could mix in the ratios of 14:16 and 14:32, they should surely be able to mix at intermediate ratios too. But if materials are made of atoms, it elegantly explains why those specific ratios mix and intermediate ratios do not. Nitric oxide is like pairing boys and girls at a dance when the ratio of boys to girls is one to one. Nitric dioxide is like pairing two guys with each girl. Intermediate ratios just don't allow any sort of consistent matching of the guys and gals.

So Democritus has been vindicated twenty-two centuries after his death: Amazingly, matter is made of atoms! I look at my hands for a moment. They seem solid and continuous. But now, for the first time, we have real evidence that they comprise trillions of little atoms. Matter is not what it seems.

"Well, this is quite a surprise, but it's great to finally know what everything is made of," I say.

I glance around the room, taking in the dozens of instruments, hundreds of test tubes, and thousands of material samples accumulated, no doubt over tens of thousands of hours of painstaking work, some of which may have been as mind-numbing as plowing is. Of all the times and places, it was here and now, in this room, that a very patient

Mancunian finally coerced nature into divulging her innermost secret—the atomic nature of matter.

I stand up and start pacing. "So, John, please tell me everything: What are these atoms like? What is the list of all atom types? How do they differ from each other? Do they have any structure? How big is each atom? How do they interact with one another?"

"Oh. Um, here is what I think we can say about atoms." Dalton somewhat sheepishly hands me a page with the following notes:

1. *The chemical elements are made of atoms.*
2. *The atoms of an element are identical in mass.*
3. *Atoms of different elements have different masses.*
4. *Atoms combine only in small, whole-number ratios like 1:1, 1:2, 2:3, etc.*
5. *Atoms can not be created or destroyed.*

I stop pacing to read the all-too-short note. "That's it? Nothing else? You don't even know the mass or size of the atoms?"

"For a few of them, I know at least the relative mass, how much they weigh relative to hydrogen."

"Huh. Why do you only know the relative mass?"

"For example, you can burn one gram of hydrogen in eight grams of oxygen to produce water. Assuming the water molecule is one hydrogen atom and one oxygen atom, which I write HO, I can conclude that water contains the same number of hydrogen and oxygen atoms. So if I make water from 1 gram of hydrogen for each 8 grams of oxygen, I may derive that the oxygen atom weighs eight times more than the hydrogen atom."

"But you can't see these atoms, can you? What if the water molecule is actually HO_2 or H_2O?" I ask.

"Yes, it is possible. But if water was, say, H_2O, it should be possible for that same oxygen to react with half as much hydrogen to produce HO. I have not been able to do that, which suggests that water is probably HO."

"Hmm. Either way, it seems like I'm going to walk out of here with proof that there are atoms but virtually no knowledge about those atoms."

My toes wiggle in frustration. Now I know that they're made of atoms, but still have no idea what those atoms are like. *This Dalton reminds me of*

Newton, who knew all the patterns of how gravity varies but didn't know how strong gravity is.

Dalton shrugs. "I am so sorry to disappoint you."

I bite my lip. "Not at all. It's all in the process, right? I'm sure your brilliant insight will eventually lead you or others to uncover the details of atoms." *I just so wish you had some more answers right here and now.* "Anyway," I try to smile, "this knowledge—that matter is made out of atoms—will this lead to new technology?"

"Technology? How?"

"Never mind, just a thought. What about light?" I ask. "Lavoisier said light was an element. Have you studied what light is made of?"

"Fizz, I am still a chemist at heart. If you want to know about light, visit Dr. Young. He is back in London."

"Dr. Young?"

"Dr. Thomas Young. He is also a Quaker from a family in Somerset. Oldest of ten kids."

"London? There's an academy for dissenters there too?"

"Actually, no. Young studied in Göttingen, Germany, and then in Cambridge."

"Did he? How?"

"I—well—" Dalton looks off the side and trails off.

"By renouncing his Quaker faith?"

He clears his throat. "Yes."

"Oh." I study his expression: uncomfortable but I don't think resentful. "And he studies light?"

"Young studies everything. Makes us all look stupid."

"What do you mean everything? No one can be an expert on everything."

"Judge for yourself. Suffice it to say that Thomas read the Bible twice by the age of four and has continued learning at that pace every since. He actually has a particular interest in studying me."

"You mean a particular interest in studying your work on atoms? I don't suppose you could give me a letter of recommendation to secure an audience with him?"

"I can. But, no, not my work, Thomas has a particular interest in studying me."

Day 11. London, England. 1800.

The midpoint of my PCC—ten days gone by, ten more to go. I'm halfway through the plowing—the brown area to my left precisely equals the green to my right, like perfectly balanced scales.

For once, last night, my hut was just a glorified horse, travelling through space without skipping any time. My sleep was disturbed by frequent thoughts about my father every time my eye fell on the little screen. *Why did he risk repeatedly time traveling to 2092, the year he left and the year I was born?* Could it be that he regrets leaving, even more than I realize? Or even... that he has thoughts of changing what he did?

Did my Dad dedicate his entire life on the Outside to building a time machine because he felt so desperately guilty about leaving his daughter? Or... am I reading far too much into the log of this hut?

As I attempt to use gold dust to buy some food, I discover that Bank of England notes and coins have taken over. Bullion now has a published price of four and a quarter pounds sterling per fine ounce, so I sell a small nugget for five shillings and use one shilling to buy some fresh bread and marmalade for breakfast. I make a mental note to buy back gold at the end of the day. Who knows if my shillings will be worth anything wherever and whenever I am tomorrow?

The letter of recommendation from Dalton secures me a brief audience with Doctor Young before he receives his first patient at 48 Welbeck Street, just north of bustling Oxford Street. Dalton's "everything" was no exaggeration. Young's waiting room is bursting with knowledge of every possible discipline, testimony to a polymath to rival the Good Doctor. Not content with being both a physicist and a physician, Young's wooden shelves are lined with books in more languages than even I know: Greek, Latin, French, Italian, Hebrew, German, Chaldean, Syriac, Samaritan, Arabic, Persian, Turkish, and Amharic. Facsimiles of Egyptian papyruses and the Rosetta Stone are strewn around the place, plastered with his handwritten notes. He apparently deciphers hieroglyphics between appointments with patients. I also see a flute and notes on techniques for tuning instruments.

As science seems to be accelerating, I wonder if anyone will ever again rival Young's ability to study all of human knowledge. *With all these other studies, what possible interest could he have in Dalton?*

But I'm here to discuss light, and Young seems happy to chat about the subject. He's in his late twenties with curly hair and the now-fashionable long sideburns framing his cute, roundish face.

"So I heard that you're oldest of ten children. I can't imagine what that's like. I'm an only child."

"Well, if the birth of a younger sibling reduces your sense of self-importance, you could say I am a very modest man."

Thomas Young

I smile. "I heard rumors of a breakthrough in understanding the nature of light?"

"Take a look." Thomas walks around shuttering the windows until the room is completely dark. I have an awkward sense of déjà vu, but it worked out well with Aristotle ten of my days ago, so I give Young the benefit of the doubt. Finally, as Aristotle did, he opens a small pinhole to allow in a beam of sunlight. But this is no camera obscura image of Welbeck Street—Young is letting in a pinhole beam of direct sunlight.

He places a thin piece of card through the length of the beam, splitting it into two tiny adjacent pinhole beams; effectively the slit becomes a double slit. He allows these two rays to mix together on a simple white screen in the dark room.

With nothing more than white sunlight streaming through a tiny double slit, magic unfolds. Two tiny rays of white sunlight mix together to produce an entirely unexpected spectrum of colored fringes:

Colored fringes from a double slit of light

I stare at the psychedelic fringes and scratch my head.

"Where on earth are those colored fringes coming from?" I ask. "Why aren't the light corpuscles—as Newton called them—producing two simple white blotches on the paper?"

"What if... light is not made of corpuscles?" Thomas says.

He almost sounds hesitant as if a hundred years after Newton, at least here in England, it is still risqué to contradict the man, almost as if Newton is the new Aristotle. Except that, cautiously, he is challenging Newton. If light isn't corpuscles, is he suggesting that light is a wave as Huygens and Hooke thought? Even if light were a wave, how would it explain the bizarre colorful phenomenon which is playing out on the little white screen in front of me?

This double slit experiment with a simple pinhole and piece of card reminds me of Galileo's chisel and Newton's prism. I want to figure this one out for myself. "Dr. Young, could you give me a moment?"

Back in the lighter anteroom, I borrow ink, quill, and paper from the receptionist and try to analyze for myself what might happen when two waves mix. The concept of light as a wave is still foreign to me, so I find it easier to imagine a water wave coming through two slits. As d'Alembert taught me, this is the incredible power of the theory of waves—one simple equation describes vibrating strings, water waves, sound, and now perhaps light. *If light is a wave, I should be able to understand light by thinking about water!*

What do I know about waves coming through two slits? I know that the waves diffract or spread out from each slit, and that the two waves from the two slits interfere—they are added to each other. I sketch the crests of a straight wave front diffracting through two slits then interfering:

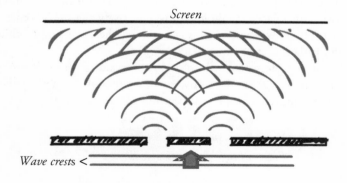

Wave crests diffract through two slits then interfere

Hmm, I can't get my head around the totality of both waves. What if I focus on just two different points on the screen and consider only the slices of the two waves that reach those two points? Suddenly my thoughts become clearer:

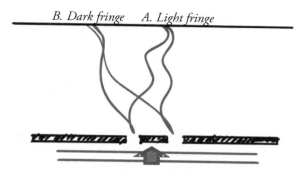

Analyzing just two specific pairs of lines of the waves:
A: Waves arrive in unison: crest-with-crest, trough-with-trough.
B: Waves cancel crest-with-trough giving zero total wave.

At the mid-point A the two waves will arrive in unison and add up together to give a big wave, or bright light. But, if I'm not mistaken, there must be a point B which is further from one slit than from the other, such that the crest from one wave will always arrive together with the trough from the other wave, since the other wave has cycled through an extra half of a wavelength—from peak to trough. Then the trough from one will arrive with the crest from the other. Strange as it seems, according to what d'Alembert said, a positive crest added to a negative trough would give no wave at all! So even with waves all around me, if I were floating in the water at point B, I would not be bobbing up or down at all.

So if these were light waves, it is logically inevitable, albeit intuitively surprising, that at point B the two light sources would add together to give complete darkness.

I grin. A simple logical analysis led me to an unexpected result: *Two waves, coming through two slits, would mix together—interfere—to give some patches of light and some patches of darkness.*

I think again of Young's demonstration. We didn't just see fringes of light and dark. Different colors appeared and disappeared at different places. So Young has not only proven that light is, after all, a wave, but he has also proven that different colors have different wavelengths—different distances from wave peak to wave peak—which explains why different colors appear and disappear at different distances from the center. *He's cracked the secret of color.*

Given those small fringes, I suppose that the wavelength of light—namely, the distance from peak to peak—must be microscopic. I make a sketch and estimate that the wavelengths of the different light colors must be less than a thousandth of a millimeter to produce the fringes I saw.

Maybe that is why the wave nature of light has been so elusive: Light waves are tiny! Atoms are probably incredibly miniscule too. No one can detect them directly, so no one can even attempt to estimate their size. So that's the secret of the "within." The universe has all kinds of stuff going on at microscopic scales—levels that, as of 1800, we can barely imagine, much less probe. *There are hidden worlds within everything.*

I find Thomas again. "Any conclusions?" he asks me.

"Yeah, I get it," I say. "You have proven Newton wrong. Light is a wave. Different colors have different wavelengths. Incredibly small wavelengths."

He smiles.

I still cannot smile. "But, Dr. Young, all of that is indirect. Light is a wave, but what is the wave? I know that water waves are disturbances in the height of the water. Galileo found that sound waves are disturbances in the position of the medium of air. What are the light waves? What is the medium and what is the disturbance?"

"I do not know, but I do know that there is more to light than meets the eye."

"More than meets the eye?"

"If you want to know more, catch a concert in Slough."

"A concert in Slough?"

"A concert in Slough. There is only one. Say hi to the musician."

I wasn't planning to spend my PCC time at concerts, but Thomas sounds adamant.

"Well, I hope that helps me." I shake my head. "I have too many half-solved puzzles. I now know that light is a wave, but a wave of what? I know that materials are made of atoms, but what are the atoms? What are electric charges? In fact, even the first and best understood law, the universal law of gravitation, is unfinished. I still don't even know the universal constant—how strong gravity is."

"Ah, about that," Thomas Young says, "just pass by the Clapham Common estate."

We walk out through Thomas' physics lab, affording me a quick insight into the wide range of interests he has even within physics. I pick up a very narrow open glass tube resting in a beaker of water. "So what's with this?"

"You know, the surface of a liquid behaves like a very thin membrane that is under tension, which we call *surface tension*. In a small capillary, or for that matter at the edge of a cup, you can see the liquid curving upward because of this tension and that pulls the entire liquid up the capillary. I've found an equation for it. Laplace is doing some related work in Paris."

"You know Laplace?"

"Oh yes. The Parisians are experts in theoretical mathematical physics. In England, we tend to be more practical. We often deride each other, but sometimes the two approaches do complement each other nicely."

I think of water seeping up through plants without any pump. Now we know how.

"And all these material samples?" I pick up a block of rubber, from an assortment of different-sized blocks of miscellaneous materials and give it a squeeze.

"Robert Hooke talked about the elasticity of a specific string or spring. I've found a way to characterize the elasticity of the material. Now engineers can just learn a single *modulus* which characterizes the elasticity of steel and then calculate the elasticity of every steel beam or screw without further measurement."

Through an open door, Thomas spots his first patient waiting and starts to fidget.

"You know, Dr. Young, it's perhaps a pity you spend your days on medicine. The world of science needs you full-time."

"Inter-disciplinary expertise has its advantages."

"Such as?"

"I only have a minute, but briefly, I have been able to apply Bernoulli's hydrodynamics to analyzing blood flow, and—"

He hurriedly pulls out a chart of the interior of the human eye and points to it with his stick. "With an understanding of optics I have been able to prove that the human eye focuses light with this lens here." He points at a lens just behind the eye's surface, labeled "cornea." "I have identified that some people have non-spherical lenses which I have called *astigmatism*."

He moves his stick to the label "retina" at the back of the eyeball. "With the new understanding of the wave nature of light I have been able to analyze the retina and understand the perception of color. You see, while light comes in many different wavelengths, the eye is only sensitive to three ranges of wavelength, which we perceive as red, green, and blue. Other color sensations are just a mixture of those three sensations. Some people are missing one of the three and perceive a reduced color palette."

"You mean they are blind to some colors?"

"Yes. I call it *Daltonism*."

There's the connection. I thank Dr. Young and take my leave. If Thomas Young had retained his faith and not attended university, would scientists still believe that light is a particle? Would engineers still measure the stiffness of every individual piece of steel? Would Dalton not know why he can't tell red from brown? *If I go back to my community, will the world of science be any poorer for it?*

From behind me I hear Dr. Young calling, "First patient, please."

A shilling hires me a Hackney Carriage for the ten-kilometer ride to Clapham Common. We start down the east side of Hyde Park and pass a particularly elegant building. "What's that?"

"Buckingham House," the cabbie cracks his whip.

"What is it?"

"The Queen's House," he says, "bought by His Majesty King George III for Queen Charlotte."

We cross the river Thames to South London and pass Battersea Park. "Clapham Common," the driver announces shortly afterwards, "estate of the Cavendish family."

Cavendish! Perhaps I will finally meet Henry Cavendish, acclaimed by Lavoisier and Coulomb. I can ask him why he never published his research on electricity.

Clapham Common is a large, flat, grassy estate, private but unfenced. I walk around for ten minutes before I finally meet the man who deciphered the secrets of electricity and then decided to keep them secret. Cavendish is in his late sixties, seated outdoors in his aristocratic dress, peering across his own grounds with a telescope. He's sitting at a table with some notebooks and a silver platter covered in an arrangement of beautifully manicured sandwiches. *Ornithology in style*, I think, stifling a giggle.

Henry Cavendish

But following the path of his telescope I see no birds. In fact, all I can see in the distance is a bizarre glass enclosure housing two massive lead spheres. I look again. Yes, he's actually observing a pair of metal spheres through a telescope.

I walk a little closer. Each sphere seems to be suspended from a torsion balance. I recognize the simple instrument from Coulomb's lab—the balls are hanging from delicate springs to measure minute forces with extreme sensitivity. But why is he observing all of this from a distance?

Then I see the two large spheres rotating. There is no one in the enclosure—this is somehow being controlled from outside. Now I spot two much smaller spheres. It seems that he is rotating the big spheres to be proximate to the small spheres.

Why is he doing all of this remotely? Then it occurs to me: *Could he possibly be measuring something so sensitive that his own body heat or breath or footsteps would affect the result?* If so, this must be by far the most delicate experiment ever attempted. But what force would be so small as to require such unprecedented, elaborate precautions? What force would require such a large, expensive lead sphere?

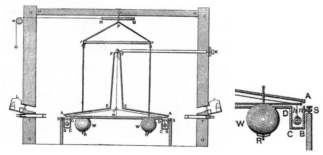

Cavendish's apparatus to measure gravity between large & small lead spheres

There is surely only one force that I've heard of which is feeble enough to require such pedantic arrangements—*gravity*. Cavendish must be measuring the gravitational attraction between the large and small lead spheres. This must be the first time that anyone is measuring the gravity of anything smaller than the Moon. *The first opportunity to confirm Newton's bold prediction that all masses experience gravity!*

I guess that measuring the gravity between two known masses would not only confirm Newton's theory that gravity is universal, but also provide the critical missing number of gravitational theory—the universal gravitational constant. And knowing the strength of gravity would in turn reveal what mass the Earth must have to create the gravity we all feel.

Interesting that such a historic experiment is being performed not in a university, but by an aristocrat in his own home with his own equipment. Of course, from what I've seen, the few universities in this time period only fund a small handful of professors, so maybe a lot of science is carried out by those gentlemen who happen to have the interest and the means.

I finally approach Cavendish. "Good morning, Mr. Cavendish, I'm Fizz. I see you're weighing planet Earth this morning?"

Cavendish immediately averts his eyes and turns away from me. He gives the slightest nod, apparently in response to my question.

"Um, Mr. Cavendish? Any results? Is there really a gravitational attraction between those spheres?"

He ignores me.

"I'm really fascinated by your work. I travelled from far away to ask you."

Finally Henry Cavendish retrieves some paper and a quill from his outdoor desk and writes something on it. He then approaches me slowly without once making eye contact. As he gets close, he turns his head away but stretches out an arm handing me the following note:

Earth's density = 5.5 times the density of water

Why is he looking away and passing me notes? Either he thinks I have the plague or he is incredibly awkward with people; or just with women.

"Mr. Cavendish. You know, I'm not as delicate as a lead sphere on a torsion balance, it's perfectly safe to come close."

He shuffles away leaving me to wonder what other unpublished secrets of nature are trapped in his head by what seems to be a pathological shyness.

But what an interesting result. Firstly Newton's outlandish prediction was correct—there really is gravity between everyday objects. Creative, logical thinking triumphs.

And now we finally know how strong gravity is, and therefore how dense the vast ball we all live on is. This density number makes me realize that I know absolutely nothing about the interior of the world underneath me. I was never allowed to ask what's inside, what the Earth is made of, and as far as I'm aware, no one as of 1800 has any way to probe the interior of the planet, beyond what they can dig with a shovel. Now Cavendish has given humanity the very first glimpse into the depths of our planet. Five-and-a-half times denser than water—one very small clue as to the composition of our very own planet—it still reveals nothing about the actual materials or structure.

I stare down at the grass between my feet. *What is down there deep underfoot?* How will we ever know the composition of the big ball that is our home?

I have some math to do. The radius of the Earth is known to be 6,400 kilometers; from this I can calculate the volume of the Earth—we learned the formula for the volume of a sphere in school. Multiplying the volume by the density—which we certainly never did at school—I find that the Earth's mass must be some 6 trillion trillion kilograms! No wonder it exerts a strong gravitational pull.

Extrapolating from the gravity of planet Earth, using the inverse square law, I also calculate that, in the base case, if I were one meter away from a mass of one kilogram, gravity would accelerate me toward that mass at an acceleration of roughly… less than a tenth of a billionth of a meter per second per second. *That is by far the smallest number I've ever seen.* So gravity is indeed feeble.

Flipping the note over, I write "Great discovery. Thank you for sharing it with me. Fizz." I hand it back to Cavendish.

I take my leave without ever once achieving eye contact. Coulomb mentioned a lonely profession. Cavendish seems to have taken that to a disturbing extreme.

It's early afternoon by the time I get back to central London. I don't have to wait long for the next westbound stagecoach toward Slough.

A team of four horses drags us along the thirty-kilometer journey to Slough, which is the first "stage" of the westbound travel route. Sitting atop the coach, facing backward, I am alongside a doctor and his wife and little girl, who are heading for a weekend in Bath. Two tradesmen en route to Wales are facing forward just behind the coachman. Three more passengers paid extra to sit inside.

The coach body is suspended on leather straps, sparing us some of the violent vibrations that the wheels below us seem to be experiencing, but instead swaying constantly, almost like Galileo's pendulum, inducing a feeling of nausea. Facing backward doesn't help matters. I fantasize about stealing one of the horses and riding on my own, as I so often did in Iceland. *This had better be some scientist I'm going to meet; or at the very least some concert.*

Trying to calm my spinning head, I scan the monotonous green hills and distract myself with reminiscences of home. After eleven days— longer than I ever expected to be away—I've learned so much, yet probably have more open questions than I set out with! I'm finally witnessing the beginning of the industrial revolution but still have not seen any signs that it is linked to science or that the Great Deterioration is all that great. A week after meeting Galileo, the very same dilemma is still tearing at me, and I feel no closer to the truth that he implored me to seek; once I complete my knowledge of physics as best I can and under- stand the consequences for human lifestyles, which of the two futures is the true one for me?

My meetings today have only confused me more. Two Quakers both found ways to perform important science—one within his community, one by leaving. *Does it even matter whether I stay or leave?* Yes, of course it does. *Don't fool yourself, Fizz: The differences between the Ecommunity and Outside in 2110 are so much starker than what Dalton and Young faced.* After all, they could meet with each other any time, not just as first- degree relatives on birthdays. Dalton's community still accepts him even after he enquired deep within. *Is anyone else facing the kind of stark choice that I am?*

Now Laplace's demon comes back to haunt me. *I don't even need to consciously choose to which life to go home.* The laws of physics will deterministically guide my brain toward a predictable decision. *How depressing.* So the laws of physics have deterministically prescribed that I should feel a bit depressed now. *Arghhhhhhh! Do I even matter?*

My thoughts are interrupted when the coachman, evidently more worried about his horses than his passengers, asks us all to get out and walk up one of the steeper hills.

Three wobbly hours later, the coach pulls in to its first stop—the Ostrich Inn, Slough. A sign boasts that the inn has been open since 1106. The doctor next to me points out to his daughter the grand brick walls of the Royal Palace of Windsor, one of the King's two primary residences, crowning a hill just a couple of kilometers south. We disembark, and the coachman switches all four horses for a fresh team and orders himself a yard of ale from the inn's bar, which turns out to be a narrow V-shaped glass almost a yard high with a round bulb at the bottom. He downs the generous dosage in less than a minute and returns to the coach. I take my leave from the other passengers while some new passenger takes my place.

Sitting down at the bar, I breathe for a few minutes, allowing my stomach to settle, then order myself a pint. It's going to be late after the concert, so I reserve a room for the night.

"All we 'ave tonight is room 11," says the innkeeper, a man in his forties. "Hope you're not superstitious."

"Superstitious?"

"Some say 'tis haunted."

"Room 11 will be fine."

I confirm my reservation and ask for directions to the concert.

Family Business

The musician, William Herschel, shows remarkably versatile talent, seducing us with an oboe concerto of his own composition, a violin concerto, and a harpsichord sonata. A small soprano soloist accompanies some of the pieces. During the applause between movements, the woman sitting next to me tells me that William, previously Friedrich Wilhelm Herschel, is one of ten children—like Young—and was an oboist in the Hanoverian Guards regiment. He first visited London with the band when the crowns of England and Hannover were united under George II. Wilhelm soon resigned from the army and immigrated to England.

William is in his early sixties. The soprano turns out to be his younger sister Caroline, now fifty, who followed him to England. At less than a meter thirty tall, or four foot three as they say here, she suffers from dwarfism due to a childhood attack of typhus. Apparently William and Caroline have performed only rarely since William became a scientist.

I don't quite know why I'm here, but for an hour I allow the unfamiliar but timeless music to wash right through me, sweeping away the disheartening train of thought that accompanied my journey here.

"Thanks, I found your concert cleansing," I say, smiling at Herschel as he walks out. He has a long face with sharp features and is dressed in a white bow tie and black tails.

"Thank you," he says, pronouncing it more like "zunk you."

"Dr. Young suggested I should talk to you."

"Dr. Thomas Young? *Ja*—that is flattering to me. About what shall we talk?" Herschel pronounces the w's as v's and the th's as z's.

"He said something about there being more to light than meets the eye? Any idea what he meant?"

"More than meets the eye?" William chuckles lightly. "I think I may. If you walk me home, I shall tell you on the way. Come, Caroline, we must be home before dark."

The three of us step outside. The last blue light of a long English summer day is still lingering into the late evening, affording us another glimpse of the royal castle. As we walk, the light seems to be dropping into the western horizon while the air temperature plummets.

"You know that one can separate white light into a rainbow using a prism?" William asks.

"Yes. Didn't Newton discover that?"

He nods. "If you put a thermometer in the sunlight, it warms up. Quite by chance I placed a mercury thermometer in the dark area just beyond the red end of the spectrum from a prism and was amazed to find that it gets even hotter in this dark area than it does in the red light."

"No kidding—it heated up in a place which was complete dark? You mean... there's light coming from the Sun beyond the red end of the spectrum? Light that is completely invisible to us?"

More than meets the eye.

We turn into Windsor Street.

"Indeed. You could call it *infrared light*. Anyhow, this is my home. I hope you have a worthwhile visit in Slough. Where are you staying?" He slows his walking, and Caroline stops too.

Right now I'm wondering why I am staying here. It's interesting to hear that there are invisible colors with wavelengths longer than red light, but surely Thomas Young could have told me that without sending me all the way to Slough. True the concert was cool, but I imagine they have good concerts in London too.

"The Ostrich," I finally answer.

"Not room 11, I hope," Caroline smiles.

These parting pleasantries are interrupted when I notice, in the near darkness, a large triangular silhouette looming behind Herschel's house, its apex towering above the house's roof.

"Excuse my curiosity, but what is that?" I wave at the scaffolding, some tens of meters high.

"Oh, my brother dabbles in astronomy," Caroline says.

"You drag your telescope way up that structure just to dabble?"

"That structure," Caroline smirks, "*is* his telescope."

My mouth gapes. "May I...?"

"Sure." William and Caroline allow me to follow them as they meander around the house to the foot of the elephantine wooden scaffolding. It supports a pipe some twelve meters long and well over a meter in diameter pointing skywards. *I could stuff three hippos along that pipe.* There is an observation deck, not at the foot of the tube but suspended precariously above the ground halfway up. *Something seems familiar about that configuration.* After a few seconds I realize why.

"Goodness, I wonder if Newton himself would recognize his reflector design."

William Herschel's 40 foot (12 meter) telescope

I arch my neck upward to take in what I imagine must be the largest scientific instrument in history. For a moment I am so distracted that I don't notice the second largest scientific instrument in history: a similarly structured telescope just some seven meters long, somewhere further along the meadow.

As the final remnants of daylight wilt away, William inspects the sky and suddenly calls out, "It is time." He and Caroline, and a couple of workmen who I did not previously notice, all seem to perk up and stride into the house. Caroline nods me in, putting her finger to her lips.

William's house immediately feels not so much like a living place for people, but more like a home for an extended family of telescopes. I see hundreds of them, of all shapes and sizes and at different stages of life: unfinished embryonic telescopes, young telescopes, ailing telescopes in repair, telescopes that have died of old age. Some telescopes have grown up and left home, remembered only by the letters of thanks hanging on the walls from their adopted families, which include Herschel's neighbor, His Majesty King George III of the United Kingdom, as well as the Emperor of Austria and the Empress of Russia.

Alongside the resident telescopes, the room celebrates the telescopes' achievements in a meticulously catalogued library of hundreds of labeled astronomical notebooks. The telescopes have accessories too—I see a shelf full of eyepieces labeled with different magnifications right up to "6000x." I recall how Galileo thought that 30x was revolutionary.

Some of Herschel's eye-pieces

Here and there, between the stargazing equipment and notebooks, I see a music stand or a sad-looking flute, instruments that—judging by tonight's concert—still perform on occasion, but in this home they are clearly playing second fiddle to the music of the universe.

I think of the connection to Thomas Young. Now that we know that light is a wave, with wavelengths in the tenths of thousandths of a millimeter, I believe Herschel must aim to shape and polish his hundreds of lenses and mirrors to avoid any imperfection greater than the tenths of thousandths of a millimeter.

While I look around, William starts talking, "We have a nice clear night. The Moon is rising around midnight so we will reluctantly get some sleep after that."

I am still trying to take it all in. The cluttered room broadcasts the story of William Herschel's celestial obsession—the sheer number of notebooks and instruments suggests that this may have been going on for decades—day after day, year after year, grinding mirrors and lenses to perfection by day, then night after night on a makeshift platform several meters above solid ground. I envision him methodically cataloging the night sky, one strip at a time, sleeping only when clouds or the Moon interfere. His family probably thinks he's crazy. I glance at Caroline to see how she is reacting to all of this; she's probably used to it.

In the indoor light I notice that William bears scars on his face and limbs. I wonder whether his wounds were sustained while smelting and grinding during the day, or groping around large heavy instruments in the dark of night. Perhaps both.

To my surprise after the quick pep talk, William hands over to Caroline, and I now notice that she herself has a nasty scar on her leg extending just below her hemline. Caroline opens a notebook and tells the workmen to adjust the forty foot telescope to an elevation of forty-three degrees in the south sky, then go home. She reads out to William a list of constellations and notable stars that will be paraded before his telescope tonight.

Apparently the unwieldy telescope will not be moved during the night. Instead, the Earth will gently rotate William and his telescope, allowing him to sweep a long strip of sky, adjacent to the strip he surveyed last night, parallel to the strip he catalogued the night before that.

Imagine plowing a field like that: somehow hovering in space holding the plow, allowing the Earth to rotate underneath me.

William's wife pops into the room with their young son, already the same height as his aunt, although he can't be more than eight years old. William welcomes "John."

"How was the concert?" William's wife asks, carrying a plate with several halved raw onions in one hand and a pile of sweaters in the other. She kisses William, and I notice Caroline cringing. Spotting the guest, she offers me the first half onion.

"No thanks."

"You do not want to be a hero out there," she says. She hands out onions to William, Caroline, and little John. They all start smearing the onion over their skin. "William suffered from malaria for years," she explains.

"Mrs. Herschel, may I change my mind?" I say sheepishly as it dawns on me that the onions are mosquito repellents, not snacks.

Suitably clothed and protected, three smelly Herschels march back outdoors with me in tow.

"Do you get used to working in this cold?" I shiver. The winters in Iceland are even colder but we don't spend the nights outside out of choice.

"Cold cannot stop us," Caroline says stoically. "Well, that's not quite true. The one time that the cold defeated our work was when my ink froze solid."

We approach the large telescope. "I have a soft spot for telescopes," I tell William arching my neck to look at the instruments looming above us, "ever since I, err, read about Galileo's discoveries of new stars and Jupiter's moons."

"Yes. I suppose Galileo," William laments, "left no major discoveries for the rest of us."

"It must be frustrating," I try to sound sympathetic, "investing so heavily in astronomy when the really big discoveries are in the past." *Less frustrating of course for those of us who were with Galileo.*

"Yes," his face drops, "deeply depressing."

We are at the base of the larger telescope, which they call the "forty-footer." "John," William says to his son, "show this young woman some trifles while we work."

Before I have time to be offended, William starts climbing a ladder and disappears into the darkness above my head. Caroline, who looks even smaller at the foot of the scaffolding, a bonnet tied tightly around her head, walks across to the "twenty-footer" and soon she too has all but disappeared.

I am left alone with John, who drags a medium-sized portable telescope out of the house and starts to adjust it expertly on its tripod.

"So, John, you like doing astronomy with your father?"

"Aha," his eye is plastered to the lens as he turns some knobs. Somewhere above our heads I hear William shouting out the word "*nebula*" followed by a list of numbers across to Caroline, who duly interrupts her own observations to note them down.

"What's a nebula? What are those numbers?" I ask John.

"A nebula is any fuzzy object in the sky. The *declination* and *right ascension* are like a longitude and latitude for the sky and the *magnitude* is a measure of brightness."

"Oh. Okay, then. I mean I knew that," I smile at the eight-year-old. "You know, my Dad is a scientist too. But he never taught me about his work."

"Aha."

"Well, you're a lucky boy. May I take a look now?"

Reluctantly, John moves aside.

I glance for a few seconds at a small disk of light with two small white dots either side of it. I look up with my naked eye and see nothing. I examine it again.

"A comet?" I ask John.

"That's what Dad thought at first, but look again."

"Yes?" I gaze through the telescope uncertainly.

"Well do you see any tail? Its orbit is almost circular—does that sound like a comet?" the precocious little boy says.

I snap my fingers.

"Okay, Dr. Herschel," I shout up at William, who is working intensely somewhere almost directly above us, "I do feel like a complete idiot." I take one more look at a discovery that could be said to dwarf anything Galileo found.

I climb up the ladder joining William on the small observation platform.

"Have you named it?" I pant.

"Oh that is *Georgium sidus* or The Georgian Star. 'The Georgian' for short." He makes it sound like he's naming a goldfish.

"Do we need to add an eighth day to the week now? Maybe Georgeday?" I smile.

This musician-cum-astronomer is the first person in history to discover a new planet, complete with two moons.

"What else have you found?"

Herschel's eye is plastered to a small eyepiece that delivers, in concentrated form, all the light that streams from distant stars into the gigantic tube besides us. He pulls away for just a minute to pass me a handheld telescope he seems to keep handy on his little observation deck.

"What else? Observe Saturn," he says, pointing up at the constellation of Cancer, then, seemingly reluctant to take the risk of missing some detail, quickly reapplies his eye to the large telescope.

I take a look, trying to ignore the threatening creaks caused by each footstep on the small wooden platform.

It's a beautiful sight. "Rings!" I say. "So those rings are what Galileo mistook for—" I stop suddenly, wondering for a second if I might be about to commit the faux pas of exposing Galileo's mistake which, for all I know, is still encrypted in the anagram to this day. "I mean, did Galileo—?"

"Yes, Galileo mistook the rings for a pair of moons. Yet, coincidentally, his anagram turns out not to be wrong. Look closely."

I look. "I see them. So you discovered that Saturn does in fact have two moons, beyond its rings?"

"Yes. Huygens discovered the first Moon, Titan. I discovered the second with that telescope, yes. With this forty-footer, I have now found seven moons. I also spotted seasonal variations in Mars' polar region—probably ice."

As we chat, William surprises me by telling me about the aliens he believes inhabit the Moon, planets, and even the Sun. This almost seems to me like a lapse back into Aristotelian thinking—assuming that the planets have a purpose rather than relying on evidence alone. Or maybe it is just healthy speculation that he fully intends to subject to empirical testing.

Moving beyond our own solar system, Herschel shows me that the North Star, technically called Polaris, is actually a double star—one of many pairs of stars that he has observed orbiting each other, bound together by their mutual gravitational attraction. He points out that this is the first demonstration of gravity beyond our own solar system. He pauses to call out a couple more nebulae, then, as they rotate out of view, he goes quiet again, straining his eye to try to discern anything at all. "Here is truly a hole in Heaven," he mutters.

"Thinking about it," I say, "naming your planet after King George might get you a knighthood but will it catch on in France? Shouldn't you pick some neutral name?"

"No," he says with a heavy hint of indignation. "The name Georgian is perfect. It will pinpoint to future generations the time in which the discovery was made."

"Hmm. So you're thinking that future generations will all be entirely familiar with when exactly George III reigned. What's wrong with the tradition?"

"Tradition? Did not Galileo himself name the Moons of Jupiter after his own royal sponsors, the Medicis?"

"How did that work out?" I ask.

"Well," he says slowly, "it is true that those moons are now better known by the names of the lovers of Zeus."

"So why not stick with the convention and name your planet after some Greek god?"

"No. 'The Georgian' is the right name," he says, seemingly closing the subject. "Anyhow, all these planets and moons are not important work."

"You called them 'trifles' before. It seems like serious science to me."

"No more than walking around Slough makes you a serious explorer. The solar system and, for that matter, all the visible stars, are just our backyard," William says. "My real goal is to understand the structure of the universe well beyond our own solar system. Galileo found that the Milky Way comprises millions of stars. My observations have confirmed the recent theory by Thomas Wright that our Sun is one of a cluster of millions of stars arranged in a fairly flat disk. Do you see, Fizz, since we are right inside a disk-shaped cluster of stars, the rest of the disk appears to us as if it were a dense ring of stars around us."

"A ring of stars around us? Oh—you mean the Milky Way?"

"Yup. The Milky Way is not what it seems. It is not a ring around us, but a disk that we are within."

"A disk with millions of stars?"

"Right. I like to call any cluster of stars, such as our own Milky Way, a *galaxy*. If you could look at the Milky Way, including our own Sun, from the outside, our Sun and the other millions of stars in the Milky Way would look something like this." He grabs a notebook from a small shelf on the observation platform:

The billions of stars of our Milky Way Galaxy viewed from outside

"So our Sun is just one dot at the center of the Milky Way galaxy?" I ask.

"Just one dot, but no, Copernicus was wrong, the Sun may be the center of our own little solar system, but it is definitely not at the center of our galaxy—let alone the center of the universe. I have been able to detect that the Sun itself is moving through space."

So Copernicus concluded that the Earth is spinning around itself and orbiting round the Sun. Now it seems that the Sun is in turn circling around in the Milky Way at even greater speeds!

"But here's the exciting part," he continues. "Take a look."

All I see in the telescope is a fuzzy spot. "That's what you call a nebula?"

"As Wright suggested," he continues, "I believe that many of these fuzzy points you can see in a telescope are actually distant galaxies. I believe the dot you are looking at may itself comprise millions of stars just like our Milky Way! I've catalogued five thousand nebulae, many of which may be galaxies."

Herschel shows me that, even though these other galaxies may each contain billions of suns, they are so distant that only one of them is at all visible to the naked eye, as a miniscule faint fuzzy white dot in the constellation of Andromeda.

My head starts to spin. It's as if the universe is expanding all around me. This man is thinking on a scale never before imagined. To him, our solar system together with all the stars visible in the night sky and the billions of others stars of the Milky Way amount to just "a galaxy." Now he's spending his time cataloging thousands of other galaxies as if each one were merely a speck of dust.

It's like a new science beyond astronomy, studying the orderly nature of the universe on scales way beyond what we can see. Studying the "cosmos," perhaps, in the Greek sense of ordered world. Maybe Herschel is the first *cosmologist*.

This is all I need. I was just feeling on the way here that I may not matter in the great scheme of things, that I'm just a small automaton in a big deterministic universe. Now Herschel is making that universe thousands of times bigger. *Thanks a bunch.*

"I have another." This time it is Caroline shouting excitedly about her observations to William. She calls out the coordinates.

"Another comet? Outstanding! Is that your seventh?" he shouts back.

"Eighth," she says.

"I shall write to Maskelyne in the morning"

"That is not really good enough is it?" Caroline shouts back.

Our observations come to an end when a three-quarter Moon rises, washing out all but the brighter stars. William and John retire to the house while Caroline, whose apartment turns out to be near the Ostrich, offers to walk me back.

"You're not really going to stay in that room, are you?" she says as we walk.

"Sure. I don't believe that rubbish about it being haunted."

"Neither do I, but I wouldn't sleep there."

I look at her. "Why? What happened?"

Caroline looks back up at me as we walk alongside each other. "In the 1600s, the owner of The Ostrich was called Jarman. He had that room specially furbished for the wealthiest visitors."

"Sounds great."

"Specially furbished with a hinged bed."

"I'm sorry?"

"The bed was a trap door. The richest guests, while they slept, would be suddenly tipped into a giant vat of boiling liquid below. Then he and his wife would rob the guest's horse and possessions. Some sixty guests were tipped to a boiling death in that room."

"Oh! I wish you hadn't told me. I'm not going to sleep a wink thinking about that."

"There may be an alternative. Are you heading to London?" she says.

"Yes. As soon as possible—first thing in the morning."

"That is not as soon as possible. Maybe you can join me?"

"Join you where?"

"I am on my way to London," Caroline stops walking.

"You mean—you can't mean right now?"

"Yes, right now. Have you ever ridden by moonlight?"

"I have. Often, actually. But why would you?"

"Maskelyne."

"What or who is that?"

"The Astronomer Royal in Greenwich."

"But your brother said he would write."

"Not good enough. Last time I discovered a comet the letter took two days by which time the weather had turned bad and Maskelyne could not observe it."

I look down in utter amazement at the short fifty-year-old German-born woman who has discovered eight comets, partnered with her brother to catalog the skies, and now wishes to ride thirty kilometers to London—then beyond London to Greenwich—in the middle of a cold night.

"I—well," I fling my arms out, "great! Certainly, I would love to save a day. Can I rent a horse and join you?"

At the Ostrich, we wake the innkeeper and negotiate a ten-shilling rental and a three-pound deposit for a horse. The innkeeper gives me a note to claim back my deposit at the stagecoach station in London, not that I know whether this currency will be valid my tomorrow.

I may not be wearing the most comfortable clothes for horse riding, but being back in the saddle feels like the most natural thing in the world. This is how I'm supposed to travel—not by stagecoach or time machine. Unencumbered by a carriage, our two horses set off at a canter along the straight road back to London. In the dark, I try to imagine myself to be in Iceland in my own time. I can almost fool myself that I'm riding Laozi along an Icelandic dirt road, traversing an endless sequence of green hills just barely illuminated by the Moon.

As we ride through the wee hours, I keep wondering what it all means. What *I* mean. I now know that I am a cluster of trillions of atoms. Each invisible little bit of me is dancing its little deterministic dance rigorously dictated by the laws of physics. Am I more than the sum of my parts?

Here I am, traversing just one of six—no, seven—planets that orbit just one of millions of stars, but even when we lift our heads high and observe the millions of stars around us, we are still like a flea who thinks that the dog is the entirety of reality. All the millions of stars I knew of until today are just one little galaxy—like one dog—amongst untold galaxies. *The universe is so much larger than it seems.* I somehow hope the discovery of other galaxies is the final humbling of mankind. I'm not sure I can take much more.

Whether in the Ecommunity or the Outside, *who am I?* I think how William Herschel will always be remembered for composing music, discovering a planet, and uncovering infrared light, while Caroline will be known for discovering eight comets. Does that give meaning to their lives? Even if it does, what chance do I have of ever making such discoveries?

Then I think about William's son John. *I may never discover a planet, but when I'm older I could have a couple of kids.* I take one hand off the reins and put it on my stomach, just where I have that strange little mark. I try to imagine myself inside my mother, her inside my grandmother stacked across the generations like Russian dolls. Do I bestow meaning upon my mother? Will my children give meaning to me?

Maybe if I have children—even if I go back to the Collective—I can secretly teach them science. No one other than me and my children would need to know; it would be our little family secret. Our little family meaning—that we understand our universe more than anyone around us. Would passing on the rich knowledge I'm gathering to the next generation add significance to my life?

"Do you have any children?" I shout across to Caroline. *Ouch,* I wonder whether her medical situation might prevent it.

"No, I am single," she replies in her Germanic accent.

Oh yeah, children have fathers—that could complicate my little plan.

A couple of hours later our horses trot into the center of London. Caroline and I chat over the slowing claps of hoofs. She explains how her mother refused her any education, even in the family tradition of musical instruments. When she followed William to England, he tutored her in music and let her assist his astronomy. After many years, William had occasion to travel to his home country of Germany, at the request of the King, and left her in charge of observations in his absence. Since then she's made her own observations as well as organizing the records of his work for publication.

"Do you ever resent your role as a woman," I ask her hesitantly, "like observing on the twenty-foot telescope while he gets the forty-footer?"

She laughs. I raise my eyebrows.

"Between us girls," she says, "the twenty-foot telescope works much better. The bigger one is not only clumsy to move, but the mirror is too big to hold a perfect shape, especially as air temperatures change."

"You mean it's blurry? So why does William use it?"

"Are you volunteering to tell His Majesty?"

"His Majesty? To tell him what?"

"That the two thousand pound sterling telescope he financed, which ended up costing four thousand pounds, is inferior to a smaller existing telescope."

"Ah. So the King finances your operation? That's why you live next to Windsor?"

"Yes. William earns a royal stipend. And as of recently, so do I. The first money I have ever earned."

I hear the pride and wonder if she is the first woman to earn a salary as a scientist.

"But the King already has a royal astronomer in Greenwich. Why does he finance you? The King has a love for pure science?"

"Well, yes, and a dislike for long social events."

"What?"

"Late in the evening, when he gets tired of hosting, he will summon William to entertain his guests with views of the planets."

I laugh. "Well, no wonder William wanted to name his planet 'The Georgian'. But seriously, how is that being received in Continental Europe?"

"It's not," she says, giving a sad smile. "Everyone else is calling it Uranus."

Ah, yes, Ouranus—god of the skies and father of Saturn.

"That fits. But loyalty prevents William from doing the same?"

Caroline half smiles. "Yes, loyalty… and contract. William did not tell me explicitly but I believe it was a condition of his position."

Finally in the wee hours, back in the hut, sitting on the bed, I think back over my packed day—and night—with mixed emotions. I've learned so much physics, delving deep within and far without. The universe is nothing like fjallagrasamjólk after all. It doesn't have a simple recipe, it has layers. And the inner layers are still a mystery: What's in the atoms? What are light waves? What is the nature of caloric?

I rewrite the label to summarize my growing but patchy knowledge as accumulated to date:

<u>ROW Label</u>

Date of manufacture: No scientific evidence!

Contents: Thousands of galaxies, each containing millions of stars. Our galaxy is the Milky Way and in it our star is the Sun which is orbited by seven planets, at least four of which have moons.

Ingredients: Matter is made of atoms. Light is a wave (of what?). Colors represent different wavelengths and extend beyond the visible red. Heat is a fluid called caloric. Details unknown.

Laws: Newton's laws of motion are the framework.

Forces: Newton's law for gravity (now complete) and Coulomb's law for the electric force between static charges. Both vary with the inverse-square of the distance.

Methods of calculation: For calculations we have calculus, the idea of potential, the wave equation.

MANY LAWS MISSING!

<u>WARNING</u>: Action at a distance!

<u>WARNING</u>: Universe is deterministic! (Laplace's demon)

My biggest frustration is that none of this physics seems to relate to the mushrooming industrial technology all around me. I have enquired deep within—about atoms—and far without—about other galaxies—and even gained a glimpse of the interior of our own Earth—at least its density— yet no calamity has resulted. It's time to get to the heart of the matter.

"Computer, find me a connection between physics and technology."

Feeling the Heat

Day 12. Oxford, England. 1847.

Another half a century nearer home.

The early summer morning sun drapes itself weakly across the V-shaped wedge of land separating the Thames and Cherwell rivers, as they flow toward their meeting point where they merge and, as one, flow eastward toward London. Oxford, England's other university town, spans the two rivers, a veritable maze of perfectly square college courtyards—which, it turns out, are known here as "quads."

Dwarfed by hordes of towering spires, I weave my way through cloistered university departments, cut across formal and informal gardens, peek inside grand gothic chapels, and pass through countless unidentified stone archways under the constant gaze of stone statues.

People's clothing and carriages, and shop windows, suggest growing wealth, which seems to have allowed the university to expand beyond anything I saw in the 1700s. I feel a little lost in the sea of fluttering academic gowns as students and college fellows stream between departments and colleges, sometimes stopping to soak up a few minutes of morning sunlight, laying down their gowns as blankets on one of the manicured lawns. I hope that by now the university has adopted Galileo's method of scientific thinking, but the college folk have not inherited his distaste for academic dress.

It's not hard to determine why the computer brought me here on this day: Several notice-boards are carrying flyers advertising James Prescott Joule's talk to the British Association meeting, here in Oxford. After touring the city for several hours, I arrive in time to secure a front-row seat for the early afternoon lecture—the first scientific lecture I've ever attended. Soon the auditorium is filling with people—with men, to be precise.

A suited gown-less gentleman of about fifty sits to my right. I notice his handsome face, framed by the now compulsory sideburns, with his graying hair parted down the center. I smile at myself. *All these gorgeous students are buzzing around and I'm sizing up this older man!*

"Hi, I'm Fizz."

"The name is Michael," he says, not looking away from the podium at the front of the lecture hall.

I turn to watch more men pour in.

"Michael, am I going to be the only woman?"

"Probably."

I shift around a little in the wooden chair. "And... is that okay?"

He shrugs, almost imperceptibly. "It is all right with me."

"Err, thank you. And with everyone else?"

He chuckles and turns to face me. "Surely I can only speak for myself. Personally, I learnt my foundations of science from Jane Marcet's textbooks. They say she would sometimes attend a lecture."

"That's a relief. So which university did you study at?"

"University?" he looks around at all the students. "I could not have dreamt of such a privilege."

Oops. I look toward the front of the lecture hall as a man who seems to be in his early thirties—presumably Joule—posts a formula and diagram in preparation for the upcoming talk.

"So who is this *Jowl?*" I ask Michael.

"It's pronounced *jewel*," he corrects me. "Would you believe that he is a beer brewer? From Salford, near Manchester. He studied under John Dalton before entering the family brewing business. Apparently, he made such a hobby of studying the brewery's steam engines, while waiting for the barley to ferment, that he earned himself an invitation to address the British Association."

"I hope he brought some samples."

Michael smiles.

"So what became of Dalton?" I ask.

"Dalton? Died three years ago at the age of seventy-seven—although not before he achieved his goal of being awarded a degree here in Oxford."

"Didn't he have the wrong religion for that?"

Michael shrugs. "It was an honorary degree; he was never admitted to the university. I remember the surprised reports that he actually turned up to the ceremony properly dressed in scarlet robes."

"Scarlet? I thought Quakers were strict about plain dress?"

"That was the surprise. But Dalton claimed that the robe appeared gray to him!"

I glance at the formula Joule has posted:

The ideal gas equation: **PV = nRT**

P=Pressure of gas. V=Volume of gas.
n=number of molecules. T=Temperature. R=gas constant.

"Michael, could you explain—"

Something brushes against my left shoulder before I can finish my request, and I turn to find a bicep big enough to bulge through a three-piece suit worn by a student with a clean-cut, well-proportioned face; he can't be much over twenty.

"I am William," he says in a strong accent, flashing me a cocky smile.

"I am... in the middle of a conversation," I reply as I turn back to Michael. "Can you explain that equation to me?"

"That one little equation, $PV = nRT$," Michael says, "captures everything there is to know about a gas—its pressure, volume, the number of molecules, and temperature, as well as how all those quantities are related to each other when you expand or heat the gas."

"Ah, whose law is that?"

"Would you believe that at least four authors participated in writing that miniature equation?"

"Four? Really?" I ask.

Michael glances at me and nods appreciatively. "Two centuries ago, Boyle demonstrated that a gas's pressure is inverse to volume. In other words, a compressed gas is more pressurized. He was responsible for the PV component of our little formula there," he points at the posted formula. "Then Jacques Charles found that, when you heat a gas, the volume is proportional to temperature—hot gases expand. He added the T. Next was Amedeo Avogadro, who discovered the surprising result that the physical properties of a gas do not depend on the type of the gas. A trillion hydrogen molecules and a trillion oxygen molecules at the same volume and temperature exert the very same pressure. Avogadro introduced the count of molecules, n, as a universal measure of the amount of gas. Finally, Émile Clapeyron and Henri Regnault combined those three laws into one compact *ideal gas equation.*"

So science has elevated itself into a pattern of international collaboration, with each physicist building on the work of others rather than always relying on the lone genius. *Scientists are becoming more like farmers than like deans.*

William's shoulder brushes against me again, beckoning me back to my left. "Excuse me...," I start, glancing at it brushing against me.

"Oh, sorry. Too much rowing I guess." William frowns at his own arm as if it were quite a nuisance to be in such good shape.

"Rowing?"

"Yes, yes, winning the Colquhoun Sculls will do that to your upper body." He shakes his head again for good measure.

Pah. I turn back to Michael and whisper, "Michael, what is the kolkuon skulls?"

Michael glances over my head to William, then leans back down to whisper, "The premier race in Cambridge for men's singles sculling—rowing with two oars."

"So what is your name?" William says rather loudly.

He reminds me of many of the guys in our Collective. *Rowing or farming, same thing. All muscle and confidence, no brains.* He's sat himself next to the only girl in the room and just had to blurt out that he's won some rowing competition. No doubt William expects my mind to flood with images of him in his sleeveless shirt, rowing solo with a powerful rhythmic pumping of his arms, speeding through the frigid river at the crack of dawn. *Forget about it.*

"Fizz," I answer coldly.

I turn to focus on Joule, who is now revealing an apparatus. I assume he has brought it with him to prove his point to what might be a skeptical audience. The apparatus stirs a copper bucket that looks to be full of water. I also see a thermometer to measure the water's temperature. Joule rigs the handle to two weights so that the falling weights will drive the stirring of the water. He posts a diagram to explain the arrangement:

James Joule's apparatus for using falling weights to stir and heat water

Joule turns to the audience. "By arranging falling weights to drive a propeller that stirs this water," he says, releasing the weight so that the handle starts to turn, "I am able to convert approximately an 800-foot-pound force of mechanical work—movement—from the falling weights into 1 British thermal unit, or BTU, of heat in the water."

All the men and myself sit quietly, allowing this claim to percolate through our minds. I look at the faces around me, some mesmerized, some skeptical. In the stunned silence, I can actually hear the water stirring.

Big deal, he stirred some water and it heated up. But I realize that, in the seventy years since Lavoisier's caloric theory—or three days for me—and in some ways since Aristotle's Fire, science has accepted that heat is an element that we cannot create or destroy. Now Joule is standing in front of the who's who of British science and making the radical claim that he is achieving the impossible right here on stage under their noses: creating heat. Specifically, he is claiming to have converted mechanical motion into heat. If he were standing at the podium and transforming lead into gold, I'm not sure that this audience would be any more surprised.

"You buying this?" I ask Michael.

"It is entirely unexpected, but myself, yes, I am struck with it. But—" Michael waves an arm as he continues his whispers, "no one cares what I think. Everyone will be waiting to see if Professor Thomson accepts it."

"Professor Thomson?"

Michael nods toward William.

I glance at William and then back to Michael. Raising my eyebrows and lowering my voice. "That poster boy for rowing is a *professor*? He's barely older than me."

"William is twenty-two. Professor for the second time. He was second wrangler at Cambridge and became a fellow there, then a professor of natural philosophy at the University of Glasgow."

"Second wrangler?"

Michael rolls his eyes. "Wrangler is some pompous term used at Cambridge for a first-class honors degree in mathematics. Senior wrangler is top of the year. So he was second top of his year in math."

I turn around and see William in a whole new light. Images flood my mind of William in his sleeveless shirt, rowing with a powerful rhythmic pumping of his arms, speeding solo through the frigid river at the crack of dawn, analyzing problems in mathematical physics in his head while he rows. *Hmm, muscles, confidence,* and *brains.*

As the talk progresses, despite myself, I seem to be glancing at William more frequently. Soon the lecture winds up and a lively discussion erupts. William speaks deliberately, carefully choosing his wording while asking questions, apparently trying to avoid any judgment about Joule's claims.

Meanwhile, at least one man, besides Michael, seems quite convinced. "I am inclined to be a Joulite," the man in his late twenties declares.

Michael seems very pleased with this. "That is George Stokes," he tells me in an undertone. "Originally from Ireland, member of the Royal Society, and Lucasian Professor of Mathematics at Cambridge—the same chair that Newton held. George was senior wrangler—first place in mathematics—in his year. He has done some important work on optics and fluid dynamics."

I wonder how often the country's top professor of mathematics, successor to Newton's chair, bestows such complements upon a manufacturer of alcoholic beverages.

As teas are passed around, it seems that increasingly many of the greatest minds in British physics *are* drinking up the ideas that this Joule is brewing.

"So is Joule the first to establish converting mechanical motion into heat?" I strike up a conversation with William, whom I now know to be Professor William Thomson.

"Not many people know that the same idea was also suggested by Sir Benjamin Thompson. Thompson with a 'p'. But nobody took it seriously until this moment."

"Who was he?"

"Thompson? A colorful man. He was born near Cambridge, Massachusetts, and heard some lectures in Harvard. Married well, but backed the wrong side in America's War of Independence, then abandoned his wife and became a spy for our side. Thompson then moved to Bavaria as aide-de-camp to the Prince-Elect Karl Theodor and was ennobled as Count Rumford. At some point during this vibrant career, in Munich, Count Rumford used horses to drive a drill into cannon barrels while they were submerged underwater, claiming that the friction caused the water to boil."

"If this Count Rumford proved it, what's the big news flash today?" I ask.

"Rumford himself had some very particular ways in which he wanted to apply his discovery. Rather than promoting this idea at scientific meetings, where it could be understood and tested, he used his scientific prowess to impress and marry a wealthy widow named Marie-Anne. Mind you, soon after the marriage she paid him to go away, which may be exactly what he was angling for."

"Marie-Anne—which Marie-Anne?"

"Widow of Antoine Lavoisier," William says.

"The very man who proposed the caloric theory that Rumford disproved!"

What intricate circles this scientific community spins.

"Indeed. In any event, it is Joule who has presented a more considered challenge to the caloric theory."

"So," I look right at him, "with this new understanding of mechanics and heat, will physics finally produce a theory for steam engines?"

William smiles at me. "It already has. I recently discovered a theory for steam engines in the little-known writings of the Frenchman Sadi Carnot. Excuse me, Fizz," he says as he stands. "It has been nice to meet you, but I must debrief Joule."

"May I join?" I try a smile.

William pauses, looking down at me. He glances at Joule, then back to me. "Well, Fizz, I think you had better read up on Carnot's cycle before you join a conversation like this."

"Oh, yes, of course," I say, nodding. "Nice to meet you William," I mumble.

I head off deflated, looking for a library, as I hear the men behind me resolve to continue their scientific banter at the Bull and Bear.

I stop a student and ask about a library. He directs me to the Bodley, which turns out to be the Bodleian Library on the nearby and aptly named Broad Street, just across from an iconic domed, round building—signed the Clarendon Building.

May I join? I cringe as I replay my lame request to William. Even so, he didn't have to turn me down. I wonder if he is one of those maddening guys who lose interest as soon as they start to get yours. Perhaps I hurt his pride with the brush-off earlier. *How was I supposed to know he's a professor?*

"Do you have any works by Sadi Carnot, please?"

The librarian consults a catalog. "Yes, we have one copy of Carnot's book, *Reflections on the Motive Power of Fire,* 1824, in the French science section. It seems we only have it by request of one of the professors—Carnot was a French military engineer, not an academic, and his work is little known. Apparently much of his work was lost too. He died of cholera at the age of thirty-six and many of his writings were incinerated for fear they were contagious."

In the French science section, I first come across the works of one Joseph Fourier. Student of Lagrange, Fourier seems to have continued the French work on waves. Of note, he found that a pure color or a pure musical note correspond to a very particular shape of wave—the sine wave—which is precisely the shadow of a spiral:

A sine wave—the shadow of a spiral—represents a pure color or pure note

I think about the concert I attended my yesterday. I already know how multiple sound waves are added together and propagate through the air from the instruments to my ear. Now I know how my ears are able to distinguish the individual musical notes—by breaking up the complex wave into sine waves, just like picking individual vegetable ingredients out of a kjötsúpa stew.

Fourier also discusses—presumably for the first time—that the Earth's atmosphere may trap what he calls "dark heat," just like a greenhouse. However, nowhere does he indicate the one piece of science I actually learned in the Ecommunity—that artificial changes to the atmosphere will amplify that greenhouse effect.

I'm annoyed that Fourier doesn't credit Herschel for the discovery of non-visible types of light. I read that in 1802, during a brief outbreak of peace between France and England, my friend William Herschel was able to visit Paris and meet Laplace, Jacques Charles, and even Napoleon, so it doesn't seem possible that Fourier was unaware of Herschel!

Apparently Fourier himself later abandoned science to become Napoleon's governor of Lower Egypt.

I move on to read about the *Carnot cycle,* feeling increasingly uneasy. Here it is, laid out in front of me in a small obscure book written by a French soldier—a direct connection between science and industrial technology—a theory of engines. And that's not all: a theory of heat pumps that I believe are known on the Outside as refrigerators and air conditioners.

The cycle itself is remarkably straightforward. Like a true theoretician, Carnot has managed to abstract away all the engineering details of an engine and analyze the simplest possible engine, a single piston:

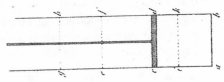

A single piston—Carnot's model of the engine and heat pump

I take some time to understand the cycle and memorize the key points. As I read it, I notice a bizarre anomaly. *Ah, an anomaly could also be the subject of a conversation with a certain brash young professor who keeps popping back into my thoughts.*

Exiting the library I walk along Broad Street as it becomes George Street, and continue into Hythe Bridge Street, which crosses an offshoot of the Thames. I've walked less than a kilometer when I hear a strange, long tooting sound accompanied by the cyclical clanging of metal. Suddenly all the carriage and foot traffic around me halts abruptly, and I stand still with everyone else. *What are we waiting for? Come on, if I don't catch William now, he'll be heading back to Scotland and I won't get another shot at him.*

With the cacophony of hoofs suddenly absent, the ominous tooting and clanging sounds are amplified. *What is that?*

The noises speak for themselves a few seconds later when a large vehicle glides along a pair of perfectly straight, parallel steel rails at a trotting pace, crossing the road right in front of me. Pedestrians, riders, and horses all track it silently with their eyes. The bright red bumper is followed by a shiny, black, tubular body topped with sparkling brass chimneys. I assume this is the engine as it is bellowing steam toward the blue sky. It is pulling several cars in matching black and red.

Watching, mesmerized, I realize I'm not alone. Everyone in the street is gazing at the train with admiration. Faces are peering back out of the train windows, clearly enjoying the attention of the crowds on the street and the views of the river and city. A child waves from one of the windows. The strange sound is almost hypnotic. *Chuga-chuga-chuga...*

"It's the Great Western Railway Star Class 2-2-2 locomotive," a boy near me exclaims.

They use artificial energy to transport themselves across unnatural distances without regard for the air pollution and global warming they are leaving in their wake.

I look again at the faces around me. I frown at the steam bellowing above the train. So here it is: the start of fossil-fuel-powered transportation, harbinger of the Great Deterioration. I glare at the brilliant black, red, and copper colors. I should hate it. I want to hate it.

But... I don't.

Chuga-chuga-chuga-chuga.

Each *chuga* is a Carnot cycle, the cycle I hope to now test and discuss with William, who will later himself be on a train heading north. As I watch the train disappear from view, I can't quite help imagining myself sitting next to William during the long journey, riding the Carnot cycle all the way to Scotland.

Heading to the Bull and Bear, which I have guessed is a beerhouse, trains—and William—are chugging through my mind. At one point along my way, I step on a small sheet of rubber, and without hesitation pick it up from the street. I later gather a small length of string. This junk is all the equipment I need to explore the cycle of engines and heat pumps—*and hopefully to explore William.*

As I walk in, male heads turn to eye me, some more inebriated than others.

The clientele all seem like university types drinking beer in their three-piece suits, many still in their gowns. There must be an unwritten law that the non-academic city inhabitants drink elsewhere. Or maybe a written law. I can distinguish the groups of professors sitting upright, sipping their first pints as they engage in rapid intellectual banter, from other groups that are slouching back, on their third or fourth round, long since moved on to college gossip. The clique of young physicists—James, George, William, and the much older Michael—seem to be verging toward the latter state.

I pull up a chair, holding the sheet of rubber and string behind my back.

"Oh hello, um, Fizz," William says in moderately slurred surprise. If he's pleased to see me, he doesn't show it.

The other young men bow their heads and give William a knowing smile. Michael touches his top hat.

"Hi, William. Well, I read all about the Carnot cycle, as you said. But I think I may have found an irregularity. I was hoping to investigate it with you?"

The other men laugh and wave William away.

"Yes, Fizz," he says as we step away from the table, "what did you want to discuss?"

"Not discuss. Investigate. Bring your glass."

The evening air in Oxford has turned cold as we step outdoors, away from the hot ambience of the beerhouse's coal fire. William and I are now standing just outside on the sidewalk, and I'm holding an empty pint glass. I stretch the small sheet of rubber over the top of the glass and tie the piece of string around the rim creating an airtight seal.

"That is some impressive scientific apparatus you have there," William says, in his heavy accent.

"Okay, let's take this cold air inside and watch the action," I say. We take the covered beer glass, full of cold outside air, into the beerhouse, and walk over to the fireplace. I set the glass down on the stone floor close to the smoldering coal fireplace. We wait as others intermittently stare at us.

I'm watching and waiting for the anticipated effect. Well, to be accurate, I'm waiting for two effects. The burning coal should heat and expand the air trapped in the pint glass, and hanging around the toasty fireplace with William should surely melt a bit of the tough-guy charade.

"So you like Glasgow?" I ask.

William breaks into a warm smile. *Good choice of question, Fizz.* "Aye, I do. I have a beautiful lab right on the river Kelvin. A bit cold though. So where are you from?"

"Iceland."

"Iceland! Then I feel like a right idiot for calling Glasgow cold."

We make small talk for another minute. Then Jacques Charles' law kicks in and the warming air trapped in the glass starts to expand, causing the membrane to bulge upward.

"It is not much, is it?" William says looking pitifully at the small bulge in the piece of rubber.

"No, but enough to prove the principle. If I understand correctly, this is a very gentle version of the piston action, right? Heat causes expansion. That expansion," I point at the piece of rubber being slowly stretched, "could push a piston that drives a train wheel. We are watching a model of a single train 'chug' in slow motion. Right?"

"Right," William nods once.

"Let's go back out."

Outside, the long English June day is heading toward its dark end. The horse and foot traffic has dwindled to a trickle. A city worker with a long pole is walking around igniting the gas street lamps. In the dark, William's black suit has all but disappeared, and his face and collar glow gently in the firelight as if suspended in midair.

We wait as the air in the glass cools and contracts and the bulging membrane gradually sinks back down.

"So now the air in the glass contains heat from the fireplace," I say softly, "and that heat is seeping through the glass and membrane into the outdoor air, correct? So effectively we are heating the outdoors. And the air and membrane are settling back to their original position. That's why it's a cycle. I guess we could repeat this as often as we like… we could keep absorbing heat by the fireplace to drive an expansion that can drive mechanical motion like a piston, and each time we could dump the heat outside, like a train expels the heat from the chimney. Then we could start all over again. So when heat flows from hot to cold you can derive mechanical energy—movement."

"Yes, yes," William says, "it is like a water mill can derive mechanical work when water flows from a high point to a lower point. The beer glass is a little heat-mill—extracting mechanical work as heat flows from high temperature to low temperature. That is Carnot's model for the engine. So, Fizz, what is the anomaly you wanted to investigate?"

"Not yet," I say, "we need to try the reverse cycle first. Come inside."

The glass is back as it started—air at cool outside temperature, membrane relaxed—as we step inside to try the reverse cycle.

Standing in a quiet corner of the pub, I grip the glass firmly around the tied piece of rubber and, bunching the fingers of my other hand, I push the membrane forcefully into the cup, compressing the cool air. The compression causes the air to heat up and I soon feel through the rubber membrane that the air inside has become quite hot, even hotter than the warm room.

I look up and am pleased to notice that William has been giving me a good look-over while I was focused on compressing the air in the glass.

I look him in the eye. "I can feel the heat," I report. William grins.

We stand there, my hand inside the beer glass keeping the air compressed, waiting for the little bit of heat I generated to flow into the already warm surrounding air and top up the heat in the room. The air in the glass, which I heated by compression to above room temperature, is slowly cooling down to the room's temperature, as the extra heat escapes.

This time we wait in silence. The buzz of surrounding chatter and clinking of glasses blur into the distant background as I focus on William and find him looking intensely right back at me. As our gazes lock, I feel a slight dizziness. At this very moment, my control of my feelings is slipping away. I'm barely even aware of the rubber taut around my hand. Right now, there is William and there is me and there are four eyes observing each other. In a couple of minutes the hot air will have cooled to room temperature and we will have to go outside to finish the cycle. Outside, where there is relative privacy, where I will have both hands free. *Just a minute or two, now.*

"Okay, William, let's take this to the next step," I finally whisper as I feel that the compressed air has cooled to room temperature.

As we exit onto the road, I release the membrane. The air, which has already cooled down to room temperature, now cools further as it expands. After a couple of seconds, I can feel that—due to the sudden expansion—it is now even cooler than the outside air. So it will slowly absorb a bit of heat from the outside making the already cold evening just a tiny bit colder.

Without taking my eyes off William, I crouch to put the cool beer glass on the sidewalk. The glass doesn't need me to hold it while it warms back up to complete the cycle. The hem of my dress crumples onto the grimy road as I bend, but I don't care, I can always print another. Let the heat flow...

As I stand back up, my eyes are just above William's powerful shoulders, his face inches away from mine, we gaze in silence for a few seconds more.

Too many seconds actually—*surely I don't have to take the lead again.*

Finally William puts a hand tenderly on my hip and leans forward.

Here it comes—my first kiss—and about time!

But attuned to his every movement, I notice his eyes dart to the side, glancing over my shoulder. *Focus, William!*

And then the trance is shattered by an exploding laugh right behind me. I recognize the voice of George Stokes, and turn to see him emerging a little unsteadily from the drinking establishment.

"So how's the carnal cycle going?" he booms.

"It *was* going fine, thank you very much, George," William says.

"It turns out there's an *anomaly* in the cycle," I stare right at George Stokes.

George is still laughing, his laugh carrying our "moment" far away. *Selfish immature idiot.*

"Seriously, William," George says, "it is time to go."

"Well, Fizz," William frowns and bends to pick up the beer glass. It is back as is started, at the same temperature of the outside air and back to the initial volume. "As you hear, I have to go. Apologies." He moves closer to George, then turns back to me. "Oh, what was the question that you had? We performed one cycle where we derived mechanical work from the flow of heat from high temperature to low temperature—the engine. In the second cycle we *exerted* mechanical effort—you pushed the membrane—and using that effort you were able to take some heat from the low temperature outside to the hotter temperature inside—depositing a little heat inside, extracting a little heat from the outside. It is similar to water. You can derive mechanical work when water flows from high to low and you can exert mechanical work to pump water from low to high. The Carnot cycles are the heat mill and the heat pump."

I sigh deeply. "Here's the problem. It's not quite like water. The two processes are not truly opposite. The energy extracted when heat flows from hot to cold isn't sufficient to pump the same heat back from cold to hot. When you finish both cycles you are left with more heat, and you have exerted more mechanical work than you ever derived."

William looks impressed. "You are absolutely right. It *is* strange and quite different from water. I have been studying that. But I am afraid it is not an issue for a quick conversation. Well, Fizz, I do hope we meet again."

He pecks me on the cheek and walks off with the other men. I find myself standing alone, glaring at his back.

As I return to my hut along the dimly lit streets, I try to forget William by reflecting on the implications of the Carnot cycle. We now have a model for steam engines and formulae for how efficient they may be.

The other cycle—the heat pump cycle—seems to have technological potential too. People could pump heat out of their homes in the summer to cool the building, all it takes is a gas that can be compressed outside and expanded inside. The gas could be pumped in and out through a pipe rather than being carried around in a beer glass. We could use the same cycle as an alternative way to heat homes in the winter, pumping heat from the cold outside to the warmer inside, as I did briefly in the beerhouse, rather than creating new heat by burning coal.

When did I start getting excited about the technological potential! The Dean's warnings regurgitate through my consciousness:

On the Outside they do not content themselves with nature's weather, which they have anyway tampered with... They require unnatural air conditioners, adapting the weather to themselves instead of themselves to the weather. They are not content with fresh food but artificially refrigerate and freeze their foodstuffs...

Technology—the potential versus the dangers. Surely I should soon have enough information to start making an informed decision about whether physics and technology should be embraced or shunned.

Inevitably, my thoughts do return to William. I've rarely seen such physical or such mental prowess, let alone both in one guy. *The charm, the smile, the physique.* Yes, I remind myself, I'm on a mission and must put this unique opportunity of time travel to good use. I sigh. It can't go anywhere. William lives not only in a different country than me, but—worse—in a different century!

Nothing to lose, I retort to myself, *no complications, no worries about commitment. He lives in a different country, better still, in a different century.*

I've been working hard and making progress. I still have up to a week available. Perhaps I've earned one day of fun! I walk into the hut, determination in my voice.

"Computer, find me a romantic rendezvous with William Thomson. And, computer, please don't tell my Dad about this!"

River Kelvin, here I come.

The Waterfall

Day 13. Chamonix, France. 1847.

I rub my eyes. *What was my agenda today? Ah, yes of course—William!* And why am I chasing William Thomson in a time machine? *Well, because he's incredibly hot.* I smile. Yes, ten out of ten, easy. Possibly one in a million.

Still lying in bed, my smile fades. *Perhaps I'm also here because I have lost my way.* I successfully hunted down a connection between science and technology, I witnessed the industrial revolution and coal-powered trains, yet still I feel no closer to a comfortable decision. I cannot possibly see myself fitting back into the Ecommunity, caging my curiosity, after it has become accustomed to running wild. Yet I also can't see myself finding happiness away from Mom, with a lifetime feeling the kind of regret that may be plaguing Dad. *Also, I haven't really seen the ultimate problems of the Outside yet.*

The thoughts swirl in my head as I rub my temples, trying to make them go away. I'm only eighteen for goodness sake; I deserve a shot at a happy life.

At the very least I deserve this day off. *But what is it about you, Fizz, that drives you to chase a fleeting relationship with William Thomson, while you always gave the cold shoulder to Zopp, and any other guy who hit on you, back home?*

I look at the screen. *Still 1847—good—but Chamonix?* Why aren't I in some romantic spot in Scotland?

Soon I swing open the door to the ROW, and any disappointment is blown away. The quaint town in front of me is nestled in a deep green valley surrounded by a thrilling view of snow-peaked mountains. It's a bright, cool summer day, so I must have travelled just a few weeks forward. Proud, rugged mountaintops glance down at me apathetically as I fill my lungs and marvel back at them. Walking into the town, a map informs me that the grandest of the pinnacles looming above is Mont Blanc, although now in the summertime only the cap is *blanc*.

I enquire for William Thomson at every inn in town and eventually find him at the Vallée. Now to play the waiting game. I pace up and down the road outside the Vallée, trying to look matter-of-fact even on the three hundredth pass.

More than an hour later, William emerges, striding with characteristic energy. I stroll away, trying to ignore the tingling in my arms, which seem to want to fling themselves around him. I then double back to pass him casually.

"Could that be William?" I paint shock, horror, all over my face.

William looks even more desirable in what, in this Victorian era, must count for casual holiday dress: a beige three-piece suit and a wide-brimmed hat.

"Hey, mukker! What a surprise." He's smiling. Hopefully my premeditated serendipity will work its magic.

"So what are you doing here? On your own?" I ask.

"On my own. A hiking holiday. Thought I would get away from everyone here! What about you, Fizz—here with your... parents? Um, husband?"

"No, just me."

He looks a little shocked, but not displeased. "Oh. Well, you know I was just on my way to—" he pauses "—to visit a waterfall, the Cascade de Sallanches. Care to join me?"

"I could be persuaded." I give a rueful smile, admiring his ability to instantly dream up a romantic destination; his fast demeanor obviously extends beyond the realms of sports and science.

"Walk this way," he says, touching the brim of his hat.

William hires a carriage and we head off on a bumpy thirty-kilometer drive, snaking through the alpine valleys to Sallanches. The scenery we pass is stunning; I could almost be in Iceland. The scenery inside the coach is captivating too.

As we chat, I strain to understand some of William's words. "You know, William, it just occurred to me that you pronounce some words just like George Stokes—'oi' for 'I', 'aaa' for 'o'."

"Certainly. We are both 'oyrish' he says."

"I thought you're from Glasgow?"

"Born in 'Doblin.' Made my life in Glasgow, though."

I spot an opportunity to deepen the conversation. "Made your life. And what is your life about? Sports? Science? What is your real passion?"

"Actually, I have a new ambition brewing. Applying science—creating new technology."

My heart skips a beat. So here it is. *Prying leads to tinkering...*

"You *have* to tell me about that. What's your idea?"

"I can't actually say."

"Can't or won't?"

"Won't."

"You know what, William? I actually don't care what your idea is. But why? Why not stick to pure science? Why do you want to develop new technologies—isn't that like tinkering with the human experience?"

"My idea—the idea I am part of—could change the world. For the better. Improve people's lives."

"Especially... your own?"

"Look, if I am part of creating something that many people benefit from, sure I'd like to profit from it too."

"But what if it's not a benefit to mankind? What if in the long term it's harmful?"

"Harmful. Why should it be?"

"Well, I don't actually know what your idea is, but I have a feeling that some inventions may have unintended consequences. Unforeseen results. In the long term. What do you think?"

"Rest assured, this invention is pure goodness."

Finally I have found a definite, premeditated connection, except that I don't know what it actually is. William offers no more information and seems to sink into his own thoughts. He rests his elbow on his vibrating knee and supports his face, covering his mouth. Once again, it really bothers me to see his mouth covered.

I touch his arm gently. "Don't," I say.

"Don't what?"

"Don't cover your mouth."

"Why not?" He raises an eyebrow.

"I—no special reason. I just don't like it."

William takes his hand off his mouth revealing a slight frown.

Why does it bother me to see his mouth covered? But soon my mind is back on the silent, unspoiled surroundings streaming past us. In England, in the mid-1800s, I witnessed the so-called Great Deterioration steaming away. Now people like William talk explicitly about the connection between science and technology. Yet out here in the Alps, nothing has changed at all. Then again, even in England, has human life changed fundamentally? Were the Dean's warnings about the woeful Great Deterioration something of a great exaggeration?

What if the Dean could see me now? I just about choke at the thought: a purebred Ecommunity girl, taking a romantic drive with a key protagonist of the Deterioration. But—*I actually feel happy.* According to my education, I should be reviling William, but his intelligence and inquisitiveness are contagious, and his ambition seems well intended. *What does he make of me?*

We arrive at Sallanches and William jumps out and runs around the coach to open my door, extending a gentlemanly arm. The touch of his hand stirs me. I've had little human contact during my time travels, and here I am—however casually—touching a gorgeous guy with all the intrigue of a different era and an opposing culture. He must feel something too, because after I step down to the ground, he seems in no great hurry to let go.

I flash a shy smile and, as neither of us takes the initiative to pull away, we find ourselves walking through the village hand-in-hand. As we pass the last house, the distant noise of splashing water gently beckons us. A couple of minutes out of the village we arrive at the foot of a majestic waterfall, where water, descending from the snowy peaks above, drops down one sheer black rock face, bounces off a small ledge, then plunges again to finally splatter right in front of us. The sight is inspiring, the random noise soothing. *William could not have thought of a better place to take me even if he had had time to plan it.*

As I watch the graceful splashes, I become aware of William gazing sideways at me. When I look at him, he has already turned back to the waterfall. This continues for a minute, until—as if by chance—our gazes meet… and… as they did yesterday, they stick. I am slipping back into the trance of last night, and this time there is no one around to interrupt. For William, it's been some weeks of course, but hopefully his memory of our interrupted moment is almost as vivid as mine. Sure enough, he leans toward me ever so slowly and now my arms finally get to wrap themselves around his neck.

"Jewel," William whispers in my ear.

Well, this is testing my language skills in a whole new way. *Quick, Fizz, think of a Victorian term of endearment intimate enough to answer "jewel" but not too soppy for a first kiss. Two seconds: Go!*

"Honeybunch?" I mutter under pressure, regretting it even before I finish the word.

"No, James Joule," he says slightly louder.

"Not now, William. Kiss now. Physics later."

"Now. Right there." He pulls away and points. Sure enough, I'm amazed to see Joule's bushy beard heading our way. The scientist is hand-in-hand with a woman. William looks as surprised as I do; Joule mirrors our surprise. William and I stand still as the other couple approaches.

"You two at it again?" Joule teases.

"Of all the places. What on earth are you doing here?" William says.

"Same as you I should think. Allow me to present my new wife, Amelia."

Amelia curtsies.

"Congratulations," William says to Amelia. He smirks at Joule. "So James, you told her this was a honeymoon outing, hah? I suppose we think alike. Great, let us do it together then," he says cryptically. "So, James, are you going on top or shall I?"

Watching Amelia turn deep scandalized red, I'm confused too. I glance from William to Joule and back, then at the waterfall. Suddenly, understanding dawns.

I cross my arms. "Okay, where are they?"

They both look sheepish.

"Go on. Whip them out."

Finally, they both reach into their jackets and a second later James and William are both holding thermometers.

As the four of us stand for a few awkward seconds, only the water dares make a sound. Here we are: James Joule, who discovered that stirring water converts mechanical work into heat; Professor William Thomson, world expert on heat, intrigued but not yet convinced by Joule's novel claim. And two naïve young women enticed to this spot by thoughts of romance, whereas these men's first love will always be physics.

I sigh and shake my head. Mother Nature is vigorously stirring water right here in front of us, as if for the two scientists' convenience. If Joule is right, the stirring must be creating a temperature difference between the water at the top and the bottom of the fall.

Finally, we all laugh and James and William break off into deep scientific dialogue. Amelia catches my eye and we exchange a look of sympathy in a way that two strange men never could. But for me, not all is lost. After all, the physics interests me as much as the physicist.

I listen in as James tells William about further experiments he has carried out, then William suggests theoretical explanations and guides James toward yet more experiments he should perform. I can feel the intellectual sparks flying as a great experimentalist spars with a great theoretician, pushing each other to—respectively—probe and analyze nature, peel back the layers, then probe and analyze ever more deeply.

Meanwhile, the waterfall keeps flowing, oblivious to the fact that these two visitors are quite unlike any of the thousands of other tourists who have stood before it. They are here not to gawk at it, not to shower in it, not to kiss under it, but to measure it and to unravel its long-kept physical secrets.

"You can not only convert mechanical work into heat," Joule says, "but electricity too may be converted into heat."

"Hmm. So maybe Thomas Young was right when he spoke about *energy*," William says. "Think about it. A single concept of energy that spans mechanics, thermodynamics, and electricity."

"Yes, one concept of energy," James says. "In fact, it is a historical aberration that we measure mechanical energy in *pounds-feet-force* versus heat in *British thermal units* or *calories*. These are just different manifestations of the same resource of energy—a concept that also extends into electricity and chemistry. In fact, we need a new unit for measuring energy, a unit that spans all disciplines."

"The *Joule?*" William teases. "Do you realize that now that you have discredited the caloric theory, and brought back kinetic theory, it is actually quite clear why the energy of a moving body—*kinetic energy*—and heat are related. Heat is movement—heat is just the movement of invisible atoms inside matter." William pauses, seeming to consider his argument further. "And the total energy remains the same—*conservation of energy*. That finally nails the coffin on the dreams of perpetual motion—you cannot generate energy out of nothing."

The excitement is palpable. Seemingly unrelated disciplines of mechanics, thermodynamics, and electricity have all been sharing a common currency without even realizing it, the commonality veiled by the use of different names and units. Yet now William and James are exposing the hidden connection, like travelers who find that their different units of money and different forms of coins are all made of the same gold. *Energy*—a natural resource that unifies seemingly unrelated phenomena.

William is thinking intensely now. He waves his hands around as if his brain needs winding up. "And the kinetic theory of heat gives us insight into the concept of *temperature*. If heat is the energy of particles moving internally within the material, then there must be a lowest possible temperature—namely, the temperature at which all movement stops. We should call that *absolute zero!*"

William is swaying slightly with excitement. "So it seems to be a historical aberration that Anders Celsius took the melting point of ice as the zero of his temperature scale, or that Daniel Gabriel Fahrenheit took the freezing point of brine as his zero. Temperature should be measured counting up from the absolute zero—where all particles stop still. We need a new unit for measuring temperature counting up from the absolute zero!"

"The Thomson?" Joule teases.

"I have a question," I say. Amelia scowls at me but I continue. "This takes me back to my question yesterday in Oxford."

"Yesterday?" William looks at me, confused.

"Err, whatever, it feels like yesterday," I brush him off. "If heat is just a form of energy, why does it always flow in one direction, from hot to cold? In the Carnot cycle, why does it take extra mechanical energy to force the heat back from cold to hot?"

"That," says William, "is a deep question. Physical processes are normally reversible. Why does heat flow from hot to cold and not from cold to hot? Why is the Carnot cycle not symmetrical?" He glances at James then back to me. "Well, we do not really know why, but we know that it is a fundamental law with many interesting consequences. In fact I am beginning to think that we can sum up the laws of thermodynamics as follows." He lifts his hand to count off the laws.

"*First law of thermodynamics:* Energy is always conserved."

"*Second law of thermodynamics:* Heat cannot flow spontaneously from a lower temperature to a higher temperature."

Wow—William's summarized a highly complex subject in two concise laws! The first law replaces the outdated idea that caloric is always conserved. Heat is not always conserved, but energy is. We can convert heat into motion or motion into heat or electricity into heat, but these are all just different forms of energy. We cannot create or destroy energy. It's like money—it moves around and gets converted from one currency to another, but the total amount of gold doesn't change.

I start replaying everyday scenarios through my mind to see how energy is conserved. "What happens when a rock drops?" I ask. "Suddenly it has kinetic energy, or movement. Where did that kinetic energy come from?"

"That comes back to Laplace's idea of *potential*," William says. "When the rock is up at a higher gravitational potential—higher altitude—that potential is a form of energy too. *Potential energy.*"

Okay, I like that. Potential energy, kinetic energy, heat energy, electric energy—all manifestations of the concept of energy.

"And when the rock hits the ground and stops, where does the kinetic energy disappear too?" I ask.

"Vibrations through the floor." Joule says.

"Sound waves in the air," William adds.

Yes, it works. Every process converts one form of energy into another, but never creates or destroys energy. There is something equitable about that. Energy is like a universal currency for the cosmos; it may be traded from one form to another, but the total never varies, as if the cosmos were granted a fixed, immutable allocation of energy.

Now, what of the second law formalizing the strange asymmetry I noticed yesterday. Heat can flow from a high temperature to low temperature, but not the reverse. Formalizing this anomaly as a law is helpful, but not really satisfying. *How come heat always flows from hot to cold?* Something fishy is going on, and I want a deeper explanation for this strange asymmetry. I add it to my mental list of open questions—the heat artifact back in the hut is mostly understood, but not quite.

William and I continue to banter while we journey back to Chamonix. Our shoulders rub against each other as the carriage shudders, generating—as we now know—a smidgen of heat. He tells me about his Christian faith, his work on the shape of the Earth, his embracing of continental mathematics at a time when most British mathematicians felt an exclusive loyalty to Newton, his development of theories for heat flow, and his increasing dabbling in the theory of electricity. He addresses all these topics with characteristic enthusiasm.

Chamonix appears on the distant horizon. The horses are tiring and slowing to a gentle trot. I decide to make one last request of my would-be suitor.

"So, William, since I probably won't see you again, why don't you tell me about the technological ambition you're harboring."

My question hangs in the air as William hesitates. Then he leans forward, gently grabs the scruff of my neck, and before I know it, he finally kisses me. *About time!* It's not so much, as I always expected, that I am simply kissing; rather, it feels more like William and I have become part of a kiss. Romance with an amazing guy from 250 years before my own time. *Zero strings attached.*

Perhaps this is his way of avoiding my question. *I don't care—it feels amazing.*

We are almost upon Chamonix, and I lean my head on William's masculine shoulder and watch the view streaming past. I sigh contentedly. Right now, I need nothing else in my life. I could quite happily forget about time traveling and leave myself right here in 1847 to slowly fall in love with William. My heart skips a couple of beats. *That may not be a bad option at all—here in 1847 I can study science openly and enjoy just a measured amount of "evil" conveniences such as the railways.*

My thought is lost as we pull in to Chamonix.

On the way back to the hut, I reflect on my time with William and try to calm my still erratic heartbeat. Eventually I focus on my mission once again. In Fizz's Place, I add William Thomson's two laws of thermodynamics to the ROW Label: conservation of energy, and the asymmetry of heat flow. I note the mystery of how that asymmetry comes about.

Lying on my bed, I stare up at another mystery: the hanging pebble. I reach up to twist it a couple of times. Something catches my attention. Each time the pebble spins, it comes to rest in exactly the same orientation. Twisting the thread gently, the pebble still holds itself in an identical direction, like some sort of miniature homing pigeon.

The meaning of this last artifact has been literally staring me in the face every night! It is not any old pebble, it's magnetic, like the magnet Mom uses to hold a cluster of sewing needles. I read once that the Greeks discovered how some stones naturally rotate to the north. Lodestones, I think they were called. The only artifact I have not even touched represents magnetism. Of course! *So what is magnetism?* I don't mind too much, so long as it doesn't join gravity and electric forces as a third case of mysterious instant action at a distance.

I tuck myself under the sheets. *Magnetism is all very interesting, but how do I get my adventure on track toward a decision?* I got closer to William Thomson than I have to any of the other physicist—or to any other guy for that matter—but did I really understand him? Do I really know whether the primary drive of his ambition is greed or selflessness? *And why didn't I really understand him?* Are my own growing scientific interests coming at the expense of fully appreciating people?

If this journey is going to lead me to the truth, I must resolve to better understand the scientists themselves, to test their motivations, not only their science.

As drowsiness overcomes me, I whisper my instructions. "Computer, I want to understand magnetism."

As I sink deeper into my well-travelled bed and let go of another day of consciousness, only one thing comes to mind, and it's the last thing I expected: *Zopp*.

Field Day

Day 14. Green Park, London, England. 1864.

Two weeks down, one to go!

I meander through Green Park, a medium-sized public garden with an expansive lawn and a crisscross of tree-lined paths sloping gently down, ending right opposite a building which I recognize as Buckingham House. Guards stand outside in ridiculously tall, flat, furry, black hats. One of them agrees to chat to me in a strange mutter, through clenched teeth, without once rattling the gold-colored chain which passes under his lip. He informs me that the "Queen's Guard" have been wearing these "bearskins"—from Canadian black bears—since the Battle of Waterloo fifty years ago. I also learn that Buckingham House had been promoted to Buckingham Palace ("Where have you been, Miss?") and is the residence of Queen Victoria of the United Kingdom of Great Britain and Ireland. Apparently Her Majesty is still distraught after being widowed three years ago. The "Royal Standard" flag is flying which, he says, informs me that the Queen is at home.

Standing outside the palace in a gown with the skirt held out by hoops to resemble a tent, I notice that amongst the other vast skirts, a few women have adopted more artistic dress, with streamlined designs in beautiful materials. So I return to the hut, between the bushes in the park, scrunch up the dress, snap the hoops, and stuff them into the recycling shoot. "Computer, you can keep printing dresses till you come up with something beautiful, appropriate *and* comfortable."

It is surprisingly easy to get directions to the nearest science lab. It seems that The Royal Institution, around the corner from the top end of the park at 21 Albemarle Street, has become well known in London society for the public science lectures it hosts. The institution itself is housed in a palatial rectangular stone building, three stories high and fourteen columns long, with the words "The Royal Institution of Great Britain" engraved proudly across the top. Sure enough, there is a lecture on today. I pay the small entrance fee and take my place in the auditorium.

Waiting for the lecture to start, I take a seat high up one side of the auditorium and survey the audience below and around me. I'm pleased to notice several woman and even a few children. Some of the men look like working men with simpler clothes and rough skin. It feels like science, for the first time, has become a matter of intrigue and perhaps national pride, well beyond the academic elite. I frown. *That might be a bad sign as well.* Science is finally spilling over into technologies that benefit the population at large, which is in turn attracting their attention.

The man who walks onto the stage below me is a much older version of none other than Michael, whom I met in Oxford! Michael takes the stage and, with what might be described as flare, albeit the special British variety which comes tightly wrapped in sober understatement, he regales the audience with demonstrations of the effect of a magnet on iron filings, electric sparks, and chemical reactions.

Michael's natural philosophy lecture at the Royal Institution

After the talk finishes and the applause dies down, Michael makes a rapid exit. I pursue him through the building.

I have not seen a lab in what would be eighty years, in normal time. Now I'm passing libraries of chemical beakers, kilometers of bookshelves, not to mention thousands of different implements with which to give Mother Nature a poke and record how she responds. I recall Galileo's lab. Galileo's innovation has grown to dimensions he could not possibly have imagined.

By the time I reach the director's office, I'm overwhelmed, my jaw hanging loose. I feel like I'm setting off to cross the Atlantic in a row boat. Could one person ever master such a vast body of scientific literature? Let alone grasp the key principles in one week? And this is just the science as of 1865. In the Outside during my own time, there will be another two and a half centuries of scientific progress to study. *What chance do I have starting from zero at age eighteen?*

"Michael?" I find the old man in his room. Minutes after the lecture he is already behind some brick stand performing some experiment:

Michael's lab

Michael is still handsome at seventy, with a full head of white hair, parted, as before, down the middle and extended by the sideburns I now know as mutton chops. *When will all this facial hair finally go out of fashion?* He may have picked up some wrinkles along the way, but this is the very same face I saw my two days ago in Oxford, looking dapper in the black bow tie and tails he wore for the lecture. If he recognizes me, I'm going to have to think on my feet. *Do men remember a girl they sat next to seventeen years earlier?*

Michael is examining me quizzically. "Sorry, do I know you? I apologize, my memory is not what it used to be."

I suppress a relieved smile. "No, no you don't, I—"

"Oh! Fizz, is it not? Yes, the only woman at that seminal lecture by Joule. The only woman I ever saw distracting William Thomson from physics... but... no, of course it's not possible; how can it be?" He frowns and waves a hand at my youthful face. Then he keeps staring, waiting for an explanation.

I too am waiting for an explanation to suggest itself. "Yes, yes... everyone says it's uncanny. It's a bit of a bore, actually. My mother has fond memories of you kindly guiding her through Joule's talk."

He looks a little confused, but... what can he do?

"Ah. So what is your name?"

"Fizz. Um, I mean I'm named after my own mother."

"Really?"

"Yes?"

"You took her name in her own lifetime?"

"No, err, sadly she died in childbirth."

The confused face deepens. "I am sorry. But did you not just say she has fond memories?"

"No, no, *had* fond memories. Um, my father mentioned it."

Unexpectedly, the confused face breaks into a provocative grin. *Why is he smiling?*

Michael keeps looking at me. "So your father... well, no wonder you have an interest in physics!"

"My father, what? Oh, no-no-no-no-no. William Thomson is not my father. I, um, don't think my Mom and he ever got that far." My goodness. *A little white lie could start the biggest scandal in the history of British science!* I had better change the conversation quickly.

"So, Michael, have you been here at the Royal Institution long?"

Michael walks out from behind the counter and we both sit at his desk. "Long? Not so long. Would you say half a century is long? That is right, I was hired in 1813, aged twenty-two. This building has been my home—literally—ever since. Can you imagine? When I started here, Doctor Thomas Young was still carrying out research down the road in Welbeck Street. William Herschel was still making telescopes in Slough."

I smile. *So he only started at twenty-two.*

"But how did you pull off a job like this? You don't have a university education do you? " *Oops—he told that to my "mother."* I quickly continue, "Were your parents well connected?"

Michael smirks. "Yes, young Fizz. You found me out. I got my big break by way of nepotism. My father was one of the best-connected poor blacksmiths in any of the little villages south of London. I have struggled my whole life to step out of the old man's long intellectual shadow."

I cringe. "Apologies. How did you get a scientific education then?"

"My first job here was washing test tubes."

"Even so? Didn't it require some background?"

"I was lucky. I had been taught to read and write. And my career up to that point gave me ample opportunity to read science."

"Oh. So you already had a career in science."

"Not exactly. I was apprentice to a bookbinder. On Blandford Street, not far from here. Seven years. I will tell you, when I close my eyes," Michael closes his eyes and sniffs, "I can still smell the glue. Sometimes my boss would allow me to read the books I was binding. Occasionally, when I could scrape together a shilling, I attended a public lecture in science—often here in this very building."

With every word, Michael sounds like he is reliving the events of fifty years earlier, and I watch and listen intently. "I'm inspired," I say. "And I suppose I should thank you for sharing your knowledge with people like me and other members of the public who didn't have the privilege to be, well, assistant bookbinders!" I smile at him. "Once you were here, did you rise rapidly to director?"

"That is right, young Fizz. I never looked back. One minute I was scrubbing beakers, and just twenty years later I found my name on that plaque."

He points at a plaque that reads *Michael Faraday Esq., Director (retired), Royal Institution.*

"You have to understand, science is a pursuit for gentlemen. I wore the wrong clothes, spoke an inappropriate dialect, and held a teacup in the most unbecoming manner. Not to mention that I knew no mathematics. Naught. Still do not."

I glance around the room at the floor-to-ceiling library of beakers and instruments. Massive Leyden jars rest on the floor. But I find none of the trimmings I would expect in the office of the director, none of the elaborate furniture and decorative art I saw in the offices in Paris. The desk is unpolished, no certificates hang on the walls, no trophies peek out from the cabinets.

"No mathematics? So how did you make it? I think you are credited with important insights into magnetism." *At least my computer seems to think so.* "Was that your breakthrough?"

"*Electromagnetism,*" he corrects me. "Electricity and magnetism turn out to be tightly interconnected. That has been my life-long study."

"Connected how? What's the connection between the spark in amber and the rotation of a lodestone?"

He smiles. "I would concede that when people studied ambers and lodestones they found no connection. But we have gone beyond that now. The new era of research started with the electric cell, or battery. It was invented in 1800 by the Italian Alessandro Volta. Volta personally presented an electric cell to my boss, Humphry Davy, and me when we visited him in Italy in 1814. Then we started producing our own batteries. Those were exciting times. Instead of sparks of static electricity, we suddenly found ourselves with chemical electric cells that could drive a sustained *electric current*—piping electric charge continuously around a circuit of metal wire."

Michael Faraday hands me a metal wire.

So electric charges can flow through a metal wire. *But what are they?*

"In 1820," Faraday continues, "Hans Christian Ørsted in Denmark discovered the first connection between electricity and magnetism. Probably quite by chance, he found that a compass placed near an electric current in a wire is deflected away from north. The current—moving electric charges in the wire—attracts a magnetic compass, just like the Earth's magnetism does. This revelation sparked an international frenzy of investigation. Just one week later, the Frenchman André-Marie Ampère published a paper with a mathematical model quantifying the magnetic force generated by electric currents. Ampère's discovery was surprising—the magnetic effect goes in circles *around* the electric current."

"So that is the connection—moving charges act as a magnet?" I ask.

"That was the first connection. Electromagnetism was born that day as a single interconnected discipline, a broad, unexplored facet of nature, a vast, empty playground where most established academics had yet to step—a setting in which a young unproven scientist might just have an outside chance of proving himself." Faraday winks at me. "But so far the connection was only from electricity to magnetism. I had an intuition that there should be a reverse connection, so I dedicated myself to finding it. For years I made thousands of trials and at least as many errors. Along the way, I developed a completely new way of thinking about electro-magnetism."

"What do you mean a new way of thinking about it?"

Faraday scratches a sideburn. "Well, I never much liked the idea of action at a distance."

My ears perk up as I remember the warning on the ROW label. "Right! Me neither!"

"Here, watch." Michael grabs a small machine and starts vigorously turning a handle. "Look, the handle rubs this silk belt against these hare furs. I get positive electric charge off one and negative electric charge off the other."

So his machine is like an automated version of the sleeve I used to rub the amber.

Michael puts on rubber gloves and removes two metal balls from the machine. I understand that the two metal spheres are now electrically charged: one positively and one negatively.

Resting on the table, Coulomb's law kicks in and the spheres start to accelerate toward one another. As they get closer, the attractive force and resulting acceleration increase greatly—the inverse square law—and finally the two metal spheres come together, first with a little blue spark between them, immediately followed by the clang of metal on metal.

"Instead of imagining these balls just magically attracting each other as some sort of action at a distance that reaches across space," Michael explains, "I like to think that each electric charge is emanating a *field* that fills the space around it, and that it is this field which in turn pushes the other charges."

"A field?"

"Yes, a field. You see, young Fizz, up to now physics was all about objects that have a specific location, like a mass or an electric charge. The field is a whole new type of physics. Think of it like an agricultural field where the stalks have a height at every single point. In the same way, the electric field permeates space having a value at every single point."

I hold back a laugh. "Did you know you were going to meet me when you chose a farming analogy? Anyway, what is this electric field?"

Michael shows me a chart of a pair of electrically charged spheres, like the pair he just demonstrated, and the electric field he is hypothesizing around them, with outbound lines for positive and inbound lines for negative:

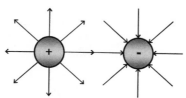

Positive electric charges emit and negative charges absorb electric field lines. The field in turn pushes or pulls other charges.

I wave at the two metal balls. "Michael, I didn't see any field."

"You saw the balls pulled toward each other, did you not?"

"Yes," I admit.

"So if we reject the idea that the charges are magically acting on each other at a distance—reaching across space to attract each other—then there must be some mechanism that is carrying the force between the charges. That is the field. I don't even know if the field is something tangible or not. It's more like a potentiality. When I say there is an electric field in some vicinity, I am saying that if you put a charge there, it will experience a force."

I look up from the table and into his eyes. *Wow! This is like a whole new way of thinking about the world.* Galileo found mathematical patterns for phenomena he observed, like a dropping object. Newton took it to a new level using one explanation—gravity—to explain apparently disparate phenomena like falling apples and orbiting moons. *But Galileo and Newton modeled what they saw!* This Faraday is transcending his own senses and proposing new invisible layers permeating the universe—fields.

I lift up the two metal spheres. "Michael, you're fabricating new worlds over here. Do you have any evidence? Anything to suggest that your fields are a better model than action at a distance?"

"Perhaps I do. All those action-at-a-distance scientists have to postulate the inverse square law—Coulomb's law that at half the distance the electric force is four times stronger. My field lines actually explain it."

"You can explain how the inverse square law comes about? That would be cool—how?"

"Ah, I was hoping you would ask that," he smiles. "Let us step into the garden."

"What?"

"Follow me."

I follow Faraday outside. It's a sunny day in London. He turns a tap and a water sprinkler shoots water in all directions, forming a big wet dome over the lawn. "Go on, step into the spray," he says.

"Pardon me?"

"You cannot truly understand the inverse square law without getting wet. Step in." The kindly old man is grinning broadly.

I have wanted to understand the inverse square law ever since Newton proposed it for gravity and even more when it popped up a second time in Cavendish and Coulomb's theory of electricity. I shrug. *Here goes nothing.* I step into the water spray fully clothed, thankful that I'm no longer wearing those hoops. The water tickles my face and dampens my beautiful outfit.

"Okay I'm wet. Now can you please explain it to me?"

"Not yet," says Michael, now laughing out loud. "Get closer. Halve your distance to the sprinkler."

"I'm pleased this is entertaining you." I'm about four meters from the sprinkler and I obediently walk forward to within about two meters of the water source. Now I'm getting drenched. My gown tugs down in protest. Water is streaming along my face. I close my eyes and shout "Now what?" over the noise of the water.

"When you halved your distance," Michael says, "did the amount of water double?"

"Are you kidding? I'm getting immersed here," I pause to swallow water. "It must be like three or four times more! You've had your laugh. Can you please explain it to me?"

"Well, young Fizz. I am not sure you would appreciate the answer if it flew toward you and splashed you in the face." Michael chuckles some more.

I'm about to say something rather unladylike when realization dawns. *Half the distance, four times more water!* The hose is an analogy for an electrically charged object—say, rubbed amber or one of those metal balls. The jets of water are Michael's imaginary electric field lines emanating from a charge. When I halve my distance, I catch four times more water. *Why?* Of course, the front surface of my body is two dimensional—so it can catch twice as many jets of water width-ways and twice as many lengthways—four times more water overall! Four times more electric attraction when you're twice as close. Last century's inscrutable inverse square law is now reduced by Michael to a simple matter of geometry!

"And you had to get me soaked to explain that?" I step out of the water spray smiling and shake like a dog, ensuring that Michael is not entirely spared.

"I have a nice chart in my office, but this was much more entertaining."

I follow Michael back inside, teeth chattering. My every shiver sprinkles water around the lab floor. "I make no apology if my wet dress damages your chair," I say slumping into a seat in his office, but I'm smiling.

Then I see the chart that could have spared me that little ordeal. At twice the distance, we need four times more squares to catch the same number of lines. So one square catches a quarter as many lines—inverse square!

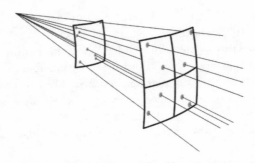

Geometric explanation of inverse square law: At twice the distance only one quarter of the field lines hit each square

"Let me see if I can summarize what you are saying." I walk over to his chalkboard, dripping water all over his floor. The cold, hard, brittle slate surface brings back childhood memories. I take some chalk and write something we would never have written in my school:

Electric field

Every electric charge emanates an electric field

The electric field in turn pushes/pulls other electric charges

(Coulomb's inverse square law is just the geometry of the field thinning out as it spreads in all directions)

Michael nods approvingly.

"Cool, what about magnetism?" I say.

Faraday walks up and grabs the chalk.

Magnetic field

Every moving electric charge emanates a magnetic field (Ampère's law)

The magnetic field in turn pushes other electric charges that move across its path, causing their movement to curve sideways

"Let me show you three examples of magnetic field lines," Michael says, pulling out a chart:

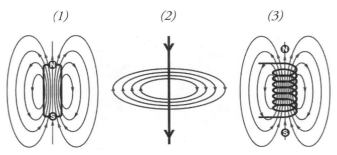

Magnetic field lines around: (1) an iron bar magnet
(2) electric current in a single wire, and (3) a coiled electric current

"Michael, how does a lodestone—or rather, your iron bar magnet—fit in? You wrote that magnetic fields are created by moving charges."

"Right," he grabs two magnetic bars and lets them snap together. "It would seem that inside an iron magnet there may be spinning charges."

"That helps," I nod in approval. "So the fields really do come down to interactions between 'charges'—whatever the charges actually are. The electric field carries force from all charges to all charges, and the magnetic field carries force from moving charges to moving charges. So what about the reverse connection you said that you found, a connection from magnetism back to electricity?"

Faraday walks back to the chalkboard.

Field–to–field interaction:

A changing magnetic field induces an electric field
(Faraday's law of electromagnetic induction).

Oh. Suddenly now the fields are interacting with themselves. *This is getting kind of abstract, especially as I don't even know what those invisible charges actually are, let alone what the fields are.* I look around the room at the pair of spheres that were charged and attracted each other earlier. The theory may sound abstract, but the results are real enough.

"Can this induction be demonstrated?" I ask.

"Give it a spin?" Michael says, gesturing at a small device on the corner of his desk.

Faraday's dynamo (generator)

I recall how Michael said it took many years to find the reverse connection. I reach over and rotate the copper wheel mounted between the poles of a horseshoe-shaped magnet. Strangely, the wires are connected to a pair of dried out shriveled—if I'm not very much mistaken—frogs' legs! The dead legs start to twitch eerily. Either Michael uses the frogs' legs as a way of detecting the presence of electric current, or, alternatively, perhaps Ampère invented this method to heat his lunch.

"Do you see why induction was so hard to find," Michael says. "No one realized that a magnet only induces electric current in a wire if the wire is moving relative to the magnet. But I was systematic. Once I happened upon the correct setup, electromagnetic induction worked beautifully. This device is called a dynamo."

On the Outside they generate vast amounts of electric energy overwhelming and devaluing our natural human energy. This little dynamo looks so quaint and innocent compared to the monstrous description of electricity painted in sermons back home.

"So," I say, my mind racing, "this right here is how you can generate a steady flow of electricity? I suppose you could make the wheel bigger? Could it be turned by a steam engine to generate a steady supply of electricity?"

I can't believe the way my mind is thinking.

Michael nods. "Yes, you could use the dynamo to continuously turn movement energy into electric current. Next I invented a device for the reverse—turning electric energy into movement. Not just twitching a compass: continuous movement. A *motor*. Look here."

Faraday points at what is clearly a small marvel of experimental ingenuity. He has dipped a wire into what I now recognize as mercury so that the wire can continue to conduct electricity through the liquid metal even as it moves:

Faraday's first electric motor

"And when I connect the wire and mercury to a Volta cell—" he flicks a switch. The hanging wire, now carrying electric current, has become a magnet, just as Ørsted and Ampère found. The wire suddenly comes to life and starts to draw circles in the mercury around a fixed magnet that is placed at the bowl's center.

On the Outside, they are not content with nature's movement. They use electricity to generate artificial movement for every tiny aspect of their lives, eclipsing their own ability to move.

Memories of sermons notwithstanding, I can't take my eyes off this tiny electric motor—a dangling wire tracing circles in a shiny bowl of mercury. I look at Faraday. He cannot possibly imagine at this moment how billions of electric motors will one day pervade the Outside world. *All because some London bookbinder was a lax—or perhaps generous?— employer.*

"So you did it," I look at the chalkboard. "Those laws explain everything!"

"Well… there is still a mystery or two. I have found a totally bizarre connection between magnetism and light. In some situations a magnet has a subtle influence on a light beam. No one knows why there should be any connection at all." He points at a block of glass balanced on top of a heavy electric coil, which I now recognize as an electromagnet.

"Magnetism and light! That's just incredible." I smile. *Where did that come from—it's like discovering that my two close friends are cousins.*

"Yes," he nods at the apparatus. "You see, young Fizz, nothing is too wonderful to be true."

When I'm seventy, I wonder if I will look back on my life and have achieved even a fraction of what this man has.

Faraday's experiment connecting magnetism and light:
a block of glass resting on an electromagnet

"So with all your discoveries and inventions—and with your marvelous new ideas about fields—the scientific establishment who doubted you must be eating humble pie," I smile.

"Feeding me humble pie, more like." Michael looks sullen. "You see, sketching field lines is all very well, but I do not know enough mathematics to elucidate and formalize my ideas. The scientific establishment has celebrated my experiments, but rejected—even ridiculed—my theories. They are sticking to the formal mathematical action-at-a-distance formulae."

"What? Michael, let me get this straight. You discovered the connection from magnetism to electricity and the connection of magnetism to light. You're the inventor of the electric motor and electric dynamo." I wave at the devices surrounding us. "And you're struggling to get your field ideas taken seriously? Goodness, maybe you should make the entire membership of the Royal Society step into your hose spray!"

He grins. "There is just one ray of hope. A certain Scottish physicist has taken an interest in my intuitions and has been laboring for years to find a mathematical model for my ideas. He was the one who helped me with the idea of a field—before that I had just called it 'lines of force.' He applied calculus—especially the work of one Gauss—to adding up the fields across space. Brilliant man. He knows all the mathematics that I do not—was second wrangler at Cambridge."

Michael gives me some sort of knowing look.

Instantaneous goose bumps. I believe that brilliant Scottish mathematician-physicist kissed me in Chamonix my yesterday evening and was almost mistaken for my father this morning.

"He has worked out much of it," Faraday says, "but there seems to be one critical piece of the puzzle missing that is frustrating us both. If he ever finishes it, my ideas—in their new mathematical guise—may finally get a serious hearing with the scientific establishment."

"Good luck. It must be slow collaborating with Scotland."

"Scotland? I said Scottish. He is now based a mile from here at the new King's College. In fact, he is visiting me this afternoon."

"Oh! He's here in London? Goodness. Michael may I excuse myself to change into something dry?"

In the hut I print myself a new dry gown. *Now what do I do?* I have to see William, but he's not going to buy this daughter-of-Fizz story. *I don't want him to.* I spend some time experimenting with makeup—maybe some pale foundation can age my skin—I must look hot and... *thirty-five!* And I absolutely have to avoid Michael or this is all going to blow up in my made-up face.

Seeing the Light

I head back to the Royal Institution to encounter an older William Thomson. Determined to avoid Michael, whom I so recklessly deceived earlier, I loiter along Albemarle Street outside the Royal Institution to hook William before he enters.

My emotions are scrambled. *What will he look like, approaching forty? Is he married? What will it feel like for him to meet me again?* I must face the fact that he might feel nothing at all—a first kiss that is still damp on my lips has probably been coated over hundreds of times by other women on his. *At the very least, perhaps I can finally discover his secret ambition.*

My muscles suddenly tense as I see, walking toward me, the one man I did not want to meet right now—*Michael*. It hadn't occurred to me that he might pop out for lunch.

"Hi, young Fizz. Yes, he should be here any moment. You look... a bit different."

"Oh, Michael, um, actually I wanted to tell you that I can't stay."

"Cannot stay? But here he comes now."

"I don't see him. Well, I'd better run. Give him my best," I say, then reconsider. "No, don't. Thanks so much for your time this morning."

"But here he is. Let me at least introduce you. Fizz," Michael says, "meet James."

"Err, how do you do," I say to the wrong dashing Scotsman. This one looks to be in his early thirties—a little younger than William should be—his pale but well-proportioned face framed with a black beard, high forehead, and thin hair, neatly combed along the top, growing longer down the sides.

"Delighted," James says.

"You are?" I say, confused.

Michael looks embarrassed. "Well, surely you recognize James Clerk Maxwell, the famous brilliant Scottish professor I mentioned? Edinburgh, Trinity College Cambridge, Aberdeen, and now King's College here in London. As I told you, I am fortunate to have such an eminent scientist working to formalize my ideas on electromagnetism. Pity you have to leave."

I exhale slowly. I guess at this moment I'm more relieved at not getting caught than disappointed at not seeing William. *Just barely, though.*

"Michael, I suppose you're right. It would be a great pity to leave. My other business will just have to wait—if it's still okay with you?"

Faraday nods. As my pulse slows, I resolve to keep a closer check on my romantic enthusiasm in the future and to avoid deceit at all costs. Now I should really make the most of the opportunity to see how Michael Faraday the experimentalist, and this James Clerk Maxwell, the theoretician, work together to tame the electromagnetic beast that has apparently tantalized the best scientific minds for decades. More importantly, I need to assess *why* these men dedicate their lives to physics.

The three of us stroll through the corridors of the Royal Institution.

"If you follow physics, it is hard to believe you have not heard of James," Michael says. "He has become famous for analyzing the rings of Saturn, completing Thomas Young's theory of color vision, and using that theory to produce the world's first color photograph."

"Really! How did you do that?"

"I thought," James explains, "that since Young found that the eye can only detect three different colors, I only need to photograph those three different colors, not the whole spectrum, so I captured three slide photographs of the same scene through red, green, and blue filters, then projected the three images back, superimposing the three photographs again through red, green, and blue filters."

"But that is not James' greatest virtue," Michael says.

"I get it. His greatest accomplishment is working on your ideas for electromagnetism."

"Not at all. I admire James most for delivering free public lectures for working men," Michael says.

"Really?" I regard James.

James seems keen to deflect the conversation. "Well, Fizz, I hear you've been lucky enough to spend this morning with the greatest experimental physicist in history." He turns to Michael. "So how is retirement?"

"As you see," Michael smiles with a gesture toward the workplace we're in.

"Do you know," James says to me, "that despite Michael's best attempts at antagonizing the royal family, Queen Victoria's husband, the late Prince Albert, provided him with a grace and favor retirement house in Hampton Court?"

"You antagonized the royal family?" I turn back to Michael.

"Well, not willfully. But I declined a knighthood," Michael smiles. "It transpires that Her Majesty is not accustomed to that."

"And," James adds, "Michael obstinately refused to advise the government on chemical warfare during the Crimean War."

Confused, I gaze at their backs as we enter the narrower corridor toward Michael's office and they march in front of me in. *Is it too much to ask that you both stop being so nice and spend some time greedily plundering Mother Nature?*

We reach Michael's lab-office and sit down.

"James, any progress?" Michael asks.

James' face leaps to life. "Yes. Not only have I found the missing piece in the electromagnetic theory, but, would you know, it has astonishing ramifications way beyond what either of us ever imagined. Startling. You see, the subtle but crucial interaction that we missed up to now is responsible—" James' speech is animated as he looks around. "Ah, perfect, who wrote all of this on the chalkboard?"

Michael, age notwithstanding, is like an alert young puppy attuned to every word. "We did," he says.

"Let me add it right here to your notes. Drum roll, please:"

...

Field interaction:

A changing magnetic field induces an electric field (Faraday's law of electromagnetic induction).

A changing electric field generates a magnetic field.

That's nice and symmetrical. A changing electric field creates a magnetic field, and a changing magnetic field creates an electric field. But this final law seems to fall short of the superlatives James heaped on it. *Does a second field-to-field interaction really change the world?*

"Hmm, I have not observed that," Michael frowns. He waves his hand around the room as if to say, "You do realize I have explored every possible electromagnetic interaction every day for tens of years?"

"I think you have observed it," James says at length. "I think you *are* observing it."

Michael drops his head into both hands.

"Michael, can you explain the implications?" I ask.

"Goodness, give me a moment here. James, I need to absorb this. Entertain her—tell her about the units," Michael says.

James obediently moves me a few paces away from Michael and whispers to me.

"Ah, yes, you know Lavoisier helped King Louis XVI to standardize the units of the *gram, meter,* and *second*. Mind you, we have not yet adopted those over here. Then they have the *Newton* as a unit of force."

James pauses briefly to smile at Michael, who is still deep in thought.

"Now we are working to standardize units for electricity, hopefully with international consensus. We are proposing the *coulomb* as a measure of an amount of electric charge, although,"—he lowers his voice even more—"chemists are proposing to use the *faraday*. I have proposed that the unit *ampere*, or *amp*, will mean an electric current where one coulomb of charge flows per second. *Ohm* is the proposed measure of electrical resistance—that is to what extent a piece of material is a conductor or insulator."

"What about units for the electric field?" I ask.

"Instead of talking about the field itself, we can talk about Laplace's idea of a potential as we do for gravity. We have proposed measuring electric potential in *volts*. So the electric field will always push positive charges from the high *voltage* to the low voltage. For example, if you have a Volta cell of nine volts, that tells you how energetically the battery will be pumping charges around your circuit from the positive to the negative terminal."

"How do you even get agreement on these names?"

"Years of politics," James exhales slowly, rolling his eyes. "We need to negotiate just the right balance of British, French, and Italian names if we want to achieve agreement."

James looks over to gauge Michael's progress.

I watch them both. This powerful English-Scottish duo reminds me so much of the fruitful collaboration I saw yesterday between another English-Scottish pair, James Joule and William Thomson. Michael reports on new experiments or intuitions to James. James comes back with fresh ideas for theoretical models. Michael absorbs them and dreams up the next experiments to test the theories and new intuitions to explain them.

"It's inspiring," I whisper to James, "to see you two collaborate. Michael's lucky to have you to respond to his discoveries and intuition and turn them into theories."

"Just like that, huh? I suppose you think I figured out these field concepts over a pint."

"Um, well, I had imagined it something like that."

James rolls his eyes again, "That would be nice, but I do not mind telling you, I have been working on these fields night and day for nine years. Even with all my mathematical training, I was completely unable to imagine Faraday's electric and magnetic 'lines of force' abstractly. Along the way, I looked for every possible analogy I could for the fields. I thought about liquids flowing through space, heat flows, space filled with elastic materials, or rotating ball bearings. I published papers that today look naïve in retrospect, but these analogies helped me get to the right abstract formalism."

"Naïve?" Michael rejoins the conversation now smiling broadly, "Illuminating. People can learn as much from our mistakes as from our successes."

"Yup. Another thing I learned from the master. Take a look." James grabs a book entitled *Experimental Researches in Electricity volume 1 by Michael Faraday* from the shelf and hands it to me. I flick through its 372 pages; volume two looks just as big and volume three much bigger. Sure enough, Michael Faraday has published his every experiment and thought—failures as much as successes, complete with diagrams.

"Newton," says James, "climbed a ladder to some lofty intellectual roof, then kicked the ladder away and said, 'I am up here, aren't I clever.' We can but speculate how Newton got there. Michael has taken the opposite approach, humbly documenting every rung of his intellectual assent, every trial and every error, for the benefit of posterity."

"Let us see if the approach works," Michael says. "Young Fizz, having been privy to our thought processes today, can you anticipate the implications of the field interaction James here discovered?"

Ouch, talk about pressure. I've got like sixty seconds to vindicate Faraday and Maxwell's efforts to educate the next generation! Think Fizz—now.

A changing electric field creates a changing magnetic field; a changing magnetic field creates a changing electric field. *Ah—what if the changing electric field could cause a changing magnetic field which could in turn cause a changing electric field—and on and on and on?*

"How about the circularity—could the two fields continuously change each other?"

"Yes," James says slowly.

"So you have discovered a new phenomenon: the electric and magnetic field can feed off each other," I continue. "It sounds like some sort of *electromagnetic wave*. If the fields feed off each other, I suppose you get an electromagnetic wave that can propel itself through space even far from the charges that originally created the fields."

They glance at each other and smile, then back at me.

"Absolutely. Just like this." Maxwell sketches it. "But I do not think it is a new phenomenon at all:"

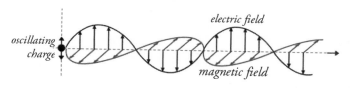

An electromagnetic wave

He doesn't continue. The ball's back in my court. *Okay, Fizz, you don't have to guess the answer, just work through the process to figure it out.* "Tell me about the characteristics of this wave. From your field equations, can you calculate the speed of an electromagnetic wave?"

James nods enthusiastically. "That is exactly what I wondered, and yes, my equations predict a speed of 300 million meters per second for electromagnetic waves."

"300,000 kilometers in one second? Well, this seems unlikely, but do any known phenomena propagate at the speed of 300 million meters per second?"

"Only one," he says.

Suddenly I touch my forehead. I met a man who tried and failed, using two shuttered lamps on opposite hills, to detect a speed of... "Light?"

"Light. The electromagnetic wave is none other than light," James confirms.

I glance again at Faraday's experiment with a block of glass over a magnet. Faraday had anticipated some sort of connection, but little had he known that light itself is a pure wave of oscillating electric and magnetic fields.

"And James Clerk Maxwell said," Michael jokes, "let there be light!"

I gawk at them for a moment. *This scientific process is so unlike what I expected.* "You're like, I don't know, Christopher Columbus!" I say to James.

"What?"

"I mean you go off looking for a new route to Asia and instead you discover America. You try to crystallize the explanation of Volta cells and iron magnets and, lo and behold, you discover light! Well, with this revelation of the nature of light, I suppose the lines of force—or rather your electromagnetic field equations—will finally triumph!"

They both sigh. "Not so fast," James says, "These ideas about fields are radical. The establishment is skeptical. We may need more evidence—new testable predictions."

"And, do you have any new predictions?"

"I do. You see, according to the equations, electromagnetic waves can form at any frequency. The visible light our eyes see completes a few hundred trillion cycles per second. We have evidence for infrared below that and for ultraviolet above, but according to my equations, there is no limit to the range. So I predict that you could make electromagnetic waves with much slower cycles—say, a few thousand or a few million cycles per second—slow enough that you could actually control the wave directly using an electric circuit. When someone finds such low-frequency electromagnetic waves, my theory will be well and truly proven." He glances at a candidate "someone."

"When someone finds those waves," Michael chuckles, "they might rip down all the telegraph cables and communicate through thin air!"

"But did you really say *hundreds of trillions* of wave cycles every second—how is such a fast wave of light even created?"

"We believe that inside every material," says James, "there are positive and negative charges. Normally they are exactly balanced. In rubbed amber, there is an excess of negative over positive. In an electric current—say, in a wire—the negative and positive charges are balanced, but the positive is moving through the wire. Or maybe the negative. Now when you heat a material to the temperatures of a flame, the atoms start to move around violently."

"That's kinetic theory," I say. "Heat is movement of the atoms."

"Right. The movement of the charges in the atoms generates changing electric fields according to my equations. So every material is transmitting electromagnetic waves at every point in time! If you make something hot enough—say in a flame—"

"The charges in the atoms," I suggest, "are jiggling hundreds of trillions of times per second?"

"Right. So you get visible light."

I break into a grin. Frayed thoughts that have been lingering awkwardly at different places in my mind—heat, atoms, electricity, magnetism, light—all come flying together, like a happy reunion of a dispersed family. I interleave both hands over my head, feeling elation.

Hot things glow because the heat is causing the charges in the atoms to jiggle around and emit changing electromagnetic fields. The changing electric and magnetic fields can feed off each other—as light—and propagate through space. Light waves are electromagnetic fields, so when they hit my retina they cause charges inside the retina to move. These tiny electric currents—moving charges—can presumably be detected by my brain.

The theories of electricity, magnetism, light, heat, and even human vision are all interrelated. It's like having many pieces and discovering for the first time that they all fit together as a perfectly planned puzzle.

I glance again at the chalkboard. It's beautiful, but just a little too abstract. "So, these fields," I ask, "is there some medium that carries the electromagnetic waves, like air carries sound, and water carries water waves?"

"That is still a bit of a mystery, but generally waves must be carried by a medium. I am calling the medium of electromagnetic waves *ether*."

"You're resuscitating Aristotle's idea that the universe is filled with aether? Wow, tell me about it."

"I know nothing about the ether. It is really just a name, a hypothesis. There must be some medium to carry the waves."

I take a step back and look at James and Michael. *I'm one of the first people to know how I see.* In fact I am one of the first people to understand how electricity, magnetism, light, and heat all fit together based on just a handful of laws written on the chalkboard. "So is this it?" I ask them both. "Is Galileo and Newton's program of mathematically modeling a causally deterministic world now nearing completion?"

"In a way," James says, "but I am also starting to realize the limitations of causal determinism. After all, you could never track every atom in practice, even if it behaves deterministically in principle. Sometimes you have to understand the world through statistics."

"*Statistics?*"

"Yes. I hope to work on that when I return to Scotland next year. If you ever find yourself up there, pay us a visit and I will tell you all about it…"

Back in Fizz's Place, feeling dizzy with excitement, I append Maxwell's equations of electromagnetism to the ROW label:

Maxwell's equations of electromagnetism

1. Every electric charge emanates an electric field.

2. An electric field exerts a force on any charge (Coulomb's law).

3. A moving electric charge emanates a magnetic field (Ampère's law).

4. A magnetic field exerts a force on any moving charge, causing its movement to curve.

5. A changing magnetic field induces an electric field (Faraday's law of electromagnetic induction).

6. A changing electric field induces a magnetic field (new law by Maxwell).

NB: 5 & 6 together imply electromagnetic waves: light/ultraviolet/infrared.

NB: Materials usually contain equal positive and negative charges. We say something is charged if there is an imbalance. An electric current means the charges are moving through the material. Heat involves jiggling charges, which in turn radiate light.

At the end of two weeks, everything is finally coming together! Electricity, magnetism, light, the overriding concept of energy, and that specific type of energy—heat, which can generate light.

Everything except one tiny, little, gaping hole! I write:

Nature of atoms? Charges?

And what about the "ocean" that carries these electromagnetic waves:

Ether?

But as to my agenda for tomorrow, I have an invitation from James Clerk Maxwell, the man who, thinking about it, mathematically modeled more of the world than anyone since Newton—maybe more than Newton. I instruct the computer. *This time I really am going to Scotland.*

I curl into bed looking at the ROW label. I have one week left to tie up the loose ends. *Then what?* I have discovered that, even after 1800, at least some of the physicists are motivated by truth, not greed. They even show humility and generosity.

But how does that really help me? In my own life there is no doubt that it's my mother, as much as I sometimes take her for granted, who's showered me with generosity.

Meanwhile, Dad abandoned me. I know it's not entirely his fault. I of all people can understand what he went through.

I think almost obsessively about that meeting with Mom and the headmistress. I was only ten. I can still hear the headmistress saying "I think Fizz is a little old to be asking negative questions in class *blah blah blah* I trust this will stop..."

I remember how I glanced at my Mom, expecting—no, *pleading*—for her support. And for that one second—less than a second, really—my mother glanced away.

Like it or not, in my mind, that one second back when I was ten years old is eclipsing eighteen years of maternal care and love.

Time's Arrow

The Sun rises in the west. The west? Yes, the west. Facing backward, I drag myself out of bed, remove my nightgown and get dressed. I walk backward out of the house and back through the town and although I never once glance over my shoulder, I successfully avoid stumbling into anything. I bend down and lift a pebble and toss it up and catch it a few times, then place it back down on the ground. I jump up and down and flap my hands around. A man passes by, walking backward in the other direction. "Gnineve doog," he says.

"You see," James says, "it all works, just as you imagine it. Admittedly walking and talking backward, or the Sun rising in the west, may not be familiar, but nothing is contradicting the laws of physics. As I said, the laws of physics are *time-reversible*—forwards or backward in time, the same laws of physics apply. If you could watch the world in reverse, nothing you observe would contradict the laws of physics."

We are sitting in the Clerk Maxwell estate in Glenair, Scotland. James and his wife Katherine seemed pleased for the company when I turned up this morning. Sizeable grassy grounds surround the house, although the interior is unpretentious. Amid the sparse furnishings are scientific apparatuses: color spinners for mixing red, blue, and green in different ratios and a large glass container connected to air pumps, apparently for observing a pendulum swing in a vacuum.

James and I are discussing the idea that time is reversible. As far as physics is concerned, the future equals the past. *Such a weird idea.*

A weird idea that I'm not buying. After all, when I later step back out into the damp, green hills, endlessly rolling through the family estate and the surrounding countryside beyond, I may well confuse north with south or east with west, but I cannot possibly imagine myself confusing the lucid memories of the past with the inscrutable future. What would that even be like? No, there *has* to be a clear physical distinction between past and future.

"James, we're missing something. I agree that when we imagined walking around town and going to bed in reverse, nothing impossible occurred. But I'm sure there are other events that can't be reversed."

"No," he shakes his head. "All the fundamental laws of physics work backward. It is a *symmetry* of the universe. Just as you and your reflection are the same, so forward and backward in time are physically indistinguishable."

I know I can contradict this, but how? What scenario, when played backward, would clearly violate the fundamental laws of physics?

My train of thought suffers a welcome interruption as Katherine sweeps into the living room behind a silver tray, carrying two steaming white, floral china teacups resting on saucers. She looks over forty, a good few years ahead of her husband, and wears a somber long black dress with her dark hair tied up. A small silver cross hangs from her neck and, as she leans gently forward to balance the tray, the cross dangles precariously above one of the cups and is coated in steam.

James and I both look up and smile at her. Maybe a cup of tea will help inspire my imagination to find a scenario that busts the claim that time is symmetric.

"Come on, Toby," Katherine says. The only other resident within a kilometer, a shaggy white dog, shuffles along, dangerously close to her heels. Katherine takes small steps. Toby walks with her, brushing her legs. And then it happens. Toby knocks into Katherine's leg just as the other foot is in the air. A horrible moment ensues at the end of which two teacups and their accompanying saucers shatter into pieces across the floor, the tea gathering in little puddles. Katherine stumbles, but catches herself and manages to stay standing, the tray still slanting in her outstretched arms.

James and I look at her in shock. "Oh, heck," she says, more like "awwww heeeeeck," in her deep Scottish accent. Katherine and James wince at each other. James and I jump up. Shamefully, I'm smiling in a way normally attributed to Cheshire cats. I try to bite my cheeks but they both notice.

"Sorry," I cringe.

"I know what you are thinking," James says, "but it is not what it seems."

"Let's play it backward," I say, "after we help clean up, of course."

Katherine sighs. "Physics first, physics second... go on, go on, I will get the mop."

James and I quickly lose ourselves in our thoughts as together we imagine the scene playing backward, talking it through moment by moment.

The Clerk Maxwells' floor is strewn with shards of white china. Here and there a small print of a rose looks up sadly from a piece of what might be a teacup. Little puddles of tea are everywhere, staining the elegant stone floor. Mrs. Clerk Maxwell is holding an empty platter at an awkward angle. James and Fizz are standing too, and everyone looks stunned. "kceh ho," Katherine says. Toby is trotting around backward, dipping his tongue in this tea puddle, then that.

After a few seconds James and Fizz sit down, still looking shocked.

Then quite suddenly James and Fizz relax their faces completely and take their eyes away from the carnage to look at each other as if they were chatting casually.

The bizarre spectacle that follows unfolds rapidly. Shards from the far reaches of the room fly toward each other and blobs of tea, wherever they are, converge rapidly into two fairly coherent lumps of tea hovering over the floor, more or less under the silver tray. The shards flying are aligned just perfectly so that they meet each other precisely along the cracks and snap together one at a time in very quick succession. Within tenths of a second it becomes apparent that the shards are self-assembling into two perfect teacups on the floor right under the tray. In parallel, the two blobs of tea each slide into an assembling teacup.

"There you are, James. Shards of pottery flying together and joining to make a teacup—impossible."

"Which law of physics does that contradict?"

"Um…"

"None," he answers for me. "It may be virtually impossible to achieve in practice, but if the shards are *perfectly* aligned when they fly together, there is nothing fundamentally impossible about them binding to each other."

"But look, shard after shard is joining together."

"Unlikely, perhaps, but not breaking the laws of physics," he says.

"Hah. Well that's not my main point anyway; it's the next moment that's impossible."

At the instant when the two teacups, two saucers and two blobs of tea have assembled—and without the slightest pause—the two newly reconstructed teacups, almost full of tea, and two saucers, spontaneously embark on an upward flight from the floor rising toward the silver tray. The teacups shoot up fast at first, but slow down as they ascend and rotate slowly all the while.

"There you are," I smile. "Teacups, tea, and saucers spontaneously flying upward. If that's 'possible' I'm the Chief Dean." I see his eyebrows rise. "Or the Queen Mother," I shrug. "My point is, that's a clear contradiction of the laws of physics."

"Of which laws?"

"Conservation of energy for one," I say. "The cups are suddenly moving upward. Where did that energy come from? And… Newton's laws of motion—the teacups can't accelerate upward without a force accelerating them."

"Not so fast," James raises his hand. "In the forward scenario, when the cups hit the ground what happened to their energy?"

"I suppose… it went into shock waves vibrating down through the floor?"

"Right. So when we play it backward?"

"*Oh*. I suppose… the shock waves come up through the floor and hit the cups, giving them the force and energy required to fly upward! But— I mean, come on, what are the odds of the shock waves all converging on the cups at one moment with *just* the right force to flick them back up to the tray."

"My point exactly. The odds are very long. But if it happened, were the laws of physics broken?"

"Well, maybe not *as such*," I finally concede.

Toby releases a bark. The cups slow down as they climb.

Admittedly, this part looks perfectly natural; gravity is working well in reverse and slowing down the cups' ascent.

By the time the cups reach the tray, they have slowed down and are completely full. Two full cups of tea and two saucers come to a halt as they set themselves gently onto the tray. Some steam flows downward into the teacups. The floor is sparkling clean.

At this point we're both up from our seats enacting the imaginary backward scene. We hold our hands on the floor simulating the scattered pieces of china. Simultaneously, we sweep our hands along the floor as if triggered by converging vibrations rising through the ground, moving up toward each other. I'm amazed to see that at each step things which we know could never happen in practice are actually physically possible. Time reversibility is holding up.

Our four hands fly toward each other as we if they were self-assembling teacups flying up and filling with tea—a scenario so contrary to human experience and yet not contrary to the fundamental laws of physics. As our four hands meet and soar upward toward an imaginary tray, we're suddenly back in the here and now, awkwardly close to each other.

At just the wrong moment Katherine emerges from the kitchen with fresh cups of tea. She briefly but pointedly glares at us. She sets the steaming tray down with extra care. "I think I'll get a third cup and join you."

Toby is still walking backward. At precisely the moment when the teacups land on the tray, Toby brushes past Katherine's leg, catching her gown on his collar.

James and Fizz start talking. "ybo T no emoc," Katherine says as she calmly backs into the kitchen carrying the tray. The cups of tea get hotter and hotter as she walks.

"Stop right there," I say, recalling William Thomson's laws of thermodynamics. "I knew there was an impossibility somewhere in the scenario. Tea spontaneously heating up—heat flowing from cold to hot. Impossible!"

"Is it?" he responds. "What is heat, Fizz? Why does heat flow from high temperature to low temperature?"

"Heat is the random movement of atoms."

"Yes. And if atoms are moving around randomly at different speeds, it could happen, by pure chance, that all the hot atoms gravitate toward the tea and the cold atoms toward the air and the tea spontaneously heats up."

"Are you serious? What are the odds of that?"

"One in a trillion. But if it happened, if tea heated up spontaneously, no fundamental law of physics would be broken. If you could observe the atoms, you would see each and every atom precisely obeying Newton's laws of motion."

"So you mean the 'law' that heat flows from hot to cold is not actually a fundamental law?"

"Right. Atoms jiggling around can arrange themselves in any way. Of course, the odds that the hot and cold atoms mix together to make two warm bodies are very high. The odds that all the hot, fast atoms go one way and all the cold atoms go another way—one in a trillion."

The translucent tea gradually turns into transparent water as delicate swirls of black tea seep into the tea leaves.

"So," I scratch my head, "the tea unmixing. That is also not fundamentally impossible either? Just highly improbable? Yes, I suppose there are many, many ways for tea and water to mix but only a very few ways for them to unmix. So the chances that tea will separate with all the tea molecules entering the leaves are like one in a gazillion."

I finally take a sip from my fresh cup of tea. It's not so hot. Should I wait a while and see if it heats up spontaneously? That would be nice, but I don't like the odds.

"Look, James, I get that, but I'm confused. I accept that you're right that the laws of physics—Newton's laws of motion and your laws of electromagnetism—are symmetric in time. If you played time backward, you would observe nothing fundamentally impossible. Each atom would obey the laws of physics. But these occurrences—tea heating up, tea unmixing, cups unbreaking—are so incredibly improbable that in practice you could legitimately say they're impossible. That's a really important part of how we understand the world—that these things don't happen in practice. Can't physics capture that? Isn't there some extra law of physics that incredibly improbable things, even if they don't break the laws of physics, never happen?"

"I think there is. *Entropy always increases.* That is the law."

"Entropy?"

"The concept of *entropy* was invented by German physicist Rudolf Clausius, but he himself never understood what it really meant. Now I, as well as an Austrian scientist named Ludwig Boltzmann, have understood that all of this is really about statistics. Entropy just means *disorder*. An assembled cup has low entropy; it is orderly, as there is only one way to have an assembled cup. Shards of pottery strewn across the floor have high entropy, high disorder, because there are trillions of combinations of ways in which shards might be scattered across a floor. So cups break because entropy is increasing and cups don't unbreak because entropy would be decreasing. It's really just a way to say that there are trillions of ways for a cup to break and only one way for it to unbreak."

"And heat? Tea mixing?"

"Same thing. There are relatively few ways to arrange atoms nicely with all the hot ones in one place and all the cold ones in another place. That scenario has low entropy. There are many more ways to have the hot and cold atoms all jumbled together. That has high entropy. So heat will flow from hot to cold until everything reaches a medium warm temperature, because that situation has the highest entropy and is therefore by far the most likely."

"Got it," I grin. "So the tea in the tea leaves and clear water—orderly, low entropy. Tea and water mixed together, disorderly, high entropy. So tea will mix but not unmix because there are so many more combinations of ways for tea to be mixed than unmixed."

This is so simple it's just brilliant. For all eternity people thought that heat flows from high temperature to low temperature because of some fundamental law of physics, rather like water flows from high to low under the influence of gravity. Lavoisier created a whole theory about the element of caloric flowing from hot to cold. Yet all along, heat was flowing from hot to cold not because any fundamental force was guiding it, but because of sheer statistics. There are simply many more permutations where hot and cold are mixed together. *Entropy always increases.*

"Awesome," I say.

"Welcome to *statistical physics*."

So this is a whole new layer of physics. Fundamental physics tells you what is fundamentally possible. Fundamental physics is time reversible. Statistical physics—including the study of heat, *thermodynamics*—tells you what things are *practically* impossible, even if they are fundamentally possible, because they are incredibly improbable. And James Clerk Maxwell has summed up the entire field in two words: *Entropy increases*.

I pace around and think it over for a minute. My smile fades. There's a depressing aspect to the law that disorder increases. "But James, we humans can counteract that, yes? What if I glue the shards into a mug or assemble a jigsaw puzzle for that matter? Then I'm decreasing entropy, right?"

"An assembled jigsaw puzzle does have less entropy, it is more orderly. But while you assemble the puzzle, your brain and muscles are generating heat that stirs the air around you and increases the entropy elsewhere in the world. So by exerting effort you can indeed decrease the entropy in one system—like the puzzle—but you are still increasing the total entropy in the world."

"Hmm. I love your elegant thought process but not so much the conclusion."

James seems to hesitate, then continues, talking a little slower. "Even so, one mystery remains in my mind. By way of analogy, theoretically, could some miniature demon dive into the teacup and guide the hot molecules toward the tea and the cold molecules toward the air? What if the demon could somehow do that without generating new heat of its own? Could the demon cause total entropy to decrease? I suppose not, but it is something to ponder."

"So what have you called this depressing law," I ask, "that entropy always increases?"

"I have called it the second law of thermodynamics."

"Wait a second." Feeling a little defensive, I take a steadying breath. "William Thomson already used that name for the law that heat always flows from hot to cold—you can't just steal his name."

I grab my teacup and take a final gulp of lukewarm tea.

"Well, my friend Sir William will forgive me for reusing the name of his law but, after all, the fact that heat flows from hot to cold turns out to be just one special case of this new more general law that entropy increases. So I am just elucidating and expanding the very same second law of thermodynamics."

Fair enough. In fact, this is the very explanation I was looking for, to really understand the second law of thermodynamics and the anomaly in the Carnot cycle. *When you increase disorder you can't reverse it.*

These laws of thermodynamics seem to have rather obscure names for such important concepts. The first law of thermodynamics says that energy is conserved—not only in thermodynamics, but also in mechanics and electromagnetism. It should surely be called the *universal law of conservation of energy.*

As to the "second law of thermodynamics," it is more of a meta-law for the world. Shouldn't it be called "the fundamental law of the macroscopic world" or "the law of why cups don't unbreak and tea doesn't unmix" or "the law of why the world is how it is" or "the definition of future versus past"?

But while these thoughts meander through my mind, my rudely awakened emotional side—just hearing William's name—is demanding the right to speak. "Just one second, though—your friend, *Sir* William?"

"Ah yes, knighted by Her Majesty earlier this year. After he finally succeeded in his crazy ambition," James chuckles. "Pity, I shan't be able to tease him about it any longer."

"Tease him about what?"

"Oh, not important," he waves his hand dismissively.

"It is to me."

"If you are really interested, sure, I have a copy somewhere. A poem I sent him last time he failed." He retrieves a sheet of paper and hands it to me.

"So how is William, I mean Sir William? Still his energetic self?"

"So you know him? Still energetic, but injured his leg back in '61. He keeps powering around even with the limp. And he's doing very well for himself. Collecting royalty payments from both sides of the Atlantic now. And busy intellectually sparring with Charles."

"Sorry to hear he's limping. Who's Charles?"

"A colleague of ours from Cambridge. Came back from the Galápagos Islands recently with some outlandish theory. William and I are both looking for physical evidence to discredit his ideas."

I thank James and Katherine several times and pet Toby. The three of them stand by the door to formally see me out. Maybe Katherine wants to make sure I leave.

"Our pleasure," James says. "It gets lonely during the long summers in Glenair—always happy to receive visitors, especially if I can discuss physics. Hope to see you again in the future," he says.

"If that even means anything," I smile, then pause. "In fact, tell me, James, if the fundamental laws of physics are the same in either direction, what in fact is the difference between the past and the future? Why is entropy low in the past and high in the future? Why—"

He shows me the palm of his hand. "You cannot ask why entropy is higher in the future. That is a definition. When we say 'past' we mean the direction in time when entropy is lower. 'The past' means the time when things are more orderly. 'The future' means the time when things are more disorderly than now. It is a convention just like 'north' by convention means polar bears and 'south' means penguins."

"But to me 'past' means the direction in time about which I have clear memories. The 'future' means the direction in time about which I have only vague intuitions."

"And why, Fizz, do you have clear memories about the past and only vague intuitions about the future? Because the past is more orderly, easier to form an understanding of. You see, the second law of thermodynamics is the *arrow of time*, the definition of past and future. When we say *entropy increases as time gets later*, perhaps we mean that we call the time 'later' if entropy has increased. So as I said, hope to see you in the future."

"Thanks again and, well, hope to see you when the universe is more disorderly!"

Traversing the grassy hills toward my hut, James's poem in hand, I start to replay the conversation, slowly absorbing James's novel insights. As my thoughts become more orderly, I know that my brain is generating heat, causing the cool Scottish summer air around me to stir and become even more disorderly. Overall, disorder is increasing.

I look back and wave once more at the three residents of Glenair who are enjoying the fresh air as they watch me leave, Katherine sitting on a rock.

Looking at them from a distance I cringe inside. *Hey, sorry I came empty-handed*, I mutter to myself. *Next time I'll bring a bottle of wine.*

I read the poem.

THE SONG OF THE ATLANTIC TELEGRAPH COMPANY

Mark how the telegraph motions to me,
Signals are coming along,
With a wag, wag, wag;
The telegraph needle is vibrating free,
And every vibration is telling to me
How they drag, drag, drag,
The telegraph cable along,

No little signals are coming to me
Something has surely gone wrong,
And it's broke, broke, broke;
What is the cause of it does not transpire,
But something has broken the telegraph wire
With a stroke, stroke, stroke,
Or else they've been pulling too strong.

Fishes are whispering. What can it be,
So many hundred miles long?
For it's strange, strange, strange,
How they could spin out such durable stuff,
Lying all wiry, elastic, and tough,
Without change, change, change,
In the salt water so strong.

There let us leave it for fishes to see;
They'll see lots of cables ere long,
For we'll twine, twine, twine,
And spin a new cable, and try it again,
And settle our bargains of cotton and grain,
With a line, line, line,—
A line that will never go wrong.

My grin at James's humor soon fades, and I start thinking about, well, demons. Laplace's demon depressed me greatly. It makes the world sound like one big predictable machine in which I have no free choice, in which the future is predetermined.

But in a way, maybe Maxwell's demon brings hope. She teaches us that the world is statistically complex and we cannot predict the future, at least not in practice. We must live to see the future.

Maxwell's demon teaches us why life is challenging: Disorder is increasing all around us. Maybe she also teaches us why life is worth living—we humans can make pockets of order within the disorder. Maybe a demon that creates order without increasing disorder is indeed impossible. *But at least we can create order where we want it and never mind the disorder that is created elsewhere.* We can reassemble pottery and assemble puzzles. We can even decipher the mysterious anomalies of heat flows and analyze the surprisingly subtle difference between "past" and "future." *Being human is cool.*

Walking into the hut, I add a law and tone down the determinism warning.

Second law of thermodynamics: Entropy (disorder) always increases ☹. But with effort we can reduce entropy locally ☺.

WARNING: Universe is deterministic (Laplace's demon). In practice, though, the universe is far too complicated to predict so we resort to statistical concepts like temperature and entropy.

Speaking of the meaning of life, my thoughts return to William, the man who gave me a first little taste of the power of love. So he really did become a key protagonist of the technological revolution, creating the first trans-Atlantic pipe for that "core evil"—artificial data. If anyone in the community hears about William and me, it will sound to them like some story about a girl who falls for a vampire.

Pity about poor William having his energy dampened by a limp. It happened in 1861, so he would have had his ability to walk compromised at the age of thirty-seven.

Same age my Dad is now.

Same age as the Dean is now.

The dean... who also limps.

The dean's mysterious limp, which no one wants to discuss.

So... the dean is the same age as my Dad, who seems racked with guilt because a contemporary of his joined him on the PCC, got hurt in a mugging, and went back to the Ecommunity.

I knock my head vigorously. *What a fool I've been!* My Dad's friend must be the very same man who warned me passionately about violence on the Outside—a warning that I dismissed as selfish and detached.

The Dean was really worried for me.

I sit on the bed and try to focus back on my quest. Running my eyes along the artifacts on the shelf, it is clear that progress is occurring. Liquids/waves—check. Gases—check. Electricity—check. Magnetism—check. Light—check. Heat—check.

The bottle of brown powdery material—well, partial check. We have physical and chemical evidence for atoms but no detailed knowledge of the actual structure and laws of atoms or how those all-important positive and negative electric charges are embedded in the atoms.

I must solve that final artifact—understand atoms. But as my understanding of physics nears completion, I have an overriding concern: *Is learning physics actually progressing my ultimate goal of choosing between technology and ecology?* I've seen massive scientific progress modeling the world. I have finally seen the beginning of science contributing to changes in lifestyle: the steam engine—now coming to a train station and factory near you. The telegraph—now apparently extending across the Atlantic thanks to William. Energy and data. The two biggest "evils" are taking root.

But so far the effect could be seen as positive, and the damage to the environment seems mild. *What am I missing?*

"Computer, show me how technology becomes a dominant force."

Most evenings I find I'm exhausted from physically walking around, from the intellectual exercise, from the emotional turmoil, but today I find myself lying awake for some time. I hold the bottle of brown powdery material in my hand, turning it over. *See the effects of technology, understand atoms, go home.* That's the plan. *But to which home?*

I had planned to test the motivations of physicists. Honestly, some of them are the nicest kind of people. Faraday and Maxwell's overt generosity actually made me uncomfortable because it belies everything I was taught. *Because it takes me a step closer to deciding to leave my Mom and friends.*

I get up and walk to the mirror to look at myself. I keep thinking about how I dismissed the Dean's concerns, how I taunted him: *And you, Dean, you know what it's like out there?*

Looking at my reflection, I think about how I turned up at the Clerk Maxwells' empty-handed.

No, Fizz. Faraday and Maxwell don't only make you uncomfortable because they are more generous than you were led to expect. They make you uncomfortable because they are more generous than you.

I run my hand through my wavy red hair and wipe a tear off my cheek. *You, Fizz, are the type of person who leaves her Mom to agonize for two weeks now about whether her only daughter, her reason for living, may be about to walk out of the door.*

Maybe I shouldn't worry so much about understanding physics or physicists. Maybe I should worry more about the motivations of the very person whom I see, thanks to the reflection of electromagnetic waves called light, staring back at me from the mirror.

Into the night, I debate family and friends versus the freedom to study and invent, trying to imagine my life in two different scenarios, questioning not the two worlds but my own motivations. I pick up the bottle of earth and worry again about the nature of matter—the atoms and charges—that must underlie everything I've learned.

As I deliberate, the strangest sensation creeps up on me. The bottle of Earth in my hands is getting heavier.

I suppose that tiredness is finally setting in. *No! I think it really is getting heavier.*

Now it's not just the bottle. *I'm getting heavier.* My head is weighing on my neck. My bum is pressed more firmly than normal against the seat. Even the skin of my face seems to be sagging just slightly. *I'm way too young for this.*

I try to stand up, but it requires the kind of effort normally reserved for climbing a ladder. I try to lift the bottle of water and the hot can—they too are heavy. I feel dizzy—my brain is confused. *Or is my heavy blood physically draining to my feet?* I lie horizontally on my bed and feel some relief.

What on earth is going on? *Does time-travel make gravity stronger?*

The Wizard

Day 16. New Jersey, USA, 1881.

I recall harvest in the Ecommunity—the first Sunday after the autumn equinox. Tiny seeds, dropped into the ground months earlier, have become fully grown shoots ready to sustain us. The first wagon of the newly reaped grain is paraded from the field to the Collective's tavern. Horses and oxen are not used—members of the Collective dance around the wagon, hand in hand, patiently waiting for their own turn—four at a time—for the honor of manually pulling the wagon.

Upon the wagon's arrival, the feast commences. The ceremonial "first wagon" is not literally the first—some grain has been quietly collected and baked into breads and cakes during the preceding days. All night, beer and wine mingle with song and laughter as we celebrate Mother Nature and the fruits of our own work.

For the duration of that night, the celebration masks the tension. In a good year, many weeks of hard labor will lie ahead—reaping, sun drying, threshing, winnowing, and finally storing and baking. For a couple of months we will all be working from dawn to dusk, seven days a week, and then some. In a bad year, there will be less work. Insects may have claimed the best of the bounty, or stems may have been lost to frost or drought. The farming workload will be a little lighter, and by the end of the winter, so will the farmers.

But whether we are facing food rationing, or merely daunting work, on that one Sunday we let our hair way down and allow our spirits to soar.

Those communal festivals seem so far away.

Standing, framed by the doorway, at the entrance to an oversized room, I survey the men working away at desks that are spread throughout the expansive workspace in front of me. My hair and shoulders are sprinkled with snowflakes.

Today is also a kind of harvest day. The abstract scientific ideas that I have seen planted by physicists—from Galileo to Faraday and Maxwell— have now germinated and grown up. What does a scientific idea grow into? Finally, I see it with my own eyes—*it's true*. Abstract scientific insights have sprouted into technologies. Someone is going to reap a lot of money. Confronted with real, heavy, science-led "meddling" for the first time, I have to figure out if it's a good year or bad.

When I asked which professor works here, the receptionist laughed in my face, but it turned out that the "boss" would be happy to chat briefly with a visitor from Iceland. He's available in an hour and I'm free to look around in the meantime. I'm not quite sure why he wants to talk to me, but I can plainly see why the computer brought me to him.

I head to the desk closest to the coal fire, allowing the snow to melt into my hair, which duly starts to frizz up. A man, working, as they all are, in a dark suit and bowler hat, adjusts a bolt with a spanner, then slides a heavy steam engine into the fire. It starts to rotate. Heat energy becomes kinetic energy: movement. As per the second law of thermodynamics, he is not able to convert all the disorderly heat into orderly rotation; some of the heat must escape to make the room, and my hair, more disorderly. Overall, disorder increases. Carnot's cycle and William's thermodynamics are being scaled up.

At the next station the movement energy—the spinning rod—from the steam engine is fed into a large machine. "What's that?" I ask.

"She's Mary-Ann. Long-legged Mary-Ann," the man gestures at the two long poles of the electromagnet.

I gaze at the machine. "My, my, how you've grown," I say to the Faraday dynamo. Michael's insight of electromagnetic induction is being applied to convert movement energy into electric energy, and this dynamo will be powering more than twitching frogs' legs.

Dynamo (generator)—'Long-legged Mary-Ann'

The next man takes the electricity from the generator and pipes it through a massive coil of electric wire wound tightly around a cotton reel the size of a boulder. He tests the output from the wire, which must be a kilometer long. *Someone is planning to distribute electricity over real distances.*

The generated electricity goes up to the ceiling, where the wire splits and spiders its way across the room, delivering electricity to every single desk. Catching a slight breeze, I turn around to see an electric fan at one of the stations—no doubt powered by a Faraday motor. *That completes the cycle*—electric energy is being converted right back into movement energy again!

"So where's the boss?" I finally ask. I'm directed to a flight of stairs in the corner.

As I ascend the first few steps, I pause to look back at the "crop" of technologies spread out below me. Here it is: Premeditated planning of industrial-scale production, transmission, and consumption of electric energy, transforming lumps of coal into artificial human convenience on a potentially limitless scale.

Useful or evil? I stare down at the bowler hats and sigh. *All I can really say is that it seems inevitable.*

The stairs take me up to a carpeted anteroom beyond which I can see another hall, as large and busy as the one downstairs. The anteroom houses a single small table, unmanned, decoratively covered in a black tablecloth with white trimmings. A wooden chair rests next to the table. I examine the bizarre contraption on its surface: At the center is a tin cylinder with a large brass tube emerging from one side and a shiny brass handle protruding from the other. The polished crank points at me invitingly, but I'm not sure if I should be touching the equipment. I hesitate. I glance around. Everyone is busy with their own work in the larger room. I sit on the chair and turn the handle quietly. The tin can rotates.

"Good morning," says a soft voice. I jump and let go of the handle. The voice stops. I laugh and turn the handle some more. "How do you do?" the crackly voice is emerging from the brass pipe, the first time I've ever heard an artificial voice. "How do you like the phonograph?"

Phonograph. Greek for sound-writing.

"Yes, I like it," I reply out loud, then feel a bit silly. This must be the first invention in history to introduce itself.

"I'm pleased to hear it," replies the same voice. I jump again as this time the voice is louder, clearer, and coming from behind me.

"Oh," I turn to face the voice. "Good morning, you must be the boss?" I clear my throat. "I hope you don't mind me trying it out."

"Thomas Edison." He extends his hand. "That's what it's here for. You're the visitor from Iceland? Come to my office. I have some questions to ask you."

The boss is surprisingly young—early thirties, I would say. He is clean-shaven and looks dashing in his three-piece suit.

"I'm Fizz. Before we go, can you show me how this phonograph works?"

"Ah, certainly. Observe," Edison takes my place on the chair and rotates the handle. "Can you see for yourself what is happening? Can you?" He stares at me.

Edison with his phonograph

I lean forward right over it. "Ah yes, I think I do."

A groove seems to spiral around the tin can and tiny protrusions are carefully engraved along the groove. A needle is brushing over the miniature dents in the groove, vibrating in a specific way and causing the air to vibrate with it. *Sound.* In a way, this is a highly sophisticated version of the sounds that Galileo produced when he agitated the air by brushing a chisel over grooves.

"My second most important invention," Edison says as he stands and puts his hand on the small of my back, leading me through the large upstairs hall.

"What about all the stuff downstairs?"

"Most of what I do starts where the last man left off—Faraday, Newcomen, Watt. But this phonograph is a brand new innovation."

"And your most important invention?"

He lets go of me and holds his arms out wide.

"What?" I say.

"This, all of this." He beckons at the room.

"Your laboratory?"

"Industrial laboratory. A factory, really."

"A factory? For... inspiration?" I try.

"*Pah.* Inspiration is overrated. Genius is one percent inspiration, ninety-nine percent perspiration. Great ideas originate in the muscles," Edison surveys his team, all hard at work.

"So a factory for what?"

"A factory for inventions. Our raw material is coffee. Our capital is brains. Our product is patents—coming up on one thousand patents," He points at a side office where clerks are engrossed in their work. "Well enough of that, I have some questions."

On the way to his office, I stop in my tracks at the amazing sight of a black-and-white moving image playing on the wall. *Awesome!* Our shadows cross the image. This picture is not coming live through any hole in the wall. Someone has actually recorded a moving image of reality.

"Dickson, the kinetograph is looking sharper today." Edison gives the man a quick thumbs-up.

And now it hits me. Downstairs was about energy: producing, transmitting, and utilizing energy. Upstairs here is about information: recording and transmitting sounds and sights. This entire place is a den of "evil"—of the two core evils of artificial energy and artificial information—as the Ecommunity would have it.

On the Outside they destroy privacy by having recording devices in every corner, not content with human memory, they want to record every sound and image...

Fortunately, that discomforting thought is interrupted by another.

"Mr. Dickson. Can that thing play the film backward?" I ask.

Dickson shrugs. "Sure."

A minute later, sitting among dozens of gadgets in his office, Edison wastes no time. He plops both elbows on his desk and starts to grill me. A photograph of the team I have just met hangs on the wall:

Edison's Menlo Park facility with team

"You are our first visitor from Iceland," he says leaning forward. "So tell me, how big is the population in Iceland? How concentrated is it? You see, so far I can only supply power up to one mile from a power station." He sighs and shakes his head. "What are their energy needs? Heating, I assume? You have long, dark nights in the winter—lighting? What energy sources are available—coal? Waterfalls? Geothermal? What about information—could Iceland be a relaying station for cross-Atlantic telegraphy? You know they're trying to get the cross-Atlantic telegraph up to one character a second! Can you imagine such a speedy transmission?"

As I bluff my way as best I can through the rapidly fired questions about life in Iceland in the late nineteenth century, from a man whose ambitions are clearly global, all I am thinking is: *This is it, I found it, where science feeds an explosion in technology.*

Yet despite all the foreboding, so far I'm more intrigued than repulsed.

Edison is focused. Just ten minutes later the barrage of question seems to be petering out when a member of staff bursts into the office. "I think we're getting there with the electric light bulb."

"Show me," Edison waves him in.

The man is holding a glass bulb with two wires sticking out. He grabs the electric wires dangling from Edison's ceiling and starts to twist them to the wires from the bulb.

I stare at the bulb, anticipating it lighting up at any second. Most of the physics I know must be in play in that tiny little light source. Downstairs, heat becomes motion becomes electricity. Now the electric energy will be converted back into heat energy in that filament. Heat is just the jiggling of atoms—and the vibrating charges in the atoms will emit electromagnetic waves—light!

And then it lights up. Edison grins.

I stare at the light as goose bumps burst onto my skin. I'm overpowered by a completely unexpected feeling of nausea. "Turn that thing off," I plead. "Please."

"Why?" Edison squints at me. "Look at it, this is beautiful light. Turns on and off without need for a flame, no messy fuel."

"Yes, yes, but please demonstrate how it turns off. Right now. If you don't mind."

Edison looks irritated, but a second later the light fizzles out on its own. Edison is disappointed. "What was that about? Wishing my light to fail."

"I—I'm sorry. I'm not sure—it's a great invention, it just triggered a painful déjà vu—"

"What déjà vu? This is a brand new invention, a piece of the future. It is not possible that you have seen this before."

"Well, you're right. I can't have seen it before. For some reason it triggered a bad feeling. It's me, not your invention. I apologize."

I glare at the extinguished bulb. *Impossible as it seems, I feel certain that I actually have seen that light somewhere before.*

The other man looks frustrated at the result and oblivious to my reaction. "Failed again. At these temperatures the tungsten atoms just float off the filament." He points to a bit of blackening on the glass.

"Not failed," Edison corrects him. "You can find ten thousand ways that don't work without failing. Keep at it. Many of life's failures are people who did not realize how close they were to success when they gave up."

As they speak, I regain my composure. *What brought on that reaction?* I focus my mind back on the technological revolution I just witnessed. "So, Mr. Edison, is your work guided by science? Do you have a scientific model for how much light that filament produces?"

"Yes and no. Physicists do have a formula for the pattern of how much light of various colors is emitted by objects at different temperatures. It's called *black-body radiation*. But the equation is purely empirical. No one can explain how that pattern emerges from Maxwell's equations—black-body radiation is a scientific mystery. There is even some talk of an adjustment to Maxwell's equations."

"Black-body?" I ask.

"Yes. It's best to study the emission of light from hot bodies that are black. You see, if a surface is for example blue, that means that blue light bounces off its surface—it cannot absorb blue light. Likewise, when you heat it, it cannot emit blue light. Black bodies can absorb or emit any color of light, so the emission of light is studied in hot black bodies. As I said, we have a formula for black-body radiation, but not an underlying explanation."

I look at the light bulb again. It represents the biggest remaining mystery of all—what are the charges that are jiggling inside it so rapidly? What medium carries the electromagnetic waves from the filament to my eyes? And now a new puzzle: Why is the amount of light—the "black-body radiation"—not consistent with underlying theory?

"Tell me one other thing," I say. "You have grand plans to generate and distribute electricity, to power everything from lights to fans, but do you actually have any clue what electricity is? What are the charges flowing in all your wires, in that bulb, powering your fans?"

"Maybe just a clue," Edison says flippantly. "For me, pure science takes a back seat. Sale is proof of utility, and utility is success. I want to sell light to people who dislike the dark, sell flowing, cool air to people who suffer from heat. You could say that discontent is the first necessity of progress. Having said that," he raises his eyebrows, "I did happen across one clue to your question, quite by chance."

Edison walks up to a shelf and retrieves a different glass bulb. This one has three wires, not two, and seems to contain two separate filaments, with a gap between them.

Edison effect—negative charge flowing through vacuum

"Look," he says, "I have found that electric current does not always require a metal wire. If I heat one of the filaments inside the vacuum of the bulb, I can make an electric current flow from one filament to the other—right through a vacuum! Up to now, scientists have moaned that electric current is invisibly buried inside amber, inside a metal conductor, but here is electric current flowing stark naked through a vacuum! Now that I've found them a naked electric current, surely one of those physicists can figure out what the electric charges actually are," he stands up to show me out. "I have just one interesting observation myself. You can only do this with current from the negative terminal of an electric cell, never with the positive."

I remember that Franklin considered positive and negative electric charges to be equivalent, symmetrical. Here is the first asymmetry: Only a negative electric charge can flow through a vacuum.

As Edison leads me out, we pass three men tapping deliberate sequences on little switches. *Tap tap... tap tap tap... tap...* They stop to make some adjustments and try again. "That used to be me," Edison chuckles, "tapping Morse code. Telegraphy will always be my first love. We have made several efforts here to improve it."

I thank Edison and take my leave. I make a small stop at the kineto-graph. "So, Mr. Dickson, about playing your moving images backward. Might you have any footage of a shattering teacup?"

Back in the hut, I puzzle again about my own reaction to the electric light. Was that just all the preaching against technology catching up with me? *No, there was something specific about the electric light that disturbed me deeply.*

I push the thought aside and take stock. I have just two pairs of mysteries left. Two are "within"—namely, what are the atoms that material is made of and, specifically, what are the electric charges inside atoms? The other two both relate to electromagnetic waves: Why does black-body radiation—the light emitted from hot objects—not obey Maxwell's equations, and what is the medium, the "ether," that carries the electro-magnetic waves? Four mysteries and an absolute maximum of five days available, leaving me a final day, if required, to digest what I've seen and make my decision.

Five days from now I will either be back in the stifling community or thrown into a new world separated from everyone I know.

I exhale. Here goes.

"Computer. Help me understand electric charges and black-body radiation."

I look at the screen. *Where and when will I be tomorrow?*

I try to relax. I start thinking again about the log that I saw on the screen, of Dad going back to 2092. He went back many times for short visits to that same year. It can't be a coincidence. *Dad must be feeling more guilt than I ever realized.*

Maybe he *should* feel guilty for leaving me effectively fatherless. *But he didn't know.*

I walk up to the mirror. *Why am I so sure it's about me?* Dad may indeed be visiting 2092 out of guilt. He may even be hoping to change the past. Yes, it's conceivable that visiting 2092 was his motivation for inventing time travel. *But who said the guilt was about me?* In fact, Dad may even be—well, pleased to have narrowly escaped a lifetime of paternal responsibility.

Let's face it, if Dad is feeling guilty about events in 2092, it could just as easily be about leaving his friend to the mercy of a violent mugger. His friend whom, unbeknownst to Dad, has recovered well and made himself a career as a dean, which seems to give him satisfaction. *Except perhaps when one of his congregants goes off on the PCC, and then stays away far longer than she promised.*

Little Jack Horner

Day 17. Bern, Switzerland, 1905.

The buildings in the center of Bern are not much different from those I saw on my last trip to Switzerland, but everything else has developed almost beyond recognition during my ten-day absence from this country. Horse-drawn carriages share the roads with electric trams and with the occasional gasoline-powered or steam-powered motor vehicle. Such vehicles are still a novelty, and people point and comment "There's a Benz horseless carriage" or "Look they fitted a Daimler-Mercedes engine in that carriage."

The tentacles of the growing electric power grid that I saw being conceived yesterday now extend into homes and shops; some streets are lit electrically, fed by a crisscross of overhead wires that remind me of Edison's workshop.

Walking under the electric streetlights, still glowing in the early morning, I'm again overpowered by an unexplained revulsion, which is even stronger with the lights glaring down at me. *What's that about?* There is no possible way I could have seen electric lights in the past, unless Mom had actually taken me to the Outside as a small child. But there is no legal way for her to have done that. Even if there was, surely my own mother wouldn't cover up such a thing. *Mom wouldn't lie to me.*

The availability of electricity is driving an explosion of appliances. I observe people crowding around a shop window, sizing up ceiling fans and a device called a vacuum cleaner. For a moment, I find myself contemplating how these new appliances could change my own life. *How quickly could I reach Reykjavík in one of those new vehicles? Could the engine be attached to a plow?* I shake my head suddenly to curtail these thoughts. *When did I start coveting technological conveniences?*

A gold nugget buys me five Swiss francs at a local bank, one franc for each 0.3 grams of gold. According to a notice in the bank, most of Europe has now adopted a single currency—the Swiss franc, French franc, Belgian franc, Greek drachma, Italian lire, and Spanish peseta may be used interchangeably—with the same gold content they differ only in name. I look at the coins. *For once my currency may actually be useful for more than one day.*

I break into my first franc over breakfast in a tearoom on Nägeligasse, where a surprising number of people are idly chatting and clinking teacups all around. No one seems to be rushing off to start tending their fields at the crack of dawn. *Leisure.* I glance uncomfortably at the men—whose work is powered by steam engines—shooting the breeze with women—who have delegated housework to appliances. None of them seem to feel that they might starve if they trim their workday.

When a distant clock chimes ten, and absent any sort of physics institution in the proximity of the hut, I walk around the train station and make my way to the University of Bern, a couple of kilometers northwest of the city center. *Perhaps the hut just couldn't find a hiding place nearer the university.*

On campus, I seek out the bursar.

"So did someone here have a new insight into electric currents—perhaps currents in the vacuum?"

"*Nein, mein fräulein.*"

"Ah, perhaps there is original research here into black-body radiation?"

"*Nein, fräulein.*"

"The composition of atoms? *Nein?* Well, is there any research in this university at all?"

His mouth gapes. "I shall have you know that we have award-winning research into…" he takes out his fingers to start counting all the wonderful departments at the university.

"*Ja, ja,* just a joke. My apologies. *Danke schön* and all that. Are there any other universities in Bern? *Nein?* Any professors of physics in Bern outside the university? *Nein?*" I exhale sharply. "May I visit the library?"

My Dad may be brilliant, but he can also be quite obtuse. Imagine making a machine that can intelligently choose a destination, based on my verbal description, and travel overnight through time and space to that destination, and after all of that not going to the trouble of having the machine display a simple message like "Welcome to Bern. Go find Prof. Ubersmart in the University of Bern, Room 345. His interests are the moons of Jupiter and race horses."

So much for "user-friendly."

The university's science library is even bigger than the science libraries I saw in the 1800s. Measured by meters of bookshelves, scientific research is clearly gaining momentum. The Bernoullis' manuscripts are now tucked away in an antique section, making room for dozens of scientific periodicals such as *Science* and *Nature.*

Great, I'm sitting in a library reading journals. I'm sure they have perfectly good libraries on the Outside in my own time—I didn't travel to the past for this. But what choice do I have?

I leaf through some papers scanning for a good summary of the decades I skipped last night and hopefully some connection to Bern. I find a comprehensive overview lecture by one Lord Kelvin dated 1900 surveying natural philosophy as of the turn of the century. The lecture is entitled *Nineteenth-Century Clouds over the Dynamical Theory of Heat and Light.* The lecture is actually extremely upbeat. The theme is that physics was completed during the 1800s!

Everything is known, the universe conquered.

As the title suggests, just two small "clouds" remain to amuse physicists in the twentieth century. One is the unexplained behavior of black-body radiation, and the other is some obscure-sounding experiment by Michelson and Morley in Ohio that failed to detect the ether—the medium Maxwell had speculated carried electromagnetic waves.

I swing back on the library chair and smile broadly at the text. *As I thought, I'm almost done.* The understanding I have gained of the world is nearly complete. I walked out of Edison's place with just two or three unsolved issues, and I now have validation that my short to-do list is still valid in 1905 and that—other than those issues—I have succeeded! *Thank you Lord Kelvin. Thank you*—I scan down to the footnotes—*Oh! Thank you the first Baron Kelvin, formerly Sir William Thomson!*

So William—now Kelvin—is still alive at eighty and appears to be a household name on both sides of the Atlantic, an authority trusted as a harbinger of the nearing completion of a project called physics.

Two clouds: black-body radiation and the failure to detect the ether. What about atoms and their charges? Are they not tiny but important unknown clouds too? Strangely, it appears that a century after Dalton, the eminent Lord Kelvin is not convinced that atoms exist.

This makes me curious about the others I have met. James and Katherine Clerk Maxwell were invited back to Cambridge, where James become the first Cavendish Professor and established the Cavendish Laboratory. I wonder how Cavendish, who was too shy to look me in the eye, would have liked having his name as a brand. Sadly, I find an obituary for James, who nursed Katherine through illness, then succumbed to cancer himself, dying childless at the age of forty-eight. The obituaries liken Maxwell's achievements in electrodynamics, thermodynamics, and beyond, to those of Newton.

Maxwell is dead, but I take some satisfaction in reading how his legacy continues to grow posthumously. Heinrich Hertz in Germany managed to produce *radio waves*—the electromagnetic waves Maxwell predicted with a frequency down in the thousands or millions of cycles per second, below infrared. At those frequencies the waves can be controlled using an electric circuit.

One person I read about who is controlling radio waves is Marconi, who has opened a radio station on the Isle of Wight. Apparently the actual signal—voice or music—is transmitted by either amplitude modulation (AM), which involves varying the strength of the signal, or frequency modulation (FM), which involves varying the frequency of the electromagnetic wave of each station within its assigned band of frequencies.

I wonder how the Dean would like the ability to broadcast to many Collectives at once. Then again, he might not like other deans being able to broadcast to us!

At the other end of the electromagnetic spectrum, one Wilhelm Röntgen, also in Germany, discovered unexplained rays that he named simply *X-rays*. These have turned out to be yet another form of electromagnetic waves with frequencies beyond ultraviolet. It seems that these waves can penetrate tissue. Röntgen asked his wife to "give him a hand," publishing the following image:

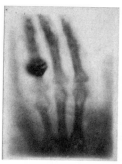

Röntgen's first "medical" X-Ray image

Some Swedish guy recently bequeathed an annual prize in physics, and Röntgen was chosen as the first recipient in 1901.

I find a nice summary of the electromagnetic spectrum and realize how little of it our eyes actually see:

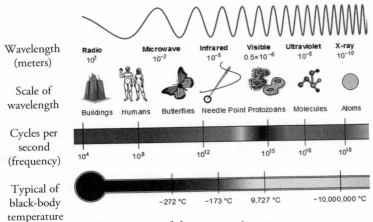

Wavelength (meters)	Radio 10^3	Microwave 10^{-2}	Infrared 10^{-5}	Visible 0.5×10^{-6}	Ultraviolet 10^{-8}	X-ray 10^{-10}

Scale of wavelength

Buildings   Humans   Butterflies   Needle Point   Protozoans   Molecules   Atoms

Cycles per second (frequency) 10^4 10^8 10^{12} 10^{15} 10^{16} 10^{18}

Typical of black-body temperature   −272 °C   −173 °C   9,727 °C   ~10,000,000 °C

The spectrum of electromagnetic waves

Exhaling, I lean back and look around the library. *Why aren't I in Germany with Röntgen and Hertz?* Here I am reading journal papers just like the other young students around me. What I need is a connection to Bern so I can get back to my own idiosyncratic method of study.

In less than five days, Fizz, you will either be cut off completely from physics, or thrown into a scary new world where you will be expected to know lots of physics. Focus, Fizz.

Okay. What about those bare negative electric currents through the vacuum that Edison showed me? Surely someone has continued that study, perhaps even here in Bern. I find that Röntgen was playing with such currents in a vacuum when he discovered X-rays. Apparently these negative electric currents are now called *cathode rays* since the negatively charged electric wire is known as a *cathode*. I come across another paper by the same Hertz, revealing that cathode rays can be produced not only by heating the cathode but also, in some metals, by shining light on it. This has been called the *photoelectric effect*. Rather like black-body radiation, it seems that no one can explain the specific patterns of the photoelectric effect.

Another "cloud" around electromagnetic waves: the photoelectric effect.

But what are the cathode rays? Finally I do find some answers in a paper by Professor Thomson—Professor Thomson who was second wrangler at Cambridge! *But not William.* This one is known as J. J.

Originally from Manchester, J. J. Thomson is now the second successor to Maxwell as Cavendish professor of physics in Cambridge.

I look up from the article and glance up at the electric fan on the library's ceiling. So *that's* what electricity is.

This Thomson found that cathode rays—in fact all electric currents—are made of particles. The particles are so small he could not detect any size whatsoever—as if they are just zero-dimensional dots. Others have named these little dots of negative electrical charge, *electrons*.

I'm intrigued. Electrons provide my first little glimpse into the nature of atoms.

The scandalous revelation about these electrons is that the very same electrons are released no matter which metal is used to produce the cathode rays. Different atoms share common components! The very word "atom" is a complete misnomer—atoms are not indivisible. The electrically negative part of the atom, the electron, can be plucked right out!

I read further and discover that the electron accounts for just 0.05% of the mass of the atoms—*ouch!* More than 99.95% of the atom's mass remains a complete and utter mystery.

This didn't stop J. J. from speculating about the rest of the atom. The atom, he suggests, may be structured like plum pudding. A big squishy positive atom with the little negative electrons stuck in like plums.

Plum pudding. I'm pleased to see physics writing has become just a little less formal since Newton's long Latin treatise. So J. J. is the guy who stuck in his thumb and pulled out a plum and said something like "what a genius am I."

J. J. Thomson's plum pudding model of the atom

Knowing about the electron seems like knowing everything about a guy's left little toe. Still, motivated by this first glimpse—and still unsure why I'm in Bern—I reluctantly scour journals for any hints as to the nature of the pudding part of the atom.

One hint is all the pudding I find. Henri Becquerel at École Polytechnique in Paris made the chance discovery that an idle sample of uranium can spoil a material called photographic emulsion, even if there is a solid object between them. Uranium spontaneously emits these mysterious rays continuously! What source of energy would allow uranium to constantly emit rays? Marie Curie from Poland, working together with her husband Pierre Curie—both now also in Paris—argue that this enigmatic radiation is somehow emerging from within the atoms. That's all we know about the pudding. The two Curies and Becquerel shared one of those Swedish prizes too.

I bury my head in my hands. Mother Nature is slipping open her kimono in front of physicists across Germany, in Paris, in Cambridge. I have a life-changing decision approaching me like a runaway wagon. *What am I doing in Bern?*

I go and wash my face. Next I pile all the science journals published this year in three large towers on the desk—English, French, and German, ignoring the funny glances sent my way. Then I get to work, plowing through the three furrows, reading the headings of the papers—language by language, journal by journal, paper by paper. I scan for the keyword "Bern" as well as for papers related to the unsolved issues of black-body radiation, the photoelectric effect, ether, and the structure of the atom.

After two mind-numbing hours I am on volume 17 of *Annalen der Physik*, a journal first published in the 1700s. I almost miss the paper that starts on page 132 of this year's sixth issue. But there it is: a paper published in Bern. The title translates to something like *On a Heuristic Viewpoint Concerning the Production and Transformation of Light*. I shrug. It's not much to go on, but it's from Bern and the title may suggest a connection to the first two "clouds" on my list.

The unknown author has only one previous publication, also from this year, explaining "Brownian motion"—a strange jiggling of pollen particles in water observed through a microscope by Scottish botanist Robert Brown almost eighty years ago. The paper suggests that random collisions with moving water atoms could explain the jiggling of the specks of pollen. *So this author is interested in atoms too.*

As I head off, I make a note to tell my Dad how I had to spend my entire morning at the university library, clueless that the guy I'm here to see is actually, according to the header of his paper, a junior clerk at the Bern patent office.

The patent office is a kilometer away in yet another perfectly rectangular beige building forming the corner of Speichergasse with Genfergasse.

If Edison's industrial research made patents seem exciting, the patent office feels more like a vast graveyard for ideas—floor upon floor, corridor after corridor, room beyond room, shelf above shelf, and volume upon volume of obscure ideas written by hopeful, but mostly naïve, would-be inventors, their names engraved on the tombstone at the top of the page.

I pull out a volume and leaf through.

In a reversible galvanic battery, the combination of an alkaline electrolyte which remains unchanged blah blah blah, a second conducting support, blah blah blah-blah-blah

Clearly most of these are not going to change humanity for better or worse. Yet people keep trying. *People want to innovate.* And one in a thousand ideas, buried alive in this labyrinth of bookshelves, might be the next telegraph or steam engine.

Navigating the maze of corridors, I pass one patent clerk after the other, finally locating the author of the paper on the third floor, room 86. The only hints of his physics hobby are small photographs on one wall of James Clerk Maxwell and Michael Faraday and a sketch of a third physicist.

A small dull thud greets me—a wooden-handled rubber stamp impacting some paper at moderate velocity. If I understand the system, some aspiring inventor somewhere has been granted a monopoly for some years, throughout the Swiss Confederation, on some esoteric improvement to some machine.

The patent clerk, one Albert Einstein, is standing at a small lectern, consulting a book, working his way through mountains of patent applications that dwarf my piles of journals. A small plaque announces his position as "technical expert third class." Apparently his position does not warrant a desk and chair. Well, perhaps if he wins one of those Swedish prizes for his ideas about light he will be promoted to second class.

Just a few years older than me—I would say mid-twenties—Albert wears his curly black hair unkempt, with a matching frizzy black mustache. He's cute looking, but even in his three-piece tweed suit and tie, his wild hair makes him look scruffier than other physicists I've met on my time travels. *Then again, he's a patent clerk, not a physicist.*

"*Guten Tag.* For 'vich' application is this?" Albert asks softly without actually looking up.

"Is that supposed to be Isaac Newton?"

"Vot?"

"That picture."

He glances at the wall then back to his paper. "*Ja.*"

"It's not much of a likeness."

Albert raises an eyebrow but doesn't look at me.

"Um, I mean not much like another sketch I saw of him."

"So, for which application are you here?"

"Ah, no. Actually I happen to be visiting Bern and heard about your paper about light—I was hoping to briefly discuss black-body radiation?"

"Well, only briefly as I am working, although it is not really a topic for such a quick discussions. You could say that the nature of light is a puzzlement wrapped in a perplexity."

"The nature of light? Surely," I say, "after Thomas Young's evidence for waves and James Clerk Maxwell's equations, that's all settled."

Finally he looks at me. "And yet despite all of that evidence for electromagnetic waves, light retains the ability to surprise us."

"Surprise us?"

"Light also behaves like a particle."

"A particle?" my eyes open very wide. *We can't be going back to Newton's light corpuscles after all of that.*

"Yes, a particle. The first clue came from Max Planck in Germany. It was he who finally explained black-body radiation, the pattern for how much light emerges from a fire or a filament at different temperatures. Planck found that he could explain the pattern perfectly based on the strangest assumption: that the jiggling electrons in a warm body always radiate light not continuously, but in specific packet sizes of energy. If you assume light is emitted in packets—or *quanta*—then all the formulae work out. You also have to assume that higher frequency light, say blue, is emitted in a larger quantum than, say, red. Based on that hypothesis, Planck could explain exactly which colors of light are radiated at each temperature."

"I don't get it, even if it explains black-body radiation. Why should a jiggling electron emit waves of light in discrete packets of energy?"

"No one knows. But it gets worse. I was trying to understand Hertz's photoelectric effect—you shine light on a metal and electrons fly off. The strange thing is that, if the light is below a certain frequency, no electrons fly off at all. For example in some metals, blue light might release electrons while red light—even very intensive red light—has no impact at all. How could that be?"

"Hmm." I frown. "So how does your paper explain that even bright red light cannot free any electrons?"

"Well, I thought, imagine we take Planck's idea to a whole new level. We do not assume merely that atoms emit light in discrete packets; rather, we assume that light by its very nature always comes in discrete *quanta*, or packets. Blue light comes in bigger packets than red light."

I look at the ceiling and think for two seconds. "Yes, I think I see what you're saying—the packets of blue light each have enough energy to knock out an electron. But each packet of red light is too small to knock out an electron, so no matter how much red light you shine there is no photoelectric effect. But—"

I try to imagine a wave that comes in discrete packets like particles. Could I imagine a wave at sea that comes at heights of 10, 20, and 30 centimeters but nothing in between? I can't quite picture it.

"—but," I continue, "sure, maybe these 'quanta' of light explain the photoelectric effect, but waves don't behave that way. And there's formidable evidence that light is a wave."

"Light is a wave. And yet," Albert says, "the evidence from both black-body radiation and the photoelectric effect prove that it is a particle. Some have called the particle the *photon*. Somehow light is both a wave and a particle! You could call it the *wave-particle duality*."

"But how? How can light be a wave and a particle?"

"As I told you, a puzzlement wrapped in a perplexity. Nothing in physics can explain this strange behavior. Perhaps this little conundrum hints that the microscopic world obeys an entirely different physics from anything we experience in the everyday world. These 'quanta' may occupy the brightest physicists for years to come. As for me, I am busy with another deep puzzle."

Not another deep puzzle—not now! Already the "clouds" on my short list seem to be merging together while turning a deeper more ominous shade of gray in the process. Both black-body radiation and the photoelectric effect are explained by the fact that light comes in quanta called photons, but that idea introduces a whole new type of physics in which things are both waves and particles. *Another deep puzzle on top of that?*

"Another," I hesitate, "um, puzzle?"

"Yes, the nature of space and time," he intones.

"What? Space and time?"

"*Ja, ja*, space and time. You know the concept of space and time since Newton—well, since forever—is not adequate. It seems that physics was developed with the wrong concept of space and time. So I'm redefining it just now. A new concept of time and space where there is no objective time and no objective space—everything is relative to the observer. So anyway—" Albert points to the pile of patents.

Wave-particle duality is bad enough. But redefining space and time— that's absurd. Where did that even come from?

"Um, *Herr* Dr. Einstein, perhaps I can buy you a cup of coffee?"

"Well," he laughs, "*nein.*"

"Oh," my face drops. "*Nein?*"

"*Nein*, not yet 'doctor'—call me Albert. But all right. Meet me at the *ratskeller* across the road after my work. Sixteen o'clock."

With that, he turns back to his lectern, apparently switching his brain from the fundamental nature of light, space, and time back to a dull pile of patents.

I watch Albert for a few more seconds before leaving. *Until this very moment I thought that plowing a field was the most boring job on earth.*

Albert Einstein at his lectern in the Swiss patent office.

The Gedankenexperiment

Outside the patent office, Speichergasse is a cobbled high street with terraced stone and cement buildings, all exactly four stories high, running continuously as far as the eye can see, creating an illusion of a road running through a deep, artificial canyon. In a flamboyant carnival of Swiss architecture, the contiguous four-story rectangular cement buildings are distinguished from each other through the use of subtly varying shades of beige, some even daring toward gray. The most ornate buildings dazzle the eyes with fine, parallel, perfectly horizontal lines ruled in the cement.

The ground level hosts cloistered shops while the upper three stories are homes and offices. On the road itself, either side of the central gutter, feet patter, hoofs clack, and motors hum.

I have a few hours to walk around town and prepare myself for this, shall we say, inconvenient turn of events. This Einstein dude may have dissipated the clouds of black-body radiation and the photoelectric effect, but he's replaced them with far more perplexing puzzles—the wave-particle oxymoron of light, and now, just when I think I'm winding up, of all the things, *a rethink of space and time!*

Passing a building site in its finishing stages, I glance at a team of builders and architects who have obviously been laboring for years, now lovingly fussing over final details of the landscaping.

I smile. Imagine Albert Einstein, a patent clerk, one evening in his spare time, walking into this building site and casually saying "*nein, nein,* why don't you just change the foundations of the building?" In the case of physics, for everyone but me, it's been three hundred years of science work painstakingly constructed above foundations that Albert is now "rethinking."

"So, remind me, your name is?" Albert says.

We're sipping coffee in a *ratskeller*—a bar below street level. Light seeps in from a narrow strip of windows just below the ceiling, illuminating the alternating red and green tablecloths, simple wooden chairs, burgundy wallpaper, and one stuffed deer head.

"My name is Fizz. Thanks for your time—if that even makes sense anymore! I just couldn't let your comment pass. What could you mean about no objective concept of space and time?"

I sip my coffee, savoring the bitter taste. *It's amazing how much I've taken to this stuff—I'd better wean myself off it in case I return to the Collective.*

"When people are saying some event happened at a certain time, or at a certain place or that some object has a certain length... well you cannot say that, it is a deficient statement."

"You can't?"

"*Nein, nein,* it is meaningless."

He says it flippantly but seems serious enough.

I try to imagine a world without a concept of space, but my head starts spinning in protest. "What can I say instead?"

"You may say 'I measured this time' or 'You measured that length,' but every person has their own clock, their own concept of space. You and I measure different times for the same occurrence and different lengths for the very same object. There is no global time; each observer—each person—must have their own subjective concept of time and their own concept of space."

"Come on... is this is a joke? You really expect me to believe that different people measure different times and lengths for the same thing? And that no one ever noticed this?"

"At everyday speeds the variance from one observer to another is negligible."

"B—but," I protest, "that would change everything. I mean, wasn't all of physics since Newton based on the perfectly reasonable assumption that there is a global concept of time and space that we all live in?" I contort my face. "Not to mention our human instincts!"

Albert waves his hand casually. "*Ja,* well physics should be redeveloped, for the new concept of time and space. Our intuitions should be adjusted."

"Oh, I see, sure, so we should just redevelop physics because you don't like the concepts of an agreed-upon space and time," I smile. "And change our conception of what it is to be human. Um, while we're examining patent applications, I suppose."

"Not during work. In the evenings."

I take a bigger gulp of coffee, willing the caffeine to stave off the oncoming headache.

Leaning forward, I look right into Albert's dark, deep eyes. "So tell me, Albert, what on earth is driving you to want to suggest redefining space and time?"

"There are some issues with the ether and the speed of light."

"You—what—I'm sorry, are you completely insane?" I chuckle. "You want to redefine the concepts of space and time and to pretty much redevelop all of physics because of 'some issues with the speed of light'?"

"Well, if you'll excuse me, I think I should be getting—" he starts to stand up.

I'm almost ready to let Albert go, but something intrigues me about him. I stand and reach for his shoulder. "No, no, no, sorry, just a joke. Please sit. I'm sure you have a great reason. Listen, can I order you some dinner?"

As Einstein sits down, I reopen the subject. "So what worried you about the speed of light? I think I learned that light travels hundreds of millions of meters per second." I recall James Clerk Maxwell linking the speed of light with the speed of his newly discovered electromagnetic waves.

"Yes, 300 million meters per second," Einstein nods. "It is usually symbolized by the letter c. My question is, 300 million meters per second relative to which medium?"

"What?"

"Okay. Imagine you are a hummingbird hovering above the sea and you drop a pebble into the sea."

"Can a hummingbird carry a pebble?" I ask.

He ignores my pedantry. "Imagine the resulting water wave spreads out in all directions in a circle at a speed of, say, one meter per second. Now consider a first scenario where you are hovering over the same point in the water medium at all times. After one second, what do you see?"

"After one second I would be over the center of a round water wave of radius one meter."

"Right." Einstein grabs a napkin and draws it. "Here you are hovering at the center of the expanding circular wave:"

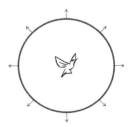

Bird that is not moving relative to water
finds itself at the center of an expanding ripple

"But," he raises a finger, "now imagine a different situation where you—still a hummingbird—are not hovering over the same point in the water but you are drifting slowly north across the water. Again you drop a pebble. Now, after one second what do you see?"

I grab the napkin. "Easy," I say. "Here, after one second I find myself north of the center of the circle:"

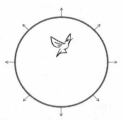

Bird that is moving relative to water
finds itself away from the center of an expanding ripple

"Correct. Now imagine that, hovering over a still sea, you do not actually know whether you are staying over the same water or drifting relative to the water. Could you tell by watching the wave?"

"Yeah, sure. I drop a pebble and wait a second. If I find myself at the center of the wave it means I am not moving relative to the water. If I find myself off-center, with one side of the water wave moving away faster from me than the other side, I know I'm moving. It's obvious. But, Albert, what has all of this got to do with light?"

"Well, light is also a wave. If I make a very quick flash of light, say I turn on an electric bulb and turn it off within a split second, what shape is the light wave that spreads out?"

Hmm, light is so incredibly fast it's hard to imagine a flash of light spreading out like the ripple from a pebble. *But in principle I suppose, it's exactly the same.* "Okay, a tiny flash of light would spread out—very fast—in a circle. Well actually, a sphere I guess."

"Now if you happen to find yourself at the exact center of an expanding circle of light what would you conclude?"

When I was over the center of the ripple from the pebble, I concluded I was stationary relative to the water that is carrying the water waves—that I was hovering over a fixed point in the water. "Okay, if I am at the precise center of an expanding ring of light, it means that I am stationary compared to the medium that carries electromagnetic waves. Stationary relative to the ether, I guess, that James Clerk Maxwell speculated about."

"*Richtig.*"

"But, Albert, how would you even measure if you are at the center or not, when the ring of light is expanding in all directions at three hundred thousand kilometers a second?"

"*Pah,*" he dismisses my concern with a wave of his hand.

I regard him. That gesture must mean something along the lines of "we are talking theory here; experimental physicists can dedicate their little lives to working out the details of how to measure it—why should I care."

The waiter interrupts. I pick up the menu. "So what can I get you, Albert?"

"Whatever," he says with considered apathy.

"Okay." I take charge and order two portions of apple röstis, some sliced meat, and zopf bread on the side.

"Great," I say. "So in theory I can tell if I'm traveling through the ether or not by seeing if I am at the center of an expanding light ring or not. What's the big deal?"

"What is the big deal?" Albert's strains his face. "This vexed me greatly because it contradicts Galileo's principle of relativity. Are you not familiar?"

I am very familiar with the principle, but the connection may not be as obvious to me as it is to you.

"Sure," I say. "Physics seems exactly the same from the perspective of someone moving with constant velocity. In the hold of a ship, you cannot actually tell if you are moving or not. In fact, it is meaningless to even say who is stationary and who is moving—I am moving relative to you, you are moving relative to me. No experiment can tell the difference."

Einstein bows his head slightly. "Now do you see the problem?"

No. I imagine myself back in the hold of the ship described in Galileo's book. "Oh, yes! I see what you're saying. Wherever I am, even in the sealed hold of a ship—even in outer space—I can make a flash of light and check whether I'm at the center of the expanding light circle or not. I'm like a hummingbird and the ether is like an ocean; *except that the ether that carries light is absolutely everywhere.* So wherever I am, I can always drop a pebble—make a flash of light—and check whether I stay at the center of the expanding light circle!" I fall back into my chair, starting to feel just a little vexed myself. "So light shatters Galileo's principle of relativity. Movement is not relative anymore because light is everywhere and some people are at the center of expanding circles of light, while others are not. You could say that the person at the center of the expanding ring of light is stationary and everyone else is moving… physics is *not* the same regardless of how you move!" I touch my forehead tenderly. "Pity, I was kind of attached to that principle."

Keeping his wrist on the table, Albert Einstein shows me the palm of his hand. "Not so fast, Fizz. Firstly, I too am fond of the principle of relativity. I do not wish to abandon it. "

"But we just said—"

"Secondly, Michelson and Morley in Ohio were actually able to perform an equivalent experiment. They made a flash of light, and as the circle expanded around them they checked whether they remained at its center or not, just like a hummingbird watching the ripple from a pebble. They expected that the Earth's rapid movement through space should be carrying us away from the center of the expanding light circle, like a hummingbird that is moving across the water."

Ah yes, I read this morning how my friend William Thomson—now Lord Kelvin—mentioned that Michelson–Morley experiment as one of the two clouds of nineteenth-century physics. I wondered why it's a "cloud." "So finally we have direct proof that the Earth is moving?"

"No. They found *nullpunkt*. Astoundingly, regardless of the time of day or season, whichever direction the Earth was moving, they still found themselves at exactly the center of an expanding circle of light."

Weird—that's like a hummingbird flying off and still finding itself at the center of the ripple. I pause to glance around at other tables. An elderly couple, a family with two children, two young lovers leaning toward each other across the red tablecloth—are any of them reexamining the fabric of our universe over dinner?

"So…?" I prompt Albert.

"So, I thought: what if light was special. If everyone is always at the center of an expanding circle of light, then Galileo's principle of relativity would be saved. No one could tell whether they were moving or not by 'dropping a pebble'—by checking their position in a light circle."

I chuckle lightly. "Sure, Albert, but what if you and I fly off in different directions—then we can't both be at the center of the same circle of light—at most one of us would be the stationary person at the center of the circle!"

"But what if we could?" he says softly. "Then Galileo's principle of relativity would be saved and the Michelson–Morley experiment would be vindicated."

"What? Well, sure it would be nice if we could both travel in different directions and still be at the center of the very same ring of light. Then again," I let out a small laugh, "it would also be nice if I could have my zopf bread and eat it. Wouldn't it be nice if I could be in seven places at one time? How nice it would be if—"

"*Ja*. Okay. And yet, this was my thought."

I look at the main entrance. *If I hadn't ordered dinner, I think I would walk out right now.* I mean, I visited Herschel to learn about infrared radiation and the existence of other galaxies, but that doesn't mean I have to accept Herschel's theory about life on the Sun. Now the computer took me to learn about the photon from this Einstein. That hardly means I have to seriously consider his musings about redefining space and time!

"Look, Albert, I think you may be... just a little confused. What you just said is like saying that two hummingbirds fly off in different directions, but after a second they are both at the precise center of the very same ripple." I look around hoping to see our food arriving.

"That is correct. I am saying that with light it is so. Everyone is at the center of every ring of light. With water waves, some birds are at the center of the water and some move relative to the water and are off-center. But with light we have no need for ether any more. There is no specific medium that carries light waves. Everyone is always at the center."

"In fact, everything is hunky dory." I glance again at the kitchen doors. "Oh yeah, except the little detail about how we can both fly off and yet be at the center of the circle."

Albert frowns. We eyeball each other for a moment.

"So this is why you redefined space and time," I break the awkward silence. "So that people shooting off in various directions can all be at the center of the very same expanding light ring?"

"Yes. That was my hypothesis."

"Well suppose—only hypothetically—that we were to, I don't know—entertain your hypothesis. How do you get from that one strange hypothesis to redefining space and time?"

"By *gedankenexperiment*."

"Sorry?"

"Thought experiment. It is not difficult. We apply our imagination to consider different scenarios and think about the implications of our hypothesis in those scenarios. Our hypothesis is that every observer always finds themselves at the center of every expanding ring of light, with each side of the ring always receding at the speed called c, three hundred thousand kilometers per second. Even if you try to chase the light ring in some direction, it still moves away from you with speed c in all directions. You are still at the center. You cannot chase light."

"Yeah, I get the hypothesis. At least I hear it. So how do you perform a thought experiment?"

Albert raises a single finger. "There is only one rule. For the duration of the thought experiment, the hypothesis is always true."

"The hypothesis is always true."

"*Ja.* You ready to try it?"

"Well, I'm a bit shy. It's, um, my first time."

"I think you are old enough, just let yourself go."

"Fizz to Albert. Communication check. Over."

"Over?"

"Oh, it's something my grandparents taught me—I guess it means 'over to you'."

"I see. Albert to Fizz. I hear you loud and clear. Um, over."

The hatch glides over my head and latches into the closed position forming an airtight seal. Through my ultra-green space goggles, I peer out of the meteorite-proof hatch glass and see Albert. He's holding some communication device to his ear and smiling at me warmly. The hyper-mega-super-engines are gently idling, ready for an activation signal. The copper walling of the spaceship is polished to reflect perfectly on the inside and out. On the exterior, the reflections are broken only by the red go-fast lightning stripes spanning the entire length. The little spaceship forms an elegant square two meters by two meters. I sit at the center, one meter from each side, one meter from the front and back. If I do say so myself, this spaceship is the very last word not only in technology, but also in style and elegance.

"Albert to Fizz. We may need to add rule number two for thought experiments: try to focus your imagination on the physics. Over."

"Sorry. Over."

"Okay," he says, "we are not going to notice any interesting implications of the hypothesis unless we go pretty fast. Stand by to accelerate to half the speed of light. Ready... I am making a very brief flash of light... *now*. Flash of light dispatched, repeat, dispatched. A ring of light is expanding around me. Proceed to chase that light beam. You are cleared to zero point five *c*. One hundred and fifty million meters per second. Bon Voyage. Over."

Pushing the throttle, the engines behind burst into action and my back is pressed violently into the seat behind me as the ship lurches forward. The world outside the hatch is a blur. $0.1c$, $0.2c$...only a few seconds have passed but already Albert is barely visible in my rearview mirror. The blood drains from my face to the back of my head, my cheeks are stretched almost to my ears, and my entire body is squashed backward like a pancake. But I relish the rush of power. $0.3c$, $0.4c$, and... $0.5c$. At half the speed of light, I cut the engine. Suddenly all the noise and vibrations cease and the ship cruises effortlessly, maintaining a constant $0.5c$. *One hundred and fifty thousand kilometers per second*. At this incredible speed, I can reach the Moon in three seconds, the Sun in sixteen minutes. Yet inside the cabin, everything is serene—there is no evidence at all of my fantastic speed. Galileo's principle of relativity is holding up: I can't feel my velocity.

"Albert to Fizz. Time for you to measure the speed of light. Confirming that the light ring from the flash I made earlier is moving away from me at the same speed *c* in all directions. I am at the center of the ring. A hundred seconds have passed so the light is thirty million kilometers away from me in every direction. But you have been chasing the light ring in one particular direction at great speed—are you any closer to one side of the ring than I am?"

"Um, how should I know? Over."

"Focus Fizz—rule number one."

"Oh, okay, yes. Fizz to Albert. Confirming that despite my chasing the light beam at an impressive speed, I am at the center of the same ring too. That light is still moving away from me at the full speed *c* in each direction. Galileo's principle of relativity is holding up—I cannot tell that I am moving even by observing a light circle. I have no idea how this could be happening though. I'm half way to Mars, how can we both be at the center of the same ring of light? Crew morale is good. Over."

"Let us proceed to explore how we are in fact at the center of that same ring. You and I are seeing the same speed for light. So what is speed? Over."

"Um, okay, speed is *distance divided by time*—meters per second. Over."

"*Gut.* Distance divided by time. So let us test whether time is playing any games. We need to set up an agreed measure of time and an agreed clock to explore time. Since our only hypothesis is about light, we should use light as a clock. So, Fizz, make a small flash of light at the center of the spaceship and put a detector on the right wall one meter away from you. When the light reaches the detector, we will call it one unit of time. Since that is the time it takes light to travel one meter we will call it one *light-meter* of time."

"One light-meter? But that would be just... 1/300,000,000 of a second!"

"So?"

"So... nothing, I guess. Okay, we will call one light-meter our unit of time."

I take a fresh paper napkin and sketch it for myself:

One light-meter tick occurs when light travels one meter from the center of the spaceship to the sensor on the wall

"Um, roger that. I have now circled around and as I fly over you"—I expertly guide the spaceship right over his unwieldy hair—"I am giving a very quick burst of light from my flashlight. I have set up a sensor that detects when it reaches the wall one meter to my right. I will send one flash after another. Confirming that we will call that one light-meter. I'm making the first flash now... my clock is counting light-meters. It is ticking forward very fast—three hundred million ticks a second. Over."

When he doesn't respond, I try again. "Albert?"

"Um, *nein* Fizz. Your clock is not counting light-meters accurately. From my perspective your clock is ticking slowly. Over."

"Based on what? Over."

"Based on the hypothesis. You see, I see myself at the center of that circle of light you made in the ship. And I see you and the spaceship moving forward. I see the light traveling more than one meter from the flash until it reaches your sensor on the wall because I see myself at the center of the ring and your spaceship moving. Standby to receive diagram on the hyper-space napkin remote-facsimile."

He draws this diagram:

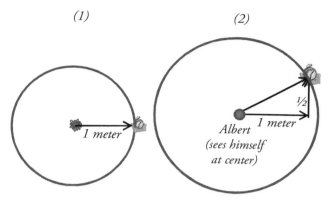

(1) Fizz sees herself at center of circle
(2) Albert sees himself at center of circle and sees Fizz moving,
so he sees light travels the hypotenuse of a triangle to the clock

"So," Albert says, "can you figure out how much slower your clock seems to me? Over."

Wow, this guy is really serious about sticking to his hypothesis. Staring at the diagram, I can't argue. Certainly from Albert's perspective, if he is really at the center of the same light circle and he sees me moving forward at half the speed of light while the ring expands, then he sees light traveling further than one meter to reach my sensor.

"Albert, I kind of follow how your hypothesis leads to the conclusion that, relative to you, my clock is slow. But I don't know any advanced math to tell you how much slower."

"You know this math."

"I do?" I squint and rack my brains. "Oh. You mean Pythagoras?"

It's just a right-angle triangle. The sides are one meter and half a meter. The square root of one squared plus a half squared is... about 1.12 meters. So Albert sees my light flash travelling 1.12 meters between ticks of my clock. He sees my clock running 12% slow!

"Fizz to Albert. I think I get it. If we assume that you are at the center of the circle then it follows that you see light traveling 1.12 meters between ticks of my clock and you conclude that my clock—my *time*—is running 12% slow. Pythagoras himself is probably turning in his grave. Over."

"Affirmative. Over."

"Good. Coming back to base. This hypothesis that we are both at the center of the same ring of light is absurd. It leads to a contradiction that you and I can't agree on what a tick of time even means. Abort mission. Over."

"Negative, please consult rule number one. Do not abandon mission. Abandon the concept of global time. You're concept of time is different from my concept of time. Time is relative. Repeat, do not abandon mission. Over."

Hmm.

"Spaceship to supreme galactic command, Fizz speaking. I have a maniac directing this mission. Request a sane replacement. Over."

"This is no time for a mutiny, Fizz."

"But this idea is entirely unprecedented!"

"Actually the idea of *time dilation* is not completely new. The idea of time changing due to movement was first proposed by the Dutchman Hendrik Lorentz and developed by Henri Poincaré to try to explain the Michelson–Morley result. However, they assumed it was at most some local effect of the clock. Now I am suggesting that time is inherently different for each observer."

Suddenly my mind is right back in the restaurant and I am staring at him. *There is method in your madness, sir.* Any normal person would have rejected the hypothesis long ago. We can't both be at the center of the same light circle when he's in the command post on Earth and I'm flying past Mars, but this is the man who reinvented the nature of light in his spare time. Perhaps he is not a normal person. And he clearly uses impeccable logic at every step. He's not actually mad, just a little... *detached.* I'm going to have to work a little harder if I want to disprove it.

"Okay, Albert, you're going too far. I'm going to find a logical contra- diction that will allow us to rule out the hypothesis and return to normality."

I had better do it on his terms, in a thought experiment. "Fizz to Albert, I have some directives of my own now. Set up your own clock—

place a sensor one meter to your side and make light circles. Count a tick when it gets to the sensor. Over."

"Confirmed. My clock is counting time-meters accurately. Over."

"Aha. Negative, repeat negative," I say. "Relative to me you are moving away at half the speed of light. I see myself at the center of the light ring you made and you and your sensor are moving through the ring. It's the very same argument the other way round! Your clock is 12% slower than mine. We have a logical contradiction—your clock is slower than mine and mine is slower than yours. That's impossible. Strike hypothesis. Abandon ship. Prepare homecoming party. Over and out."

"That's negative to your negative, Fizz. Yes, your clock is slower than mine relative to me and my clock is slower than yours relative to you. This does not contradict the hypothesis. It just means that time is a *relative* concept. This is our first major conclusion. When two people are moving relative to each other, each one sees the other one's time as slow. Time dilation is mutual. Proceed. Over."

"Goodness, you're persistent. All right we will proceed for now, but I'm going to show you that this bizarre world we're in is full of contradictions."

Back in the cockpit, dinner is served and I munching some zopf, trying to avoid dropping crumbs on the delicate controls. I check that my speed is still $0.5c$ and prepare for a dangerous maneuver.

"Okay, Albert to Fizz. Prepare for another flyby. Over."

"Flyby? Okay, proceed. Over."

"My spaceship is two meters long," I say. "Light covers two meters in two clicks, but I am traveling at half the speed of light, so expect flyby to last four light-meter clicks of my clock. Do up your jacket buttons, Albert—flying right over you at $0.5c$... now. Good, maneuver complete. Confirming it took me four clicks of my clock to fly by you. Over."

"Roger. Over."

"But, Albert, my friend, unfortunately relative to me you're clock is ticking slow, I was able to see that on your slow clock the flyby took less than four clicks. On your clock the flyby took 12% less time than I measured, about three and a half clicks. This contradicts the assumption that I am traveling at half the speed of light, so the hypothesis must be wrong. Over... and out?"

I take a slice of meat, allowing myself a slight grin as he frowns in thought. In the spare seconds I take my spaceship for a spin around Venus and confirm Copernicus' hypothesis that it is circling the Sun.

"Albert to Fizz. Confirm length of ship. Over."

"Confirming two meters. Over."

"Negative. The length was two meters before you started your journey, but you passed me at half the speed of light in less than four clicks. It follows that the length of your ship must have contracted by 12%. Your ship's length is 12% shorter. Relative to me, that is."

"What? Double negative back to you, that's ridiculous. Length of ship unchanged. Over."

"Albert to spaceship. Agreed, length of ship unchanged relative to you. Length of ship now 12% shorter relative to me. As we have seen, it follows from the hypothesis. We can only both be at the center of the same ring of light if your ship's length is contracted from my perspective and vice versa, I am contracted from your perspective. Your flyby has shown us that we must abandon the concept of an objective measure of length. As a logical consequence of the hypothesis, we must each have our own subjective concepts of space. I see you contracted, you see me contracted. Relative to me, your ship is—well, a bit flat. Over."

My grin is gone. "What are you saying now?" I say through a full mouth. "When I move at half the speed of light, relative to me everything else is 12% smaller? Is Saturn suddenly 12% closer to me? Will I see Jupiter itself not quite round but flattened by 12% in the direction I am traveling?"

"Affirmative," he says, "we have reached our second major conclusion—namely, that everyone has their own perception of distance—that is, length and position. Distance is a relative concept that depends on the frame of reference. Our thought experiment has reached its logical climax. The hypothesis has helped us understand the relative nature of space and time."

Albert sighs, sits back and lights up a pipe. The thought experiment has left me dizzy yet strangely satisfied. After a minute we both start picking lazily at our cold food.

I'm staring at a crumb in his moustache. "So that's a *Gedankenexperiment*?"

"*Ja*. Was it good for you?"

"Mind blowing." I laugh. "I need some time to digest this. Care for drinks in a half hour?"

"Your half hour or mine?"

E=M

Strolling through Bern, I enjoy the warm evening light and cool air. After some two hundred meters, I cross the pedestrian Waisenhausplatz, marked by a bronze pillar that functions as a slightly pathetic water fountain. For a moment I watch the water trickling over layer upon layer of rust and moss as it has probably been doing for centuries.

I used to think that science builds up just like that—layer upon layer. Today I learned that sometimes the fundamentals get completely shaken up.

Behind the damp pillar I get a view of the lush green trees that flank the River Aare as it winds right around this small city. Another four hundred meters bring me to the intersection with Kornhausplatz and a view of one of the river bridges opens to the left.

Two hundred meters. Four hundred meters. Height, width, depth. Far, near, big, small, high, low, area, volume. Spatial distance is so fundamental to every aspect of life. How can I even imagine a world without an objective measure of distance—where my big is someone else's small, someone's far is my near, somebody's twenty meters is my two meters?

What gave this maverick young man the audacity to take his hypothesis to such lengths, flying in the face of everything that was ever thought about the most intuitively obvious concepts of space and time?

Could it really be that no one has ever understood the nature of space and time simply because no one has ever travelled at speeds approaching the speed of light? In a world where travelling at close to the speed of light was common, would our intuition be based on relative time and space? *Would we find the concept of absolute time and space unintuitive?*

Talk about not what it seems!

Walking south on Kornhausplatz for a hundred meters—at least a hundred meters relative to me—I am now treated to a view of Zytglogge tower and its stunning old town clock.

The clock face boasts a colorful fresco of Adam and Eve's eviction from Paradise by an angel. Ringing Adam and Eve are large gold roman numerals from I to XII; decorated golden hour and minute hands point to the digits. The message is clear: Time has always been with us, all the way back to the beginning of humanity. As if to reinforce the message, suspended above Adam and Eve is an image of Chronos, the mythical personification of time. Little does Chronos realize that he is being blasphemed by a patent clerk just around the corner.

Walking through the gateway in the tower, I emerge under the eastern façade to find another clock face. On this side, under this timepiece is another instrument: an intricate astronomical clock with dozens of dials in gold, red, and blue. There is a calendar, a small sun indicating the Sun's position in the zodiac cycle, Moon phases, and times of sunrise and sunset. A frieze over the astronomical clock is painted with the likenesses of the heavenly bodies, a fitting headline for the stunning clockwork underneath. *Of course.* The clock is celebrating the relationship between time and astronomy. After all, we measure time in days, months, years— all celestial concepts.

I listen to the ticking. *Time.* The primordial concept so essential, so taken for granted, so uncontrollable. Time permeates every aspect of the human experience. What is time? Time, after all, is "of the essence." Time is... a great healer, time is money, time is ripe, time flies. We have me-time, downtime, timeout, time off. We give the time of day and do things when it's high time, just in time, or in the nick of time. Although times may change, since the beginning of time, people have taken time, wasted time, made up time, waited some time, and spent time till they're out of time. Until their time comes.

The concept of time is surely timeless.

I make an honest effort to imagine a world without an agreed-upon concept of time, where there was no global clock and each person experienced his or her own personal time. Where no one could say "meet me in half an hour for drinks" or "meet me at four o'clock" or even "at sixteen hundred hours." Where we couldn't say that this takes five minutes, or even say that one event happened before the other. Every time I try to imagine such a world, my head spins as if to avoid the thought. My mind is brewing an idea for another challenge. Will I—or others—find the fatal flaw in Einstein's ideas or will he win out?

Only time will tell.

As I walk back, it starts drizzling and I take cover in the bar, a couple of minutes early. Albert walks in a few minutes later. His hair is damp, but it could hardly get frizzier.

"So, Albert, about your ideas for time and space."

"My ideas, building on the thoughts of Lorentz and Poincaré."

"Yeah. Who are they, by the way?"

"Lorentz is Dutch. Poincaré is French, famous for *chaos theory*."

"Chaos theory?"

"It is a mathematical theory which sheds light on the limitations of physics. Poincaré found that even when you have deterministic equations of motion, it may be impossible to predict the future. Some systems are *chaotic*: The most microscopic change in the initial conditions can completely transform the outcome. So even though in theory the system is deterministic, you cannot predict its behavior in practice because you can never measure the starting situation to perfect accuracy."

I churn the thought for a moment. I glance at the rain outside. Every molecule of air and water vapor is obeying the deterministic laws of motion, but weather is so hard to predict, especially in the long term. It certainly seems chaotic at times. Perhaps the equations are such that the tiniest change now—say the flapping of a butterfly's wings—could lead to a tornado in a month's time. That would make accurate long-term prediction impossible in practice since you can never measure every molecule. *Interesting, but not our subject.* I order us two half-liters of Feldschlösschen.

"Albert, what happens to your equations when you get really close to the speed of light?" The barman presents us with a couple of half-liters of lager.

"The phenomena that we saw are taken to the extreme. The length of a moving object, relative to a stationary observer, contracts to near zero, clocks virtually stop. It is not a pretty sight," he shakes his head.

"Aha, as I thought. Let's try just one more *gedankenexperiment* this evening."

"Fizz to Albert. Speed is $0.5c$. Going to full throttle, repeat full throttle. Speed is $0.6c$, $0.7c$, $0.8c$, $0.9c$. Confirming my speed is 90% of the speed of light. Doing a quick Pythagoras calculation. My length relative to you is less than half the normal length, my clocks appear to you to be running less than half their normal speed. Confirming I am going to continue accelerating. Am planning to exceed the speed of light! Over."

"Stand by. Albert to Fizz. No problem, proceed with full throttle. We will monitor your speed from here. $0.9c$, $0.91c$... $0.98c$... $0.99c$—your length is now just one seventh of the normal length! Continue throttle. $0.991c$, $0.992c$, $0.993c$, $0.994c$, $0.995c$. The length of your elegant two-meter spaceship is now contracted to just twenty centimeters. You are in a flying pancake—at least, relative to me. Do you see what is happening to your speed? Over."

"I don't get it. I am continuing to apply full engines, why has my speed not exceeded c yet? Over." *When I get this thing above the speed of light I'll create some theory-busting contradictions, like clocks going backward or the ability to look back and see myself by overtaking the light.*

"Your speed is now progressing by much smaller increments. As you approach the speed of light the same amount of force is giving you less and less acceleration. Over."

"The same force giving less acceleration?" I think back to the laws of motion. "Impossible! Newton's second law of motion tells us that the acceleration is simply force divided by mass. The same force should always give the same acceleration—force divided by mass..."

But the hypothesis is always right—how will he wiggle his way out of this one? Uh-oh—*mass.*

"Albert to Fizz, it seems that the same force is creating one tenth of the acceleration it did previously. I conclude your mass has increased tenfold. Confirming your weight is now ten times more than your normal weight. Relative to me of course."

Does he charm all the women this way? "But Albert, mass is a constant property of a body!"

"Not anymore—it seems that if all observers are at the center of a circle of light, it follows that mass is also relative. As you approach the speed of light, your time approaches standstill, your length contracts to nothing, and your mass gets infinitely big—relative to me. Do you see Fizz? No amount of force would be enough to get you all the way to the speed of light c because you get heavier and heavier. Nothing can exceed the speed of light."

"So now mass is relative? Mass increases when energy increases!"

Einstein sips his beer thoughtfully.

"Well, *ja*... mass increases when energy increases. But I think it is much deeper than that. When I see two things increasing in unison—like mass and energy—I get suspicious. Why should two separate quantities increase in unison?"

"Um, why?"

"Well, perhaps they are one quantity. You see, I think mass *is* energy. Mass and energy are the same thing. You could just call it *mass-energy.*"

"But that's impossible—even if you're right that the mass increases when energy increases, what about when a body stops? Then it still has mass, but no energy! Those can hardly be one and the same."

"Or so we thought. But if my instinct is correct, that mass and energy are the same, it would follow that a body at rest, which has mass, does have energy. Mass and energy should be replaced by one concept: *mass-energy*." He grabs a napkin. "I checked the equivalence in my formulae and found that the mass m and energy E are related simply by $E=mc^2$, where c is a constant number—the speed of light."

"Aha, then they're not the same—you have to multiple by c^2."

"Well, c is just a constant number. It is a historical relic. You see, Fizz, up to now people did not realize that space and time were so intertwined. So, historically, we measure space in meters and time in seconds. But relativity teaches us that space and time are closely related and should be measured in the same units. From my perspective, measuring space in meters and time in seconds is as absurd as measuring north-south in meters and east-west in feet."

Measure space and time in the same units? What could he mean? Okay, I recall how Albert defined a light-meter of time to be the time taken for light to travel a meter. *So we can measure time in meters!*

Come to think of it, we could do it the other way round too and measure space in seconds. A light-second of space would be the distance light travels in a second. A *light-year* would be the distance light travels in a year—*we could measure distance in units of time or time in units of distance.*

"Well, okay, I suppose fundamentally we could measure both time and space in meters—so?"

"Yes, Fizz, that is how nature intended it. We should measure space and time in the same units. Now, if we measure both space and time in meters, what is the speed of light?"

"Um, by definition—light can travel one meter in one light-meter of time, so in these novel units, light travels one meter *per meter. One.* The speed of light is just $c=1$ in your 'natural' units!"

"Right. If you pick the right units of space and time, the speed of light is 1. And then $E=mc^2$ becomes $E=m$, plain and simple. Energy is mass. You see, Fizz, historically, just like we picked different units for space and time, we measured mass in kilograms, and energy in joules or sometimes in kilowatt-hours or calories. But now that we know that energy and mass are the same, it would be more natural to measure both energy and mass using the same units, say kilograms."

"One second there, did you say we measure energy in *joules*?"

"*Ja*, a *joule* is a measure of energy. And a *watt* means one joule of energy per second."

I recall the conversation at the waterfall near Chamonix and smile. "So, do we measure temperature in Thomsons?"

"What?"

"Never mind. Okay, so then from your perspective, c^2 is just a conversion ratio between different historical units for what is fundamentally the same concept. So let me check the conversion ratio. Based on $E=mc^2$, if m is one kilogram and c is three hundred million meters per second then mc^2 is... c times c..." I put down my beer and use my fingers to count zeros but have to cycle over my fingers more than once.

My jaw drops as I count. "Oh my goodness, Albert, one kilogram is just another way of saying *one hundred trillion Joules of energy!*" I pick up my drink and take a big gulp. "According to your equivalence of mass and energy, there would be enough energy in this glass of beer to power, to um—"

"To annihilate a city."

I slump back in my chair, and we stare at each other in silence.

After a few moments, I say, "I don't know about you, but that thought experiment wasn't so good for me."

Walking back to the hut, I look around. Everyday matter contains apoplectic amounts of energy, and we never knew it.

The electric street lights spontaneously turn on above my head, distracting me from Einstein's physics. I find myself reeling from the artificial light, attacked by feelings of nervousness and insecurity. *Why?* I look down and watch my feet stepping one in front of the other, again and again.

Slowly my mind returns to the physics I have learned. $E=mc^2$. Or if you pick the right units for time and space, just $E=m$.

The full extent of the irony dawns on me slowly. *No one ever noticed that mass was energy precisely because mass is so much energy.* Lavoisier declared the conservation of mass; Joule, and others, described the conservation of energy—as if it were a separate law. No one ever noticed that mass and energy are one and the same, precisely because c^2 is such a big number—mass is energy all right, it's just an unimaginably big dollop of energy. *Mass-energy.*

It starts to drizzle again. *It's as if no one ever noticed that the rain and the ocean are both made of water.* People watched rain falling into the ocean and didn't see the ocean rising because the ocean is just too big. Similarly the mass-energy, in a half-liter of beer is so immense that when one adds a tiny bit more mass-energy—by heating the beer, burning the alcohol or just squirting it—one doesn't even notice that you are adding more mass.

So people called the mass-energy inherent in material *mass* and all the other much smaller forms of mass-energy—heat, chemical energy and movement energy—were called *energy.* But it wasn't what it seemed: Mass and energy are in fact one and the same.

Finally I reach the small, unlit, densely wooded area behind Brückenstrasse where my hut is hidden. In one of the clearings between the trees, now some distance from the artificial city lights, the constellations are clearly visible. *Technology really does obfuscate nature.* I take a moment to gaze up at Mother Nature in all her nighttime glory, masquerading as a serene scattering of white dots, cloaking layer upon layer of invisible mystery.

Here am I marching toward the unavoidable fork in the road of my life. Trying to postpone the decision—the schism—until the last possible moment. *Yet I know that the moment is approaching me like a falling glacier which cannot be sidestepped.*

My insides spasm at the thought of it. This no gentle fork in the road with two paths diverging gradually away from each other. No, I'm approaching a stark T-junction.

To the right, a familiar and peaceful life engulfed in the love of my Mom and friends, with the Dean who understood me more than I was willing to acknowledge. *In an intellectual prison, where they will continue pumping me with slogans about greedy scientists.*

With Mom who loves me unconditionally, but… doesn't quite get me. *And whom I feel, every time I see an electric light, must be hiding something from me.*

To the left, an intriguing and foreboding life of intellectual freedom, where the only human being I know is a father whom I think feels guilty about inadvertently abandoning the unborn me he didn't know about, but who doesn't necessarily want me as a permanent feature in his life. *An unfamiliar life with no certainty of love.*

And there is Mother Nature, standing arrogantly at the crossroads, looking me in the eye as I approach, taunting me with her hidden layers, threatening to withhold so many secrets that I will never satisfy my curiosity and will have no choice but to turn left.

My upward gaze morphs into a glare.

What's your game up there—are you actively conspiring to deceive me? If the Earth is spinning, why work so hard to make it feel stationary? If behind the specks I can see there are millions more stars and beyond that entire other galaxies, just bring them out and show them! Why con us into feeling that we're made out of continuous and solid material if we're made of atoms? Why are you guarding the secret of atoms so closely that a century after Dalton proved their existence, only the puny electrons have been uncovered?

And in your most sinister deception of all, if time, space, and mass-energy are amorphous, subjective quantities, changing relative to each and every observer, why did you work so hard to disguise them as absolute quantities?

And if, Mother Nature, you are so big and complex and crafty, what importance do you even attach to little me?

Back in the hut, I think back to the *theory of relativity,* attempting to absorb it well enough to write it up. My mind is still rejecting the concepts of relative time and space as if they were foreign bodies. I hold my forehead. It's like—*revenge!* Galileo was forced to answer to the unfair court of the Inquisition and their literal reading of Genesis. But now the biblical concepts of time and space are being dragged in front of the court founded by Galileo Galilei—the principle of relativity.

But who asked for the theory of relativity? Unlike previous theories, this relativity doesn't illuminate any phenomena that I experience. Maybe it explains some obscure experiment in the 1880s in Ohio or some subtlety in Galileo's principle of relativity, but for me it actually obfuscates my understanding of the universe in which I live.

What gives Einstein the confidence? Other than Michelson–Morley, what experiments can validate this theory?

I see the note on my door. "Warning: Instant action at a distance." Instant action at a distance—Newton's controversial idea, inspired by alchemy, that eventually gained wide acceptance. But then Faraday and

Maxwell did away with action at a distance for electromagnetism, replacing it with electromagnetic waves. The stain of action at a distance remains only in the theory of gravity.

Opening the door, I glance once more out into the ROW. My feet are firmly on the ground, attracted to planet Earth. The Moon is orbiting above, trapped by the attraction of planet Earth.

"Which is it?" I say aloud. "Is gravity affecting me and the Moon instantly, or can nothing travel faster than the speed of light?"

I should not be expected to live in an ROW with such a contradiction.

"Computer, take me to when Einstein found a theory of gravity consistent with his relative space and time."

I close the door firmly.

While the hut starts its time travel, I lie awake doing mental battle with the new reality. Will anything ever go fast enough to measure these effects directly as we did in the thought-experiment spacecraft? Will we ever witness the obscene amount of energy—or rather mass-energy—apparently buried inside everyday objects?

How different the world would be if we could indeed travel very close to the speed of light, if we could experience time dilation, if our clocks could slow down. What would the world even be like if our clocks could slow so much that many years for other observers would be like... *one night!*

I sit up sharply as my brain suddenly reevaluates its instinctive hostility to relative time and space. Maybe Einstein's ideas are not so obscure, so irrelevant, to my everyday experience after all. Maybe there is somebody who does travel routinely at close to the speed of light and regularly experiences time dilation.

Could it all be as simple as that—does this hut travel at 99.99% of the speed of light all night in order to "transport" me to the future? *I am not "jumping" to the future at all—just experiencing the intervening years at a highly contracted rate due to fast travel.* My Dad didn't invent time travel, Einstein discovered it here in 1905. My Dad just figured out how to drive this box extremely close to the speed of light! So simple...

But how did I jump back in time?

As I sit up pondering, I feel an urge to lie back down. *Not an urge—a pull.* Yes, I am getting heavier again.

Relative mass. Of course—when I travel fast, I get heavier! *No, no, no... mass is relative—I am heavier relative to others—I myself should never actually feel a change in my own space, time, or mass.* That's Galileo's theory of relativity—I can't feel my own steady movement.

So why do I feel heavy?

Then again, to cruise through space at a speed close to *c*, we first have to *accelerate*. To approach the speed of light we have to accelerate *a lot*. I clasp my heavy hands. *This hut is not just moving, it must be accelerating upward.*

I think about what happens when a carriage accelerates forward—I get thrown back in the seat. That must be why I feel heavier, upward acceleration is throwing me down toward the floor. *I mistook it for stronger gravity, but it's just acceleration.*

Finally, I feel drowsy. I don't know to where or when I'm travelling, but for the first time I know how. After the acceleration continues for quite some time, I approach the speed of light. From my perspective, time and space feel normal, but if anyone were around to see this hut from the outside, they would see it contracted as flat as a sheet of paper but weighing thousands of times its normal mass, with its clock ticking thousands of times slower than theirs. *They could observe me their whole life and die of old age while they jealously watch me catching just a few hours' sleep.*

What is powering the staggering acceleration I am experiencing right now? I somehow don't think its coal and steam or an electric battery. What would provide enough energy to accelerate this hut to such incredible speeds even as the hut gets heavier and heavier? Here too, Einstein has provided at least a hint to the answer: $E=mc^2$. One kilogram of mass is equivalent to about a hundred trillion joules of energy. Not equivalent—*is*.

In the morning I wake earlier than usual. As I stretch, I notice that I still feel heavy. *Surely by now we are decelerating down from the lofty speed of light toward a soft landing.* Shouldn't I be sticking to the ceiling? It occurs to me that, if the hut turned during the night and is now travelling back to earth floor-first, then the braking would once again be throwing me toward the floor, once again simulating an increased weight. Dad thought of everything: he even had the hut aligned so I would be pushed against the floor, not the ceiling, during both the acceleration and the declaration each night.

I rub my eyes and print myself an outfit. Today I will find out how Einstein reconciled gravity with relativity. I will then have just three days left to crack Mother Nature's final two secrets: the nature of atoms and the "quantum"—the wave-particle duality.

Watch out Mother Nature—I might just be winning.
But then what?

Attractive Curves

I emerge into a green world: lush, soggy grass underfoot; a dense forest canopy overhead; a small pond just in front of me, its water green either from algae or from reflecting the leaves. I fill my lungs with the smells of nature and start marching. Gravity pulls my feet into the undergrowth with every step—now I need to know how. All I know is that the Earth's mass can't be acting on me instantly from a distance, as Newton would have it, because the concept of "instant" no longer makes any sense in the new relative world.

After a few minutes, a deer appears between the trees perched on the rocks, its antlers raised proudly. Water is squirting all around it. Soon I'm a little disappointed to find that the deer is a life-like sculpture and the fountain turns out to be the meeting point of a star of five ruler-straight roads that cut through this forest.

Crossing the tree line, views open up along the five roads. Open-top motorized vehicles, with shiny brass grills and elegant leather benches, mingle with horse-drawn carriages, each vehicle driving down one of the five roads, around the deer, and up another road. From one of the open automobiles, a windswept Alsatian barks at me, its tongue and tail wagging in the wind, and I can't help but smile back.

My eyes gravitate toward an imposing gate standing grandly a couple of kilometers along one of the routes. Twenty minutes later, now joining a crowd of pedestrians, I walk through the gate, crossing between a dozen large Greek-style columns under a bronze likeness of a triumphant Roman Goddess Victoria parading victoriously in a four-horse chariot.

Near the gate—the Brandenburg Gate, according to a sign—I purchase a pretzel from a small kiosk. Asked for a university, the old baker directs me to follow the main thoroughfare one kilometer east of the gate. Along the way I pop into one of the many shops to buy a small gift.

Back home I battle Mother Nature's threats of drought, parasites, crop diseases. But right now I'm doing mental battle with Mother Nature's disguises—her deceit—I have four days left to figure out what's really going on out here in this ROW.

I'm also battling the feeling that I'm just one insignificant speck on just one insignificant planet somewhere deep inside an entirely unremarkable galaxy.

Suddenly I smile. Maybe, in a way, the theory of relativity is my friend. *At least I have my own unique concept of time and space. No one else in the entire universe experiences time and space in exactly the way I do!*

At the university, another bronze-green horse greets me, this time carrying a likeness of Frederick II of Prussia under the shade of a lone soaring tree in an expansive courtyard. I enter the palatial four-story white building of the University of Berlin and ask for Professor Einstein.

The receptionist points at a man sitting in a tiny office, barely more than a closet, with no door.

"*Nein*, that's not him. *Herr* Professor Albert Einstein," I say.

"*Bitte schön*," she points at the man again.

I walk into the closet-office to talk to the man. He doffs his flat cap.

"You're not Einstein. Can you direct me to Professor Einstein, *bitte*?"

"*Ja*." With that he reaches into a crack in the wall and pulls a metal handle.

A crisscrossed bronze gate slides in front of me, separating me and the man from the lobby and I find myself in what can only be described as a cage. Holding the panic at bay for a second, I quickly scan the plaques on the wall of the little room for any hint of why the receptionist and this capped man are colluding to lock me up. I see the words "Siemens Elevator." While I try to think quickly what an elevator could be, the man turns a shaft and the cage starts to—well—elevate.

Before long, I arrive safe and sound on one of the higher stories. Laughing with relief, I step out into the Kaiser Wilhelm Institute for Physics. Consulting the notice board, I find that Einstein is now a full professor free of any teaching obligations.

"Couldn't hold down the patent job?"

Albert must be in his early thirties now, but I have to say that he looks poorly. Given that the computer took me to 1915, it must have taken him ten years to figure out how to make gravity consistent with special relativity—ten years for a man who completed a Ph.D., the theory of Brownian motion, the theory of the photon, and the theory of special relativity all in his spare time in just one miraculous year, 1905.

Albert doesn't recognize me immediately but I can almost see his mind working to place my face while he mumbles answers to my question. "Actually I was able to hold down the job for several years. I even made technical expert second class—"

"Congratulations. What has changed since then?"

"I quit the patent job in 1909 to become a professor at Zürich, then here in Berlin. I married, had some kids, separated ... okay I think I have placed you. Fizz, correct? Goodness you do not look a day older than you were—it must have been ten years ago!"

"Ah, well, what is ten years?" I say, shrugging. "Ten years relative to whom? For all you know, I've been traveling close to the speed of light since then. Perhaps, relative to me, it really isn't a day since we last met."

Einstein gives a hearty chuckle.

I clear my throat nervously. "Here, Albert, I brought a small gift." I hand him the little gift-wrapped package.

"*Danke*. What is it?"

"Nothing big. Something I was sure you could use. It's... a hairbrush," I smile.

Einstein laughs out loud. "Does it come with instructions?"

He slowly unwraps the colorful gift paper and then several layers of tissue paper—right now he probably doesn't know whether I'm joking or not.

Finally he nods. "Ah! This I know how to use."

Einstein removes the cherry wood smoking pipe and rotates it appreciatively in his hands. I watch him, beaming. *That wasn't difficult.*

"So, Albert, what I really wanted to know is whether you found a theory of gravity consistent with your theory of relativity? Gravity without action at a distance."

"Ah yes, I believe I have. It took many years of hard work. You know, it all started with a *gedankenexperiment*. You remember how that works?"

My muscles tense reflexively. "I do. You hold on for dear life to some bizarre hypothesis and you don't let go, even as common sense is blown to smithereens all around you."

I try to coerce my muscles to relax and my mind to open wide.

He smiles. "So. Imagine you are in a sealed box. You start feeling that you are a little heavier than usual. What would be your conclusion? Would you conclude that gravity has increased?"

Einstein starts to stuff tobacco into his new pipe.

"Seriously? That, I can imagine easily. I wouldn't necessarily conclude that gravity has increased—it could also be caused by the box accelerating, thereby pushing me toward the floor."

Albert looks up from his tobacco. "Oh. Outstanding. Um, how did you imagine that so easily?"

Oops. "Well—err—I just rode up here in the elevator."

"You noticed your weight increase from the acceleration in that thing?" He glances out the door.

"I—um—I'm very sensitive to my weight increasing."

"Well, you are correct. When you feel heavier inside a box, it could either be because of gravity—say if someone brought a new planet nearby—or it could be due to upward acceleration of the box. So, interestingly, downward gravity and upward acceleration feel equivalent. In fact, at this very moment we think we're sitting firmly in our chairs because of the Earth's gravity, but without looking outside we cannot really be certain that there is any gravity at all—we could be in a room in outer space that is accelerating. Let me demonstrate it to you another way. Close your eyes."

"Sorry?"

"Close your eyes. Tightly."

I close my eyes. I can hear Albert walking around behind my chair; he is almost breathing down my back. Suddenly I feel him tilt my chair backward. My body jerks and I spin around almost causing him to lose his grip.

Albert is grinning. "It is okay, Fizz, be relaxed. Keep your eyes closed."

"This was supposed to be a *thought* experiment," I say. "Well, go ahead."

I close my eyes again and focus hard on trying to trust Albert. My chair is tilting backward and, with my eyes sealed, I feel my weight gradually shifting from the seat to the back of the chair. Eventually, all my weight is on the chair-back. A very small thud suggests that my seat is now flat on the floor, facing the ceiling. It is fortunate that the skirts in this time period are long.

"So, what do you feel?" Albert says.

"I feel the blood rushing from my legs to my head."

"*Gut.* And what is your conclusion—just from the forces you feel now?"

"That there is a planet somewhere behind my back exerting a gravitational force from behind me."

"Or?"

"Alternatively, based on what I feel, my chair might be accelerating forward, and that acceleration could be throwing my weight back into the chair."

"Right. That is my *equivalence principle*. In a sealed room, gravity and acceleration feel equivalent."

"Okay, I think I see where you're going with this."

Einstein is taking Galileo's principle of relativity to the next level. Galileo said that, if you're in the hold of a ship and the ship is moving at a constant speed, you cannot feel the movement in any way. However, if the ship is accelerating, then you do feel that—you get thrown against one of the walls.

Einstein is adding a new twist: Even if you get thrown against a wall, you can't be sure that the ship is accelerating—it might be gravity— maybe you are thrown against a wall because someone brought a new planet nearby!

"So, Albert, you don't have a clue as to how to model gravity directly, huh?"

I smile. *This equivalence principle is a cunning mental maneuver.* Einstein doesn't have a theory for gravity, so he hypothesizes that gravity is equivalent to the more familiar situation of acceleration!

Knowing Albert, once he has hypothesized the equivalence of gravity and acceleration, he will stop at nothing—and I do mean nothing—to defend this hypothesis.

I hear Einstein saying "Bring me some matches." There's no one else in the room, so I peek through my closed eyes and see him talking to a small box with a button attached to a wire. *Perhaps someone has figured out how to send more than Morse code over an electric wire.*

"Albert to Fizz. Shine a beam of light from your right hand to your left. Over."

I'm still lying on my back, eyes closed. The elevated blood pressure in my brain may be enriching my imagination. I have no idea whether I feel pressure on the back of the chair because I am lying on my back near the planet Earth or, alternatively, because I am in a room, like my hut at night, which is accelerating through space.

"Fizz to Albert. I'm holding my two arms out in front of me. Let's assume I'm accelerating. I am shining a light beam from my right hand toward the left—now. Hold on... okay, the thing is that I'm accelerating so fast forward that by the time the light crosses from my right hand to my left, my left arm has accelerated forward and the light is hitting my left elbow instead of my left hand. Over."

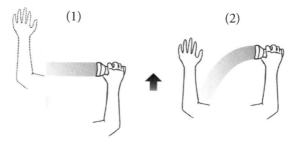

A light beam crossing an accelerating room:
(1) View from outside—left arm accelerates while light crosses
(2) From person's point of view, light seems to be curving.

"Albert to Fizz. Good. Now assume gravity."

I hesitate. "Um, Fizz to Albert, we may have a problem here. If I'm *not* accelerating, then the light behaves differently: It passes directly from my right hand to my left. Actually by shining the light, I can probably tell whether—"

"Fizz!"

"Oh, oops, I'm sorry—rule number one." I clear my throat. "Fizz to Albert. Exactly the same thing happens under gravity. I shine a light from my right hand toward my left, but somehow it curves down and hits my left elbow. Over."

"And so?"

"And so, um—*ah*—gravity attracts light! The light beam is 'falling' toward the gravitational attraction of Earth!"

"Affirmative. That is our first conclusion. Gravity attracts light."

I open my eyes. "So Albert, this radical conclusion that gravity curves light—can we test it experimentally?"

"I think it should be possible. For example, during an eclipse of the Sun, the sky darkens and you can observe stars adjacent to the Sun. We should be able to detect that the light from those stars is slightly bent by the gravity of the Sun. In fact, I have issued a challenge to experimental physicists to test that during an upcoming eclipse."

"That's exciting. Will they?"

"Obviously, right now, I have no communication with physicists outside Germany, and physicists here cannot travel far."

"Obviously?"

He shrugs. "You know."

"Um, of course."

"Now, Fizz, close your eyes again. And look at your watch."

"Err, I'm not wearing a watch. And my eyes are closed."

"Fizz—"

"Okay, sorry." I physically hold my wrist somewhere in front of my closed eyes and imagine I'm reading a watch. *What do I even call that direction, given that I am imagining I don't know that planet Earth is behind my back?* Well whether my back is pulled down by gravity or acceleration, the direction against the pull feels like "up." "Confirmed I'm looking at my watch which is 'above' my face."

"Does it appear to be ticking normally?"

"Yes?"

"Think, Fizz, are you accelerating forward very dramatically?"

"Hmm, well, I suppose that between two ticks I'm accelerating toward the watch, so as the light from the second tick travels toward me, I accelerate toward the light and see the second tick within less than a second. So my watch appears to be ticking fast! If there was another watch right next to my face, it would appear to be ticking more slowly than the watch above my face."

"So—"

"So… if the pull I'm experiencing is actually gravity and my wrist is higher than my face—based on the hypothesis of equivalence—I would have to see the same thing: I would see a watch that is higher up ticking fast, which means that a clock that is lower—closer to a source of gravity—must… tick slower?"

"*Wunderbar.* Another testable conclusion. I predict that time passes slower in a valley than it does up a mountain—another form of time dilation. Not easy to test, since the differences with Earth's gravity are small, but testable."

I open my eyes and look at Albert. "Seriously? Gravity makes light bend and makes clocks slow down?"

"*Ja.*"

Ja. That means: *Yes, Fizz, I am dismantling whatever was left of human intuition.*

Still lying on the floor, I look at Einstein. "But what *is* it? What is gravity?"

With a smile, he gestures for me to resume a normal seated position at his desk.

"The curving light gave me the critical clue as to the enigmatic nature of gravity. Allow me to illustrate by way of a little story. Imagine two tiny beads, Alice and Bob. Alice and Bob live their entire life in a one-dimensional world, along a long, thin wire. The wire is their universe; they have no conception of a three-dimensional world. For Alice and Bob, life is moving left and right only. There is not even any way for them to pass each other. Like two obstinate politicians, Alice will always be to the left of Bob. And, perhaps again like politicians, they have no capacity to imagine a three-dimensional world because they have no experience of such things. In Alice and Bob's world, there is a gravitational attraction between them. Bob is heavy set, Alice is petite. They both feel pulled toward one another, but Alice is accelerating toward the heavier Bob more intensely than Bob toward Alice."

Alice and Bob's world sounds incredibly dull. I try to imagine a conversation with Alice. Could I explain to her about three dimensions? *"Alice, there are other directions you could move in, perpendicular to the one direction you've been moving in up to now."* I don't think Alice would be able to grasp that. *I myself can barely imagine a life on the Outside in 2110.* Maybe I could describe three dimensions mathematically to Alice in terms of Descartes' x, y, and z axes, but I doubt she would be able to visualize those dimensions.

I look back to Einstein. "Okay, go on," I say.

"Alice and Bob start life with Alice on the left and Bob on the right of their one-dimensional world. Due to gravitational attraction, they start drifting toward each other. Bob is lonely and is quite excited when Alice drifts close enough for him to see her. But Alice gets shy when she sees Bob; she starts propelling herself vigorously to the left away from Bob, overcoming gravity. Bob is still drifting slightly leftward after her. After a while, Alice gets tired and thinks, 'Well, what the heck. I will give Bob a chance.' So she stops propelling herself and they both drift toward each other under the influence of gravity. Our story ends in a romantic cliff hanger, with Alice drifting rapidly rightward toward the heavy Bob and Bob drifting more slowly leftward toward Alice."

"Albert, please don't stop, I can't take the suspense." I sniff the scent of tobacco in the air.

"Now," Albert says, "do you think you can draw the story, not just one moment—but the whole story?" He hands me a sheet of paper and a pen.

I think for a moment. "Yes, I think I can. I can use the height of the page for time and draw Alice and Bob's position at an early time across the bottom of the page, and their positions later at the top like this:"

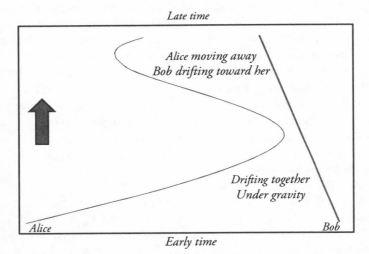

Late time

Alice moving away
Bob drifting toward her

Drifting together
Under gravity

Alice

Bob

Early time

The world lines of Alice and Bob:
A one-dimensional world, plus time, drawn as two dimensions

"Good. Do you see what you have achieved? Alice and Bob live in one dimension of space, but time is also a dimension. When you add the one dimension of their space to the dimension of time, you actually get two dimensions of space and time, which you have just drawn on a two-dimensional sheet of paper. Your diagram is called a *spacetime* diagram. Those lines are the *world lines* of Alice and Bob as they live their life through spacetime."

Big words, but a simple concept, really. I used up and down on the page to represent time.

Albert points at my diagram. "You could think of our world the same way—three dimensions of space and one dimension of time, giving four dimensions of spacetime. In terms of Descartes' axes, every event is described not only by three numbers x, y, and z but actually by four numbers: x, y, z, and t for time. For example, near Earth you can describe an event with the four numbers of *longitude, latitude, altitude,* and *time.*"

Hmm. I can't visualize four-dimensional spacetime, but I accept that it takes four values to describe an event. *So I guess that is four dimensions.*

"But, Albert, what's all of this spacetime got to do with gravity?"

Albert takes the sheet of paper and curves it into a kind of trough.

"Look: Alice and Bob thought they were drifting toward each other because of a gravitational *force*, but all along they were drifting toward each other because—" he pauses to give me a chance.

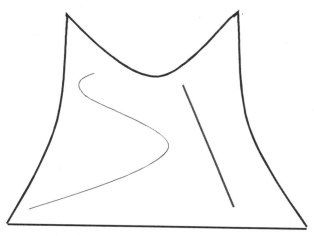

Gravity is a curvature of spacetime

My eyebrows spring up. Albert's every thought is more radical than the one before. "Because their spacetime is *curved*? They didn't even realize they were living in a curved spacetime?"

I suppose that for us, looking in from the outside on their two-dimensional spacetime, it is easy to observe Alice and Bob's two-dimensional world being curved, but Alice and Bob could never imagine that. *They would probably think that their mutual attraction is some mysterious action-at-a-distance gravity rather than what it really is: a curvature of spacetime!*

Unless, of course, one of them had the unusual mind of an Albert Einstein.

Albert shows me a diagram visualizing the fact that each mass bends the spacetime around it.

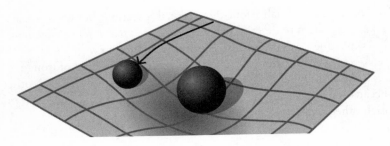

Gravity: Each mass curves spacetime, in turn attracting other masses

"I get the idea. But are you suggesting that *we* are living in a curved four-dimensional spacetime?" I massage my temples. "I can't imagine it."

"Do not try. The human mind cannot visualize it. But when I started doing research, I found that mathematicians in the nineteenth century were busy creating geometries for studying such curved spaces."

"Were they—why?"

"Out of sheer mathematical curiosity. You see, the ancient Greek Euclid had formulated geometry in the flat plane. Two parallel lines never meet, etcetera. Much more recently, mathematicians such as Gauss and Riemann created mathematics for geometry of curved spaces and for any number of dimensions. Their math was waiting there, ready for me—once I finally understood the need to model curved four-dimensional spacetime."

I wonder if mathematicians like Riemann would be excited to see their abstract models at the heart of a physical theory of the world or if those pure mathematicians would perhaps actually be upset that their theoretical musings were being dragged away from the realm of the hideously abstract and dirtied in the real world!

"So, no more action at a distance?" I want to breathe a sigh of relief, but I hadn't counted on this cathartic process where all my human intuitions are cleaned out together with action at a distance.

"Action at a distance is dead. That is a great achievement of my theory. And there is another advantage. You know how heavy and light objects fall at the same rate?"

I nod—*how could I forget*. I also remember that Newton's explanation, something to do with the extra force being cancelled out by the extra mass to give the same acceleration, seemed a little contrived.

Of course! Objects are not falling because they are pulled down, they are just taking the shortest most natural path through a curved spacetime—so it is completely natural that objects of different masses follow the same path!

Once again, the universe is hopelessly different from what it seems. In the normal course of events, I wouldn't stand a chance of deciphering the universe's twisted secrets—literally twisted apparently—in the dwindling time available to me. *With this Einstein in my corner, maybe I have a small fighting chance.*

My mind is racing now. *Curved spacetime!* For physicists, this must be like a child being presented with a new set of building blocks. With the curvature of spacetime, all kinds of universes must be possible. Are there any limits?

"Albert, what would happen as gravity became stronger and stronger? Is there a limit to the curvature?"

"According to my theory, there is no limit. In fact, if a star is massive enough, it must eventually collapse into a mass that is so dense, it will curve spacetime to the point that even a light beam cannot escape. A *black hole*—gravity is so strong that nothing, not even light, can escape. Time is curved too by a black hole. An observer from the outside sees time standing still for someone approaching a black hole, so you never actually see them crossing the point of no return—known as the event horizon—into the abyss! Somewhere within the black hole the curvature becomes infinite and my equations break down. Such an infinite point is known as a singularity."

I try and pretty much fail to imagine such a nefarious place as a black hole, which sucks in everything and lets nothing out, which bends spacetime so extremely that time as seen from the outside comes to a standstill and spacetime on the inside reaches a singularity of infinite values.

"Goodness. Black holes are way weirder than Laplace ever anticipated. Albert, what are you calling this theory?"

"The *general theory of relativity*. The previous theory, which I now call the *special theory of relativity*, deals with relative space and time in the special case where there is no gravity. The general theory of relativity explains gravity by introducing curvature into spacetime." Albert frowns. "But there is still one serious open problem—"

"You mean besides the problems of the theory being too abstract to conceptualize, too bizarre to be true, and as of yet unsubstantiated by any evidence?" I smile.

"Um, yes. Besides that, there is the issue that, when you consider the overall cosmology of general relativity—the total structure of spacetime—it turns out that spacetime cannot be static. The equations suggest the strange situation that the universe must be either expanding or contracting. I am looking for a solution to this oddity. I may have to modify the theory to make it consistent with the fact that the universe is static. I'm thinking of adding a *cosmological constant* to the equation to explain a static universe."

"Yes, please, a stable universe would be kind of important."

I pick up the sheet of paper with the world lines of Alice and Bob. This two-dimensional analogy is as close as I can get to an intuitive understanding of Einstein's new general theory of relativity. I bend the paper and consider how heavier masses cause more curvature, thereby affecting other masses. I imagine beams of light following the shortest path through the curved spacetime. I visualize different masses falling at the same rate because their fall is guided not by any force, but by the pure geometry of spacetime.

Then I try out some more extreme situations. Albert has claimed that, when there's sufficient mass—perhaps a large collapsing star—black hole monstrosities are inevitable. So I try to depress a point in the paper to create a curved well of spacetime so deep that even light cannot escape. Of course, paper doesn't stretch very well and I rip it slightly. *Well, perhaps this small fissure is a reasonable analogy for the infinite singularity inside a black hole.*

Curvature opens a world of new possibilities. I twist and turn Alice and Bob's two-dimensional spacetime as if I were a god. I curl it into a tube. Could their one-dimensional wire actually be a loop, a world where if you travel enough to the left you might come back from the right? *Could our world be a loop?*

Now I curl the sheet along the time direction, bringing the edge of the paper representing the end of the story alongside the edge representing the start. Could their time be circular: history repeating itself again and again?

I start to get more creative. I can't quite do it without tearing the paper, but I imagine a two-dimensional spacetime where not all of time repeats, but maybe a tunnel links two different times at a particular place.

I freeze for a moment.

"Quick, Albert, give me a pen. This curvature opens up the strangest possibilities." I sketch furiously. "Look at this, Albert." I plant a finger firmly on my drawing. "Tell me, could you have this kind of tunnel in spacetime?"

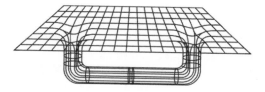

A wormhole in spacetime

Albert responds to my flustered sketching and questioning with his characteristic calm. "Yes, the equations might permit such a wormhole—although even if the equations permit it, that does not mean it necessarily exists."

My mind is elsewhere. I must be looking right through him as I say, "It does. Tunnels in spacetime exist."

On my way back along Unter den Linden toward the gate, I smile at a single-file procession of little boys, not more than ten or eleven years old, heading my way, chanting. They're wearing an assortment of formal clothes—some sort of uniforms—with decorated flat caps, long coats, short trousers, and thick tights. Every one of the boys holds an identical black-and-white placard up high as they march cutely down the high street.

As the kids march closer, the words come into view and my smile fades fast: *wer kriegsanleihe zeichnet verkürzt den krieg*. It means something like "supporting the war bonds shortens the war."

I watch the little kids, now shocked and saddened to see them being used to raise money for a war about which they, like me, probably understand nothing. Soon I find another boy selling newspapers and purchase a copy of *Berliner Tageblatt*. Nervously, I unfold the wide, thin sheets of paper.

My muscles tense as my eyes scan one war story after another, slowly piecing together the scale of the conflict. Apparently the German Empire is allied with Austria-Hungry and with the Ottoman Empire. The "enemies" include the British Empire, the Russian Empire, France, and recently the United States, among others. I'm horrified to read about German *unterseeboots*, or U-boats, currently tightening a siege which they promise will starve the British Isles.

I glance up from the paper to see a convoy of dark green, motorized trucks drive right past me, packed with armed, uniformed men wearing dome-shaped metallic helmets. The boys, now past me, wave their placards and cheer.

For just a second the sounds of the trucks' engines distract me from the alarming site: The pitch of each truck's engine sounds higher when approaching me and lower when it drives away. *Why is that?*

Then I hear another motor, this time from directly above me. I look up and see a bright red aircraft flying overhead; it has a stack of three sets of wings and carries a black cross prominently on each wing. I wonder if the aircraft too is part of the war.

I turn back to the newspaper as pangs of despair flood me. Shells are being aimed using Newton's equations of motion and calculus. Right in front of me truck engines are employing the Carnot cycle to carry troops and weapons. Above me aircraft are lifted by Bernoulli's effect. I recall how Einstein ordered matches and wonder whether commands are being dispatched to armies using electric currents.

The newspaper starts shaking in my hands. *I've been enjoying a chat about physics, unaware that physics is empowering a huge outbreak of the Great Deterioration, engulfing and destroying the world around me.* I toss the paper and run much of the way back to the forest, scared and lonely. It's true—the world has become a machine for transforming physics into death. *And I was wondering why Einstein can't collaborate with physicists outside Germany right now.*

Only a couple of hours later does my mind tire of worrying about the fighting and gradually turn back to the new pliable spacetime physics I learned of today. I remove the sign "Warning: Instant action at a distance" from the ROW label—a warning that has been with me—with the world—for the 250 years since Newton in the 1660s. The world may have relative space and time, the world may have *curved* spacetime, the world may even have tunnels through spacetime, but the world does not have instantaneous action at a distance. *Good riddance.*

I add a brand new section to the ROW label:

Context: The world plays out in four-dimensional spacetime. Space and time are relative to the observer. ~~Mass~~ Mass-energy causes spacetime to curve, and the effects of this curvature appear as gravity (general relativity).

I read it again. Space and time were not even mentioned on my label up to now. Einstein has promoted space and time from the passive background to active participants in the dynamics of the world. *Einstein is like an artist who, after years of painting over the canvas, suddenly decides that the fabric of the canvas may itself become an active part of the creation.*

I survey the label—it is almost complete. But I think of the war raging around me and feel no satisfaction in my achievements. The stakes have been raised again on both sides. The Outside really does have awful wars fueled by science. Yet in the Ecommunity, I will miss out on intellectual discoveries way more exciting than I could possibly have imagined—like curved spacetime.

I take the warning about action at a distance and write on the other side:

Warning: Physics can empower warfare.

I look at the artifacts, willing them to distract me. If Dad was determined to interfere, he might have given me a heads up about this relative curved spacetime thing! *But then I would not have had the pleasure of meeting Einstein and discovering it myself.* I put the lens and the bottle of earth in the center of the desk and put the rest of the artifacts back in the box. I know a lot about light, but there is still the mystery of the wave-particle duality—how can light be a wave yet come in "quanta"—discrete patterns called the photon. Then of course there is the atom, which—other than the little electron and some radiation from uranium—has kept itself entirely concealed. My agenda for the last three days is clear—atoms and the wave-particle duality.

The next two to three days is about all that is clear in my life.

"Computer, let's crack this atom mystery. Somewhere peaceful."

The Modern Alchemist

Day 19. Whitworth Park, Manchester, England. 1919.

How apt to wake up in this particular city this morning. Dalton proved the existence of atoms in Manchester 120 years ago. J. J. Thomson travelled from Manchester to Cambridge to reveal the first piece of the puzzle—the electron. Today, I hope that the computer brought me back here to witness the secrets of the atom finally being exposed.

I count myself lucky that I had to endure the frustration of knowing that atoms exist, but knowing nothing about them, for only ten days. *For everyone else, it has been four generations.*

Whitworth Park turns out to be almost adjacent to the University of Manchester, but I walk around a block or two on the way, perhaps to reassure myself that the war is over. On Wilmslow Road, I'm amazed by the variety of shops and goods—I suspect the frenzied development of this city has continued while I was busy touring London, Bath, Chamonix, Glenair, Bern, and Berlin. As I walk past store after store, my own feeling of excitement gradually returns.

I pass a store selling beautiful dresses, all far more practical and comfortable-looking than anything I've worn on my journey so far. The middle-aged shopkeeper is standing in the doorway; like me, she's wearing a tunic over a long underskirt. She catches me ogling the incredible variety of goods in the window and starts chatting to me.

"I'm just amazed by the amount of stuff available in this city," I say.

"They don't call it 'Cottonopolis' for nothing," she says. "So what brings you to warehouse city—the shopping I hope?"

"No, sorry. To me Manchester will always be 'atom city,'" I say, and take my leave.

"It was ten years ago. It was quite the most incredible event that has ever happened to me in my life. It was almost as incredible as if you fired a 15-inch shell at a piece of tissue paper and it came back and hit you."

When I finally arrived at the university, the department of physics' notice board informed me that the chair in physics is held by a "Nobel" laureate who is also a knight of the realm. So I'm now talking to Sir Ernest Rutherford, a prim man who's pushing fifty. *He really needs to lose that moustache.* I listen to him recalling the experiment he performed with his students ten years ago.

Ernest, I have learned, was born a "kiwi" to British ex-pats. In New Zealand, he studied first in Canterbury College, then at the University of New Zealand, before moving to the UK to Cambridge University. Later, his first professorship was at McGill University, Montreal, but he told me how he much prefers teaching here at the University of Manchester.

"I find the students here regard a full professor as little short of Lord God Almighty," he told me earlier, "it is quite refreshing after the critical attitude of Canadian students." Manchester must be delighted too as after arriving here in 1907 Rutherford brought home that Nobel Prize in 1908. The award may have actually been premature as Sir Ernest is now telling me about his monumental discoveries in 1909.

"Um, what shell, what tissue paper?" I ask.

"I had my students Geiger and Marsden shoot the radiation emanating from radium atoms through a very thin leaf of gold. The particles were so fast and the gold leaf so thin that we expected the particles to easily penetrate straight through. And mostly, that is precisely what occurred." He points at a picture of the experiment on the wall:

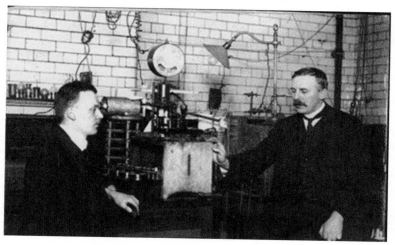

Geiger and Rutherford bombarding a thin leaf of gold with alpha particles

"Mostly?"

"Mostly. But once in a while we were shocked to find a particle backscattering straight back at us!"

"So you mean—those particles must have been hitting something pretty hard to bounce like that?"

"Right."

"Oh. So," I say, "atoms are not much like plum pudding after all?"

"Atoms turn out to be nothing at all like any kind of pudding. We realized that the unexplored positive part of each atom must be very small and concentrated. I christened it the *nucleus*. The electrons must be orbiting around a small hard positive core, not suspended within the positive charges."

"Orbiting *around?* Then what's between the nucleus and the electrons?"

"Absolutely nothing. That was the real scandal. We discovered, by analogy, that if an atom were a soccer field, the nucleus, which carries 99.95% of the mass of the atom and all the positive charge, would be smaller than a pea at the center of the field. The electrons, with the negative charge, would be minuscule specks around the outside of the field, comprising less than one thousandth of the mass. Or if Manchester were the nucleus, the entire British Empire would be the atom; a sheep in New Zealand would be an electron."

"And the rest?"

"By volume, some 99.99999999999% of the atom is void. Solid materials are mostly nothingness."

What? I stare at Rutherford as he rummages around in piles of old papers and finds me a chart:

J. J. Thomson
plum pudding model

Rutherford atomic
nucleus (1909)

I pinch the corner of the desk in front of me. It feels solid enough, but apparently it is overwhelmingly empty. *Matter doesn't seem like it is.*

I return my attention to Rutherford. Everything I've learned about physics has always been overshadowed by the question of what stuff is made of. For the first time the answers—however unintuitive—seem to be within grasp. *Did he go that critical one step further?* I lean forward and look straight at him.

"So, Sir Ernest. This atomic nucleus—what is it? Do you know what it's made of? Does each element have its own unique nucleus?"

"Ah, no. The world turns out to be much more elegant than that."

"Well go on, do tell," I say.

"I have recently found evidence that all the different nuclei are constructed of the very same *subatomic particle*. I call it the *proton*. This proton is the positive charge in materials. You see, the hydrogen atom has a nucleus of just one proton; helium has two, and so on up to uranium, which has ninety-two. All the atomic nuclei are just bunches of the same proton."

He pulls out another chart from higher in the pile:

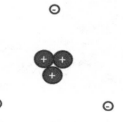

Rutherford's model of the atom after discovery of the proton (1919)

Rutherford describes the proton in a tone which would sound more appropriate if he were detecting a hint of ginger in his lunchtime soup. I have to remind myself that this man has discovered the fundamental ingredient of 99.95% of everything, an unknown that has surely baffled every thinker that ever lived.

So that's it: Matter comprises positive protons clumped into nuclei. That's what we are. Plus some much less massive negative electrons orbiting them.

"Let me show you the *periodic table*," he says. "Russian chemist Dmitri Mendeleev started to organize the atoms back in 1869 based on shaking test tubes. He found that as you count through the atoms, some of the properties repeat themselves periodically. But Mendeleev had no idea that what he was really doing when he enumerated the atoms was counting protons. Here is one of several modern versions of the periodic table—this one's by Nodder:"

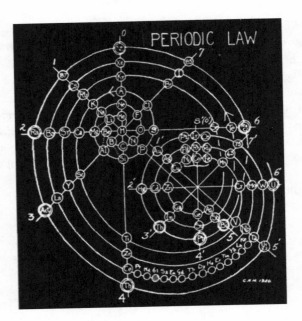

Nodder's periodic table

"So if all the elements are made out of the same protons," I ask, "why indeed can't we change one element into another? Doesn't lead plus a few protons give gold?"

"Turn one element into another? Lead into gold? *Really!*" Rutherford chuckles. "Did you come here from the middle ages?"

I hesitate, then decide to hold my ground. "Well, but why not?"

Rutherford smiles and points at a small metal cylinder fed by glass tubes. "I'm joking. Look. I put some nitrogen in here and bombard it with the radiation emanating from radon atoms—which seems to comprise protons. What do I get?"

Rutherford's apparatus for transmutation of nitrogen into oxygen

"One sec—" I grab the periodic table. If we really could add one proton to the nucleus of the nitrogen atom, we should get the next element in the periodic table: "Nitrogen is N? You must have obtained some O atoms. You created—I guess—oxygen?"

Ernest gives a modest grin. *So he's the first real alchemist in history.* He's turned one of nature's "fundamental" elements into another.

"In principle you could transmute a few atoms of lead into gold too but... I'm not sure it would be economical."

"Also," I say, "there's the small matter of a tortuous death sentence."

"Um, I think they repealed that," he laughs.

"Yeah. So this little experiment here is really the first time one element changed into another?"

"The first time it's been achieved artificially. But some nuclei, mostly big ones, seem to be naturally unstable and change on their own. That's what we now call *radioactivity*." He hands me two lumps of metal. "Feel these: uranium and radium."

The intense weight of the silvery metals takes me by surprise.

"You see," Rutherford says, "some atoms have unstable nuclei as found by Becquerel and the Curies. We don't fully know why. I have found three types of radiation that may be spontaneously emitted by an unstable nucleus. I called them *alpha, beta,* and *gamma* radiation before I had any idea what they were. My investigations now suggest that alpha particles may be pairs of protons, beta may be fast electrons, and gamma radiation may actually be a new type of electromagnetic radiation more powerful even than X-rays."

"So how do these atoms stick together to make material?" I ask.

"It seems that the electrons in one atom attract the protons in the next atom, causing atoms to bond together very tightly into molecules, and causing the molecules to be attracted to each other to form a solid. At higher temperatures, the atomic movement overcomes these electromagnetic bonds, and you get a liquid in which the molecules can slip past each other. At still higher temperatures the molecules break loose of each other and fly around independently—a gas. A gas may expand and contract because the molecules are not bound together so they have no fixed spacing."

Having thanked Rutherford, I find myself jogging the short distance back to Fizz's Place in Whitworth Park. Back "home," I gingerly shred the

ROW label and start again. *This time I'm going to distill the label down to the fundamentals—now that the fundamentals have finally been exposed.*

ROW Label

Ingredients: Protons (heavy, positive); Electrons (light, negative)
Interactions: Electromagnetism (Maxwell's Field Equations)
Context: Curved relative spacetime (curvature=gravity).
Framework for laws: Equations of motion

I take the marker, cap it, and place it down firmly on the desk. *Fundamentally, after peeling back the layers, that is all there is to say about the world!*

Everything else follows: electromagnetism binds the electrons and protons into atoms, the atoms into molecules, and the molecules into gases, liquids, and solids. The gases, liquids, and solids form plants, people, buildings, planets, and stars. The electrons move around electromagnetically to create electric currents and jiggle randomly as heat, emitting electromagnetic radiation—light.

Gravity—the curved spacetime of general relativity—clusters the stars into galaxies and ties the planets to the suns they orbit and the moons to the planets.

The entire cosmos is just electrons and protons interacting according to electromagnetism within a curved spacetime!

I place my hand on the door handle and swing the door open. I stand in the doorway, regarding the outside. "Fjallagrasamjólk," I say. And I stride into the Rest of World with a confidence I have never once felt before.

Soon I find myself back at the fashion shop on Wilmslow Road. This time I do walk in.

Among hundreds of dresses I spot a simple one in flowing light natural colors. *My mother would love that dress.* She wouldn't need to know that it is mass-produced. No one else in the Collective will have it. My mother and I are similar sizes. I try on the dress. Can I get away with sneaking just one dress back to the future?

I look at myself in the mirror. I am jarred to see myself, for the first time in three weeks, almost looking like an Ecommunity girl. *But with my commanding knowledge of the universe, I feel nothing like an Ecommunity girl.*

"Um, Miss, would you like the dress?"

"Yes, please. For my Mom."

I walk on in a trance, the dress—wrapped in brown paper—under my arm. Leave or stay? The devil or the deep blue sea? A rock or a hard place? *Why do I have to start my adult life with such an impossible choice?*

Sitting on a park bench, I place the package on my lap, unwrap the dress, and find myself staring down at it, feeling increasingly melancholy. A gentle curvature in spacetime, caused by the nearby mass of planet Earth, drags a tear—comprising electrons and protons—down my cheek, and drops the salt water onto the dress.

Dad told me not to take items from one period of time to another. What am I doing with this dress?

Surely this situation is special. This dress is a gift. This dress might just be… a parting gift.

Until this very moment, I have so carefully avoided thinking explicitly about the consequences of parting, but let's face it: *I will never fit back into the Collective.* I don't think right, I don't act right.

I try to play out the scene in my mind. Is my mother weeping inconsolably and exclaiming, "Fizz, how can you do this to me?" over and over again? Or is she sniffling and saying "I love you and support you, whatever you choose." And, if the latter, silently inside her mind, is Mom saying "Fizz how can you do this to me?" over and over again?

Can I do it to her?

Only later does my mind slowly return to digesting the physics I learned this morning, if only as a way to avoid more difficult thoughts.

Protons. So simple. There are ninety-two elements in the world because the number of protons in a nucleus can be one, two, or three up to ninety-two. People have been systematically investigating atoms for more than a century since Dalton. *How come no one ever noticed that the mass of the different atoms are just multiples of the hydrogen atom's mass?*

Another thing—protons are positive. Like charges repel. *How do those protons bind together in the atomic nucleus if they repel each other?* And the periodic table—why is it periodic? As the number of protons goes up from one to ninety-two, why do some chemical properties repeat themselves?

Hmm, perhaps I don't understand the world quite as thoroughly as I thought. Not to mention the mystery of the wave-particle duality.

I head back to the university and catch Rutherford on his way to a lecture.

"Sir Ernest, do you mind if I ask a couple of quick supplementary questions? Not that I want to burst your bubble or anything, but isn't it obvious? You said that the helium nucleus is just two protons where hydrogen is one. A lithium atom has three. Why didn't people notice long ago that a lithium atom weighs three times more than hydrogen?"

"Ah, but it doesn't. There is mystery yet in those atoms. The larger atoms weigh more than the sum of the weight of the protons. Perhaps there is something else in there."

"Oh," I sigh. "Another thing: How do the protons stick together in the nucleus? Don't they repel each other? Does gravity hold them together?"

Ernest laughs at me.

"What's so funny?"

"The electromagnetic repulsion between two protons is about a trillion trillion trillion times stronger than the gravitational attraction."

"Ah. So maybe it's not gravity then?"

"Maybe not," he smiles. "There must be an entirely new strong force holding those protons together. We know nothing about it. The microscopic world of nuclear physics has its own laws waiting to be explored."

"Hmm. And the *nuclear radiation*—those powerful rays that Becquerel and Curie discovered shooting out of some big atoms—you said that the 'alpha rays' are protons, which makes sense. But the 'beta rays' are electrons—how do electrons emerge from inside a nucleus that is made purely of protons?"

"Yes, yes, good questions. Look Fizz, no one said our work is quite finished. In fact, the biggest mystery of all is the behavior of the electrons in the atoms. They seem to absorb and emit light in very specific colors. The electrons also seem to be arranged in layers, or shells, that lead to the periodic table. Why do bound electrons exhibit these behaviors? So, good news, there is still some work left for you younger physicists. Good day."

With that, Sir Ernest Rutherford walks into the lecture hall.

The pressure is on. I will have to use my last two days very efficiently if I am going to finish this mission successfully.

Walking toward the exit of the university, I try to energize myself to plan my last forty-eight hours of PCC, but I fail. As I open the door of the university I watch my own feet and find that they're dragging. I look up at the evening sky. The ROW is not as familiar as fjallagrasamjólk after all—a couple of ingredients remain unknown. Deep inside the atoms, fundamental questions remain unanswered. Maybe I can answer them in the next two days and choose a life from some sort of position of strength—although it will still be the devil's choice; or worse, maybe I'll be left with pressing mysteries that add to the pressure on me to leave home.

I sulk into a pub and sit at a table, placing the wrapped dress on a seat next to me. The pub's dark floral wallpaper is depressing. *Mom wouldn't like it.*

Finally, a tall waitress comes over carrying a menu. I decline the menu and order a half-pint of lager, paying her little attention. But from the vantage point of my low padded seat, I can hardly ignore her protruding belly which is almost in my face.

As the waitress turns to get my drink, I call her back. "Hey, hang on a second. You're pregnant, yes?"

"Yeah."

Now I look up and notice the pretty face and long dark-hair above me. "Oh. Congratulations. How far along are you?"

"Six months." Her Manchester accent makes it sound like "moonts."

"You don't say." I stare at her tummy for a little longer than seems polite, then back at her face. "And... everyone can tell?"

She looks displeased. "You did. Depends wha' I wear I guess. Be gettin' your lager then—"

"Wait. But someone who knew you well could tell for sure?"

"I 'spose. Look I'm not tryin' to hide it or notin'. I'm married an' all."

"Give me that menu," I blurt out, almost grabbing it. My finger rapidly scans down the dull list of British pub foods. It must be here somewhere...

"Here. *Strawberry tart.*"

She regards me strangely. "*Yeees...* Would 'ya like a tart with your lager, miss?"

"No. The strawberries are fresh?"

"'Course ma'am. First lot this season. 'Ya want one or not?"

"And it's summer soon? I *know* it's a stupid question—just tell me what month it is."

"It's May. Look, miss, don' take this wrong an' all, but maybe you 'ad enough already—"

Of course, there are no strawberries before May.

"I was born in July," I say.

"And?"

"So much for truth…" I mutter to myself.

"Miss?"

"No tart. Just make it a full pint."

Three pints later I'm too inebriated to talk clearly or walk quite straight, but, unfortunately—given that this was my goal—not intoxicated enough to forget that my own father, whom I have been thinking more and more may be the parent I spend my life with, must have left the Ecommunity knowing full well that Mom was pregnant with his child.

Whatever useless alcohol they use in Manchester doesn't even suppress the unfortunate thought that my Dad, at age eighteen, may even have left the community *because* he knew full well that Mom was pregnant with his child.

When I get back to the hut, I'm still just about sober enough to remember—before I collapse—what Rutherford identified as the central unsolved mystery of physics.

"C-c-computer, f-find me an explanation for how electrons behave inside atoms."

Let the Cat Out

Another new European city. With a bit of luck Brussels will have just one university and one expert on electrons.

It's a bright, cold fall day in Brussels as I emerge into another spacious city park, somewhere and sometime in curved four-dimensional spacetime, with a bit of a headache. The grassy hills rise to the horizon in most directions. *Perhaps urbanization is not quite as intense as the Dean lamented.*

Starting my morning, again, walking through soggy grass, the squelching this time is punctuated by the occasional crunch of a red-brown leaf.

The park is built around a serene pond, as green as the one in Berlin. An old man is leaning on a stick, feeding breadcrumbs to the various winged fauna in the area. He tells me proudly that this pond in Leopoldspark is home to mallards, moorhens, coots, Egyptian geese, and rose-ringed parakeets.

I get chatting to him in French. "So tell me, mister," I say, "may I ask you about a subject that interests me? You look like you've got some experience of life. How has technology affected you over the years?"

He shrugs.

"Do you have electricity in your home?"

"No," he shakes his head slowly. "I hear that new homes have electricity but I do not really see the point."

"Do you have a horseless carriage? Have you flown in an airplane?"

The man smirks. "No, of course not. But my son has some dream about taking a train to Paris then flying to London. I am trying to talk him out of it."

"So all the exciting new developments during your lifetime have not affected you at all?"

"Well, maybe one thing."

"Yes?" I try to encourage him.

"Chaplin. I do love Charlie Chaplin."

"Oh. Who's he?"

As I march across the lawns I pass a cluster of three elegant buildings embedded within the park. I'm annoyed that the city allowed construction in this green oasis, but all is quickly forgiven when a large banner across the gate to the buildings greets me with the words *Fifth Solvay Conference on Physics: Electrons et photons*. With only a day to spare, I've hit the jackpot—the answer to all my open questions, right here within the park. A conference where they will undoubtedly discuss the photon of light with its wave-particle duality as well as the electrons in the atom with their strange energy levels and the unexplained repetition of their properties in the periodic table.

The electron and the photon.

I talk my way in as a science journalist. "I risked my life travelling all the way from the North Atlantic to report on this conference—are you really going to turn me back?" I say, then feel a bit guilty and bite my tongue.

Inside, the attendees are mingling over coffee under a large chandelier in a staid, wood-paneled room. I order myself a cup too, and gulp it down but keep hold of the cup, if only to occupy my hands as I approach strangers.

My first impressions are disappointing. There are at most some thirty attendees. Perhaps it's a local Belgian affair. I see only one other woman, but at least there's one. This seems far short of the major international gathering that I hoped I was lying my way into.

There is something somber about the gathering. Almost everyone is wearing three-piece black suits with either a black necktie or black bowtie under black hats. Moustaches and goatees are popular. One man strikes a lone blow for casualness with a light gray two-piece suit. The woman, white-haired, seemingly in her sixties, fits right in with a black dress, black coat, black shoes, and black hat. She wears no jewelry, although she has allowed herself to break the blackness with a delicately patterned scarf tied around her hat.

It could almost be a funeral.

I pluck up the courage to start my investigative journalism by striking up conversations with random "mourners." There's nothing like starting at the top. *"Bonjour.* I'm Fizz from Iceland. Science journalist," I say to the old man wearing the "chairman" pin.

"Welcome. I am Hendrik Lorentz from Arnhem in The Netherlands."

An international visitor—that's good. *But from where do I know that name?* Oh, of course—the man Einstein credited with the idea of time dilation and space contraction before Einstein himself realized that space and time are always relative to the observer. Where else did I see the name Lorentz? Ah yes, winner of the second Nobel Prize in physics after Röntgen.

"Congratulations on your Nobel Prize," I say.

Lorentz waves his hand. "Well, at this event most of us have won them."

"Really!" I smile. "So those who don't feel kind of inferior do they?"

"I hope not," he says kindly. "Anyway, one attendee has been awarded two Nobels, so that keeps up the averages."

"Two?"

"In physics and in chemistry. Albeit that attendee is still refused membership of The French Academy of Sciences."

"Refused! Why?"

"Apparently the French Academy considers two Nobel Prizes to be a poor substitute for the requirement of possessing two testicles."

Finally a woman. As I make a beeline for the only woman delegate, I spot the name *Max Planck* on a nametag—the man who explained black-body radiation by saying that light is emitted in packets, before Einstein then suggested that light is always "quantized" in the packets now known as photons.

The woman's name is Marie Curie and I recall reading about her research on mysterious rays from within the atoms which Rutherford would later identify with the nucleus and classify as alpha, beta, and gamma nuclear radiation.

"Bonjour, Madame Curie. I've already heard a lot about your physics research. So what did you achieve in chemistry?"

"Two new elements—radium and polonium."

"Radium? From *radius*—a ray?"

"Yes, since radium is radioactive. Polonium for my country of birth."

"How do you even discover a new element?"

"It is considerably worse than finding a needle in a haystack," she sighs. "The 'haystack' was one ton of pitchblende, a natural mineral rich in uranium. The 'needle' was just one tenth of one gram of what we would now call radium chloride. To find it, I had to get past all the 'decoy needles'—barium atoms which chemically resemble radium. Once I proved it was a separate element, I placed radium directly below barium in the periodic table. Perhaps today we will finally find out why the properties of electrons repeat themselves periodically—why radium mimics barium."

I look at her in admiration, then look around. "So tell me, Rutherford didn't make it?" I ask.

"No, but his former student Niels Bohr is here. In fact," Curie lowers her voice and points subtly, "Bohr is the man to watch here. He also studied under J. J. Thomson in Cambridge, and now heads up a world-famous physics institution in Copenhagen with his own students."

Soon the attendees file into the plenary room. I'm planning to take an inconspicuous place at the back of the auditorium, but am mortified to find that this exclusive conference meets sitting around a large mahogany table. I hesitate. I don't quite have the gall to take a place with all the laureates, so I grab a chair and sit in a corner to observe the meeting.

The meeting starts. Lorentz sets the agenda. Einstein's theory of relativity is not even mentioned. Evidently relative spacetime is already taken for granted.

Even tucked away in the corner, I'm self-conscious. *I'm like a lightweight electron, lonely and out of place, orbiting a room full of heavyweight protons.* I wonder how many hours it will take to get to the crux of the issues that concern me.

My luck changes when a frizzy ball of salt-and-pepper hair makes its late entrance into the room, preceded by a familiar-looking cherry wood smoking pipe.

"The ever-youthful Fizz! What brings you here?" he whispers. I stand to greet him and he air kisses me on both cheeks, almost setting fire to my hair with his pipe.

"Um, I've taken up science journalism." Lying to someone I know, someone who has been kind to me, feels even worse.

The delegates pause for a second in deference to Einstein.

"Well, come and join us at the table then," he says to me.

Sheepishly, I follow Albert Einstein to sit among the Nobel laureates.

The meeting resumes. Arthur Compton—a tall, mustached man in his mid-thirties who states that he's at Washington University in St. Louis, Missouri—presents the latest evidence for photons, this time photons in X-rays and gamma rays. Compton is careful to credit Max Planck and Albert Einstein for the idea that light is quantized in packets called photons. After all, they are both sitting at the table.

Niels Bohr, who looks about forty, clears his throat. I perk up—Curie told me to follow him.

"Just as light is not only a wave, but also a particle," Bohr declares in a Scandinavian accent, "the electron is not only a particle but also a wave. I believe the same is true of a proton."

Some in the room may have heard it already, but for me it's a bomb-shell. *Everything is a wave and a particle!* Bohr has gone "all in." If we can't understand how something can be both a wave and a particle, we won't be able to truly understand anything at all.

But why does he think an electron is a wave? And what is it a wave of? The mystery of the electron is how electrons in atoms have very specific energy levels. If an electron is a wave, does that help?

"When you put a wave in a box," Bohr explains, "it becomes con-strained to vibrate at the specific wavelengths that fit into the box. For example, when you tie a guitar string, it vibrates with a specific note and multiples of that note, known as *harmonics*. When you capture air in a flute, that air resonates at the specific harmonics that fit into that cavity. The distance of peak-to-trough in the wave is adjusted to either the length of the cavity or a half or a third of that, etcetera."

Bohr sketches it on the blackboard:

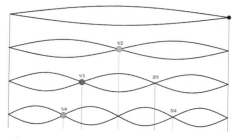

Harmonics of constrained string—analogy for an electron in an atom

"It is precisely the same with electrons," Bohr declares with flair. "An electron is a wave. When you tie an electron wave into an atom, it's like pinning a guitar string—the electron can only vibrate at the specific wavelengths that fit into the dimensions of the atom. So electrons in an atom have very specific energy levels corresponding to the wavelengths that fit in the atom."

Now I've heard it all. The same wave equation for guitar strings and for electrons in an atom. *But what are electrons waves of?*

Bohr hangs a chart on the wall. "The specific colors radiated when we electrify, for example, neon, are simply determined by conservation of energy. The electrons in the hydrogen atom have specific energy levels, like rungs of a ladder. When an electron drops from one rung to the next, the lost energy becomes a photon—a packet of light. The amount of energy in the photon determines the color of the photon as Planck and Einstein found. So now my theory can predict exactly which colors of light will be radiated by hydrogen."

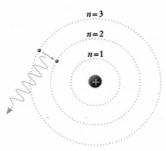

An electron dropping between discrete energy levels in an atom emits a photon of light with characteristic color

Some people are smiling; the mystery of the electron's energy levels in the atoms has been solved. However, I notice that others are frowning, perhaps uncomfortable with this strange wave-particle duality or wondering—as I am—what the electron is actually a wave of.

Murmurs erupt around the table.

Finally someone I don't recognize asks a question. "That is very well for the simple case of hydrogen with just one electron. But why is the periodic table periodic? When you have a heavier atom with many electrons, why don't all the electrons settle down into the lowest energy level?"

A younger man comes to the rescue. *"Guten Tag.* I am Wolfgang Pauli from Austria. I would like to propose that the universe has an *exclusion principle*. No two electrons can ever occupy the same state. So, as you go up the periodic table to atoms with many protons and many electrons, the lower energy levels are occupied and the extra electrons are forced into higher energy levels. These outer electrons create the characteristic chemical properties of the periodic table."

More murmurs. Some people think that helium with two protons and two electrons does, in fact, have both electrons in the lowest energy level.

Pauli is ready to refine his exclusion principle. "*Ja, ja,* but I have found that electrons have *spin.* That is the origin of magnetism in materials like iron. Remember that a rotating charge creates a magnetic field. Well, in iron, the spins of the electrons are all aligned so that all the tiny spinning electron magnets add up to make a magnetic field."

He sketches his idea on the board:

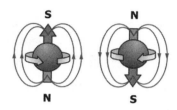

Electrons spin up or down creating tiny magnetic fields

"Spin in an electron," Pauli continues, "is not like a spinning top. An electron cannot spin fast or slow, and it can never stop spinning. It can spin up, that is clockwise in the up direction, or down, that is clockwise in the downward direction. Up or down, or left or right, that is it. Now since an electron can spin in two ways—up or down—it is possible to have two electrons in the same energy level: one spinning up and one spinning down. But only two—you can never find more than two electrons in the same energy level. Lithium must have one of its three electrons in a higher rung of energy, which explains its different chemical properties."

More muttering and nods occur around the table. *But how does the universe prevent two electrons from having the same state?* It's like a new type of physics—not predicting how electrons will move, but rather prescribing what they cannot do.

Hmm. Electrons are waves, and some mystical law prevents two electrons from having identical energy levels. But the same question keeps bothering me. Sound waves are waves of movement of air molecules, water waves are displacement of the level of the water. *What are electron-waves a wave of?*

A few moments later, Erwin Schrödinger—also from Austria and now at the University of Zürich—presents his new *quantum wave equation.* He has applied d'Alembert's general wave equation in the most unexpected context: to give the precise details of the wave of an electron. These scientists are thirsty for mathematical rigor. Some already know about this equation and refer to it as *Schrödinger's equation* while others seem to be hearing about it for the first time, eagerly jotting down the mathematics on their notepads.

So now we have an equation for the wave and we still don't know what it's a wave of! And if an electron is a wave, how does an electron sometimes have a clear, definite position like a particle?

A brash young scientist is ready with an answer. Werner Heisenberg, mid-twenties, clean-shaven, introduces himself. He was educated at the University of Göttingen—which I remember Thomas Young attended—and is now a lecturer under Niels Bohr in Copenhagen. "A particle can have a position or a momentum, but it can never have both," Heisenberg announces.

What? I recall that momentum is closely related to inertia and speed. He seems to be saying that an electron can have a definite position or a definite speed, but not both. Now *everyone* looks perplexed. Heisenberg marches to the board.

"You see, an electron is a wave. When the electron wave looks like a nice sine wave—" Heisenberg sketches:

Wave equation for an electron with definite momentum (speed)

"—then the electron has a definite speed and momentum. But as you can see, this electron's wave is spread out across space! It does not have a definite position! It is somehow in a *superposition* of all different positions just like a wave at sea does not have one specific position. Now, when the electron's wave looks more like a *shock wave* with a specific position, like a sonic boom or a tsunami wave hitting the shore, like so—"

Wave equation for electron of definite position and indefinite speed

"—then the electron does have a definite position. But the momentum is determined by the wavelength and, in this case, there is no defined wavelength. So the momentum and speed are completely uncertain!"

Heisenberg senses people are lost and tries to sum up his point.

"When the electron has a definite position, say when it makes a track in a photographic emulsion, its momentum is undefined. It is a superposition of all possible momenta. Conversely, when an electron has a definite momentum and speed, its position is blurred across space."

A confused ruckus erupts. How can an electron not have a definite position? What if I measure the position and momentum at the same time? Heisenberg remains standing and fields the questions confidently. He shows the audience that every experiment measures either position or momentum; no experiment can be configured to measure both simultaneously. But more deeply, he says, the electron cannot actually have a definite position and a definite momentum at the same time, because a wave cannot be both a shock wave with a definite position and a sine wave with a consistent wavelength. Either it is a sharp wave with no definite wavelength or a sine wave with no definite position.

"You agree with this, Albert?" I whisper.

Einstein seems deep in thought and puts a finger to his lips to shush me.

I think about my own situation. *Maybe I'm a bit like an electron—I can have the love of my Mom and friends, or intellectual freedom, but never both.*

Finally, someone shouts the obvious question. "All right, all right, but a wave of *what*? And how can an electron not have both a definite position and a definite momentum? What if an electron has definite momentum? You claim it has no position, but if I go ahead and measure its position, what result would I get?"

Most of the brilliant heads in the room are nodding in agreement. What is that wave?

Another man lets out a loud "Ah." Everyone turns to him expectantly. They are hungry for someone to make sense of this. Max Born, who appears to be in his forties, introduces himself—he's also visiting from the University of Göttingen in Germany. He stands and basks in the spotlight for a few seconds. "I think we are all impressed how modeling an electron as a wave explains the energy levels in atoms and the colors of neon lights. But I think that what we want to know is what is the electron a wave of, right? And what happens when an electron has no definite position and we go ahead and measure its position?"

Could you spit out the answer, if it's not too much trouble...

"I surmise that the electron wave is a wave of *probability*," Born says dramatically. "Do you see? The wave tells me the probability that the electron will be in a given place if I measure its position. So, if you have an electron with a definite momentum there is an equal probability that it will be any place. If I then measure the electron's position, the universe will randomly choose some position for the electron based on the probabilities in the wave equation." The observer—the measurement—always has an effect—you can't observe a system without affecting it.

He sketches this idea on the blackboard:

An electron with definite momentum—a sine wave—has equal probability of being in any place. Measuring its position forces the electron to randomly choose one position.

Albert is shaking his head sadly. Back home, the guys played rugby; what breaks out now can only be described as the academic equivalent of a rugby pile-up. Nobel laureates are waving their programs and shouting.

"Probabilities—what probabilities?"

"The universe is not a casino!"

"The very purpose of physics is to find definite laws, not probabilities."

"What does a 'wave of probability' even mean? How can the result of an experiment be random?"

But Born is armed with evidence and waits patiently for the opportunity to present it. "If you have an electron with definite momentum and you measure its position—say, using a simple photograph emulsion to expose the electron's tracks—you get a different position every time. Although the experiment is set up identically, you always get a different result. At best you can assign a probability to each result."

Lorentz is losing control of the discussion and proposes a coffee break. Fierce debate continues as everyone shuffles out.

"But, Albert," I ask over the background noise, "didn't Maxwell and Boltzmann already use statistics in physics?"

"Sure, sure, they used statistics, but only as a shorthand for describing all the atoms in a hot gas, as a way of statistically summarizing the definitive behavior of each atom. Fundamentally, each particle must behave deterministically. The universe is deterministic. Maxwell never doubted that. This randomness from Bohr, Heisenberg, and Born is too bizarre."

I burst out laughing.

Einstein takes umbrage. "What is amusing?"

"You, Albert. You're amusing me. You, who proposed that light comes in packets, that space and time are relative to each observer, that energy and mass are one and the same and—wait for it—that spacetime is four-dimensional and curved. You find this bizarre?"

"Well, yes, my theories may have been innovative, but curved spacetime still follows clear laws. Reality is definite. You know, I like to think that the Moon is there even if I am not looking at it. Why should an electron not have a position just because I do not measure it? And a random position? I tell you, Fizz, God does not play dice with the cosmos."

Bohr is passing by, looking rather pleased with himself. He overhears Einstein and puts a hand on his shoulder. "Einstein, don't tell God what to do," he quips.

The small crowd seems to be aligning into two distinct camps. The conservative camp led by Einstein and Schrödinger say that this *quantum mechanics* might be useful, but it is not complete. The electron with a definite momentum also has a definite position; it may just be hidden from us so it *appears* to be random. Measuring the electron's position reveals a hidden position that was always definite—the universe never makes a random choice. The universe is deterministic.

Bohr is leading the maverick camp with Heisenberg and Born—soon someone coins the term *Copenhagen camp*. They seem excited to abandon the very scientific program that Galileo and Newton started more than three centuries ago: the program of finding laws for a deterministic universe. Bohr is pleased by the incredulous reactions. "Anyone who is not shocked by quantum theory has not understood it," he says. To my surprise, the Copenhagen camp and its radical ideas seem to be gaining momentum.

I look around. *This conference is indeed a funeral.* A funeral for *classical physics*. A funeral for determinism. A burial of the concept of an objective reality that does not depend on how we observe it. An internment of what little common sense has survived Einstein. But the Copenhagen camp is shedding no tears. Bohr is beaming, almost dancing on the grave.

Before lunch, Lorentz invites everyone to step outside for a conference photograph. Einstein beckons me to join, but I insist on standing on the side to observe something I've never seen—some photographer snapping a photograph.

Piccard, Henriot, Ehrenfest, Herzen, DeDonder, Schrödinger, Verschaffelt, Pauli,
...Heisenberg, Fowler, Brillouin
Debye, Knudsen, Bragg, Kramers, Dirac, Compton, deBroglie, Born, Bohr
Langmuir, Planck, Curie, Lorentz, Einstein, Langevin, Guye, Wilson, Richardson

Discussions continue throughout lunch. People are struggling to grasp the concepts that have been flying around. What does Schrödinger's wave equation mean? What does the exclusion principle mean? What does Heisenberg's uncertainty principle mean?

Bohr and Einstein continue their debate in a quiet corner while they digest lunch. They seem no closer to agreement. Someone photographs them:

Bohr and Einstein

My stomach is busy trying to digest this new more abstract type of physics. Up to now, physics modeled the world directly. No one ever asked to interpret the meaning of Newton's law of gravity—the law prescribes the gravitational attraction, which governs the movement of two masses.

But now there is a Schrödinger wave equation, and it is valuable because it can predict complex physical phenomena, but no one is quite sure what it means. The only proposal on the table for an interpretation—Born's idea that it is a wave of probability—is highly controversial. Reveling in the debate, Bohr is making ever-more radical statements. "It is not the role of physics to model the world, but only to predict the results of experiments. Physics does not provide an ontology—a model of what *is*—but only an epistemology—a model of what is *known*. It is all about *complementarity*, he says. The wave picture is complementary to the particle picture; definite position is complementary to definite momentum. You can never have both."

Albert seems to sense the tide turning against him and has become contemplative. But he holds firm in his belief that the probabilities of the newly emerging quantum mechanics are just approximations for a definite hidden theory of physics.

Lorentz struggles to herd the physicists back to the table. The afternoon agenda is to progress from discussing a single electron to discussing two or more electrons. This time, Schrödinger grabs a seat on the other side of Einstein. The shrinking conservative camp is regrouping and planning its comeback. Schrödinger whispers to Einstein something cryptic along the lines of "I will attack on indefiniteness and you go for the non-locality." Einstein seems to perk up a bit. They feel that the *Copenhagen Interpretation* will run into trouble when considering multiple electrons.

A lot of the discussion now centers on the electron's spin as an example. Spin is nice and simple—up or down, left or right. But Pauli explains that *Heisenberg's uncertainty principle* applies to spin as well. If the electron's spin is definitely up or definitely down, then it has no defined left/right spin; it is in a mixture, or *superposition*, of left and right. If an electron has a definite left or right spin, then it is in a superposition of up and down. It's a simpler example of the uncertainty principle. If one type of spin is defined, the other is uncertain or in fact undefined.

I'm very slowly catching on to this fanciful new reality. Measuring up/down spin messes up left/right spin and vice versa. If an electron is spinning up and I measure the left/right spin, the universe selects left or right entirely randomly.

Paul Dirac from Cambridge has something to say. In his mid twenties, he's one of the younger attendees. "I want to report some progress with making the wave equation consistent with relativity and a surprising result—"

"No, no," Bohr interrupts. "Show them your notation."

"I would really like to explain about relativistic quantum mechanics."

"Paul, your notation. Please."

"Oh, um, okay." He walks to the board. "If an electron is spinning left, we can write its state as a ket:"

$$|electron\ left>$$

"A ket?" someone asks.

"Sure. The '>' is the ket and '<' is the bra."

There are some smiles.

"An electron that is spinning left," Dirac continues, "is in a mixture or superposition of up and down spins. We can write that fact simply as follows:"

$$|electron\ left> = |electron\ up> + |electron\ down>$$

"Now if I *measure* the up/down spin, the electron will jump randomly to either the $|electron\ up>$ or $|electron\ down>$ state.

"I can summarize the question that we are debating this afternoon— the issue of two electrons—using my bra-ket notation: What if there are two electrons, both spinning left, and I measure the total up/down spin of the system and obtain a result of zero? If the total up/down spin is zero, then we must have one up and one down. Our pair of electrons could be:"

$$|electron\ 1\ up>|electron\ 2\ down>\ \mathbf{or}\ \ |electron\ 1\ down>|electron\ 2\ up>.$$

"Those are the two ways we can get a total spin of zero. But what I really wanted to tell you about—"

Bohr is on his feet. "Wrong! We did not measure the spin of each electron, so each electron does not have a definite up/down spin. The total system has definite spin, but each electron does not have definite spin. What we have is a mixture of both those two states." Bohr steps up to the board, crosses out the word "or," and writes "plus" instead:

$$|electron\ 1\ up>|electron\ 2\ down> \text{ ~~or~~ } \underline{plus}$$
$$|electron\ 2\ down>|electron\ 1\ up>.$$

I'm now completely and utterly perplexed beyond anything I have encountered to date. I whisper to Albert, "He's lost me. Surely each electron has its own state. I can just about accept than one electron is in a superposition of two different states like $|up> + |down>$. But Bohr seems to be talking about the two electrons as if their states are mixed together and dependent on each other. If one is up, then two is down; and if one is down, then two is up—but neither one of them is actually up or down?"

"That is exactly what he is suggesting," Albert confirms, "that the two electrons have *entangled* states. And... he has completely lost me too. In fact," Einstein actually winks at me, "he may just be digging his own grave."

I smile.

But Bohr is dead serious. "No particle in the universe has its own independent state. No particle has its own wave equation. We have one big, complicated universe where any one particle may be in a state entangled with any other."

At last Schrödinger stands up for the defense. "*Ja, ja.* So the states of two separate electrons may be entangled. I would ask my esteemed colleague Bohr to consider what would happen if, instead of two electrons, we have an electron and a cat! Yes, an electron and a cat sealed in a box. The electron starts off spinning $|left>$. Also in the box is a device that measures the up/down spin of the electron: if the result is $|up>$ the nefarious device releases a deadly poison. You claim there is a 50% chance this experiment results in $|up>$. So the state inside the box will be one of:"

$$|electron\ up>|cat\ dead> \text{ \underline{or} } |electron\ down>|cat\ alive>.$$

"But 'no', you say!" Schrödinger says, mimicking Bohr's Scandinavian pronunciation. "After all, the box is sealed and we did not yet measure if the cat is alive or dead. Why should the cat be alive or dead?" He crosses out his own "or". "I suppose the contents of the box will be in a superposition:"

$$|electron\ up>|cat\ dead> \text{ ~~or~~ } \underline{plus} |electron\ down>|cat\ alive>.$$

"That's right, the cat is neither alive nor dead." His subtle smile suggests that he truly enjoys the irony. "Naturally the poor kitty is in a superposition of alive and dead, entangled with the spin of the electron."

This thought experiment sets the cat amongst the pigeons, as it were. Electrons are one thing, but can a cat inside a box be in a superposition of dead and alive until the experimenter gets curious and opens the box? Does curiosity kill the cat?

Albert allows himself a gentle smile. For once, Bohr is not ready with an immediate answer. Soon there are as many opinions as there are physicists. Maybe these *superpositions* apply only to microscopic particles like electrons, not to cats, someone suggests. But isn't a cat just a collection of electrons and protons—why shouldn't the same principle apply to a cat as to an electron? But if the same laws apply why doesn't the whole world decay into a weird superposition? Why does anything have a definite position?

What happens when the box is opened, someone asks, taking the thought experiment another step further. Maybe the experimenter becomes part of the superposition? Is the state, after the box is open, something like:

|electron up> |cat dead> |experimenter charged with animal abuse>
plus *|electron down> |cat alive> |experimenter off the hook>*.

There are some smiles. The conservatives have had a good rally.

"No," Bohr replies eventually, "once there is an observation, the universe will randomly pick one definite value or the other. There will no longer be a superposition of an alive and dead cat."

"But isn't the observer just a collection of electrons and protons too?"

"Why isn't the cat counted as an observer?"

"In fact, going back to the original example, why isn't the second electron counted as an observer?"

"What is an observer—what counts as a measurement and what doesn't?"

Einstein is being surprisingly quiet as the debate rages on. I'm lost at sea.

Finally, Einstein stands up. There still seems to be a modicum of respect for the man who laid the foundations for the very same quantum theory now being debated. An uneasy quiet breaks out.

"Let us go back to those two electrons with total up/down spin of zero. According to you, Niels, they are in a superposition state—" Einstein points at the formula still on the board:

|electron 1 up>|electron 2 down> **plus** *|electron 2 down>|electron 1 up>*

"—until I measure the spin of one or the other. Only then will the universe pick a definite state for the both of them, which you have written as:"

|electron 1 up>|electron 2 down> **or** *|electron 2 down>|electron 1 up>*

Bohr nods.

Albert speaks softly but confidently. "But suppose I take those two electrons and carefully transport them to different sides of the universe without ever measuring their individual spin. Then I measure one of their spins. Does the universe only then pick a definite spin for the other distant electron?

Bohr and Heisenberg are nodding their agreement—only then.

Albert goes for the kill. "Well, that means that my measurement of one electron is instantly causing its distant 'entangled' twin electron to take on a definite state. That would be instant action at a distance!"

There is a tense silence. Everyone here knows that it was Einstein who cured the world of the blemish of instant action at a distance. Even I know that Einstein's theory of relativity forbids travel or communication faster than the speed of light.

Bohr gets up and starts pacing. Heisenberg buries his head deep in his hands. Everyone else glances uneasily from Einstein to Bohr and back again. Einstein glances around the room. The tension is palpable.

"Yes," Bohr finally breaks the silence. "That is right. Entanglement means that a measurement on an electron here can instantly cause an electron on the other side of the universe to collapse into a definite state."

Einstein is incredulous. "You want to bring back spooky action at a distance? The theory of relativity prohibits instant interactions—"

"I believe if you check the theory of relativity," Bohr smiles, "you will find that it prohibits instant communication or movement. This is not communication. Measuring one electron causes the state of the other to collapse, but it does not communicate any information."

Suddenly two core axioms of classical physics—the determinism and locality that characterized physics before quantum mechanics—are both being assaulted. Things are not definite, they are random. Influences are not local; observing an electron here can instantly affect an electron at great distance. Einstein is now trying to fight two enemies: "God playing with dice" as well as "spooky action at a distance." Someone makes a comment I don't get about the atom being like a rabbit hole—inside the atom we find a completely different type of world.

Paul Dirac clears his throat. "Ahem." He has been waiting patiently and finally gets the audience's attention for whatever it was he wanted to say in the first place. "As I was going to say earlier, I have succeeded in combining the wave equation with the space and time of special relativity." There are nods. All physics nowadays should be set in relativistic space and time. "There was a surprise in the mathematics, though," Paul tells the room. "Negative values, as well as positive—as if you can have minus electrons as well as electrons. Studying my equation, it is almost as if an electron should have an anti-electron counterpart. The equations suggest that every type of matter should have an *antimatter* companion!"

Yet again the conference breaks into a dozen muttering conversations. Some quite like the symmetry of every matter having its antimatter, but can we really trust some quirk in Dirac's mathematical formula to make such an unexpected and unsubstantiated prediction? If there really is matter and antimatter, why is our world made of matter and not of antimatter? What happens when matter and antimatter meet each other?

As the dust settles, it seems to me that Schrödinger's cat has the last purr. Perhaps, it may just be possible that the universe is random, not deterministic. It is even conceivable that distant electrons can have entangled states. But cats are not simultaneously alive and dead. People are not here and there. If you measure the spin of an electron and use that to decide whether to build a city, that city will not be forever both built and unbuilt. Somehow, somewhere, the vague superpositions of the subatomic world become definite states of the macroscopic world. *Someone had better figure out how.*

Back in my hut, I reflect that perhaps the greatest collection of geniuses in history, when brought together in one room, managed to dismantle almost everything that has ever been achieved. After centuries of work on deterministic models for predicting the behavior of the universe, they are arguing that all the fundamental processes of the universe are completely random. After Maxwell and Einstein painstakingly did away with action at a distance and found nice "local" theories for electromagnetism and gravity, after Einstein proved that instantaneous travel and communication are impossible, quantum mechanics has brought back entanglement between distant particles and instantaneous action at a distance when one of the entangled particles is measured.

It's a cold autumn evening, and I take the warm can from the box and hold it in my hands while I reflect. *Just one more day.*

My mission to understand physics is almost complete. Quantum mechanics now explains the behavior of the protons, electrons, and photons that everything else is made of. *It's just so different from what it seems.*

I add a brand new section to the ROW label:

Nature of reality: Everything—the electron, proton, and photon—is both a wave and a particle. The nature of this "quantum mechanical" wave is abstract, but the wave seems to give a probability for the particle being at a certain location in case you measure its position. Some particles, such as electrons, obey an exclusion principle and have an intrinsic spin.

I add new fewer than three major new warnings:

WARNING: Non-locality: Different particles may have their states entangled even when they are distant; measuring one can instantaneously affect the state of the other (a new type of action at a distance!)

WARNING: Randomness: The world is inherently random, not deterministic.

WARNING: Indefiniteness: Nobody knows what exactly constitutes a "measurement" that causes quantum "superpositions" to finally collapse into definite macroscopic states (Schrödinger's cat).

Stepping outside, I look up at the familiar night sky and shake my head slowly, with newfound respect for an old adversary. *Fact is so much stranger than fiction.* Who could have possibly believed that hidden under the surface of the definite, predictable, local physical world we observe is this cosmic casino, where everything is random and indefinite and where entanglements create instant links at a distance.

Closing the door, I again pick up the warm can. I have started to take for granted that it is always there to warm my hands. But now I recall what I asked when I first held it. How is this can still warm almost three weeks after I left home? If it were preheated, it would have cooled down in minutes. A chemical reaction would have fizzled out in hours.

There is only one possible answer. *The can I am holding must be radioactive.* The atoms inside it have unstable nuclei. Perhaps it contains radium or uranium.

I think of my Dad and hold the can tighter. What subtle clues he left me. The can never represented heat—heat, after all, is not a fundamental phenomenon—it is just the statistical collection of the random movements of the electrons. Nuclear forces—now that is a mysterious fundamental phenomenon of the universe. I have one more day available and one final set of mysteries to explore—the interior of the atomic nucleus: how protons bind together and how electrons sometimes shoot out of a nucleus.

"Computer. Find me an explanation of the interactions within the nucleus."

Warning: low on fuel

I gawk at the screen. *What the—? Low on fuel! Where did that come from? This hut uses fuel?* I have been taking the availability of time travel as a given. Have I overstayed my welcome? I mean, I told my Dad two or three days. Even so, he might have warned me if I have a quota. Perhaps he thought I would only travel back a few decades—did I overdo it with Ancient Greece? Did I stay too long? Did I make too many stops?

I shout at the computer. "What does 'low' mean?"

No answer.

"Just enough for tonight's journey and then the long trip home, right?"

No answer.

"Computer would it be safer to go home right now and not make one more stop?"

Still no answer.

I toss and turn in my bed all night. Being mostly awake, I get to feel the accelerations that I believe are taking me to the brink of the speed of light where I can benefit from time dilation, then the decelerations back to rest on Earth. In any event, this next stop must be my last one as my three weeks are up. *I'd better have enough fuel for tonight and for tomorrow's trip home because—well, because I signed a disclaimer!*

MED

Day 21. MED.

MED? The screen is even terser than usual. *Or truncated due to the fuel shortage?* What could MED be short for? It's like one of the geography quizzes back home. Medford, Oregon? Medan, Indonesia? Mediterranean Sea?

21 days. The legal limit. MED will be my very last stop. Next time I wake up that screen will say "2110, Iceland." Assuming of course—I swallow—that I have enough fuel to get there.

Tomorrow I say my goodbyes and... start a brand new life. With this thought poisoning not only my mind but also my stomach, I stagger to the little bathroom and discover that indoor toilets are very convenient when you have a sudden unexpected need to vomit.

How do I prepare myself for such a change? I can't even say I'm making the decision full-heartedly; in addition to the painful personal changes, I did witness the fringes of the Great War, so the Ecommunity's warnings were not entirely unfounded. Science does come with big risks. But that war seems to have been a big blot on a generally positive process.

I have also realized that my Dad knowingly abandoned the unborn me and... lied to me about it. He may be racked with guilt, but then again, for all I know he's quite relieved to have dodged all the diapers and was experimenting with traveling to 2092 to try to save the Dean.

But for all of that, I just cannot return from this trip to a lifetime of plowing and to sermons about evil scientists.

One thing is certain: today is my last chance to equip myself with the knowledge that will be expected of me for my career on the Outside. I glance at the ROW label—yes, it's almost complete. Everything except the forces within the atom's nucleus. There are several warnings about the world being non-deterministic and non-local and the question about the measurements that introduce definiteness. *But heck, that's just the strange world we live in.*

Breathing heavily, I step outside.

Dressed in a knee-length pleated skirt and a simply cut blouse, I find myself on a campus. I scan the signs on the different buildings; they're all dedicated to theoretical physics. Not just any theoretical physics—the whole complex seems to be focused on the final frontier—the nucleus of the atom. *A sizeable campus entirely dedicated to studying something a few trillionths of a millimeter wide!*

The weather is sunny and warm. People are walking around in an atmosphere that is business-like, but relaxed and occasionally jovial. Here and there, scientists huddle around a white board scribbling formulae, engaging each other in scientific banter. Others sit alone with pen and paper or consult a book. I pass an extensive library and then a handful of small labs with people—men, pretty much—in white coats fussing over various apparatus.

After Brussels, I have a little practice at working a group, so I introduce myself to a couple of people, trying to identify the lynchpins. My impression is that this may be no lesser a group than the group I encountered my yesterday in Parc Léopold! At least this will be a great place to crown my three week crash course in physics. *Hoping, of course, it doesn't end up literally as a crash course.*

"I'm a new physics intern here. Who can bring me up to speed?" I ask some young academic in a double-breasted gray suit.

"I'm Richard Feynman. But you should really speak to James Chadwick," Richard points, "his work—Nobel-winning work—was key to starting all the research here."

"It all started in Rutherford's team in Manchester and then Cambridge," Chadwick tells me in a relaxed British accent. He must be in his fifties, his face wide at the forehead drawn a little sharply around the chin.

"Ah, how is Sir Ernest?"

"How is he? Oh. I'm sorry to be the one to tell you that the First Baron Rutherford of Nelson—as he became—has passed away."

"I'm so sorry; I—I've been somehow out of touch. What happened?"

"You could say he died of nobility."

"Of nobility?"

"Rutherford suffered an umbilical hernia in 1937. It was operable, but unfortunately protocol was that only a titled doctor could operate on a 'peer of the realm'—a Lord. The doctors in Cambridge actually watched Lord Rutherford die rather than operate, while awaiting a suitably ennobled doctor. Yes, very sad," he says, shaking his head. "Anyway, once Rutherford discovered—"

"Wait, wait. What did you say? What was that word?"

Chadwick looks confused. "Which word? Ennobled? Hernia?"

"Yes—hernia! I think I've heard that word once. What is that?"

"You know, when some of the intestines protrude. Dangerous if untreated, but operable. As I was saying... um, are you all right?"

I'm not all right, and I'm not listening. Distant but painful memories are perforating my mind struggling to reassemble themselves. Without thinking, I whip my blouse out of my skirt revealing my tummy, and the small mark which I don't like showing. "This little mark right here? This... scar. Could it be from a hernia? From a hernia operation?"

Chadwick squints at me. "Fizz, I'm not a surgeon. Surely you would know that? I would guess that a hernia scar would probably be bigger than that."

"But if surgical techniques improved?" I say.

"What? Fizz..."

But my mind is no longer in the present.

"Mom and daughter time," Mom says. "A trip to Reykjavik."

I'm small, my eyes barely reach Mom's waist as she tells me. I would estimate I'm three years old.

In Reykjavik there is none of the fun touring I expected. We're indoors. People in white coats talk to Mom. They keep glancing down at me while they talk. Several times I hear a word I don't understand—hernia.

Then I'm sleepy, so incredibly tired, but for one short moment—and with great effort—I manage to fight my heavy eyes open. I look up. Bright lights like I've never seen—unnatural lights—are shining down on me, blinding me, scaring me. Around the lights, I see people's faces. Adults without mouths, two, no—three people, all mouthless, all with their mouths covered.

"This won't hurt," one of the covered mouths says, but then for a second he does hurt me with a sharp jab to my shoulder... then nothing...

Back home in bed, Mom looks blurred as she says, "You got sick on our little trip. Stay in bed for a couple of days. No, don't undress..."

I shake my head. "You're right, I do know. It is a hernia. I was only little. No one ever told me."

"Well then, it looks like someone took good care of you," Chadwick tries to sound reassuring.

"No..."

"No?" He looks confused. "You survived, didn't you? With a surprisingly mild scar."

I look down at my midriff for a while. Then become aware of him staring at me and tuck my blouse back in. "That's not the scar. The scar is up here." I tap my head.

Chadwick frowns. "Look I don't know you, but someone saved your life. You're upset they didn't tell you about it? I guess you were young, they probably thought you didn't remember, thought that it would upset you."

"They lied to me."

"Well, seems to me like a white lie to protect a small child."

"No! You don't understand! Not the operation. They lied to me about technology! About medicine! Everything they said is tainted with hypocrisy! What else did they lie about? No doubt they greatly exaggerated the evils of technology!"

It doesn't even matter anymore—in a strange way, since I'm leaving anyway, this may even be helpful.

Chadwick shifts awkwardly. "Listen, Fizz, shall I brief you tomorrow?"

I draw a deep breath or two. "No," I say with as much definiteness as I can muster. "Please go on. Strangely this strengthens my interest."

"Are you sure?" He watches my reaction carefully. "All right. Once Rutherford discovered the atomic nucleus, he drove all of us around him in the Cavendish Lab to probe it relentlessly," Chadwick tells me. "Year after year, element after element, experiment after experiment, we scrutinized those little things. Over the course of more than twenty years our experimental apparatus improved too. It was in 1932 that two of Rutherford's other students first managed to split an atom artificially— split the nucleus itself—finally making a total nonsense of the very name 'atom.' It was in the same year that I made my big discovery. Sure you are all right?"

"Yes. Your discovery was?"

"I was investigating a new type of nuclear radiation. It did not seem to fit into any of Rutherford's three categories of nuclear radiation, which he had called alpha, beta, and gamma."

"Delta radiation?"

Chadwick smiles. "By then we had the apparatus to explore the radiation rather than just stick another Greek letter on it. I identified that this new radiation comprised an entirely new unknown particle that weighed the same as a proton, but was electrically neutral, not positive."

"What is that?"

"It was an unexpected discovery—a third fundamental particle for the world alongside the proton and the electron—an electrically neutral version of the proton! I called it the *neutron*."

"Hmm," I frown. "Sounds like an unwelcome complication. A fifty percent increase in the ingredients of matter."

"That was our first reaction too. But once we came to understand the neutron, we welcomed it as a long lost friend. It solved two major open problems."

"Ah," I say. "Is that the extra mass in the nucleus? Are there neutrons in the nucleus?"

"Right. And there was an even bigger mystery. J. J. Thomson had in the meantime discovered that some neon atoms are heavier than other neon atoms. These two versions of the same atom have been called *isotopes* of the atom. Chemically the isotopes are identical, but their mass is different. With my discovery of the neutron, it all made sense. A neon atom always has ten protons, but it may have either ten or twelve neutrons. Nowadays we call these isotopes discovered by Thomson *Neon-20* and *Neon-22*, because the total number of protons plus neutrons in the nucleus is twenty in one case and twenty-two in the other."

"Okay, so the world is made out of electrons, protons, *and* neutrons. Please tell me that's it."

"One last mystery remained. When we looked at the products of the radioactive decay of an atom, there was some momentum unaccounted for. There had to be some extra invisible particle at play. The next year Wolfgang Pauli proposed the *neutrino,* which solved that puzzle."

I recall Wolfgang Pauli at the table my yesterday, presenting his exclusion principle and electron spin.

"The neutrino is devilishly hard to detect," Chadwick continues, "because it is so light and doesn't interact much. It can fly through the entire planet without interacting with a single atom. In fact, trillions of neutrinos from the Sun pass through you every second."

My eyebrows shoot up as if trying to dodge the stream of neutrinos. *Recently physics is sounding more like a horror story than a science.* "So, back to Aristotle? Four constituents of matter?" I'm almost pleading.

"Almost. In the meantime," Chadwick continues as I sigh, "Carl David Anderson at the California Institute of Technology discovered *antimatter*. Andersen found the antimatter version of the electron. The anti-electron is now called a *positron*. He found the positron in the cosmic rays—the constant stream of particles splattered out by the Sun.

Now that antimatter is confirmed, we assume that there are anti-protons, anti-neutrons, and anti-neutrinos too."

Wow—it worked. I remember Dirac showing some esoteric equation in Parc Léopold that happened to have negative solutions. He boldly predicted that every particle has an anti-particle—probably the first person to predict a brand new type of matter purely based on a formula. *And he was right.* The world has a new symmetry: matter and antimatter.

"And then all the mysteries were solved?"

"Ah, yes," Chadwick leans back. "I have to say that in 1933 we all felt very smug. The universe was our oyster. We were able to explain pretty much all known phenomena. Matter was made of electrons, protons, neutrons, and neutrinos. The interactions were electromagnetism, based on the photon, and gravity, governed by general relativity. And we started to understand the interactions within the nucleus too. For some years, we all felt that physics was pretty much complete. Theoretical physicists advised their students to seek other careers."

Chadwick smiles. "Then—"

"Wait. Give me a few seconds."

"What?"

"Look, you had some years to enjoy the feeling that everything is known. Can I at least have a few seconds?"

"Feel free." He shrugs and tilts his head sideways as if looking at me from an angle.

I close my eyes. All physical processes are known and understood. The ROW is familiar, it's label complete. Comfortable. Satisfying.

Boring.

"Please go ahead," I open my eyes. *Do I even want everything to be known?*

"Then came the *muon*. It's like a heavy version of the electron. As someone quipped at the time, '*Who ordered that?*' The universe just tossed the muon out there as if to say, 'Hello, I'm not quite finished here, I have a surprise or two left up my sleeve.'"

Chadwick leans forward. "Now, for your work here, you will need to be up to speed on nuclear physics. Our everyday world," he waves around, "has two interactions—electromagnetism and gravity. But the world inside the nucleus has two fundamental interactions of its own: the *strong interaction* and the *weak interaction*."

"The strong interaction binds the protons together in the nucleus?" I ask.

"Indeed."

"So without the strong interaction, the universe would be a cloud of hydrogen with no heavier atoms! And the weak interaction?"

"The weak interaction is more esoteric. It plays no clear role in our everyday lives. The weak interaction can actually change a neutron into a proton, electron, and anti-neutrino—and that's an important process in some nuclear reactions and in the radioactive decay of some nuclei. Anyway, what interests us here is one conundrum, in particular, of the nucleus."

"Conundrum?"

"The mass of a neon-20 nucleus, say, must be the sum of the masses of the ten protons and the ten neutrons that it's made of. Right?"

"Obviously," I nod.

"Wrong," he smiles. "The mass of an atom's nucleus is up to *ten percent less* than the mass of its constituents. There is a mass deficit in the atoms."

"Less?"

"Less."

I scrunch up my face. Mass is conserved. Assembling protons and neutrons into a nucleus must result in as much mass as what was put in, yet this Nobel laureate is sitting here claiming that all everyday matter weighs less than the sum of its building blocks!

"So the universe is skimming some off the top, huh?" I say. "We should demand more accountability."

"Well, yes," Chadwick says, "but you see the strong interaction is, as its name might suggest, rather strong. At least at extremely small distances."

I want to understand this one myself. I imagine myself holding two protons—aka hydrogen nuclei—one in each hand. They are both electrically positive, so they repel one another, but I am determined to fuse them together. I push them closer and closer. The closer they get, the more electromagnetic repulsion there is. But I keep pushing. As they get really close, the repulsion is overwhelming. I break into a sweat. My arm muscles shudder. Soon my whole body is shaking, but I call on hidden strengths and still I'm pushing those two protons closer and closer and closer. I'm exerting energy...

One centimeter. One millimeter. Down to a thousandth of a millimeter, or a micron, where the inverse-square electric force has grown a million-fold stronger than at a millimeter. And still I'm pushing! A millionth of a millimeter, a billionth of a millimeter...

Finally, I get those two protons to within one trillionth of a millimeter of each other. Mere words cannot begin to describe the intensity of the repulsion.

Suddenly it happens. At around a trillionth of a millimeter separation, the protons enter a whole new world where new interactions rule. *The strong interaction*—and its attraction is a hundred times stronger than the electromagnetic repulsion that seconds earlier seemed so overwhelming.

I lose my grip of the two protons as the strong interaction snaps them together with super-violent intensity. The protons crash together so violently that a shower of high-energy photons—X-rays—and other particles come shooting out. In fact, the amount of energy released in the final crunch is far greater than all the energy I exerted in pushing them together.

Energy is released.

Suddenly I realize my mistake. Einstein taught me that energy is more correctly thought of as mass-energy. *Mass-energy is released.* For the first time I am hearing about a phenomenon—the *fusing* of protons by the strong interaction—that is so energetic that we can actually notice the energy change even in terms of mass.

Einstein's incredible suggestion that $E=mc^2$ is vindicated inside each and every atomic nucleus!

I rub my hands together. "So are you saying that when protons and neutrons fuse into a nucleus, so much mass-energy is released that their own mass-energy—their actual weight—is reduced by several percent?"

"Precisely. You'll do well here."

Hmm. I recall how the number c^2 in $E=mc^2$ is so huge that each kilogram of mass is some hundred trillion joules of energy. Now Chadwick has said that when one kilogram of protons—that is hydrogen—is assembled into bigger atoms, ten percent of that mass-energy is released. That ten percent would be ten trillion joules for each kilogram of matter—*a calamitous dollop of energy.*

"Now, this is important," Chadwick says. "The biggest mass-energy deficit is in the medium-sized nuclei. So if you can take small nuclei like hydrogen atoms and fuse them together, that releases energy. If you take a big atom like uranium and split it—*fission*—that releases mass-energy too, because middle-sized atoms have the biggest mass-energy deficit."

"Got it. *Fusion* of small nuclei and *fission*—splitting—of big nuclei; both release huge amounts of mass-energy. So that's what you're exploring here?"

"Yes. Others are expert on each subject." Chadwick waves to a colleague walking past. "Hans, Fizz here is just getting started. Come give her the quick once over on nuclear *fusion*." Then he says to me softly, "Hans Bethe from Germany."

"Nuclear fusion," says Hans with an air of importance, "is the most important process in the universe."

I smirk. He's the expert—I'm sure fusion is the most important process in his universe. *To a hammer, the most important thing in the world is a nail.*

"Hans, I already understand that if you can press protons and neutrons to within a trillionth of a millimeter of each other, the strong interaction snaps them together, releasing incredible amounts of mass-energy. But how would you ever get them that close when they repel so strongly?"

"I actually discovered the only known way to fuse hydrogen. You take a lot of protons—a ball of about a million trillion trillion kilograms of hydrogen. That's about a billion trillion trillion trillion trillion protons."

"Hans, can we just say 'a lot'?"

"*Ja.* You take a lot of hydrogen. You see, at that incredible size the sheer gravity within your vast ball of hydrogen becomes so intense that the hydrogen nuclei at the center of the ball will be crushed together by the gravitational attraction, despite their electric repulsion, and they will start to spontaneously fuse into helium. The fusion will release energy— 'a lot' of energy."

Again I find myself smirking. "Oh right. You performed this experiment, did you, with a zillion kilos of hydrogen? In one of the labs here perhaps?"

"Well, I didn't so much perform the experiment as observe it. In that lab over there." Hans points out of the window. "You know, I was out with my girlfriend the evening when the insight into fusion occurred to me. She was just saying 'Look at the stars twinkling'—"

Where is he going with this?

"—and I answered 'yes, and right now I'm the only person in the world who knows how they twinkle.'" Hans looks at me and smiles. "Yeah, that's the confused face my girlfriend made—just like that."

Fortunately my confused face doesn't last long. Stars twinkling? *Don't I feel stupid.* Perhaps he wasn't exaggerating after all! I pace to the window and glance up at Hans' "lab." And from the sky, Hans' lab of nuclear fusion shines down brightly on my face.

"So," I sum up, "the Sun is just a big ball of hydrogen being fused into helium under its own sheer weight?"

Hans nods. "Same for all the stars, all fusing hydrogen as they fly away from us. Nuclear fusion powers the cosmos."

I linger by the window for a second and feel the warmth of the Sun on my face. The fusion inside that big ball of hydrogen is so energetic that I can feel it from a hundred and fifty million kilometers away—with a delay of eight minutes of light-travel time. The same warmth from the Sun illuminates our planet and makes plants grow and water evaporate to provide rain and wind. *Nuclear fusion really is powering every aspect of life on Earth.*

"Wait one second, Hans, did you say that the stars are flying away from us?"

Bethe frowns. "Goodness, where do we recruit these days? Surely you know about Hubble's discovery?"

"Err... remind me please."

"Edwin Hubble at the Mount Wilson Observatory near L.A. You know how hydrogen atoms emit and absorb some very specific colors?"

I recall Bohr's explanation of the electron waves in the atoms being like constrained guitar strings.

"Astronomers observed those same colors absorbed in the Sun and stars. That is how we know that the Sun and other stars are made of the simplest atom: hydrogen. But Hubble found that the hydrogen in distant galaxies always appears redder than it should. So they're all flying away from us."

"Back up a sec. Why does redder mean they're traveling away from us?" I smile. "I saw red lights on the back of automobiles—I don't suppose stars have that feature."

"*No.* It's the Doppler Effect. If they're moving away, the wavelength gets stretched. Like the noise of a car."

I noticed that in Berlin—the noise of the truck engines did sound lower when they were driving away from me. I close my eyes and think about a hummingbird dropping a series of pebbles as it moves. *Of course*, the wavelength—the distance between the wave peaks—would effectively be stretched if the source of the wave—the hummingbird—is moving away from me, and contracted if it's moving toward me. That's why the engine noise sounds higher when approaching and lower as it recedes. But stretching light to the point where it literally appears redder! Those galaxies must be receding pretty quickly.

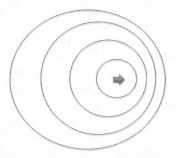

Doppler Effect: When the source of a wave is moving away, the wave in its wake is stretched—light from a receding source appears redder.

"What's more," Bethe continues, "the further galaxies are flying away fastest. The universe is stretching—expanding."

"The universe is expanding? Wow. So Einstein was wrong in believing that he was wrong?"

"What? Oh yes," Bethe grins, "Einstein spent years trying to 'fix' general relativity to reconcile his equations with a static universe. In fact, he had inadvertently made an important discovery: that the universe cannot be—and is now confirmed not to be—static."

It's kind of depressing though—everything in the universe is distancing itself from us.

"Hans, if the universe is expanding, then it used to be... smaller?"

"Right, given the rate of expansion now, it would appear that everything originated from one point billions of years ago. The universe started with a *Big Bang* and is expanding to this very day."

My mind is spinning. The universe started from a point and expanded in a Big Bang. And we can see all the galaxies flying away from each other still today.

I thank Bethe.

I catch Chadwick again. "I don't see trillions of kilos of hydrogen here on campus, so obviously you're not working on fusion here."

"No. Although one of the guys, Ede Teller—or Edward in English—does have an idea for pursuing fusion here on Earth. But as you guessed, you will mostly be working here on splitting large atoms—fission. That also releases energy and it's much easier to achieve because big atoms are fairly unstable and amenable to being split."

"But how do you—do we—split atoms?"

"Okay, it's critical you understand that well. Let me get Fermi. He's from Rome, also a Nobel Prize winner."

Chadwick returns soon and introduces me to Fermi, in his forties. "Enrico Fermi here, with Leó Szilárd from Budapest, both now at the University of Chicago, figured it out. Then Szilárd and Einstein proposed our research program in a letter to President Roosevelt." Chadwick introduces us, then leaves us alone.

"*Si*, well, the idea was simple," Enrico tells me. "If you have a big atom like uranium, it is unstable. Occasionally a uranium atom will spontaneously split, and then you get neutrons flying out as Chadwick discovered."

"Okay," I say, "but does a single atom splitting achieve much?"

"A single atom splitting could barely move a speck of dust. But what, we thought, if those neutrons from the one splitting atom in turn hit other atoms and cause them to split? Do you see? Now we have a few atoms splitting. And what if those splitting atoms released yet more neutrons. Pretty soon you have trillions of atoms splitting! We called that scenario a *chain reaction*—each splitting atom releases neutrons and triggers more splitting atoms like links in a very big chain. Actually, it is more like bowling: one pin knocks down two, knocks down three—the number keeps increasing."

"Bowling?" I ask.

"You know, ten-pin bowling."

I nod uncertainly. "But does that happen? Does uranium exhibit such a chain reaction?"

"Natural uranium does not chain react, but about one percent of natural uranium atoms are the U-235 isotope. If you can separate out those U-235 atoms, and if you get enough of them, a *critical mass*, you get a chain reaction. But it's extremely difficult to separate that rare U-235 isotope because the two isotopes are chemically identical and the difference in masses is slight. But if we can—well, come and see."

He walks me over to a chart hanging on one of the walls showing the hypothesized chain reaction of U-235 uranium, once enough of it is *enriched* out of natural uranium:

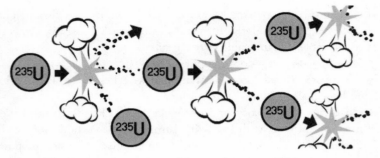

Chain reaction—continued fission of uranium-235 atoms

"Another possibility," Fermi continues, "is that in a nuclear reactor you can add protons to uranium atoms and transmute them into *plutonium*. Plutonium doesn't exist in nature—it's an artificial atom with ninety-four protons. A critical mass of plutonium will chain react too."

Rutherford changed one natural element into another. These physicists have changed one natural element into a brand new element, a new atom, that doesn't even exist in nature—plutonium.

"So," I say, "this chain reaction sounds all very well in theory. Does it really work? Have you tested it?"

"We did a full-scale test with plutonium a month ago. It made one big pop. The U-235 uranium will be tried out any time now. It's been years of intense research—all of us are on tenterhooks, waiting to see how well it works."

I marvel at the process. Years of scribbling formulae on a blackboard, years of theoreticizing about the delicate balance between the electro-magnetic repulsion and the strong nuclear attraction acting on the 235 protons and neutrons in a U-235 atom—all of this coming together in one dramatic experiment.

I thank Fermi and Chadwick. *I think I've achieved pretty good under-standing of the final frontier, the strong and weak interactions within the nucleus.* This afternoon I must write up my notes and polish off the label. I think I'm as well prepared—at least intellectually—as I can be for my new life. *Assuming of course that there's enough fuel to get back there.* I head to the library.

Entering the library, I almost trip over a pile of newspapers. The *Santa Fe New Mexican.* So I'm in the state of New Mexico. I pick up the top copy, dated Saturday, August 4, 1945. Two photos appear on the front page: A large group of wounded veteran soldiers has returned from Europe; a nurse tenderly leans over one of the mutilated soldiers. My stomach lurches at the image of another major war. In the other picture, one President Truman is shaking hands with King George VI of the United Kingdom in Plymouth, England. The caption states that the US president is en route home from the "Big-Three Conference," whatever that is, in Germany.

Reading further, the conference involved the three victors discussing the future of a war-ravaged Europe. It seems that every one of the beautiful cities I have visited these last three weeks, with the possible exception of Bern and Basel, has been decimated by air raids and battles. The US was not spared. *Food Shortage to Last Into 1946* reads a smaller headline. In other parts of the world, the war is not over. *Not a Safe Spot in Japan: Surrender or die* reads the main headline, which seems more like propaganda than news.

I'm holding back the tears. Back home in 2110, we are told about terrible wars on the Outside in the previous century, but why did I have to land—for the second time—right in the middle of one? My stomach churns. I look around the library at the various academics. Their whispered conversations about obscure issues in nuclear physics suddenly seem irrelevant, in fact horribly insensitive. I hold up the newspaper and want to shout across the library: *Why didn't you all tell me there's a brutal war going on? Why don't you all forget about the strong interaction and do something about the fighting?*

A morbid fascination drives me to continue reading the articles in the newspaper and to pick up papers from a couple of previous days. Even as the dark feelings deepen, I read on. The majority of the world's nations have been at war for six years—the scale of the war seems to dwarf even the Great War that I was near in Berlin in 1919. One hundred million people have been directly employed in the conflict, and the majority of the world's population is indirectly involved in economically and logistically supporting the worldwide combat. Tens of millions have perished in fighting and genocide, possibly more than all the wars in history combined.

The articles and pictures make it clear how this war grew to monstrous proportions, far greater than even the recent Great War. *Science and technology.* A small headline states that the US produced 4,800 aircraft in the single month of July. *4,800 a month!* So the Bernoulli effect is now lifting many tens of thousands of airplanes. The radio waves predicted by Maxwell and discovered by Hertz are being used for wireless communication across the globe as well as for RAdio Detection And Ranging, or radar, identifying and shooting down those aircraft as rapidly as they can be manufactured. Every single aspect of the war—the factories, planes, trains, trucks, boats, and submarines—is powered by artificial energy and controlled by artificial communications.

As I turn page after page of horror, my skin turns cold and clammy. The Great Deterioration, greater than I ever imagined. A world I would never want to live in. *What do I do now?*

While I'm standing somberly, I notice some men running around outside. There's some shouting. One man bursts into the library and dumps down a pile of newspapers. "They dropped it on Hiroshima," he says.

All the men around me in the library stand up spontaneously. Some are grinning—beaming with satisfaction. Two guys hug each other. Others stand silently—serious, somber. One man sheds a tear. I still don't know what "it" is, but "it" can provoke incredibly strong and entirely contradictory emotions in grown men.

I grab today's newspaper from the fresh pile: *Santa Fe New Mexican*, Monday August 6, 1945.

ATOMIC BOMBS DROP ON JAPAN. Then the subheadings: *Deadliest Weapons in World's History. Utter Destruction… Power more than 20,000 tons of TNT… 2,000 times more than the largest bomb ever used before… Mr. Truman added: "It is an atomic bomb. It is a harnessing of the basic power of the universe."* There is some commentary on the front page as well, which seems horribly optimistic in the circumstances: *May Be Tool To End Wars; New Era Seen.*

Below these items, the front page carries a short report on *Tomato Juice off Rationing* as well as the weather.

More men pour into the library. I look around, stunned, for any guidance of how to conduct myself.

"A historic blunder," one man is muttering repeatedly.

"Celebrations?" suggests another.

"I just tried, La Fonda Hotel is sold out for dinner," someone replies.

Then come the three words that pierce my mind more sharply than any others. "We did it."

I grab the Santa Fe paper again and scan the large front-page frantically. There it is in another subtitle: *Los Alamos Secret Disclosed by Truman… Made In Santa Fe Vicinity.*

Amongst the chaos, I spot Chadwick. "P—Professor Chadwick, what—what is this place? I thought it was a research institute. Is all this research some sort of weapon design?"

He looks at me, perplexed. "Of course it is. You were admitted onto campus. How could you not know that?"

"But I only see theoretical physicists here, I don't see weapons."

He stares at me. "Fizz, in addition to us physicists, the MED project employs 130,000 people across the US who carry out our ideas for enriching uranium and synthesizing plutonium. The vast majority of them don't even know that they have been working to produce the atomic fission bombs like the one dropped today in Japan."

"M—MED?"

"Sure, that's the official name," he's starting to squint at me. "You know, the Manhattan Engineering District or Manhattan Project. Manhattan is where it started, before we came here to Los Alamos."

"And they really dropped this awful bomb without ever doing a full-scale test?"

"Even with 130,000 people, the entire project could only enrich enough uranium-235 for one critical mass. So the first test was for real."

"W—what are the implications?"

I ask, but I'm not really focused on Chadwick's answer.

"Maybe some 100,000 casualties. An initial shock wave of sound and heat, fires raging for kilometers around… aftermath of radiation sickness… an arsenal of plutonium bombs in case they don't surrender after today's uranium bomb—we are still manufacturing more… Ede Teller here wants to start developing a hydrogen bomb… He thinks he can use a uranium fission bomb as a trigger to reproduce the temperatures of the core of the Sun and use that to start hydrogen fusion for greater energies—"

I'm hearing but not listening. Instead, my mind is listening—as it never listened before—to words from the Dean's sermons, now reverberating through every cell in my brain. *Prying leads to tinkering… leads to meddling… insatiable greed for greater energies… the lust for power… applying technology for evil… unimaginable weapons of mass distraction…*

Why didn't they tell me explicitly about the atomic bombs destroying a city? And still Teller is dreaming about bigger weapons? How did my father let me out into this horrific world? Why didn't Mom physically hold me back?

I need to be home right now. *Home—to my real home, to safety, to the home in my Ecommunity that will be unattainable after midnight.* I need my mother by my side, my friends, holding me, telling me everything will be okay. I promise to never again question the blissful isolation of the Collective and the remoteness of the Ecommunity. I want to completely obliterate any memories of this ill-conceived mission and of any thought I ever had of leaving.

I'm only vaguely aware of Chadwick asking if I am all right as I turn and start running through the campus in the now baking midday desert sunshine. I pass a row of physicists phoning in their reservations for dinner. I try very hard to think about home, to fill my mind with images of fields and waterfalls and hot springs and moss-padded hills and community songs—to occupy my thoughts so completely that there is not the smallest bit of room left for images of the inferno that must be raging, consuming life right this second in Hiroshima, Japan.

In the hut, I slam the door shut and stagger over to the desk, perspiring and panting.

"Computer, take me home to my Collective. 2110. Right now."

Error: Insufficient energy for 165 years of time travel.

My worst nightmare is presented to me, impersonally, on a small screen.

"Just help me, damn it," I sob, "get me out of this place; find me someone who can get me home."

Very Nearly Everything

Day 22. White Valley, Jerusalem. 2011.

The night is a blur of nightmares, and I wake up, my skin sticking to the sheets, to find that the computer has only managed a meager sixty-five years of time travel, depositing me a full century—ninety-nine years to be precise—prior to my own time.

If my time travel comes to an abrupt end here in 2011, and if I get to live a full life, the most contact that I could hope for with my own time period would be, as an elderly woman, to meet my grandparents as little kids. Perhaps I can tell my young grandparents that, when they grow up and have a son, they should tell him that Fizz says sorry about the hut. Or that Fizz says thanks for nothing. Or perhaps when they become grandparents they should tell their granddaughter not to push her luck with too much time traveling—or better not to time travel at all. *Whatever; I may have a lifetime to think about what to say to my little grandparents.*

The only slight hope is that I asked the computer to find someone that can help me. *But am I not beyond help?* And even if I do get back to 2110, my three-week PCC has expired and I'll be branded a "deserter" and barred from home. *Still, living in a violent world in my own time has got to be better than being banished to some random historic period.*

Today the war and atomic explosion of yesterday seem no less horrific, but my survival instinct focuses my thinking on my own problems. After staring at the screen, blinking my damp eyes for quite some time, feeling desperately sorry for myself, I finally request some period-appropriate clothes, which turn out to be heavy-duty pants labeled Levis, and a T-shirt. I drag myself into the ROW.

I emerge half-way up what I suppose is a pretty valley nestled between several sizeable hills. The hillsides grow wild, but the flora is mostly limited to small shrubs, some greenish, some thistly and yellow, as if limited rain has stilted natural growth. The hut is hidden in one of a few small patches of pine trees. I watch a family of three carefree, wild gazelle bouncing elegantly from rock to rock.

While the slopes are natural, some of the hilltops around are capped with dense residential construction. At a far end of the valley, a couple of giraffe are peering over a wall of what must be a zoo. One of the further hills has a high concrete wall snaking ominously around a village. *More conflict.*

Only a single one of all the homes built uphill from my location has access from below and, with no other options available, I find myself entering what seems to be a private apartment through the small garden.

A white Labrador jumps all over me, her tail wagging wildly, depositing hairs all over my clothes. *At least someone is happy.* I pet her.

Then a tall, dashing man of about forty greets me. "Good morning, Fizz," he says in an accent that sounds kind of British.

What the—I stand gaping. "How do you know my name?"

"Come inside."

I hesitate. *What else can I do?*

The man leads me through sliding glass doors into the lounge of the home, from where there is a panoramic view of the valley I just landed in.

"Who are you? How do you know my name? Can you get me home?" I demand.

"Perhaps, but I would prefer that you help yourself get home."

"I will take whatever help I can get, thank you very much. How can you help me? Are you a famous physicist?"

"I wish. For me physics is a hobby at best."

"A fellow time traveler? A time machine mechanic?"

The man clears his throat. "I believe you're not supposed to discuss your time machine in an age when it's not yet been invented."

How does he know so much? "To hell with that." I squint at him. "So who are you, and can you help me—yes or no?"

"We'll see. But first you must catch up with physics in 2011."

"I must—says who?"

"Look, Fizz. Maybe today you're scared and confused, but I'm betting your curiosity is still there. 1945 was a low point—take a couple of days to get a more balanced view. Indulge your curiosity a little further. Who knows? It might help you get home."

"Home? So you think... I have a chance of getting home?"

"A chance, yes."

I stare at him for a long while.

"Is there some world war going on I should be aware of?"

"No. Much of humanity has been at peace since 1945, albeit with a few nasty exceptions. Mind you, you wouldn't know it living in this particular city."

A girl my age and my height, also with wavy red hair—*his daughter?*—walks by. For a split second we eye each other.

I look back to the man. "You got any food?"

"Sure," he smiles.

I wash down some cornflakes with a few gulps of orange juice.

"There's something I want to show you." The man places in front of me a slim matte-silvery metallic box with a glowing icon of a white apple, minus one bite, at its center. He then presses a tiny latch and unfolds the box into two. The lower half has a few dozen metallic-colored buttons bearing letters of the English alphabet. The top half seems to be a bright colorful screen that keeps moving and changing, like nothing I've ever seen before.

The man presses some buttons rather quickly, and somewhere near the top of the psychedelic screen there appears a strange sequence of letters *w... i... k...* forming the cryptic message *wikipedia.org*. He hits a larger button labeled "Enter" and suddenly the whole screen changes, showing a globe-shaped jigsaw puzzle and a list of languages. At the top of the list "English" appears, with some claim about more than three million "articles."

"This little pad here is called a mouse, never mind why," he points below the keyboard. "Moving your finger here controls that pointer there, and if you position the pointer in this rectangle you can type any subject that interests you using these keys."

I stare down at the device. "Maybe I could, if you hadn't jumbled up the alphabet."

"Take your time."

"Since you're being so obtuse, can this device tell me who you are?"

He rolls his eyes.

I slowly poke at the letters. *I... C... E... L... A... N... D.* Sure enough I am treated to an article all about my home country. Pictures of the familiar cliffs and mountains prompt a wave of nostalgia, as I fight back the tears. The Langjökull glacier in one of the images looks so much bigger than I know it—like witnessing history in reverse—a global cooling.

I gaze at the photographs. *If I'm stuck in 2011, shall I go live in the familiar scenery of Iceland?* Maybe spend my life hiding notes to the future me?

Reading on, I learn how last year an eruption of the Eyjafjoell volcano closed air travel across Europe. *Hah.*

"So you have articles on three million topics inside this little box?" *More efficient than my notebook at home.*

"Access to three million articles. Scroll down."

There's a word I've not heard since Aristotle.

At the very bottom of the long article on Iceland are two underlined words: "About Wikipedia."

"You can 'click' those underlined words with the mouse," he says.

Now I read about Wikipedia. "Written collaboratively by largely anonymous Internet volunteers who write without pay."

"What's an Internet?"

"Like a more advanced telegraph. Millions of data pipes—electric currents in wires, light pulses in fibers of glass, radio waves through the air—designed to take ones and zeros from any point in the world to any other. People have found ways to transmit text, pictures, sound, and video all digitized into ones and zeros. In total there is about a zettabyte of data available."

"Zettabyte? Like a zillion bite-fulls of data?"

"It's a real word—a trillion gigabytes—a trillion billion characters."

"Okay, 'a lot.' And people in 2011 just volunteer to share their knowledge with strangers around the world?"

"Yes," he nods.

"That's nice," I sniff. "Why are you showing me this?"

"Let's say I feel responsible for your predicament."

"Who are you?" I point at him but he arrogantly ignores my question. "Whoever you are, just leave me for a while to read a few of the zetta-bytes."

Alone, I lean back into the burgundy, corduroy sofa, and as I place the warm little machine on my lap, I type in some topics of interest. *Aristotle. Relativity. World war. Time travel. History of the twentieth century.* Each one brings up a considered article on the requested subject apparently synthesized by thousands of anonymous strangers in distant countries.

As far as physics goes, I read how—in the century since Einstein—humanity has changed tactics in the battle of wits against Mother Nature. The world no longer waits passively for the lone intellectual warrior to materialize and fight the intellectual fight. Rather, the intellectual battle against Mother Nature has been elevated to a whole new scale by battalions of thousands of physicists armed with multi-billion-dollar space telescopes and with particle accelerators the size of a city. It seems that, day after day, these physicists systematically prod the cosmic pockets and rip open the cosmic seams.

For just a second, I do wonder what this well-equipped army of twentieth century physicists has uncovered.

But what of the Great Deterioration? Not all the news is bad. I read how the world has set up welfare, communications, and aid. Famine is rare, life expectancy up, and some nasty diseases extinct. But world populations are mushrooming, natural resources are dwindling, the atmosphere is being artificially altered, and the world has stockpiled sufficient atomic bombs to destroy life many times over. In addition to uranium and plutonium fission bombs, I read that Teller realized his dream—*nightmare, really*—of hydrogen fusion bombs, which use an atomic fission bomb like the one that destroyed Hiroshima my yesterday as a mere trigger to recreate the temperatures at the center of the Sun, and those temperatures are then used to fuse hydrogen into helium, just as the Sun does, for even greater destructive energies.

I need to get out of here.

"So do you want an update on physics?" the man walks back in and asks.

"No. Unless—can it help me?" I demand.

"It's your only chance."

He's right—only physics can get me home. "Well, yeah," I shrug. "How about the conceptual problems. Did they sort out the weirdness of quantum mechanics? What came of the debates about non-locality and randomness? Most of all, what about the measurement problem of Schrödinger's cat—how does indefiniteness become definiteness?"

"Come, Fizz, I'll tell you on the way. You should have enough fuel to reach Geneva in the present time."

"What—why Geneva?"

"We can see there what Germany, France, the UK, Italy, and sixteen other European countries can achieve when they're working with each other."

"Yeah, right. Like I'm just going to let you into my hut and follow you to Geneva without knowing who you are?"

"As you like." He shrugs and walks toward the little garden somewhere beyond which is the hut—my hut.

I glare at his back. *What on earth do I do now?* I follow.

"The argument between Einstein's camp and the Copenhagen camp that you saw in the 1920s raged on until the sixties," the man says as we travel in the hut.

He's sitting at the desk while I'm cross-legged on the bed for the short trip to Geneva in the present time.

"Some of the greatest minds of all times grappled to grasp the significance of the weird microscopic behavior uncovered by quantum mechanics. It was a battle of wits to determine, deep down, what our universe is all about. Some embraced quantum mechanics and the reality of a universe that is fundamentally random, is non-local, and has indeterminate superpositions of states like a cat that is alive and dead. Einstein and others continued to insist that there must be an underlying theory that respects locality and is deterministic."

Who is this man and what is he doing in my hut? For the moment, I try to forget my problems, and my suspicion, and focus on what the man's saying. "I'm with Einstein."

"Many were. But Einstein was wrong. That finally became clear in 1964, after his death."

"What happened in 1964?"

"Someone dreamt up a new thought experiment—a thought experiment that the likes of Bohr, Einstein, Schrödinger, and Heisenberg had all missed despite spending their lives sweating the issue. John Bell, perhaps more than anyone else whom you have met, teaches us that the world is not as it seems. Bell also teaches us that the 'little guy' can sometimes produce a single brilliant insight that humbles the recognized intellectual giants. Bell was from Northern Ireland, but based in the European Center for European Research—CERN—which is exactly where we're heading right now."

He pauses. "Well?" I prod.

"Einstein and others had shown that, according to quantum mechanics, two distant electrons can appear to be in an entangled state like $|up>|down>$ *plus* $|down>|up>$. Einstein thought that was a limitation of the theory—that in reality the pair of particles are either in the state $|up>|down>$ or in the state $|down>|up>$ but not both. Einstein thought the electrons are each in a definite state that happens to be unknown to us until we measure at least one of the electrons.

"But Bell thought of a way of configuring the experiment such that no possible hidden state could explain the result. *Bell's Theorem* proves conclusively that distant electrons can be entangled. Measurement of one electron really can instantly affect the state of another distant electron. For decades, Bell's Theorem was purely a thought experiment, but in recent years some physicists claim to have carried out the experiment for real."

"Ouch," I blow out some air. "I had better leave that warning about non-locality up." I gesture at the warning on my ROW label. "What about randomness?" *Like the randomness of me being stuck in the period of time where I happened to run out of fuel.*

"There is no proof-positive that the universe is random, but there is a ton of evidence. As we investigate deeper and deeper into the nucleus of the atom and deeper still into the internals of the protons and neutrons, we find that pretty much everything seems random. Identical experiments regularly produce different results. We'll see that in CERN today. So modern physics is largely about probabilities. Often scenarios that are classically impossible—such as an electron tunneling through a wall that should be thick enough to stop it—have a non-zero probability in quantum mechanics. Such classically impossible scenarios are observed regularly."

"That's just unbelievable," I shake my head. "So it's really true, when you look at the universe up close it is completely random and has influences that are non-local. But the very same universe on everyday scales is predictable and local! You know, I still don't get how those two world pictures can co-exist. What about Schrödinger's cat? Surely that is the deepest mystery of all. How can things be indefinite when they're not observed? That's just too absurd to be true."

"Is it?" The man stares at me for a while. "Actually, I don't think that should seem all that mysterious. Especially to you, Fizz."

I shoot back a menacing look. "What do you mean especially to me? Who are you?"

"My name is Zvi."

He pronounces it *tsvee*.

"But who are you?" I try to insist.

"Later."

Jerk. I would very much like to press him further—about both his identity and about Schrödinger's cat—but we are interrupted as the small screen announces our arrival.

CERN near Geneva, Switzerland

I look at the screen, then regard Zvi. *Why did I let him into Fizz's Place?* "So what are we doing here?" I ask him.

"Getting up to date on physics."

"That's what I'm doing here. I meant what are *you* doing here."

"I'm here to teach you."

"Mister, you've got to do better than that."

He looks taken aback. "Better? Why?"

"Why?" I look at the hut ceiling. "Let's be honest, you're a complete stranger, from a different country and from a different era to me. You told me your knowledge of physics is amateurish, certainly you're nowhere in the league of the great physicists I've been meeting. You seem to have your own life, your own family. How do you know so much about me? Why are you 'kindly' volunteering your time to travel with me and teach me physics?"

"Look, Fizz, you're trapped in time, a situation that only physics can get you out of, and here I am, offering to try to figure it out with you. You interested or not?"

"You're not off the hook," I point my finger right at him. "Eventually you're going to have to tell me what's going on here. But... yes, if there is any chance whatsoever that physics circa 2011 can pave my way home, I'm interested."

I open the door to peek outside the hut and am greeted by cold, damp air, contrasting with the sunshine we left behind in Jerusalem just an hour or two ago. Towering over the trees that surround us is a large rust-colored globe. Way behind it, through the drizzle, I can just about make out the grey silhouette of some mountains, presumably the Alps.

CERN exhibition center

"So this globe," I say, "is it some sort of climax to my journey? The physicists' equivalent of the crystal ball? Does it reveal the ultimate theory of everything?"

"That's just an exhibition center. But to the best of my understanding, physicists do indeed have a theory of very nearly everything, and this is the best place to learn about it."

"This theory-of-very-nearly-everything was developed here?"

"No, better still, this is where the theory is subjected to its most rigorous and vigorous testing. The extreme experiments carried out here in CERN may further confirm the theory or may expose the flaws that hint at a still deeper theory."

I nod. In my quest for truth, inspired by Galileo, I have certainly come to admire the creative process of conjuring up new theories, but I've also learned that making predictions and testing them experimentally is the only sure way to separate fact from fiction. *Does the world in 2011 really have a theory-of-very-nearly-everything?* It sounds like a bombastic claim. But if true, a theory-of-very-nearly-everything must surely include some mechanism for time traveling home. *If I got here, there must be some way to get back—maybe physics has found a new source of energy or a new mechanism of time dilation.*

"I'm going to take a look on my own," I say. I make a mental note to drill down on that suspicious "very nearly" qualifier he slipped in. I leave Zvi and walk out of the hut following signs that take me around the globe and across a road. I look around at the cars—now in multiple colors—and people; a large aircraft cruises overhead. *Get used to it, Fizz—this may be the world you live your life in.*

For just a moment I wonder if I should be in some way relieved that I have found myself in 2011 prior to the Ecommunity split. Staying here I won't face the choice between my Mom and Dad and their respective worlds. *No, living in the wrong century, with both my parents mourning me in the future, is way worse than being trapped in the wrong community—I absolutely must get back.*

I follow signs to the main reception, which is in building 33 of what I am realizing is a huge, sprawling campus. Here I follow a short corridor to the CERN Microcosm exhibition.

Come on Fizz, this is worth focusing on: the theory-of-very-nearly-everything. My head tries to sidestep thoughts of my predicament and performs an imaginary drum roll for the theory of very-nearly everything.

I step into the exhibition and walk from display to display. At each stop, another piece of the jigsaw puzzle falls into place, a picture of the universe taking shape one step at a time in my mind. As the image assembles, the theory's astounding simplicity becomes apparent, almost a cubist-style model in which a cosmos, appearing infinitely complex to the untrained eye, is distilled down to a tiny number of basic ingredients.

In my mind's eye I see molehills and mountains, puddles and oceans, beetles and redwoods, moons and planets, and stars and entire galaxies, all being stripped down to their basic skeletal building blocks. As the analysis proceeds, their charades of intricacy and uniqueness and differentiation dissipate. *Deep down, everything is the same.*

Three particles: the *up-quark, down-quark,* and *electron.* All matter from the virus to the supernova is constructed of the very same three building blocks. My body, the core of the Earth, and the moons of Jupiter are all just lumps of up-quarks, down-quarks, and electrons. *That's it.*

Even the subatomic proton and neutron are built of quarks. The proton is two up-quarks and a down-quark. The neutron is two down-quarks and an up-quark. The proton and the neutron are made of the very same stuff as each other, and they in turn combine with the electrons to make all the atoms that make—*well, everything.*

Meanwhile, a fourth constituent of matter, the neutrino, plays no role as a building block, but streams through space with complete independence, only very rarely interacting at all with the other forms of matter that it flies through effortlessly. In total, four elements. *Aristotle would be proud.*

How do scientists even examine the basic building blocks of matter? I read how scientists from the 1930s onward studied *cosmic rays*—energetic particles hurled at us by the Sun. When they exhausted the analysis of the natural laboratory of cosmic rays, physicists started building particle accelerators to artificially collide electrons or protons at even higher energies than the core of the Sun.

I wonder how physicists detect fundamental particles, some of which apparently live for only billionths of a second. I read how emerging from a violent collision, these particles are typically travelling near the speed of light; during their short lifetimes, the particles have time to leave a trail in a photographic emulsion or a bubble chamber rather like the froth in beer or—more recently—in electronic detectors made of silicon.

I read how physicists use the cunning little trick of placing their detectors inside a magnetic field so that any particles that are electrically charged spend their ever-so-short lifespan performing a telltale pirouette. One exhibit shows a historic picture of particles streaming through a CERN bubble chamber:

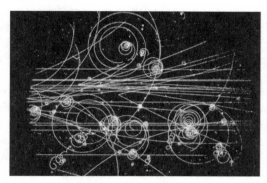

Tracks of fundamental particles in historic CERN bubble chamber

Those are the same particles that I'm made of! That would be a photograph of me if all the quarks and electrons that form me hadn't been cooled and then carefully bonded together, layer upon layer, into protons and neutrons, that form atoms, that combine into molecules, that build cells, that form organs, that are my functioning body. *Which is currently trying to understand the quarks and electrons.*

I read a little about the history of the tortuous route scientists took to the discovery of quarks. *It's fortunate that I never visited the 1950s and early 1960s.* Apparently during that time, physicists uncovered—in cosmic rays and particle accelerators—what they themselves termed a "menagerie" of new fundamental particles. The muon, μ, was joined by the kaon, K, the pion, π, and different flavors of the Ξ, Λ, Ω, and Δ. Scientists started worrying that they would run out of Greek letters! Finally in the 1960s, American physicist Murray Gell-Mann at Caltech, along with others, noticed some telltale patterns that hinted at these "fundamental" particles' secret—they are all just pairs or triplets of the same quarks. Gell-Mann picked the name *quarks*—apparently he intended it to be pronounced "kworks."

So how do the quarks, electrons, and neutrinos interact? Again reading about the "dynamics," I discover relative simplicity underlying the apparent varied complexity of everyday life. Just the four interactions that

I have already heard about govern the universe. They tend to act in independent realms.

Gravity, explained by Einstein's general relativity, rules the cosmic scale—it controls the evolution of galaxies and stars, right down to the behavior of falling objects in the vicinity of a planet.

Electromagnetism is the monarch of the everyday scale. It provides a single model for almost all everyday interactions from the chemical reactions of home cooking to the properties of materials such as elasticity and plasticity, friction, heat, color, and of course electric currents and magnetism.

Finally, two more interactions govern the interior of the nucleus.

The strong interaction glues the quarks into protons and neutrons and glues the protons and neutrons into atomic nuclei.

Then the oddball of physics: the weak interaction. I read how, although the effects of this weak force are more esoteric, the Sun and stars would not burn without the weak interaction's ability to transform a proton into a neutron. The weak interaction is something of a delinquent breaking some of the symmetry laws we so take for granted. For example, the other three interactions look exactly the same in the mirror, but the weak interaction actually works differently to the right and to the left!

So all of the world's phenomena are disguised versions of just four interactions. The Big Bang, the supernova, the photosynthesis and metabolism of life, painting a picture, baking bread, bouncing a ball—all of these are just quarks and electrons interacting via gravity, electromagnetism, the strong interaction, and—occasionally—the weak interaction.

Zvi walks into the exhibition.

"Oh, you," I say. "Well, I think I've got it. Once upon a time, in an expanding four-dimensional spacetime, there lived up-quarks, down-quarks, electrons, and neutrinos. The spacetime had a curvature known as gravity. The particles interacted with each other in three other ways: the electromagnetic interaction, the strong interaction, and the weak interaction. The end."

He gives a strange grin—I try to interpret it. *That grin almost looks like... pride.*

"So who are you?"

"That's it in a nutshell," he laughs, ignoring my question. "That's the *standard model.* Well, to be accurate, there are some other particles besides those four, but they're not stable—they fleet into existence in high-energy collisions for a fraction of a second."

"Pity," I say "there should never be more than four elements."

"That's just how it is. There are two heavier pairs of quarks besides the up and down: the *strange* and *charm* quarks and the *top* and *bottom* quarks. Similarly, there are two heavier siblings of the electron: the *muon* and *tau*, and two other neutrinos too. And all particles have antimatter counterparts."

"So be it. But saying that there are four interactions that govern those particles is all very well," I say. "Does this standard model give details of the interactions? Does it make predictions?"

"Absolutely. To fully understand the interactions of matter, physicists such as Hans Bethe and Richard Feynman in the US, both of whom you came across in Los Alamos—"

"You're doing it again!" I shout into the quiet exhibition space. Other guests look at me.

"Doing what?"

"How were you spying on me in Los Alamos? You couldn't have even been born yet! Have you been time traveling to follow me?"

"No. Do you want to know about the nature of the interactions?"

"Yes, but—"

"So," he continues, "physicists including Bethe and Feynman took quantum mechanics to a higher level. Instead of applying quantum mechanics to individual particles, they treated the field itself—initially the electromagnetic field—using quantum mechanics. It's called *quantum field theory*. Quantum field theory is the basis for all of modern physics.

"Remember Heisenberg's uncertainty principle—that in quantum mechanics the position or momentum of an electron is undefined? Well, in quantum field theory, uncertainty goes beyond individual particles. Often we are uncertain how many particles exist or which particles. One particle can transform into another! It's madness—everything is random and indefinite."

I shake my head vigorously. "So 'quantum field theory' is a fancy euphemism for 'cosmic anarchy'," I say. I look at my hands. *Deep inside my own hands there is a random carnival of particles fleeting in and out of existence.*

"More like a cosmic casino," Zvi says. "There are still rules of what's allowed and what isn't, and you can calculate probabilities, but it's certainly weird. In quantum field theory, there is not even such a thing as a perfect vacuum. There is always some probability that particles will appear out of nothing, then self-annihilate. It takes some getting used to. And the equations are horrendous. There are infinites that have to be mathematically finessed."

So maybe nature does abhor a vacuum—there is never a perfect vacuum if particles can just materialize!

"That's madness. How does anyone make predictions with this stuff?"

"It was Richard Feynman who finally made quantum field theory comprehensible by replacing the equations with diagrams." Zvi points at another chart:

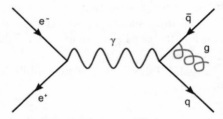

Feynman diagram of a quantum field theory scenario:
An electron e⁻ and positron e⁺ meet and annihilate into a photon γ; the photon decays into a quark q and an anti-quark; the anti-quark emits a gluon g

"Do you see? This diagram shows one possible scenario. Thousands of other scenarios are possible too, and for each possible scenario we can draw a diagram and calculate a probability. In quantum field theory, everything is described as an interaction of particles, and everything is probabilistic."

"Everything?" I ask. "The strong and weak interactions are also based on a 'quantum'—they are modeled with particles too?"

"You got it. The weak interaction is carried by the *W* and *Z* particles and the strong interaction by the *gluon*."

"Hmm. So gluon particles—the strong interaction—somehow hold the quarks together inside the proton or neutron?"

"Yup. It's the very same strong interaction—the exchange of gluon particles—that binds quarks into protons and neutrons, and binds protons and neutrons into atomic nuclei. The model for the strong force is known as *quantum chromodynamics*. By way of analogy only, physicists like to imagine that the three quarks inside a proton, or neutron, are red, blue, and green:"

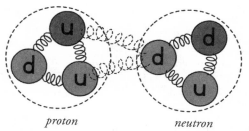

proton   neutron

The strong interaction, modeled by quantum chromodynamics, works by exchange of gluon particles. It binds quarks into protons and neutrons, and protons and neutrons into atomic nuclei.

I take a moment to absorb the standard model—the theory-of-very-nearly-everything. *Where concealed in this model of the world is my ticket home to 2110?* I look around me at the exhibits and other visitors.

"But, Zvi, look around us. How does a probabilistic model of the quarks and electrons deep inside the atoms tell us about 'very nearly everything'? How does it tell us about our everyday world? How does the standard model help Fizz to get home?"

"Layer upon layer," he says. "Just like bricks make a wall, and walls make a house, and houses make a city—but the city is still made of bricks. First the strong interaction explains how protons and neutrons are made."

"Does it explain how protons and neutrons combine to make atomic nuclei?"

"Yes, that's *nuclear physics.* But for convenience, nuclear physicists usually ignore the quarks and think about protons and neutrons, just like city planners think about houses and ignore the bricks."

I nod. *Layer-upon-layer.*

"And beyond that," I say, "Atoms combine into molecules?"

"Yup, that's chemistry. Chemists 'abstract' away the details of the nucleus and treat the nucleus as if it were a point."

I keep pressing. "Biology, psychology—also quarks?" *Those are subjects we actually studied a little back home.*

"Sure. Those are all higher level shorthand for thinking about quarks and electrons interacting."

"Astronomy, cosmology?" I say.

"Yes. Well—"

"Well, what?"

"Well," he repeats, "the standard model covers many aspects of cosmology, but there are a few places where it breaks down."

"Aha. Hence the 'very-nearly' epitaph?"

"Right."

"Never mind where it breaks down. Where in this standard model is a source of plentiful energy I can use to power my hut home? Does the standard model introduce any new mechanisms of time dilation?"

"No."

I sigh. "I remember from Rutherford that physics has realized the alchemists' dream of converting lead into gold. Maybe physics also provides an elixir of life so I can live till 2110?"

"Sadly not," he says flatly.

"Yeah, I was joking. But this isn't actually funny. What if nothing in the standard model can help me?" I exhale. "What about this 'very-nearly' limitation?"

"The biggest limitation of the standard model is that no one has figured out how to make the general relativity theory of gravity—with its complex curved spacetime—work with the other interactions. There's a disconnect. There are certain very extreme situations that will only be fully understood when someone finds a theory that combines the theory of gravity and the theory of the other interactions."

"And no one has done that?"

"No. There have been some interesting attempts, such as *string theory*, but none have succeeded."

"That's a disaster. What if my getting home requires combining gravity with quantum field theory? That may be solved in 2110, but if my Dad used such a theory, I don't stand a chance in 2011!" I shiver. "Any other limitations I should be aware of?"

"Not necessarily. But there are two other issues. The standard model is still somewhat complex, especially when you include all those other unstable siblings of the quarks and electrons. Physicists still hope there may be a simpler underlying theory, maybe even a single particle and a single interaction that explain everything. And finally there is one prediction of the standard model that has yet to be experimentally confirmed."

"Which is?"

"The standard model requires one more particle, known as the *Higgs boson*, to make everything work. Quantum field theory doesn't explain the mass of the quarks and electrons. Peter Higgs, from England, suggested there might be one more particle that acts as a ball-and-chain for the other particles to create their mass. That is one of the final unconfirmed predictions of the standard model. It is one of the goals here at CERN to find the Higgs. So here are all the particles in the standard model—the stable with the unstable:"

	matter (fermions)			force carriers (bosons)
quarks	up	charm	top	photon (light)
	down	strange	bottom	Z (weak force)
leptons	electron	muon	tau	W (weak force)
	neutrino	neutrino	neutrino	gluon (strong force)
				Higgs (unconfirmed)

Particles in the standard model. The four particles in the left-most column are stable and appear in matter. The four particles in the right-most column carry the three interactions (gravity excluded).

"They have nicknamed the Higgs the 'God' particle," he continues.

"Because no one has ever seen it?"

He lowers his voice. "Actually, I think they're trying to hype the importance of the Higgs in the press. They have a multi-billion euro budget to justify to the public."

"What's a Euro?"

"It's a European unit of currency—"

"What's it worth? How much is a cow?" I ask.

"I—well I've never bought a cow. I would have to guess a few hundred Euros." We start strolling between the exhibits.

"Goodness. This place costs tens of millions of cows? The same money could feed a medium-sized country! European States spend that kind of money on a physics experiment?"

"Better than the other thing, right?"

I stop walking. "Good point," I say. "My yesterday, the same countries were spending way more than that killing each other. But what do they do here?" *And what are you doing here?*

"Let's take a look."

He leads me out of the exhibition, out of the reception building, past the rust-colored globe, which I now see is in Galileo Galilei Square, and along a short path signposted: "To ATLAS."

"We talked about the limitations of the standard model," Zvi says. "The beginning of the Big Bang, some 13.7 billion years ago, is a good example of where the standard model breaks down. Imagine all the mass in the universe compressed into one tiny point of infinite density and temperature. Can you? Well, at that apoplectic moment, gravity and the other interactions were all acting at once with unimaginable intensity. No one will be able to model exactly what happened at the moment of the Big Bang until we have a theory that combines general relativity with the other interactions."

"Hah. So in fact this 'very-nearly-everything' is pretty arrogant right? There are periods of time and scenarios that the standard model cannot capture—situations that we are unable to test!"

"Well, fortunately, though, the universe was expanding and cooling at the Big Bang. Eventually the universe would reach temperatures that are recreated every day right here in CERN. At those temperatures the standard model is tried and tested."

"What temperatures are those?"

"A few thousand trillion degrees."

I raise my eyebrows. "Kind of toasty, then. And how long did it take the universe to cool down to a few thousand trillion degrees?"

"About a trillionth of a second," he says smugly. "From the age of one trillionth of a second onward, the physics of the cosmos is much clearer."

Wow. They can recreate the temperature of the trillionth-of-a-second-old universe right here? *Maybe "very-nearly" is justified.* "Still, there could be entire unexplored worlds at scales below a trillionth of a meter or temperatures above a few trillion degrees."

"It's possible," he concedes.

"So, what was the universe like at that ripe old age?"

"Let's take a look."

It's still drizzling as we arrive at a large concrete building. It would be particularly ugly if it weren't for a vast psychedelic mural covering two of its sides:

ATLAS experiment at CERN

"Is that a picture of what's inside?"

"Yes. ATLAS is one of four main experiments here at the LHC, the Large Hadron Collider. LHC creates two beams of protons—basically hydrogen atoms—each moving at 99.999999% of the speed of light. At such speeds according to $E=mc^2$, each proton weighs 7,500 times more than its normal mass, so they're actually not all that light! One of our days is just a few seconds for the protons."

"Hah, I must be going that fast on a good night. Although perhaps no longer," I slump my shoulders.

"ATLAS is one of the places where they collide the two beams of protons head on. Ah, we may be in luck—there's the director."

Zvi points to a woman striding into the ATLAS building.

"Dr. Gianotti," he says to her, "might you have a couple of minutes to tell a visitor from Iceland about ATLAS?"

"Sure," says the woman, in her late forties, in a familiar Italian accent. "We collide the energetic protons from the LHC head on. We create for one instant a superhot, super-dense soup of quarks like in the Big Bang, and then immediately the quarks cool and coalesce in various combinations: pairs and triplets of quarks that are called *hadron* particles, including the familiar protons and neutrons. All these particles shoot out in every direction at nearly the speed of light. In ATLAS we've constructed a detector the size of an apartment block, filled with magnets, electronic sensors, and 3,000 kilometers of cables. It weighs 7000 tons, like a hundred 747s."

"One of the largest passenger aircraft," Zvi interjects.

"Staggering. All that equipment is right here in this building?" I ask.

"Not exactly. The ATLAS experiment that you see in the mural is occurring one hundred meters below us. Yup, imagine, we had to lower 7,000 tons of extremely delicate and expensive equipment down a 100-meter shaft and assemble it underground, calibrating the sensors to one hundredth of a millimeter! Up here is the control room for the mini-big-bang that is occurring right now way below our feet."

We take a few steps to the other side of the entrance hall and see the ATLAS Control Room through a large glass window:

ATLAS control center monitors collisions of energetic protons

I gawk at all the bright screens. "But, I thought when particles interact, fundamentally everything is random? Aren't there many possible resulting scenarios from colliding two protons?"

"Ah yes, billions of scenarios. So we are carrying out trillions of collisions and tracking each and every one. Maybe one in a few million collisions will produce a Higgs particle. Better still, maybe we will produce something entirely unexpected."

"So no Higgs yet?"

"We had Peter Higgs visit here," she smiles. "He's over eighty now. No Higgs particles yet, but we're just getting started, we hope to find it in his lifetime. If it's there."

"But… the amount of data you're describing!"

"Ah, yes, the data. The raw data is about a petabyte per second—a million billion characters. Very quickly we filter out the uninteresting events and distribute the data to a 'grid' of tens of thousands of computers worldwide. 3,000 scientists in 38 countries working at 174 universities and labs analyze it. And ATLAS is just one of several experiments around the LHC."

"3,000 collaborators on one experiment? So the lone genius scientist is a faint memory?"

"You could say that. Still, the conceptual breakthroughs are often the brainchild of individuals. Such as Higgs."

"What is the LHC?"

"The LHC is the factory that supplies a beam of high-energy protons to ATLAS and the other experiments. You should go and take a look at the LHC for yourself."

The statistics of this experiment make me dizzy. *The Big Bang doesn't sound quite so abstract when you know that some of its processes are being recreated below your own feet.* But I still don't understand how the quark soup of the Big Bang evolved into the stars and planets and people we have today—and whether somewhere along the way there was some process that can help me power my own time travel home.

"Can we see this LHC?" I ask Zvi.

"I will try to make an appointment. Why don't you go and get yourself a drink, then meet me back here in an hour?"

When we meet back, the necessary arrangements have been made. We step into another of the many CERN buildings and take an elevator labeled LHC. It has only one button—down—and only one stop. Unlike the metal grid I saw in Berlin, the elevator doors are automated and opaque. As we descend through the long windowless underground shaft, it occurs to me that I am not only descending a hundred meters, but—in a way—going back 13.7 billion years to witness the quark soup that occurred when the universe was a trillionth of a second old.

We emerge at the entrance of a generously sized tunnel with a thick blue pipe running through its center.

"I thought protons are subatomic. A person could swim through that pipe."

"The beams of protons are tiny. The pipe is full of magnets and liquid helium. You wouldn't want to swim in that stuff. It's cold."

"I've swum in some pretty cold rivers."

"This helium is at 1.9K," he says.

"K?"

"1.9 *Kelvin*. 1.9 degrees above absolute zero. That's -271C or -456F."

Kelvin! I recall Joule's quip about "the Thomson." *He had the right idea, just the wrong name.*

"Why cool it so dramatically? Does that keep the protons fresh?"

He rolls his eyes. "At those temperatures, some metals become *super-conductors*. They carry electric current perfectly. If you start electric current spinning around a loop of superconducting wire, it will just keep spinning, creating a really powerful magnet. This entire pipe is colder than outer space. You could say that this pipe is the coldest place in the galaxy."

"Until they actually collide the protons!"

"True. Then you get—briefly—by far the highest temperature in the galaxy, a hundred thousand times hotter than the core of the Sun!"

CERN Large Hadron Collider (LHC) tunnel

A technician in plastic goggles and white overalls emerges from the depths of the tunnel on a bicycle, panting heavily. I look at him.

"Um, Zvi, how long is this tunnel?"

"Twenty-seven kilometers."

"What?"

"Yup. Once the protons approach the speed of light they complete this twenty-seven kilometer circuit 11,000 times every second, crossing from France to Switzerland and back each time."

I place a hand on the blue pipe. "So this is a torture chamber for protons! They take them down to this underground dungeon, spin them around viciously, then smash them about with extreme violence until they finally reveal their deeply hidden secrets."

Zvi laughs. "You could say. The final torture occurs here on the Swiss side. Fewer issues with EU human rights laws that way."

I'm not sure what EU means, but I smile politely at his joke and lead the way back to the elevator. "You've convinced me that they're making a jolly good effort to check the limits of the standard model. Enthralling stuff. But how does it help me? Maybe if I understood how the universe got from the quark soup reproduced here to what it is today, I could find an idea for how I'm going to travel from today to 2110."

"Yes, now that you're armed with the standard model theory of very-nearly-everything, you're missing one last piece: the story of the cosmos. I have an idea how we can both recreate the story..."

Bang

We're sitting inside the rusty globe that CERN calls an exhibition center. The large interior is pitch-black with a scattering of white orbs, illuminated in gentle bluish light, hovering over the floor and below the ceiling. *Spooky.* Zvi and I sit opposite each other inside the dimly lit shiny, white swivel chairs, shaped like eggs with one side sliced off.

"Go ahead, interview me," Zvi says.

"Pardon?"

"I'm a 13.7 billion-year-old quark, veteran of the Big Bang. Interview me. You must have some questions."

"You're weird."

"That's not actually a question. Fine I'll start. Would you like to know about my start in life?"

"No."

"Good, because I can recall almost nothing about my first trillionth of a second. All I have is this vague recollection of extreme pressure, as if all the mass-energy in the universe was infinitely condensed around me. But I'm not sure that I was really me. I was part of an intense amorphous ball of mass-energy, not really composed of any stable set of particles. All the interactions were unified. Then expansion. I have this fuzzy memory of everything expanding very rapidly, maybe exponentially. Expanding faster than the speed of light."

"That's impossible," I sigh.

"No. It's impossible to move through spacetime faster than the speed of light. But spacetime itself was stretching and expanding. General relativity imposes no speed limit on the expansion of spacetime. Go on, interview me."

I look nervously at a couple of other visitors who are quietly examining various exhibits in the dim light. I lower my voice. "Ok, quark, what was your life like after one trillionth of a second?"

"The next millionth of a second was the '*quark epoch*' named after my friends and me—not because it was a good era for us quarks, though—truthfully, it was hell—but because the universe was filled with a dense soup of quarks, expanding together with the universe. Of course there were also electrons and the like and lots of interaction particles like photons and gluons, but we quarks are heaviest, so we dominated that era."

"I get that, it's like what is going on right below us in the LHC."

"Yup. I don't mind telling you, those were aggressive times. Particles violently interacting with other particles at astounding rates. Even then, I barely had a real identity. Quarks were being created and destroyed at an incredible clip."

"Not much fun then."

"No fun at all. It came to an end when the universe reached the ripe old age of one millionth of a second. Believe it or not, in some ways I would come to miss that first millionth of a second of the quark epoch. There was some freedom in that violence—freedom I have never again tasted throughout my billions of years. It all came to an abrupt end the moment the temperature dipped below a few trillion degrees."

"I suppose that's freezing relative to thousands of trillions of degrees. What changed?"

"It turns out that the extreme temperatures were exactly what had allowed us quarks to interact freely. None of us knew it at the time of the quark epoch, but it soon turned out that roaming freely is not at all natural for us quarks. Suddenly as the universe cooled, all us quarks were snapping together into pairs and triplets, known as hadrons. Eventually most of us would be bound into the most stable triplets—proton and neutron."

I clear my throat. "OK quark, what happened to you, specifically?"

"I'm a down quark—although I've always resented that choice of epitaph. I was passing by a couple of up quarks and making some casual comment about how temperatures seemed to be dropping and, before I knew it, the strong interaction had the three of us tied together using gluons. Suddenly two other quarks and I snapped together into a proton. We were simply no longer moving fast enough to break apart. I was in denial for a long while, but eventually I had to face the fact that I would likely be bound in a threesome of quarks for eternity. It was degrading really. The final blow was to come one year around 13,700,000,000, the year which humans call 1919, when Rutherford 'discovered the proton' with not a single mention of the individual quarks within it. I still *hate* that collective label."

He grits his teeth. I smirk.

"I'm so sorry. But on the positive side, it sounds like—bound in the proton—things were more stable?"

"Stable? Hah. You're forgetting that at the age of one millionth of a second, the universe contained almost as much antimatter as matter.

Protons and anti-protons started annihilating each other at an incredible rate, producing bursts of light and other energy. For a while, I thought there would be no quarks left at all, but by some good fortune there must have always been a small excess of protons over anti-protons so that at the end of the day—or rather by the end of the first second—all the anti-protons and most of the protons were gone, leaving a balance of protons. We lost so many fellow quarks in that second. I—or rather the three of us—were amongst the few survivors."

He fakes a sniff.

"After that first second, things did become more stable for us quarks in the proton. In the meantime, the electrons and anti-electrons—positrons—continued to annihilate each other for about another ten seconds. After ten seconds the positrons became extinct, and a few electrons were left. So at ten seconds old, the universe was mostly filled with the very same protons, neutrons, and electrons that everything is still built of today."

"So those basic ingredients haven't changed since the age of ten seconds!" I say. "What became of all the energy that was produced in all those annihilations?"

"Ah, exactly. There was light. A lot of photons. Beyond the first ten seconds, the universe was one big bright *plasma*—a mixture of light and matter—very much like the tiny plasma pixels you saw in those bright plasma monitors in the ATLAS control room around the corner. Don't you see? If the ATLAS experiment simulates the quark epoch, the plasma screens in the ATLAS control room actually resemble the later *plasma* stage of the embryonic universe. Yes, the universe was one big plasma television dominated by photons. It was the *photon era*."

Zvi waves his arms in a pointless attempt to demonstrate hot bright plasma filling all of space. "And now, over to you."

"Over to me what?"

"Over to you to role-play a photon," he says.

"Do me a favor," I look up at the domed ceiling.

"I insist. You cannot get a balanced history of the universe from the perspective of a quark; we must balance it with your perspective as a photon."

"Okay, okay. I'm a photon in a hot plasma interacting with protons, neutrons, and electrons. Now what?"

"You and I—the quarks and electrons—are brushing up against each other, interacting electromagnetically for four hundred thousand years.

The universe is expanding and cooling all the while. Then, after what seems like an eternity, everything changes one Monday afternoon."

I swivel a full circle in my chair. "Changes how?"

"The universe dips below four thousand Kelvin. Suddenly, as the electrons cooled, we discovered that we and the electrons are electrically attracted; we had never even noticed the attraction when we were all buzzing around at higher temperatures. There we were, the three of us quarks—a four-hundred-thousand-year-old proton—set in our ways, and suddenly an electron binds to us! Now the three of us have a little electron, an unwelcome fourth wheel buzzing all around us."

"Ah, you become an atom!" I say. "You were—and I suppose you still are—a hydrogen atom."

"Indeed, we were. And most of the hydrogen atoms from back then are still hydrogen atoms today—most of the matter in the universe today is hydrogen. But not us. We'll see soon. So, photon, how did this affect you?"

"What?"

"After four hundred thousand years of hot plasma, when all the electrons and protons suddenly bonded into hydrogen atoms, how did it affect you?"

"I... well..." My mind gropes through three weeks of learning, searching for relevance, finally honing in on Bohr's speech in Parc Léopold my three days ago. "Of course, once the electrons are bound in an atom, like guitar strings, they can no longer emit and absorb photons. Err, us photons. Except for very specific frequencies. You guys—the matter in the universe—suddenly become *transparent*. We photons could roam freely."

"Right! Matter and light, which were interacting so intensely in the plasma, now barely interacted at all. We entered the *cosmological dark ages*, very boring and some 150 million years long. The universe was an expanding, thinning cloud of hydrogen, including me, and streaming through it, but without any contact, a stream of light, including you."

"Would we ever meet again?"

"Ah yes," he spreads his hands dramatically. "Would you believe that the light from the Big Bang plasma continues to fill the universe till this very day? It's compelling evidence for the Big Bang. As the universe expanded, you photons were stretched from visible light photons and the like into radio wave photons, specifically the type of radio waves we call *microwaves*. The universe today is still filled with microwaves from the

Big Bang, the *cosmic microwave background*. As to your question, you and I would meet again in the year which humans call 1965. But first, how did we get from the dullness of the dark ages to today's lively universe?"

He waits for an answer.

"Give me a clue," I say.

"For many eons, I was part of one atom in a large hydrogen cloud. I thought our cloud would continue expanding and thinning forever. The other hydrogen atoms around us were getting further and further away. But another force—weak, but very long-reaching—was slowly but steadily working its magic on all us quarks."

"Gravity?"

"Gravity," he gives a sagely nod. "Gravity very slowly collapsed the hydrogen under its own weight. One day we noticed that the hydrogen atoms that had been moving away from us were getting closer again. Soon the hydrogen all around me was clumping into clusters of thicker hydrogen with empty pockets between them. Each huge ball of hydrogen would in the fullness of time become a galaxy, and within each galaxy the hydrogen coagulated into denser spheres that would become stars. Suddenly pressure was no longer decreasing; it was increasing—gently at first, then rather intensely, then crushing pressures the likes of which we had not experienced since our youth. Until one day…"

I recall Bethe's little speech. "You fused with another hydrogen atom?"

"Yes! I found myself fused by the brute force of gravity with another proton and a couple of neutrons. They literally became stuck to us."

Despite myself, I'm getting more absorbed in the story. "Aha," I smile, "you found yourself at the center of a newly formed star and became— with another proton—part of a helium nucleus!"

"Right. Suddenly after 150 million years of peaceful darkness, at lunchtime one Tuesday, the first star ignites. Then another, and another. Soon there are hydrogen-fusing stars dotted all around the sky. The modern era had dawned."

"The modern era—but still no atoms larger than helium? No planets, no life?"

Zvi makes a dismissive wave. "Those details are of little consequence to cosmology."

"Even so, humor me."

"If you insist. Billions of years later, the star I was in exhausted all of its hydrogen. So it started fusing helium into heavier atoms. After billions of years as a helium atom, I found myself fused into a carbon atom of six protons and six neutrons. It was crowded. Soon my star depleted all its fuel and underwent an almighty explosion."

"A supernova? Like the one Galileo and Kepler witnessed?"

"Correct," he says, "I was lucky to be one of the atoms that was spewed out into space by the supernova explosion. Some of my friends had it much worse. In the fullness of time, gravity would hook me up with other heavy atoms in outer space, and we would coalesce to become part of an inconsequential planet named Earth that was captured in orbit around a brash young upstart star known as the Sun. Then the heavier atoms forming Earth, heated by the Sun, started participating in some fresh—but entirely marginal processes—like chemistry, which led to biology, and eventually psychology, economics, and other processes that are of no cosmological importance whatsoever."

He looks at me, waiting for another question. I look back and wait for him to continue—eventually he does.

"The carbon atom I am part of connected to other carbon atoms and some hydrogen and oxygen and other atoms to form a molecule known as a protein. That 'molecule' was the final humiliation of this long suffering quark. Think of it from my point of view. First I become one third of a proton, then the proton becomes part of an atom, then part of a bigger nucleus with other protons and neutrons, and finally—the ultimate ignominy—just one of many atoms in a protein that is just one of trillions of molecules in some organism. Specifically, I ended up in the retina of the eye of some biological creature that apparently is known as Arno Penzias."

"So what happened to your less fortunate quark friends?"

"Let me first tell me about our happy reunion—you and I—in 1965. In that year Arno Penzias, whose body included yours truly, and Robert Wilson were working as engineers at Bell Labs in New Jersey. Penzias and Wilson had a huge horn-shaped microwave antenna, but they were annoyed to find that it kept producing an unexpected signal, no matter which part of the sky it pointed at. They could not explain where the microwave 'noise' was coming from, so they climbed inside the antenna. In the interior they found a family of pigeons. Penzias later described how he attributed the mysterious signal to a 'thin layer of white dielectric material' that he found deposited on the inside of the antenna. They 'put down' the source of that 'white dielectric material.' But the unexplained signal persisted."

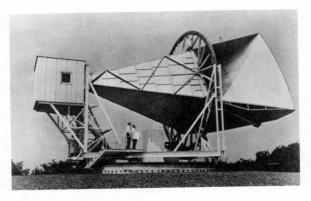

Arno Penzias and Robert Wilson's microwave antenna, Bell Labs NJ

"Okay, I get it," I grin. "There in the picture is me, a photon left over from the plasma of the Big Bang. After thirteen billion years of steaming ghost-like through space at the speed of light, I finally happened by pure chance into an antenna on planet Earth and interacted with an electron that registered a signal in the retina that you are part of! You and I had a cosmic rendezvous for the first time since the big bang. Penzias and Wilson had discovered the Big Bang but the misinterpreted it as, well, pigeon dung!"

"Right. Later Penzias and Wilson hooked up with some theoreticians who identified the microwave signal as the light from the Big Bang plasma. Hey, you can see the microwaves from the Big Bang too."

"Really? You have a microwave antenna here?"

"Yes. Come take a look."

He marches over to one of the screens showing a video about CERN. Zvi looks around and, as no one else is watching, he presses a button labeled "tuning" and seems to set the screen to some completely random frequency.

"Look," he says, "the television is a microwave antenna, and some of this noise is microwaves left over from the Big Bang:"

He resets the television set and we sit down.

"So, quark," I say, "what happened to the less fortunate quarks that remained in the remnants of your star after you were spewed out by the supernova?"

Zvi looks at his feet. "You're asking about the dark side of physics—the death of stars. The quarks and other particles that didn't escape collapsed under their own gravity. In a small star, they would have ended up as a harmless *white dwarf*. In a bigger star, though, gravity would be strong enough to break the electric repulsion between the protons, and the entire star would be crushed into one vast atomic nucleus, a *neutron star*. That's one big nucleus without the 99.99999999999% of void that we normally have between atoms in matter. A sugar-cube-sized chunk of neutron star would weigh more than all eight billion human beings combined."

"No kidding. Kind of dense, then. Is that what became of the star that you were in?"

He bows his head. "Tragically not. The star I was in was too massive to create a stable neutron star, it weighed several times more than the Sun. It seems inevitable that what remained of my star must have collapsed into—"

Suddenly I recall my chat with Albert Einstein in Berlin and jump out of my seat. "A black hole!" I almost shout.

"Yes, a black hole," he says softly, looking up at me quizzically. "One thing is for sure, we'll never see those other quarks again. Nothing can escape from that black hole, not even light. Any information my fellow quarks had would have been erased when the black hole formed."

An idea grabs me and won't let go. I start pacing around. *Of course, why didn't I think of it before?*

My pacing slows. *No it is not possible... even if it is possible, it's too dangerous... and even if it's not too dangerous, what I need probably doesn't exist... or exists but is too far.*

"Quick, what do we know about black holes?"

"Black holes are... tricky," Zvi says. "I told you that it would take a combined theory of gravity and the standard model to really understand the first trillionth of a second of the Big Bang. I'm afraid the same could be said of black holes. The intense gravity, the singularity—they require a more complete theory than we have. And as you know by now—"

I slump back into my egg-shaped chair, which starts to swivel under my weight. "Don't tell me: There is no such theory. No one has reconciled Einstein's general theory of relativity with the three quantum field interactions of the standard model."

The shot of adrenalin is starting to dissipate.

"But," he says slowly, "since you ask, there is a physicist who is not afraid to speculate about how general relativity and the standard model would interact around a black hole. Although there isn't a complete theory, he has some good ideas."

I stand up again. "Where?" I demand.

"Cambridge."

"It's worth a shot. Let's go—now."

I march out of the globe and toward the hut, Zvi following behind.

Day 23. Cambridge, England

The man's cheek twitches rhythmically.

The cheek is gently but invisibly illuminated by infrared light, from a tiny light emitting diode, or LED, just a millimeter or two in size. The LED is always hovering just above the cheek—I can see that it's connected to the man's glasses using some pretty advanced apparatus—a paperclip and some glue.

As Zvi explains to me, the LED is a simple device—a tiny piece of silicon. Silicon, apparently, is a semiconductor—it conducts some electricity, but it does not allow electrons to roam as freely as in a metal. Different parts of this silicon have been *doped* with non-silicon atoms. The electrons "falling" from one part of the silicon to another emit energy in the form of infrared photons. Apparently this is a good example of how the theory of quantum mechanics has led to the technology of electronics. *Prying leads to meddling leads to destruction.*

The infrared light reflects off the man's cheek, in accordance with the wave equation. Some of the bouncing photons are detected by a second tiny piece of silicon, a photo diode, glued adjacent to the LED. Here the opposite process occurs—photons release electrons that form a tiny electric current flowing through a circuit and into a computer where the current is processed by millions of silicon transistors.

The computer translates the facial gestures into English words, which appear on a small screen that comprises thousands more LEDs. The available choices of words on the screen are scanned by the man's eyes, which then feed electrical signals into a biological computer, his brain, which decides whether to twitch the cheek again and for how long.

And so the biological brain and the silicon brain collaborate back and forth—nature and technology in a duet. "Hello" is a common word and is selected with just a few twitches. "Fizz" is spelled out by gestures of the cheek, one painstaking letter at a time. *F... I... Z... Z.*

I wait patiently. If this man can live his whole life communicating this way, I'm not going to complain about one conversation. Eventually, gesture-by-gesture, the two words "Hello Fizz" appear on the screen. One more movement of the face and the words are passed to some sort of artificial voice. The man is British, but the awkward metallic pronunciation of the words "Hello Fizz," when it finally emerges from the computer, sounds American.

"Good morning, Professor Hawking," I reply.

We are at Cambridge's Department of Applied Mathematics and Theoretical Physics, housed in a series of modern buildings arranged in a U shape, surrounded by greenery. I learned that Professor Stephen Hawking retired two years ago from the chair of Lucasian Professor of Mathematics, a position previously held by Isaac Newton, Charles Babbage, George Stokes, and Paul Dirac.

Apparently Professor Hawking likes to joke that the Lucasian "chair" had to become motorized for his benefit as his eyes, cheek, and one weak finger are the only working parts of Professor Hawking's slumped body, which has been decimated by motor-neuron disease.

"I... hear... that... you..."

I'm almost moved to tears by this man's courage in overcoming such a devastating disability to become an important professor. I hold it in—he doesn't look like he's feeling sorry for himself, so I assume he doesn't want my sympathy.

I think of home. In the Collective, kids would bring Hawking fruit every day. But I'm not sure we could give him any way to communicate, let alone become a professor.

"... are... visiting... us... from... the... future?"

"You know that?"

I wait patiently while he pieces together his response which emerges unpunctuated.

"So I was told but I am skeptical that it is possible to travel back in time even though there are wormhole solutions to general relativity. Forward time dilation is easy of course."

"Professor Hawking, I'm really sorry, could you excuse me for just one minute." This time I don't wait for a response.

I go back to Zvi, who is waiting in the other room.

"Zvi, is this visit some sort of emotional manipulation? Show Fizz how much technology can help one man? Help her get over the atom bomb? Help Fizz adjust to her bitter fate of being stuck in 2011?"

"If it is, is it working?"

"Well... only very slightly."

"It's not. It's an attempt to help Fizz get herself home. Ask him about his work."

"Okay, then. Why aren't you coming in?"

"Professor Hawking and I met in unfortunate circumstances."

"What were those?"

"As a student, I flung open a door once and almost knocked him out of his wheel-chair. I'm a little embarrassed to see him."

"Oh, ok." I sigh. "I'm going to figure out how he can help me."

Back in the room, I press on. "Professor Hawking, never mind if you're skeptical about how I got here. Can you help me get home?"

"I am a physicist not a travel agent."

"Physics is exactly what I need for this particular journey. May I ask what your expertise is?"

"Cosmology especially black holes."

"Oh. Einstein told me that the curved spacetime of general relativity could in theory lead to black holes. Do they exist in practice?"

"It appears so I lost a bet on that point," the metallic computer voice says, at the command of Professor Hawking's cheek.

"That's great news! Well, for me, not for you. What did you wager?"

"A subscription to *Penthouse* magazine."

What's the connection? Well, I suppose some physicists are interested in real estate too.

"But if black holes are black, how do we know they exist?"

"Firstly indirectly. The spacetime curvature around a black hole forms a gravitational lens which distorts our view of the galaxies behind the black hole in a characteristic way."

I wait patiently as he continues entering the information for his next thought to be spoken out loud through the computer.

"Secondly I proposed that black holes may not be so black. If you imagine combining general relativity with quantum field theory you realize that matter-antimatter pairs might appear out of the vacuum right at the event horizon of the black hole and due to the intense gravity one particle might fall into the hole while the other radiates out and escapes before they can annihilate."

I recall that the event horizon is the point of no return, where time comes to a standstill. So Hawking has realized that subtle quantum effects must occur at that crucial boundary between the outside universe and the abyss of the black hole. "Wow. So even without a theory that fully reconciles general relativity with quantum field theory, you've realized that quantum field theory should cause light and particles to radiate from the event horizon that envelops a black hole!"

"Yes my *Hawking radiation* solves a major paradox. Scientists wondered whether when something disorderly like a broken vase or hot soup falls into a black hole the entropy was lost to the world."

"Wouldn't that contradict the second law of thermodynamics?"

"Precisely. But Hawking radiation solves the paradox. Quantum effects at the event horizon allow entropy to escape the black hole."

My mind is spinning. Radiation emerging from black holes? Now I've heard it all. *But could Hawking radiation be the beacon I desperately need to guide me home?*

As I thank Professor Hawking, my mind is elsewhere.

"Zvi, where is the world's largest telescope?"

"As luck would have it, it's just ten minutes away."

Zvi and I are in the back of a taxi heading west out of Cambridge. I'm fidgeting with nervous excitement. It takes a cat on the sidewalk to remind me that there is one key conceptual problem overshadowing all of this modern physics which I have not yet addressed.

"All right," I say, "While we drive, last issue: Schrödinger's cat. Everything at a microscopic level is indefinite. Fundamental particles are always in superpositions like $|up> + |down>$, $|left> + |right>$, $|alive> + |decayed>$. Does that extend to cats? How does anything ever become definite? How can unobserved parts of the world be indefinite—the very idea sounds crazy!"

"As I said yesterday, you, Fizz, should find that easy to understand."

"What does that even mean? Why me?" As I raise my voice, I catch the cabbie glancing at me in his mirror.

"Well, remember yesterday, while I arranged access to the LHC tunnel, I told you to go get a drink for an hour."

"Sure."

"What did you do during that hour?"

I pull an indignant face. "None of your business."

"True. But tell me anyway."

"Why, did you follow me?"

"No. No one followed you at all. That's my point. Tell me—what did you do?"

"No."

"Fine. Tell me just one thing, did you buy a drink?"

"I suppose I did."

"You suppose you did? Okay, what drink did you buy?"

"Whatever." A strange nausea is overwhelming me.

"Don't say 'whatever.' Which was it? A coke? Orange juice? Double Scotch?"

As I look at him, I feel my stomach wrenching. My head is throbbing—I scratch my scalp rigorously—*what did I do?* Finally I drop my head and look down at my lap. "I… I… don't know."

"Right, Fizz." He holds my arm. "It's okay, of course you don't. No one was observing you during that hour so everything you did is indefinite. It's undefined. At most we can assign probabilities to the different possible scenarios."

We are leaving Cambridge now. The world outside is a blur as Barton Road passes over the M11 motorway by the village of Barton and becomes Cambridge Road heading southwest through more flat grassy countryside. Trees line the road.

"Who are you? What are you?" Silence. "Look, Zvi, stop avoiding my questions. This is getting way too weird."

"I wouldn't say 'weird'," he says. "I prefer 'metaphysical.'"

"Call it what you please. I don't like it one bit. Catching up on physics may just save me after all, but I'm totally fed up having you around making me feel extremely uncomfortable."

"It's not me making you uncomfortable. The world, when we look at it closely enough, makes us all uncomfortable. At the scales of quantum mechanics, physics meets metaphysics. Colliding protons make us reassess whether the world we live in is deterministic or random, local or non-local, and whether things have a definite state even when they're not observed."

"And what is the answer? If fundamentally things are so indefinite, how do macroscopic things become definite? Even people are just clusters of subatomic particles. Why should people be definite?"

"It's the biggest mystery of all, is it not? Sometimes it's known as the *measurement problem*. Quantum mechanics says that when an observer performs a measurement, the state becomes definite. But what distinguishes a measurement from any other interaction? What constitutes a measurement that can cause a superposition of indefinite states to become definite?"

"Well?"

"There have been several suggestions. Bohr's Copenhagen interpretation sidestepped the issue by suggesting that physics just predicts the results of experiments and does not—cannot—provide a model for the world: epistemology, not ontology. Some have suggested that, as in Descartes' dualism, humans have a consciousness that is not physical, but rather our consciousness acts like an external observer of the physical world. Maybe it is observation by human consciousness that forces the world into a definite position."

"Now I've heard it all," I shake my dizzy head.

"No you haven't. A physicist named Hugh Everett made an even more radical suggestion that there are infinitely many worlds—one for each possibility! Maybe in one world you bought a bottle of mineral water, in another you had an iced coffee, while in a third world you had a few pints and threw up on the LHC pipe."

I pull a face. "That's ridiculous. I can't even imagine this being one of many worlds."

"Why, Fizz, why can't you imagine that? You think yours is the only world? Sure, it may feel like that. But try to imagine, if you can, that your entire world were just a story in a book, and that, unbeknownst to you, that book was in a bookstore, on one of the shelves full of thousands of alternative books, each one of them containing a world just as real as yours."

My headache tightens still further. "I think I'd rather not. But is it true, does quantum mechanics teach us that there are many parallel universes?"

"Not necessarily. The many-worlds proposal captured many people's imagination, but it is pretty vague, not to say, uneconomical. Ockham would not have approved. In the meantime it is just one proposal, but you could say that the measurement problem, or the indefiniteness problem captured by Schrödinger's cat, remains unsolved."

"Hmm. Maybe they solved it in the future. If I get home I'll ask Dad."

Zvi hands the driver a twenty-pound note and we emerge in the shadow of the biggest cereal bowl I have ever seen—it must be over thirty meters across. The sign says "Mullard Radio Astronomy Observatory."

We stand in its shadow looking up. I'm still thinking about the observer effect. *As I stand here under the telescope observing the sky, is it possible that anything is looking down at me?*

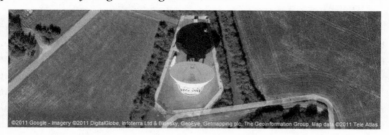

Mullard Radio Telescope—part of an international grid

"So this dish," I point up, "is a Newtonian reflector?"

"It is, but not for observing light. It observes the radio waves from the sky—a *radio telescope*. Astronomers observe the sky using the entire spectrum of electromagnetic radiation: gamma rays, X-rays, ultraviolet, infrared, and various ranges of radio waves."

"And this is the world's largest telescope?"

"Far from it."

"What are we doing here? This is serious, I need the best shot at getting home and I thought you said—"

"Ah, this dish is part of the world's biggest telescope. It's wired with other radio telescopes across the UK and Europe with hookups into Russia and the US. This big dish is one component in a virtual radio telescope with the diameter of the entire planet. Compare that to the largest optical telescope, which is a mere ten meters across. This network of telescopes could read a watch on the Moon while the best light telescope could barely make out a football pitch. More importantly for us, this array of telescopes can observe the light from those first galaxies— light that has been traveling almost thirteen billion years across a distance that, by definition, is some thirteen billion light-years."

"Some of which contain black holes," I say.

We step into the building and look at some images. I read the label and question one of the guys hanging around—he's wearing heavy-duty blue pants a bit like my "Levis," but his are ripped at the knees.

"So this image is of a galaxy which is thirteen billion light-years away?" I ask. *Unbelievable.*

Galaxy 13 billion light-years away seen by radio telescopes as it was in the early universe, 13 billion years ago

"No," he smiles. "We're seeing it as it was in the early universe thirteen billion years ago. Back *then* it was thirteen billion light-years away. But while the radio-wave light you see here made its long journey from that galaxy to us, the universe continued expanding. By now that galaxy must be some forty-five billion light years away, at the very edge of the observable universe."

Another image shows what's left today of Kepler's supernova of 1604.

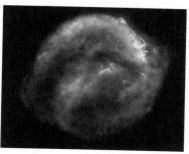

Remains of Kepler's Nova

I remember fondly how the chance appearance of this supernova within our own galaxy helped shake up almost two thousand years of lazy Aristotelian thinking—the supernova was a harbinger of the Renaissance scientific revolution. And now I've learned how this supernova is right now spewing into space the heavy atoms that will make tomorrow's planets and life forms, leaving behind it an astoundingly dense neutron star or—worse—a black hole, that may assist some future time traveler.

"Zvi, could I take a look at some of the data from this network of radio telescopes."

He gives me a knowing smile. "I think that could be arranged."

I settle down in front of a computer and spend the entire afternoon looking, as it were, for a needle in a cosmic haystack—the needle that may pave my way home, even with the minimal energy reserve that remains in my hut. I exhale deeply. *The odds are probably much worse than a needle in a haystack—if I succeed I'll be more like Madame Curie finding a tenth of a gram of radium in a ton of pitchblende.*

The Abbey

Mid-afternoon I finally extricate myself from the immense stacks of astronomical data. "I'm going home," I announce. I draw a sharp breath. "Or, I'm going to die trying."

"Really?" Zvi asks.

"Not really home, no. But I'm really going to attempt to get back to 2110. If I don't make it, my remains will be forever erased from the world. If I do, I just hope for the best in my exiled life on the Outside."

"I tried to show you that technology has some advantages," he says.

I sigh. "What difference does it make? It's not like I have a choice. It is what it is. Whatever my future, if I have one at all, I will cherish these last three weeks. I don't know if anything else in my life will ever seem as significant." I glance at the door.

"Well, good luck."

I hesitate. "You know, Zvi, I'm desperate to get back but I'm not quite ready to end my trip. It's like I need to say goodbyes or something." *Plus my journey home is going to be terrifying.*

"Ahh. Goodbye, Fizz." Zvi holds out his arms.

"Not to you, idiot. To the great physicists I met. Look, to me they are all fresh acquaintances. Some pretty much became friends. I guess my brain needs to somehow adjust to relegating them to long-gone historic figures."

He recovers quickly. "I may just have an idea for you; care to make one quick stop before you leave? It's just an hour away in London."

On the train I ask to borrow his little computer again.

"More Wikipedia?" he asks.

"Yes," I say simply.

This time I register myself as Wikipedia user *fizz2092*. I glance through the pages on the physicists I met and make the odd correction. I edit the page of William Thomson, First Baron Kelvin and insert missing information about his injury. Here and there I improve the language or correct a fact.

I share.

An hour or so later our train rolls into King's Cross Station, London, platform eight. Next to where we emerge, a small brass sign reads

"Platform 9¾" and half a trolley is seen as if being pushed through a brick wall.

"What's that about?" I ask.

"A joke. The station management put it there as a tribute to a famous story."

It now turns out that the one hour of travel didn't include another forty-five minutes riding the "tube"—or subway—around the Circle Line to Westminster.

"Next time we're travelling by hut," I say.

Mind you, what's the hurry? I'm only going to travel once more by hut and likely as not it will kill me.

I glance up at the colorful diagram of the London Underground, which maps out the entire subway system. "There's something reassuring about having a model of everything. Besides the first trillionth of a second, I mean."

"About that," he says.

I turn to him. "What?"

"When it comes to the interactions of matter, the standard model is indeed a good model of very-nearly-everything. But as to the understanding of the big scale of the cosmos, the situation is, well, less good."

"Oh. How so?"

"You see people have been weighing galaxies. They can do that by measuring the speed at which stars orbit the galaxies. Scientists have been adding up the mass they can see in all the stars, and it doesn't add up."

"Now you drop this little bombshell? How much mass in the galaxies is unaccounted for by the stars?"

"Quite a bit."

"How much, Zvi?"

He looks sheepish. "Well, all the stars and other mass we can see only account for, um, about five percent of the total mass we know is there."

"Just five percent!"

"Err, yes."

I wave my arms around and raise my voice. "You're trying to tell me that all of these networks of radio telescopes and optical telescopes and space telescopes and your detailed account of every split second of the Big Bang and the rest of this sounding-like-we-know-everything, and all along ninety-five percent of the universe's mass is unaccounted for? Ninety-five percent!"

"Yes, it's a bit depressing I'm afraid. There's a lot of *dark matter* out there."

"But besides adding gravitational mass to the galaxies, this dark matter is entirely passive? That's why we can't see it?"

"Well, not entirely passive."

"Spit it out, what effect does it have?"

"You see, the universe's expansion is accelerating," Zvi whispers back.

"Accelerating?" I shriek.

The British travelers sitting opposite pretend to be reading the boring little adverts above my head, ignoring my inappropriate volume.

"Yes. In recent years evidence has accumulated that the expansion is accelerating."

"Shouldn't gravity slow down the expansion?"

"Yes."

"What do you mean 'yes'? So why is the expansion accelerating?"

He mumbles something.

"Pardon?"

"*Dark energy.*"

"Dark energy makes the universe's expansion accelerate?"

"Yes. At least part of the dark matter is a 'dark energy' that drives expansion."

"And what is dark energy?"

"We don't know"

"'Dark energy' means 'no clue'?"

"There are some clues, but no more than that. You may recall that Einstein thought of adding a *cosmological constant* to general relativity. The cosmological constant represents some inherent tendency of spacetime to expand or contract. After Hubble's discovery that the universe is expanding, Einstein happily dumped the cosmological constant, calling it his own 'worst blunder.' But maybe there is a cosmological constant after all, explaining the accelerated expansion of the universe; maybe the cosmological constant represents some inherent tendency of spacetime to expand."

"But there is no direct evidence for a cosmological constant or explanation for why it comes about with the specific value we see?"

Zvi sighs. "No. Well, the universe's expansion is accelerating, that is the only evidence."

"Let's just make sure I got this straight. Ninety-five percent of the galaxies' mass is dark matter and dark energy and there is only speculation as to their nature."

"Yes. The neutrinos may be part of it or..." he trails off.

We ride in silence for some minutes through dark tunnels deep under the East End of London—Barbican, Moorgate, Liverpool Street. This tube ride is almost an analogy for modern cosmology. All I'm seeing of East London is a handful of underground platforms. I have reason to believe there is a city above my head, but what I observe is just the fringes that happen to be visible to me. Astronomers, with all their equipment, see just five percent of the mass of the universe—just the tube stations as it were.

"And with all that unknown dark stuff, can cosmology answer our fundamental questions, like whether the universe is infinite and what is its ultimate fate?" I ask.

"Probably. All observations suggest that at the large scale, spacetime seems flat. That suggests it may be infinite. But it is not impossible that over an extremely large scale spacetime curves into a closed loop."

I remember how I wrapped Alice and Bob's two-dimensional spacetime into a tube.

"So, if I travel far enough in one direction, I may loop around and come back where I started."

"It's possible."

"And the fate of the universe?"

"That has become pretty clear. When I was younger, people assumed that eventually gravity would win the day and reverse the Big Bang, bringing all of matter back together in a Big Crunch. But now that we have found that the expansion of the universe is accelerating—it is clear that the universe is destined to keep expanding. Eventually all the stars will fizzle out and the universe will become a big expanding frozen relic."

I roll my eyes. "What a party."

We alight at Westminster into the evening shadow of Big Ben, a vast, sand-colored, limestone-clad clock tower that my Welsh grandmother had once told me about. I also spare a glance for the bronze statue of Boadicea, Queen of the Iceni, across the road. Two galloping bronze horses, their veins protruding from their faces, draw her two-wheeled carriage, no doubt leading her Celtic tribe in another battle against the Romans.

"Follow me," Zvi says.

Cutting across Parliament Square, we face a majestic gothic church. To my surprise, Zvi crosses the road and strides straight up to the grand entrance of the Collegiate Church of Saint Peter at Westminster. A sign reads "Westminster Abbey, Founded 960," and informs us that the current building dates back to the 1200s.

Westminster Abbey in the evening

"A church?"

"A church," Zvi confirms.

"You don't seem like the type. You thought I would want to pray before my dangerous journey home?"

"No."

"You thought I would like to finish my trip with a discussion about physics and God."

"Not necessarily."

"So why come all the way to London to visit a church, beautiful as it might be? They have some cool chapels in Cambridge."

"Closure."

"Closure?"

"Follow me."

Zvi walks up to the cashier. Pulling out a fifty-pound note, he turns and hands it to me.

"Um, thanks?"

"No, just take a look."

I see a picture of James Watt, the engineer who perfected the fossil-fuel-powered steam engine and lent his name to the unit of power in physics. The man who perhaps, as much as anyone else in history, unleashed the power of technology—now commemorated on the currency that powers the modern economy he helped to create—the economy I still have mixed feelings about. I hand the note back to Zvi, who buys two entrance tickets to the Abbey.

"When I was younger, we had Isaac Newton on the one pound note and then Michael Faraday on the twenty," he explains.

We are swallowed into the swarms of tourists, from every corner of the globe, and are swept along with them through the ornate stone archways, into the endless hollow of the Abbey. As we strain our necks to observe the decorated ceiling so far above us, all of us experience the very emotion that the architects no doubt intended—a feeling of insignificance, like we are mere specks passing briefly through an endless and timeless building, lost in the infinite stonework, the countless architectural features, turrets, cloisters and archways, the marble statues, stained glass windows, wooden beams, and gilded plaques. If I make it back to my own time, no doubt this Abbey will not have changed one bit, and perhaps my Dad and I can visit it again.

As if to further emphasize our human mortality, and contrast it with the supposed eternalness of the church, I find that the very floor under our feet and the walls looming all around us are packed with buried human remains, the final resting place for ten centuries of kings and queens, knights and dukes, and poets such as Chaucer and Shakespeare.

Stepping from one tombstone to another, I suddenly stop dead in my tracks. I find myself standing on a black tombstone, flush with the floor: the resting place of Sir Isaac Newton.

Overlooking the tombstone is one of the most elaborate commemorative monuments in the entire Abbey. Under a decorated golden arch, the marble statue comprises a figure of a man reclining on top of a sarcophagus, his right elbow resting on a pile of books, his left hand pointing to a mathematical scroll. Above him are a pyramid and a celestial globe showing the signs of the zodiac and the path of a comet. A relief panel depicts a telescope and a prism.

I take a second to read the Latin inscription that translates more or less as "Here is buried Isaac Newton, Knight, who by a strength of mind almost divine, and mathematical principles peculiarly his own, explored the course and figures of the planets, the paths of comets, the tides of the sea, the dissimilarities in rays of light… Mortals rejoice that there has existed such and so great an ornament of the human race."

Tomb of Newton; in floor: grave of Newton surrounded by other physicists

Goodbye Isaac Newton—I'm so sorry we parted the way we did.

Newton's greatest legacy, I soon realize, is commemorated not in the monument but rather under my feet buried in the floor directly around him—the scientists he inspired to model the world. The men—alas here they are all men—to whom Newton bequeathed not only curiosity and technique but also the very tools of the equations of motion and the calculus, which were like the hammer and chisel for future generations of scientists.

Buried in the floor next to Newton is William Thomson, Lord Kelvin 1824-1907. The man I kissed just my two weeks ago, buried a few paces from the man he labored to discredit, Charles Darwin. The tombstones of the physicists bask in the delicately colored light pouring through a stained glass window dedicated "In memory of Kelvin of Largs. University of Glasgow."

Goodbye William.

Around Newton and Kelvin rest Sir Joseph John (J. J.) Thomson 1856-1940, master of Trinity College Cambridge, who discovered the electron, and his student, Ernest Rutherford of Nelson 1871-1937, who unraveled the atom and died of a treatable hernia.

There is a memorial for Faraday, who no doubt snubbed the Royal Family one last time in his death, refusing the honor of a burial in this Abbey. Plaques commemorate the other men I met in Oxford: James

Joule, and Sir George Gabriel Stokes, First Baronet, successor to Newton's chair in Cambridge. There is a memorial to James Clerk Maxwell.

Sir John Frederick William Herschel, First Baronet, who as a small child showed me Uranus, is also buried here next to a tribute to his father William Herschel: "He broke through the confines of the heavens."

The most recent burial in 1984, right between Newton and Rutherford, is Paul Dirac, with a small tombstone in a more modern diamond-shaped green slate. Other than his name and date, Dirac's memorial stone reads simply: $i\gamma\cdot\partial\psi=m\psi$, a formula I recognize from his presentation at Parc Léopold. It takes just those few characters to sum up perfectly Dirac's life achievement—the relativistic quantum wave equation which reconciled the two pillars of modern physics—special relativity and quantum mechanics—while introducing the spectacular prediction of antimatter.

Elsewhere I find a marble tablet dedicated to Thomas Young, "A man alike eminent in almost every department of human learning."

Here lie the heroes who led the battle of wits against Mother Nature. Closure.

Zvi rejoins me. "You expressed a need to say goodbyes. I hope this was meaningful."

"Very much," I sniffle, "thank you. I only wish I had the opportunity to say goodbye to some of the others. What became of Copernicus?"

"Nicolaus Copernicus was buried with full honors in the Frombork Cathedral by the Primate of Poland."

"Oh that is nice," I nod. "You know, I didn't get the impression he was afforded much respect by the Church."

"The burial was in May of last year. 2010."

"Oh. There's nothing like instant gratification. Galileo?"

"Galileo Galilei was completely rehabilitated by the Church. A statue was erected in his honor in the Vatican and the Pope praised his achievements. In 2008. That is the same year in which the Church of England apologized to Darwin."

"At least for me it's been less than three weeks. Of course, I miss Einstein too. But while we're here in this monumental edifice..." I hesitate.

"Yes?"

"Well, I do have a question. What does physics have to say about God? The Ecommunity worships nature, but I have sometimes wondered if nature itself must have been created by a single all-knowing, all-powerful deity. Does physics shed any light on that question?"

"Are you trying to get me into trouble?"

"I wouldn't mind at all. But isn't it a legitimate question?" I say.

"Indeed. Well, science rules out a literal reading of the Bible. The Sun does not orbit the Earth, the world is not thousands of years old, and humanity doesn't have a recent common ancestor such as Noah or Adam and Eve. But, beyond that, science presents little direct evidence as to whether the universe was created by a god or not. Even so, there are some interesting hints both ways."

"I'm listening."

"The standard model includes about twenty-six parameters—numbers—such as the masses of the quarks and the *leptons*—the electron and its siblings—and the relative strengths of the four interactions. The standard model just assumes these numbers; it has no way to predict them. The theory is like a guitar with twenty-six strings that can be tuned. We have no particular explanation why the world has been tuned to those specific twenty-six values."

"Surely we hope that not all of those numbers are arbitrary—that an even deeper theory will one day be able to predict some or all of those twenty-six numbers?"

"That's true, we do hope that. But as of now, the standard model includes many arbitrary parameters."

"So?"

"So… some of those parameters seem to have been fine-tuned with incredible accuracy to make life possible. If the strong interaction, for example, were just a couple of percent stronger or a couple of percent weaker, it would change everything. Atoms and therefore life as we know it would be impossible. But the most dramatic case of fine-tuning is the cosmological constant or the amount of dark energy in the universe. Some have argued that the number must have been fine-tuned to one part in 1,000,000,000,000,000,000,000,000,000,000,000,000,000, 000,000,000,000,000,000,000,000,000,000,000,000,000,000, 000,000,000,000,000,000,000,000,000,000 in order to allow life to develop." He stops to takes a breath. "Yes, we might yet find that it is all an inevitable consequence of some unknown more fundamental law, but in the meantime, it makes you wonder. Maybe somebody knew what they were doing when they fine-tuned that value so carefully. But then again…" he trails off.

"Then again what?"

"We are biased observers. All we see is our own universe. Maybe there are many universes. Maybe infinitely many. Why are the laws of physics so fine-tuned to allow life? Perhaps they're not. Perhaps there are other universes with other values. In most universes, there may be no life. Once in trillions of times a universe pops up that happens to have the conditions for life. Then that life evolves and starts asking: Why is our universe fine-tuned for life? Perhaps it was pure chance. It's called the *anthropic principle*. We shouldn't wonder why our universe is fine-tuned for life. The fact that humans are here to ask the question means that our universe had to be tuned in that way. Whenever a universe is not suitably tuned for life, there is no one around to notice."

"That's confusing. Why not assume that a single all-powerful being created the universe?"

"As you have seen, Fizz, science teaches us that making assumptions without evidence is dangerous. In the case of your world, for example, that assumption is definitely false."

I stand up from the pew and glare at him. "What do you mean *my* world? And how can you be sure that a single all-powerful being didn't create my world?"

"Because I did. And I had help."

"What?" I shriek again. "Who the hell are you?"

"I'm the author."

"What does that mean? That you created my universe?"

"Kind of, yeah."

"You said to trust nothing without evidence. Prove it."

Zvi snaps his fingers. Suddenly I'm floating high in the atrium of Westminster Abbey, tens of meters above the pews, suspended head-down. Nothing could prepare me for a shock like this, and I have to admit that I find the evidence instantly convincing. Fortunately, I'm wearing pants.

"If I die inside Westminster Abbey," I scream down to Zvi, the voice echoing around the atrium, "do I get the honor of being buried here?"

"So you think our universe was designed for life? Take a look at some of the other universes," he shouts back.

Zvi snaps his fingers again. I am in a different universe with a higher cosmological constant. I watch the Big Bang, following which the universe flies apart so rapidly that the hydrogen is dispersed and never coalesces into stars. The universe dies a rapid, cold death. No intelligent beings ever evolve to take note of this universe's existence.

Snap. I'm in a universe with a lower cosmological constant. Following the Big Bang, the universe expands for just milliseconds before being pulled back together into a big crunch. The universe is annihilated with no chance of anyone noticing.

Snap. I'm in a universe with a different strong interaction. The atoms that appear don't resemble the atoms I am used to, but a bizarre fuzzy form of life has evolved with no resemblance to the life on Earth.

Snap. Now I am in a universe with seventeen dimensions, not four. Five of the dimensions are infinite, and twelve dimensions are finite, wrapping around like the circumference of a pipe.

Snap. I'm back sitting next to Zvi on a pew in Westminster Abbey, with a splitting headache.

We sit in silence for a long time.

"So," he finally says, "what's it like to have met your creator?"

I look deeply into his eyes for another moment. "Frankly, I'm disappointed."

He looks down. "Yeah, I know."

"So there I was," I say, "thinking that my world was the ultimate purpose, and that perhaps some all-powerful creator had designed me. At times I wondered whether He might be following my progress, willing me to do good. And all along my entire world was just some creative writing project you took on to celebrate your mid-life crisis?"

For a moment he looks hurt, almost angry. I fear I may have provoked his wrath. But some seconds later his merciful side shines through and he emits a hearty chuckle.

"So you took me on a lightning tour of other worlds you imagined just to show me that you can?"

"Just to show you that unsubstantiated assumptions, especially self-centered assumptions like ours-is-the-only-universe or the-universe-was-tuned-for-us or we-are-the-purpose-of-the-universe, are—well—unsubstantiated."

"You barged into my world to make that point?"

"Amongst others. An outside perspective can be helpful."

"Helpful, but extremely irritating. Frankly I wish I'd never met you. You make me feel, I don't know, insignificant, almost unreal."

"How do you think I feel? Just one of billions of people," he gestures at the crowds all around us, "all of whom comprise just one of millions of species living on one of probably billions of planets, in what might be one of an infinity of universes."

"Well too bad for you. So you invade my universe in some vain attempt to make yourself feel more significant?"

"I, well—I thought it would be a good demonstration of the observer effect. And that I could help you, of course."

I glare at him. "And what qualifies you to appoint yourself as my teacher?"

His head droops slightly. "I—well—not much."

"Have you met Galileo, Newton, or Einstein, like I have?"

"Sadly, no."

"So, Zvi, I repeat, what credentials do you have to appoint yourself as my physics tutor?"

"It's not exactly like that."

"What is it exactly like?"

I don't get an answer. We sit there for a while, the last of the honeyed evening light streaming in through the stained-glass windows all around. Tourists swarm. From time to time one of them takes the opportunity to kneel in prayer. The bodies below and around us remain oblivious to all the attention they're getting. The muffled sound of a distant Big Ben striking seven p.m. reverberates gently through the hollow of the Abbey.

I look at Zvi. "You know, Zvi, I think I know what it's like. I mean you and me."

"You do?"

"Yes, I don't think your goal is to teach me, you're barely qualified for that anyway." I notice him wincing. "I think it may be the very opposite."

"The opposite?"

"Yes. I think I'm teaching you. You're some sort of voyeur, surreptitiously watching me discuss physics with the giants, because you can't. Because you want to get your own thoughts in order. That is how I read our 'metaphysical' interaction."

He stares at me. "I think I'll leave you now."

"That would be nice. I have a dangerous maneuver to attempt. It's bad enough knowing you're looking over my shoulder the whole time, without having you traveling in my hut."

"Bye, Fizz. I'm rooting for you," Zvi says. And the author gives me a metaphysical hug.

Eternal Mystery

"Computer, listen very carefully. You don't have enough fuel to get me back home by traveling at close to the speed of light. Instead, I want you to put us in a tight orbit around a relatively nearby black hole." I read out the coordinates of a black hole that I identified by detecting the Hawking radiation with the worldwide network of radio telescopes. "Do not—I repeat—do not cross the event horizon, or we'll be trapped in the time-space warp of the black hole forever. Get close enough that we can experience the time dilation predicted by general relativity around an intense source of gravity. Stay in orbit just outside the event horizon for long enough that one hundred years will have passed on Earth—it should only be hours for us. Preserve enough fuel to pull us out of the orbit and get me home to Iceland."

I watch the screen. It gives no indication of whether it has understood my instructions, no updates on our progress. But soon I'm feeling some pretty intensive accelerations—or perhaps gravitational attractions—which first crush me down into the floor, then disappear, leaving me to float weightless in the air—*awesome!*—and then gradually push me against the ceiling which soon becomes the new "floor."

The hut has no windows so I can only hope that we're performing the highly dangerous maneuver of precariously orbiting in the highly curved spacetime close to an intense source of gravity, zipping through the years as the last remains of fuel dwindle. I should be panicking. Or praying. *Or something.* But I mostly feel numb, so I try to focus my blank mind on digesting all that I've learned.

Somehow my thoughts just refuse to arrange themselves on a label. Instead, one thought—one word—comes to the forefront of my mind, as if to help make sense of it all: *layers.* The world is just too complex for a single-leveled label. Our universe must be understood in layers.

So walking on a surface which till recently was "one of the walls," but which now seems to be attracting me, I grab a pad with several sheets of paper, and start to write on them in such a way that each sheet represents a layer in our view of the universe, each sheet resting on the sheet below it, building on the ideas of that lower layer but abstracting away the details. I sit cross-legged on the wall with my bed providing a cushioned back rest.

On the first and lowest sheet I write:

ROW Label level O:

Fundamental theory of everything (doesn't exist yet).

If I make it home safely, I will have a lifetime, banned to the Outside, in which to find out what progress has been made toward such a theory. I imagine the dream of one elegant theory of everything continues to motivate physicists like my Dad in 2110. *Unless they already found it.*

As of 2011, I learned a theory, which is a little more complex than we would ideally like, but which seems to perfectly model virtually everything right down the sub-nuclear quarks and right back to the first hundredth of one millionth of a second of the Big Bang:

ROW Label level 1: The standard model

Context: Spacetime is relative to the observer and is curved by masses (manifests as gravity — called general relativity)

Ingredients:

Up quark, down quark (and four unstable siblings)

Electron (and two unstable "lepton" siblings)

Neutrino (and two siblings)

Higgs boson (unconfirmed)

Antimatter counterparts (that quickly annihilate)

Interactions (quantum field theory):

Electromagnetism (carried by photon)

Weak interaction (carried by W and Z particles)

Strong interaction (carried by gluon, binds quarks)

Arrow of time: Entropy always increases

Warnings:

Measurement problem: what is the magical "measurement" that turns indefinite superpositions into definite states (Schrödinger's cat)?

Universe appears random (God plays with dice)

Non-local effects of a measurement (Bell's theorem)

Standard model too complex: 26 fine-tuned parameters

No theory combining general relativity with standard model
In cosmology—dark matter, dark energy

In theory, my pad could stop right there! Everything else in the universe is really just the study of quarks and leptons interacting according the laws of the standard model.

But you would not get very far trying to analyze a human thought, or planet Mars, or the Big Bang, quark-by-quark and electron-by-electron.

So I create some more placeholder layers for my ROW label, each one building on the layer below and creating shortcuts for analyzing really complex combinations of quarks and electrons:

Level 2: Nuclear physics: Studies the protons and neutrons in the nucleus (abstracting the details of the quarks within them)

Level 3: Atomic physics: Studies the atom—nucleus and electrons (while abstracting the internals of the nucleus)

Level 4: Chemistry: Studies the interactions between atoms as they bind into molecules

Level 5: Solid-state physics: Studies the behavior of solids composed of trillions of atoms, including semi-conductors

Level 6: Thermodynamics: Ignores the behavior of individual atoms and treats overall statistical concepts such as temperature and entropy

Level 7: Mechanics: Studies the macroscopic movement of objects. Here we ignore the atoms completely and treat materials as if they were smooth solids (framework is Newton's equations of motion)

I flip up and down the layers and shake my head. *It's astounding that the universe looks so different at different resolutions.* By the time we get to mechanics—like bridges and billiard balls—the universe is perfectly deterministic and local, and couldn't care less that materials comprise atoms, let alone quarks.

<u>Higher levels outside physics:</u> Biology, psychology, philosophy, law, economics, arts...

Then at the grandest level of all, we can ignore trivial details like planets, life, and civilization and we're back in the realm of physics studying the overall structure of a universe full of quarks, electrons and microwave photons.

<u>Level (top): Cosmology</u>
<u>Date of manufacture:</u> Big Bang ~13 billion years ago
<u>Contents:</u> The primordial "soup" of the Big Bang expanded and cooled leaving:
(1)   Microwave background radiation
(2)   A thin soup of hydrogen that has clumped under the influence of gravity into galaxies and stars within those galaxies. In stars, gravity fuses hydrogen into helium.
(3)   Dark matter, and dark energy that drives accelerated expansion.
Exploding stars at their end of life—supernovas—have created the heavier atoms that have formed planets.
Large, dead stars collapse into neutron stars (a vast nucleus) or black holes. Black holes radiate Hawking radiation from their event horizon.

And one more:

<u>Level multiverse:</u> Is our universe one of many?

I shift to lie on the ceiling and flick through the labels again and again, distracting myself from some pretty violent changes in my weight. *Just three weeks ago I knew zero science—I've not done badly.*
In addition to learning physics, I've discovered how technology started without physics, but how physics supercharged technology, boosting it to both bright and dark places.
If I have to be marooned on the Outside, I've certainly given myself the best foundation I can in terms of physics.

And now my human skills are facing their greatest test ever.

Iceland Ecommunity Visitors' Center. 2110.

I made it.

The wave of relief at seeing this final message on the little screen lasts for about as long as a positron lasts in a container full of electrons, before my mind is possessed with the situation I must now face.

I sulk out of the hut on to the launching pad. The cool summer evening air and a beautiful sunset welcome me home to Iceland. I stand for a while watching some PAT emerge from the orange-pink western sky shooting rapidly toward me, fracturing the serenity of the sunset as it breaks sharply and parks just a few meters away. I regard the oddly dressed Outsider as she emerges, ready to deposit her gadgets and make a rushed annual visit to some relative in the Ecommunity before the Visitor's Center closes for the night. I keep staring at the stranger as she climbs the path toward the Visitors' Center, the warm evening colors illuminating her back with photons of electromagnetic radiation.

I wonder if she's here to visit her mother. What kind of relationship do they have meeting just once a year? Is there any possible way I can get dispensation to visit my mother once a year even though I overstayed the three weeks?

I realize that I'm still wearing jeans and T-Shirt from 2011. Back in the hut, I retrieve my own Collective clothes from the shelf. Closing the hut door gently I carefully remove the "Fizz's Place" plaque and take it with me.

My feet drag themselves up toward the Visitors' Center. The Outside Relations Office upstairs will have to send word to Dad that I'm back and ready for him to collect me. By now he must have realized that I'm coming home with him. I don't suppose they will let me go to Mom personally, but hopefully they will send word on my behalf, with the next horseman going in her direction, that I'm waiting here for her to come and say a final goodbye. *By now she may think I'm dead—she could even be relieved to see me.*

Perhaps Mom is right here keeping vigil.

Snaking up the hill, I have time to wonder. *What would I choose at this very moment, if I still had the choice?* No answer presents itself. Well, I have a lifetime on the Outside to torture myself with that very question. Now I must focus on saying my goodbyes and building a new life. *How will I learn the ways of my new world? How long will it take to make new friends? How will guys respond to a red-headed chick who is completely green in the ways of their world?*

At least I will have my Dad. *If he wants me.* My already unsettled stomach tightens further.

Finally, I open the door of the Visitors' Center and slowly I walk in. Both Mom and Dad are right here at a table. It's the very first time that I've seen them together. They present quite a contrast, her loose plain off-white clothes, his more colorful tailored attire. Not to mention their diametrically opposite worldviews—philosophies as fundamentally incompatible as an electron's position and momentum.

At least I can say goodbye to Mom in person. Much as a note would be easier, this way is right.

Has Dad, who finds it torturous to wait for an hour, waited the entire three weeks for me? If so, he's going to be wound up like... like some oversized uranium atom, ready to violently explode at a random moment. *What a way to start.*

Mom stares for a couple of seconds then runs across the room to embrace me. We hug tightly, Mom whispering "Fizz" again and again. *I've broken her heart.* Raising me has been her life for eighteen years and I'm turning around and abandoning her—just because I couldn't stay home and keep a lid on my own juvenile curiosity. Or because, when I did take the trip, I allowed myself to become enamored with shiny steam engines and oversized telescopes and didn't wind up my journey after a few days as planned. *Now I have a lifetime to regret my greedy, ill-conceived decision to take—and prolong—my time traveling trip.*

Still holding Mom, I glance over her shoulder at the white and red doors of the clinic and put a hand on my stomach.

"Fizz, thank goodness," Mom is whispering, "I was livid with your Dad. I thought I'd lost you. But I should never have doubted your promise."

I loosen my grip slightly. "Which promise?" I whisper back.

"You promised to come back to me in a couple of days. I'm so relieved you did."

Still embracing my Mom I turn her slightly to get a view of Dad. He winks at me. I glare at him; my head feels like it will physically explode. *You manipulated my time travel... and now you break the news with a rueful wink!*

I could kick myself too. After everything I've learned about space and time, why would I assume, just because more than three weeks have elapsed for me, that the same is true relative to those who remained in Iceland?

I release Mom and stumble to grab the nearest chair.

Right now in my personal life too, nothing at all is as it seems.

Dad comes and stands over me, resting a hand on my shoulder and talks casually. "So Fizz, what was it like? I'm sure you have many experiences to share with us."

"Certainly, many adventures—revelations—*dangers*. This time yesterday I didn't think I'd ever make it back. But I can't think about all of that now. Apparently, I've got a decision to make."

Mom's face collapses. "Decision? Fizz, you swore—"

I can barely breathe. I get up and walk out.

Pacing away from the building, I find myself marching to the nearby beach. I lie on my back in the sand and try to control the dizziness of emotions that has come over me. I watch the now familiar ritual of the stars emerging. I try to transport myself, this time emotionally, three and a half weeks back, to that night when I slept on the beach, the last night before I dreamt up my fateful time voyage. *Back when there was less entropy—more order—in the universe—in my universe—although it sure didn't feel that way at the time.* I look up at the stars. How much more I now know about what they are, how they work, where they come from. Yet how much deeper are the dilemmas I face. *If now really was back then, would I embark on the journey all over again?*

I close my eyes and try to replay the past, but my mind is obsessing over the future. I lie here, fighting the tension, battling with the options, trying to pin down turbulent thoughts, not quite able to weigh up the alternatives rationally.

A slight shift in the sand jolts me. Both my parents are towering above me, visible only as silhouettes against the backdrop of twinkling stars. Without a word, the two of them lay down in the sand on either side of me. *Dad's not allowed out here, but that's the least of my worries right now.*

"Hello?" I say weakly.

"Dad and I spoke, Fizz," Mom whispers from my left.

"You spoke?"

"Yes. Fizz, it's so hard for me to say this, but I see you're hurting. So I want to tell you that whatever is good for you, I'm behind you."

My eyes well up. "Thank you, Mom, you don't have to say that."

"I think I do. Mainly because you will make up your own mind any-way."

With Mom and Dad next to me I'm finally forming an instinct—vague and weak, but an instinct nonetheless—for how to play my life.

"Yes. I suppose I need to speak to you both. But first Mom, is there any way to send word with the next southbound horse going to tell the Dean to come here first thing in the morning?"

"You Fizz? You want the Dean?"

"Yes. And Zopp."

"The Dean? Zopp? Fizz, what's going on?"

"Please, Mom, trust me. Just send word before it's too late."

"I can't just summon them."

"No. But you can ask. If you tell them I'm back here, I think they'll come."

"I—well, all right." Mom gets up and walks off along the dark sand.

"What is going on?" Dad asks.

"Let's wait for Mom."

We lie on the sand in silence.

Ten minutes later, Mom returns and I beckon to her to join us in the sand.

"Well Fizz?" she breathes.

"Dad," I turn to my right. "I want to be with you."

I hear a gasp from behind my head. In the dim light, I study Dad's reactions from inches away. He's clearly shocked.

"That—well—that could be very exciting. But are you... sure?"

I keep tracking his face as he shifts slightly—I think he's trying to ensure that my head obscures his line of sight with Mom at this particular moment. I study his every facial muscle.

I don't think he's displeased.

"Yes, Dad, I'm sure. I want you to be my father and I want to be with you. In this Visitors' Center, on every second of July."

Now Mom is exhaling down my neck.

Sorry Mom. I just couldn't resist the opportunity to see Dad's reaction.

"Dad. The world you live in is absolutely fascinating. And scary as hell. But I love you. And I forgive you."

"You f—forgive me? Um, for?" he says.

"For abandoning me."

"I—well—I—" Dad hesitates. "I'm so sorry, Fizz. I was young."

"Well you gave me the gift of life, that's something. And I've decided that I can't judge decisions you made when you were eighteen. I know another eighteen-year-old who's made some rash decisions."

"But—I'm not sure you fully understand," Dad says.

"I think I do. You knew, right?"

"I knew what?"

"And even so I forgive you. Truly Dad, I do. I don't judge you, not anymore."

"You forgive me? I..." Dad trails off, then takes my hand and holds it tight for a while. "Thank you, Fizz. That means so much to me."

"Whatever decisions you made at eighteen, I don't want you to have to live with any guilt."

Now Dad swallows. "If only," he mutters.

"The mugging?"

His dimly lit eyes pop wide open. Then he looks away. "Yes."

"There's a chance I can help with that too. I believe your friend from your PCC escaped with an injury to his leg. He made a full recovery except for a slight limp and found a profession that gives him a lot of satisfaction—warning people about the Outside. He should be on his way here. Who knows, maybe he's ready to forgive you too. Seeing his stray young congregant safely back island-side may put him in the right mood."

Dad stares at me amazed, perhaps... proud. In the meantime I can almost feel Mom's eyes boring through the back of my head.

"And Dad, as much as we can, I want a real relationship with you."

"Of course, I would treasure that."

"Starting tomorrow. Before you leave, I'm hoping you'll take a minute to meet my new boyfriend. You know, play the Dad card, size him up for me. Give him the speech about treating me right."

"Fizz—what century do you think—" he waits for a second then continues very seriously. "I mean, sure, it would be my honor. Yes, it would be my fatherly pleasure."

Gravity pulls a tear sideways from his eye to the sand.

"You can skip the bit about not knocking me up," I say.

Dad sniffs and smiles awkwardly. "Fizz, I don't know what to say."

"Don't say anything. Just kiss my forehead."

Dad kisses my forehead.

It's nice, but it's not quite the same.

Mom clears her throat. Turning, I see she's crying too. "Fizz—"

"Mom, I love you. I wouldn't be anywhere else. But there is a condition."

She pauses. "Of course, Fizz. You can keep your secret little physics book." She watches my eyebrows rise. "I'm sorry, but when you took off like that, I had to do a bit of exploring of my own."

"Here's the thing, Mom. My notebook won't be secret anymore. I don't care what the Dean or anyone says. I'm going to keep asking questions. And when I can't answer them myself, I'm going to save them up for Dad."

"Well, Fizz. No one can physically stop you. But you know that the Collective won't accept it. I don't want that for you, being an outcast."

I shrug. "I prefer the term 'maverick.' Anyhow, that's how it's going to be. At least I'll get to see who really loves me."

Mom gazes at me in the starlight. Then she takes my hand. "Count me in, of course. But why, Fizz? What about everything you've been taught? Curiosity leading to exploitation."

"That piece of my education is—well—true; truer than I could ever have imagined. For centuries it wasn't. Even into the early 1800s. So much so that when I saw people like William making the connection, I kind of denied it. Until the connection became so violent that it couldn't possibly be ignored—"

"Who's William?" Mom asks.

"Yet, understanding the world we live in is also human nature. Irrepressible. It's an insolvable dilemma that I'll just have to muddle through."

The three of us lie in silence. I wonder what Mom and Dad are thinking. I'm greatly relieved to have made a decision with which I feel kind of comfortable.

Eventually Dad breaks the lull. "Beautiful," he intones.

I smile for the first time in some hours, and turn to see which of us he's looking at. But Dad is looking at neither Mom nor me. He's gazing straight up at the unpolluted night sky. "In all the years, I completely forgot—really spectacular."

Another silence.

"So what is it?" Mom says.

"What is what?"

"The sky. The stars. All of it, Fizz. What is it?"

"Mother? Are you asking me about astronomy?"

"Fizz, if it's part of your life, it's part of mine. Anyw___ u and your father don't have a monopoly on curiosity, you know."

"Yes, of course, Mom." I take my Mom's arm and slowly I lift it to point. "Look Mom—that bright dot is Jupiter. That red spot over there is Mars—those are planets. They are kind of like Earth's siblings, orbiting the Sun, just as we do. They're our own backyard.

"Every other white dot you see, each star, is actually like our Sun—a vast ball of hydrogen left over from the first seconds of the universe, now collapsing under the force of gravity, which is a curvature of space-time, to the extent that some of the hydrogen crushes into helium and eventually into heavier atoms, releasing energy in the form of light, which is electromagnetic waves, but comes in packets called photons, that travel for many years to reach our eyes. The very atoms we were made of were manufactured by dying stars."

"Oh. Um, I think you are going to have to explain that to me more slowly. There's time enough for that. What's that white strip?"

"That is actually millions more stars, a disk of stars that we are within. But everything you see, all of it, is just our own suburb, the Milky Way. With just one exception, that is."

"Which exception, Fizz?"

I gently move Mom's arm. "Those stars there are known as the constellation of Andromeda. Do you see four bright stars in a line? Just north of them, do you see a tiny faint white smudge? That 'little' smudge is the Andromeda galaxy. In it are a trillion stars, more than the entire Milky Way. That barely visible dot is bigger than everything else you can see combined."

Dad smiles proudly. "Makes you feel pretty small, doesn't it?"

I think for quite a while before answering.

"No, I'm not sure it does," I say at length.

Mom puts down her arm and takes my hand again. She turns her head to me. "No?"

"Not really. Sure, the universe is large, but it isn't all that complex. It took an impressive series of geniuses, but now that the secrets have been exposed, the universe is not so hard to fathom. During my journey I learned how a few dozen laws of the standard model govern virtually every fundamental process in the entire cosmos. Strangely, I think that some mechanisms within the universe—like you and me—are much more complicated than the universe itself. You know, it is easier to understan[...]ig Bang and galactic evolution than it is to understand human tho[...]s and emotions."

"Like ho[...]e resolve tough dilemmas," says Mom.

"Yeah, like that."

"If it's not all that complicated," Mom says, "why all this dramatic time travel, Fizz? You could have sat with your Dad and studied a physics book for a week."

"I certainly offered," Dad says.

"Yes, Mom, I could have studied physics from a textbook. But I have to tell you, I don't regret the journey. Reliving how it all developed, seeing the insights firsthand, chatting with the personalities—somehow studying a textbook would just not have been the same."

I gaze up at the universe and for a second it feels like it may be gazing back at me, perhaps with a modicum of respect for how many of its secrets I've uncovered.

"The most amazing thing about this place," I say, "is how the universe is simple enough that it lends itself to analysis, yet complex enough to give rise to intelligent beings with the motivation and means to analyze it."

Dad takes my other hand. "Did you meet Albert Einstein, Fizz?"

I smile. "Yes, I did, several times."

"It's like he said, isn't it?"

"Yes, Dad. I was just thinking the very same thought. As Einstein said, 'The eternal mystery of the world is its comprehensibility.'"

Epilogue

The three of us wake up on the beach, and Dad asks to give his time machine the once-over before the Dean and Zopp arrive. After all, he says, I've put it through its most vigorous testing to date. We leave Mom in the Visitors' Center and walk together to the launch pad. The idea hits me as we walk.

"Dad, could you take a picture of me?"

"Sure." He stops walking, looks at me, and blinks. "Done."

"What is the time?"

"About eleven."

"No, the precise date and time." I believe he can see a virtual clock on demand.

"July 5, 2110, 11:02:30."

"Thanks."

"Err, sure."

We arrive at the hut and step in.

"Oh. So I see you opened the box, Fizz, was everything okay?"

"At first I resented you putting the box in there," I say, "but actually those artifacts came in handy."

"I'm not sure how, you don't seem to have used them much," Dad says as he starts to remove the objects one at a time. "You were okay for food?" I nod. Dad opens the jar of brown powder, scoops his finger in, and licks it. "You know when I travel in this thing I'm always tempted to eat the cake mix, food emergency or not…"

He keeps unpacking the box. "Emergency drinking water—intact," he seems to be going through a formal checklist that only he can see, presumably in his inter-cranial computer. "I see you traveled well… sick bag—unused… so how did you find navigating with a lodestone? I'm sorry that I couldn't have you walking around the ancient world with a GPS."

I stare at him, then at the artifacts. So the lens represented neither the celestial spheres nor the phenomenon of light; it was probably there for lighting a fire in an emergency. The amber represented neither quintessence nor electricity; its electrical spark must be for lighting a fire at night.

Dad keeps examining them one at a time. "Anyway, what were that photo and time-check all about?"

"I was thinking that with the knowledge I've accumulated I'm ready to experience today's Outside life for a bit. Are you game?"

"What—you mean right now?"

"Right now. For a few weeks."

"But Fizz, your Mom is expecting you back any minute! And you know your Collective won't accept you back once the PCC expires."

"Don't you have some spare fuel somewhere? Would they ever have to know?

Dad laughs nervously. "Fizz!" He takes some sort of thick safety glove out of his bag and uses it to pick up the warm can. "Yes, of course. In fact there's enough enriched uranium fuel right here for a few hundred years of time travel. But are you sure?"

I step outside and gaze at the sunrise. *It's not the sun rising at all—we're the ones rotating.* Out of the sunrise emerges a PAT no doubt carrying today's first visitor. *What's it like traveling in those things? Right now I'm not sure I care.*

"No, Dad, cancel that. I'm staying right here."

Why not share/review
your experience of Fizz

www.fizz-book.com

Thanks

My first thanks are to my wife and editor-in-chief, Rina, for her love and encouragement, and for patiently and repeatedly reviewing and discussing each chapter. My children Keren and Daniel were devoted and astute reviewers, Eitan happy to bounce ideas around, and Joel full of encouragement and suggestions. Thanks to Keren for modeling Fizz for the cover. Fizz is dedicated to these five special people.

I'm blessed with a talented, supportive extended family. While my parents, David and Ruth Schreiber, never loaned me a time machine, they provided me with every other opportunity and encouragement to develop my own curiosity. Mum ploughed through the manuscript twice making copious comments. My sister Tamar (hokeycroquis.com) was Fizz's official historic fashion consultant and sis Avital (avitalschreiber.com) my typographical/graphical advisor. Both tried to help my desperate attempts to fathom the mind of a teenage girl. Brothers Benji and Arye also provided feedback.

It is doubtful if I would have persevered beyond some rather poor early drafts if it wasn't for people like my brother Daniel Schreiber and Karin Berkman's ability to spot the potential buried rather deeply therein and to provide much needed encouragement and insightful criticism.

During the past year, the Jerusalem Malcha Writer's Group was a source not only of valuable constructive criticism, but also a forum to vent my own frustrations by critiquing others. My thanks to Michael Loftus, Anna Levine (annalevine.org), Ben Dansker, Sara Halevi, and June Leavitt (spiritualityteaching.com) and best of luck to characters Ben Zona, Andi, Jacov, and Evie, or their successors.

I'm grateful to Dr. John Hubisz for his detailed expert comments, and, for their feedback, to Heather Schwaber, Victor Ofstein, Tracy Stevens, Lori Kaufman and author Daniel Levin.

This was an international effort. Written in Jerusalem and printed in the US and Lithuania, the cover art for Fizz was by Ricardo Jorge Martins in Portugal, the web site and cover edits by Robertus Ricky Zakaria from Indonesia, the diagram graphics by Khalil Hanna in Palestine.

For valuable publishing industry tips and introductions, I'm indebted to Avi Gross, author Jonathan Tropper, Shany Moore, Jonny and Mindy Ebbrahimof, Charlotte Paisner, and Yadin Kaufman.

The all-important finishing touches owe much to editors Nanette Day and Julia Denton (XpertEditor and EditrixJD at EditAvenue.com).

Wikipedia was an invaluable resource throughout and everyone who contributes to that wonderful project deserves my gratitude too.

Historical notes and credits

Fizz, her background, and all the specific scenes and conversations are obviously fictional. The physicists she meets are all based on their historical (or contemporary) namesakes and the scientific discoveries and insights, as well as most of the settings, are based as closely as possible on historical reality. Where possible, personality traits are often inspired by history but come with no warranty of authenticity.

I have prioritized conceptual clarity over historical detail. At times where the contemporary scientific nomenclature is too confusing to the modern ear, I unashamedly place modern terminology into historical mouths. This includes the use in most cases of the metric units of meters (1 meter equals approximately 3 feet) and kilograms (1 kilogram weighs 2.2lb), which are today the official standard in every country of the world except Burma, Liberia, and the USA.

Insights or experiments presented in the same scene may have developed a couple of years apart. Some arguments are embellished with nuances that may have in fact been conceived later. I hope that these small anachronisms increase clarity without significantly misrepresenting the general thrust of the historic development of physics.

When people reviewed the book I sometimes got comments like "that sounds nothing like what Einstein might have said" or "this occurrence is not credible." It turns out that most such comments actually related to direct quotes of Einstein or historic facts. Fact, as they say, is stranger than fiction. So while Fizz is clearly not intended as a detailed or accurate historical work, for those readers who want a better idea of history versus fiction in the story, I offer these brief notes.

3 Greek to Me

This chapter is set at a time when Aristotle was indeed on the island of Lesbos, widowed and living with his daughter, before heading to Macedon. I did not find a record of young Pythias' actual age at the date of this chapter, and her eavesdropping is purely fictional. Aristotle did make a detailed study and sketches of sea creatures found in fishing nets while in Lesbos, including discovering the cephalopods' so-called hectocotylus arm (whatever that is), a discovery which was doubted until it was rediscovered in the nineteenth century. I have no idea whether he actually sat in the harbor. Aristotle did wear a more decorated Chiton and rings and had his hair fashionably short, leading J. Barnes to describe him as "a bit of a dandy." There is limited evidence of Aristotle's personality, but scholars point to some indications in his will and elsewhere of his being kindly, generous, and family-oriented although his detractors accused him of being arrogant.

I did not find specific records of Aristotle's home in Lesbos, so I describe my impression of a typical high-end ancient Greek home and meal. Aristotle made contributions to all the topics described in his library and documents the earliest description of a camera obscura. Amazingly, Aristotle did describe women as colder, having fewer teeth, and not being fully human, although he did attribute importance to women's happiness.

4 Center of the World

German was common around Frombork, and there has been some nationalistic debate about whether Copernicus' mother tongue was Polish or German, although he was clearly fluent in both in addition to Latin. Krystian is a purely fictional character representing the typical response Copernicus faced from the Church.

Copernicus was a bachelor and something of a loner. He first circulated his ideas on heliocentrism among a small circle of friends in some written notes in or shortly before the year when the chapter is set, 1514. His authoritative work on the subject, *Revolutionibus Orbium Coelestium* (On the Revolutions of the Heavenly Spheres), was published, after many years of hesitation, during the year of his death, 1543. Legend has it that Copernicus received a printed copy of the book on the day of his death.

According to some sources, he lived in one of the towers of the cathedral, and the description of the contents of the room is based on a reconstruction of one of his rooms that is currently exhibited in Frombork.

The photograph of the Frombork cathedral and surrounding castle walls is a modern one, although to the best of my knowledge there has not been much change.

During his life, Copernicus' ideas were met with skepticism, but the Church did not officially censor his book until long after his death in 1620 when others, particularly Galileo, had started building on the "heretical" ideas to the point where they became more threatening to Rome.

The following quotes from Copernicus' book *Revolutionibus* inspired a couple of passages of dialogue:

All this is suggested by the systematic procession of events and the harmony of the whole Universe… if only we face the facts, as they say, 'with both eyes open.'

If perchance there should be foolish speakers who… because of some place in the Scriptures wickedly distorted to their purpose, should dare to assail this my work, they are of no importance to me, to such an extent do I despise their judgment as rash.

For, in this most beautiful temple, who would place this lamp in another or better position than that from which it can light up the whole thing at the same time? For the sun is not inappropriately called by some people the lantern of the universe... Thus indeed, as though seated on a royal throne, the sun governs the family of planets revolving around it.

The following quote, placed in the mouth of Copernicus, was appropriated from Vatican librarian Cesare Cardinal Baronio and quoted by Galileo: *I believe the purpose of Holy Scripture is to guide us how to go to heaven, not how the heavens go.*

5 Father and Sun

Galileo performed all the experiments described in the lab at one time or another, including creating the first thermometer and discovering the time-keeping properties of the pendulum and the nature of sound. I believe it is fair to describe his workshop as the world's first physics lab.

Marina Gamba was Galileo's long-term mistress and bore him two daughters, who, being illegitimate, were considered unmarriageable and sent off to a convent for life. Their son Vincenzo was later legitimized.

I chose to set this and the next chapter in Pisa, since this city was so important to Galileo's life. As mentioned in the chapter, in 1610 Galileo was not living in Pisa, but rather was in the process of moving from Padua to Florence, although he was a professor at the University of Pisa and did visit Pisa during that year to show the planets of Jupiter to his sponsor the Grand Duke in the tower of the Medici Palace, where the night scene is set.

Galileo published an anagram with a hidden claim that Saturn is three-bodied, i.e. has two moons. In fact, the fuzziness he was observing was, of course, Saturn's rings.

Galileo made all the astronomical observations described in the chapter during the months of late 1609 and during 1610. He by no means made all the discoveries in one night, although each time he created a more powerful telescope the discoveries came in quick succession, probably many on a single night. Galileo did observe the Sun through his telescopes, and there is speculation that this contributed to his blindness later, although others have argued that Galileo was able to safely project the image of the Sun onto a screen.

The story, recounted by his pupil Vincenzo Viviani, of Galileo dropping weights from the Leaning Tower of Pisa may well be a legend, so I have limited this activity to Fizz.

I enjoyed reading *Galileo's Daughter* by Dava Sobel in writing the Galileo chapters and also benefited greatly from a walking tour of Pisa "in the footsteps of Galileo" with tour guide Ilaria Marchetti.

In several places I refer to Aristotle being unchallenged for almost two millennia. In fairness there were occasional thinkers, including churchmen, who questions Aristotle. However none of them successfully proposed alternatives, neither did successfully instill the principle of scientific verification, so that, until Galileo, the challenges were of marginal significance.

6 Nature's Beat

In earlier years, Galileo was disciplined for refusing to wear academic robes. He wrote a controversial poem criticizing academic dress in Pisa and included the argument that such robes made it impractical to visit brothels. I do not know for certain whether he still refused academic dress in 1610.

There is a story also recounted by Vincenzo Viviani, quite possibly apocryphal, that Galileo discovered the properties of the pendulum watching the chandelier in the cathedral.

Stillman Drake in the '70s speculated that Galileo may have used singing as a timer (since his water clocks and pulse would have been too crude to provide some of the more detailed measurements found in his notes). I came across this in *The Ten Most Beautiful Experiments* by George Johnson. Since it is pure speculation, I again limited use of this technique to Fizz. Galileo himself, by the way, probably first found the square law studying balls rolling down a plane (which exhibit a similar pattern) rather than by directly measuring vertical freefall.

7 Relative

The watercolors of the Moon and chart of Jupiter's moons are facsimiles of Galileo's originals.

The following is an approximate quote:

If Aristotle himself rose from the grave, he would honor the evidence of his senses... They wish never to raise their eyes from the pages of Aristotle's works as if the universe had been written to be read by nobody but Aristotle, and his eyes had been destined to see for all posterity.

The letter from Kepler is fictional, but Kepler did discover the three laws of planetary motion that still bear his name, argued that the Moon causes tides, and authored what might be the first-ever science fiction story about a journey to the Moon. Kepler used the term *telescopium* while Galileo used *telescopio*.

Galileo objected obstinately (and incorrectly) to Kepler's theory of tides and elliptical orbits. It seems like a reasonable speculation that part of the reason Galileo rejected Kepler's lunar theory of tides was that he desperately needed the tides as evidence for the Earth's rotation.

It has been reported that Galileo complied with the censor's instruction to cross out sections of Copernicus' book but that he indeed did so with a light touch.

Galileo had the relationship described with the Cardinal-cum-Pope. The following are quotes from letters from the cardinal/pope to Galileo.

I pray the Lord God to preserve you, because men of great value like you deserve to live a long time to the benefit of the public

As your brother

We embrace with paternal love this great man whose fame shines in the heavens and goes on Earth far and wide

Galileo was summonsed to Rome on charges of heresy in 1633 as described, having his appeal on medical grounds turned down by a committee chaired by the Pope. The text of the summons is fictional.

8 *Them Apples* & 9 *Instant Attraction*

These two chapters describe Newton's key physics and mathematics insights in quick succession. The thoughts probably developed over a couple of years around the time that Cambridge was closed for the plague and shortly thereafter.

Curiously, Galileo died in January 1642 according to the Gregorian calendar then in use in Italy, and Newton was born in 1642 according to the Julian calendar still in use in the UK. However these events did not fall in the same year in either the Gregorian or Julian calendars.

It is believed to be true that Newton was inspired by a falling apple (the apple falling on his head is a common embellishment).

Newton did perform alchemy and physics experiments in a small brick lab in the secret garden described. The lab was probably in the specific location described, although it may have been a few meters away from there. See *Investigating the site of Newton's laboratory in Trinity College, Cambridge* by P E Spargo, South African Journal of Science 101, July/August 2005. That paper also directed me to the historical images of Trinity College.

The same walled garden is now no longer surrounded by a high wall and can be observed from the street. At its center is an apple tree that, according to college tradition as relayed to me by a modern day porter, is descendent from the apple tree that inspired Newton.

There is no record of Newton exhibiting any sexuality, and there has been speculation that he was homosexual or asexual.

10 *Fluxions*

"Fluxions" was the name Newton used for the analysis now known as calculus. I weaved in the later name *calculus* for easier recognition. Newton and Leibnitz spent many years in a bitter priority dispute over ideas which Newton had not published and which the two almost certainly invented independently. It is apparently true that Newton wrote the Royal Society report that ruled in his favor.

Alchemy was punishable by a tortuous death in England in the 1600s. Robert Boyle did lobby for repeal of the law (although I am not aware at what date he did so), and the death penalty was later repealed by King Charles II, although the King was still entitled to confiscate any gold produced.

Newton wrote more about alchemy and biblical hermeneutics than about physics. He discussed alchemy with Boyle, a keen alchemist, in London. The Cambridge economist John Maynard Keynes, who acquired many of Newton's writings on alchemy, commented that "Newton was not the first of the age of reason: He was the last of the magicians."

Newton's lab, with twenty years of notes, was indeed burned down, although at a later date. There is a well-known legend that this was caused by a dog named Diamond upsetting a lantern.

11 Fluid

This chapter is based on the true story of Daniel Bernoulli's father plagiarizing his son's work and back-dating it. Bernoulli indeed proposed the kinetic theory, which was later discredited, then reestablished.

12 Waving

This chapter is set a few years before the French Revolution when d'Alembert headed the academy in the Louvre and the next-door Tuileries palace was still standing (there is now a park there). D'Almbert's famous students Lagrange and Laplace (Laplace is sometimes referred to as the Newton of France) were based elsewhere in Paris at that time, but the story has them visiting on that day. I admit to having found little about the personalities of these men. At this time, there really was quite a political divide between mathematics in England and that of continental Europe.

Laplace was the first to speculate about black holes even though he had no conception of Einstein's General Theory of Relativity, which eventually led to a robust theory of black holes.

13 The Good Doctor

Benjamin Franklin was Ambassador to France during the American Revolutionary War, representing, as of 1783, the thirteen founding states plus Vermont. He was a popular figure in Paris and was often referred to as the Good Doctor based on his honorary doctorate.

A volcano in Iceland in 1783 caused months of fog in Europe, and Franklin is credited with recognizing the connection between the volcano and the foggy weather that led to drought in Europe. Franklin invented bifocal glasses. It is not known for certain if he ever performed the experiment he suggested of flying a kite in a thunderstorm. Franklin's choice of positive and negative was completely arbitrary, although the reference to a coin flip is fictional. The choice was unfortunate: to this day electrical diagrams show electricity flowing from positive to negative even though we have long known that physically the electrons drift from negative to positive.

Coulomb and Lavoisier made the scientific contributions described, and Lavoisier was a partner in a tax-collecting consortium. Coulomb's comments about a lonely profession have no connection to his historic personality.

14 In a New Light

I placed the brief insights on the industrial revolution into Dalton's mouth for pure convenience. I don't even know to what extent people at the time were conscious of those insights into the changes around them, although the term *industrial revolution* had indeed been coined before 1800 by a French envoy.

The chart entitled *Elements* is an image of Dalton's. Note that he uses outdated names such as azote for nitrogen but in the text I use nitrogen for the convenience of modern eyes and ears.

Dalton's five laws of atoms starting with *1. The chemical elements are made of atoms* are quoted verbatim from a paper he published in 1805.

Dalton failed to synthesize hydrogen peroxide (HO) and therefore did assume incorrectly that water is HO rather than H_2O, leading him to miscalculate the ratio of the hydrogen to oxygen atomic masses. Dalton was the first man to document his color blindness, which was explained by Thomas Young and is sometimes known as Daltonism.

Thomas Young's paper on the double-slit experiment was published in 1803, so the suggestion that he had tried the basic experiment in 1800 is speculative.

Young was an incredible polymath and is the subject of a book entitled *The Last Man Who Knew Everything* by Andrew Robinson. Among other achievements, Young played a key role in deciphering Egyptian hieroglyphs, performed all the experiments recounted here, and was fluent in all the languages mentioned.

Henry Cavendish was incredibly shy, especially of women, and it's reported that he was unable to talk to the maids in his household and would pass them notes.

His famous experiment focused on the density of the Earth. This density easily implies the mass of the Earth (as the radius of the Earth was known) and the universal gravitational constant, but there is no record of Cavendish making these simple calculations himself. Others calculated these numbers later based on Cavendish's results, which is why these calculations are confined to Fizz's thoughts.

The experiment is set here in 1800, although, to be accurate, Cavendish published his results in 1798.

As referenced in this and the previous chapter, Cavendish found many important results in electricity and published none of them. He was actually the first to discover "Coulomb's Law" and "Ohm's Law" as well as ideas of electric potential, capacitance, and more. In the previous chapter, there is an implication that Coulomb had some awareness of Cavendish's priority—I am not sure if that is true. Cavendish's extensive work on electricity was only fully revealed and edited later by James Clerk Maxwell.

15 Family Business

Herschel did achieve all the musical feats described, although once he obtained a royal stipend for astronomy I'm not sure whether he ever gave concerts again.

Herschel made all the scientific discoveries attributed to him in the story, and he did try to insist on the name *Georgium sidus* for what was already in his lifetime called Uranus by others. He was later knighted all the same. Herschel himself referred to the discovery of Uranus and his other discoveries in the solar system as "trifles" compared to the real work of mapping out the structure of the cosmos. Even so, during his lifetime the interpretation of nebula as galaxies (or other "universes" in his words at the time) was still speculative, and Herschel himself suggested alternative explanations too. The matter was only fully resolved scientifically by Hubble in the 1930s, so Hubble competes for the title of the first cosmologist.

Caroline's mother refused to teach her music, let alone science, thinking her fit for nothing other than housework. With help from William she later taught herself music and sang soprano at his concerts. She became his astronomical assistant and finally an important astronomer in her own right. Apparently she really did ride all the way to Greenwich at night to inform a startled Astronomer Royal about her eighth comet find, which more accurately was in 1797, not 1800.

William had many scrapes with death while making and using telescopes, and Caroline sustained a serious injury to her leg. She bitterly resented William's wife during their first years of marriage. William did use onions to repel mosquitoes but contracted malaria nonetheless (although that occurred at an earlier time when he lived nearer the Thames). Apparently their ink really did freeze on one occasion.

William Herschel's son John, later Sir John Frederick William Herschel, 1st Baronet, went on to become senior wrangler at Cambridge (the honor which Stokes achieved and which William Thomson, James Clerk Maxwell, and J. J. Thomson all narrowly missed) an important astronomer, scientist, and an inventor of photographic techniques.

The Ostrich Inn really has been open since the 1100s and was the first stage for westbound stagecoaches; they claim the history of Jarman's sixty murders using a hinged bed as true. Today the Inn is still a layover for travelers—passengers coming through London's Heathrow airport.

Here is truly a hole in Heaven is a quote.

I enjoyed the book *The Georgian Star* by Michael D. Lemonick in writing this chapter.

16 Feeling the Heat

Apparently Dalton really did turn up in scarlet robes to receive his honorary degree, which would normally contradict his religion, citing his color blindness as an excuse.

Joule's seminal talk did take place in Oxford that summer and Faraday, Thomson, and Stokes did attend. The following are direct quotes:

I am struck with it

I am inclined to be a Joulite

Thompson was instrumental in publicizing Carnot's important work. The piston diagram is from Carnot's book.

The pub scene is imaginary, although the men described did talk after the lecture.

17 The Waterfall

Several weeks after the Oxford lecture there really was a chance meeting between Thompson and James Joule, who was on honeymoon as described, in Chamonix. They did discuss measuring the temperature at the top and bottom of the waterfall but apparently never made the measurement. In one of Thompson's accounts of the chance meeting he says he met Joule, "thermometer in hand," although this may have been an embellishment.

18 Field Day

Faraday's background and achievements are all factual. He was the son of a blacksmith and apprentice to a bookbinder, and later he had traveled with Davy to Europe and received an electric cell from Volta in 1814. That trip was traumatic for Faraday in that Davy's wife treated him as something of a servant. I do not know whether Faraday kept an office at the RI, which had been his home and workplace for decades, once he officially retired, or if he still gave any public lectures at the exact time described, although he certainly did for many years before that, most famously a Christmas lecture.

It was common in those says to use frogs' legs to detect electric current, and one common friction machine for electrostatic generation designed by N. Rouland rubbed silk against hare fur; I don't know whether Faraday used that specific machine.

The electric motor and dynamo are real. The water sprinkler is purely fictional.

Quotes:

Nothing is too wonderful to be true

19 Seeing the Light

Maxwell developed his watershed theory of electromagnetism over many years, building on Faraday's experiments and intuitions about lines-of-force. As described, Maxwell suggested the extra field-to-field interaction that led to his insight about light. The two men did meet while they were both in London, although the details of the specific meeting are purely fictional.

20 Time's Arrow

The scene is set at a time when James and Katherine lived in Glenair and around the period when Maxwell and independently Boltzmann started to understand entropy in terms of statistics. I'm not sure whether Maxwell thought in terms of "time reversibility" and whether he made the connection with the psychological arrow of time (we remember the past, not the future), or if those particular thoughts were added later. I'm also not sure if the Maxwell's dog, Toby, was alive and with them in that particular year.

The question about the demon decreasing entropy was indeed posed by Maxwell, and *Maxwell's demon* spurred a lot of interesting research and has perhaps been finally resolved in recent decades.

21 The Wizard

Edison worked on all the devices and processes described and produced over a thousand patents. The logical layout of the tables is fictional. He was sometimes referred to as the "wizard of Menlo Park."

The following are quotes:

There is no substitute for hard work

I start where the last man left off

Genius is one percent inspiration, ninety-nine percent perspiration

Great ideas originate in the muscles

I can find 10,000 ways that don't work without failing.

Many of life's failures are people who did not realize how close they were to success when they gave up.

Sale is proof of utility, and utility is success

Good morning. How do you do? How do you like the phonograph? (recording on the first phonograph)

22 Little Jack Horner

It's worth noting that "plum pudding" was J. J. Thomson's own analogy and that this proposal, later discredited, is referred to by physicists as the *plum pudding model of the atom*.

The use of the word *photon* for the quantum of light in this chapter is an anachronism introduced for clarity, as that word was in fact coined later by Gilbert Lewis in 1926.

Einstein did like to keep photos of Newton, Faraday, and Maxwell, although I don't know whether he had those in the patent office.

23 The Gedankenexperiment

This chapter is set in 1905, Einstein's so-called *annus mirabilis*—year of wonders. There is no exaggeration here—Einstein published his Ph.D., his theory on Brownian motion, his theory of special relativity, and his theory of the photon, (which was the corner-stone of quantum mechanics) all in one year while holding down a full-time job as a mid-level patent clerk.

One point which has been debated at length was how aware Einstein was of the Michelson-Morley experiment. At some point Einstein denied that he was aware of the experiment when he thought of the special theory of relativity. But historians have shown fairly conclusively, I think, that whether or not he had that specific experiment in mind, Einstein was certainly aware of its results, namely that experimentally the Earth's movement does not carry us away from the center of an expanding circle of light. The experiment was not actually carried out with a full circle of light—that just made the description easier—but rather with light beams in two specific directions.

There has been a headline-grabbing claim that Einstein had Asperger's Syndrome. Others counter that he was simply too intelligent to be responsive to small-talk. If at points in the chapter Einstein is oblivious to the mundane, I hope this somehow approximates a true aspect of his personality.

24 E=M

Poincaré indeed discovered the phenomenon of chaos. However, the name "chaos theory" and much of its development came later. Fizz's thoughts about the weather being chaotic are here anticipating work by Edward Lorenz (unrelated to Lorentz) in the 1960s. Lorenz initially discovered accidentally that when the starting value for his computer model of the weather was rounded from 0.506127 to 0.506, the predictions changed dramatically—the system has extreme sensitivity to starting conditions. Philip Merilees in 1972 suggested, *Does the flap of a butterfly's wings in Brazil set off a tornado in Texas?* This led to the coining of the "butterfly effect." A detailed treatment of chaos theory was not a priority for the book, but I took the liberty of allowing Fizz to anticipate a couple of its important concepts.

25 Attractive Curves

The discussion of black holes and wormholes is anachronistic. These concepts are indeed enabled by Einstein's general relativity of 1915, but those particular topographies were only studied during the following years by Schwarzschild and others. The term *wormhole* was only coined in 1957 by John Archibald Wheeler.

In 1919, after the war, Arthur Eddington led a mission to carry out the experiment Einstein suggested, observing the effects of the gravity of the Sun on the star light passing near the Sun during a total eclipse. This mission produced the first dramatic evidence for general relativity.

26 The Modern Alchemist

The terms *Cottonopolis* and *Warehouse City* were apparently known nicknames for Manchester.

At that time there was a lot of experimentation with creative ways of displaying the periodic table (search for "The Internet Database of Periodic Tables").

The following are quotations:

It was quite the most incredible event that has ever happened to me in my life. It was almost as incredible as if you fired a 15-inch shell at a piece of tissue paper and it came back and hit you.

I find the students here regard a full professor as little short of Lord God Almighty.

27 Let the Cat Out

The Fifth Solvay Conference was indeed a watershed in the development of quantum mechanics. All the people described were at the conference and had the insights ascribed to them. Most attendees were, or later became, Nobel laureates. Marie Curie had at that time really been awarded two Nobel prizes but had been refused membership of the French Academy.

I have taken the liberty of having each person briefly present their discoveries of the immediately preceding years, although I do not know whether they did in fact present a recap of those ideas at the conference. While Einstein and Schrödinger did object to the non-determinism and non-locality at the conference, the specific thought experiments of Schrödinger's cat and Einstein's argument regarding non-locality of the entanglement of two distant electrons were described in the following years, in Einstein's case in the famous "EPR paradox" coauthored with Podolsky & Rosen in 1935. I have slightly simplified the details of some of the arguments while, I hope, being true to their essence. For example, the quantum wave equation actually requires a combination of two numbers at each point—the mathematical concept of *complex numbers* are usually used—so the wave equation for definite momentum would require at least two sine waves to represent its values along one line. Physicists did largely divide into the Copenhagen and conservative camps as the strange ideas of quantum mechanics emerged around the time of this conference, but the way this develops in one day at the conference in the text is obviously something of a caricature.

Einstein Quotes:

Objecting to *Spooky Action at a Distance*

I like to think that the Moon is there even if I am not looking at it

He does not throw dice paraphrased here as in many places as *God does not play dice with the universe*

Bohr quotes:

Einstein, don't tell God what to do with his dice (disputed quote)

Anyone who is not shocked by quantum theory has not understood it

Dirac really proposed the now widely used bra-ket notation.

28 MED

Manhattan Engineering District (MED) was the official name of what is commonly called the Manhattan Project. Apparently Hans Bethe really reported that discussion with his girlfriend about how stars twinkle. All the details are based on historical fact, including the reactions to the news of Hiroshima—Otto Frisch reported that several colleagues made celebratory dinner reservations at the La Fonda hotel while Szilard, one of the key initiators, called it *one of the greatest blunders in history*. The newspaper quotes are from the actual *Santa Fe New Mexican* of the date described. Ede (Edward) Teller went on to create the hydrogen bomb project. The MED project cost $22bn in today's terms, with 135,000 employees creating only enough enriched uranium for one full chain reaction, which occurred over Hiroshima. The bomb dropped on Nagasaki comprised plutonium.

29 Very Nearly Everything

I have captured details of the LHC and ATLAS experiment at CERN as accurately as I can. The encounter with Dr. Fabiola Gianotti is of course pure fiction and without her approval. Arno Allan Penzias and Robert Woodrow Wilson are both alive, and Penzias did not give me permission to pose as a quark inside his retina and did not endorse anything that the quark said.

30 Bang

The encounter with Professor Hawking is, of course, entirely fictional, and Professor Hawking did not approve or endorse this story. Hawking is a famous cosmologist best known for Hawking radiation from black holes, and he communicates by moving his cheek, ever since his finger became too weak to control a joystick. Hawking indeed conceded a bet about the existence of black holes and bought a subscription to Penthouse magazine for a fellow physicist. It's true that as an undergraduate I swung open a door in the math department very nearly knocking his wheel-chair, although I missed narrowly and am hopeful that he does not recall that encounter.

32 Eternal Mystery

Einstein quote:
> The eternal mystery of the world is its comprehensibility

Time travel

Forward "time travel" by moving at close to the speed of light is entirely possible and proven. Nevertheless, the time travel in this story, while demonstrating real physical ideas, is bordering on science fiction. Traveling forward centuries or decades for Earth during just one night for the traveler is exaggerated, because the accelerations required to reach that close to the speed of light in just a few hours would be crushing beyond the mild weight-increase described in the book.

While the general theory of relativity is consistent with wormholes for backward time travel, most physicists assume that this is not in fact possible for reasons that have to do with physics theory, commonsense preservation of cause-and-effect, and the lack of tourists from the future. If it is possible to create wormholes at all, it may only be possible to travel back to the point of creation of the wormhole.

Fizz's final forward time travel by orbiting a black hole is certainly possible, although I'm not sure that, in reality, achieving time dilation by traveling to a black hole, into orbit, breaking out of the orbit, and traveling home would actually require less energy than simply travelling at close to the speed of light. Orbiting near a black hole has other problems due to the steep changes of gravity, even from one side of the hut to the other, although this might not be an issue around a very large black hole. Again, achieving this maneuver in one night of Fizz's time is probably impossible without experiencing crushing accelerations or gravity.

Despite the exaggerations and the speculative nature of the backward time travel, I do hope that Fizz's time travel not only facilitates the story but also, in itself, demonstrates real physical phenomena of time dilation, the possibility of wormholes in curved spacetime, and the gravity-acceleration equivalence.

Image details and credits

p.48 *A chart of constellations:* Generated with John Walker's Home Planet software.

p.62 *Frombork Cathedral with Vistula Lagoon in background:* Photograph by Holger Weinandt licensed under the Creative Commons Attribution-Share Alike 3.0 Germany license. Source: Wikipedia. This is a modern photo although as far as I know the cathedral has not changed much.

p.80 *Galileo Galilei:* Painting by Domenico Robusti, 1605. Widely reproduced.

p.92 *An eye piece of one of Galileo's telescopes and view of the cathedral and tower from the Medici Palace:* Eye piece picture widely reproduced, source unknown. Distant photograph of Pisa Cathedral and Leaning Tower taken by the author from the tower of the former Medici palace. I would like to thank the museum in the former Medici Palace for allowing me to access the tower, which is usually closed to the public.

p.93 *The Medici Palazzo Reale, and the tower :* Photograph by the author.

p.96 *A panorama of the Milky Way:* By Digital Sky, LLC. Licensed under the Creative Commons Attribution-Share Alike 2.5 Generic license. Source: Wikipedia.

p.97 *Jupiter and its four "Galilean" moons through a small telescope:* By Rob Glover, licensed under Creative Commons Attribution-ShareAlike 2.0 Generic. Source: Flickr user Robbo-Man.

p.100 *Galileo's sketch of sunspots:* Circa 1612, widely reproduced.

p.103 *Pisa's Piazza dei Miracoli: Baptistry, cathedral, leaning bell tower:* Engraving from Francesco Fontani, pictorial journey of Tuscany, Florence, Vincenzo Batelli and Co., 1827. Public Domain—copyright expired. Source: Wikipedia—Italian.

p.113 *Galileo:* Detail from Portrait of Galileo Galilei by Justus Sustermans painted in 1636. National Maritime Museum, Greenwich, London. Public domain—copyright expired. Source: Wikipedia.

p.114 *Galileo's sketches of the lunar phases:* From a folio attached to a manuscript of Galileo's *Sidereus Nuncius* (Starry Messenger) of 1610. Found in the The National Library in Florence. Widely reproduced. Either watercolor or sepia ink.

p.118 *One of Galileo's telescopes:* Telescope from 1609. Widely reproduced.

p.119 *A fragment of Galileo's records of Jupiter's moons:* Apparently from 1610. Widely reproduced.

p.127 *Great Gate, Trinity College, Cambridge:* From Ackermann R. (1815). *A History of the University of Cambridge, its Colleges, Halls and Public Buildings,* 2 vols. (Text by William Combe.). London. Public domain—copyright expired.

p.130 *Trinity College Cambridge in the 1600s:* Etching from *Cantabrigia Illustrata,* David Loggan, 1690. Public domain—copyright expired. The Wren library was edited out of this image since it was not yet built when the scene is set in 1667.

p.155 *Newton's reflector telescope:* Photograph © Andrew Dunn, November 5, 2004. Licensed under the Creative Commons Attribution-Share Alike 2.0 Generic license.

Source: Wikipedia. This replica of the second telescope presented by Newton to the Royal Society is in the Whipple Museum of the History of Science in Cambridge, England.

p.173 *Newton's Principia:* Photograph by Paul Hermans. Licensed under Creative Commons Attribution-Share Alike 3.0 license. Source: Wikipedia. Copyright of book expired.

p.190 *Two-dimensional waves: two sets of water ripples:* Photograph by Claudiodivizia. Licensed by Pixmac.

p.198 *Benjamin Franklin:* Portrait of 1785 by Joseph-Siffred Duplessis. Oil on canvas. Public domain—copyright expired. Source: Wikipedia.

p.200 *Leyden jar for storing electric charge:* Photographed at Museum Boerhave, Leiden, Netherlands, by Wikipedia user Alvinrune. Licensed under the Creative Commons Attribution-Share Alike 3.0 Unported license.

p.210 *John Dalton:* Frontispiece of *John Dalton and the Rise of Modern Chemistry* by Henry Roscoe. Henry Roscoe (author), William Henry Worthington (engraver), and Joseph Allen (painter). Public domain—copyright expired. Source: Wikipedia

p.213 *John Dalton's list of elements:* A lecture diagram prepared by John Dalton, 1806-1807 (Dalton used these symbols from at least 1803). Widely reproduced, probably originally from the archives of the Manchester Literary and Philosophical Society. Public domain—copyright expired.

p.219 *Thomas Young:* From *Popular Science Monthly* Volume 5, July 1874, from a slab in Westminster Abbey, the work of Chantrey. Public domain—copyright expired.

p.225 *Cavendish's apparatus to measure gravity between large & small lead spheres:* Cavendish, H. (1798), *Experiments to determine the Density of the Earth* in McKenzie, A.S. ed. Scientific Memoirs Vol.9: The Laws of Gravitation, American Book Co. 1900, p.62. From Google Books. Copyright expired. Detail from Henry Cavendish's 1798 paper published in Philosophical Magazine. Source: Wikipedia. Public domain—copyright expired.

p.238 *The billions of stars of our Milky Way Galaxy viewed from outside:* Sketch made by Lord Rosse of the Whirlpool Galaxy in 1845. Public domain—copyright expired. Source: Wikipedia.

p.232 *William Herschel's 40 foot (12 meter) telescope:* From *Leisure Hour*, Nov. 2, 1867, p.729. Public domain—copyright expired. Source: Wikipedia.

p.233 *Some of Herschel's eye-pieces:* Photograph by the author at the London Science Museum.

p.247 *James Joule's apparatus for using falling weights to stir and heat water:* Apparatus from 1845. Photograph from Science Museum, London, released to public domain by Gaius Cornelius. Engraving from Harper's New Monthly Magazine, No. 231, August, 1869 (arrows added). Source: Wikipedia.

p.251 *A sine wave—the shadow of a spiral—represents a pure color or pure note:* Photograph by the author.

p.252 *A single piston—Carnot's model of the engine and heat pump:* This is Fig. 1 from *Réflexions sur la puissance motrice du feu* (Reflections on the motive power of fire) by Sadi Carnot, 1824. Public domain—copyright expired.

p.270 *Michael's natural philosophy lecture at the Royal Institution:* Lithograph of Michael Faraday delivering a Christmas lecture at the Royal Institution by Alexander Blaikley. Public domain—copyright expired. Source: Wikipedia.

p.271 *Michael's lab:* Painting by Harriet Moore. Public domain—copyright expired. Source: Wikipedia.

p.280 *Faraday's dynamo (generator):* By Émile Alglave. From Émile Alglave & J. Boulard (1884) *The Electric Light: It's History, Production, and Applications,* translated by T. O'Conor Sloan, D. Appleton & Co., New York, p.224, fig.142. From Google Books. Public domain—copyright expired. Source: Wikipedia.

p.281 *Faraday's first electric motor:* Public domain—copyright expired.

p.282 *Faraday's experiment connecting magnetism and light:* Exhibit at the Royal Institution, London, photographed by the author.

p.309 *Dynamo (generator)—'Long-legged Mary-Ann':* Edison made these dynamos from 1879; the specific one pictured is apparently dated 1884. This design was nicknamed the long-legged Mary-Ann, then apparently renamed the long-waisted Mary-Ann out of modesty. Image widely reproduced, source unknown. Public domain—copyright expired.

p.311 *Edison with his phonograph:* Photograph by L.C. Handy 1877. Public domain—copyright expired. Source: Library of Congress

p.313 *Edison's Menlo Park facility with team:* Source: U.S. Department of the Interior, National Park Service, Edison National Historic Site. Public domain—copyright expired.

p.315 *Edison effect—negative charge flowing through vacuum:* Source: National Edison Historic Site.

p.321 *Röntgen's first "medical" X-Ray image:* The first "medical" X-ray, of Anna Bertha Roentgen's hand. Demonstration print made to give to academic colleagues, December 22, 1895. Public domain—copyright expired. Source: Wikipedia.

p.322 *The spectrum of electromagnetic waves:* By NASA, edited by Wikipedia user Inductiveload (plus minor edits and cropping by the author). Licensed under the Creative Commons Attribution-Share Alike 3.0 Unported.

p.323 *J. J. Thomson's plum pudding model of the atom:* Contributed to public domain by the author, Wikipedia user Fastfission.

p.328 *Albert Einstein at his lectern in the Swiss patent office:* 1904. Public domain—copyright expired. Source unknown—widely reproduced.

Thanks to Barbara Wolff, Einstein Information Officer at the Albert Einstein Archives of the Hebrew University of Jerusalem for the archive's consent to use images of Einstein in appropriate context.

p.371 *Geiger and Rutherford bombarding a thin leaf of gold* : Photographed in the University of Manchester Schuster lab around 1912. Widely reproduced. The print was found in the estate of Prof H Stansfield.

p.374 *Nodder's periodic table*: From C. R. Nodder *A convenient form of the periodic classification of the elements*, Chemistry News 121, 269, December, 1920. Reproduced in Quam & Quam, *Types of graphic classifications of the elements*, 1934. Public domain—copyright expired.

p.374 *Rutherford's apparatus for transmutation of nitrogen into oxygen:* Replica of 1919. On loan from Cavendish Laboratory Cambridge. Source: royalsociety.org.

p.385 *Harmonics of constrained string—analogy for an electron in an atom:* Released to public domain by its author Y Landman and edited by W. Axel. Source: Wikipedia.

p.392 *Piccard, Henriot, Ehrenfest, Herzen, DeDonder, Schrödinger, Verschaffelt*, Pauli, ...Heisenberg, Fowler, Brillouin: Conference photograph by Benjamin Couprie, Institut International de Physique de Solvay. Public domain—copyright expired. Source: Wikipedia.

p.392 *Bohr and Einstein:* This photograph was not actually taken at the conference but was taken by Paul Ehrenfest at his home in Leiden; the occasion was most likely the 50th anniversary of Hendrik Lorentz' doctorate (December 11, 1925). Public domain—copyright expired.

p.426 *CERN exhibition center:* Photograph by the author.

p.429 *Tracks of fundamental particles in historic CERN* bubble chamber: Historic picture from CERN liquid hydrogen bubble chamber. Copyright CERN. Used with permission of CERN subject to the CDS Conditions of use.

p.105 *Feynman diagram of a quantum field theory scenario:* Licensed under the GNU Free Documentation License by author Joel Holdsworth (Wikipedia:Joelholdsworth).

p.437 *ATLAS experiment at CERN:* Photograph by the author.

p.438 *ATLAS control center:* Photograph by the author.

p.440 *CERN Large Hadron Collider (LHC) tunnel:* Copyright CERN. Used with permission of CERN subject to the CDS Conditions of use.

p.448 *Arno Penzias and Robert Wilson's microwave antenna, Bell Labs NJ:* The 15-meter Holmdel horn antenna at Bell Telephone Laboratories in Holmdel, New Jersey, was built in 1959. Photograph released to the public domain by NASA. Source: Wikipedia.

p.456 *Mullard Radio Telescope—part of an international grid:* Google Maps. Reproduced according to Permission Guidelines for Google Maps and Google Earth.

p.457 *Galaxy 13 billion light-years away seen by radio telescopes*
as it was in the early universe, 13 billion years ago: Image of quasar 0014+813 by the EVN+VSOP network of radio telescopes which includes the Mullard Radio Telescope. Gurvits L.I., et al. Source: http://www.evlbi.org.

p.457 *Remains of Kepler's Nova:* X-ray, optical & infrared composite of Kepler's supernova remnant (known to astronomers as Supernova 1604) by NASA/ESA/JHU/R.Sankrit & W.Blair.

Index

Key: **People** *Places* Concepts

Physicists by chapter

Greek to Me: Aristotle

Center of the World: Nicolaus Copernicus

Father and Sun: Galileo Galilei

Them Apples—Fluxions: Isaac Newton (Hooke, Huygens, Boyle)

Fluid: Daniel Bernoulli

Waving: Jean le Rond d'Alembert, Pierre-Simon Laplace, Joseph-Louis Lagrange

The Good Doctor: Benjamin Franklin, Charles-Augustin de Coulomb, Antoine Lavoisier

In a New Light: John Dalton, Thomas Young, Henry Cavendish

Family Business: William & Caroline Herschel (John Herschel)

Feeling the Heat—The Waterfall: James Joule, William Thomson—Lord Kelvin (Stokes, Carnot, Fourier)

Field Day: Michael Faraday (Volta, Ørsted, Ampère)

Seeing the Light: Michael Faraday, James Clerk Maxwell

Time: James Clerk Maxwell (Clausius, Boltzmann)

The Wizard: Thomas Edison

Little Jack Horner: Albert Einstein, (J. J. Thomson, Röntgen, Hertz, Becquerel, The Curies, Planck)

The Gedankenexperiment—Attractive Curves: Albert Einstein (Lorentz, Poincaré)

The Modern Alchemist: Ernst Rutherford (Geiger, Marsden)

Let the Cat Out: Niels Bohr, Einstein, Schrödinger, Heisenberg, Born, Dirac, Pauli, Marie Curie (Lorentz, Compton)

MED: Chadwick, Bethe, Fermi, (Feynman)

Very Nearly Everything: (Higgs, Feynman)

Bang: Stephen Hawking

The Abbey: (Recap of British physicists)